Fred

A Full Collation of the Codex Sinaiticus with the Received Text of the New Testament

SALZWASSER
VERLAG

Frederick Henry Scrivener

A Full Collation of the Codex Sinaiticus with the Received Text of the New Testament

Reprint of the original, first published in 1864.

1st Edition 2022 | ISBN: 978-3-75259-360-0

Verlag (Publisher): Salzwasser Verlag GmbH, Zeilweg 44, 60439 Frankfurt, Deutschland
Vertretungsberechtigt (Authorized to represent): E. Roepke, Zeilweg 44, 60439 Frankfurt, Deutschland
Druck (Print): Books on Demand GmbH, In de Tarpen 42, 22848 Norderstedt, Deutschland

A

FULL COLLATION OF THE CODEX SINAITICUS WITH THE RECEIVED TEXT OF THE NEW TESTAMENT:

TO WHICH IS PREFIXED A CRITICAL INTRODUCTION

BY

FREDERICK H. SCRIVENER, M.A.

1864.

ADVERTISEMENT.

THE following pages comprise a collation, as full and exact as my best pains could make it, of the text of Stephens' Greek Testament of 1550, as reprinted in the series of "Cambridge Texts" (1862), with Tischendorf's larger and smaller editions of the Codex Sinaiticus, compared with each other and with his *Notitia Editionis Cod. Bibl. Sinait.* It is hoped that this manual will not only prove a good substitute for Tischendorf's publications to students who may not possess them, but will be found of some use to those who do. I am enabled to produce it in the present form by the considerate liberality of the Rev. Christopher Wordsworth, D.D., Canon of Westminster; who, being aware that I had been hindered from undertaking it by prudential considerations, first engaged my services to collate the Codex Sinaiticus for his forthcoming new edition of the Greek Testament, and afterwards allowed me to take stereotyped plates of the printed pages for my own purpose. I gladly avail myself of this opportunity of thanking him for this and other acts of kindness, which I have been privileged to receive from him during a long course of years.

September 29, 1863.

INTRODUCTION.

About four years ago, when the textual criticism of Holy Scripture was fast regaining its proper rank as a branch of theological study, the general attention of the learned was directed to it by the unexpected announcement that Tischendorf had found at Mount Sinai a Greek manuscript of the whole New Testament and a portion of the Old, at least as ancient as any yet known to us. Nor has the public interest in this important subject in any way diminished as the details of Tischendorf's discovery, the external appearance of the Codex Sinaiticus as a palaeographic record, and its internal character as a witness to the sacred text, have become gradually and at length completely known to us: while the strange attempt of Dr. Simonides to establish his claim to be the actual writer of a document pronounced by competent judges to be fifteen hundred years old has arrested the curiosity of many who, but for his adventurous boldness, would never have been led to think about Biblical manuscripts at all, much less to regard them, as what in truth they are, *the very title-deeds of our Christian inheritance.*

It is the design of this little volume to represent, in a convenient and accessible form, every variation, however minute or insignificant, of the Codex Sinaiticus from the commonly received or standard text of the Greek Testament

(Stephens' of 1550); distinguishing by an arbitrary mark (✓) mere errors of the scribe or peculiarities in the spelling, from other changes which more or less affect the sense of the sacred authors. This method seems at once the simplest and the best for enabling students of the original to estimate, each one for himself, the extent and value of the contributions made by this manuscript, now first brought to light, to the previously existing fund of materials for amending or confirming the text as usually printed. In the course of this Introduction the editor will offer some suggestions bearing on that point which have occurred to him in the prosecution of his work, and as clear and full a description of the Codex Sinaiticus and its history as the limits within which he is confined may allow.

CHAPTER I.

ON THE DISCOVERY AND PUBLICATION OF THE CODEX SINAITICUS.

THE services rendered to this department of Biblical literature by Aen. F. Constantine Tischendorf of Leipsic far exceed in extent, and probably in importance, those of any man now living. While he was travelling in 1844 in search of ancient manuscripts, under the patronage of his own sovereign, King Frederick Augustus of Saxony, he was so fortunate as to pick out of a basket of *papers*, destined to light the stove in the convent of S. Catherine on Mount Sinai, forty-three *vellum* leaves containing portions of the Septuagint version, chiefly from 1 Chronicles and Jeremiah, with Nehemiah and Esther complete, bearing every mark of extreme antiquity, in oblong folio, written with four columns on each page.

How these precious fragments came into such a place is not easily understood, the rather since we have been recently assured that the manuscript of which they formed a part had long been in the library of the monastery, and inserted in the old catalogues[1]. The forty-three leaves thus rescued he of course easily got for asking; but on finding that further portions of the same work (containing Isaiah and 1. 4 Maccabees) yet survived, he told the monks that their probable date was as remote as the *fourth* century, and thereupon they were immediately withdrawn from his view: he was only permitted to copy one leaf, comprising the last page of Isaiah and the first of Jeremiah. Thus baulked for a while, he brought to Europe the portion he had secured, which he published in 1846 as the *Codex Frederico-Augustanus*. It has since been noticed that he gave at the time no account of the manner in which the leaves had been obtained; but such information he has withheld in several other instances[2], and in this case he could scarcely have afforded it without frustrating his hope of getting the rest of the volume on some future visit. When at S. Catherine's for the second time in 1853, he could gain no tidings of the leaves he had left behind, and concluded that they had been carried off by some richer or more favoured collector: accordingly, in mere despair, he published in his *Monumenta Sacra Inedita*, vol. i. 1855, his transcript of the two pages he had copied in 1844. At the beginning of 1859, however, he went for the third time into the East, being on this occasion under the protection of the Emperor of Russia, the great champion of the Eastern Church. He had been for five days the guest of

[1] See Callinicos of Sinai's letter to Mr. J. S. Davies, in the *Guardian* of May 27, 1863.

[2] E. g. Evan. ΓΘΛ and Act. lo^{ti}.

the convent, and was on the eve of departure on the 4th of February, when on their return from a walk, during which the conversation had turned on the Greek text of the Old Testament, the Steward (*οἰκόνομος*) brought out to him from a corner of his own cell a manuscript of Scripture written on loose leaves and wrapped in a red cloth, such as the Orientals usually employ for that purpose. To Tischendorf's deep joy and astonishment, he had now before him the treasure he had so long been searching for; and that night there was no sleep for him:—*quippe dormire nefas videbatur*. It was found to contain much more than he had thought or hoped for:—a further portion of the Septuagint version (but this had become a secondary matter); the New Testament absolutely entire; the Epistle ascribed to the Apostle Barnabas, and certainly written not much later than his age, now for the first time found in the original Greek throughout; a large fragment of the Shepherd of Hermas also in Greek; these two books having been publicly read in the congregation before the canon of Scripture was finally settled, towards the close of the fourth century. Barnabas he transcribed that same night, and soon obtained a letter from Cyril the librarian to the superiors of the monastery at S. Catherine's in Cairo, which procured for him permission to copy the manuscript in the latter place, to which it was brought for that purpose on February 24. Two months were devoted by Tischendorf to this task, the book being doled out to him by quaternions, or eight leaves at a time, his assistants being two natives, a doctor of medicine and a druggist. As might have been expected from so much haste and such helpers, the result of their labours proved but loose and unsatisfactory, especially as regards the numerous changes in the original writing made by various hands at different periods.

By this time, however, Tischendorf had devised a more

promising scheme. He had persuaded the brethren that such a monument of ancient piety and learning would be a fit present for their patron the Emperor Alexander II.; and although the proper arrangements for completing the gift could not be made while the see of Sinai was vacant by reason of the death of its archbishop, the ex-patriarch Constantius, he was provisionally entrusted with the Codex Sinaiticus at Cairo on the 28th of September (though not without some opposition, as he tells us), at least for the purpose of preparing a correct edition of its contents. He submitted it early in November at St. Petersburg to the Emperor of Russia, who liberally undertook to defray the cost of a splendid edition of 300 copies, which should appear in 1862 as a memorial of the thousandth anniversary of his kingdom. With the exception of a few leaves left at St. Petersburg for the purpose of making *facsimiles*, Tischendorf took the manuscript to Leipsic in May, 1860, where his edition, for which special type had now been cast, was commenced forthwith. The codex was studied at Leipsic by at least two English scholars in the summer of 1862, and we believe that it has since been given up to the Emperor of Russia, and remains in his possession at St. Petersburg. The reader will perhaps see hereafter that our narrative of the foregoing events, though particular, is not unnecessarily prolix or irrelevant.

Before quitting this part of our subject, it is right to state that the manuscript must have been inspected by two persons at Mount Sinai during the interval between its being first seen by Tischendorf in 1844 and its removal from the convent in 1859. In 1845 or 1846 the Russian Archimandrite Porphyrius examined it, observed that the New Testament formed a part of it, and published a tolerable account of its contents and the character of its text at St. Petersburg in 1856. This book, being written in the Russian language, was unknown to Tischendorf until it was shown to him at Constantinople in August 1859, by Prince Lobanow, the Russian embassador there. It subsequently appeared that Porphyrius brought with him from Sinai some fragments of the Codex Sinaiticus itself, containing portions of Genesis and of Numbers v.—vii., which had been applied long before to the binding of some other books. Again, a little later than Porphyrius, Major Macdonald glanced at what seems to be the same copy:—it was kept wrapped up in a cloth: there were several columns on each page (three at least, perhaps four), and it was affirmed by the monks that the manuscript, which opened at some part of the New Testament, was of the fourth century, the very date which Tischendorf in 1844 had taught them to assign to it. Of these two witnesses in confirmation of Tischendorf's narrative, perfectly independent of him and of each other, Porphyrius, who is by far the more explicit, is the rather entitled to regard, inasmuch as he has since become involved in a controversy with Tischendorf, on his part angry and unintelligent enough, as to the merits of the text of this manuscript, which would certainly render him unwilling to lend his adversary support, any further than truth and the exigency of the case might compel.

To satisfy the reasonable curiosity excited among Biblical students by the report of his great discovery, Tischendorf put forth at Leipsic, about the end of 1860, his *Notitia Editionis Codicis Bibliorum Sinaitici;* but of its 124 pages only 44 relate to that manuscript, the rest being devoted to a description of other precious documents which he had brought to Europe, chiefly to enrich the imperial library of St. Petersburg. He afforded us some notion of what we might expect from the publication of the whole, as well by means of a *facsimile* of a portion of one page (Luke xxiv. 24—53), as from a transcript of eighteen pages in ordinary Greek type (nine of them taken from the New Testament), and less safely from a loose *sylva lectionum* culled almost at random from the other parts of the New Testament. By the end of 1862 his splendid *editio major* of the whole manuscript in four thin folio volumes was ready, and was first seen in England early in January, 1863. Of the 300 copies of which it is composed, 200 seem to have been absorbed as presents from the Emperor to various public bodies (chiefly in his own dominions) and to a few learned men. The rest were given up to Tischendorf for sale, their price being fixed by him at 230 thalers, or 34*l.* 10*s.* Those beyond whose reach such a work is placed, must yet needs confess that it is one of the most magnificent ever given to the world. The 345½ leaves of the original (199 of them containing portions of the Septuagint version) comprise three volumes (ii.—iv.) printed on paper at once thick and fine, the ink being made to resemble that of the original in colour, and the type being greatly varied, so as to imitate the various shapes and sizes of the letters employed by the scribe: the very spaces too between the letters have been carefully measured and represented with all faithfulness. The first volume contains (1) the Dedication to Alexander II.: (2) Prolegomena (13½ leaves), which through pressure of time are neither so full nor so elaborate as Tischendorf could easily have rendered them: (3) a Commentary or body of notes on the text exhibited in the other three volumes (45½ leaves), describing 15,000 changes made by contemporary or later hands, and other such matters: (4) twenty-one admirable *facsimile* plates, seventeen comprising whole pages of the manuscript [3],

[3] Those who use our collation may wish to know what pages are given in *facsimile*, the rather as we have employed them to check and correct the readings of the printed editions: they are Tobit ix. 2—x. 12. Isa. lxii. 11—lxiv. 6. Ps. cxviii. 169—

two containing numerous characteristic specimens of changes by later hands (a novel and most interesting feature of this edition), and the other two plates being covered with *fac-simile* specimens of other chief manuscripts, for comparison with the style of the Codex Sinaiticus. Finally, in April 1863, was published a cheap manual or popular edition, containing the New Testament, Barnabas and Hermas alone, in ordinary Greek type, with the Prolegomena and notes pertaining to the New Testament, &c., somewhat altered and slightly improved, accompanied by one *facsimile* plate (Heb. xii. 27—xiii. 25). This handsome volume, for all practical purposes, is amply sufficient for the use of those who have access to the larger edition as a book of reference. It is to be regretted, however, that the text of the smaller work, and more especially the notes of both, are rather inaccurately printed. Such errors as we have detected are placed at the end of this Volume, and that in no carping spirit as directed against Tischendorf, whose merits indeed are beyond all praise, but purely as a matter of necessity and duty to the reader [4].

cxxiii. 2. Cant. viii. 8.—Sapient. i. 11. Matth. v. 22—vi. 4: x. 17—xi. 5. Marc. xvi. 2—Luc. i. 56. Johann. v. 37—vi. 23. Gal. iv. 12—Eph. i. 9. Hebr. xii. 27—xiii. 25. Act. ii. 28—iii. 9. 1 Johann. v. 5—2 Johann. 7. Apoc. vii. 12—ix. 5: xxii. 19—Barnab. 2. Pastor Vision. 1. We have also been allowed to use Tregelles' collation of the Catholic Epistles with the Codex Sinaiticus itself, made at Leipsic in June, 1862 (see above, p. ix), and have carefully indicated the places in which Tregelles and Tischendorf differ.

[4] A fuller account of the circumstances attending the discovery of Cod. Sinaiticus is given in Tischendorf's "Aus dem heiligen Lande" (Leipzig, 1862).

CHAPTER II.

PALAEOGRAPHICAL DESCRIPTION OF THE MANUSCRIPT.

The Codex Sinaiticus consists, as we have before stated, of 345½ leaves of very fine and beautiful vellum, probably fabricated from the skins of antelopes or asses, each leaf being even at present as large as 13½ inches in length by 14⅞ inches high, although marginal notes have sometimes been partially cut off by the ancient binder. The volume was originally arranged by quaternions, each consisting of four sheets or eight leaves, one animal contributing only a single sheet or two leaves of such unusual size. The writing on each page is distributed into four columns, an arrangement quite unique so far as we know, each column containing 48 lines of from 12 to 14 letters each, the characters being *uncial* or capitals, formed separately and unconnected with each other, without spaces between the words or breathings (except ἁ Gal. v. 21), or accents, or the iota *ascript* or *postscript*; the marks of punctuation also being exceedingly few. Our *Facsimiles* (1) and (2)[1] will convey some notion

[1] It may help some readers if we print these passages in common type: (1) is the celebrated passage 1 John v. 6—9: *τω ῦδατι μονον|αλλ εν τω ῦδατι|και τω αιματι και|το π̄ν̄ᾱ εστιν το|μαρτυρουν οτι το|π̄ν̄ᾱ εστιν η αλη|θεια οτι οι τρεισ ει|σιν οι μαρτυρου̅|τεσ το π̄ν̄ᾱ και το ῦ|δωρ και το αιμα|και οι τρεισ εισ το|εν εισιν ει την μαρ|τυριαν του θ̄ῡ λαμ|*. Here we see the familiar abridgement *π̄ν̄ᾱ* for *πνευμα* in two places, ˉ over *υ* at the end of l. 8 stands for *ν*: *των ανων* (i. e. *ανθρωπων*), for *του θ̄ῡ* (i. e. *θεου*), is a later correction, about which we shall speak hereafter.

(2) is John vi. 14, 15: *ησεν σημειον ελε|γον· ουτοσ εστιν| αληθωσ ο προφη|τησ ο εισ τον κοσμο̅|ερχομενοσ·|ισ ουν γνουσ οτι|*

of the square, plain, yet noble style of the hand-writing, which bears the closest resemblance in shape to that of the Herculanean papyri, none of which can be dated below A.D. 79; although the letters in the Sinai manuscript (while they vary in size on different pages) are always decidedly the larger and more bold. The scribe is never careful to end a word at the close of a line, since even *εν*, *επ*, *απ*, and *ου|κ* or *ου|χ* are habitually found divided: yet he scarcely ever places any other letter at the end of a line than one of the vowels or liquids, or *σ*, or gamma when it stands before another consonant[2], except very rarely in the case of proper names, as *φιλιπ|πος*, Acts viii. 5. 30: *ιοπ|πην*, xi. 13: *αγριπ|πα*, xxv. 26; xxvi. 19: *ατ|ταλιαν*, xiv. 25. Where lists of names or an

μελλουσιν ερχε|σθαι και αρπαζειν|αυτον και αναδι|κνυναι βασιλεα| φευγει παλιν εισ το|οροσ μονοσ αυτοσ. Here we find three stops, one in the middle (l. 2), one upper (l. 5), one lower (l. 12), all by the first hand: ¯ again stands for *ν* at the end of the line (l. 4): all the changes are by a later hand, except probably $\overline{\text{NA}}$ and Δ in the right margin, which are in red ink in the original MS. Of these $\overline{\text{NA}}$ (51) is the proper number of the Ammonian section, Δ (4) the corresponding Eusebian Canon. (Scrivener's *Plain Introduction*, pp. 50—53.)

[2] See *Journal of Sacred Literature for April*, 1863, No. V., p. 8. We may note a few such cases as *εχ|θροι*, Matt. x. 36; *κλαυθ|μος*, *ibid.* xxii. 13; Luke xiii. 28; *σαβ|βατων*, Acts xvi. 13; *αριθ|μον*, Apoc. ix. 16. It has also been remarked that no line in the Cod. Sinaiticus begins with any combination of letters which might not commence a Greek word, unless it be *θμ* in Matt. viii. 12; xxv. 30; John vi. 10; Acts xxi. 35; Apoc. vii. 4. Inasmuch as *θμ* is found at the beginning of *Coptic* words (Herod. ii. 166, &c.), it has been ingeniously suggested that this apparent exception to the scribe's general practice is a proof that he copied line for line from an *Egyptian* papyrus, to the writer of which such forms would be familiar.

enumeration of several particulars occurs, each member mostly forms a separate line, *versus*, or *στίχος* proper (e. g. Luke iii. 24—38; Rom. viii. 35. 38, 39; Gal. v. 19—23; Acts vi. 5; Apoc. xviii. 13), determined by the sense. There are no letters larger than the rest at the beginning of sentences, though the continuity of the text is much broken by a line being left incomplete (sometimes it will contain only two or three letters), in which case the first letter in the next line mostly stands out of the range of the column, encroaching on the margin (*see Facsimile* 2, *ll.* 5, 6). This manuscript must have been derived from one more ancient, in which the lines were similarly divided, since the writer occasionally omits just the number of letters which would suffice to fill a line, and that to the utter ruin of the sense; as if his eye had heedlessly wandered to the line immediately below. Instances of this want of care will be found Luke xxi. 8; xxii. 25, perhaps John iv. 45; xii. 25, where complete lines are omitted: John xix. 26; Heb. xiii. 18 (partly corrected); Apoc. xviii. 16; xix. 12; xxii. 2, where the copyist passed in the middle of a line to the corresponding portion of the line below. It must be confessed, indeed, that the Codex Sinaiticus abounds with similar errors of the eye and pen, to an extent not unparalleled, but happily rather unusual in documents of first-rate importance; so that Tregelles has freely pronounced that "the state of the text, as proceeding from the first scribe, may be regarded as *very rough*" (N. T. Part ii. p. 2). Letters and words, even whole sentences, are frequently written twice over, or begun and immediately cancelled: while that gross blunder technically known as Homoeoteleuton (*ὁμοιοτέλευτον*), whereby a clause is omitted because it happens to end in the same words as the clause preceding, occurs no less than 115 times in the N. T., though the defect is often supplied by a more recent hand. We have thought it right to record all such clerical errors in their proper place for the reader's information; but while they must be admitted to deform the face of this exquisite relique of the primitive ages of our faith, they need not be held to detract materially from its intrinsic value, much less ought they to militate against our conviction of its very high antiquity.

In the deliberate judgment of Tischendorf, who has of course the best right to be heard on such a point, no less than four different hands were employed on the Codex Sinaiticus. He believes that the scribe by him called A wrote the fragment of Chronicles, 1 Maccabees, the last 4½ leaves of 4 Maccabees, Barnabas' Epistle, and the whole N. T. excepting about six leaves. To B he ascribes the Prophetical Books and Hermas' Shepherd: to C the Poetical Books of the Old Testament, written in *στίχοι* or verses clause by clause, according to the sense, with but two columns on a page, just as in the great Codex Vaticanus, which in all other parts has three columns, but in the Poetical Books only two. To D he gives Tobit, Judith, the first 3½ leaves of 4 Maccabees, and in the N. T. leaves 10 (Matt. xvi. 9—xviii. 12), 15 (*ibid.* xxiv. 36—xxvi. 6), 28, 29 (Mark xiv. 54—Luke i. 56), 88 (1 Thess. ii. 14—v. 28), 91 (Heb. iv. 16—viii. 1), and possibly the first 32 lines of the Apocalypse (i. 1—5 to $\overline{\iota\upsilon}$ $\overline{\chi\upsilon}$, fol. 126*), the last mainly upon grounds expressly assigned, which we shall speak of hereafter. He further states that A and B much resemble each other, as also do C and D. On the other hand Tregelles, who by Tischendorf's permission examined the manuscript for three whole days in 1862, has observed no such diversity in the writing as would necessarily lead us to refer the several portions to different scribes; and we know that Woide has suspected the same change of hands in the portion of the Codex Alexandrinus which he edited, and others too, with still greater show of probability, in the case of Codex Augiensis; though there is little doubt that each of these is the work of but one penman, whose hand would naturally vary a little with the quality of his materials, and as he became familiar with or weary of his task [3].

Those who have not inspected the manuscript for themselves are scarcely entitled to express an opinion on a matter like this. We may venture, however, to say, that the published *Facsimile* plates (for the moveable type of the larger edition can hardly be relied upon in a question so delicate) show no such diversity as would have suggested to us Tischendorf's conclusions. Notice, however, the peculiar shape of *omega*, with its tall central stroke, represented in our *Facsimile* (7). This form occurs in none of Tischendorf's plates, by him assigned to C or D, or in those portions of the N. T. in moveable type which are imputed to D, but eight times in the two he ascribes to B (II. XVII.), six times in one of A's (V), only once in A's other nine, always towards the end of lines, mostly reduced in size, and except on Plate V. mixed up with the more familiar ω [4]. We must add too, that the

[3] A writer in the *Christian Remembrancer*, April, 1863, No. cxx. p. 399, otherwise well-informed, can have had no practical experience on this head when he said, "If it be decided that Professor Tischendorf is mistaken, this must of course diminish our confidence in his judgment." Why so? The formal style maintained in uncial codices admits of much less *individuality* of character than the free running-hand which the ancients as well as ourselves used in common life; yet in our law courts persons who have made the subject their special study, and whose honesty is beyond suspicion, perpetually give the most contradictory evidence about hand-writing, and that in cases where men's honour and liberty, almost their lives, are at stake.

[4] It is quite worthy of notice, that although > is sometimes placed in the margin of the New Testament to point out quotations from the Old, and that too by the first hand, e.g. Acts

few leaves of the N. T. ascribed by Tischendorf to D are much freer from *itacisms*, or instances of false spelling, than those on either side of them: the transition is quite remarkable from leaf 9 of A to leaf 10 (Matt. xvi. 9—xviii. 12) of D, and then back again to leaf 11 of A, as the reader may see for himself by consulting our collation. These remarks, so far as they extend, would seem to suggest *two* scribes, A being identical with B, and possibly C with D; the members of which pairs Tischendorf declares to be much alike; but whether the actual penmen be one, or two, or four, is of the less importance, as (in the N. T. certainly, and most probably in the Old) the whole work was clearly executed at the same time, and transcribed from the same older copy.

Nearly all Biblical manuscripts abound in changes brought

xxvi. 23; though more frequently by later scribes, as in Matth. i. 23; ii. 6, &c.: this mark is never met with in the N. T. at the end of a line for the mere purpose of filling up a blank space (which is its usual office in the Old Testament portion of Cod. Sinaiticus and in some other manuscripts), except in the leaves assigned to D, *on every one of which it repeatedly occurs*, viz. 219 times in the other six leaves, four times in Apoc. i. 1—5 (*see* p. xvi). Elsewhere > is found in only four places which have suffered correction (Matth. vi. 28; xxii. 9; Luke xi. 36; xii. 58), being used, like — in 1 Cor. xv. 22, merely to cover erasures. Moreover, the apostrophus, though frequently employed in the Old Testament to divide syllables in the *middle* of a word, is never so used throughout the N. T. itself; while in the Shepherd of Hermas, which closes the volume, and is referred by Tischendorf to the scribe B, we read **αγ'γελια, αγ'γελον, αλ'λα** thrice, **μελ'λοντεσ, πολ'λουσ, ελατ'τονι, εχ'μαλωτισμον**, &c., and > several times at the end of lines. These minute points, insignificant as they may seem, go far to support Tischendorf's notion that the manuscript is the work of several distinct hands. See also p. xxxii, note 7.

by more recent critics into the text, varying widely in age and value, all which an editor is bound to record and discriminate with his utmost care. Speaking generally, the most venerable documents, as having passed through many hands during a long course of ages, may be expected to cost the greatest labour in this particular: Codd. Bezae and Claromontanus, for example (in the latter Tischendorf detects nine different emendators), are full of corrections, which again will often be withdrawn by yet later scribes; so that much patience and fixed attention are needed to discover the original reading, and to trace the successive changes the text has undergone. It is no slight proof of the early date of Codex Sinaiticus, that it is covered with such alterations, brought in by *at least* ten different revisers, some of them systematically spread over every page, others occasional or limited to separate portions of the manuscript, many of them being contemporaneous with the first writer, far the greater part belonging to the sixth or seventh century, a few being as recent as the twelfth. A glance at our collation will show both the extent and character of these emendations, and that the reader may the more easily judge of their relative weight and importance, we shall give some account of each class separately, illustrating our description by the annexed *Facsimiles* (Nos. 3 to 15).

(1) Corrections by the original scribe, *primâ manu* (*p. m.*) as they are termed, can hardly be deemed various readings. The penman, proceeding with his monotonous task rapidly and perhaps a little heedlessly, falls into some clerical error, which he immediately discovers and proceeds to set right; in a few manuscripts (e. g. Codex Bezae) by washing out the writing fluid, which was rather a kind of paint than ink, so that what he first copied can only just be perceived under his amended reading: in others, as in Codex Sinaiticus, by

placing points or some such marks (e. g. ' ') over the letters or words he wishes to revoke. To give one instance out of thousands. In Act. iv. 3, the text being *την αυριον ην γαρ*, while he was writing the first *ην*, the copyist allowed his eye to wander over *αυριον* to the second *ην*, and so he begins to write *γαρ*: finding out his mistake as soon as *γ* is finished, he simply places a point over that letter to cancel it, and proceeds with *αυριον ην γαρ* as if no error had been made. We have expressly recorded all these lapses, trifling as they are.

(2) The next class of corrections is far more important. When a manuscript was completely written, it seems to have been subjected to two several kinds of revision. It was collated with the copy from which it was derived, in order to eliminate whatever mere clerical blunders had not been noted at the time of writing; the person who executed this office was named the *comparer* (*ὁ ἀντιβάλλων*), being usually the scribe himself. The second process was that of the *διορθωτὴς* or *corrector*, seldom the same person as the comparer, whose business was to revise the text, often by the aid of a second manuscript varying a little from that first employed[5]. From a careful examination of the hand-writing and reddish-brown colour of the ink, Tischendorf is led to believe that the duty of *corrector*, at least in the N. T. portion of Cod. Sinaiticus, was performed by the scribe D[6], who wrote those six or seven leaves of the N. T. text itself (see p. xvi), and he

[5] See Tischendorf, *Cod. Sin. Prolegomena*, fol. 9, edit. maj.; Tregelles' *Horne's Introd.* vol. iv. p. 85; Scrivener's *Plain Introduction*, pp. 46-7, 388.

[6] Chiefly it should seem from Tobit v. 6, Tab. XIX., which he judges to have been written by D, and where he considers the marginal *εισ γαρρασ κ.τ.λ.* as p. m.

assigns to him *as corrector* the symbol A*[7], as being contemporaneous and the most authoritative of them all. Our *Facsimile* (3) θουσ και βρεχι επι δικαιουσ και αδικουσ (ϗ for και twice), Matt. v. 45, affords a fair specimen of A* in all but the shade of the ink; θουσ alone is by the first scribe, yet but for the smaller writing in the margin, και βρεχι επι would hardly be distinguished from it. The line placed under θ is intended to mark the close of an Ammonian section, and is probably by a later pen. The most important addition ascribed to A* is John xxi. 25, which (as Tischendorf holds) was omitted in the original draught. If the Homoeoteleuton supplied in 1 Cor. xiii. 1, 2 be truly referred to the same corrector, he must have done his work before the running titles were added at the head of each page, inasmuch as προσ κορινθιουσ α is much displaced by it: but this note contains (if we may trust the type of the larger edition) no less than four examples of that form of ω which is not found in the *Facsimiles* of D (see p. xvii).

(3) The corrector indicated simply by A, though separate (as it would seem) from A*, is described by Tischendorf as "et formis et atramento primam manum tantum non adaequans" (N. T. *note* 14—18 on fol. 48*): his writing is hardly less ancient or elegant, and occurs throughout the whole N. T. except the Apocalypse (and only four times in the Catholic Epistles), chiefly to amend gross and obvious mistakes, or to supply words and clauses omitted, whether through Homoeoteleuton or otherwise. Occasionally his changes are made over the original text itself, in letters of the same size, and very like it in appearance (e. g. John

[7] This is the ultimate designation given to him by Tischendorf: in some places however (e. g. Matth. v. 45; 1 Cor. xiii. 1, 2) he is merely called A.

ii. 3), but far more frequently they are found in the margin, or at the top or bottom of the columns (referred to their proper places by the words *ανω* or *κατω*), in minute and very neat characters. Our specimen *Facsimile* (4), *ο ευρων την ψυχην αυτου απολεσι* (i. e. *-σει*) *αυτην*, Matt. x. 39, stands at the foot of a column, the anchor-shaped obelus to the left referring to a similar mark in the margin of that part of the column where the words are to be inserted, the numerals *in red ink* Ϙϛ (97) and *γ* (3) being respectively the proper Ammonian section and Eusebian canon, also referred to their right place by ·/·

(4) A obliq. is represented in *Facsimile* (5) by *εαυτουσ* between *αλλα αυτοι εν εαυ* and *τοισ μετρουντεσ*, 2 Cor. x. 12. The letters are oblique, leaning slightly to the right, and are somewhat inferior to those of A proper both in elegance and date.. Only fifteen instances of A obliq. are met with, all in St. Paul's Epistles, from fol. 77 to fol. 89.

(5) The corrector B is a full age below A, and may be conjecturely placed at the end of the sixth century. From *Facsimile* (6) Matt. ix. 10 (where he supplies *ελθοντεσ* in the margin after *και αμαρτωλοι* of the scribe) it will be seen that the strokes of B are thicker, more firm, but less neat than those of A. Occasionally B's writing is much larger than in our *Facsimile*, e. g. *απηλθον* added to the *text*, John vi. 22. This corrector has only touched the Gospels, and especially the early chapters of St. Matthew. Indeed, he has much deformed the first leaves of the N. T. by adding breathings, accents, stops, and apostrophi, till after a few pages he gradually got tired of his useless labour.

(6) B[a] is employed to indicate an ancient scholar-like hand, met with only in the early pages of St. Matthew, which fluctuates in appearance between A and B, and is

probably different from each of them. In *Facsimile* (7), Matt. iii. 13, 14, *ιωαννησ* in the margin, with the ω shaped as described above (p. xvii) is referred by the marks ⸪ ./· to its place in the original text *του ὁ δε διε*, where the aspirate was added by B.

(7) Far the greater part of the changes throughout the whole manuscript belong to C, of about the seventh century, before breathings and accents became habitual [8]. The frequent repetition of the note (C *cum* Steph.) in the ensuing collation will prove that one object of this corrector was to assimilate the Codex to manuscripts more in vogue in his time, and approaching far nearer to our modern Textus Receptus. For his style of writing (not at all remarkable for its beauty) see our *Facsimile* (8), Luke xxiv. 51, ϗ (*i. e.* *και*) *ανεφερετο εις τον* $\overline{ουνον}$ (*i. e.* *ουρανον*), which stands at the head of a column, and is referred to its proper place by the sign ⊬. Moreover, the later alterations seen in *Facsimiles* (1) (2) are all the work of C, viz. the faint interlinear *ων ανω̄ν* (*i. e.* *ανθρωπων*), 1 John v. 9, and the marginal *ῒνα ποιησωσιν*, the interlinear *ανεχωρησεν*, and the dots over the words he rejects in John vi. 15.

The following hands C^b, C^c, C^{c*} are little posterior to C in date. C^b is much used in the Old Testament, occasionally in the Gospels; C^c in John xiii. 26, and 33 times in the Apocalypse (wherein C occurs no less than 290 times); C^{c*} five times in the Apocalypse. In the Gospels and Apocalypse Tischendorf indicates C by C^a, by way of distinction, reserving C for a few cases, wherein, we presume, he is doubtful by which member of this class the change was made.

[8] C contains a few of them, e. g. ἣ John ix. 31; 2 John 12; ἐν John xvii. 22; ὅτι Acts xv. 7: yet even the first hand has ἃ Gal. v. 21, and *possibly* A^a in John xxi. 25.

(8) *Facsimile* (9), Matt. xxiii. 35, supplies an example of the style of C[b], where to the reading of the text *αιματοσ ζαχαριου* is appended in the margin *ῡιου βαραχιου*. This person's hand is easily known by his appending to *ρτυφ* and sometimes to *ι*, tails which make with the vertical lines of the letters at their bottom an obtuse angle to the left. He often recalls a reading of the original scribe, which C[a] had banished, so that he had before him a text somewhat different from C[a]'s, to which he corrected the manuscript.

(9) C[c] seems to have had familiar access to the Codex Sinaiticus for many years, as specimens of his hand-writing (somewhat like that of C[b]) are scattered over its pages in inks of various shades. He would now and then place the abridgment *ωρ* for *ὡραῖον*, "beautiful," in the margin of passages he piously admired. See *Facsimile* (10).

(10) C[c*] is rude, but, like the rest of its class, is without breathings or accents. See *Facsimile* (11), Apoc. xi. 1 *margin* : ·/. *ϗ* (*i. e. και*) *εστηκει ο αγγελοσ* [*λεγων not in Facsim.*]. C[c*] occurs also in Apoc. xi. 3; 8; xii. 6; xviii. 11, and he probably wrote *τελοσ* at the end of the Church lesson, Act. x. 16.

By this time the primitive writing, especially on the smooth side of the vellum which had been nearest the animal's body, became so much faded through age, that (as in the case of the great Codex Vaticanus and others) it was thought necessary to retrace the original strokes, which seems to have been done carefully and faithfully, if not with all possible regard for neatness. The renovator now and then introduces, perhaps by mere accident, some slight change into the text, whether correcting an error of the scribe (e. g. Act. iv. 15 *κελευσαντεσ*), or bringing in one of his own (e. g. Mark i. 7 *ειμη* for *ειμι ι*). This retracing of the lines of the text must have been accomplished about the eighth century;

for while the work of all the correctors we have yet enumerated is occasionally covered by the operation, it never touches the notes of the reviser we shall next name (if indeed he is not the same person), whose style bespeaks the 8th or 9th century.

(11) D much resembles in manner Cod. Y of the Gospels, and Cod. B of the Apocalypse. His corrections are not found in the N. T., but (if the hand be the same in all places) twenty times in the Shepherd of Hermas (the first sixteen lines of which he has defaced by coarse breathings and accents), and in the Old Testament. *Facsimile* (12) ·/. κάτω ἐμβλέψονται ꝁ is from Isaiah viii. 22. To him (D[a]) may be ascribed some Arabic scrawl spread over the manuscript, earlier than the elegant note in that language at the foot of the three columns containing Apoc. vii. 12—viii. 12.

(12) The last corrector E appears but three times in the N. T., and seems full as late as the twelfth century. Besides his placing θὲ above οσ in the great text 1 Tim. iii. 16, *Facsimile* (13) το τησ ευσεβειασ μυστηριον οσ (θεὸσ E) ε, this critic puts ἄνῳ (*i. e.* ἀνθρώπῳ *with* ι *subscript*) after γοντεσ ει εξεστῑ (*i. e.* εξεστιν) in *Facsimile* (14) Matth. xix. 3, and probably supplies παίδα in Act. iii. 13.

It will readily be imagined how vastly the labour and anxiety of a critical editor must be enhanced by so extensive a mass of alterations, many of them being corrections of corrections, in such different hands and spread over the course of many centuries. Patient toil, nice tact, and ripe experience have enabled Tischendorf to decide with reasonable confidence on the date and character of the great majority of these changes: but he is occasionally obliged to confess his doubts and perplexity, or even to change in the larger edition the decision he had given in the *Notitia*, in the smaller edition (which we have followed), the verdict of the larger. Meanwhile we are thus presented with a kind of history of the sacred text and of the changes it underwent from time to time; not to mention that the occurrence of so many hands, in such various shades of ink, and so diversified in style, forms a powerful argument for the high antiquity of the copy to which these annotations are appended.

Tischendorf affords us specimens of about four other persons' writing, scattered throughout the margin of this manuscript, but having no bearing upon the criticism of the text. Such are our Arabic notes appended to the Apocalypse, less rude in style than D[a] (p. xxv), and not earlier than the tenth century, and several subscriptions of about the twelfth century; one by a monk named Dionysius (vol. ii. fol. 16), given in our *Facsimile* (15)[9], a signature by one Hilarion (vol. ii. fol. 41*), and three by one Theophylact (vol. ii. fol. 42; vol. iii. foll. 73*; 112*). Tischendorf conjectures that these three were brethren of the Convent of St. Catherine, whither the Codex may have been brought on its foundation by the Emperor Justinian, about A.D. 530.

If we turn from the earliest of these second-hand emendations to the original manuscript, the contrast is great enough to impress the least instructed reader. There is a primitive simplicity about its whole appearance which is very striking[1],

[9] This subscription is full of those abridgments, which by the twelfth century had become habitual. It runs *μνήσθητι κύριε τὴν ψυχὴν τοῦ ἁμαρτωλοῦ διουνυσίου μοναχοῦ ὅταν ἔλθησ ἐν τῇ βασιλείᾳ σου.* We find *α* with *χ* over it thus used for *μοναχου* in Act. lo[ti]. (Brit. Mus. Add. 20,003) fol. 57a, and elsewhere.

[1] As in Cod. Bezae, and most other of our old documents, the

and when we come to scrutinize each letter separately, the result is much the same. Such testing characters as *Alpha*, *Delta*, *Epsilon*, *Pi*, *Sigma* are as unadorned as possible, without flourishes, knobs, or thickened points at their extremities [2]. The only apparent exceptions which can be alleged is the less usual shape of *omega* mentioned above (pp. xvii, xxi, xxiii) as peculiar to Tischendorf's scribes A and B (though even this occurs in the Codex Vaticanus, *see* Cod. Sinait. Tab. XX.), and that form of *mu* frequent through the Cod. Sinaiticus (*though only at or near the end of a line*) which is represented in our *Facsimile* (2), line 4. Something approximate to this *mu* may be seen at times in the running hand of Mr. Babington's papyri of Hyperides, and it is quite ordinary in Cod. Z of the Gospels, whose date is the sixth century. So far as we know (for who will venture to answer for the Codex Vaticanus?) our copy is the oldest which exhibits it, and that only towards the end of lines, in which place all known scribes are prone to quit the conventional hand prevailing in formal documents, for the more familiar manner of common life; being naturally led to that practice by the use of those smaller letters, employed in all the uncial copies at the close of some lines, in order to economize the space [3]. Both the *mu* and *omega* of this shape are frequent in the titles and sub-

regularity of the writing is maintained by means of lines previously ruled on one side of the blank leaf, and easily seen through the vellum, the spaces having been accurately measured and noted with a needle or bodkin (*acus*).

[2] *Sigma*, however, has the knob at the lower curve of the second C in *αναστασεωσ* Act. ii. 31, Tischendorf's Tab. XIII.: see also our *Facsimiles* (2), (9); and a few other such cases occur.

[3] Thus some codices which have a very primitive look are

scriptions to Codd. Sin. and Vatic., but these in Cod. Vat. are doubtless a little later than the text.

As regards the extreme scarcity of marks of punctuation, also, the two manuscripts are near akin. In the Hyperides papyri are no stops at all, in the Herculanean very few: the labours of so many renovators and correctors render the question more difficult as regards Codd. Sin. and Vatic., yet some in both copies are certainly by the first hand, though oftentimes a blank space will be found without any. In our *Facsimile* (2) the upper, middle, and lower single point, all occur, where the middle point seems to have the least power, though this distinction is far from constant. Occasionally, especially at the end of books, two points (:) will be found, as is represented by our collation in *αμην*: Apoc. vii. 12; xxii. 21. In all later codices the stops are much more numerous and their system more complicated and regular.

We have already referred to the use of > both for noting Scripture quotations in the margin and as a flourish at the end of lines to fill up a blank space (*see* p. xvii, note 4): it is used for the latter purpose in the Hyperides, the Herculanean rolls, in the Sarravian Octateuch of the fourth century [4], and in a few codices of later date, as the Coislin Pentateuch of the sixth century, Codd. Augiensis, Sangallensis and its con-

detected as bearing a later date than would at first sight be imagined, by the cramped and more modern shape of the small final letters of a line. Tregelles (*Horne's Introd.* vol. iv. p. 202) notes this of Cod. U of the Gospels: but, except in the possible case of *mu*, no suspicion of the sort attaches to Cod. Sinaiticus.

[4] This precious manuscript is unfortunately scattered among different libraries, one leaf of Judges being at St. Petersburg, some leaves at Paris, the rest at Leyden. A fine *Facsimile* is given by Silvestre, *Paléographie Universelle*, No. 61; another by Tischendorf, Cod. Sin. Tab. XX.

tinuation Cod. Boernerianus of the ninth, Cod. M. Paul. of the tenth. The employment of the apostrophus also, to which we have before alluded (p. xviii, note 4), forms no objection to its early date, although it is sometimes added by a later hand. We often find it, as in Cod. Bezae, at the end of a proper name, though not very frequently *primâ manu* : Codd. Sinaiticus and Alexandrinus, &c., employ it besides at the end of words ending with *rho* (e. g. Cod. Sin. Mark xvi. 8); in certain portions of the former it is used to divide syllables, as it also appears in Cod. Claromontanus (e. g. *απ' ορφανισθεντεσ* 1 Thess. ii. 17); instances such as *τουτο'* (fol. 145, col. 4) and *οραματα'* (fol. 146*, col. 3), both in the "Shepherd," are more peculiar, if we may not say unprecedented.

The shape of the characters, the simplicity of the punctuation, and the employment of the marks just described, all tend to make us believe that the Codex Sinaiticus is coeval with its rival in the Vatican, and consequently a record of the fourth century of the Christian aera. The same inference may be fairly drawn from the absence of letters larger than the rest, employed, like our *capitals*, at the beginning of clauses or paragraphs. As early as the opening of the fifth century they were used by the writer of Codex Alexandrinus at the commencement of each Ammonian section, and elsewhere. Just as freely do they occur in Cod. Ephraemi, which is almost contemporary with Cod. Alex., and oftener still in later manuscripts. They are wanting only in Codd. Sinaiticus and Vaticanus; apparently in the Vatican Dion Cassius and in a fragment referred to the fourth century, containing some sixteen verses of St. John (Evan. N^b) underlying two several pieces of Syriac writing in the British Museum (Addl. MSS. 17,136); and certainly in the celebrated Sarravian Octateuch, which accord in this particular with the Herculanean and early Egyptian *papyri*.

Still more striking is the likeness which Cod. Sinaiticus bears to these records of the first century in respect to its outward form and arrangement. The latter are composed of narrow slips of the papyrus, the writing on which is seldom more than 2 or 2½ inches broad, glued together in parallel columns, and kept in scrolls which were unrolled at one end for the purpose of reading, and when read rolled up at the other. This fashion still prevails in the most venerated copies of the Old Testament on skins preserved in Jewish Synagogues; and the appearance of the Sinai manuscript, with its eight narrow columns (seldom exceeding two inches in breadth) exhibited on each open leaf, suggests at once the notion that it was transcribed line for line from some primitive papyrus, whether written in Egypt or elsewhere [5]. If high antiquity has been plausibly claimed for the great Vatican Bible because that, in common with the Vatican Dion Cassius and a few other books, it has *three* columns on the page, the argument is far more cogent when applied to the Sinai volume, which stands alone in containing *four*.

Nor, in estimating its date, must we forget the quality of the material on which it is written, or its present look and condition. The vellum leaves, now almost yellow in colour, are not only the largest, but among the finest and smoothest yet known; if not quite so thin as those of the Codex Claromontanus of St. Paul's Epistles, the skins of none but the very oldest documents can be compared to them in beauty The original ink, which varies in hue according as it was impressed on the rough or smooth side of the skin, where it has not been covered by the strokes of the renovator (*see* p. xxiv), is for the most part of a yellowish brown, occasionally of an

[5] The reader will please to weigh what has been alleged on this head above, pp. xiv, xv, and note 2.

ashy tinge; the emendations of A[a] (*see* p. xx) are of a reddish cast; the shades of ink observable in the countless corrections of different scribes through a period of several centuries, are beyond the reach of language to discriminate: those indicated by D and E look very black, as in Tischendorf's *Facsimiles.* Many pages, especially on the inner and smoother side of the vellum, have suffered much from age, and yet scarce a single word is absolutely illegible. Hence, though the general semblance of the whole work is somewhat less worn than that of Cod. Vaticanus (whose extensive hiatus prove how carelessly it has been kept), when it comes to be contrasted with such a manuscript as the illustrated Dioscorides at Vienna (whose age is fixed by internal evidence at about A.D. 500), that interesting and valuable manuscript looks comparatively quite fresh and modern [6].

The contents also of the Cod. Sinaiticus lend further credibility to our persuasion of its early date. Out of its 345½ leaves, 199, or reckoning as we ought the 43 leaves of the Cod. Frederico-Augustanus (*see* p. vii) 242, are taken up by the Septuagint version of the Old Testament, and comprise (we name them in the order wherein they stand) portions of the books of Chronicles, Ezra, Nehemiah, Esther, Tobit, and Judith, the first and fourth books of the Maccabees, Isaiah, Jeremiah, Joel, Obadiah, Jonah, Nahum, Habakkuk, Zephaniah, Haggai, Zechariah, Malachi. Then follow the poetical books, written in στίχοι, *versus*, or parallel clauses, regulated by the sense (*see* p. xiv), with but two columns on a page (herein also resembling the Codex Vaticanus), and that as a

[6] For this, and some other statements in my Introduction, I rest on the evidence of Dr. Tregelles, who bore testimony to them as an eye-witness on the occasion of a lecture I gave on the Codex Sinaiticus to the Plymouth Institution, Oct. 8, 1863.

matter of necessity by reason of the length of the *στίχοι*. These books are the Psalms, Proverbs, Ecclesiastes, Canticles, Wisdom, Ecclesiasticus, and Job. That the earlier portion of the Old Testament was once contained in this manuscript appears as well from the small fragment of the Pentateuch possessed by Porphyrius (*see* p. x), as from the numerals set in the outer margin at the head of the quaternions, which, though the work of a later hand, have evidently been substituted for others cut off in the binding[7]. The first extant leaf is the last of the thirty-fourth quaternion, so that 271 leaves must have perished before it, if each *quaternion* consisted of eight, which is not always the case[8]. The last numeral is 92, on the first page of the Shepherd, of which but seven leaves survive, thus making the number of leaves down to the place where Hermas breaks off 724 at the utmost.

[7] In Cod. Bezae and many other copies these numerals stand at the foot of the *last* page of a quaternion. Besides these more recent numbers in very black ink, in parts of the Old Testament and after the Gospels in the New, an older set (elsewhere cut off), in red ink, of the eighth or ninth century, occur at the top of the inner margin, each number being greater by unity than the corresponding one in black ink (e. g. 82 for 81 &c.); a difference which is probably accidental. In connexion with these quaternions we obtain another argument for the six leaves assigned to D (*see* pp. xvi, xviii, note 4) being written by another hand from the rest of the manuscript. *Each neighbouring pair of these leaves comprises one skin or sheet:* viz. foll. 10 and 15 the 2nd sheet of quaternion 74; foll. 28 and 29 the 4th sheet of quaternion 76; foll. 88 and 91 the 3rd sheet of quaternion 84. This cannot be the result of chance.

[8] E. g. the 78th consisted of but seven leaves, the 91st of two, the 80th and 90th of but six, and were more properly called *ternions*. Eusebius recognizes both arrangements (*τρισσὰ καὶ τετρασσὰ Vit. Const.* iv. 37).

But our main concern is with the N. T., which this precious record alone contains entire among all manuscripts possessing any real claim to antiquity. The four Gospels stand in their usual order, then follow St. Paul's Epistles,—that to the Hebrews preceding the four Pastoral Letters, then the Acts and Catholic Epistles in their usual order, then the Apocalypse. In postponing the Acts to the Pauline Epistles, our manuscript is only followed by four comparatively modern copies[9]; but this position of the Hebrews is found in all other codices of the first rank excepting the Claromontanus:—such are the great uncial Codd. Alexandrinus, Vaticanus, Ephraemi, and (according to Tischendorf) Coislin. 202 (ABCH), not to insist on at least nine later MSS. written in cursive letters. Since Epiphanius, who flourished towards the end of the third century, testifies that the Epistle to the Hebrews stood before the first to Timothy in some copies extant in his time, we cannot but regard this order as one presumption the more in favour of the remote antiquity of the Codex Sinaiticus, the rather as it is therein countenanced by the oldest and best authorities hitherto known.

A yet stronger argument to the same effect may be drawn from the supplementary matter appended in this copy to the N. T., so as indeed to form an integral portion of it. It is well known that down to as late a period as the middle of the fourth century the canon of Scripture, *in respect to a few books more or less*, was rather unsettled[1], nor was it until

[9] Yet three of these exhibit a very remarkable text:—the Leicester (Evan. 69), Montfort's (Evan. 61), and Faber's (Evan. 90): the fourth (Bodl. Canon. 34) is uncollated, except in the Apocalypse (k^{scr}).

[1] Eusebius, *Eccles. Hist.* iii. 25, is the well-known leading passage on this subject. He divides the books into four classes,

the decrees of the Council of Laodicea (364 or 366), and of two or three yet later (e. g. Carthage 397), became generally received, that the Church laid aside the primitive custom of reading publicly in the congregation certain works which had never been regarded quite in the same light as Holy Scripture itself. Hence it is reasonable to infer, that manuscripts which contain compositions of such doubtful authority were written before the close of the fourth century, by which time they would have become mere cumbersome additions to a volume already large. It is one considerable proof of the venerable age of the Codex Alexandrinus that it contains the only known copy of Clement of Rome's celebrated Epistle to the Corinthians, though the force of the argument may be a little impaired by its being followed by part of a second Epistle which can hardly be genuine. Codex Sinaiticus exhibits to us moderns for the first time in full, commencing on the same page as the Apocalypse ends, the original Greek of the Epistle attributed to the Apostle Barnabas, and placed before the Apocalypse and the Acts in the curious and very ancient catalogue (doubtless drawn up some centuries before), still preserved in the Cod. Claromontanus of the sixth century. This same catalogue ends with "the

with the last of which, mere heretical works, *ἄτοπα καὶ δυσσεβῆ*, we have no concern. His first class comprises the *acknowledged*, *ὁμολογούμενα*, the Gospels, Acts, St. Paul's Epistles, 1 John, 1 Pet.: his second the *disputed*, *ἀντιλεγόμενα*, James, Jude, 2 Pet.; 2, 3 John: his third the *spurious*, *νόθα*, Acts of Paul, the Shepherd, Revelation of Peter, Barnabas, Apostolic Institutions. Clement is not named: the Apocalypse is placed with an expression of doubt both in the first and third class. In the third division (*also* termed by him that of the *ἀντιλεγόμενα*) some place the Gospel to the Hebrews. These *ἀντιλεγόμενα* however were read in churches (iii. 31), and "approved by most," *γνώριμα τοῖς πολλοῖς*.

Shepherd, the Acts of Paul, the Revelation of Peter:" while, in remarkable correspondence with it, Codex Sinaiticus closes with a fragment of Hermas' Shepherd, much of which we could previously read only in an old Latin translation. Add to this, that between the end of Barnabas and the beginning of Hermas are lost the last six leaves of quaternion 90, which might have contained either of the other books named in the Claromontane list, though the space would not suffice for Clement's Epistle, which does not appear in it.

Nothing can be more brief than the Titles and Subscriptions to the sacred books (all written by a contemporary of the scribe: *see* p. xxi), as found in Cod. Sinaiticus, and if they did not proceed from the original writers, they must yet needs be more ancient than the longer inscriptions we read elsewhere [2]. Thus the Gospels are headed only by ΚΑΤΑ ΜΑΘΘΑΙΟΝ, ΚΑΤΑ ΜΑΡΚΟΝ &c. in the Codd. Sin. and Vat., instead of ΕΥΑΓΓΕΛΙΟΝ ΚΑΤΑ Μ. of Codd. Alex. Ephraemi and the rest: the end is just as simple, and in St. Matthew Cod. Sin. has no subscription whatever. In the Acts the title of Cod. Sin. is merely ΠΡΑΞЄΙC, as contrasted with *πραξεισ* (Cod. Bez. *πραξισ*) *αποστολων* even of Codd. Vatic. and Bezae. The Epistles (as our collation will show) have only ΠΡΟC ΡѠΜΑΙΟΥC &c., like the other oldest manuscripts, in the room of the elaborate titles and full subscriptions attributed to Euthalius (A.D. 458), and seen in more recent copies. To ten of St. Paul's Epistles (as our collation will show) are appended notes expressing the number of *στίχοι* they respectively contain, and to Philemon *στιχων* only without numerals; but these annotations are all by a second though almost as ancient hand [3]; and although

[2] The titles at the heads of the pages in Cod. Sin. are often neglected through oversight.

[3] Of about the same date, *secundâ manu* yet early, are the

the numbers somewhat resemble those reckoned by Euthalius in the fifth century, they precisely coincide but in one case (Ephesians 312), and must have been derived from some earlier system (for such no doubt existed) which Euthalius may have modified to form his own.

Those larger chapters (*κεφάλαια* majora) with their corresponding *τίτλοι*, or summaries of contents, which appear in all the copies of the Gospels written from the fifth century downwards (including Codd. Alexandrinus and Ephraemi), are wanting in Codd. Sinaiticus and Vaticanus alone, from which defect also we infer their higher date.

Nor will the conclusions to which we are thus led on, step by step, be at all weakened by the fact that Cod. Sinaiticus, in this particular disagreeing with Cod. Vaticanus, exhibits the Ammonian sections and Eusebian canons in red ink in the margin (*see Facsimile* 2, *and* p. xiv, note 1), of which Cod. Alexandrinus had hitherto supplied the earliest example. These numerals are very possibly by the hand of the original scribe, but must have been added by a contemporary, perhaps by the *διορθωτὴς* or *corrector* (*see* p. xx), since to the eye they look quite as old, and here and there the arrangements of the manuscript in respect to breaks and initial letters (*see* p. xv) are plainly adapted to them [4]. Nor

lemmata or short summaries of contents (in no wise resembling those of Euthalius) which stand at the head of columns in 25 places throughout the Acts. Tischendorf's Tab. XIII. over Acts iii. 1 contains one specimen in very small and elegant letters: *τα περι τον πετρον κ̧ ῑωαννην κ̧ του εκ κοιλιασ χωλου* (*sic*). They are all found in Tischendorf's *Annotationes*.

[4] Notice, however, that except from Ammonian section 40 to 49 of St. Matthew, the numeral employed throughout is invariably shaped like the *mu* in *Facsimile* (2), line 4 (*see* p. xxvii); that is, if we may trust the moveable type of the larger edition.

will it make at all for the early or late origin of these rubric numerals, that after ρε (105) Luke ix. 57 they disappear altogether until St. John's Gospel begins[8]. There are many well-known cases in which the first hand has thus left the sections and canons unfinished; while in Cod. Bezae, where a decidedly more recent scribe has inserted the sections without the canons, they end at Mark xv. 16 σζ (207), and are not carried on to the end of SS. Matthew and John. One inference we may safely draw from the presence of these contemporaneous marginal numerals, that since Eusebius, who constructed his harmonical canons on the earlier sections of Ammonius, died A.D. 340, Codex Sinaiticus ought not to be dated before the middle of the fourth century: nor on the other hand need it be placed later. Caesarius (d. A.D. 368) and Epiphanius (writing A.D. 374) testify that his ingenious scheme was already well known in their time. Jerome, addressing Pope Damasus (A.D. 384), would fain have introduced it into his revised Latin version; not to add that the suspicion, not altogether unjust, in which Eusebius' memory was held, would have hindered his canons from obtaining the general acceptance with which they were honoured, had they not been favourably received when he was in the flower of life and reputation. The coincidence of this manuscript with certain readings known to have been approved by Eusebius (of which we shall speak in the next chapter) renders it very credible that Codex Sinaiticus was one of the fifty volumes of Holy Scripture, written "on skins in ternions and quaternions" (*see* p. xxxii, note 8),

[8] The two leaves 10 and 15, forming one sheet, and written by the scribe D (*see* pp. xvi—xviii and p. xxxii, note 7), are also void of their proper sections and canons: but these appear in leaves 28, 29, which were also written by D.

which he prepared A.D. 331 by Constantine's direction for the use of the new capital; and these would naturally contain the canons he cherished with so much honest pride.

The Gospels in Cod. Vaticanus are divided into chapters on an entirely different principle, and since nothing of the kind had been met with elsewhere, they were at one time urged in proof of the pre-eminent antiquity of that manuscript; nor need the argument be much impaired by Tregelles' recent discovery of the same divisions in the margin of Codex Zacynthius (Evan. Ξ), a fragment of St. Luke, edited by him, and assigned to the eighth century. Now in the Acts of the Apostles Cod. Vatican. has two independent sets of 36 and 69 chapters respectively, the marginal numerals indicating the larger number being considered as somewhat later than the others. These smaller chapters up to 42 are found in the margin of Cod. Sinaiticus, written by a very old hand, and together with their slight variations from the sister manuscript are recorded at the end of our collation of the Acts. Since no traces of these chapters have been discovered elsewhere, this remarkable coincidence not only powerfully strengthens our judgment, derived from internal evidence (*below* Chap. III.), of a real, though perhaps indirect connexion between the two codices, but affords some presumption that they are not unlike in their age or critical value.

We would close our palaeographical description of this manuscript by a few miscellaneous statements, having no very obvious bearing on its date, to determine which our attention has hitherto been chiefly addressed.

Iota and *upsilon*, when used alone, and *upsilon*, when the first vowel of the diphthong *υι*, often have over them two points as a mark of *dialysis*, and that by the first hand: yet it is often far from easy, as well in this manuscript as in

Cod. Bezae and others, to distinguish such original points from those subsequently added. Instead of the two points a short straight line is sometimes promiscuously substituted in Cod. Sinaiticus (compare our *Facsimile* (1), lines 1 and 2), as in the N. T. portion of Cod. Ephraemi, but scarcely in any other known copies[6].

The ordinary abridgements usual in the earliest Biblical manuscripts appear here with some slight variations. We read $\overline{\theta\sigma}$, $\overline{\kappa\sigma}$, $\overline{\iota\sigma}$, $\overline{\chi\sigma}$, $\overline{\pi\nu\alpha}$ and its compounds in all their cases invariably: $\overline{\iota\upsilon}$ and $\overline{\iota\eta\upsilon}$ in consecutive lines of Apoc. xxii. 20, 21: $\overline{\chi\rho\upsilon}$ Rom. vii. 4, but mostly $\overline{\chi\upsilon}$: sometimes $\overline{\upsilon\sigma}$, $\overline{\pi\eta\rho}$, $\overline{\mu\eta\rho}$, $\overline{\sigma\rho\sigma}$ (i. e. $\sigma\omega\tau\eta\rho o\sigma$), $\overline{\sigma\tau\rho\sigma}$ (i. e. $\sigma\tau\alpha\upsilon\rho o\sigma$), $\overline{\alpha\nu o\sigma}$ (i. e. $\alpha\nu\theta\rho\omega\pi o\sigma$), $\overline{o\upsilon\nu o\sigma}$ (i. e. $o\upsilon\rho\alpha\nu o\sigma$), $\overline{\delta\alpha\delta}$ (*vel* $\delta\alpha\nu\epsilon\iota\delta$), sometimes the words at full length. There occur quite indiscriminately $\iota\epsilon\rho o\upsilon\sigma\alpha\lambda\eta\mu$, $\overline{\iota\eta\lambda\mu}$ and $\overline{\iota\epsilon\lambda\mu}$ (this last not in the N. T.); $\iota\sigma\rho\alpha\eta\lambda$, $\overline{\iota\eta\lambda}$, $\overline{\iota\sigma\lambda}$, $\overline{\iota\sigma\eta\lambda}$, each of them with or without the dialysis and final apostrophus. At the end of a line — over the last letter denotes *nu*; a similar line is mostly set over letters employed as numerals. Other *compendia scribendi* are ϗ for $\kappa\alpha\iota$ perpetually: in the Septuagint alone ⁊ ·θ for -$\tau\alpha\iota$ and -$\theta\alpha\iota$. Two other forms placed at the end of lines, found too in the Herculanean rolls, should also be noticed, viz. μ̊ for $\mu o\upsilon$ 29 times in the N. T., and very seldom (*never* in the N. T.) π̊ for $\pi\rho o\sigma$ or $\pi\rho o$[7]. As in Cod. Bezae and nearly all uncial codices, μ ν and π often coalesce with η and with each other, as in our *Facsimile* (4) of the corrector A.

[6] In a Lectionary, at Christ Church, of the eleventh century (Wake 12), we remark that the two dots in the dialysis often glide into one straight line.

[7] This symbol seems to have been more common in earlier books, and to have been the source of the various reading $\pi\rho o\sigma\epsilon\lambda\theta\omega\nu$ for $\pi\rho o\epsilon\lambda\theta\omega\nu$ Matth. xxvi. 39; Mark xiv. 35; Acts xx. 5; 13.

Lastly, short straight lines are frequently put over the first letters of a line at the commencement of an Ammonian section (*see Facsimile* 3) or of a paragraph, *secundâ manu* as it would seem[8], for Tischendorf mostly omits them in his printed text. Occasionally however they are retained (e. g. John i. 21; 25; iv. 10; James ii. 23), as if in his judgment they were by the first hand. Such original marks occur as well in other places (Rom. viii. 5; 1 Cor. xii. 29—31, &c.), as ten times in the Acts, in one place (x. 23, 24) apparently for the purpose of mutual reference. The slight neat arabesques (sometimes touched with the red paint) at the end of each book also seem the work of the first scribes, as in Codd. Vatican., Alexandrin., Bezae, &c.

CHAPTER III.

ON THE INTERNAL CHARACTER OF THE TEXT OF CODEX SINAITICUS.

We have tried to lay before the reader as full a description as possible of the palaeographic appearances presented by our manuscript, but any thing approaching to a complete view of its internal character as a witness to the sacred text would carry us far beyond the limits assigned to the present Introduction, and indeed would introduce us to enquiries as difficult as they are involved and obscure. We must there-

[8] In John i. 9; xiv. 25 ⲧ is set in the margin in red to the right of the numerals of the section and canon; in the latter place : in red stands in the text before the first word of the section by way of reference, as also in John xix. 40; xx. 2, and constantly in Cod. Bezae, *s.m.*

fore content ourselves with stating a few of the leading facts of the case, from which the student will readily gather both the *independent* value of Codex Sinaiticus as a critical record, and the *extreme antiquity* of the readings it preserves, even where we may not on the whole be inclined to adopt them as the genuine words of the inspired penmen.

I. We will first ascertain whether it be an independent document, that is, one which exhibits a text not immediately drawn from any other still extant.

As soon as Tischendorf published his *Notitia Cod. Sin.* we minutely compared the passages of the Gospels he therein gave in full[9], and which may be presumed to be fair specimens of the whole, selected to favour no individual prejudices, with the corresponding parts of the other four great manuscripts, Cod. Alexandrin. (A), Cod. Vatican. (B), Cod. Ephraemi (C, but sadly mutilated throughout), and Cod. Bezae (D), and that with the following result. Of the 312 variations from the common text noted therein, Cod. Sinaiticus (א)[1] stands alone in 45, in 8 agrees with A B C D united, with A B C together 31 times, with A B D 14, with A B 13, with D alone 10, with B alone but once (Mark i. 27), with C alone once: with several authorities against A B 39 times, with A against B 52, with B against A 98. So far as this investigation goes Cod. B is not much upheld by Cod. א in its peculiar and characteristic readings, while the mutual

[9] They are in all four pages, containing Matth. xxvii. 64—Mark i. 35; John xxi. 1—25; Luke xxiv. 24—53, this last incomplete.

[1] Thus Tischendorf in the exercise of his undoubted right has been pleased to indicate this MS., whether by way of asserting its pre-eminence, or in allusion to the place of its discovery: but it has been found very inconvenient to break the range of type by a Hebrew letter.

divergencies of the very oldest authorities become more visible and perplexing than ever.

Much the same consequences would ensue from an analysis of the various readings in the Apocalypse, wherein the divergency from our printed text is very considerable throughout every known manuscript. Here we have Codd. A C as before; that now denoted Cod. B is no longer the great Vatican copy, but another in the same library, some four centuries younger. Besides these and Cod. Sinaiticus no other uncial copy contains this book, except one of the eighth or ninth century, just found at St. Petersburg by the indefatigable Tischendorf, and as yet unpublished. All the variations, whether from the Textus Receptus or each other, which occur in Cod. ℵ when compared with Codd. A B C throughout the 239 verses wherein Cod. C is extant, are 993 in number. Out of these 310 are peculiar to ℵ, 188 are in all four, in 64 ℵ A B agree, in 170 ℵ A C, in 96 ℵ B C, in 24 ℵ A, in 89 ℵ B, in 52 ℵ C. The *lectiones singulares* of A B C we did not note, but in most of its 310 Cod. ℵ was countenanced by cursive manuscripts, often in considerable numbers, sometimes by only a few, or even one or two of the best (e.g. i. 16; 17; iii. 16; vi. 9; vii. 1; 14; x. 3; 4; 8; 9; xi. 4; 8, &c.), such as Codd. 38 and 95 (g^{scr} at Parham). As a general result Cod. ℵ leans more towards C than B, though it contains fewer of C's peculiar readings: it separates most from A, and is manifestly independent of them all.

Let us now take the Epistle to the Colossians, the only one of St. Paul which is found nearly complete[2] in all the five great uncials, Codd. ℵ A B C D,—D being no longer Cod. Bezae, but its younger contemporary of the sixth cen-

[2] Cod. C alone is deficient in chap. i. vv. 1, 2 partly, where we have past over the readings of Cod. ℵ.

tury, Cod. Claromontanus. On examining the 126 variations set down in the following pages (we do not meddle with clerical errors, &c. denoted by ✓, or with changes by later hands), it appears that A B C D all unite with ℵ 26 times, while ℵ differs from the other four 23 times: ℵ accords with A B C 10 times, with A B D 5, with B C D 3, with A C D 14, with A B only 4, with A C 15, with B C 6, with B D and C D twice each, with A D never; with A alone 6 times (e. g. I. 23; 25), with B alone five (e. g. II. 2 παν πλουτος; 13; IV. 12 σταθητε), with C alone thrice, with D alone twice (II. 10; III. 14). Of the whole 126 places B is with ℵ 61 times (in the Epistle to the Romans we have calculated the higher proportion of 176 out of 325), A in 80, C in 79, D in but 54. Speaking generally, no two of these authorities of the first order so far resemble each other as to enable us to dispense with the rest, or with all other available sources of information; yet Cod. ℵ approximates nearer to A or C, or A C united, than it does to B.

II. When from this wider survey we come to scrutinize individual passages, it must not be dissembled that the affinity of Codd. ℵ and B is closer than would have been at first sight anticipated. The connexion between the two, indirect perhaps yet not imaginary, which the identity of the chapters in the Acts had previously suggested (*see* p. xxxviii), is sufficiently proved by their coincidence in peculiar readings, and those of much importance, for which the two together comprise the principal, sometimes (notwithstanding the seeming abundance of our critical materials) the only *positive* evidence. Now these readings are cleared from all suspicion of being mere arbitrary changes, unduly foisted into the two manuscripts, by the evidence of Christian authors that lived in or before the times when they were written, who tell us that those self-same readings were actually found in some or in most of the copies to which they had access. It is plain that such accordant testimony, proceeding as it sometimes does from widely different sources, is a powerful corroboration both of the antiquity of the text exhibited in these venerable codices, and of their general value as instruments of criticism.

The two chief places, out of many that might be cited, wherein the united testimony of Codd. א and B is supported by the weighty authority of contemporary writers, are Mark xvi. 9—16 and Ephes. i. 1. For the omission of the whole paragraph containing the last twelve verses of the second Gospel we have indeed no other direct manuscript evidence than theirs, and even the scribe of Cod. B betrays a certain consciousness of an omission by leaving blank the column immediately following the end of St. Mark, this being the only perfectly vacant column throughout the whole volume. Cod. א presents no such peculiarity; but Cod. L (Paris 62, of the eighth century) exhibits the passage in such a shape as plainly shows that its writer regarded vv. 9—20 as of very questionable authenticity. About thirty of the later or *cursive* manuscripts, though they contain the whole passage, either mark it with an asterisk, or append scholia which throw more or less doubt upon it, as an integral part of the Gospel. In fact, after having been cited as genuine by the Fathers of the second and third centuries, from Irenaeus downwards, the difficulty of harmonising their narrative with the other Gospels (a circumstance which ought to plead in their favour) brought suspicion upon these verses, and caused their omission in some copies seen by Eusebius (*Quaestiones ad Marinum*), whose influence over the Scripture codices of his age we have seen to be very considerable (*see* p. xxxvii).

The omission of ἐν ἐφέσῳ in Eph. i. 1 after τοῖσ οὖσιν is

another point in which Codd. א B (attended by the margin of Cod. 67, B's close ally) stand alone among manuscripts, and in both the words are added by later hands: in Cod. א the corrector is C, of the seventh century. This shorter reading was in the manuscripts used by Origen, who resorts to a mystical interpretation of the expression τοῖσ οὖσιν, and very possibly in those of the heretic Marcion a century earlier: it was known and approved by Basil in the middle of the fourth century, both from tradition, and as found by him in the oldest copies (ἐν τοῖς παλαιοῖς τῶν ἀντιγράφων): Jerome, as usual, repeats Origen to the echo. The truth is that this Epistle, so singularly void of personal allusions or salutations (in that respect contrasting with its sister letter to the Colossians) was a *circular* addressed to other Asiatic cities besides the capital Ephesus,—to Laodicea perhaps among the rest (Col. iv. 16); and that while some codices may have contained the name of Ephesus in the first verse, others may have had another city substituted, or the space after τοῖσ οὖσιν left utterly void (*see* Bp. Middleton on the *Greek Article* in loc.).

To these celebrated texts we annex a few others, less known, yet very instructive, in which Codd. א B agree together against the mass of critical authorities: some of their coincidences (e. g. Matth. x. 25; 1 Cor. xiii. 3; James i. 17) can hardly have been accidental. It will be borne in mind that no opinion is implied respecting the probable genuineness of any of the readings cited below for the purpose of exhibiting the character of Codex א, unless that opinion be expressly stated.

Matth. i. 25 αυτησ τον πρωτοτοκον is omitted by Codd. א B Z (sixth century, at Dublin), two first-rate cursives (1. 33), Cureton's Syriac, the Egyptian (πρωτοτοκον only), some Old Latin versions, and (after them) twice by Ambrose.

Ibid. vi. 1 *δικαιοσυνην* for *ελεημοσυνην* is in Codd. א B D (though an early hand changed א's reading into the poor gloss *δοσειν*, i. e. *δοσιν*), three cursives (including Cod. 1), the scholia of two others, the Vulgate and Old Latin versions, the Peshito[3] and Philoxenian Syriac, Origen, Isidore of Pelusium, Hilary, and Jerome ("justitiam, hoc est, eleemosynam vestram"). Internal evidence pleads strongly in its favour.

Ibid. x. 25 *βεεζεβουλ* Codd. א B *only:* so xii. 24; 27 (not Mark iii. 22 in א); Luke xi. 15; 18; 19.

Ibid. xi. 19 *εργων* for *τεκνων* is here read by Codd. א B *p.m.* and the valuable cursive 124, by copies known to Jerome, the Peshito and Philoxenian *in the text* (but not Cureton's Syriac), the Memphitic, Aethiopic, and Armenian MSS. But in the parallel place Luke vii. 35 Cod. א stands alone in maintaining *εργων*, though Ambrose in his Commentary on Luke states that "plerique Graeci" thus read it here.

Ibid. xiv. 30 *ισχυρον* is wanting only in Codd. א B *p.m.* 33 and the Memphitic version. We shall recur to this passage in Chap. IV.

Ibid. xxvii. 49. At the end of this verse the wretched scholium from John xix. 34 *αλλος δε λαβων λογχην ενυξεν αυτου την πλευραν και εξηλθεν υδωρ και αιμα*, though as certainly spurious as the latter portion of Matth. xxvii. 35 drawn from the same source (John xix. 24), is found in substance in Codd. א B C L (*see* p. xliv) U (*see* p. xxvii, note 3),

[3] I once said (*Supplement to the Authorised Version*, p. 153, 1845) that "the Peshito is of necessity neutral, since ܙܕܩܬܐ would very well answer to either Greek word," but the subsequent discovery of Cureton's Syriac makes it pretty certain that the Peshito read *δικαιοσύνην*, since wishing to render *ἐλεημοσύνην* Cureton's version gives ܡܘܗܒܬܐ.

five cursives, the Aethiopic, Jerusalem Syriac, and two MSS. of the Latin Vulgate, and Fathers named by the scholiast in Cod. 72. To the same purpose Chrysostom (Hom. in Matth. 88, tom. ii. p. 526, Field) speaks expressly, and others after him: but this interpolation, which would represent the Saviour as pierced while yet living, is a good example of the fact that some of our highest authorities may combine in attesting a reading unquestionably false.

Mark vi. 20 *ηπορει* for *εποιει* is found only in Codd. ℵ B L and the Memphitic version.

Ibid. xiv. 30; 68; 72. Here we have a set of passages which bear clear marks of wilful and critical correction, thoroughly carried out in Cod. ℵ, and only partially in Cod. B and some of its compeers, the object being so far to assimilate the narrative of Peter's denials with those of the other Evangelists, as to suppress the fact, vouched for by St. Mark only, that the cock crowed twice. In Cod. ℵ *δισ* is omitted in vv. 30, 72, and *και αλεκτωρ εφωνησε* in v. 68. The last change is countenanced by Codd. B L, one Lectionary, one Old Latin copy (*c*), and the Memphitic version: the former *δισ* is rejected by C (*p.m.*) D, one Moscow cursive copy, several of the Old Latin and Vulgate, by the Armenian and Aethiopic: the latter by fewer still, perhaps by C *p.m.*, by two later MSS. (Δ. 251), the Aethiopic, and some Old Latin copies.

Luke iii. 32 *ϊωβηλ* for *ιωβηδ* is found in ℵ, and in B also according to Mai's larger edition, which in many places is known to be more accurate than the second and smaller one. In D *ωβηλ* is the reading of the first hand.

Ibid. vi. 1. The perplexing *δευτεροπρωτω*, which they could not understand, is consequently omitted by Codd. ℵ B L, seven cursives (including 1. 33. 69), by some Lectionaries (but these last usually omit such notes of time at the beginning of a lesson), and by some versions, including the Peshito Syriac, some Old Latin copies, the Memphitic and Aethiopic, and the margin of the Philoxenian.

Ibid. xi. 4 *αλλα ρυσαι ημασ απο του πονηρου* is omitted by Codd. ℵ B. 1, and above eight other cursives, by scholia in six more, by the Armenian, the Vulgate, Jerome, Cyril, perhaps Tertullian, and very expressly by Origen and Augustine.

John i. 18. The minute but weighty variation *θσ̄* (i. e. *θεοσ*) for *υσ̄* (i. e. *υιοσ*) is supported by Codd. ℵ B C (*p.m.*) L. 33, the Peshito and margin of the Philoxenian, the Memphitic, Roman Aethiopic, and a host of Fathers.

Ibid. iii. 13 *ο ων εν τω ουρανω* is omitted in Codd. ℵ B L. 33, the Roman Aethiopic, a Memphitic MS., by Origen, and apparently by Eusebius.

Acts i. 5 *εν πν̄ι βαπτισθησεσθε* (*-αι* ℵ) *αγιω* is the order in Codd. ℵ B and lo[ti] (*see* p. xxvi, note 9) alone of all known copies.

Ibid. i. 19 *ιδια* is omitted in ℵ B (*p.m.*) D, the Vulgate, Thebaic, and Armenian (if versions can be trusted), and in Augustine.

Ibid. iii. 6 *εγειραι και* omitted in Codd. ℵ B D and the Thebaic version alone.

Rom. iv. 8 *ου* for *ῳ* appears only in Codd. ℵ B D (Claromontan.) *p.m.* G (but not in its sister manuscript F, or its own Latin version), and the margin of 67 (*see* p. xlv).

1 Cor. xiii. 3. The very strange reading *καυχησωμαι* for *καυθησωμαι* or *καυθησομαι* is found in Codd. ℵ A B, one cursive (17, the important Evan. 33), some Greek copies known to Jerome, one MS. of the Memphitic, Ephraem, and possibly the Aethiopic: it may be presumed by way of moderating our estimate of the critical worth of the consent of our very best codices.

James i. 17 *αποσκιασματοσ* for *ἀποσκίασμα* seems to make

utter nonsense of the passage, yet such is the reading of Codd. א B. This single instance goes a good way to prove a connexion, real if not direct, between the two oldest documents.

Cod. Bezae (D) has been found in company with Codd. א B several times in the preceding list. We subjoin a few passages out of many in which א and D stand together, with no other ally among the great uncials: yet it must be added that א is perfectly free from the bold interpolations of D, especially those which abound throughout the Acts.

Matth. ix. 9 *ηκολουθει* (for *-θησεν*) Codd. א D. 1, and two other cursives; *ibid.* xv. 36 *και* is prefixed to *ευχαριστησασ* in א D. 1. 13. 33? 72. 124. 346? and (*me teste*) Wake 34[4] at Christ Church, together with the Latin, Syriac, and Memphitic versions; Mark iii. 11 *λεγοντεσ* for *λεγοντα* Codd. א D K 69 (*not* 61 in Dobbin) and two Lectionaries; John i. 4 *εστιν* for the first *ην* is found only in Codd. א D, Greek MSS. known to Origen, six copies of the Old Latin, Cureton's Syriac, the Thebaic, Irenaeus, Cyprian, Hilary, and one or two others; *ibid.* xii. 32 *παντα* for *παντασ* Codd. א D, one cursive, the Gothic, the Latin versions with Augustine expressly ("omnia"), Ambrose, and Jerome, possibly other versions if *παντα* be singular (Peshito ܟܠܡܕܡ : and thus perhaps the Memphitic, Thebaic, Aethiopic). In Col. ii. 10 Cod. א favours a very peculiar reading of D of St. Paul and its transcript E, *εκκλησιασ* for *αρχησ και εξουσιασ*: א however retains *αρχησ*, and the Latin versions of D E have the common reading. In Heb. ix. 17 *τοτε* for *ποτε* is found only in Codd. א D *p.m.*, but Isidore of Pelusium (about A.D. 412) speaks of it as the reading of *old* copies.

[4] Wake 34, hitherto unknown except in the Apocalypse (27), in the fragment of the Gospels it contains (ending Luke vi. 42) strikingly resembles Codd. B D Z, and especially 1.

A or C or some others also frequently side with Cod. א against nearly all the rest: Matth. xxv. 33 *αυτου* omitted after *δεξιων* by Cod. A, one Lectionary, perhaps two other copies, with the Aethiopic and Cyprian (א alone adds *αυτου* at the end of the verse); Mark viii. 25 *δηλαυγωσ* in C L Δ (at St. Gall, IXth century) for *τηλαυγωσ* (*δηλωσ* of Cod. 33 is the connecting link); *ibid.* xv. 1 *ετοιμασαντεσ* for *ποιησαντεσ* also in C L only; Luke vi. 35 *μηδενα* for *μηδεν* only in Cod. Ξ of Tregelles, Scrivener's w, and the Syriac versions (ܐܢܫ Peshito); *ibid.* xxiv. 13 *εκατον* stands before *εξηκοντα* in two early (11 N) and one later (K) uncial, the margin of one cursive (34), some Latin and Syriac MSS., in Jerome and in Eusebius, who so often resembles Cod. א. Sometimes, as in the case of Cod. B, these copies accord with א in reading what is palpably untrue: e. g. Acts vi. 5 *ανδρα πληρησ* א A C D E H &c.; in 1 Pet. i. 23 too notice the absurd *φθορασ φθαρτησ* for *σπορασ φθ.*, through the mere wandering of the eye from *σπ* to *φθ* in א A C. Just the same kind of blunder, *πεπτωκαν* or *-κασιν* for *πεπωκασι*, is found in all the uncials of the Apocalypse xviii. 3 (א A B C) and in many cursives.

Most interesting of all are the cases wherein Cod. א follows readings which ancient writers or versions testify to have been found in their copies, though they have quite disappeared from those at present extant: instances like these much enhance our estimate of the value of the text which preserves them. With this part of the subject Tischendorf has taken unusual pains, and from his Prolegomena (with some modifications) are derived the following examples: Matth. vii. 13 *η πυλη* omitted by Clement and Origen often, by Eusebius, seven Latin copies and Latin Fathers; *ibid.* xviii. 24 *πολλων* for *μυριων* with Origen four or six times, Juvencus, and both Egyptian versions; Mark i. 15 *και λεγων* omitted by Origen and two Latin copies (*c. mt.*); *ibid.* vii. 3 πυκνα for πυγμη, with four Old Latin MSS., the Vulgate ("crebro"), the Memphitic, Gothic, the Philoxenian text, and Aethiopic; John ii. 2 the original reading of Cod. ℵ in this place is supported only by three Old Latin copies, the Philoxenian Syriac margin, and the Aethiopic; *ibid.* vi. 51, the omission of ην εγω δωσω is supported by many, but the transfer of η σαρξ μου εστιν to the end of the verse is peculiar to Cod. ℵ, Tertullian, and *m* of the Old Latin, the well-known Speculum of the 6th century published by Mai; *ibid.* xiii. 10 ουκ εχει χρειαν νιψασθαι omitting η τουσ ποδασ with Origen six times, Tertullian, and four MSS. of the Latin Vulgate; *ibid.* xvii. 7 εγνων for εγνωκαν, a variation noticed but repudiated by Chrysostom; *ibid.* xix. 38 ηλθον ουν και ηραν with only five copies of the Old Latin, the Thebaic, Jerusalem Syriac, and best Armenian edition; Rom. v. 7 μογισ for μολισ with Origen only; 2 Pet. i. 4 την εν τω κοσμω επιθυμιαν φθορασ with Jerome only.

For many readings Cod. ℵ has no support; some of these may possibly be arbitrary alterations: Mark x. 42 μεγαλοι αυτων is changed into βασιλεισ; *ibid.* xiv. 58 ειπεν is substituted for ημεισ ηκουσαμεν αυτου λεγοντοσ; Luke i. 26 ιουδαιασ stands for γαλιλαιασ, and a Moscow cursive (255) has ιουδα; *ibid.* ii. 37 εβδομηκοντα τεσσαρων; *ibid.* iii. 5 τροχιαι for τραχειαι by the first hand; John viii. 57 εωρακεν σε for ἑωρακασ; Acts viii. 5 καισαριασ for σαμαρειασ (on account of viii. 40 and xxi. 8); *ibid.* xi. 20 ευαγγελιστασ for ἑλληνιστασ; *ibid.* xiv. 9 ουκ inserted before ηκουσεν; Heb. ii. 4 θερισμοισ for μερισμοισ; *ibid.* iii. 8 πιρασμω for παραπικρασμω; 1 Pet. iv. 1 αποθανοντοσ for παθοντοσ, to correspond with ii. 21, where a few, and to iii. 18, where even A C read απεθανεν.

Lastly: as the reviser of a manuscript often had another

copy before him, by whose aid he corrected the text (*see* p. xx), so it would sometimes seem as if the original scribe mingled together two separate readings, both of which were found in the documents to which he had access: thus in 1 John iv. 17, where the alternative forms *μεθ ημων* and *εν ημιν* are both retained: so in Apoc. iv. 11, while some copies have *κ̅ε̅*, some *ο κ̅σ̅ και θ̅σ̅ ημων*, Cod. ℵ gives the latter after the former. Tischendorf cites to the same purpose as our examples Tit. iii. 2; 1 Pet. ii. 12; 2 Pet. ii. 15.

With regard to those *itacisms*, or substitutions of one vowel or diphthong for another, which prevail more or less in all manuscripts, whatever be their date, it will be seen from the following collation (in which they are all registered and indicated by the symbol √) that Cod. Sinaiticus abounds in them as much as any known copy. Since they are in fact nothing better than instances of mis-spelling, or accommodation of the orthography to the sound, it is not surprising that their frequency should vary in different parts of the same copy, especially where (as is surely the case with this manuscript) more than one person has been engaged on the task (*see* pp. xvi, xvii, and especially note 4). The Epistle of Barnabas, and yet more the Shepherd of Hermas, which is in other respects more inaccurately written than the N. T., are full of the harshest and most unusual itacisms (e. g. *τεσ* for *ταῖσ*, *αιαν* for *ἐάν*, *ανδραισ* for *ἄνδρεσ*). Elsewhere in Cod. Sinaiticus the most ordinary interchange is between *ι* and *ει*, which is indeed perpetual in Codd. Alexandrinus and Ephraemi, and we should probably add in Cod. Vaticanus also if we knew its contents more minutely. Next to *ι* and *ει* we find *ε* substituted for *αι* and *vice versâ* in all the four codices; in some parts of Cod. ℵ more frequently than in others. In such words as *ηνοιγη*, *σοι* &c. the diphthong *οι* is often turned into *υ*: some of the other changes observable in later copies (e. g. between *η* and *ει* or *ι*[5], *η* and *ε*) are more rare in ours, though *υ* and *η* are transmuted about 12 times, chiefly in the plural of personal pronouns; *ου* and *ω* 20 times in the termination of verbs; even *ο* and *ω* 68 times, which last may tend to illustrate the readings in Rom. v. 1; 1 Cor. xv. 49.

The most ancient manuscripts of the N. T. hitherto known depart from the common grammatical inflections, and are assimilated to those forms which pertain to the Alexandrine modification of the Hellenistic, or debased dialect of the Greek current among Jewish converts in the first century. It is not necessary to infer from this peculiarity that all the oldest codices were written at Alexandria (a supposition not very likely in the case of such as have parallel Latin versions, e. g. Cod. Bezae), but rather that they approximate to the primitive orthography of the sacred penmen, whose style would naturally be moulded on that of the Septuagint version; while later scribes have gradually softened down its harshness and brought it into closer conformity with the usage of their own times. Hence the prevalence of these Alexandrine terminations in a manuscript has been reasonably held a presumptive proof (valid so far as it goes) of its high antiquity: and it will appear from the ensuing summary that no document is more fully entitled than Cod. ℵ to the benefit of such an argument. Our observations are limited to the N. T. portion of the manuscript (though the Old Testament precisely resembles it in character), and we take no notice of

[5] Yet Cod. ℵ has *χρηστιανοσ* in all the three places, Acts xi. 26; xxvi. 28; 1 Pet. iv. 16, but changed *s.m.*

the corrections brought in by later hands, chiefly by C (*see* p. xxiii).

(1) The oldest copies of Scripture so constantly exhibit the appended *ν* before a consonant in the third person singular of verbs ending in -*ε*, and in the dative plural of nouns and adjectives in -*ι*, that modern editors have somewhat hastily regarded this *ν* ἐφελκυστικὸν (as it is termed) the normal form, proper to be represented throughout their printed text of the N. T. Now Cod. ℵ (as will be seen by the perpetual use of the symbol ✓ in our collation) is found to retain the *ν* as a general rule: the exceptions (which also we have duly noted) do not exceed 208 for the whole N. T. (in about three of which an hiatus is caused by the omission of *ν*), whereof 134 occur with verbs, 29 with nouns, 45 with adjectives (chiefly *πασι*) or participles.

(2) In the same way the weak *σ* is retained in *ουτωσ* before a consonant: Cod. ℵ has *ουτω* but 14 times in the N. T.

(3) The accusative of the third declension often ends in -*αν* for -*α*: Matt. ii. 2; 10; xii. 49; John iv. 46; xx. 25; xxi. 18; Acts xxi. 7; xxii. 23; 1 Pet. v. 6; Apoc. vi. 9; ix. 4; in Barnabas and Hermas each seven times: also in -*ην* for -*η* from adjectives in -*ησ*, John v. 11; Rom. iv. 5.

(4) The second person plural of the second aorist may terminate in -*ατε*: Matth. vii. 13; xi. 7; 8; 9; xxv. 36; xxvi. 55; Mark xiv. 48 (-*αται*, so Luke vii. 24; 25; 26); Luke xi. 52; Acts ii. 23; Col. i. 7; Apoc. xviii. 4 (-*αται*). Sometimes the first person sing. middle second aorist is in -*αμην*, Acts xxiii. 27; the third in -*ατο*, Acts vii. 10; 21; xii. 11; 2 Thess. ii. 13. Thus also the first pers. pl. act. in -*αμεν*, Luke xvii. 10 (*imperf.*); Acts iv. 20; xxvii. 5; xxviii. 14; and the participle in -*αμενοσ* Luke xxii. 44.

(5) Also the third person in -*αν* for -*ον*: *ειπαν* 68 times in

the N. T., and other verbs in Matth. v. 1; vii. 27; xiii. 17; xvii. 6; Mark vi. 40; 50; viii. 7 (*imperf.*); xiv. 46; Luke v. 7; ix. 32; x. 24; xxii. 63 (*imperf.*, so κατεκοπταν in Hermas *vis*. 3); John iv. 27; 46; vi. 10; ix. 10 (*imperf.*); 12; x. 20; xi. 36; 47; 56; xviii. 6 *bis;* Acts viii. 10; ix. 18; x. 24; 39; 45; xii. 7; 10; xiv. 19; xvi. 40; xxi. 27; xxvii. 36; xxviii. 2; 15; Rom. xv. 3; 1 Cor. x. 8; Apoc. v. 4; ix. 8; xxi. 1: also in -αν for -ασι in the perfect tense, Acts xvi. 36; Rom. xvi. 7; Col. ii. 1; Barnabas once. So we read ειπα Matth. xxviii. 7; Mark ix. 18; Acts xxii. 8; επεσα Acts xxii. 7; Apoc. xix. 10; ειδα *ibid.* xvii. 6; and -οσαν for -ον, imperfect or second aorist: John xv. 22; 24; 2 Thess. iii. 6; Apoc. iv. 8.

(6) In the imperative second aorist -ατω stands for -ετω: Matth. vi. 10; x. 13; xxvi. 39; Mark xiii. 15; Luke xi. 2.

(7) The augment is used for the reduplication: John xv. 18; xviii. 30; Acts viii. 16; xxvii. 41 (?); 1 John v. 10 *bis* (so εποιηκασ Hermas *vis*. 2): or a double augment is put Matth. xii. 13; Mark iii. 5; viii. 25; Luke vi. 10: the augment is wholly neglected Matth. xiii. 17; Luke iv. 4; v. 3; x. 24; John ii. 20; Acts ii. 25; vii. 10; 17; x. 39; xviii. 14 (?); xxvii. 36; Col. ii. 20; James ii. 22 (?); 1 Pet. ii. 25: or the preposition is augmented Matth. vii. 22; xi. 13; xv. 7; Mark vii. 6; Luke i. 67; John xi. 51; Acts xix. 6.

(8) Verbs in -εω used instead of -αω: Matth. xv. 23; Mark iv. 10; xiv. 5; John xi. 38: and *vice versâ* Acts xx. 37; xxviii. 6; Philem. 18; Jude 22; 23.

(9) For ουκ is put ουχ and *vice versâ:* Matth. xx. 13; Luke vi. 2; xxiv. 3; John vii. 25; viii. 44; Acts ii. 7; iii. 6; xii. 18; xiv. 28; xix. 23; 24; 1 Cor. xiv. 2; James ii. 5; 1 Pet. iii. 3; 1 John i. 10 (*see* our collation, Acts xiv. 28).

(10) In λαμβανω and its compounds and derivatives μ is

always inserted before ψ, e. g. *λημψομαι, προσωποληημψια.* *Ιωανησ* and *μωσησ* are found much less often than *ιωαννησ* and *μωυσησ*. We read *δεδωκασ με* for *μοι* John xvii. 4. Other unusual or anomalous forms are *εφιορκησεισ* Matth. v. 33; *εφ ελπιδι* Acts ii. 26; Rom. viii. 21; *καθ ιδιαν* Matth. xxiv. 3; *εξεδετο* Matth. xxi. 33; Mark xii. 1; Luke xx. 9; *εξεκρεμετο ibid.* xix. 48; *διεδιδετο* Acts iv. 35; *ηδυνασθη* Mark vii. 24; *διελεγχθησαν ibid.* ix. 34; *εκεκραξα* Acts xxiv. 21; *αφεονται* Luke vii. 47; 48; 1 John ii. 12; *φιμοιν* 1 Pet. ii. 15; *καταπιν* 1 Pet. v. 8, so *πιν* often; *επαναπαησεται* Luke x. 6 (so *παηναι* Hermas *vis.* 1); *αναπεσε ibid.* xiv. 10; xvii. 7; *εραυναω* John v. 39; vii. 52; Rom. viii. 27; 1 Cor. ii. 10; 1 Pet. i. 10; 11 (*not* Apoc. ii. 23); *συλλαβουμενοι* Acts xxvi. 21; *εμελλεν* (for *ἔμελεν*) *ibid.* xviii. 17; *εορακ.* 1 Cor. ix. 1; Col. ii. 1; 18; *αποδοι* 1 Thess. v. 15; *ρ* for *ρρ* 2 Cor. xi. 25; 2 Tim. iv. 17; Heb. ii. 1; ix. 19; 21; 1 Pet. v. 7; *αλα* for *ἅλασ* Matth. v. 13 *bis;* Mark ix. 50 *bis;* Luke xiv. 34 *bis; κραβακτον always*, except Acts v. 15 *κραβαττων;* *λαιλαψ masc.* Mark iv. 37; *λιμοσ fem.* Luke xv. 14; Acts xi. 28; *πλουτοσ neut.* Phil. iv. 19; Col. ii. 2; *μαχαιρησ* Heb. xi. 34; 37; Apoc. xiii. 14; *μαχαιρη dat.* Matth. xxvi. 52; Luke xxii. 49; Acts xii. 2; *τετρααρχ.* Matth. xiv. 1; Luke iii. 1; 19; Acts xiii. 1; *τεσσερεσ* mostly; *δρακυον* Apoc. vii. 17; *δρακυ ibid.* xxi. 4; *μετοξυ* Luke xi. 51, and Barnabas once: nor is the final consonant in *εν, παλιν, συν* often changed before another consonant in composition.

The present chapter may close with a slight notice of two or three out of a multitude of interesting questions which the study of this manuscript suggests to a thoughtful reader.

(1) In Matth. xiii. 35 Cod. ℵ is upheld by five of the best cursive MSS. (1. 13. 33. 124. 253) in putting *ησαιου* between *δια* and *του προφητου*, and Eusebius testifies that in his time some copies, but not the best (*τοῖσ ἀκριβέσιν*) inserted that

prophet's name, which is also found in the Clementine Homilies attributed to the second century. The true reference is beyond doubt Psalm lxxviii. 2, though Isaiah xlviii. 3 has also been cited by some. Porphyry the philosopher, the most acute and formidable adversary our faith encountered in ancient times (d. 304), alleges this misquotation (if such it be) as an instance of St. Matthew's ignorance, and is met by Jerome in language which proves that ἠσαΐου was not read in the copies before him; for he conjectures that the original word before τοῦ προφήτου was *Asaph* (the reputed author of Psalm lxxviii. according to the Hebrew title), that *Asaph* was changed into *Isaiah* through a misapprehension of the copyists who knew nothing of Asaph, and that Isaiah had been subsequently withdrawn "a prudentibus viris," who became aware of the error. Since Cod. ℵ retains two other readings (Mark i. 2 τω ησαϊα τω προφητη; John vii. 8 ουκ αναβαινω) which Jerome tells had been harassed by the "bark" of Porphyry, an intelligent writer has urged the three readings taken together as a strong proof that our manuscript was written before Porphyry's time, in the course of the *third* century. "It is scarcely conceivable," he remarks, "that any one forging a manuscript in the design to pass it off as of very early date, would thus forfeit for it the credit of conformity with the most venerable uncials, and at the same time expose it to the assaults of an early heathen writer[6]." I cannot profess to understand the

[6] I quote a little pamphlet, to which are appended the initials D. W. The writer also lays some stress on the fact that the Evangelist describes the citation as "spoken" (ῥηθὲν), not "written" by the prophet, as if it were some verbal message, like that alluded to in 2 Kings xiv. 25, and retained by tradition. But ῥηθὲν is thus used *habitually* by St. Matthew, at least nine times in this Gospel.

force of this argument. The readings of Cod. ℵ in Mark i. 1, and (in a less degree) in John vii. 8, are too well supported by other authorities, most venerable uncials too, to warrant any such inference as has been drawn from them; and Matth. xiii. 35 only shows that the fourth century penman faithfully transcribed the older model before him, in which ησαΐου occurs, without regarding or perhaps without having heard of the cavils of Porphyry.

(2) In Matth. xxiii. 35 Cod. ℵ accords with the parallel passage Luke xi. 51 in rejecting του βαραχιου after ζαχαριου, though it was subsequently added by C^b (*see Facsimile* 9 and p. xxiv) some centuries later. Only three Lectionaries (6. 13. z^{scr}) of the tenth or eleventh centuries, and Eusebius (whose correspondence with the readings of Cod. ℵ we have noticed several times before, pp. xxxvii, xliv, xlviii, l *bis*, lvi) by his silence, countenance the omission of the words, which are found in every other known manuscript, and were known even to Irenaeus in the second century, to Origen in the third: in the fourth they perplexed Jerome, as well they might, but he has no better solution than the statement that for "Barachiah" the apocryphal Gospel used by the Nazarenes substituted "Joiada." That our Saviour refers to the well-known Zechariah son of Jehoiada the High Priest, whose murder in the court of the Lord's house, and whose dying words are recorded 2 Chron. xxiv. 20—22, cannot be seriously doubted; but the father of the prophet Zechariah (respecting whose death nothing is known) being named Berechiah, "the name of the father has been since added, or changed, by some one, who took it from the title of the prophecy, which happened to be better known to him than the history in the Chronicles" (Paley, *Evidences*, Pt. ii. Ch. vi.). The fancy that the Baptist's father is the person meant is idle enough; and as our Lord's words clearly relate

to something past, they cannot be supposed to foretell the slaughter of Zacharias the son of Baruch, an eminent private citizen, killed by the zealots near forty years afterwards (A. D. 68), and singularly enough, within the precincts of the Temple (Joseph. *Bell. Jud.* iv. 5). Here therefore, for once, Cod. ℵ with a very small minority of copies must preserve the Evangelist's genuine reading.

(3) John xxi. 25 has been regarded by Tischendorf as a subsequent appendage made to the Gospel by the contemporary reviser A[a], whom he believes to be the original scribe D (*see* p. xx): the ink he considers to resemble that of the addition in Matth. v. 45 in its reddish tinge, the characters to be more slender than in the context. The latter peculiarity is quite observable in Tischendorf's *Facsimile* (Tab. XIX.); but we cannot much rely on *Facsimiles* for a point so delicate. Tregelles, to whom the German critic showed the original passage, is convinced that the hand-writing is the same as that in the rest of the chapter, only that the scribe, when he had completed v. 24, dipped his pen afresh into the fluid, which afterwards flowed more freely. No extant manuscript favours the omission of v. 25 [7], although the

[7] Tischendorf cites for the omission Cod. 63, a tenth century MS. at Trin. Coll. Dublin (A. 1. 8). Aware that his only authority must be Mill's note "versum hunc omittit Usser. 1," I wrote to Dublin to ascertain whether the last leaf of the MS., which once contained John xxi. 25, might not have been lost. The Assistant Librarian Dr. Lottner favoured me with a reply which proves the truth of my suspicion. The text on the last extant page ends with *ἡ μαρτυρία αὐτοῦ·* v. 24, the stop being only a colon, not (:—) as at the end of the other Gospels in this MS. Then, after a small space, comes the following fragment of a commentary, which can only relate to v. 25 *τοῦτο φησίν· ἐκ μυρίων γὰρ θαυμάτων τὰ μόνα πρὸς πίστιν καὶ ἀρετὴν ....* The

hyperbole it contains caused it to be suspected by some, as we learn from the Scholia to Codd. 36. 237 and others. But it is quoted without the least misgiving by a long array of Patristic writers from Origen (who alleges it five times over) and Pamphilus downwards; and it is exactly in St. John's simple manner to assert broadly that which cannot be true to the letter, leaving its necessary limitation to the common sense of the reader (*see* John vii. 39; 1 John iii. 9).

CHAPTER IV.

WAS THE CODEX SINAITICUS WRITTEN BY CONSTANTINE SIMONIDES?

THE first impression conveyed to Tischendorf by the loose leaves of the Codex Friderico-Augustanus was the assurance that their date must be referred to the fourth century; and after a prolonged and intimate acquaintance with the whole manuscript, the investigations of himself and other competent judges by no means prejudiced in his favour, have led them, with little or no hesitation or wavering, to the same deliberate conclusion. The singularly fine quality and venerable appearance of the vellum—the fact that it is the only known manuscript containing eight columns on the open leaf, as if in imitation of the older *rolled* books:—the very simple, yet graceful shape of the uncial characters, the rare occurrence even of a single point for a stop, the total lack of capital letters, all these particulars closely resembling the Herculanean papyri:—the brevity of the titles and subscrip-

last leaf, of course, contained v. 25 and the rest of the commentary upon it.

tions, and some of these too by a second hand :—the absence of the larger chapters and their titles of contents; the presence, on the other hand, of the Ammonian sections and Eusebian canons in the Gospels and of the Vatican chapters in the Acts :—the unusual order of the books of the N. T., especially of the Epistle to the Hebrews :—the presence of the works of Barnabas and Hermas, as a portion of canonical Scripture :—the various corrections the primitive text has undergone from ten or more different hands, with inks of many various shades, in different ages, yet nearly all before breathings and accents came into common use :—above all, the peculiar character of the original text itself, which is of the most ancient type, thoroughly independent in its general current, often standing quite alone; often countenanced only by Cod. Vaticanus or Cod. Bezae, or perhaps by a single later or cursive copy; or by one very old version; or by a single Greek or Latin Father, Eusebius, Basil, or Chrysostom; Ambrose, Jerome, or Augustine :—all these facts, true beyond dispute, every one of them of some weight, several of them of great importance, when taken all together, *with nothing considerable to set in the opposite scale*, persuade us by their accumulated influence that our manuscript is inferior to no copy yet known (hardly excepting the Cod. Vaticanus itself), whether in age or in critical value.

In the face of reasoning thus strong, and to our mind quite irresistible, Constantine Simonides asserts that he wrote the Codex Sinaiticus with his own hands twenty-four years ago, without the wish, or design, or indeed the smallest expectation, of misleading the most ignorant and unwary as to the true character of his work. This strange and startling claim had been whispered about for some time before, but was first publicly asserted in a letter to the *Guardian* newspaper, which appeared Sept. 3, 1862. The name of Dr.

Simonides was already well known to the literary world. According to a Biography of this ingenious person, written by Mr. Charles Steuart of Brighton, but distributed among his friends with his own hands, he is a Greek native of the isle of Syme, on the coast of Asia Minor, born about the hour of sunrise November 11th, 1824. For full ten years he has been well known as the discoverer of some and the possessor of other documents, Biblical, Patristic, Historical, Hieroglyphical, and Archaeological, bearing a semblance of antiquity which the learned in general have not been willing to allow to them. We will here mention only two of the most remarkable of Simonides' treasures, the *palimpsest*[8] of Uranius and the Liverpool papyrus fragments of St. Matthew. The History of the Kings of Egypt from the remotest ages to the reign of Ptolemy Lagus, by Uranius of Alexandria, son of Anaximenes, a perfectly novel work on a subject of deep interest, was offered by Simonides to the celebrated Professor Lepsius in or about 1855; and though for the moment accepted by him and Professor Dindorf, was soon rejected as spurious by them both and all other German scholars: some of those who have since examined the *palimpsest* by the microscope profess to trace the faint outlines of Uranius' history *above* the writing which ought to be more modern. The Biblical fragments were found by Simonides in 1860 when engaged in unrolling masses of papyri (supposed to have come from Egypt) in the Museum of Mr. Mayer, a Liverpool merchant. One of these papyri,

[8] In times when vellum was scarce, it was usual to wash out an original work in order to substitute in its room something later and more popular: the primitive writing being left just legible *under* that of the later hand. Such *palimpsests* are Codd. C and N^b (*see* pp. xxix, xli).

in the subscription to St. Matthew's Gospel, proclaims itself to be the very copy dictated by the Evangelist himself to the deacon Nicolas (Acts vi. 5) his scribe, in the fifteenth year after the Lord's Ascension. Among other marvellous facts which may serve to modify our wonder at such a discovery of the very autograph of the earliest Gospel, our author assures us that he has seen a transcript of this same Gospel, in the monastery of Mount Sinai, "with the inscription of the date of publication extremely clear," which purports to be one out of fourteen copies written by Hermodorus, a disciple of the Lord, sixty-five years after the Ascension, and fifteen after the Evangelist's death. Of this papyrus Simonides has afforded us one exquisite *Facsimile*, and promises the whole Gospel in due time[9]. We are not aware that the Mayer papyri have as yet found a Lepsius sanguine enough to accord to them even a provisional assent. By most scholars they have been held to be condemned by the very extràvagance of their claims on our belief, and those who have felt it their duty to scrutinize them patiently have certainly seen no cause to vary from the verdict which first impressions would suggest.

Such is a brief outline of the previous career of the extraordinary man who on being shown Tischendorf's *Facsimile* of the Codex Sinaiticus (it could have been none other than the portion of Luke xxiv., *see* p. x) annexed to the *Notitia*,

[9] We derive these facts respecting Codd. Nicolai et Hermodori from Dr. Simonides' "Facsimiles of certain portions of the Gospel of St. Matthew and the Epistles of SS. James and Jude, written on papyrus in the first century, and preserved in the Egyptian Museum of Joseph Mayer, Esq., Liverpool," by Constantine Simonides, Ph. D., 1862. No one who has not studied this book can form any adequate notion of the writer and his labours.

which appeared late in 1860, at once pronounced it the work of his own hands. How it was that he had not long ago put in the same claim to be the scribe of Codex Friderico-Augustanus, a part of the self-same copy, which was edited in 1846 (*see* p. vii), especially since he might have seen the original leaves when at Leipsic some years before, is one of the most perplexing parts of his case. Even after he had asserted that Cod. Sinaiticus was his work, he allowed "two years" to elapse before the appearance of his public letter of Sept. 3, 1862.

Simonides' account of the origin of the manuscript is, in substance, the following:—About the end of 1839, when he was living with his uncle Benedict, head of the monastery of Panteleemon on Mount Athos, that venerable dignitary was anxious to send to the Emperor Nicholas of Russia some gift, in dutiful acknowledgment of the benefits he had conferred, from time to time, on that society. Not possessing any thing he deemed acceptable, Benedict resolved to provide a copy of the Old and New Testaments in vellum, in uncial letters of the ancient form. As Dionysius, the professed calligrapher of the monastery, was afraid to undertake the task[1], Simonides commenced it at the request of his uncle, who provided him with that edition of the Greek Bible which the brothers Zosimas, wealthy Russian merchants, had defrayed the cost of publishing at Moscow. This Moscow Bible, after having been collated with three ancient manuscripts and the printed edition of the Codex Alexandrinus, so as to be cleared from many errors (the old spelling however remaining unaltered), was given to Simonides to transcribe. He obtained the vellum from an old book in the convent library, which

[1] As he very well might be, if the scrawl in our *Facsimile* (15) were his veritable hand-writing.

was almost blank, the material being very clean and beautifully finished. He thus copied out both the Old and New Testaments, the Epistle of Barnabas, and the first part of Hermas; he would have completed the whole of the Apostolic Fathers, but that the parchment was now exhausted and Benedict dead. He therefore ended his task by simply writing *Σιμωνιδου το ολον εργον*, gave it over to the binder, and retaining the dedication to the Emperor at the beginning of the book, he sought for another patron who might be disposed to value it.

This patron was found in Constantius, ex-Patriarch of Constantinople and Archbishop of Sinai, at whose residence in the isle of Antigonus, the Patriarch being absent, he left the volume in 1841. Constantius accepted the gift in a gracious and fatherly letter, with which he sent 25,000 piastres (about £1300 we believe [2]) and his benediction. It may well be presumed that the prelate whose benediction to a young scholar amounted to something approaching the fee-simple of his bishopric is now in the number of the blest: he was already dead, as Tischendorf tells us, early in 1859 (*see* p. ix); but in 1844 Simonides heard from his own lips that he had long ago sent the Codex to Sinai, and there accordingly its writer found it (though now imperfect and with an older appearance than it ought to have had) on the occasion of two visits he made there in 1844 and 1852: in 1852 he vainly questioned the librarian about its history.

This strange narrative naturally excited great curiosity, and was subjected to searching criticism. On one leading point, his visits to Sinai, he has been met with a direct contradiction: Callinicos, a monk of Sinai, in a letter dated from that

[2] We can find no authority for putting the Turkish or any piastre at a lower value than between 12 and 13 pence.

convent April 13, 1863, addressed to the late British chaplain at Alexandria, and forwarded through his successor, declares in the name of the brotherhood, including him who held the office of librarian from 1841 to 1858, that no such person as Simonides was ever known there[3]. It was, moreover, soon observed, that if Mr. Steuart's Biography might be trusted, his hero could have been only just fifteen years old when he undertook this very considerable task; and that as barely nine months elapsed between his arrival at Athos in November 1839 and the death of Benedict in August 1840, even had he begun his work immediately on his arrival, he must have proceeded at the rate of 20,000 uncial letters daily, to have advanced thus far in so short a time. To these objections Simonides rejoined that he laboured on some time after his uncle's decease; and that, as regards his age, he was nineteen years old in 1839, having been born, not (as Mr. Steuart alleges) "about the hour of sunrise, Nov. 11, 1824"—that was the birthday of his brother Photius—but on Nov. 5, 1820, the sixth hour before noon. This last correction he supports by publishing a letter to Mr. Steuart[4], complaining of the error, dated as far back as Jan. 16, 1860.

One most serious defect in Dr. Simonides' case is his utter lack of living witnesses, except indeed Mr. Steuart, and that only for the authenticity of the letter dated Jan. 1860. Constantius the Patriarch, whose evidence would have been very important, is unquestionably dead:—of the several persons incidentally mentioned in his narrative, not one has presented himself to corroborate his statements. One person,

[3] His rude but vigorous Greek admits of no mistake: *ὅτι δηλονότι οὐδέποτε Σιμωνίδης τις ἐφάνη εἰς τὸ Μοναστήριον τοῦτο.*

[4] In the *Literary Churchman*, Sept. 1, 1863. We have thought it due to Dr. Simonides to regard this, his last published statement, as his version of the whole transaction.

indeed, respecting whom Simonides had hitherto said nothing, Callinicos, a Greek priest of Alexandria, has borne testimony by letter most strongly and explicitly in his favour; but all attempts to trace his existence in the city whence his letters were dated, and in the community (alas! a small and persecuted flock) of which he is represented to be a distinguished ornament, have hitherto proved unavailing. Until their writer is produced, his letters must go for nothing.

One single circumstance, not hitherto dwelt upon so far as we know, but which seems to tell somewhat in favour of Simonides, ought not to be suppressed, even though we may not think it of any great weight. Hermas, whose treatise closes the Codex Sinaiticus, well as he was known and esteemed in the ancient Church, has attracted comparatively little notice in modern times. Now it certainly is remarkable that Simonides, some years since, brought to Leipsic from Mount Athos, together with the palimpsest of Uranius, one genuine fragment of the Shepherd in Greek, and the transcript of a second made by him from a manuscript in the same place, both which materially assisted Tischendorf in his edition of the Patres Apostolici. It is true that Simonides has been accused of unfair dealings even with regard to these manuscripts of Hermas (*see Prolegom. Cod. Sin.* pp. xl—i, edit. min.), but we do not purpose to enter on that debate, though it has undoubtedly embittered the relations between him and Tischendorf. We merely wish to point out, as a curious coincidence, his having brought from Athos, about 1855, genuine codices of that self-same early treatise, which he now alleges that he copied at Athos in 1840 as an integral part of the Codex Sinaiticus.

We have submitted to the reader a summary of the statements of Dr. Simonides, and of the chief objections which have been urged against their truthfulness: every one will form his own judgment on the facts here placed before him, as we would fain hope, with no undue bias or prepossession. If on the whole it shall be thought that we are under no logical necessity to deny that he wrote in 1839-40 some such manuscript as he has described, one thing appears quite certain, that the manuscript he may have then written neither is nor can be the Codex Sinaiticus.

We consider this last point fully established by the following arguments, each of which we trust will be found to have some force when considered separately, and two or three to prove our conclusion beyond all possibility of doubt.

I. Simonides inscribed on his work when completed *Σιμωνιδου το ολον εργον*, and these words were read on it (whether in 1844 or 1859) by *his* correspondent, the Alexandrian Callinicos. Indeed his whole narrative is grounded on the assertion that he was the only scribe engaged, although Benedict and Dionysius made a few marks or notes in several places. Now even though Tischendorf may be wrong in supposing that so many as four different hands were employed upon Cod. Sinaiticus (*see* p. xvi), it is nearly impossible to maintain, in the face of the internal proofs we have accumulated (*see* p. xvii and note 4, p. xxxii note 7, p. xxxvii note 5), that the whole is the labour of one scribe. Hence the Cod. Simoneidos, as its author calls it, cannot be identical with Cod. Sinaiticus.

II. Again, Simonides transcribed from a Moscow Bible, whose text Benedict had altered by means of his three manuscripts and the printed Cod. Alexandrinus. Cod. Sinaiticus, on the contrary, must have been derived from a model whose lines were similarly divided with its own, that is, in a manner totally unlike what any printed Bible would represent. This is evident from the not unfrequent instances wherein its scribe suffers his eye to wander over a line, or from one line to another, to the utter destruction of the sense. The reader will perceive our meaning if he examines narrowly the examples cited above, p. xv.

III. Yet further, how could *itacisms*, which are nothing better than mere blunders in the spelling, find their place in the transcript of a printed book? Codex Sinaiticus is so full of them, those too of the oldest type (*see* p. lii), that the bulk of our collation is materially increased thereby. Certainly we are told in the letter of Sept. 3 "that the old spelling remained unaltered" when the learned Benedict, by means of his manuscripts, cleared his printed text from errors: but is it likely that he, or any sane person, would have deliberately and systematically changed the true spelling of the Moscow Bible into the false fashion prevailing in the oldest manuscripts? Yet he must have undertaken such a preposterous task if Cod. Simoneidos and Cod. Sinaiticus are one document. The same observations apply, though with less force, to the grammatical peculiarities enumerated in pp. liii—lvi.

IV. Benedict had before him the Codex Alexandrinus, and right glad we are to be told that so ripe a work of western scholarship has penetrated the recesses of the Greek monasteries. How came he then to adopt the Ammonian sections and Eusebian canons of that manuscript, while he rejected the notation of the larger *κεφάλαια* and the titles or headings it also contains; the rather since all known manuscripts except Codd. Sinaiticus, Vaticanus, and Bezae are believed to exhibit them? Then again, as to capital letters larger than the rest: only four documents on *vellum* besides Cod. Sinaiticus are known to be void of them: why not have followed Cod. Alexandrinus and all later manuscripts in this respect also? Why conform to the contrary practice, which had long since become obsolete, when capitals would have so much better enabled Simonides to exhibit his exquisite skill as a calligrapher?

V. From what source too did Benedict derive those divisions in the Acts which are peculiar to Codd. Sinaiticus and Vaticanus alone among all extant copies? Simonides never intimates that either his uncle or he had taken the trouble to ascertain the readings of Cod. B, nor have we seen one word in his subsequent works which would make us think that he even knew of its existence. Add to this that the chapters in Cod. Sinaiticus, though evidently the same in substance as those of the sister manuscript, differ from it (as may be seen by the note appended to our collation of the Acts) sufficiently to prove that the connexion between them is too remote for one to have been derived immediately from the other.

VI. Let us now recall to mind the numerous marks of extreme antiquity on the face of the Cod. Sinaiticus, which have persuaded every competent scholar who has examined it, or received its description on the word of others, that it is a genuine relique of the primitive ages of the Church. It would be very difficult for the most skilful palaeographer living to fabricate a manuscript of but a few leaves in extent, so perfectly like an ancient document in respect to material, and form, and shape of the letters, and the various shades of inks, of different ages and from different hands, as seriously to perplex competent and careful judges: to palm on them a forgery of any considerable length we hold to be quite impracticable. But even were this not the case, such an attempt would necessarily imply experience, adroitness, special information, in a word, *design* and fraudulent intention on the part of the writer of the document. That a boy of fifteen, or a youth of nineteen, who many years afterwards has exhibited surprising ignorance of much which even sciolists are presumed to know, should have executed within the compass of a few months a volume of 1400 pages, comprising nearly four millions of uncial letters; and that too in such a fashion that WITHOUT THE SMALLEST INTENTION TO DECEIVE, or to pass off his performance as an ancient work, he has actually misled the best critics in Europe: —this proposition we must confess to be so unlikely and indeed incredible, that we could not receive it on any evidence whatever.

VII. Finally, the text afforded by the Codex Sinaiticus can never have been derived from the meagre sources described by Simonides, though they might amply suffice for the very limited purpose Benedict had in view. About the character of his three manuscripts used at Athos he is silent, but nothing has ever been brought from the Holy Mountain which much exceeds a thousand years old. To Codex Alexandrinus also that of Sinai approximates less than to most of the same rank, especially in the Gospels and Apocalypse (*see* pp. xli, xlii). But in truth, its text is manifestly derived from an original of the highest interest and authority. Had Benedict been the most acute and accomplished Biblical scholar in Christendom he could not have anticipated in 1839 the results of the discoveries of the last twenty years; no one who in his time sat down to construct an ancient text, which should resemble that of the earliest manuscripts, versions, and ecclesiastical writers, could possibly have been led to the results embodied in the Cod. Sinaiticus; not even though to their deep and comprehensive learning be added the fortunate daring of a Bentley, the tact and ripe judgment of a Griesbach. One example will illustrate our meaning as well as a thousand, which the student may readily find for himself in the following collation. In Matth. xiv. 30 Cod. Sinaiticus omits *ισχυρον* after *ανεμον*: in 1839 no other document, manuscript, version[5], or Father was known to countenance such a variation: it has no such inherent probability as to have suggested itself to Benedict, or to any one else. When Rulotta's revised collation of the Cod. Vaticanus was brought to light again in 1855, it first became known that that venerable authority contains the word *only in a later hand;* in 1857 Tregelles published his collation of the important cursive Cod. 33, made seven years before: this copy also omits *ισχυρον*. Thus, were we now engaged in forming a text that should seem ancient, here is just such a various reading as we should adopt for our purpose; it could not have been so employed twenty-four years ago, since the omission in any one codex was completely unknown, and would not have been conjectured.

Such are the grounds of our firm conviction that Codex Sinaiticus is a monument of the Biblical scholarship and pious skill of the fourth century of our aera. On its happy discovery we congratulate the Christian world, and respectfully thank Professor Tischendorf for the care and diligence he has bestowed upon editing it.

[5] Mill, indeed, in the Appendix to his N. T. (1707), observes "omittit *ἰσχυρὸν Copt.;*" but this, like so many of his best readings, was neglected by the later editors, Wetstein, Griesbach, and Scholz: no one will think that Benedict borrowed the hint from Mill's note.

COLLATION

OF

THE CODEX SINAITICUS

WITH SCRIVENER'S REPRINT (1862) OF STEPHENS' TEXT OF THE NEW TESTAMENT (1550).

N.B. + placed before a reading denotes that it is an addition to Stephens' text.

— placed before a reading denotes that a portion of Stephens' text is wanting in Cod. Sin.

√ is placed after all readings which are only itacisms, instances of ν εφελκυστικον and σ appended, or mere errors of the scribe.

[ ] Doubtful readings in which Stephens' text and Cod. Sin. agree are placed within these brackets.

p.m. indicates readings of the original scribe:

l.m. those of later correctors: viz. A^a, A, A obliq., B, B^a, C (C^a, C^b, C^c), D, E.

κατα μαθθαιον.

CAP. I. 1. δᾱδ *ferè passim*√. 2. εγεννησεν *ter* (*sic passim*
vv. 3. 4. 5. 6. 7. 8. 9. 10. 11. 12. 13. 14. 15. 16)√. ϊσακ *bis* (ϊσαακ'
B).—δε *prim.* (*habet* B). 4. [αμιναδαβ *prim.*]. αμιναδαμ *secund.*
5. βοεσ *bis.* ϊωβηδ *bis.* 6. δαυειδ *secund.*√. —ο βασιλευσ. σα-
λομων (*pro* σολομωντα: σαλωμωνα B). [σολομων: *at* σαλωμων B].
7. αβιασ *secund.* (B *cum* Steph.). ασαφ' *bis.* 9. οζειαν (B *cum*
Steph.)√. [οζιασ]. [αχαζ *prim.*: *at* αχασ A *vel* B]. αχασ *secund.*
[εζεκιαν]. 10. [εζεκιασ]. (μανασση *pro* μανασσησ B). αμωσ *bis.*
ϊωσειαν (-σιαν B)√. 11. ϊωσειασ√ (*caetera cum* Steph.). 13.
αβιουτ: *prim.* (-ουδ' B *bis*). 14. σαδωχ *bis* (B *cum* Steph.).
(αχιμ *bis* B). 14, 15. ελιουτ (-ουδ' B). 15. [ματθαν *bis*, ματ'θαν
B]. 17. ῑδ *ter.* 18. [ῑυ χ̄υ]. γενεσισ. μνηστευθισησ *sic in
textu*; μνηστ. *in annotationibus* (-εισησ B)√.—γαρ. συνελθιν√.
19. παραδιγματισαι (δειγματισαι B). απολυσε√. 20. ϊωσηφ'√. 21.
—αυτου *prim.*, *ut videtur* (αυτου ῑν αυτοσ *rescripsit* A). σωσι√.
22. —του *prim.* (ησαΐου *adnotat* B, *citationis signis* > > *additis*:
sic ii. 6). 23. εξι√. τεξετε√. (τεξεται B). καλεσουσιν√.—αυτου

(cf. v. 21: αυτου εμ'μα *rescripsit* A). εστιν√. [ο θ̅σ̅]. 24. εγερθεισ.—ο *prim.* παρελαβεν√ (*addidit* μαριαμ Cª? *sed prorsus erasum est*). γυνεκα (γυναικα B)√. *fin.* (εαυτου B). 25. ετεκεν ϋϊον (—τον).—αυτησ τον πρωτοτοκον. εκαλεσεν√.

II. 1. ημερεσ (-αισ Cª?)√. (του *improbat* B, *restituit* C). ϊσ (εισ C)√. 2. ϊδομεν (ειδ. B, *non* C)√. αστεραν (—εν) *p.m.*, *ut videtur* (A *vel* B *cum* Steph.). 3. ο βασιλευσ ηρωδησ. 4. (αρχιϊερεισ B). γεννατε (-ται B)√. 5. ειπαν (—αυτω B? *non* C). ουτωσ√. 6. εξου (*pro* εκ σου)√.—γαρ (*habet* B). ποιμανι (-ει B). 7. ηκριβωσεν√. 8. ειπεν√. εξετασατε ακριβωσ. πεδιου√. απαγγιλατε√. 9. ϊδον (ειδον B)√. προηγον *primò* (-εν *forsan p.m.*). εσταθη. 10. αστεραν (ν *eras.* B?). 11. ϊδον (*pro* ευρον: ειδον B). 12. την εαυτων χωραν (την χωραν αυτων B). 13. [φαινεται κατ οναρ]. ζητιν το πεδιον√. απολεσε√. 14. [παρελαβε, *sic* v. 21]. πεδιον√. εκι√. 15. —του *prim.* (εν αριθμοισ *adnotat* B, *additis signis*). 16. ενεπεχθη√. λειαν (λιαν B)√. αποστιλασ ανειλεν√. [πασι]. ηκριβωσεν√. 17. δια (*pro* υπο: Bª *cum* Steph.). 18. —θρηνοσ και. ηθελεν√. εισιν√. 19. φαινεται κατ οναρ. 20. τεθνηκασιν√. πεδιου√. 21. εγερθισ√. εισηλθεν. 22. —επι. τοὺ π̅ρ̅σ̅ αυτου ηρωδου. 23. [ναζαρετ]. (υπο Bª *pro* δια).

III. 1. ημερεσ√. παραγεινεται (-γιν- B)√. [ιωαννησ *passim*]. ιουδεασ√. 2. *init.*—και. ηγγικεν√. βασιλια (-εια B)√. 3. ρηθισ√. δια (*pro* υπο). ευθιασ√. ποιειται (-ειτε B)√. 4. ειχεν√. ην αυτου. 5. ϊουδεα (-δαια B). και πασα η *rescript. p.m.*? 6. [-οντο εν]. + ποταμω (*post* ιορδανη).—υπ αυτου (*habet* Bª). 7. —αυτου (*habet* Bª). φυγιν√. 8. καρπον αξιον. 9. λεγιν√. εγιραι (-ειραι B)√. 10. —και *prim.* 11. + γαρ (*post* μεν). ϋμασ βαπτιζω (*at* B *habet* εν ϋδ. *ante* βαπτ.). βαπτισι√. 12. [-κην το δε]. κατακαυσι√. 14. —ιωαννησ (*habet* Bª). χριαν (χρει- B)√. βαπτισθηνε (-ναι B)√. 15. ειπεν√. [προσ αυτον]. [ουτω, *at* -ωσ B]. ημασ (*pro* ημιν: B Cª *cum* Steph.). 16. βαπτισθεισ δε (—και). ευθυσ ανεβη. [ανεωχθησαν].—αυτω (*habet* Bª). ειδεν√. π̅ν̅α̅ θ̅υ̅ (—το *et* του).—και *ult.* (*habet* Cª). 17. ηϋδοκησα (ευδ- B, *non* C).

IV. 1. [ο ι̅σ̅]. ϋπο του π̅ν̅σ̅ εισ την ερημον. πιρασθηναι (πειρ- B)√. 2. ημ. τεσσερακοντα και τεσσερακοντα νυκτασ. επινασεν√. 3. -θων ο πιραζων ειπεν αυτω. (ειπον ινα B). 4. (ο δ B). ειπεν√. γεγραπτε (-ται B)√. + ο (*ante* α̅ν̅ο̅σ̅). [επι]. 5. παραλαμβανι√. εστησεν. 6. (ειπεν *pro* λεγει B: Cª *cum p.m.*). εντελιτε (-λειτε B Cª)√. αρουσιν (-ρουσι B)√. 7. εκπιρασεισ√. 8. δικνυει. βασιλιασ√. 9. ειπεν (*pro* λεγει). σοι παντα. 10. λεγι√. [ῦπαγε σατ.]. προσκυνησησ. λατρευσισ√. 12. —ο ι̅σ̅. ἴωαννησ οτι (οτι ἴωανν. A B). 13. ναζαρεθ (ναζαρα B). καφαρναουμ. παρα θαλασσαν (-σιαν *p.m. vel* B). 16. σκοτι (-τια B)√. φωσ ἴδεν (φ. ειδεν B). ανετιλεν√. 17. κηρυσσιν (-σειν B)√. λεγιν√. ηγγικεν√. βασιλια (-λεια B)√. 18. —ο ι̅σ̅. ειδεν√. (καλουμενον *pro* λεγομενον B). αλεεισ (αλιεισ B Cª). 19. [αυτοισ δευτε]. αλεεισ (γενεσθαι αλιεισ B). 21. ιδεν√. (εαυτου A, αυτου B). 22. + αυτων (*post* πλοιον: *delet* B). 23. ο ι̅σ̅ εν τη γαλιλαια (— ολην: ο ι̅σ̅ ολην την γ. B). + αυτουσ (*post* διδασκων: *improbat* B). βασιλιασ√. 24. εξηλθεν (*pro* απηλθεν). πασαν (*pro* ολην). βασανουσ (-οισ A *vel* B). [και] δεμονιαζομενουσ (δ *et* μο *rescript.*: *forsan* σ λη *p.m. quasi vellet* σεληνιαζομενουσ, δεμο A *vel* B, δαιμο Cª)√.

V. 1. προσηλθαν (-ηλθον B) [αυτω]. 3. βασιλια (-εια B)√. 4, 5. [*ordo cum* Steph.]. 4. (+ νυν *post* πενθουντεσ B). 5. κληρονομησουσιν√. 6. πινωντεσ√. 8. καρδια (ρ *rescript. p.m.*)√. 9. ἰρηνοποιοι√.— αυτοι. 10. βασιλια (-εια B)√. 11. διωξουσιν√. ειπωσιν π. πον. καθ υμ. (— ρημα). [ψευδομενοι]. 12. χαιρεται√. ουτωσ (*sic* vv. 16. 19)√. 13. ῦμισ√. αλα *prim.* (σ *addit* C, *at eras.*). αλα *secund.* βληθεν εξω καταπατισθε (— και). 14. εσται√. 15. κεουσιν√. λαμπι√. πασιν√. 16. δοξασωσιν√. τον *super ras. p.m., bis*√. 18. (κερεα√ B). 19. κληθησετε√. βασιλια√.— οσ δ αν ποιηση *ad fin. vers. ob* ὁμοιοτελευτον (*supplet* A). 20. ῦμων η δικαιοσυνη. πλεον (πλιον B, *at* Cᵇ? *cum* Steph.). εισελθηται (-τε B)√. βασιλιαν√. 21. οτι ερρεθη τοισ αρ *in rasurâ rescript. ab* A?√. 22. (οτι *improbat* B).— εικη (*habet* Cᵇ). εστε *prim. et tert.*√ ραχα (-κα B). 23. [κακει]. εχι√. 24. εκι√. 25. μετ αυτου εν τη οδω.— σε παραδω *secund.* 26. εκιθεν√. 27. [ερρεθη: *sic* vv. 21. 31. 33. 38. 43].— τοισ αρχαιοισ. μοιχευσισ√. 28. επιθυμησε√.— αυτησ (*habet* Bª). *fin.* [αυτου]. 29. σκανδαλιζι (*sic* v. 30)√. συμφερι (*sic* v. 30)√. 30. η (*pro* και μη: B *cum* Steph.). εισ γεενναν απελθη (*pro* βληθη εισ γ.). 31. — δε (*habent* B C).— οτι. 32. πασ ο απολυων (*pro* οσ αν απολυση). πορνιασ√. μοιχευθηναι. οσ αν (εαν B) απολελυμενην γαμηση. μοιχατε (-ται B)√. 33. εφιορκησεισ. αποδωσισ√. 34. εστιν (*sic* v. 35 *bis*)√. 36. (μηδε B, μητε *p.m. et* C). τριχαν (B *cum* Steph.). λευκην ποιησαι η μελαιναν. 37. [εστω]. 39. αντισταθηναι. ραπιζι√. εισ (*pro* επι: Cª *cum* Steph.).— σου. 40. λαβιν√. τουτω (*pro* αυτω: B? Cª *cum* Steph.). *fin.* + σου. 41. εαν ενγαρευση (*pro* αγγαρευσει). 42. σοι (*pro* σε: B *cum* Steph.). δοσ. δανισασθαι√.

44. —ευλογειτε *usque ad* μισουντασ υμασ. προσευχεσθαι√.—επηρεαζοντων υμασ και. **45.** ανατελλι√.—και βρεχ. *ad fin. vers.* (ὁμοιοτ.): *habet* A, *legens* βρεχι√. **46.** —ουχι (*habet* Bª). [το αυτο]. ποιουσιν√. **47.** ποιειται√. εθνικοι το αυτο (*pro* τελωναι ουτω). **48.** ϋμισ τελιοι√. ωσ (*pro* ωσπερ). ουρανιοσ (*pro* εν τοισ ουρανοισ). τελιοσ εστιν√.

VI. **1.** +δε (*post* προσεχετε). δικαιοσυνην (*pro* ελεημοσυνην: δοσειν A, *at* B *cum p.m.*). θεαθηνε√.—τοισ (*habet* Cª). **2.** ποιησισ *forsan p.m.* τεσ συναγωγεσ (Cª *cum* Steph.)√. αμην *bis legit p.m.* (*improbat alterum* Cª). απεχουσιν√. **3.** ελαιημοσυνην√. **4.** ελεημοσυνη η (*pro* η ελεημ.: B *cum* Steph.).—αυτοσ. αποδωσι (*sic* vv. 6. 18)√.—εν τω φανερω (*sic* vv. 6. 18). **5.** [προσευχη *p.m.*]. ουκ εσεσθε (*at* ουκ εσεσθε ω *p.m. rescript.*, *quae sequuntur* σ οι *spatium occupantibus antea vacuum, o in* ουκ *pro* σ *reposito: hinc constat* προσευχησθε *primò scriptum fuisse:* Cª *habet* προσευχησθαι). ωσ (*pro* ωσπερ). πλατιων√. προσέυχεσθε (*pro* -θαι)√. —αν. φανωσιν√.—οτι. [απεχουσι]. **6.** προσευχησ (σ *eras.*)√. ταμιον. κλισασ√. σου προσευξε *rescript. p.m.*√. —εν τω φανερω. **7.** βατταλογησηται. εθνικοι (θ *rescript.*)√. δοκουσιν√. **8.** οιδεν√. +ο $\overline{θσ}$ (*post* γαρ), *at eras.* χριαν√. **9.** προσευχεσθαι√. °εν (ο *p.m.*). **10.** ελθατω. βασιλια√.—τησ. **12.** οφιληματα√. ημισ√. αφηκαμεν (Cª *cum* Steph.). οφιλεταισ√. **13.** πιρασμον√.—οτι σου κ.τ.λ. *ad finem versûs.* **14.** αφηται√. αυτων (α *supplet* A)√. αφησι (*sic* v. 15)√. **15.** —τα παραπτωματα αυτων. ϋμιν (*pro* υμων *prim.*). **16.** *init.* +και (*improbat* A *vel* B). ωσ (*pro* ωσπερ).—οι (*habet* Cª). [αφανιζουσι]. το προσωπον (Cª *cum* Steph.). [αυτων *prim.*]. [φανωσι]. +γαρ (*post* αμην: *improbat* Cª).—οτι. απεχουσιν√. **17.** αλιψε√. **18.** [τοισ $\overline{ανοισ}$ νησ.]. κρυφαιω (*pro* κρυπτω *prim.*). —σου *secund.* (*habet* Bª). κρυφεω (B -αιω, *pro* κρυπτω *secund.*). —εν τω φανερω. **19.** διορυσσουσιν√. κλεπτουσιν√. **20.** διορυσσουσι και (*pro* -ουσιν ουδε). **21.** σου (*pro* υμων) *bis.* εκι√. [και]. **22.** [-μοσ εαν].—ουν. η ο οφθαλμοσ σου απλουσ. φωτινον εστε√. **23.** η ο οφθαλμοσ σου πονηροσ (B *cum* Steph.). σκοτινον√. εστιν√. **24.** [δυσι]. ει (*pro* η *prim.*). μισησι√. αγαπησι (-ει B)√. ανθεξετε√. μαμωνα. **25.** μεριμναται√. φαγηται√.—και τι πιητε (ὁμοιοτελ.).—υμων *secund.* (*habet* Bª). [εστι]. **26.** εμβλεψαται√. πετινα√. σπιρουσιν√. (+τασ *ante* αποθηκασ). τρεφι√. διαφερεται√. **28.** μεριμναται√. καταμαθεται√. αυξανουσιν. κοπιωσιν. νηθουσιν· (*ab* αγρου *ad fin. vers. rescript. p.m.*, *salvâ lectione*). **30.** ϊ (*pro* ει)√. **32.** ταυτα γαρ παντα. επιζητουσιν.

οιδεν√. +ο θσ (*post* γαρ: δε *pro* γαρ Cª, *qui improbat* ο θσ) cf. v. 8. —ο ουρανιοσ. 33. —του θυ [την β. και την δ.]. 34. μεριμνησι√.—τα.

VII. I. κρινεται√. 2. κριθησεσθαι√. μετριται μετρηθησεται. 3. βλεπισ√. την δε δοκον την εν τω σω οφθαλμω (Cª *cum* Steph.). 4. λεγισ (*pro* ερεισ: B Cª ερισ). +αδελφε (*ante* αφεσ). εκ (*pro* απο). 5. εκ του οφθαλμου σου την δοκον. διαβλεψισ√. εκβαλλειν. 6. κυσιν√. [καταπατησωσιν]. 7. κρουεται√. 8. [ανοιγησεται]. 9. στιν *in* εστιν *p.m. rescript.*√.—εαν (*habet* B). αιτησει. επιδωσι (*non* v. 10)√. 10. *init.* η και ϊχθυν αιτησι. 11. ϋμισ√. οιδαται√. 12. —ουν (*habet* B). εαν (*pro* αν). θεληται√. ϋμειν (ει *p.m. in rasura*)√. ουτωσ√. ϋμισ ποιειται√. 13. εισελθατε. πλατια√.—η πυλη (*habet* B). απωλιαν√.—εισιν (*habet* B). (Cª *pro* εισερχομενοι *legere voluit* πορευομαινοι? *at revocavit*). 14. *init.* [οτι: *at* τι B? Cª]. [η πυλη]. 15. προσεχεται√.—δε. [ενδυμασι]. εισιν√. 16. σταφυλασ. 17. [ουτω]. 18. ποιειν *prim. rescript. p.m., lectione non mutatá.* ενεγκειν (*pro* ποιειν *secund.*: B Cª *cum* Steph.). 19. [παν δενδ.]. 20. [απο]. επιγνωσεσθαι√. 21. βασιλιαν√. τα θεληματα (B *cum* Steph.). +τοισ (*ante* ουνοισ). 22. ερουσιν√. επροφητευσαμεν. δεμονια πολλα (B *improbat* πολλα). εξεβαλλομεν (-αλομεν Cª). δυναμισ√. 24. [τουτουσ]. ομοιωθησεται (*pro* ομ. αυτον). ωκοδομησεν√. αυτου την οικιαν. 25. [ηλθον]. προσεπεσεν (-σαν B). εκινη (*sic* v. 27)√. επεσεν (*sic* v. 27)√. *fin.* +και πασ *p.m. at erasit, sequente* και (v. 26) *in rasura scripto*√. 26. ωκοδομησεν αυτου την οικιαν. (*fin.* ψαμμον Cª? *at* ψ *erasum*). 27. ηλθαν.—και επνευσαν οι ανεμοι (ὁμοιοτ.: *supplet* A). [προσεκοψαν]. 28. ετελεσεν. εξεπληττοντο (-σσοντο B). επι τη διδαχη αυτου οι οχλοι (B Cª *cum* Steph.). 29. *fin.* +αυτων *tantum.*

VIII. 1. [-βαντι δε αυτω: *at* -βαντοσ δε αυτου B]. 2. προσελθων. 3. εκτινασ√. +αυτου (*post* χειρα: *improbat* B, *non* C). —ο ισ. —ευθεωσ (*habet* B). [εκαθ.]. 4. ειπεν (*pro* λεγει: Cª λεγι). αλλα. διξον√. [προσενεγκε]. προσεταξεν√. μωϋσησ. 5. εισελθοντοσ δε αυτου (—τω ιυ). καφαρναουμ. εκατονταρχησ (-χοσ B). 6. —κυριε (*habet* B). δινωσ√. 7. [και]. λεγι√.—ο ισ. +ακολουθι μοι (*ante* εγω: *improbat* Cª). 8. αποκριθεισ δε (—και: B C *cum* Steph.). εκατονταρχησ (-χοσ B). ειπεν (*pro* εφη: B *cum* Steph.). λογω. 9. +τασσομενοσ (*post* εξουσιαν). πορευετε√. ερχετε√. 10. εθαυμασεν√. ειπεν√. [*caetera cum* Steph.]. 11. ηξουσιν√. ϊσακ. 12. εξελευσονται *ut videtur p.m.* (A *cum* Steph.

εκβλη.). εστε√. 13. εκατονταρχη (-χω B).—και *secund.*—αυτου. [εν τ. ω. ε.]. *fin.* + και ϋποστρεψασ ο εκατονταρχοσ εισ τον οικον αυτου εν αυτη τη ωρα ευρεν τον παιδα ϋγιαινοντα (*uncis improbat* B, *sed rursus unci eraduntur*). 14. ειδεν√. 15. χιροσ√. ^{n}εγερθη ϗ διηκονι (^{n} *etiam* η ϗ *per* B: εγερθισα *p.m., ut videtur*). *fin.* αυτω (-οισ B). 16. εξεβαλεν√. 17. ασθενιασ√. ελαβεν√. 18. —πολλουσ (*habet* C^a, *fortasse pro* οχλουσ). 20. εχουσιν√. πετινα√. κατασκηνωσισ√. εχι√. 21. —αυτου. θαψε (*sic* v. 22)√. 22. —ισ̄. λεγι (*pro* ειπεν). ακολουθι√. 23. [το: *improbat* B, *restituit* C]. μαθητε√. 24. σισμοσ√. [το]. καλυπτεσθε√. εκαθευδεν√. 25. —οι μαθηται αυτου. ηγιραν√.—ημασ. 26. λεγι√. διλοι√. εγερθισ επετιμησεν√. τω ανεμω (B *cum* Steph.). θαλλασση√. 27. [και *prim.*]. αυτω ϋπακουουσιν. 28. ελθοντων αυτων (ελθοντοσ αυτου B). γαζαρηνων (*pro* γεργεσηνων: C^a *cum* Steph.). δεμονιζομενοι (δαιμ. C^a)√. μνημιων√. εκινησ√. 29. — ιησου. ϋιε *rescript. per* B? (ῡε *p.m.*?)√. ημασ απολεσαι προ καιρου (ημασ βασανισαι ημασ προ κ. B). 31. εκβαλλισ√. αποστιλον ημασ (*pro* επιτρεψον ημιν απελθειν). 32. [αυτοισ ϋπ.]. απηλθον εισ τουσ χοιρουσ (—την αγελην). ωρμησεν√.—των χοιρων *secund.* (απεθαναν B). 33. απηγγιλαν√. 34. ϋπαντησιν του ιῡ. ειδοντεσ√. [οπωσ].

IX. 1. —το. διεπερασεν√. 2. [προσεφερον]. ειδων√. ειπεν√. αφιενται. σου (*pro* σοι). *fin.* —σου. 3. [ειπον]. 4. [ιδων]. —υμεισ. καρδιεσ (-ιαισ C^a)√. 5. αφιονται (αφιενται C^a). σου (*pro* σοι). εγειρε.—και (*habet* B). περιπατι√. 6. εχι√. [εγερθεισ]. πορευου (*pro* υπαγε: C^a *cum* Steph.). 8. εφοβηθησαν (*pro* εθαυμασαν). 9. —εκειθεν (εκιθεν B). (+ εκι C^a *ante* καθημενον: *sed erasum*). μαθθαιον.—και *secund.* (*habet* B). λεγι√. ακολουθι√. ηκολουθει (*pro* -θησεν). 10. —εγενετο αυτου. ανακειμενων (*at* και εγενετο ανακιμενου αυτου C^a).—και *secund.* τελωνε (-ναι C^a)√. —ελθοντεσ (*habet* B). συνανεκιντο√. μαθητεσ√. 11. ελεγον (*pro* ειπον). 12. —ιησουσ.—αυτοισ. χριαν√. ϊατρων. [αλλ]. 13. μαθεται√. ελεοσ. αλλα.—εισ μετανοιαν. 14. ημισ√.—πολλα (*habet* C, *at* πυκνα A *vel* B). νηστευουσιν√. 15. —ελευσονται δε *usque ad* νυμφιοσ (ὁμοιοτ.: *supplet* A, *legens* νυμφειοσ). 16. παλεων√. αιρι√.—αυτου (*habet* B). γεινεται√. 17. εκχειται (κ *forsan a* B *suppletum*)√. απολλυνται. αλλ οινον νεον εισ ασκουσ καινουσ βλητεον. αμφοτεροι. 18. αρχων προσελθων (+ εισ *post* αρχων B C^a: ελθων C^a). προσεκυνι√.—οτι. 19. ηκολουθει. 20. αιμαροουσα (αιμοροουσα C^a). 21. ελεγεν√.—μονον (*habet* B). 22. —ιησουσ (*habet*

B). στραφεισ. ειπεν θαρσι√. [θυγατερ]. σεσωκεν√. εκινησ√. 24. ελεγεν (— αυτοισ). αναχωριτε√. απεθανεν *prim.*√. *fin.* + ειδοτεσ οτι απεθανεν (*improbat* Cª). 25. εκρατησεν√. χιροσ√. 26. αυτησ (*pro* αυτη). 27. [αυτω]. κραυγαζοντεσ. [ϋϊε]. 28. *init.* εισελθοντι δε αυτω (ελθοντι δε αυτ. Cª). [προσηλθον]. + δυο (*ante* τυφλοι : *improbat* Cª).— ο (*habet* Cª : *at p.m. etiam* ισ *omisit primò*). + ϋμιν (*ante* τουτο ποιησαι : A Cª *improbant*, B *habet*). 30. [ανεωχθησαν].— αυτων (*habet* Cª). ενεβριμηθη. μηδισ√. 31. — ολη (*habet* B). 32. — ανθρωπον. 33. — οτι. 34. — εν (*habet* B). δεμονια√. 35. πολισ√.— και *tert.* (*habet* B). [εν τω λαω : *delet* B]. *fin.* + και ηκολουθησαν αυτω (*delet* B). 36. εσκυλμενοι (*pro* εκλελυμενοι). εριμμενοι. [ωσει]. 37. λεγι√. μαθητεσ√. εργατε√.

X. 1. ιβ (*sic* vv. 2. 5)√. εκβαλλιν√. 2. εστιν√. + και (*ante* ϊακωβοσ : *at eras.*). 3. βαρθολομεοσ√. μαθθεοσ.— και λεββαιοσ ο επικληθεισ (και *tantum habet* B). 4. [κανανιτησ]. ο ιουδασ ο ϊσκαριωτησ (B *cum* Steph.). (παραδιδουσ B : *at* δι *eras.*). 5. απεστιλεν√. παραγγιλασ√.— λεγων (*habet* B).— εθνων (*habet* B). απελθηται√. σαμαριτων√. εισελθηται√. 7. βασιλια√. 8. νεκρουσ εγειρεται λεπρουσ καθαριζεται (*literae* νεκ *p.m.*, *at in rasurâ scriptae, fortasse* λεπ *primò* : νεκρ. εγ. *improbat* A *vel* B ; *postea restitut.*). 9. κτησησθαι√.— μηδε αργυρον (ὁμοιοτ. : *habet* B). 10. [ραβδον]. *fin.* — εστιν. 11. εισελθηται εξετασαται√. εν αυτη τισ. εστιν√. μινατε√. εξελθηται√. 12. *fin.* + λεγοντεσ ειρηνη τω οικω τουτω (*improbant* B ? C ; *postea restitut.*). 13. ελθατω. ϊρηνη *bis in versu*√. εφ (*pro* προσ). 14. αν (*pro* εαν). + εξω (*ante* τησ οικιασ).— τησ *secund.* + η κωμησ (*post* πολεωσ). εκινησ√. + εκ (*ante* των ποδων). 15. + γη (*ante* γομορρων). πολι εκινη√. 16. ο οφισ (οι οφισ Cª). ακαιρεοι√. 17. παραδωσουσιν√. 18. βασιλισ√. αχθησεσθαι√. 19. παραδωσιν. εκινη√. *fin.* λαλησητε. 20. ϋμισ√. 21. παραδωσι√. αδελφοσ (*pro* αδελφον : ν C ?)√. γονισ√. 22. υπομινασ√. 23. πολι√. φευγεται√. ετεραν (*pro* αλλην : *nihil additum*). πολισ√. [του].— αν (*at* ου Cª). 24. εστιν√. + αυτου (*post* διδασκαλον). 25. [τον οικοδ.]. βεεζεβουλ. επεκαλεσαντο (επεκαλεσαν Cª). [τουσ οικιακ.]. 26. εστιν√. αποκαλυφθησετε√. γνωσθησετε√. 28. φοβισθε (*pro* φοβηθητε) *bis in vers.* : *sic* v. 31. αποκτεννοντων. αποκτιναι√. και ψυχην και το σωμα (την ψυχ. B). απολεσε√. 29. πωλειτε√. πεσιται√. 30. ηριθμημενε εισιν√. 31. φοβισθε. διαφερεται ϋμισ√. 32. ομολογησι√. [εν ουρ. : *sic* v. 33]. 33. [δ αν]. αρνησομε√. καγω αυτον. 34. νομισηται√. ϊρηνην βαλιν *prim.* βαλιν ϊρηνην *secund.*

37. εστιν *bis in versu* (*sic* v. 38)√. 38. ου λαμβανι. ακολουθι. 39. — ο ευρων *usque ad* και *inclusum* (*supplet* A, *legens* απολεσιν√). ευρησιν√. 40. δεχετε *bis in vers.*√. ο δε (*pro* και ο: Cª *cum* Steph.). αποστιλαντα√. 41. λημψετε *bis in vers.* δικεου *secund.*√. 42. [εαν].

XI. 1. ιβ√. διδασκιν√. κηρυσσιν√. 2. δια (*pro* δυο). 4. αποκριθισ√. (ο ισ: *sic* Tischend., *at deest annotatio: nec lucem affert facsimil.* Tab. VI.). απαγγιλατε√. + τω (*ante* ϊωαννη: *improbat* B). 5. αναβλεπουσιν και. περιπατουσιν√. καθαριζοντε και. ακούουσιν√. + και (*ante* νεκροι). εγιροντε και. ευαγγελιζοντε√. 6. [εαν]. 7. λεγιν√. εξηλθατε (*sic ferè* vv. 8. 9). θεασασθε√. 8. εξηλθαται. ανον ϊδιν (ϊδιν ανον B). — ιματιοισ. [βασιλεων]. — εισιν (*habet* Cª). 9. εξηλθατε. προφητην ϊδιν (ϊδ. πρ. C). 10. — γαρ. εστιν√. [εγω]. [οσ]. κατασκευασι√. 11. εγηγερτε√. γυνεκων√. μιζων *bis in versu*√. βασιλια (*sic* v. 12)√. [αυτου εστιν]. 12. βιαζετε√. βιαζστε (*primò* βιαζετε: B? ζε *in* ζσ *mutat*)√. 13. επροφητευσαν. 14. δεξασθε√. ερχεσθε√. 15. [ακουειν]. 16. εστιν√. παιδιοισ καθημενοισ εν τεσ αγορεσ (ταισ αγοραισ Cª) α προσφωνουντα τοισ ετεροισ λεγουσιν (— αυτων και). 17. — υμιν *secund.* 18. ηλθεν√. λεγουσιν√. δεμονιον (δαιμ. Cª)√. 19. φιλοσ τελωνων. εδικεωθη√. εργων (*pro* τεκνων). 20. ονιδιζειν√. πλισται√. δυναμισ (*sic* v. 21)√. 21. χοραζειν√. βηδσαϊδαν (ν *eras.*). (ει η εν B, *at ipse delet* η)√. + καθημενοι (*ante* μετενοησαν). 22. εστε√. 23. καφαρναουμ μη εωσ ουνου ϋψωθηση. [καταβιβασθηση]. εγενηθησαν (*pro* εγενοντο). δυναμισ√. [αι γενομεναι εν σοι: *at* σοι *ab* A *super rasuram scriptum:* ϋμιν *p.m., ut videtur*]. εμεινεν. 24. — οτι (*habet* B, *at eras.*). ανεκτοτερον εστε γη σοδομων. 25. εκινω√. αποκριθισ√. εκρυψασ. 26. ευδοκια εγενετο. 27. — μου (*habet* B?). ουδισ√. επιγινωσκι *bis in versu*√. βουλητε ο υσ αποκαλυψε. 29. — απ εμου (*habet* A). πραϋσ. ταπινοσ√. ψυχεσ√. 30. [χρηστοσ].

XII. 1. εκινω√. σαββασιν√. μαθητε√. επινασαν√. τιλλιν√. 2. ειπαν. εξεστιν (*sic* vv. 10. 12)√. 3. εποιησεν√. δαδ (*sic* v. 23)√. επινασεν√. — αυτοσ. 4. εφαγον. [ουσ]. φαγιν√. ϊερευσιν√. 5. ϊερισ√. βεβηλουσιν√. εισιν√. 6. μιζον. 7. ελεοσ. 8. εστιν√. — και. 9. εκιθεν√. 10. — ην την. χιρα√. σαββασιν (*sic* v. 12)√. θεραπευσε. 11. [εσται]. εξι√. πεση (ενπ. B). κρατησασ εγερει αυτο (— και). 12. διαφερι√. 13. λεγι√. εκτινον σου την χειρα (+ σου C, *at eras.*). εξετινεν√. απεκατεσταθη. — ωσ η αλλη. 14.

8

εξελθοντεσ δε οι φαρισεοι συμβουλιον ελαβον κατ αυτου. 15. εκιθεν√.—οχλοι. 16. [φαν. αυτ.]. 17. ἵνα (*pro* οπωσ). 18. —εισ (*habet* B). ηΰδοκησεν. 19. τεσ (ταισ Cᵃ) πλατιαισ√. 20. σβεσι√. 21. —εν. ελπιουσιν√. 22. [προσηνεχθη]. [δαιμονιζομενοσ τυφλοσ και κωφοσ]. αυτουσ (*pro* αυτον: Cᵃ *cum* Steph.).—τυφλον και. —και (*ante* λαλειν: *habet* Cᵃ). βλεπιν√. 24. εκβαλλι (*sic* v. 26)√. βεεζεβουλ (*sic* v. 27). δεμονιων (δαι- Cᵃ)√. 25. ἴδωσ (ν *eras. super* σ: ν *per* B?).—ο ιησουσ. βασιλια (*sic* vv. 26. 28)√. μερισθισα *bis in versu*√. 26. σταθησετε√. 27. εκβαλλουσιν√. κριται εσονται ὑμων. 28. εν πνι θυ εγω. δεμονια (δαι- Cᵃ)√. 29. εισελθιν√. [διαρπασαι]. *fin.* διαρπαση. 30. εστιν√. σκορπιζι√. *fin.* + με. 31. αφεθησετε *bis in versu* (*sic* v. 32 *bis*)√.—τοισ ανθρωποισ *secund.* 32. εαν (*pro* αν *prim.*). ου μη (*pro* ουκ: B? C *cum* Steph.). [εν τουτω τω]. 33. ποιησαται *prim.*√. αγαθον *forsan primò*, *at* καλον *secund. p.m.* γινωσκετε√. 34. γεννηματα (τα *p.m.*?). λαλιν√. 35. —τησ καρδιασ. [τα]. 36. λαλησουσιν (—εαν). αποδωσουσιν (απο *improbat* B?, *sed postea restitut.*). 37. δικεωθηση√.—σου *secund.* 38. + αυτω (*ante* τινεσ). φαρισεων√. σημιον ιδιν√. 39. αποκριθισ√. σημιον *ter in versu*√. επιζητι√. δοθησετε√. 40. τρισ *ter*, γ̄ *semel.* εστε√. 41. νινευειτε√. αναστησοντε√. κρισι (*non* v. 42)√. 42. εγερθησετε√. κατακρινι√. ακουσε√. σολομωνοσ *bis in versu.* 43. διερχετε√. (ζητουν: ω A *vel* B: *sed deletum*). 44. λεγι√. εισ τον οικον μου επιστρεψω.—ελθον (*habet* A). + και (*ante* σεσαρ.). 45. πορευετε√. παραλαμβανι√. [επτα ετερα]. κατοικι εκι√. γινετε√. εκινου χιρονα√. εστε√. 46. —δε. (αυτου *secund. punctis notat.*, *sed restitut.*). ἵστηκισαν√.—ζητουντεσ *usque ad fin. versûs sequentis* (*supplet* A, *legens* v. 47 ειπεν δε τισ των μαθητων αυτου ἴδου η μηρ σου και οι αδελφοι σου εξω ζητουσιν σε: cf. Marc. iii. 32). 48. ειπεν√. λεγοντι (*pro* ειποντι). 49. εκτινασ√. χιραν *p.m.*, *ut videtur*.—αυτου *prim.* (*habet* A). 50. [ποιηση].

XIII. 1. —δε. εκινη√. εκ (*pro* απο). 2. —το. καθησθε√. ἵστηκι√. 3. σπιρων. σπιρε√. 4. σπιριν√. επεσεν√. ηλθεν τα πετινα και. 5. ειχεν√. εξανετιλεν√. εχιν (*non* v. 6)√. [βαθοσ γησ]. 6. ανατιλαντοσ√. 7. επνιξαν. 8. *fin.* λ̄√. 9. —ακουειν (*habet* Cᵃ). 10. μαθηται ειπαν. αυτοισ λαλεισ (B *cum* Steph.). 11. —αυτοισ. γνωνε√. βασιλιασ√. εκινοισ√. 12. δοθησετε√. περισσευθησετε√. εχι *prim.*√. αρθησετε√. 13. παραβολεσ (-αισ Cᵃ)√. βλεπουσιν√. συνιουσιν. 14. —επ. προφητια√. βλεψητε. 15. ωσιν αυτων *prim.* ἴδωσιν√. (+ αυτων *post* ωσιν *secund.* B). ακουσωσιν√. συνωσιν√. επιστρεψωσιν√. ϊασομε√. 16. βλεπουσιν√. [ϋμων *secund.*]. ακουουσιν√. 17. —γαρ. προφητε√. δικεοι (-αιοι C^{a})√. ϊδιν√. ιδαν. ακουσε√. 18. υμισ√. σπιραντοσ (-ροντοσ C^{a}). 19. βασιλιασ√. ερχετε√. αρπαζι√. σπαρισ (*sic* vv. 20. 23, *non* 22)√. 21. εχι√. εστιν√. 22. —τουτου (*habet* B?). συνπνιγει. γινετε√. 23. την καλην γην. συνιεισ. καρποφορι√. ρ̄. ξ̄. λ̄√. 24. βασιλια (*sic* v. 31, *non* 33)√. σπιραντι. 25. καθευδιν√. επεσπαρκεν (επεσπειρεν B). 26. εποιησεν√. 27. εσπιρασ√. εχι τα ζ. (B *delet* τα). 28. δουλοι λεγουσιν αυτω (—ειπον). θελισ√. 29. φησιν (*pro* εφη). 30. συναυξανεσθε√. αχρι (μεχρι B? *sed* αχρι *restitut.*). [τω καιρω: τω *delet* B? *sed restitut.*]. θεριστεσ√. [εισ δ.]. κατακαυσε√. [συναγαγετε]. 31. εσπιρεν√. 32. εστιν *bis in versu*√. (αυξηση C? *sed restitut.*). γινετε√. [κατασκηνουν]. 33. + λεγων (*ante* ομοια). 34. ουδεν ελαλησεν (*at* ουκ ελαλι C^{a}). 35. + ησαϊου (*post* δια: *delet* B). παραβολεσ (*pro* -αισ)√. [κοσμου: *delet* C, *sed restitut.*]. 36. αφισ√. εισηλθεν√.— ο ιησουσ. προσηλθον *p.m.*, *at* -εν *primò*. μαθητε√. διασαφησον (*pro* φρασον: C^{a} *cum* Steph.). 37. —αυτοισ. σπιρων√. 38. βασιλιασ (*sic* v. 41)√. 39. ο σπιρασ αυτα εστιν. —θερισμοσ *usque ad* οι δε (ὁμοιοτ.: *supplet* A, του *omisso ante* αιωνοσ, *quod supplet* C^{a})√. 40. συλλεγετε√. [κατακαιεται]. εστε√. συντελια√.—τουτου. 41. αποστελι√.—αυτου *prim.* 42. βαλλουσιν (λ *prius eras.*). εκι√. εστε (εσται B?)√. 43. δικεοι (δικαιοι B?)√.—ακουειν (*habet* C^{a}). 44. —παλιν. (+ δε *post* ομοια B). βασιλια (-λεια B)√.—εν τω αγρω (ὁμοιοτ.: *supplet* A). εκρυψεν√. ϋπαγι√. πωλι παντα οσα εχι√. εκινον√. 45. βασιλια (*sic* v. 47)√.—ανθρωπω (*habet* B). 46. ευρων δε (—οσ). πεπρακεν√. ειχεν√. 47. βληθιση√. 48. [επι τον αιγιαλον και: *at* και επι τ. αι. B? *sed prior lectio restitut.*]. αγγη. εβαλλον (εβαλον B?). 49. εστε (*sic* v. 50)√. συντελια√. εξελευσοντε√. [αφοριουσι]. 50. βαλλουσιν (βαλουσιν B?). 51. —λεγει αυτοισ ο ισ̄.—κυριε. 52. [ειπεν]. μαθητευθισ τη βασιλια (—εισ). ομοια (ομοιοσ A *vel* B, *itemque* C)√. 53. εκιθεν√. 54. αντιπατριδα (πατριδα A *vel* B). εκπλησσεσθε. δυναμισ√. 55. ουχ (*pro* ουχι). λεγετε√. ϊωσηφ (-σηφ A *in rasura*: ϊωαννησ *p.m.*, *ut videtur*). 56. εισιν√. [ταυτα παντα]. 57. —ιησουσ. εστιν√. ϊδια πατριδι (—αυτου). 58. εκι√. δυναμισ√.

XIV. 1. $^{\beta}$ηκουσεν ηρωδησ ^{a}εν εκινω τω $^{/}$καιρω ($^{\beta\ a\ /}$ B *vel forsan p.m.*). τετρααρχησ. ειπεν√. 2. δυναμισ√. 3. —αυτον (*habet* A). και εν φυλακη απεθετο (εν τη φ. και απ. C^{a}). [φιλιππου]. 4. ελεγεν√.—αυτω (*habet* C^{a} *post* ϊωαννησ).—ο. εξεστιν√. εχιν√.

5. αποκτιναι√. 6. γενεσιοισ δε γενομενοισ (*pro* γενεσιων δε αγ.). ηρεσεν√. 7. μετα. [εαν]. 8. προβιβασθισα√. (*Post* αυτησ *forsan scripsit* B ειπεν, *at rursus eras.*) 9. [ελυπηθη]. [δε]. συνανακιμενουσ√. εκελευσεν√. 10. απεκεφαλισεν (—τον: *habet* Cª). 11. ηνεγκεν√. 12. πτωμα αυτου (*pro* σωμα: αυτου *deletum, et restitutum*). αυτον (*pro* αυτο: B? *cum* Steph.). απηγγιλαν√. 13. ακουσασ δε (—και). εκιθεν√. πεζοι. 14. —ο ισ. ειδεν√. επ αυτοισ. εθεραπευσεν√. 15. [προσηλθον]. μαθητε√. —αυτου. παρηλθεν ηδη. +ουν (*post* απολυσον). χωρασ (*pro* κωμασ: Cª *cum* Steph.). 16. —ισ (*habet* Cª). χριαν√. απελθιν√. υμισ φαγιν√. 17. αρτουσ ει μη πεντε (Cª *cum* Steph.). 18. ειπεν√. ωδε αυτουσ. 19. εκελευσεν. του χορτου. [και λαβων]. ε̄ *et* β̄√. ευλογησεν√. εδωκεν√. 21. ωσι (ωσει B? Cª)√. [γ. και π.]. 22. —ευθεωσ (*habet* B). ηναγκασεν (—ο ισ).—αυτου. εμβηνε√. [το]. προαγιν√. 23. —απολυσασ τουσ οχλουσ (ὁμοιοτ.: *supplet* A). προσευξασθε√. 24. [μεσον τησ θ. ην]. 25. ηλθεν.—ο ισ. την θαλασσαν. 26. ἰδοντεσ δε αυτον (—και *et* οι μαθηται: *at* οι δε μαθ. ἰδον. αυτ. A). τησ θαλασσησ. εστιν√. 27. ευθυσ. [αυτοισ].—ο ισ (*post* ελαλησεν *ponit* A). θαρσιτε√. φοβισθε√. 28. αποκριθισ√. [αυτ. ο πετ.] ειπεν. ει συ ει κε, ελθιν προσ σε. 29. —ο *secund.* ελθιν ηλθεν ουν (*pro* ελθειν: ηλθεν ουν *improbat* C). 30. —ισχυρον (Cod. B. *in marg.*). καταποντιζεσθε εκραξεν√. 31. ευθυσ. εκτινασ√. 32. αναβαντων. 33. —ελθοντεσ. 34. επι (*pro* εισ). +εισ (*ante* γεννησαρετ). 35. απεστιλαν√. εκινην√. 36. εσωθησαν.

XV. 1. προσερχοντε√.—οι. φαρισαιοι και γραμματεισ. 2. μαθητε√. παραβενουσι√. χιρασ (χειρ. B).—αυτων. 3. —και (*habet* C). παραβενετε√. 4. ενετιλατο λεγων (Cª ειπεν: *at* ενετ. λ. *restitut.*).—σου. 5. υμισ√. ουδεν εστιν (*pro* και: *improbat* ουδ. εσ. A *vel* B). [τιμηση].—η την μητερα αυτου. 6. τον νομον (*pro* την εντολην: Cª τον λογον, *at* νομ. *restitutum*). 7. επροφητευσεν√. 8. —εγγιζει μοι.—τω στοματι αυτων και. χιλεσιν√. 11. +τουτο (*ante* κοινοι *prim.*: *improbat* Cª). 12. —αυτου. ειπαν. 13. αποκριθισ ειπεν√. φυτια√. εκριζωθησετε√. 14. οδηγοι εισιν τυφλοι (—τυφλων: *at* Cª τυφλοι εισιν οδ. τυφλων, *sed prior lectio restituitur*). πεσουντε *primò, at* -ται *p.m.*?√. 15. —ταυτην. 16. —ισ. υμισ√. 17. [ουπω]. νοιτε√. χωρι√. +τον (*ante* αφεδρωνα). εκβαλλετε√. 18, 19. —εξερχεται *usque ad* καρδιασ (ὁμοιοτ.: *supplet* A). 19. πορνιαι√. 20. εστιν√. χερσιν φαγιν√. 21. εκιθεν√. 22. εκινων√. εκραξεν (*pro* εκραυγασεν: Cª εκραζεν).

11

—αυτω. [υιε δαδ]. δαιμονιζετε√. 23. ηρωτουν. 24. αποκριθισ (non vv. 26. 28)√. 25. προσεκυνι√ (C προσεκυνησεν). βοηθι√. 26. εστιν καλον. λαβιν√. βαλιν√. 27. ειπεν√. 28. θελισ√. εκινησ√. 29. εκιθεν√. ηλθεν√. 30. κυλλουσ κωφουσ. εριψαν. αυτου (pro του ιυ). 31. τον οχλον. θαυμασε√.—κυλλουσ υγιεισ. + και (ante χωλουσ). εδοξαζον. 32. —αυτου. (+αυτοισ post ειπεν A). σπλαγχνιζομε√. [ημερασ γ προσμενουσι]. εχουσιν√. φαγωσιν√. απολυσε√. νηστισ√. μη (pro μηποτε). 33. —αυτου. χορτασε√. 34. λεγι√. ειπαν. 35. παραγγιλασ τω οχλω (pro εκελευσε τοισ οχλοισ). αναπεσιν√. 36. init. —και. ελαβεν. + δυο (ante ιχθυασ: improbat C[a]). + και (post ιχθυασ). εκλασεν√. εδιδου. μαθητεσ (-ταισ A?)√.—αυτου. μαθητε (-ται A?)√. τοισ οχλοισ. 37. [ηρ. το π. των κλ.]. πληρισ√. 38. ανδρεσ ωσι τετρακισχιλιοι. πεδιων και γυνεκων. 39. [ενεβη]. μαγαδαν (μαγεδαν C[a]).

XVI. 1. (+οι ante σαδδ. C[a]). πιραζοντεσ√. (ηρωτησαν C[a], sed prior lectio restituitur). σημιον√. επιδιξε√. 2. —οψιασ γενομενησ usque ad finem v. 3. 4. σημιον ter in versu.√. δοθησετε√. —του προφητου. απηλθεν√. 5. —αυτου. 6. —αυτοισ (sic v. 8). 8. —αυτοισ. εχετε (pro ελαβετε). 9. —ουδε μνημονευετε (ὁμοιοτ.: habet C[a], at -εται√). 10. ζ√. [σπυριδασ]. 11. αρτων. προσεχετε δε (pro προσεχειν). φαρεισαιων hic√. 12. Rescript. p.m. usque ad τησ ζ. ειπεν√. των φαρεισαιων και σαδδουκαιων (pro του αρτου: at των αρτων corrigit C[a]). αλλα. διδασκαλιασ (pro διδαχησ: C[a] cum Steph.). φαρεισαιων secund.√. 13. καισαριασ√. οι ανοι ειναι λεγουσιν (—με: at λεγ. ειν. C[a]). 14. [ειπον]. ιωανην. [αλλοι]. 15. [αυτοισ υμεισ]. 16. ειπεν√. 17. αποκριθεισ δε (—και). απεκαλυψεν√. αλλα. [τοισ]. 19. init.—και. κλιδασ (κλισ C[a]). [ο εαν bis in versu]. την γην prim. (τησ γησ C[a]). [δεδεμενον]. 20. [διεστειλατο].—αυτοισ.—ισ (habet C[a]). 21. ισ χσ (—ο: improbat utrumque C[a]: ο ισ C[b]?). δικνυειν√. εισ ιεροσολυμα απελθειν. 22. [επιτιμαν αυτω]. ειλεωσ√. 23. ειπεν (sic v. 24)√. ει εμου (ει μου C). 25. εαν (pro αν prim.). 26. ωφεληθησεται. (οταν pro εαν C[a]: at εαν restitut.). [λλ]. 27. τα εργα (pro την πραξιν: C[a] cum Steph.). 28. +οτι (ante εισιν√). [των ωδε]. εστωτων. [γευσωνται]. ϊδωσιν√. (pro βασιλεια C[a] habet δοξη του πρσ).

XVII. 1. τον ιακωβον και ϊωανην. 2. ελαμψεν√. 3. ωφθη. μωυσησ. ηλειασ. συνλαλουντεσ μετ αυτου. 4. ειπεν√. ποιησω. μωϋσει. ηλεια μιαν. 5. [ευδ.]. ακουετε αυτου. 6. επεσαν. 7.

προσηλθεν. και αψαμενοσ (*pro* ηψατο).— και (*ante* ειπεν). 8. — τον (*ante* ι̅ν̅). + αυτον (*ante* μονον). 9. εκ (*pro* απο). [αναστη]. 10. ^{ε}πηρ. (ε *p.m.*)√.— αυτου. ηλειαν. 11. — ι̅σ̅. [αυτοισ]. + οτι (*ante* ηλειασ).— πρωτον. 12. ηλειασ. ηλθεν√. [αλλ].— εν. ουτωσ√. 13. ιωανου. 14. — αυτων. αυτον (*pro* αυτω). 15. — κυριε. εχει (*pro* πασχει). 17. ο δε αποκριθεισ (— ι̅σ̅: *at* C^a τοτε αποκρ. ο ι̅σ̅). + αυτοισ (*post* ειπεν). μεθ υμων εσομαι. 18. — ο παισ. 19. ειπαν. 20. — ι̅σ̅. λεγει (*pro* ειπεν). ολιγοπιστιαν. μεταβα. ενθεν (*pro* εντευθεν). 21. *Deest versus* (*habet* C^b, *legens* εκβαλλεται *pro* εκπορευεται). 22. συστρεφομενων. γαλειλαια√. 23. [εγερθησεται]. 24. καφαρναουμ. [-χμα *bis in versu*]. (ειπαν C^a). — τα *secund.* (*habet* C^a). 25. εισελθοντα (*pro* οτε εισηλθεν: *sic* C^b? *at* ελθοντα C^a?). λαμβανουσιν√. 26. ο δε εφη (*pro* λεγει αυτω ο πετροσ). + ειποντοσ δε απο των αλλοτριων (*post* αλλοτριων). 27. σκανδαλιζωμεν.— την. [αναβαντα].

XVIII. 1. [ωρα]. 2. — ο ι̅σ̅. 3. εισελθη^{τ}ε (τ *p.m.*)√. 4. ταπινωσει. 5. [εαν]. παιδιον εν τοιουτο. 6. μεικρων (*sic* v. 10)√. περι (*pro* επι). πελαγι√. 7. [εστιν].— εκεινω. 8. εξελε (*pro* εκκοψον: C^a *cum* Steph.). αυτον (*pro* αυτα): cf. v. 9. κυλλον η χωλον. 9. εστιν√. 10. [εν ουρανοισ *prim.*]. [βλεπουσι]. 11. *Deest versus.* 12. αφισ√. ενενηκονταεννεα (*sic* v. 13).— επι τα ορη (*habet* A). ζητι√. 13. ευριν√. χαιρι√. 14. εστιν√.— εμπροσθεν. [υμων]. εν (*pro* εισ). 15. — εισ σε.— και *prim.* 16. μετα σεαυτου ετι. δυο η τριων μαρτυρων. 17. ειπον. 18. ο^{α}σ εαν *prim.* (^{α} *p.m.*?).— να εν *prim. rescript. ab* A *vel forsan p.m.* δεδεμενον, *ut videtur, primò.* τοισ ουρανοισ *prim.*— και (*habet* C). αν (*pro* εαν *secund.*: B C *cum* Steph.). λυσηται√.— τω *secund.* 19. [παλιν (*sine* αμην)]. συμφωνησουσιν εξ υμων. αυτοισ γενησεται. 20. (οπου *pro* ου B?: C *et p.m.* ου). εισιν√.— η (*habet* B). γ̅√. 21. — αυτω (*habet* C^a). ο πετροσ ειπεν√. αμαρτησι√. 22. λεγι√. [αλλ]. 23. βασιλια√. βασιλι√. ηθελησεν√. 24. συναιριν√. [προσηνεχθη]. εισ αυτω (C^a *cum* Steph.). οφιλετησ√. πολλων (*pro* μυριων: C^a *cum* Steph.). 25. αποδουνε√.— αυτου *secund.* πραθηνε (-ναι C^a)√. γυνεκα (-αικα C^a)√.— αυτου *tert.* πεδια (*pro* τεκνα). ειχεν√. αποδοθηνε√. 26. + εκινοσ (*post* δουλοσ). προσεκυνι√. [κ̅ε̅]. [επ εμοι: *sic* v. 29]. αποδωσω σοι. 27. σπλαγχνισθισ√. εκινου√. δανιον√. 28. εκινοσ√. ωφιλεν√. επνιγεν√. — μοι. ει τι οφιλισ. 29. — εισ τουσ ποδασ αυτου. παρεκαλι√.

—παντα (*habet* C^a). 30. και (*pro* αλλα: C^a *cum* Steph.).—ου. αποδη (αποδω C^a). οφιλομενον (*sic* v. 34)√. 31. ουν (*pro* δε: C^a *cum* Steph., *at* ουν *restituitur*). [οι συνδ. αυτ.]. (γεινομενα *prim.* C^a, *at* ι *eras.*). οι δε (*pro* και). εαυτων. 32. λεγι√. οφιλην εκινην√. επι√. 33. ελεησε√. καγω. 34. οργισθισ√. [εωσ ου]. (αυτω *improbatur et rursus restituitur*). 35. ουτωσ√. ουρανιοσ. ποιησι√.—τα παραπτωματα αυτων.

XIX. 1. [τησ γ.]. και ηλθεν *bis script. prius notatum* ' '√. ϊουδεασ (-δαιασ C^a)√. 2. εκι√. 3. φαρισεοι πιραζοντεσ√.—αυτω *secund.*—ανθρωπω (E *habet* ανφ). απολυσε√. γυνεκα√. 4. —αυτοισ. [ποιησασ]. 5. ενεκα. καταλιψι√. προσκολληθησετε√. γυνεκι (-αικι C^a)√. εσοντε√. 6. εισιν√. μια σαρξ. 7. [μωσησ: *at* B C μωυσησ]. ενετιλατο√. δουνε√. απολυσε (*non* v. 8)√.—αυτην. 8. λεγι√. + ο ισ (*ante* οτι). μωυσησ. ουτωσ (*sic* v. 12)√. 9. [οτι]. γυνεκα (-αικα C^a)√.—ει. πορνια√. μοιχατε *prim.*√.—και ο απολελ. *ad fin. vers.* (ὁμοιοτ.). 10. —αυτω (*habet* C^a).—αυτου.—ει (*habent* C, *anteriores*). γυνεκοσ (-αικοσ C^a)√. συμφερι√. 11. [χωρουσι]. [τουτον]. δεδοτε√. 12. εισιν (—γαρ: *habet* C^a). χωριν χωριτω√. 13. προσηνεχθησαν. πεδιαι (*sic* v. 14)√. χιρασ√. προσευξητε√. μαθητε√. 14. + αυτοισ (*post* ειπεν). ελθιν√. εμε. βασιλια√. 15. επιθισ τασ χιρασ επ αυτουσ. 16. αυτω ειπεν. —αγαθε. ποιησασ ζωην αιωνιον κληρονομησω (—ινα). 17. τι με ερωτασ περι του αγαθου εισ εστιν ο αγαθοσ (*pro* τι με λεγεισ *usque ad* θσ). θελισ√. εισ την ζωην εισελθιν. [τηρησον]. 18. ποιασ φησιν (*pro* λεγει αυτω ποιασ). ειπεν√. φονευσισ√.—οι μοιχευσεισ ου κλεψεισ (ὁμοιοτ.: *supplet* A, *legens* μοιχευσισ√). ψευδομαρτυρησισ√. 19. —σου *prim.* 20. λεγι√. [παν. ταυ.]. εφυλαξα.—εκ νεοτητοσ μου (*habet* C^b). 21. [εφη]. θελισ τελιοσ√. γενεσθε (*pro* ειναι: C^a *cum* Steph.). [δοσ πτ.]. [ουνω]. ακολουθι√. 22. —τον λογον. απηλθεν√. 23. ειπεν√. πλουσιοσ δυσκολωσ. εισελευσετε√. βασιλιαν (*sic* v. 24)√. 24. + οτι (*post* υμιν). εστιν√. [καμηλον]. τρηματοσ (*pro* τρυπηματοσ: *habet* C^a). εισελθιν (*pro* διελθειν). [του θυ]. *fin.*—εισελθειν. 25. —δε (*habent* A C). —αυτου. δυνατε σωθηνε√. 26. —παρα ανθρωποισ (*habet* A). εστιν *prim.*√. δυνατα παντα. *fin.*—εστι *secund.* 27. ημισ√. 28. ϋμισ *prim.*√. παλινγενεσια. καθησεσθε. αυτοι (*pro* υμεισ *secund.*). ιβ *bis*√. 29. οστισ (*pro* οσ).—οικιασ η. [η πρα η μρα η γυναικα]. (+ η οικιασ *post* αγρουσ A). ενεκα του εμου ονοματοσ. [εκατονταπλασιονα]. λημψετε√. κληρονομησι√. 30. εσοντε√. εσχατοι πρωτοι και πρωτοι εσχατοι.

XX. 1. βασιλια√. μισθωσασθε√. 2. απεστιλεν√. 3. —την. 4. και εκεινοισ. ῡμισ√. + μου (*post* αμπελωνα). δικεον (-καιον Cª)√. 5. + δε (*post* παλιν). ενατην. 6. —ωραν. εξηλθεν *primò* (εξελθων *p.m. vel potius* A).—αργουσ. 7. ουδισ√.—ημασ (*habet* A). ῡμισ√. *Post* αμπελωνα *caetera in versu desunt*. 8. λεγι√.—αυτοισ. 9. [και ελθοντεσ]. 10. [ελθοντεσ δε]. πλιονα√. λημψονται. το ανα δηναριον και αυτοι. 12. —οτι. (εισουσ Cª, ε *rursus deleto*)√. αυτουσ ημιν. [βαστασασι]. 13. ενι αυτων ειπεν. ετερε√. ουχ (*pro* ουκ). 14. ᵀω εσχ. (τ *p.m. vel* A). συ (*pro* σοι)√. 15. *init*. [η]. εξεστιν√. ο θελω ποιησε. η (*pro* ει). 16. εσοντε√. —πολλοι γαρ *ad fin. vers*. 17. αναβενων√. ισ (εισ Cª)√. παρελαβεν√. ιβ̄√.—μαθητασ. και εν τη οδω ειπ. 18. αναβενομεν√. ῑσ (εῑσ Cª)√. παραδοθησετε√. αρχιερευσιν√. γραμματευσιν√. *fin*. εισ θανατον. 19. εμπεξε√. μαστιγωσε (-σαι Cª)√. σταυρωσε√.—και *quart*. (*supplet* A *vel forte p.m.*). εγερθησετε (*pro* αναστησεται). 20. [παρ]. 21. θελισ√. λεγι√. [ουτοι].—σου *prim*. + σου (*post* ευωνυμων). βασιλια√. 22. αποκριθισ√. αιτισθε√. πινιν√.—και το βαπτισμα *usque ad* βαπτισθηναι. 23. *init*.—και. λεγι√.—και το βαπτισμα *usque ad* βαπτισθησεσθε.—μου *tert*. εμον δουνε. 24. [και ακουσαντεσ: *at* Cª ακ. δε]. ηρξαντο αγανακτιν (*pro* ηγανακτησαν). 26. —δε. εστε *prim*.√. [εαν]. γενεσθε√. εστε (*pro* εστω: Cª *cum* Steph.). 27. αν (*pro* εαν). εστε (*pro* εστω). 28. ηλθεν√. διακονησε√. δουνε√. 29. [ῑεριχω].—αυτω (*habent* A? C). 30. οᵀᶦ (τι C, *forsan etiam vetustiores*). ελεησον ημασ ῑῡ ῡῑε δᾱδ (—κυριε). 31. [σιωπησωσιν]. πολλω μαλλον (*pro* μειζον). εκραξαν. κ̄ε ελεησον ημασ ῡῡ δᾱδ (*at* ῡε̄ *etiam ante* Cª *correctum*). 32. ειπεν√. (Cª *habet* ῑνα *post* θελετε). 33. ανυγωσιν οι οφθαλμοι ῡμων (*at* ημων Cª). 34. [οφθαλμων]. αυτου (*pro* αυτων *prim*.: A *cum* Steph.).—αυτων οι οφθαλμοι *secund*.

XXI. 1. ῑσ ιερ- (εισ ῑερ- Cª)√. ηλθεν (ηλθον Cª). [βηθφαγη προσ]. ελεων√. ο ῑσ̄ απεστιλεν β̄. 2. πορευεσθε. κατεναντει. ευθυσ. [αγαγετε]. 3. αυτου (*pro* αυτων). χριαν√. ευθυσ. αποστελι√. 4. —ολον. 5. ερχετε√. [πραῡσ και]. + επι (*ante* πωλον). (ῡιον *improbat* A *vel* B: *sed restituitur*). 6. [προσεταξεν]. 7. *init*. (+ και A?: *sed rursus extinctum*). επ (*pro* επανω *prim*.). —αυτων *secund*. (*habet* A). εκαθισαν (*pro* επεκαθισεν: Cª επεκαθισαν). + επ (*post* επανω *secund*.: *at* αυτον[?] *sine* επ Cª).

8. πλιστοσ√. εστρωσαν (*pro* εστρωννυον : C^a *cum* Steph.). 9. +αυτον (*post* προαγοντεσ). υ̅υ̅ω̅ δ̅α̅δ̅√. 10. ελθοντοσ (εισελ. C^a). ῒσ√. εσισθη√. 11. ο προφητησ ι̅σ̅. ναζαρεθ. γαλιλεασ√. 12. —ο (*habet corrector, sed rursus eras.*).—του θ̅υ̅. εξεβαλεν√. [λλ]. κατεστρεψεν√. 13. λεγι√. κληθησετε√. ὓμισ√. ποιειτε. σπηλεον√. 14. προσελθοντεσ (προσηλθον *s.m.*)√. 15. αρχιερισ√. γραμματισ√. εποιησεν√. +τουσ (*ante* κραζοντασ). 16. ειπαν. λεγι√. —οτι. *fin.* ενον (C^a αινον)√. 17. —εξω τησ πολεωσ (*habet* A). 18. πρωι δε επαναγαγων (C^a *cum* Steph.). επινασεν√. 19. —ευρεν (*habet* A?). [αυτη μηκετι]. γενοιτο. 20. μαθητε√. 21. ορι√. γενησετε√. 22. [αν]. λημψεσθε√. 23. ελθοντοσ αυτου. εδωκεν√. 24. [δε]. και εγω *bis in vers.* 25. +το (*ante* ῒωαννου). η (*pro* ην : C^a *cum* Steph.). [παρ]. 26. ωσ προφητην εχουσι τον ῒωαννην. 27. ειπαν. ο ι̅σ̅ (*pro* και αυτοσ). 28. α̅ν̅ο̅σ̅ ειχεν τεκνα β̅. —και (*habet* C^a). ειπεν√.—μου. 29. —δε *secund.* (*habet* C^a). μεταμεληθισ απηλθεν√. 30. προσελθων δε (—και). ετερω (*pro* δευτερω : C^a *cum* Steph.).—ο δε αποκριθεισ ειπεν (*habet* C^a, *sed* αποκριθισ√). απηλθεν√. 31. β̅ εποίησεν√.—αυτω. [πρωτοσ]. λεγι√.—οτι (*habet* C^a). τελωνε (-ναι C^a)√. βασιλιαν√. 32. ηλθεν√. ῒωαννησ προσ ὓμασ. δικεοσυνησ (δικαι- C^a)√. τελωνε√. ὓμισ√. ειδοντεσ√. [ου]. 33. —τισ. περιεθηκεν√.—εν (*habet* C^a). ωκοδομησεν√. εξεδετο (-δοτο C^a). 34. απεστιλεν√. και λαβον *primò, ut videtur, e* v. 35 (*pro* λαβειν *p.m.*)√. 35. εδιραν√. απεκτιναν (*sic* v. 39)√. 36. *init.* +και (*improbat* C^a). απεστιλεν (*sic* v. 37)√. πλιονασ√. 38. αποκτινωμεν√. σχωμεν. 39. εβαλον. 40. ποιησι√. εκινοισ√. 41. απολεσι√. εκδωσετε√. 42. τεσ γραφεσ (C^a ταισ -φαισ)√. κ̅ω̅ (κ̅υ̅ C^a *cum* Steph.). εστιν√. 43. —οτι. αρθησετε√. βασιλια√. δοθησετε εθνι√. *fin.* αυτου (*pro* αυτησ : C^a *cum* Steph.). 44. συνθλασθησετε√. λικμησι√. 45. ακουσαντεσ δε (—και). αρχιερισ√. φαρισεοι (-σαιοι C^a)√. 46. τον οχλον (τουσ οχλουσ C^a *cum* Steph.). επι (*pro* επειδη). εισ (*pro* ωσ).

XXII. 1. παραβολαισ αυτοισ (—εν : *habent* A? C^a). 2. βασιλι√. εποιησεν√. 3. απεστιλεν√. καλεσε√. ελθιν√. 4. απεστιλεν√. ητοιμακα. 5. [ο μεν *at*] οσ δε. επι (*pro* εισ *secund.*). 6. απεκτιναν√. 7. ο δε βασιλευσ (—ακουσασ). απωλεσεν√. φονισ εκινουσ√. ενεπρησεν√. 8. λεγι√. 9. ο>δ *in* οδων *rescripsit p.m. vel* A : ψ . ., λτ *primò*??). εαν (*pro* αν). 10. εκινοι√. ουσ (*pro* οσουσ). νυμφων (*pro* γαμοσ). ανακιμενων√. 11. θεασασθε√. ανακιμενουσ√.—εκει (*habet* C^a). 12. λεγι√. 13. ο βασιλευσ ειπεν. χιρασ√.—αρατε αυτον και. +αυτον (*post* εκβαλετε). εκι εστε√. 14. εισιν√. 15. φαρισεοι√. —ελαβον (*habet* Cᵃ). —εν λογω (*habet* Cᵃ). 16. λεγοντασ. ι (*pro* ει : C ει)√. αληθια√. μελι√. βλεπισ√. 17. [ειπε]. δοκι εξεστιν√. 18. ειπεν√. πιραζετε√. επιδιξατε√. 20. λεγι (*sic* v. 21)√. [αυτοισ τινοσ]. ϊκων√. [αυτ. και η επιγρ.]. 21. λεγουσι (—αυτω). κεσαροσ *bis in vers.* [*at* καισαρι]√. 22. [απηλθον]. 23. *init.* +και (*improbat* Cᵃ). εκινη√. —αυτω (*habet* Cᵃ). —οι (*habet* Cᵃ). 24. [μωσησ]. τεκνα επιγαμβρευσι√. γυνεκα (-αικα Cᵃ) *sic* v. 25√. αναστησι√. 25. γημασ. ετελευτησεν√. αφηκεν√. 27. απεθανεν (—και). 28. αναστασι ουν. εστε√. 29. και αποκριθισ (—δε)√. πλανασθαι√. ϊδοτεσ√. 30. αναστασι√. γαμουσι. γαμιζονται.—του. +τω (*ante* ουνω). εισιν√. 32. —ο *secund.*, *tert.*, *et quart.* ϊσακ (ϊσαακ Cᵃ).—θσ *quart.* 34. φαρισεοι (-σαιοι (Cᵃ)√. [εφιμωσε]. σαδδουκεουσ√. 35. πιραζων√. —και λεγων. 37. —ισ. εφη (*pro* ειπεν). αγαπησισ (*sic* v. 39)√. —τη *prim.* (*habet* Cᵃ). 38. εστιν η μεγαλη και πρωτη. 39. —δε (*habet* Cᵃ). 40. ταυτεσ τεσ (-ταισ ταισ Cᵃ)√. εντολεσ (-λαισ Cᵃ).—ολοσ (*habet* Cᵃ). κρεμαται και οι προφητε (-ται Cᵃ). 41. φαρισεων√. 42. δοκι√. εστιν√. —του *secund.* δαδ *passim*√. 43. λεγι√. καλι κν αυτον. 44. —ο. ϋποκατω (*pro* υποποδιον). 45. καλι√. εστιν√. 46. αποκριθηνε (-ναι Cᵃ) αυτω. ετολμησεν√. εκινησ√. επερωτησε√.

XXIII. 1. [ο]. ελαλησεν√. μαθητεσ (-ταισ Cᵃ)√. 2. μωυσεωσ. φαρισεοι√. 3. εαν (*pro* αν). —τηρειν τηρειτε και. ποιησατε (*pro* ποιειτε *prim.* : Cᵃ *addit* και τηρειτε). λεγουσιν√. ποιουσιν√. 4. δεσμευουσιν√. δε (*pro* γαρ). +μεγαλα (*ante* βαρεα). —και δυσβαστακτα. αυτοι δε τω (*pro* τω δε). θελουσιν κινησε√. 5. ποιουσιν√. θεαθηνε√. [πλατυνουσι]. γαρ (*pro* δε *secund.*). [μεγαλυνουσι]. —των ιματιων αυτων. 6. [φιλουσι]. δε (*pro* τε). (τασ πρωτοκλισιασ Cᵃ). διπνοισ√. τεσ συναγωγεσ (ταισ -γαισ Cᵃ, *at* -γεσ *restitutum*)√. 7. τεσ αγορεσ (ταισ αγοραισ Cᵃ)√. καλεισθε√. 7, 8. —ραββι ραββι υμεισ δε μη κληθητε (ὁμοιοτ. : *supplet* A ϋμεισ δε μη κληθητε ραββει). 8. ραββει√. [καθηγητησ : Cᵃ διδασκαλοσ, *sed* καθηγ. *restituitur*]. —ο χσ. ϋμισ√. 9. ϋμων ο πηρ. ουρανιοσ (*pro* εν τοισ ουρανοισ). 10. εισ γαρ εστιν ϋμων ο καθ. 11. μιζων√. —υμων *secund.* 12. ταπινωθησετε√. ταπινωσει√. ϋψωθησετε√. *Deest* v. 13. 14. (+δε *post* ουαι A?). γραμματισ (*sic* v. 15)√. ϋποκριτε (*non* v. 15)√. κλιετε√. βασιλιαν√. αννω (ανων C)√. ισερχεσθε (εισερχ. C)√. 15. ποιησε√. γενητε√. 16. +οι (*ante* τυφλοι: οι *eras.*). χρυσω του ναου *rescript. ab* A. οφιλει√. 17. [τισ]. μιζων√. αγιασασ. 18. αν (*pro* εαν). οφιλι√. 19. —μωροι και. μιζον√. 20. ομνυϊ (*sic* v. 22, *non* v. 21)√. [πασι]. 21. [κατοικουντι]. 23. γραμματισ (*sic* vv. 25. 27. 29)√. ϋποκριτε (*sic* vv. 25. 27. 29)√. το ελεοσ. [ταυτα εδει] ποιησε κακινα μη αφινε√. 24. [οι: *eras. ante* C: *et rursus restitut.*]. 25. φαρισεοι (*sic* v. 27)√. κε (*pro* και *secund.*). [εξ]. κε (*pro* και *tert.*: C[a] και) cf. vv. 26. 27. 28√. [ακρασιασ]. 26. [και τησ παρ.]. κε το εντοσ αυτων (C[a] *cum* Steph. και το εκτοσ αυτων). 27. κε *bis in vers.* (και B?)√. [παρομοι.]. —οιτινεσ (*habet* C[a]). φενοντε ωρεοι√. 28. ουτωσ κε (και C[a]) ϋμισ√. φενεσθε√. δικεοι (C[a] δικαιοι)√. εστε μεστοι. κε (*pro* και *secund.*)√. 29. φαρισεοι (-σαιοι C[a])√. κοσμιτε√. μνημια√. δικεων (-καιων C[a])√. 30. λεγεται√. ημεθα (*pro* ημεν *bis in vers.*). τεσ ημερεσ (ταισ -ραισ C[a])√. [κοινωνοι αυτων]. 31. μαρτυριτε√. 32. ϋμισ√. 33. οφισ√. 34. γραμματισ√. —και *tert.* αποκτενιτε√. εξ αυτων και (*ante* μαστιγωσετε: C[a] *cum* Steph.). τεσ συναγωγεσ (ταισ *tantum* C[a])√. 35. (+αν *post* οπωσ: C[a]). —παν (*habet* C[a]). δικεον (-καιον C[a])√. εκχυννομενον. —υιου βαραχιου (*habet* C[b]). 36. ηξι√. [τ. π.]. 37. —η. τουσ προφητασ αποκτενουσα (η αποκ. τουσ προφ. C[a] C[b]). επισυναγειν (C[a] *cum* Steph.). ορνισ επισυναγι (-γει C[a]). αυτησ (*pro* εαυτησ: C[a] *cum* Steph.). [πτερυγασ και]. 38. [ερημοσ].

XXIV. 1. απο του ιερου επορευετο. μαθητε√. επιδιξε√. 2. αποκριθεισ (*pro* ῑσ). ταυτα παντα, *at* —παντα *p.m.*? (*addidit* A?). —μη *secund.* 3. ελεων√. μαθηται καθ ιδιαν. εστε√. σημιον√.—τησ *secund.* συντελιασ√. 5. ελευσοντε√. πλανησουσιν√. 6. δι (*pro* δει)√.—παντα. εστιν√. 7. εγερθησετε√. επ εθνοσ. βασιλια√. βασιλιαν√. εσοντε σισμοι και λιμοι (—και λοιμοι). 9. —παντων (*habet* C[a]). [των]. 10. +εισ θλιψιν (*post* παραδωσουσιν).—και μισησουσιν αλληλουσ. 11. πολλουσ πλανησουσι. 12. πληθυνθηνε (-ναι C[a])√. ψυγησετε√. 13. ϋπομινασ√. σωθησετε√. 14. κηρυχθησετε√. βασιλιασ√. εισ ολην την οικουμενην. [πασι]. εθνεσιν√. ηξι√. 15. (δε *pro* ουν C[a]). [δαν]ιηλ (δαν A, *at super sex ferè literas erasas*)√. [εστοσ]. 16. ϊουδεα (-δαια C[a])√. [επι]. 17. καταβατω (-βητω C[a]? *at rursus emendatum*). το (*pro* τι: C[a] τα). 18. αρε (αραι C[a])√. το ιματιον√. 19. εχουσεσ (-σαισ C[a])√. θηλαζουσεσ (-σαισ C[a])√. εκινεσ (-ναισ C[a]) ταισ ημερεσ (-ραισ C[a])√. 20. χιμωνοσ√.—εν. 21. εστε√. ουκ εγενετο. γενητε√. 22. εκιναι *bis in vers.*√. εκολοβωθησαν (*pro* κολοβωθησονται: C[a] *cum* Steph.). 23. [πιστευσητε]. 24. ἰ ψευδοχριστοι (ι *improbat p.m.*)√. ψευδοπροφητε√. δωσουσιν σημια√. πλανηθηναι. 26. —ουν (*habet* C^b). εστιν√. ταμιοισ√. 27. εξερχετε√. φαινετε√. εστε√. —και *secund.* 28. που (*pro* οπου: ο *prim. supplevit corrector jam ante* C).—γαρ. σωμα (*pro* πτωμα: C^a *cum* Steph.). εκι συναχθησοντε√. 29. εκινων√. σκοτισθησετε√. δωσι√. εκ (*pro* απο). δυναμισ√. 30. φανησετε√. σημιον√.—τω.—τοτε *secund.* (*habet* C^a). κοψοντε√. πασε ε φυλαι (-σαι αι φ. C^a)√. οψοντε√. 31. αποστελι√.—φωνησ. επισυναξι (*at* -ξουσιν C^a). δ̅√. [εωσ ακρ.]. 32. γενητε√. ^τα^ φυλλα (τα *p.m. vel* A). 33. ουτωσ√. ὑμισ√. ταυτα παντα. 34. [υμιν ου μη].—αν. γενητε√. 35. *Deest versus* (*supplet* C^a, *legens* [παρελευσονται] *et* παρελθωσιν√). 36. —τησ *secund.* +ουδε> ο υιοσ (*ante* ει μη: *delet* C^a? *sed restituitur*). —μου. 37. [δε].—και.—του υιου (*habet* C^a) ὁμοιοτ. 38. ωσ (*pro* ωσπερ). [ημεραισ ταισ προ]. πεινοντεσ√. (+και *ante* γαμουντεσ C^a). γαμιζοντεσ. εισηλθεν√. 39. ȯ εωσ (ο *notat. p.m.*)√. [και η παρ.]. 40. εσονται δυο (C^a *cum* Steph.).—ο *bis.* παραλαμβανετε (*non* v. 41)√. αφιετε (*non* v. 41)√. 41. μυλω. 42. ημερα (*pro* ωρα). 43. ειασεν√. διορυχθηναι. 44. ου δοκειτε ωρα. 45. καταστησει (cf. v. 47).—αυτου *prim.* οικιασ (*pro* θεραπειασ). δουναι. 46. ουτωσ ποιουντα. 47. πασιν√. 48. —εκεινοσ (εκινοσ√ C^a). εαυτου (*pro* αυτου). μου ο κ̅σ̅.—ελθειν. 49. + εαυτου (*post* συνδουλουσ). εσθιη. πινη.

XXV. 1. [αυτων]. ὑπαντησιν. 2. πεντε δε εξ αυτων ησαν μωραι και πεντε φρονιμοι. 3. αι γαρ (*pro* αιτινεσ).—εαυτων. 4. αγγιοισ√. —αυτων *prim. fin.* εαυτων. 6. —ερχεται.—αυτου. 7. εαυτων. 8. [ειπον]. 9. [ουκ αρκεση]. ὑμιν και ημιν.—δε *secund.* 10. εκλισθη√. 11. [και]. 13. —εν η ο υ̅σ̅ *ad fin. vers.* 14. εκαλεσεν√. 15. εδωκεν√. 16. —δε (*habet* C^a). ^τ^αλαντα *prim.* (^τ^ *p.m.*)√. ηργασατο (ειργ. C^a). (εκερδησεν *pro* εποιησεν C^a *et* C^b). [ταλαντα *secund.*]. 17. —και *prim.* (*habet* C^a). εκερδησεν (—και αυτοσ). 18. [εν λαβ.]. γην (*pro* εν τη γη). εκρυψεν. 19. πολυν χρονον. λογον μετ αυτων. 20. —ταλαντα *prim.* [*habet quart.*]. —επ αυτοισ (*sic* v. 22). 21. —δε. 22. —δε (*habet* C^a). [λαβων]. ειπεν (*sic* v. 24)√.—κυριε. 24. ανθρωποσ αυστηροσ ει (*pro* σκλ. ει ανθ.). 26. [πονηρε δουλε]. 27. σε ουν. τα αργυρια (C^a *cum* Steph.). τραπεζειταισ√. 29. του δε (—απο). 30. αχριον√. εκβαλετε. 31. —αγιοι. 32. συναχθησονται. αφορισει (*pro* -ριει: -ριεει C). 33. —αυτου (*post* δεξ.). *fin.* +αυτου. 35. επινασα (*sic* v. 42)√. 36. ηλθατε προσ εμε. 37. [ειδομεν]. 39. [ασθενη].

40. [των αδ. μου]. 41. ϋπαγετε (*pro* πορευεσθε). — οι. 43. — γυμνοσ και ου περιεβαλετε με (ὁμοιοτ.: *habet* C, *legens* περιεβαλεται√ *sine* με). 44. αυτωοι (*sic p.m. pro* αυτω και αυτοι: και αυτοι C^a *sine* αυτω). πινωντα (*non* v. 37)√. ουκ ηδιηκονησαμεν (*pro* ου διηκ.)√.

XXVI. 1. ειπεν (*sic* vv. 15. 25. 26. 49)√. 3. — και οι γραμματεισ. 4. δολω κρατησωσιν. 7. εχουσα αλαβαστρον μυρου πολυτιμου. τησ κεφαλησ. ανακιμενου√. 8. — αυτου. απωλια√. 9. εδυνατο. — το μυρον. [-ναι πτωχ.]. 10. γυνεκι (-ναικ- C^a). — γαρ (*notat. et restitut.*). ηργασατο (ειργ. C^a) cf. xxv. 16. 11. [*cum* Steph.]. 13. λαληθησετε√. 14. πορευθισ√. ιβ√. αρχιερισ√. 15. ι (*pro* τι) *p.m.* τ *s.m.*√. θελεται√. δωνε√. και εγω. λ√. 16. εζητι ευκεριαν√. 17. — αυτω. θελισ√. [-σωμεν]. φαγιν√. 18. δινα√. εστιν√. 20. ανεκιτο√. *fin.* ιβ μαθητων. 21. λεγι (*pro* ειπεν). παραδωσι (*non* v. 23)√. 22. λεγιν√. εισ εκαστοσ (— αυτων). 23. αποκριθισ (*sic* v. 25)√. την χιρα εν τω τρυβλιω. 24. ϋπαγι√. εκινοσ√. 25. ραββει√. + ο ισ (*ante* συ). 26. — τον. εκλασεν√. εδιδου$^{\sigma}$ (··· *et* σ A *vel* C: εδιδου *p.m.*, δουσ *s.m.*, *ut videtur*). μαθητεσ (-ταισ C^a)√. — και *tert.* εστιν (*sic* vv. 28. 39. 48. 66)√. 27. — το. [και ευχαρ.]. 28. — το *secund.* — καινησ. εκχυννομενον. 29. — οτι. — του (*habet* C^a). γενηματοσ. εκινησ√. κενον√. 31. λεγι (*sic* vv. 35. 36. 40. 45)√. ϋμισ√. σκανδαλισθησεσθαι√. διασκορπισθησοντε (-νται C^a)√. 32. εγερθηνε√. 33. — ει και (*habet* C^a). [εγω ουδεπ.]. σκανδαλισθησομε (-μαι C^a)√. 34. με απαρνηση (C^a *cum* Steph.). 35. αποθανιν√. [ομοιωσ και]. 36. γεθσημανι. + αυτου (*post* μαθηταισ). — αυτου (*ante* εωσ). — ου (*ante* απελθων). εκι προσευξωμε√. 37. ζεβεδεου√. λυπισθε√. αδημονιν√. 38. [αυτοισ περιλ.]. μινατε√. γρηγοριτε (*non* v. 41)√. 39. προσελθων. [μου]. παρελθατω. 40. ερχετε√. ευρισκι√. γρηγορησε√. 41. εισελθηται√. πιρασμον√. 42. (A *vel* B *addit* ο ισ *ante* λεγων, *sed rursus eras.*). δυνατε√. — το ποτηριον. παρελθιν√. — απ εμου. 43. παλιν ευρεν αυτουσ. 44. αφισ√. παλιν απελθων√. τον αυτον εκ τριτου (C^a *cum* Steph.). + παλιν *iterum* (*post* ειπων). 45. ερχετε√. — αυτου. [το λ.]. χιρασ√. 46. παραδιδων (-δουσ C^a), *non* v. 48. 47. ιβ ηλθεν√. μαχερων√. 48. σημιον√. εαν (*pro* αν). κρατησαται√. 49. ραββει√. 50. — ισ. ο (*pro* ω). χιρασ√. 51. εκτινασ√. χιρα√. [απεσπασε]. αφιλεν√. 52. την μαχαιραν σου. μαχαιρη. απολουντε (-νται C^a)√. 53. — αρτι. παρακαλεσε√.

ωδε αρτι πλειω (*pro* πλειουσ: αρτι πλειουσ C^a).—η *secund.* λεγιωνων (-γαι- C^a). (αγγελων *p.m. et* C^a: *at* -ουσ *in rasura* A, *potius quam p.m.*). 54. γραφε (-αι C^a) *sic* v. 56√. ουτωσ√. δι (δει C^a)√. γενεσθε√. 55. εξηλθατε.—προσ υμασ εν τω ιερω εκαθεζομην διδασκων. 56. πληρωθοσιν? *p.m.* (-ωσιν A *vel* B)√. [-ται παντ.]. 57. γραμματισ√. 58. ηκολουθι√.—απο. 59. οι δε αρχιερισ.—και οι πρεσβυτεροι. θανατωσωσιν√. 60. —και *secund.* προσελθοντων ψευδομαρτυρων.— ουχ ευρον *secund.* β̄√.—ψευδομαρτυρεσ. 61. ειπαν. καταλυσε√. αυτον οικοδομησαι. 62, 63. —ουδεν αποκρ. *usque ad* ειπεν αυτω (ὁμοιοτ.: *supplet* A *vel* B *jam ante* C, *at eras.*: *habet* C, *sed* αποκριθεισ v. 63 *omisso*). 65.— ο (*habet* B?). διερρηξεν√. και λεγει ἴδε (*pro* λεγων οτι: C^a λεγων *tantum*). εβλασφημησεν√. χριαν√. μαρτυριων.— αυτου *secund.* 66. ειπαν (-πον C^a). 67. εραπισαν. 69. εκαθητο εξω. γαλιλεου√. 70. [-θεν παντ.]. 71. —αυτον *prim.* [λεγει τοισ εκει].— και *secund.* 72. μετα.—οτι. 74. καταθεματιζειν. [ευθεωσ]. εφωνησεν√. 75. —του *secund.*— αυτω. εκλαυσεν√.

XXVII. 1. αρχιερισ√. 2. —αυτον ποντιω. 3. [παραδιδουσ]. μετεμεληθη και εστρεψεν (μεταμεληθισ εστρεψεν C^a). λ̄ (*sic* v. 9)√. [αρχιερευσι].—τοισ *secund.* 4. [αθωον]. [ειπον: *sic* vv. 6. 21]. οψη. 5. + λ̄ (*ante* αργυρια). εισ τον ναον. ανεχωρησεν√. 6. εξεστιν βαλιν√. [κορβαναν]. επι√. εστιν√. 8. εκινοσ√. 9. και (*pro* τοτε: C^a *cum* Steph.). [ἴερεμιου του πρ.]. 10. εδωκα. συνεταξεν√. 11. εσταθη. ° ηγεμων (ο C *et jam antea*).— αυτω. λεγισ√. 12. κατηγορισθε√.—των *secund.* 13. λεγι (*sic* v. 22)√. καταμαρτυρουσιν√. 14. θαυμαζιν√. 15. παρητουντο (*pro* ηθελον: C^a *cum* Steph.). 16. τοντε (*pro* τοτε: ν *improbat p.m.*?)√. [βαραββαν *passim*]. 17. ο *p.m. at in rasura scriptum.* 18. ηδι√. 19. απεστιλεν√. εκινω√. 20. αρχιερισ√. επισαν√. 21. β̄√. + τον (*ante* βαραββαν). 22. λεγουσιν (— αυτω). 23. —ηγεμων. περισσω (C^a *cum* Steph.). 24. ωφελι√. γεινεται√. χιρασ√. [απεναντι]. [αθωοσ]. [του δικαιου]. + δε (*ante* οψεσθαι√: *improbat* δε C^a). 25. αποκριθισ√. ειπεν√. 26. [φραγελλ.]. (+ αυτοισ *ante* ἵνα C^a, *at erasum*). 27. σπιραν√. 28. (εκδυσ. *p.m. at* ν *pro* κ C^a: κ *restituit* C^b *vel forsan* C^a: cf. Cod. B). χλαμυδα κοκκινην περιεθηκαν αυτω. 29. τησ κεφαλησ. εν τη δεξια. ενεπεξαν√. [ο βασιλευσ]. 31. ενεπεξαν. εκδυσαντεσ.—και *secund.* 32. κυρηνεον√. 33.—λεγομενον (*habet* C^a). ο εστιν κρανιου τοποσ λεγομενοσ (C^a *notat* λεγομενοσ: *sed restituitur*). 34. πιν (πιειν C^a)

bis in versu. οινον (*pro* οξοσ). ηθελησεν (ηθελεν√ Cᵃ: *at* -ησεν *restituitur*). 35. βαλοντεσ.—ινα πληρωθη *ad fin. vers.* 37. ϊουδεων√. 38. ληστε (-ται Cᵃ)√. 40. [ει του θυ]. + και (*ante* καταβηθι: *improbat* Cᵃ). 41. —δε και. αρχιερισ√. εμπεζοντεσ√. των πρεσβυτερων και γραμματαιων. 42. —ει. εστιν√. *fin.* πιστευσωμεν επ αυτον. 43. [τον θν].—αυτον *prim.* θελι√. ειπεν√. 44. συνσταυρωθεντεσ συν αυτ. *fin.* αυτον. 45. —επι πασαν την γην (*habet* A εφ ολην την γην). ενατησ. 46. ενατην. [ανεβοησεν]. ελωι ελωι λεμα σαβαχθανει. τουτεστιν√. [εγκατελιπεσ]. 47. εστηκοτων.—οτι. φωνι√. 48. —εξ αυτων. 49. [ελεγον]. σωσαι (*pro* σωσων: Cᵃ *cum* Steph.). *fin.* + αλλοσ δε λαβων λογχην ενυξεν αυτου την πλευραν και εξηλθεν ϋδωρ και αιμα. *Sic* Cod. B. 50. αφηκεν√. 51. [εισ δυο].—απο. εσισθη√. 52. —και τα μνημεια ανεωχθησαν (ὁμοιοτ.: *habet* Cᵃ, *legens* μνημια√). ηγερθησαν. 53. μνημιων√.—εισηλθον.—και *secund.* 54. εκατονταρχησ. σισμον√. [γενομενα]. υσ ην του θυ (Cᵃ *cum* Steph.). 55. κακει (*pro* εκει). 56. —μαρια η μαγδαληνη και (*habet* Cᵃ). η μαρια η ιωσηφ (*pro* ιωση μητηρ: Cᵃ *habet* η ιωσ. μητηρ). μαρια η (*pro* μητηρ *secund.*: Cᵃ *cum* Steph.). ζεβεδεου√. 57. εμαθητευθη. 58. αποδοθηνε (-ναι Cᵃ).—το σωμα *secund.* 59. [αυτο σινδ.]. 60. —αυτο. μνημιω√. [μεγαν τη θ.]. μνημιου√. 61. μαριαμ (*pro* μαρια *prim.*). καθημενε (-ναι Cᵃ)√. 62. εστιν√. 63. εκινοσ√. τρισ√. εγιρομαι√. 64. —αυτου.—νυκτοσ. κλεψουσιν. ειπωσιν√. χειρον√. 65. [δε]. ασφαλισασθαι√.

XXVIII. 1. ηλθεν√. μαριαμ (*pro* μαρια *prim.*) cf. xxvii. 61. 2. σισμοσ√. + και (*ante* προσελθων). [απεκυλισε].—απο τησ θυρασ. 3. —ην δε η ιδεα αυτου (ὁμοιοτ.: *habet* A, *legens* ειδεα)√. ωσ (*pro* ωσει: *at* ωσ η Cᵃ). 4. εσισθησαν√. εγενηθησαν ωσ (*pro* εγενοντο ωσει). 5. ειπεν√.—ταισ γυναιξι (*habent* A? Cᵇ, *at* γυναιξιν√). φοβηθηται (Cᵃ φοβισθαι). ϋμισ√. 6. ειπεν√. ειδετε√. —ο κσ. 7. πορευθισαι√. οψεσθαι√. ειπα (*pro* ειπον: Cᵃ *cum* Steph.). 8. απελθουσαι (*pro* εξελθουσαι). μνημιου√. απαγγιλαι√. 9. —ωσ δε επορ. απαγγ. τοισ μαθηταισ αυτου.—ο. ϋπηντησεν (απηντησεν Cᵃ *cum* Steph.). 10. ϋπαγεται απαγγιλατε√.—μου (*habet* Cᵃ). ελθωσιν (απελθωσιν Cᵃ *cum* Steph.). και εκει. 11. αηγγιλαν. 12. εποιησαν (*pro* λαβοντεσ: *addit* A και λαβοντεσ: Cᵃ *improbat* εποιησαν και, *sed rursus restituuntur*). 13. οτι ειπατε (*pro* ειπατε οτι). 14. [επι].—αυτον. ποιησωμεν. 15.—τα (*habet* C). (καθωσ *pro* ωσ Cᵃ). εφημισθη. εωσ (*pro* μεχρι: Cᵃ *cum* Steph.). 17. —αυτω. 18. —αυτοισ (*habet* Cᵃ). [επι γησ].

19. —ουν. [βαπτιζοντεσ]. 20. τηριν✓. ενετιλαμην✓. ειμι μεθ υμων.—αμην.

Deest subscriptio.

κατα μαρκον.

Cap. I. 1. —υιου του θ̅υ̅ (ὁμοιοτ.: A *supplet* υ̅υ̅ θ̅υ̅). 2. καθωσ (*pro* ωσ). τω ησαϊα τω προφητη (*pro* τοισ προφηταισ). [εγω]. αποστελω. *fin.* —εμπροσθεν σου. 3. ευθιασ✓. 4. *init.* + και (*improbat* C[a]). + ο (*ante* βαπτιζων). [και κηρ.]. 5. ϊεροσολυμειτε (C[a] -ται)✓. παντεσ εβαπτιζοντο (—και *tert.*: C[a] *habet post* παντεσ). ϋπ αυτου εν τω ϊορδανη ποταμω. 6. και ην (*pro* ην δε). + ο (*ante* ϊωαννησ). εσθων (εσθιων C[a]?). 7. εκηρυσσεν✓. (*Pro* ειμι ι[κανοσ] *p.m.*, *instaurator habet* ει μη[κανοσ]✓). [κυψασ]. 8.—μεν. —εν *prim.*—υμασ *secund.* (*habet* C[a]). [εν *secund.*]. 9. *init.* [και εγεν.]. [ναζαρετ]. εισ τον ιορδανην ϋπο ϊωαννου. 10. ευθυσ. αναβενων✓. εκ (*pro* απο). ειδεν✓. ωσ (*pro* ωσει). + και μενον (*ante* επ). 11. —εγενετο (*habet* C[a]). σοι (*pro* ω). [ευδ.]. 12. [ευθυσ]. 13. —εκει. μ̅ ημερασ. πιραζομενοσ✓. 14. [δε]. [ο ι̅σ̅].—τησ βασιλειασ. 15. —και λεγων (λεγων *habet* A?). ηγγεικεν✓. βασιλια✓. πιστευεται✓. 16. και παραγων (*pro* περιπατων δε). ειδεν (ιδεν C)✓. σιμωνοσ (*pro* αυτου). αμφιβαλλοντασ.—αμφιβληστρον. 17. γενεσθε✓. αλεεισ (*non* v. 16). 18. ευθυσ.—αυτων. 19. [εκειθεν].—ολιγον (*post* προβασ *habet* C[a]). ϊδεν✓. ζεβεδεου✓. 20. ευθυσ. ζεβεδεον✓. 21. καφαρναουμ. ευθυσ. εδιδαξεν εισ την συναγωγην (—εισελθων: *at* εδιδασκεν C[a]). 22. [*cum* Steph.]. 23. +ευθυσ (*ante* ην). [—εν *secund.*, *teste* Tischendorf. Notitia Ed. Cod. Sin. p. 31: *habent* εν *editt. mai. et minor*]. ανεκραξεν✓. 24. —εα (*habet* C[a]). απολεσε (-σαι C[a])✓. οιδαμεν. 25. —λεγων (*habet* A). 26. φωνησαν (*pro* κραξαν). [εξ]. 27. απαντεσ. συνζητιν✓.—προσ. [αυτουσ]. εστιν✓. διδαχη καινη (*pro* τισ η διδ. η καιν. αυτη οτι). [π̅ν̅α̅σ̅ι̅]. επιτασσι✓. 28. και εξηλθεν (—δε). —ευθυσ (C[a] ευθυσ πανταχη *habet*). ϊουδαιασ (*pro* γαλιλαιασ: C[a] *cum* Steph.). 29. ευθυσ (*at* C[a] *pro* και ευθυσ *habet* ευθυσ πανταχη και, *et ante* εισ ολην v. 28 *transponit*: *postea vero* και ευθυσ v. 29 *restituit*). [εξελθοντεσ ηλθον]. 30. ευθυσ. 31. χιροσ✓. —αυτησ. —ευθεωσ. 32. [εδυ]. 32—34. —και τουσ δαιμονιζομενουσ *usque ad* ποικιλαισ νοσοισ (ὁμοιοτ. *ob* κακωσ εχοντασ: *supplet* C[a], *legens* ην ολη η πολισ επισυνηγμενη *et* εθεραπευσεν√). 34. εξεβαλλεν. [ηφιε: *at* ηφιεν√ C[a]]. λαλιν√. ηδισαν√. *fin.* (+ τον $\overline{\chi\nu}$ ειναι C[a]). 35. εννυχα. λειαν√. εξηλθεν√. κακι√. 36. κατεδιωξεν. — ο. 37. ευρον αυτον και (*pro* ευροντεσ αυτον). ζητουσιν σε. 38. αγομεν. + αλλαχου (*post* αγομεν). κωμοπολισ√. εξηλθον (*pro* εξεληλυθα). 39. ηλθεν (*pro* ην). κηρυσσιν (κηρυσσων C[a]). εισ τασ συναγωγασ. 40. [και γονυπετων].—αυτον *tert.*— και *tert.* (*habet* C[a]). [οτι]. δυνασε (-σαι C[a])√. 41. και (*pro* ο δε $\overline{\iota\sigma}$). εκτινασ√. αυτου ηψατο (*pro* ηψ. αυτ.). — αυτω. 42. — ειποντοσ αυτου. ευθυσ. [εκαθαρισθη]. 43. ευθυσ. 44. — μηδεν. αλλα. σαυτον διξον√. προσεταξεν√. μωϋσησ. 45. κηρυσσιν√. διαφημιζιν√. δυνασθε (-θαι C[a]) αυτον (*pro* αυτον δυνασθαι). εισ πολιν φανερωσ εισελθιν. [αλλ]. επ (*pro* εν). [ην]. παντοθεν (*pro* πανταχοθεν).

II. 1. εισελθων παλιν. καφαρναουμ. — και *secund.* εν οικω. εστιν√. 2. — ευθεωσ. χωριν√. 3. φεροντεσ προσ αυτον παραλυτικον. $\overline{\delta}$√. 4. προσσενεγκαι (*pro* προσεγγισαι) *sic.* [χαλωσι]. κραβακτον. οπου (*pro* εφ ω). 5. και ϊδων (— δε). + μου (*post* τεκνον: *improbat* C[a]). [αφεωνται]. σου (*pro* σοι). *fin.* — σου. 6. καρδιεσ (*sic* v. 8)√. 7. ουτωσ√. βλασφημει (*pro* βλασφημιασ). 8. ευθυσ ο $\overline{\iota\sigma}$ επιγνουσ. [οτι ουτωσ]. λεγει (*pro* ειπεν). 9. αφιενται. σου (*pro* σοι). εγειρε και. τον κραβακτον σου. ϋπαγε (*pro* περιπατει). 10. εχι√. επι τησ γησ αφιεναι. 11. εγειρε σοι λεγω αρον (— και). κραβακτον (*sic* vv. 4. 9. 12). 12. και ευθυσ (*pro* ευθεωσ και). εμπροσθεν (*pro* εναντιον). δοξαζιν√. [λεγοντασ]. ουτωσ ουδεποτε. εφανη εν τω $\overline{\iota\eta\lambda}$ (*pro* ειδομεν: C[a] *cum* Steph.). 13. εξηλθον (-θεν C[a] *cum* Steph.). εισ (*pro* παρα: C[a] *cum* Steph.). αυτουσ (*pro* αυτον: C[a] *cum* Steph.). 14. ειδεν√. λευει (λευειν C[a]). ακολουθι√. 15. γινεται κατακισθαι (— εν τω). συνανεκιντο√. ηκολουθουν. 16. — οι *prim.* των φαρισαιων (*pro* και οι φ.). + και (*ante* ϊδοντεσ). οτι ησθιεν (*pro* αυτον εσθιοντα). [τελ. και αμαρ. *bis in vers.*]. διατι (*pro* τι οτι).— και πινει. *fin.* + ο διδασκαλοσ υμων. 17. χριαν√. [ουκ].— εισ μετανοιαν. 18. [νν *bis*]. φαρισαιοι (*pro* των φαρ.). + μαθηται (*post* οι *quart.*). μαθηται σου (*pro* σοι μαθ.). νηστευουσιν√. 19. εστιν√. εχουσι τον νυμφιον μετ αυτων. 20. εκεινη τη ημερα. 21. *init.* — και. ουδισ (*non* v. 22)√. [ρακουσ. αγν.]. επιραπτι√. ιματιον παλαιον.— το *prim.* + απ (*ante* αυτου). γεινεται√. 22. ρηξει.— ο νεοσ. — βλητεον (*habet* A). [*caetera cum* Steph.]. 23. αυτον εν τοισ σαββασιν παραπορευεσθε. οι μαθηται αυτου ηρξαντο. [οδ$\bar{o}$ ποιειν: $^{-}$ *p.m.*

et C]. 24. —εν. [εξεστι]. 25. λεγει (*pro* αυτοσ ελεγεν). εποιησεν δαδ√. χριαν εσχεν√. επιναсεν√. 26. [πωσ].—του *secund.* εξεστιν φαγιν√. ϊερεισ (*pro* ιερευσι). εδωκεν√. ουσιν√. 27. + και (*ante* ουχ).

III. 1. εισηλθεν√.—την *prim.* [ην]. 2. [παρετηρουν]. ει εν τοισ σαββασι θεραπευει. [-σωσιν]. 3. τω την ξηραν χιρα εχοντι. εγειρε. 4. εξεστιν√. αγαθον ποιησαι. αποκτιναι√. 5. συνλυπουμενοσ. καρδι (ασ *omissum*)√. εκτινον√. χιρα√. [σου]. εξετινεν√. απεκατεσταθη. χιρ√.— υγιησ ωσ η αλλη. 6. ευθυσ. εποιησαν. απολεσωσιν√. 7. μετα των μαθητων αυτου ανεχωρησεν προσ. και απο τησ ϊουδαιασ ηκολουθησαν (—αυτω). 8. —και απο τησ ιδουμαιασ (*habet* Cª).— και οι (*ante* περι: και *tantum habet* Cª). ακουοντεσ [οσα εποιει]. 9. ειπεν√. 11. εθεωρουν προσεπιπτον. εκραζον λεγοντεσ. 12. [αυτ. φ.]. ποιησωσιν√. 13. οι δε (*pro* και *ultim.*). 14. εποιησεν√. + ουσ και αποστολουσ ωνομασεν (*post* ιβ). [ωσι]. 15. —θεραπευειν τασ νοσουσ και. 16. *init.* και εποιησεν τουσ ιβ και επεθηκεν ονομα τω σιμωνι. 17. βοανηργεσ. 18. ανδραιαν (-ρεαν Cª)√. [ματθαιον *hic*]. καναναιον (*pro* κανανιτην). 19. ισκαριωθ. [παρεδωκεν: *errat* Scrivener]. ερχεται (*pro* ερχονται: Cª *cum* Steph.). 20. (+ ο *ante* οχλοσ Cª). [μητε]. φαγιν√. 24. σταθηνε (-ναι Cª)√. 25. δυνησεται η οικια εκεινη σταθηναι. 26. εμερισθη και (*pro* και μεμερισται: και εμερ. και Cª). στηναι. 27. *init.* αλλ ου δυναται ουδισ εισελθων εισ την οικιαν του ϊσχυρου τα σκευη αυτ. 28. αφεθησετε τοισ ϋϊοισ των ανων τα αμαρτηματα (ϋϊοισ *in rasura, p.m.*). και αι βλασφημιαι οσα αν. 29. εχι (*non* v. 30)√. αλλα. εσται (*pro* εστιν). αμαρτηματοσ (*pro* κρισεωσ). 31. *init.* και ερχεται (—ουν) η μηρ αυτου και οι αδελφοι αυτου. σταντεσ. απεστιλαν√. καλουντεσ (*pro* φωνουντεσ). 32. προσ αυτον οχλοσ (περι *pro* προσ Cª). και λεγουσιν (*pro* ειπον δε). [*Deest* και αι αδελφαι σου]. ζητουσιν√. 33. αποκριθεισ αυτοισ λεγει. και οι αδελφοι μου (—η). 34. τουσ περι αυτον κυκλω. ειδε√. 35. [γαρ].— μου *secund.* εστιν√.

IV. 1. διδασκιν√. συναγεται (*pro* συνηχθη). πλιστοσ (*pro* πολυσ). εισ πλοιον εμβαντα (—το). καθησθε√. *fin.* ησαν. 2. πολλα εν παραβολαισ. 3. σπιρων√.—του (*habet* Cª). 4. σπιρειν√. επεσεν√. ηλθεν√. πετινα√.— του ουρανου. 5. και αλλο (—δε). τα πετρωδη (Cª *cum* Steph.) οπου. ειχεν√. ευθυσ. εξανετιλεν√. εχιν (*sic* v. 6)√. [βαθοσ γησ]. 6. *init.* και οτε ανετιλεν ο ηλιοσ [εκαυματισθη]. 7. αλλοσ (σ *delet* Cª). [εισ]. εδωκεν√. 8. αλλα (αλλο

Cᵃ, *sed ipse rursus delevit* ο). αυξανομενα. εφερον εισ $\overline{λ}$ και εισ $\overline{ξ}$ και εισ $\overline{ρ}$. 9. —αυτοισ. οσ εχει (ο εχων Cᵃ *cum* Steph.). 10. και οτε (—δε). ηρωτουν. $\overline{ιβ}$√. τασ παραβολασ. 11. το μυστηριον δεδοται (—γνωναι). βασιλιασ√.—τα. γεινεται√. 12. [βλεπωσι. ἴδωσι. ακουωσι: *at* -σιν *ter* Cᵃ]. συνιωσιν√. επιστρεψωσιν√.—τα αμαρτηματα. 13. γνωσεσθαι√. 14. σπιρων√. σπερει. 15. σπιρεται√. ευθυσ. αρπαζει (*pro* αιρει). εν αυτοισ (*pro* εν τ. κ. αυτ.). 16. ομοιωσ εισιν. σπιρομενοι (*sic* v. 18)√. ακουσωσιν√. ευθυσ (*sic* v. 17). 17. [εχουσι: *at* -σιν Cᵃ]. 18. αλλοι (*pro* ουτοι *prim.*). επι (*pro* εισ). ακουσαντεσ τον λογον. 19. —τουτου. *Post* πλουτου *legit* συνπνιγει τον λογον και αι παρα (περι Cᵃ) τα λοιπα επιθυμιαι εισπορευομεναι (A *addit* συνπνιγουσιν τον λογον) και ακαρποσ γεινεται. 20. εκεινοι (*pro* ουτοι). [ακουουσι]. εν $\overline{λ}$ και εν $\overline{ξ}$ και εν $\overline{ρ}$ (cf. v. 8). 21. [*Deest* οτι]. ερχεται ο λυχνοσ.—ινα *prim.* (*habet* Cᵃ). τεθηναι (τεθη Cᵃ). ϋπο (*pro* επι). *fin.* τεθη. 22. εστιν√ [τι]. εαν μη ἵνα (—ο). ελθη εισ φανερον. 24. μετριτε√. προστεθησετε√.—τοισ ακουουσιν. 25. εχει (*pro* αν εχη). 26. —εαν. 27. εγειρεται. [βλαστανη]. 28. —γαρ.—ειτα σταχυν (*habet* Cᵃ). ειτεν πληρη σιτον (*at* ειτ' εν Cᵃ, *sic, pro* ειτα *secund.*). 29. παραδοι (Cᵃ *cum* Steph.). ευθυσ. 30. ελεγεν (+ αυτοισ A)√. πωσ (*pro* τινι). *fin.* εν τινι αυτην παραβολη θωμεν. 31. [κοκκω]. —οσ (*habet* Cᵃ). ο μικροτερον ον (*pro* μικροτεροσ: ο *delet* C). —εστι. [των ε. τ. γ.]. 32. αναβαινι√. γεινεται μειζον παντων των λαχανων. πετινα√. *fin.* [-νουν]. 33. [ηδυν.]. 34. ἴδιοισ μαθηταισ (—αυτου). επελυεν√. 35. εκινη√. 36. —δε. πλοια ησαν (*pro* πλοιαρια ην). 37. γεινεται√. μεγασ (μεγαλη Cᵃ) ανεμου. και τα κυματα επεβαλεν (—δε).—ωστε αυτο ηδη γεμιζεσθαι (A *habet* ωστε ηδη γεμιζεσθαι το πλοιον). 38. αυτοσ ην. εν (*pro* επι *prim.*). εγιρουσιν. μελι√. 39. επετιμησεν√. ειπεν√. 40. (λεγει *pro* ειπεν Cᵃ). ουπω (*pro* ουτω πωσ ουκ). 41. (οι ανεμοι Cᵃ, *sed restituitur* ο ανεμοσ). αυτω υπακουει (υπ. αυτω Cᵃ *et* Cᵇ).

V. 1. *fin.* γερασηνων (γεργεσηνων Cᵃ). 2. εξελθοντοσ αυτου. ευθυσ ϋπηντησεν. μνημιων√. 3. μνημασιν (*pro* μνημειοισ). ουδε (*pro* ουτε). [αλυσεσιν]. + ουκετι (*ante* ουδεισ). εδυνατο. 4. δι (*pro* δια το: *at* δια τουτον *pro* δια το αυτον Cᵃ). [αλυσεσι]. αλυσισ√. παιδασ√. ουδισ ἴσχυσεν αυτον (—δαμασαι: *habet* Cᵃ). 5. μνημασιν και εν τοισ ορεσιν. 6. και ἴδων (—δε). εδραμεν√. [αυτω]. 7. λεγει (*pro* ειπε). 8. και ελεγεν (—γαρ). [εκ]. 9. [επηρωτα]. ονομα σοι. λεγι αυτω (*pro* απεκριθη λεγων). λεγιων (-γαιων Cᵃ). [μοι οτι]. 10. [παρεκαλει]. αυτον αποστιλη√. 11. προσ τω ορι (—ορι *p.m.*: *supplet*

Α). (βοσκομενων Cª). 12. [παρεκαλεσαν].—παντες οι δαιμονες. 13. —ευθεωσ ο ισ.—ησαν δε. 14. και οι (—δε). αυτουσ (*pro* τουσ χοιρουσ). απηγγιλον. (Cª ηλθον *pro* εξηλθον). εστιν√. 15. ηρχοντο (*pro* ερχονται: Α? Cª *cum* Steph.). [θεωρουσι].—και *tert.* λεγιωνα (-γαιωνα Cª). 16. [και διηγησαντο]. 17. παρακαλιν√. απελθιν√. 18. εμβαινοντοσ. μετ αυτου η. 19. και (*pro* ο δε ισ). απαγγειλον. ο κσ πεποιηκεν σοι. ηλεησεν. 20. απηλθεν (*sic* v. 24)√. δεκαπολι√. 21. εισ το περαν παλιν. 22. —ιδου. ϊαϊροσ. πιπτι√. 23. παρακαλει. τασ χιρασ αυτη. ϊνα (*pro* οπωσ). ζηση. 24. ηκολουθι√. 25. —τισ. δωδεκα ετη. 26. [εαυτησ]. ωφεληθισα√. 27. + τα (*ante* περι: *improbat* C). οπιθεν (οπισθεν Α? Cª). 28. ελεγεν (*sic* v. 30)√. οτι εαν αψωμαι καν του ϊματιου αυτου. 29. ευθυσ (*sic* v. 30). 31. λεγισ√. 33. φοβηθισα√. + και (*post* τρεμουσα: *improbant* Α? Cª). ϊδυϊα√.—επ. ηλθεν√. αληθιαν√. 34. [ο δε ειπ.]. [θυγατερ]. σεσωκεν√. ϊρηνην√. 35. απεθανεν√. 36. —ευθεωσ. παρακαουσασ (α *notatum p.m.*, παρ *improbatum a* Cª ?, *sed rursus restitutum*). 37. μετ αυτου (*pro* αυτω). [συνακολουθησαι]. + τον (*ante* πετρον). 38. ερχονται. + και (*ante* κλαιοντασ). 39. καθευδι√. 40. αυτοσ δε (*pro* ο δε). παντασ.—ανακειμενον. 41. χιροσ√. πεδιου√. κουμ. εστιν√. εγειρε. 42. ευθυσ. περιεπατι√. + ωσει (*ante* ετων). ιβ√. + ευθυσ (*post* εξεστησαν). εκστασι√. 43. διεστιλατο√. μηδισ√. [γνω]. ειπεν√. φαγιν√.

VI. 1. εκιθεν (*sic* v. 10, *non* v. 11)√. ερχεται (*pro* ηλθεν). 2. διδασκειν εν τη συναγωγη. [και πολλ.]. + παντα (*post* ταυτα). δοθισα√. τουτω (*pro* αυτω).—οτι. + αι (*ante* δυναμισ√). (αι τοιαυται αι Cª). *fin.* γινομεναι. 3. + τησ (*ante* μαριασ). και ο αδελφοσ (—δε). ϊωσηφ. 4. και ελεγεν (—δε). εστιν√. εαυτου (*pro* αυτου *prim.*: *at* ιδια πατριδι αυτου Cª).—τοισ συγγενεσι και εν (ὁμοιοτ.: *habet* Α τοισ συνγενεσιν και εν). *fin.* [αυτου]. 5. [ηδυν.]. ποιησαι ουδεμιαν δυναμιν. χιρασ εθεραπευσεν√. 6. εθαυμασεν. + ο ισ (*post* περιηγεν). 7. ιβ√. αποστελλιν√. 7, 8. —εξουσιαν *usque ad* παρηγγειλεν αυτοισ (ὁμοιοτ.: *habent* Α C^b). 8. αρωσιν. μη αρτον μη πηραν. 9. αλλα. [ενδυσησθε]. 10. [ελεγεν]. [εαν]. μινατε. 11. *init.* και οσ αν τοποσ μη δεξηται.—αμην λεγω κ.τ.λ. *ad fin. vers.* 12. εκηρυξαν αυτοισ (*pro* εκηρυσσον: αυτοισ *improbat* Α?). μετανοησωσιν. 14. [ελεγεν]. [νν *passim*]. εγηγερται εκ νεκρων. δυναμισ√. 15. + δε (*post* αλλοι *prim.*).—ελεγον *secund.*—εστιν η. 16. ελεγεν (*pro* ειπεν).—οτι. ουτοσ ϊωαννησ

27

(*sic etiam* A).—εστιν· αυτοσ (—εστιν *tantum* A: ῑωαννην ουτοσ ηγερθη *tantum* C[a]).—εκ νεκρων. 17. (ο γαρ ηρωδησ C[a], αυτοσ *omisso, sed recepta lectio restituitur*). αποστιλασ√. [εκρατησε]. —τη. 18. ελεγεν√. εξεστιν√. εχιν√. 19. [ηθελεν]. αποκτιναι√. 20. ηπορει (*pro* εποιει). ηκουεν√. 21. [οτε]. διπνον√. εποιησεν√. 22. ελθουσησ (εισελθ. C[a]). αυτου (*pro* αυτησ τησ). ηρεσεν (*pro* και αρεσασησ). ο δε βασιλευσ ειπεν. αιτησαι. 23. —με. 24. και (*pro* η δε *prim.*). ειπεν *bis in versu*√. αιτησωμαι. *fin.* βαπτιζοντοσ (*non* v. 25). 25. ελθουσα (εισελθ. C[a]). ευθυσ (*sic* v. 27). εξ αυτησ δωσ μοι. 26 [συνανακειμενουσ]. αθετησαι αυτην. 27. ευθυσ. αποστιλασ√. σπεκουλατορα. ενεγκε. 28. —ο δε απελθων *usque ad* την κεφαλην αυτου (ὁμοιοτ.?). 29. ακου. (σ *pro* α *p.m.*?)√. [ηλθον]. αυτον (*pro* αυτο).—τω. μνημιω√. 30. απηγγιλαν√.—και *tert.* —οσα *secund.* (*habet* C[a]). 31. λεγει (*pro* ειπεν). ῡμισ√. (επ *pro* εισ C[a]). αναπαυεσθαι√. ευκαιρουν. 32. εν πλοιω εισ ερημον τοπον. 33. ῑδον√.—οι οχλοι. [επεγνωσαν]. αυτουσ (*pro* αυτον *prim.*).—και συνηλθον προσ αυτον. 34. —ο ῑσ. οχλον πολυν. αυτουσ (*pro* αυτοισ).—ωσ προβατα (*habet* C[a]). διδασκιν√. 35. γινομενησ.—αυτω (*habet* C[a]). [αυτου]. ελεγον (*pro* λεγουσιν). 36. βρωματα (*pro* αρτουσ) τι φαγωσιν (—γαρ *et* ουκ εχουσιν). 37. φαγιν *prim.*√. δηναριων διακοσιων. δωσωμεν. 38. [αρτ. εχ.].—και *prim.* ελθοντεσ (*pro* γνοντεσ: C[a] *cum* Steph.). λεγουσιν πεντε. 39. ανακλιθηναι. 40. ανεπεσαν.—πρασιαι *semel.* κατα (*pro* ανα) *bis.* ν̄√. 41. ευλογησεν√. κλασασ (*pro* κατεκλασε). —και (*ante* εδιδου: *habet* και C[a]).—αυτου. παρατιθωσιν (C *cum* Steph.). β̄ *secund.*√. εμερισεν πασιν√. 43. κλασματων ῑβ̄ κοφινων πληρωματα (—πληρεισ). + δυο (*ante* ῑχθυων). 44. —τουσ αρτουσ (*additurus erat* C, *sed delevit*). ωσ (*pro* ωσει). 45. ευθυσ. [ηναγκασε].—το *prim.* απολυει. 48. ῑδων (*pro* ειδεν). ελαυνιν√. εναντιοσ ο ανεμοσ.—και *secund.* ηθελεν√. 49. επι τησ θαλασσησ περιπατουντα. οτι φαντασμα εστιν (*pro* φαντ. ειναι). 50. ειδαν. ο δε ευθυσ (—και *secund.*). ελαλησεν√. 51. —εκ περισσου.—και εθαυμαζον. 52. αλλ ην αυτων η καρδια (—γαρ). 53. επι την γην ηλθον εισ γεννησαρετ. προσωρμηθησαν (-μισθησαν C[a]). 54. ευθυσ [*nihil additum*]. 55. περιεδραμον. χωραν (*pro* περιχωρον). + και (*ante* ηρξαντο). εν τοισ τοισ κραβακτοισ (*sic*: επι *pro* εν C[a] *cum* Steph.: τοισ *secund. improbato*). ηκουσθη.—εκει. εστιν√. 56. εαν (*pro* αν *prim.*). + εισ (*ante* πολισ√ *et* αγρουσ). + η (*post* αγρουσ). ετιθεσαν. ηψαντο (*pro* αν ηπτοντο).

VII. 1. γραμματαιων√. 2. τινεσ (C[a] τινασ). + οτι (*ante* κοιναισ). χερσιν√. εσθιουσιν αρτον.—εμεμψαντο. 3. πυκνα (pro πυγμη). εσθιωσιν. 4. [απο]. ραντισωντε (Cª -νται, pro βαπτισωνται). εσθιουσιν (sic v. 5)√. κρατιν√.—και κλινων (ὁμοιοτ.). 5. και (pro επειτα). γραμματισ√. ου περιπατουσιν οι μαθηται σου. κοιναισ (pro ανιπτοισ: Cª cum Steph.). 6. —αποκριθεισ.—οτι in loco. επροφητευσεν. + οτι (ante ουτοσ ο λ.). χιλεσιν√. 7. σεβοντε (Cª -νται)√. 8. —γαρ.—βαπτισμουσ ξεστων κ.τ.λ. ad fin. vers. 9. αθετιτε√. 10. μωϋσησ. ειπεν√. 11. λεγεται√. εστιν√. 12. —και. αφιεται√. ποιησε (Cª -σαι)√.—αυτου bis. 13. παραδοσι√. πολλα τοιαυτα. 14. παλιν (pro παντα). [ακουετε].—μου παντεσ. [συνιετε]. 15. επ (pro εισ: Cª cum Steph.). κοινωσαι αυτον. εκ του ανου εκπορευομενα (—απ αυτου).—εκεινα. εστιν√. κοιναυντα (° forsan p.m.: C reposuit super a raso)√. 16. Deest versus. 17. εισηλθον. + τον (ante οικον). την παραβολην (—περι). 18. [ουτω: at Cª ουτωσ√]. ὑμισ√. ουπω (pro ου). ου κοινοι τον ανον (pro εισ τον ανον κ.τ.λ. ad fin. vers.). 19. εισπορευετε√. εκβαλλετε (pro εκπορευεται). καθαριζων. 20. ελεγεν√. εκινο√. fin. ανο (Cª ανον)√. 21, 22. πορνιαι κλοπαι φονοι μοιχιαι. 22. ασελγια√. 23. κακεινα (pro και). 24. εκειθεν δε (—και). ορια. [και σιδωνοσ].—την. ηθελησεν. ηδυνασθη. λαλειν (pro λαθειν: Cª cum Steph.). 25. αλλα ευθυσ ακουσασα (—γαρ). ειχεν√. —αυτησ. εισελθουσα. προσεπεσεν√. 26. η δε γυνη ην. συροφοινικισσα. γενι√. εκβαλη. 27. και ελεγεν (pro ο δε ισ ειπεν). εστιν καλον. τοισ κυναριοισ βαλειν. 28. —γαρ. εσθιουσιν αποκατω (ὑποκ. A, etiam p.m. τ scripsit primò pro κ, sed correxit) τησ τραπεζησ. 29. εξεληλυθεν εκ τησ θυγατροσ σου το δεμονιον[13] ([13] Tischendorf., sed deest annotatio). 30. εαυτησ. ευρεν το παιδιον βεβλημενον επι την κλινην και το δαιμονιον εξεληλυθοσ. 31. ηλθεν δια σιδωνοσ (pro και σιδ. ηλ.). εισ (pro προσ). 32. + και (ante μογιλαλον). fin. τασ χιρασ (Cª την χιρα√). 33. κατ ιδιαν απο του οχλου. ελαβεν (Cª εβαλεν√).—αυτου prim. 34. εστεναξεν√. (εφφεθα Cª, sed εφφαθα restitutum). εστιν√. διανυχθητι√. 35. —ευθεωσ. ηνυγησαν. + ευθυσ (ante ελυθη). 36. διεστιλατο√. λεγωσιν (pro ειπωσιν).—αυτοσ. + αυτοι (ante μαλλον). περισσοτερωσ. 37. πεποιηκεν√.—τουσ secund. λαλιν√.

VIII. 1. παλιν πολλου (pro παμπολλου). φαγωσιν√.—ο ισ. —αυτου. 2. σπλαγχνιζομε√. ημεραι τρισ. [προσμενουσι μοι]. [εχουσι]. φαγωσιν√. 3. νηστισ√. και τινεσ (—γαρ). + απο (ante μακροθεν). ηκασιν√. 4. —αυτω. + και ειπαν (ante ποθεν). δυνη-

σετε√. 5. ηρωτα. αρτουσ εχετε (*αρ rescriptum*). ειπαν ζ̄. 6. παραγγελλι√. τουσσ ζ̄ (*σ eras.*)√. [-τουσ ευχ.]. εκλασεν√. παρατιθωσιν√. 7. ειχαν. *fin.* και ευλογησασ αυτα παρεθηκεν (— ειπεν *et* και *ultim.*: *at* A *pro* παρεθηκεν *habet* ειπεν και ταυτα παρατιθεναι). 8. και εφαγον (— δε). + παντεσ (*post* εφαγον). + τα (*ante* περισσευματα). σφυριδασ (*non* v. 20). 9. — οι φαγοντεσ ωσ. 10. ευθυσ. [εμβασ εισ]. + ο ισ̄ (*post* ηλθεν: *improbant* Cᵃ Cᵇ). 11. συνζητειν. + ϊδιν (*post* σημιον√). πιραζοντεσ√. 12. ζητι σημιον. σημιον *secund.*√. 13. αφισ√. παλιν εμβασ.— εισ το πλοιον. 15. διετελλετο (Cᵃ διεστ.). [ορατε βλ.]. 16. — λεγοντεσ. [εχομεν]. 17. [ο ισ̄: *delet* Cᵃ].— ετι. 18. βλεπεται√.— και *prim.* (*habet* A). 19. + και (*ante* ποσουσ). κλασματων πληρισ. ιβ̄√. 20. οτε και (— δε). + αρτουσ (*post* επτα). και λεγουσιν (*pro* οι δε ειπον). 21. ουπω (*pro* πωσ ου). 22. [ερχεται: *at* Cᵃ ερχονται]. 23. εξηνεγκεν (*pro* εξηγαγεν). χιρασ√. [βλεπει]. 24. ειπεν (*pro* ελεγε: Cᵃ ελεγεν√). [*caetera cum* Steph.]. 25. επεθηκεν√. χιρασ√. διεβλεψεν (*pro* εποιη. αυτ. αναβλ.). απεκατεστη. εβλεψεν δηλαυγωσ (Cᵃ ενεβλεπεν τηλ.). *fin.* απαντα. 26. απεστιλεν√. εισ οικον αυτον αυτου (— τον: Cᵃ *cum* Steph.). μη (*pro* μηδε *prim.*: Cᵃ *cum* Steph.).— μηδε ειπησ *ad fin. vers.* 27. καισαριασ√. αυτουσ *primò* (*pro* αυτοισ *p.m.*?; αυτοισ *punctis notatum, sed rursus deleta sunt*). 28. ειπαν αυτω λεγοντεσ (*pro* απεκριθησαν). + οτι (*ante* ιωαννην: *delet* Cᵃ). ηλειαν. οτι εισ (*pro* ενα). 29. επηρωτα αυτουσ (*pro* λεγει αυτοισ). λεγεται ειvε (Cᵃ -ναι)√. [αποκρ. δε, *sine* και]. *fin.* + ο υσ̄ του θῡ. 30. λεγωσιν√. 31. διδασκιν√. αποδοκιμασθηνε (Cᵃ -ναι)√. ϋπο (*pro* απο). + των (*ante* αρχιερ. *et* γραμμ.). 32. [αυτ. ο πετρ.]. 33. επιστραφισ√. επετιμησεν√. — τω. και λεγει (*pro* λεγων). φρονισ√. 34. μαθητεσ (Cᵃ -ταισ)√. ει τισ (*pro* οστισ). [ελθειν]. εαυτου (*pro* αυτου *secund.*). ακολουθιτω√. 35. εαν (*pro* αν). απολεσει (*pro* -ση)√. [την ψυχ. αυτ. *secund.*].— ουτοσ. 36. ωφελι ανοσ̄ (Cᵃ ανον̄). κερδησαι (— εαν). ζημιωθηναι. 37. *init.* τι γαρ δοι ανοσ̄ (Cᵃ δω). [λλ]. 38. εαν (*pro* αν). επαισχυνθησετε√.

IX. 1. εισιν√. των ωδε εστωτων. [γευσωνται]. ιδωσιν√. βασιλιαν√. 2. μετα. παραλαμβανι√. [τον ιωαννην]. αναφερι√. + λιαν (*post* ϋψηλον). 3. [εγενετο].— ωσ χιων. [γναφ.]. + ουτωσ (*ante* λευκανε√, *at* Cᵃ -ναι). 4. μωυση. λαλουντεσ (*pro* συλλ.). 5. ραββει√. γ̄ σκηνασ. μωυσει. 6. ηδι√. απεκριθη (*pro* λαληση). εκφοβοι γαρ εγενοντο (— ησαν). 7. επεισκιαζουσα√. εγενετο εκ

τησ νεφελησ φωνη (—ηλθε).—λεγουσα. (*Post* αγαπητοσ Α *habet* εν ω ευδοκησα). ακουετε αυτου. 8. [εξαπινα]. ει μη (*pro* αλλα). 9. και καταβαινοντων (—δε). [απο]. διεστιλατο√. α ειδον διηγησωνται.—ει μη (*habet* Α). 10. συνζητουντεσ. εστιν√. 11. [επηρωτων]. [οτι *prim.*]. + οι φαρισαιοι και (*post* λεγουσιν). γραμματισ (*non* v. 14)√. δι√. 12. εφη (*pro* αποκριθεισ ειπεν). [μεν]. (πρωτοσ C^a^). αποκατασταννι (C^a^ αποκαθισταννι). εξουθενωθη. 13. —οτι (*habet* C^a^). εληλυθεν√. (+εν *ante* αυτω C^a^). ηθελον. γεγραπτε√. 14. ελθοντεσ (*pro* ελθων). ειδον. συνζητουντασ. προσ εαυτουσ (*pro* αυτοισ: C^a^ προσ αυτουσ). 15. ευθυσ. ϊδοντεσ. εξεθαμβηθησαν. 16. επηρωτησεν αυτουσ (—τουσ γραμματεισ). συνζητειτε. *fin.* εαυτουσ (αυτουσ Α?, *at* ε *restitut.*). 17. απεκριθη (*pro* αποκριθεισ). + αυτω (*ante* εισ). —ειπε. 18. —αν (C^a^ *habet* εαν).—αυτον *secund.*—αυτου. ειπα. [εκβαλωσι]. 19. αυτοισ (*pro* -ω). *fin.* εμε. 20. το $\overline{\pi\nu\alpha}$ ευθυσ συνεσπαραξεν. 21. επηρωτησεν√. (εξ ου *pro* ωσ C^a^). ειπεν εκ παιδ. 22. και εισ πυρ αυτον. εβαλεν√. αλλα. δυνη. 23. δυνη (C^a^ δυνασαι). —πιστευσαι. 24. [και]. —ευθεωσ (*at* ευθυσ *pro* και C^a^). —μετα δακρυων. ελεγεν√.—κυριε. 25. +ο (*ante* οχλοσ). επετιμησεν√. το αλαλον και κωφον $\overline{\pi\nu\alpha}$.—εγω (*habet* C^a^). επιτασσω σοι. [εξ αυτου]. 26. κραξασ. σπαραξασ. (αυτον *punctis notatum rursus erasis*). εξηλθεν√. +τουσ (*ante* πολλουσ). 27. —αυτον *prim.*, *at* τησ χιροσ αυτου. 28. εισελθοντοσ αυτου. κατ ιδιαν επηρωτων αυτον. ημισ√. 29. δυνατε√.—και νηστεια (*habet* C^b^). 30. κακειθεν. [παρεπ.]. γνοι. 31. εδιδασκεν√. χιρασ√. αποκτανθισ√. μετα τρισ ημερασ. 33. ηλθον. καφαρναουμ.—προσ εαυτουσ. 34. διελεγχθησαν [εν τη οδω]. *fin.* +εστιν. 35. εφωνησεν√. $\overline{\iota\beta}$√. εστε (C^a^ -ται)√. 36. ειπ εναγκαλ. (··· *p.m. et* C)√. 37. αν (*pro* εαν *prim.*). παιδιων τουτων (*pro* τοιουτων παιδ.). δεξητε *prim.*√. εμε δεχετε (*pro* εαν εμε δεξηται). δεχετε (*pro* -ται *secund.*)√. αποστιλαντα√. 38. εφη (*pro* απεκριθη δε). [ο ϊωανν.]. —λεγων. +εν (*post* τινα).—οσ ουκ ακουλουθει ημιν. εκωλυομεν. οτι ουκ ηκολουθι ημιν. 39. ειπεν√. ουδισ√. δυνησετε√. 40. εστιν *bis in versu*√. ημων (*pro* υμων) *bis in versu*. 41. εαν (*pro* αν) *non* v. 42. —τω. [μου: *improbat* C^a^]. εμον εσται (*pro* $\overline{\chi\upsilon}$ εστε: *at* C^a^ $\overline{\chi\upsilon}$ *pro* εμον). +οτι (*ante* ου μη). [απολεση]. 42. +τουτων (*post* μικρων). [πιστευοντων].—εισ εμε. περικιται√. μυλοσ ονικοσ (*pro* λιθ. μυλ.). βεβλητε√. 43. σκανδαλιση. εστιν σε (*pro* σοι εστιν). εισελθειν εισ την ζωην. εισελθειν (*pro* απελθειν: C^a^ *cum* Steph.). (εισ το πυρ το ασβεστον *punctis notata a* C^a^? *rursus deletis*).

44. *Deest versus.* **45.** σκανδαλιζει (*non* v. 47)√. εστιν σε (*pro* εστι σοι). εισ την ζωην εισελθιν. + κυλλον η (*ante* χωλον). εισ την γεενναν βληθηναι. — εισ το πυρ κ.τ.λ. *usque ad fin.* v. **46.** **47.** σε εστιν (*pro* σοι εστι). — εισελθειν (C[a] *habet* εισελθιν√). ζω σιλιαν (βα *pro* ζω C[a])√. — την *secund.* — του πυροσ. **49.** + εν (*ante* πυρι). — και πασα θ. *ad fin. vers.* (ὁμοιοτ.?). **50.** αλα *secund. et tert.* (C[a] αλασ). ιρηνευετε (ειρ. A?)√.

X. **1.** και εκειθεν. και (*pro* δια του). συνπορευονται. **2.** [οι]. επηρωτων. πιραζοντεσ√. **3.** μωϋσησ. **4.** ειπαν. επετρεψεν μωϋσησ. **5.** ο δε (*pro* και αποκριθεισ ο). **6.** — ο $\overline{θσ}$. **7.** καταλιψι√. ανθρωπ$\overline{ω}$ (*pro* $\overline{ανσσ}$)√. — και προσκολληθησεται προσ την γυναικα (αυτου *sequente ad* $\overline{μρα}$ *juncto*). **8.** εισιν√. σαρξ μια. **10.** εισ την οικιαν. — αυτου *prim.* τουτων (*pro* του αυτου). επηρωτων. (αυτον, ν *partim rescriptum*)√. **11.** αν (*pro* εαν). μοιχατε (*non* v. 12)√. **12.** αυτη απολυσασα (*pro* γυνη απολ.). γαμηση αλλον (*pro* και γαμηθη αλλω). **13.** αυτων αψηται. επετιμησαν. αυτοισ (*pro* τοισ προσφερ.). **14.** ηγανακτησεν√. ερχεσθε√. [και μη]. βασιλια√. **15.** αν (*pro* εαν). δεξητε√. βασιλιαν√. πεδιον (C[a] παιδ.)√. **16.** κατευλογει τιθεισ τασ χιρασ επ αυτα (— αυτα *semel*). **19.** — μη μοιχευσησ (*addit* A *post* φονευσησ). *fin.* + σου (*improbat* C[a]). **20.** εφη (*pro* αποκριθεισ ειπεν). [τ. π. εφυλαξαμην]. **21.** ετι εν σε ϋστερι. [τοισ πτωχ.]. ακολουθι√. — αρασ τον σταυρον. **22.** απηλθεν√. **23.** ελεγεν (λεγει C[a] *cum* Steph.). βασιλιαν (*sic* v. 25, *non* v. 24)√. εισελευσοντε√. **24.** [τεκνα]. εστιν. — τουσ πεποιθοτασ επι τοισ χρημασιν. **25.** εστιν√. τρηματοσ (*pro* τησ τρυμαλιασ τησ: C[a] τρυμαλιασ). [εισελθειν *prim.*]. εισελθιν *secund.*√. **26.** αυτον (*pro* εαυτουσ). **27.** — δε. ειπεν (*pro* λεγει: C[a] λεγι). [-ποισ αδυν.]. — τω *prim.* — εστι. **28.** *init.* — και. ηρξατο λεγιν ο πετροσ. ημισ√. [ηκολουθησαμεν]. *fin.* + τι αρα εσται ημιν. **29.** εφη αυτω ο $\overline{ισ}$ (*pro* αποκριθεισ δε ο $\overline{ισ}$ ειπεν). ουδισ√. [η πατερα η μητερα]. — η γυναικα. — εμου και (*post* αγρουσ *addit* C[a] ενεκεν εμου και). **30.** απολαβη. — οικιασ κ.τ.λ. *usque ad* διωγμων (*habent* A C[a], *legentes* μητερα, *cui addit* C[a] και $\overline{πρα}$: *sed* και αγρουσ μετα διωγμων *omittit* A). **31.** — οι. **32.** οι δε (*pro* και *tert.*). $\overline{ιβ}$√. λεγιν√. συμβαινιν√. **33.** αναβενομεν ϊσ√. [αρχιερευσι]. — και τοισ γραμματευσι (*habet* C[a], *at* -σιν√). εθνεσιν√. **34.** εμπεξουσιν√. και εμπτυουσιν (-σουσιν C[a]) αυτω και μαστιγωσουσιν αυτον. — αυτον *secund.* μετα τρισ ημερασ. **35.** παραπορευονται (C[a] προσ-). [οι]. + αυτω (*post* λεγοντεσ). **35—37.** — ο εαν αιτησωμεν *usque ad* δοσ ημιν ινα (ὁμοιοτ.: *supplet* Cª, *legens* αιτησομεν σε . . . θελεται με ποιησω . . *at* ποιησαι Cᵇ *vel* Cª *corrector*). 37. εισ σου εκ δεξιων. εισ σου εξ ευωνυμων. 38. οιδαται√. αιτισθε√. δυνασθαι√. η (*pro* και). βαπτιζομε (*sic* v. 39)√. 39. ειπαν.— μεν. 40. η (*pro* και).— μου *secund. fin.* + ὑπο του πατροσ μου (*delet. et rursus restitut.*). 41. + και (*ante* περι). 42. και προσκαλεσαμενοσ αυτουσ ισ̅ (— ο δε: Cª *habet* ο ισ̅). βασιλεισ (*pro* μεγαλοι αυτων). 43. ουτωσ√. εστιν (*pro* εσται *prim.*). αν (*pro* εαν). μεγασ γενεσθαι. εστω (*pro* εσται *secund.*). υμων διακονοσ. 44. [αν]. εν υμιν ειναι (*pro* υμων γενεσθαι). 45. ηλθεν√. 46. [ερχονται]. [ιεριχω *prim.*]. ιερειχω *secund.* + ο (*ante* ὑιοσ].— ο (*ante* τυφλοσ). + και προσαιτησ (*ante* εκαθητο).— προσαιτων. 47. [ναζωραιοσ]. υιε̅ (*pro* ο υιοσ). δαδ̅ (*sic* v. 48)√. 49. φωνησατε αυτον (*pro* αυτ. φωνηθηναι). [φωνουσι]. εγειρε. 50. αναπηδησασ (*pro* αναστασ). ηλθεν√. 51. αυτω ο ισ̅ ειπεν (— λεγει). σοι θελεισ ποιησω. ραββουνι. 52. (και ο *pro* ο δε Cª, *sed illud restitutum*). σεσωκεν√. ευθυσ. ανεβλεψεν√. αυτω (*pro* τω ιυ̅).

XI. 1. ιεροσολυμα εισ βηθφαγη και εισ βηθανιαν. ελεων√. [αποστελλει]. 2. λεγι√.— την κατεναντι υμων (*habet* Cᵇ). ευθυσ. ουδισ ανθρωπων ουπω εκαθισεν (σεν *in ras., est autem p.m.*). *fin.* λυσατε αυτον και φερετε. 3. [ποιειτε τουτο]. [οτι]. χριαν√. ευθυσ. αποστελλει παλιν ωδε. 4. και απηλθον (— δε). [τον]. [την]. 6. [ειπον]. ειπεν (*pro* ενετειλατο). 7. αγουσιν (*pro* ηγαγον: *at* φερουσιν Cª). επιβαλλουσιν. αυτων τα ἱματια αυτω (Cª αυτω τα ἱμ. εαυτων). *fin.* εκαθισαν επ αυτον. 8. και πολλοι (— δε). [εισ την οδον *prim.*]. στιβαδασ κοψαντεσ. αγρων (*pro* δενδρων).— και εστρωννυον *ad fin. vers.* 9. — λεγοντεσ. 10. — εν ονοματι κυ̅. δαδ̅√. 11. ἱσ (*pro* εισ *prim.*)√.— ο ισ̅ και. οψε. ιβ̅√. 12.— επεινασε (A? *habet* επινασεν√). 13. + μιαν απο (*post* συκην). τι ευρησι. φυλλα ο γαρ καιροσ ουκ ην συκων. 14. — ο ισ̅. εισ τον αιωνα εκ σου μηδισ. 15. ἱσ (*pro* εισ *prim.*: Cª εισ)√.— ο ισ̅. + τουσ (*ante* αγοραζ.). [λλ]. κατεστρεψεν και τασ καθ. των πωλ. τασ περιστ. (κατεστρεψεν *post* περιστερασ *ponit* Cª, *cum* Steph.). 17. εδιδασκεν√. και ελεγεν (*pro* λεγων).— αυτοισ. [οτι]. πασιν√. [εποι. αυτ.]. 18. οι αρχιερισ και οι γραμματισ. απολεσωσιν. [αυτον *secund.*]. πασ γαρ (— οτι). εξεπλησσοντο. 19. οταν (*pro* οτε). [εξεπορευετο]. 20. παρεπορευετο πρωι και ἰδον (Cª παραπορευομενοι πρωϊ ἰδον). 21. αναμνησθισ√. ραββει ειδε√. 22. + ο (*ante* ισ̅). + ει (*ante* εχετε). 23. — γαρ.— οτι. ορι√. πιστευη. ο λαλει (*pro* α λεγει). εστε (*sic* v. 24)√.— ο εαν ειπη. 24. — αν. προσευχεσθε και (*pro* προσευχομενοι). αιτισθε√. ελαβετε. 25. στητε. αφιεται√. εχεται√. 26. *Deest versus.* 27. ϊσ (Cᵃ Cᵇ εισ)√. γραμματισ√. 28. ελεγον (*pro* λεγουσιν). η (*pro* και *secund.*). εδωκεν την εξουσιαν ταυτην. 29. — αποκριθεισ. [ϋμασ καγω]. (καγω Cᵃ *pro* και *ante* ερω: *addiderat* υμιν, *sed ipse delevit*). 30. + το (*ante* ϊωαννου). ποθεν ην εξ ουρανου (*pro* εξ ουρ. ην). 31. προσελογιζοντο (Cᵃ διελογ., *sed* προσελογ. *restituitur*). [ουν]. 32. αλλα (— εαν). οχλον (*pro* λαον). παντεσ (Cᵃ *cum* Steph.). [οτι].— οντωσ (*habet* Cᵃ *ante* οτι). 33. τω ιυ λεγουσιν. [ο ισ].— αποκριθεισ. λεγι√.

XII. 1. λαλιν (*pro* λεγειν)√. ανθρωποσ εφυτευσεν. περιεθηκεν√. ωκοδομησεν√. εξεδετο. απεδημησεν√. 2. απεστιλεν√. λαβοι (Cᵃ *cum* Steph.). των καρπων. 3. και (*pro* οι δε). απεστιλαν καινον√. 4. απεστιλεν (*sic* vv. 5. 6)√.— δουλον (*habet* Cᵃ).— λιθοβολησαντεσ. εκεφαλιωσαν και ητιμασαν (— απεστ. ητιμ.). 5. — παλιν. απεκτιναν√. ο^α^λλουσ (α *p.m.?*)√. ουσ (*pro* τουσ) *bis in versu.* αποκτεννοντεσ (Cᵃ κτινυυντεσ). 6. — ουν. ειχεν υν. — αυτου. — και. εσχατον προσ αυτουσ. 7. εκινοι√. προσ εαυτουσ ειπαν. αποκτινωμεν√. εστε√. 8. απεκτιναν αυτον. [-λον εξω]. 9. [ουν]. 11. εστιν√. 12. ειπεν√. 13. αποστελλουσιν√. αγρευσωσιν√. 14. και (*pro* οι δε). μελι√. βλεπισ√. [αλλ]. διδασκισ εξεστιν√. δουναι κηνσον καισαρι. 15. ϊδων (*pro* ειδωσ: Cᵃ ϊδωσ). πιραζετε√. + ωδε (*ante* ϊνα: *improbat* Cᵃ). *fin.* ειδω. 16. οι δε ειπαν. 17. ο δε (*pro* και αποκριθεισ ο). [αυτοισ]. τα καισαροσ αποδοτε. εξεθαυμαζον. 18. επηρωτων. 19. μωϋσησ. καταλιψη. μη αφη τεκνα (Cᵃ τεκνον, *sed* να *restitut.*).— αυτου *secund.* 20. ζ αδελφοι. (A *habet* παρ ημιν *post* ησαν: *improbat* C). εισ (*pro* πρωτοσ: A C *cum* Steph.). ελαβεν√. αφηκεν√. 21. απεθανεν√. μη καταλιπων (*pro* και ουδε αυτοσ αφηκε). 22. — ελαβον αυτην.— και *secund.* αφηκεν (Cᵃ -καν)√. εσχατον. και η γυνη απεθανεν. 23. — ουν.— οταν αναστωσι. 24. εφη αυτοισ ο ισ (*pro* και αποκρ. ο ισ ειπ. αυτ.). πλανασθαι√. 25. — ουτε γαμουσιν (*supplet* A). γαμιζονται.— οι. 26. ανεγνωται√. μωϋσεωσ. του (*pro* τησ). πωσ (*pro* ωσ). [ο *quater in versu*]. ισακ (A ισακ', Cᵃ ϊσαακ'). 27. [ο]. — θσ *secund.*— υμεισ ουν. (Cᵃ πλανασθαι√). 28. συνζητουντων. ϊδων (Cᵃ ϊδωσ). απεκριθη αυτοισ. εστιν εντολη πρωτη παντων. 29. απεκριθη ο ισ (— δε).— αυτω. εστιν (*pro* πασων των εντολων).

εστιν√. 30. —αυτη πρωτη εντολη. 31. *init.*—και. δευτερα αυτη εστιν αγαπησισ (—ομοια). + δε (*post* μειζων). *fin.* εστιν√. 32. ειπεσ (C[a] -πασ). εστιν *prim.* (—θεοσ)√. 33. +σου (*post* καρδιασ).—και εξ ολησ τησ ψυχησ.—τησ (*ante* ϊσχυοσ: *habet* C[a]). + σου (*post* πλησιον: *improbat* C). σεαυτον. περισσοτερον (*pro* πλειον). εστιν√. [των θυσ.]. 34. ειδων√.—αυτον.—ει (A? C[b] *habent*, C[a] *post* θ̅υ̅ *ponit*). βασιλιασ√. ουδισ√. επωρωτησε αυτον (C[a] αυτ. επερ.). 35. ελεγεν√. γραμματισ√. δ̅α̅δ̅ εστιν. 36. —γαρ. δ̅α̅δ̅ (*sic* v. 37)√. [ειπεν ο κ̅σ̅]. [καθου]. [ϋποποδιον]. 37. —ουν. πωσ (*pro* ποθεν: C[a] *cum* Steph.). [υ̅σ̅ αυτου] εστιν.—ο. ηκουσεν. 38. εν τη διδαχη αυτου ελεγεν (—αυτοισ). γραμματαιων√. περιπατιν√. 39. διπνοισ√. 40. [κατεσθι.]. λημψονται. 41. —ο ι̅σ̅. [κατεναντι]. θεωρει (C[a] εθεωρ.). +τον (*ante* χαλκον). εξεβαλλον (*pro* εβαλλον: C[a] *cum* Steph.). 42. +γυνη (*ante* χηρα). [εβαλε]. [εστι]. 43. ειπεν (*pro* λεγει). πλεον. εβαλλεν (C[a] εβαλεν: *pro* βεβληκε). βαλλοντων.

XIII. 1. [εισ των]. ‘διδασκαλε’ διδασκαλε (‘ ’ A C *improbantes*). 2. —αποκριθεισ. βλεπισ√. + ωδε (*ante* λιθοσ). επι λιθον. ου κατα λυθησετε (—μη *secund.*: C[a] *cum* Steph.). 3. επηρωτα√. + ο (*ante* πετροσ). (ϊωανησ A, *sed* νν *postea restitut.*). 4. ειπον. σημιον√. μελλη ταυτα συντελισθαι παντα. 5. ηρξατο λεγιν αυτοισ (—αποκριθεισ). 6. —γαρ. 7. [ακουσητε]. + ορατε (*ante* μη: *improbatum sed rursus restitutum*). (θροεισθαι√ C[a]). —γαρ (*habet* C[b]). 8. εγερθησετε (C[a] -ται)√. επ εθνοσ.—βασιλεια επι (*habet* C[a], *at* -λια√).—και *secund.* σισμοι√.—κατα τοπουσ *usque ad* και ταραχαι (C[b] *supplet* κατα τοπουσ εσονται λιμοι *tantum*). αρχη. 9. —εαυτουσ (*habet* C[b]). παραδωσουσιν√. [γαρ]. (σταθησεσθαι√ C[a]). 10. προσ τον λαον δει *primò*, πρωτον δει *sine* λαον *s.m.* (C[b] &c.), *forsan etiam p.m.* 11. και οταν αγωσιν (—δε). προμεριμναται√.—μηδε μελετατε. [εαν]. λαλιτε√. ϋμισ√. 12. και παραδωσει (—δε). γονισ√. 13. υπομινασ√. 14. —το ρηθεν υπο δανιηλ του προφητου. εστηκοτα. δι√. 15. [ο δε].—εισ την οικιαν. εισελθατω. [αραι τι]. 16. —ων.—εισ τα. 18. —η φυγη υμων (*habet* C[b]). χιμωνοσ√. 19. γεγονεν√. ην (*pro* ησ). 20. εκολοβωσεν κ̅σ̅. εκολοβωσεν *secund.*√. 21. ειδε (*pro* ϊδου) *bis in versu.*—η. πιστευετε. 22. δε (*pro* γαρ). [ψευδοχριστοι και]. ψευδοπροφητε√. δωσουσιν σημια√.—και *ultim.* 23. [ϊδου]. 24. αλλα. δωσι√. 25. εσονται εκ του ουρανου πιπτοντεσ. 26. [πολλησ και δοξησ]. 27. αποστελλι. [αυτου *bis in vers.*]. 28. ηδη ο κλαδοσ αυτησ.

[γινωσκετε]. 29. ουτωσ√. ϋμισ√. ϊδητε ταυτα. 30. μεχρι (—ου). ταυτα παντα. 31. [παρελευσονται *prim.*]. *fin.* παρελευσονται (*pro* παρελθωσι). 32. [και τησ ωρασ].—οι *secund.* 33. αγρυπνιτε√. [και προσευχεσθε]. οιδαται√. 34. αφισ√.—και *secund.* ενετιλατο√. 35. γρηγοριτε (*non* v. 37)√. + η (*ante* οψε). μεσονυκτιον. 36. εξεφνησ√. 37. ο (*pro* α). πασιν√.

XIV. 1. αζυμα (α *prius p.m., sed in rasurâ scriptum*)√. αρχιερισ√. γραμματισ√. αποκτινωσι (*sic*)√. 2. γαρ (*pro* δε). εσται θορυβοσ. 3. —τη (*habet* C[a]). ηλθεν√.—και *secund.* τον (*pro* το, *at* την C[a]).—κατα. 4. αυτουσ (*pro* εαυτουσ: C[a] *cum* Steph.). —και λεγοντεσ. απωλια√. 5. το μυρον (*pro* τουτο). δηναριων τριακοσιων. δοθηνε√. [τοισ πτ.]. ενεβριμουντο. 6. +γαρ (*post* καλον). ηργασατο εν εμοι (C[a] ειργ.). 7. δυνασθαι√.—αυτουσ (*at* αυτοισ παντοτε C[a]). 8. εσχεν.—αυτη. εποιησεν√. προελαβεν√. το σωμα μου. 9. + δε (*post* αμην). εαν (*pro* αν).—τουτο. 10. —ο *prim. et secund.* ισκαριωθ (C[a] ο ϊσκαριωθ' ο). απηλθεν√. αρχιερισ√. αυτον παραδω. 11. απηγγιλαντο (επηγγ. C[a] *et jam ante eum?*). εζητι√. αυτον ευκαιρωσ [παραδω]. 12. θελισ√. 13. αυτουσ (*pro* αυτου: · *p.m.*)√. ϋπαγεται√. απαντησι√. 14. [εαν]. εστιν√. +μου (*post* καταλυμα). 15. αναγαιον. [ετοιμον]. κακει (*pro* εκει). ετοιμασαται√. 16. —αυτου και ηλθον (και ηλθον *habet* C[a]). 17. γενομενουσ (C[a] -νησ)√. 18. ο ισ̅ ειπεν. 19. —οι δε. λυπισθαι√. λεγιν√. κατα (*pro* καθ).—και αλλοσ μη τι εγω (ὁμοιοτ.?). 20. —αποκριθεισ.—εκ. [εμου εισ]. 21. *init.* +οτι. ϋπαγι√. εκινω√. [ην]. 22. [ο ισ̅ αρτον: *at* ο ισ̅ *delet* A *vel forsan p.m., restituit* C?]. εκλασεν ευλογησασ. ειπεν√.—φαγετε. εστιν (*sic* v. 24)√. 23. —το. 24. —το *secund.*—καινησ. εκχυννομενον υπερ πολλων. 25. —ουκετι. γενηματοσ. 27. σκανδαλισθησεσθαι√.—εν εμοι εν τη νυκτι ταυτη. τα προβατα διασκορπισθησονται. 29. ει και. 30. [οτι σημερον]. ταυτη τη νυκτι (—εν).—η δισ (cf. vv. 68. 72). με απαρνησει. 31. εκπερισσωσ ελαλει (—ελεγε μαλλον). με η (δεη με *pro* με η C[a]). συναποθανιν√. απαρνησωμε. ομοιωσ (*pro* ωσαυτωσ: C[a] *cum* Steph.). 32. [ου το]. γεθσημανει. 33. —τον (*ante* πετρον: *habet* C[a]). —τον *secund.* μετ αυτου. αδημονιν√. 34. μινατε√. 35. [προελθων]. επιπτεν.—ινα.—εστι (C[a] εστιν√). παρελθιν. 36. παρενεγκαι√. τουτο απ εμου. 37. καθευδισ√. 38. προσευχεσθαι√. ελθηται (C[a] εισελθ.). πιρασμον√. 40. παλιν ελθων (*pro* υποστρεψασ).—παλιν *in loco suo.* αυτων οι οφθαλμοι. καταβεβαρημενοι (C[a] καταβαρυνομενοι). ηδισαν√. αποκριθωσιν αυτω. 41. [το λοιπον]. χιρασ√. 42. ηγγισεν. 43. ευθυσ. παραγεινεται ϊουδασ εισ. — ων. — πολυσ. — των *ultim.* (*habet* A). 44. [παραδιδουσ]. συνσημον√. εστιν√. απαγετε. 45. ευθυσ. + και (*ante* προσελθων: *improbat* C^{a}). ραββει *semel*, *deest semel*. 46. επεβαλαν. — επ αυτον. τασ χιρασ αυτων (αυτω *pro* αυτων C^{a}). 47. — τισ. και επεσεν (*pro* επαισε: και *improbat* C^{a}). αφιλεν√. ωταριον. 48. εξηλθαται. συλλαβιν√. 49. εκρατησαται√. 50. εφυγον παντεσ. 51. νεανισκοσ τισ (— εισ). συνηκολουθει. — οι νεανισκοι. 52. — απ αυτων. 53. — αυτω. αρχιερισ√. [και οι πρ. και οι γρ.]. 54. συνκαθημενοσ. [το]. 55. [ευρισκον]. 56. (C^{a} εισαι, *sed restitutum* ϊσαι). ουκ' (*sic* v. 61)√. 58. ειπεν (*pro* ημεισ ηκουσαμεν αυτου λεγοντοσ). 60. — το. επηρωτησεν√. 61. + ι̅σ̅ (*ante* εσιωπα). ουκ' απεκρινατο ουδεν (*pro* ουδεν απεκρινατο). θ̅υ̅ (*pro* ευλογητου: C^{a} C^{b} *cum* Steph.). 62. εκ δεξιων καθημενον. 64. *init.* + ϊδε νυν. [τησ βλ.]. ενοχον ειναι. 65. αυτου το προσωπον. ελαβον (*pro* εβαλλον). 66. κατω εν τη αυλη. παιδισκη (*pro* των παιδισκων). 67. μετα του ι̅υ̅ ησθα του ναζαρηνου. 68. ουτε (*pro* ουκ). ουτε (*pro* ουδε). συ τι. — και αλεκτωρ εφωνησε. 69. ηρξατο παλιν. παρεστωσιν. 70. — και *prim.* (*habet* C^{a}). μεικρον√. γαλειλαιοσ√. — και η λαλια σου ομοιαζει. 71. [ομνυειν]. — τουτον ον λεγετε. 72. + ευθυσ (*post* και *prim.*). — εκ δευτερου. εφωνησεν√. το ρημα ωσ (*pro* του ρηματοσ ου). — δισ. τρισ με απαρνηση. *fin.* εκλαυσεν (C^{a} εκλεεν√).

XV. 1. ευθυσ. — επι το. ετοιμασαντεσ (*pro* ποιησαντεσ). + των (*ante* γραμματεων). — τω. πειλατω. 2. πειλατοσ (*sic* vv. 4. 9. 12. 14. 15. 44). αυτω λεγει (*pro* ειπεν αυτω). 3. [*nihil additum*]. 4. [επηρωτησεν]. — λεγων (*habet* C^{a}). *fin.* κατηγορουσιν. 5. πειλατον (*sic* v. 43). 6. ον παρητουντο (*pro* ονπερ ητουντο: C^{a} *cum* Steph.). 7. στασιαστων. στασι√. + τινα (*ante* πεποιηκεισαν). 8. αναβασ (*pro* αναβοησασ: C^{b} *cum* Steph.). — αει. 10. εγνωκει (*pro* εγινωσκε: C^{a} *cum* Steph.). [παραδεδ.]. 12. παλιν αποκριθεισ. ελεγεν (*pro* ειπεν). — θελετε. [ον λεγετε]. + τον (*ante* βασιλεα). 13. [*cum* Steph.]. 14. — αυτοισ (*habet* C^{a}). [κακον εποιησεν]. περισσωσ. [εκραξαν]. + λεγοντεσ (*ante* σταυρωσον *plenè*). 15. ποιησαι το ϊκανον τω οχλω. παρεδωκεν√. [φραγελλωσασ]. σ̅τ̅ρ̅θ̅η̅√. 16. εστιν√. συνκαλουσιν. 17. ενδιδυσκουσιν√. 18. + και λεγειν (*ante* χαιρε). [βασιλευ]. 20. τα ϊδια ϊματια αυτου. [εξαγουσιν]. [σταυρωσωσιν]. *fin.* — αυτον. 21. εγγαρευουσιν (C^{a} αγγαρ.). [*caetera cum* Steph.]. 22. τον γολγοθαν. — τοπον (*habet* C^{a}). οπερ (*pro* ο). εστιν (*sic* v. 42)√. 23. — πιειν. οσ δε (*pro* ο δε). ελαβεν√. 24. [σταυρωσαντεσ αυτον]. διαμεριζονται. ἑαυτου (˙ *p.m. notatum*). 27. σταυρουσιν√. 28. *Deest versus.* 29. κεινουντεσ√. [ουα: *punctis notat* Cᵃ? *rursus deletis*]. [εν τρ. ημ. οικοδ.]. 30. καταβασ (*pro* και καταβα). 31. — δε. 32. — του. ϊσραηλ *plenè*√. [πιστευσωμεν και]. + συν (*ante* αυτω). 33. και γενομενησ (— δε). ενατησ. 34. τη ενατη ωρα.— λεγων.

γ
[ελωϊ ελωϊ]. λεμα σαβακτανει (Cᵃ σαβαχθανει). εστιν√. εκατελιπεσ με (γ *p.m., postea instauratum*). 35. παρεστωτων. ϊδε ηλειαν. 36. τισ (*pro* εισ). [και].— τε. αφεσ. ηλειασ. 37. εξεπνευσεν√. 38. [απο]. 39. ουτωσ (— κραξασ). ουτοσ ο ανθρωποσ. θ̅υ̅ ην. 40. — ην. η ϊακωβου (— του). (Cᵃ *habet* ϊωσητοσ *pro* ϊωση). 41. — και *prim.* γαλειλαια√. 42. οψειασ√. [προσαββατον]. 43. ελθων (*pro* ηλθεν). αρειμαθαιασ (-θιασ Cᵃ?, *sed* -θαιασ *restitutum*). — οσ (*habet* Cᵃ). εισηλθεν√. + τον (*ante* πειλατον). 44. εθαυμαζεν. τεθνηκεν√. [παλαι]. απεθανεν√. 45. πτωμα (*pro* σωμα). 46. — και *secund.* ενειλησεν√. εθηκεν. μνηματι (*pro* μνημειω). προσεκυλισεν√. + μεγαν (*post* λιθον). 47. — και μαρια ιωση *usque ad* η μαγδαληνη xvi. 1 (ὁμοιοτ.: *supplet* Cᵃ, *legens* η ϊωσητοσ *pro* ιωση . . . τεθιται . . . η μαρια η μαγδαληνη).

XVI. 1. — του (*ante* ϊακωβου: *habet* Cᵃ). αλιψωσιν√. 2. τη μια των (*pro* τησ μιασ). μνημα (Cᵃ μνημιον√). ανατιλαντοσ√. 3. [εκ]. 4. — οτι. ανακεκυλισμενον τον λιθον. 5. [εισελθουσαι]. [ειδον]. 6. — τον ναζαρηνον (ὁμοιοτ.: *supplet* A). 7. αλλα. γαλειλαιαν. 8. — ταχυ. ειχεν√. γαρ (*pro* δε). [ουδεν]. γαρ'√. *Post* γαρ' v. 8 *in quartâ secundae columnae lineâ folii* xxix *explicit Evangelium Marci, cum nullo omissionis* vv. 9—20 *vestigio.*

Subscr. ευαγγελιον κατα μαρκον.

Ad caput tertiae columnae folii xxix *legitur* κατα λουκαν.

Cap. I. 1. επεχειλ *primò, at* ρ *pro* λ *p.m. ut videtur*√. 3. [εδοξε]. ακρειβωσ√. 4. επιγνοισ (Cᵃ *cum* Steph.). ασφαλιαν√. 5. — του. γυνη αυτω (*pro* η γυνη αυτου). 6. εναντιον. δικαιωμασιν√. 7. καθ' οτι (*sic*). ην η ελεισαβετ. 8. εναντιον. 9. [ελαχε: Cᵃ -χεν√]. 10. ην του λαου. 13. ειπεν (*sic* v. 18)√. ελεισαβετ (*sic* vv. 24. 36. 40. 41 *bis, non* v. 5)√. σου (*pro* σοι) *primò, at* σοι *p.m. ut videtur.* ἰωανην. 14. γενεσει. 15. — του. 17. ηλεια (*pro* ηλιου). 21. [αυτον εν τω ναω]. εδυνατο. 22. διεμενεν√. 23. λιτουργιασ√. 25. ουτωσ√. — ο. [επειδεν]. — το. 26. απο (*pro* υπο). ιουδαιασ (C^a γαλιλαιασ *cum* Steph.). [ναζαρετ]. 27. εμνηστευμενην (C^a μεμν., *sed* μ *prius rursus erasum*). + και πατριασ (*ante* δαδ). 28. προσ αυτην ο αγγελοσ ειπεν. — ευλογημενη συ εν γυναιξιν. 29. — ιδουσα. επι τω λογω διεταραχθη (— αυτου). 30. [αυτη]. μαριαμ' (*sic* v. 46)√. 31. συλλημψη. 32. δαδ√. 34. ειπεν (*sic* vv. 38. 46)√. 35. [γεννωμενον αγιον]. 36. συγγενισ. συνειληφεν. γηρει. 37. του θυ (τω θω C^a *cum* Steph.). 39. [μαριαμ]. επορευετο. ορινην√. 41. τον ασπασμον τησ μαριασ η ελεισαβετ'. + εν αγαλλιασει (*post* εσκιρτησεν: *improbat* C^a). 42. ανεβοησεν (*pro* ανεφωνησε). [φωνη]. γυναιξιν√. 43. *fin.* εμε (C^a με). 44. [εν αγαλλ. το βρ.]. 47. ηγαλλιασεν√. 48. ταπινωσιν√. μακαριουσιν√. 49. εποιησεν√. μεγαλα (C^a -λια, *sed* ι *rursus erasum*). ελεοσ (*pro* ονομα: C^a *cum* Steph.). 50. γενεαν και γενεαν (*pro* γενεασ γενεων). 51. εποιησεν√. (διανοιασ C^a, *sed* σ *ipse delevisse videtur*). 52. καθειλεν√. ὕψωσεν√. 53. εξαπεστειλεν√. 55. ελαλησεν√. 56. εμεινεν√. ωσ (*pro* ωσει). 58. συγγενισ√. εμεγαλυνεν√. 59. τη ημερα τη ογδοη. περιτεμιν√. 60. [ιωαννησ: *sic* v. 63). 61. ειπαν. ουδισ√. εκ τησ συγγενιασ. 62. καλισθε√. *fin.* αυτο. 63. εγραψεν√. εστιν√. [το]. 64. ελαλι√. [*caetera cum* Steph.]. 65. εγενετο δε (— και: C^a *cum* Steph.). ορινη√. δια (*pro* διελαλειτο παντα: A *cum* Steph.). 66. + γαρ (*ante* χιρ.√). 67. επροφητευσεν (C^a προεφητευσεν√). 68. εποιησεν√. 69. ηγειρεν√. εν (*sic p.m.*)√. — τω. δαδ√. — του. 70. ελαλησεν√. — των *secund.* αυτου προφητων. 73. ωμοσεν√. 74. δουνε (C^a -ναι)√. χιροσ (*non* v. 71)√. — των. — ημων. 75. [πασασ τασ ημερασ]. — τησ ζωησ. 76. + δε (*post* συ). ενωπιον (*pro* προ προσωπου). 77. αφεσι√. 78. επισκεψεται (C^a *cum* Steph.). 79. σκοτι√. ιρηνησ√. 80. ηυξανεν√. εκρατεουτο (*non* ii. 40)√.

II. 1. εκιναισ εξηλθεν√. αγουστου. απογραφεσθε√. 2. αυτην απογραφην (*punctis notavit* ·· *p.m. vel potius* A: αυτη η απογραφη C^a). εγενετο πρωτη (C^a *cum* Steph.). [κυρηνιου]. 3. — παντεσ (*habet* C^a). εκαστοσ απογραφεσθε (C^a *cum* Steph.). εαυτων (*pro* ιδιαν: C^a εαυτου). 4. ναζαρεθ. + την (*ante* πολιν: *improbat* C^a). δαδ *bis in versu* (*sic* v. 11). 5. απογραφεσθαι (C^a απογραψασσθαι√). εμνηστευμενη (C^a μεμν., *sed* μ *prius rursus erasum*) cf. i. 27. — γυναικι. ενκυω. 6. τεκιν✓. 7. ετεκεν✓. επν φατνη (— τη: επι *primò, at* εν *etiam p.m.*) cf. v. 12. 8. ποιμαινεσ✓. [τη αυτη]. 9. — ιδου. (θυ *pro* κυ *secund.* Cᵃ). επελαμψεν αυτοισ (*pro* περιελαμψεν αυτουσ: Cᵃ *cum* Steph.). 10. φοβισθε✓. εστιν (*pro* εσται: Cᵃ *cum* Steph.). 11. εστιν✓. πολι✓. 12. ημιν (Cᵃ υμιν)✓. σημιον✓. ευρησεται✓. εσσπαργανωμενον επν φατνη (— κειμενον: *at* και κειμενον A *ante* επν, *de quo* cf. v. 7). 13. εξεφνησ✓. [ουρανιου]. 14. ϊρηνη✓. ευδοκιασ (σ *notat. et eras.*). 15. — και οι ανθρωποι οι (A *addit* οι *post* αγγελοι). ποιμαινεσ✓. ελαλουν (*pro* ειπον). + λεγοντεσ (*post* αλληλουσ). 16. [ηλθον]. (ανευραν A, ευραν Cᵃ, *forsan alii*). 17. εγνωρισαν. 19. μαρια (Cᵃ μαριαμ). συνετηρι✓. συνβαλλουσα. *fin.* εαυτησ (ε *p.m. vel* A). 20. ϋπεστρεψαν. ποιμαινεσ✓. ϊδον✓. 21. περιτεμιν✓. αυτον (*pro* το παιδιον). [και εκλ.]. λεχθεν (κληθεν Cᵃ *cum* Steph.). συλλημφθηναι. αυτην (*pro* αυτον *ante* εν τη κ: αυτον A ? Cᵃ). 22. (επληρωθ. Cᵃ, *sed* Cᵇ *cum p.m. et* Steph.). [αυτων]. μωυσεωσ. παραστησεται (Cᵃ -στησαι)✓. 23. [εν νομω]. διανοιγων (Cᵃ -γον). 24. + τω (*ante* νομω). νοσσουσ. 25. ανθρωποσ ην. + αυτου (*post* ονομα: *improbat* Cᵃ). ευσεβησ (*pro* ευλαβησ: Cᵃ *cum* Steph.). ην αγιον. 26. ϊδιν✓. εωσ αν (*pro* πριν η: Cᵃ πριν η αν). 27. — ιν (*habet* Cᵃ). 28. + δε (*ante* εδεξατο: *improbat* A). — αυτου. ευλογησεν✓. ειπεν (*sic* vv. 34. 48. 49)✓. 29. απολλυεισ (λ *prius improbat* C). 33. ο πατηρ αυτου (*pro* ιωσηφ). (αυτου *post* μητηρ *improbat* A). 34. ηϋλογησεν. — εισ (*ante* σημιον✓: *habet* Cᵃ). 35. [δε]. *fin.* + πονηροι (*improbat* Cᵃ). 36. (και αυτη Cᵃ, *sed* και *rursus deletum*). + χηρ (*ante* ζησασα: *nempe* χηρευσασα *primò ut videtur: correxit* ζησασα A *vel p.m.*). μετα ανδροσ ετη ζ. 37. εωσ (*pro* ωσ: ε *erasum*). εβδομηκοντατεσσ. (Cᵃ ογδοηκοντατεσσ.). εκ (*pro* απο: εκ *deletum et rursus restitutum*). νηστιασ *p.m.* (-ιαισ A ? C). δεησιν *p.m., ut videtur* (δεησεσιν✓ A). 38. — αυτη *prim.* ανθωμολογιτο✓. θω (*pro* κω). πασιν✓. — εν (*ante* ιηλμ). 39. ετελεσεν (Cᵃ -σαν). παντα. — τα. επεστρεψεν (Cᵃ *cum* Steph. υπεστρεψαν). — την *prim. et secund.* (*habet* Cᵃ). πολιν εαυτων ναζαρετ'. 40. ηϋξανεν✓. — πνευματι. (σ *in* σοφιασ *erasum*). 41. γονισ✓. εθοσ (*pro* ετοσ: A *cum* Steph.). ϊσ (*pro* εισ: Cᵃ *cum* Steph.)✓. ϊηλμ✓. 42. οτων *primò* (ε *correct.*). + και (*post* ιβ: *improbat* Cᵃ). αναβαινοντων. — εισ ιεροσυλυμα. 43. τελιωσαντων✓. — ισ (*habet* Cᵃ). [ιερουσαλημ *plenè: sic* v. 45]✓. εγνωσαν οι γονισ (*pro* εγνω ιωσηφ και η μητηρ). 44. ειναι εν τη συνοδια.

συγγενεσιν√. — και εν τοισ γνωστοισ (*habet* Cª, εν *omisso*). 45. — αυτον *prim.* ῑσ (C εισ)√. (αναζητουντεσ C). 46. μετα. επηρωτωντα (ε *pro* η C *et jam antea*)√. 47. συνεσιν√. 48. ειπεν προσ αυτον η μητηρ αυτου. ζητουμεν (Cª εζητ.). 49. ζητειτε (Cª εζητ.). δι√. ειναι (Cª -ναι)√. 51. [ναζαρετ *hic*]. διετηρι√. [παντα τα ρημ.].—ταυτα (*habet* Cª). (+συμβαλλουσα Cª *ante* εν τη καρδια). *fin.* (εαυτησ Cª *pro* αυτησ). 52. +ο (*ante* ῑσ: *improbat* Cª). προεκοπτεν εν τη σοφια και ηλικια. θῡ και ανθρωποισ (—παρα: Cª *cum* Steph.).

III. 1. ετι√. (δε *prim.*: *puncta imposita sed rursus erasa*). [πιλατου *hic*: cf. Marc. xv.]. — τησ ιουδαιασ (*habet* Cª). τετρααρχουντοσ (Cª τετραρχ.) *ter in versu.*— και *ante* τετραχωνιτιδοσ (Cª και τραχων.). *Ab* ϊτουραιασ *usque ad* λυσανιου *rescripta in rasurâ per* A. 2. επι αρχιερεωσ. [καιαφα]. [ϊωαννην]. — του. 3. [την]. 4. — λεγοντοσ. ευθιασ ποιειται√. 5. ταπινωθησετε√. εστε√. ευθιαν√. τροχιαι (Cª τραχιαι√). λιασ√. 7. ελεγον (Cª ελεγεν). [νν]. ϋπεδιξεν√. 9. [καλον]. 10. ποιησωμεν (*sic* vv. 12. 14). 11. ελεγεν (*pro* λεγει). 12. [ειπον]. 13. — ειπεν προσ αυτουσ (*habet* Cª). 14. τι ποιησωμεν και ημισ. [ειπεν√ προσ αυτουσ]. μηδενα (*pro* μηδε: Cª *cum* Steph.). αρκισθαι√. 15. (εαυτων A). [νν]. 16. λεγων πασιν (πασ. λεγ. Cª) ο ϊωαννησ. [ϋμασ ερχεται]. ιμι√. — αυτοσ (*habent* A Cᵇ?). 17. διακαθαρε (— και: και διακαθαριει A). συναγαγειν (A συναξαι: C *cum* Steph.). (αυτου *tert.*, *puncta imposita sed rursus erasa*). κατασβεσι (A κατακαυσι√). 18. ευηγγελιζε (A *cum* Steph.). 19. τετρααρχησ (Cª τετραρχησ), cf. v. 1. — φιλιππου. — και (*habet* Cª). παντων των πονηρων ων εποιησεν (των *punctis notatum rursus deletis*: ων εποιπον. C). 20. προσεθηκεν√. [και *prim.*]. πασιν√. — και *secund.* (*habet* Cª). κατεκλισεν√. [νν]. — τη. 21. παντα. ανεωχθηνε√. 22. ειδι√. ωσ (*pro* ωσει). —λεγουσαν. ευδοκησα. 23. —ο. αρχομενοσ ωσει ετων λ̄. ων ϋϊοσ ωσ ενομιζετο ιωσηφ'. ηλει. 24. μαθθαθ (μαεθαθ *vel* μαθεαθ *primò*: *ambiguè* Tischendorf. "θ *medium ex* ε"). λευει. μελχει. ιανναι. 25. [ματταθιου: *sic* v. 26]. εσλει. 26. σεμεειν. ϊωσηχ. ϊωδα. 27. ϊωναν (ιωαναν A C). νηρει. 28. μελχει. αδδει. κωσα (κωσαμ Cª). ελμαδαμ. 29. ϊησου (*pro* ιωση). ελιαζερ (ελιαιζερ Cª). ϊωριμ. μαθθααθ (μαθθαθ Cª). λευει. 30. ϊωναμ. 31. μεννα. ναθαμ (ναθαν Cª *et forsan anterior*). δᾱδ√. 32. ϊωβηλ (ϊωβηδ Cª: -ηλ Cod. D, *forsan etiam* Cod. B). βαλλσ (λ *secund. p.m. notatum*: Cª βοοσ). σαλα (*pro* σαλμων: Cª *cum* Steph.). 33. αδαμ (*pro* αμιναδαβ: Cª *cum* Steph.). αδμιν του αρνει (*pro* αραμ). [εσρωμ]. 34. ϊσακ (ϊσαακ Cᵃ). (θαρρα Cᵃ). 35. σερουχ. [φαλεκ]. 36. καιναμ (καϊναμ Cᵃ): *sic* v. 37. 37. ιαρετ. μελελεηλ (μαλελεηλ Cᵃ). καιναμ (καϊ- Cᵃ).

IV. 1. πληρησ πνσ αγιου. —υπεστρεψεν (*habet* A). ηγετο το εν τω πν.√. εν τη ερημω. 2. ημερασ μ. ουδεν ' ουδεν ' (' ' A)√. συντελεσθισων√. —υστερον. επινασεν√. 3. ειπεν δε (—και). ι (*pro* ει: Cᵃ *cum* Steph.)√. 4. αποκριθη (απεκρ. Cᵃ, *forsan etiam anterior*). προσ αυτον ο ισ. —λεγων. —αλλ επι *ad fin. vers.* 5. —ο διαβολοσ. —εισ οροσ υψηλον (*habet* A). εδιξεν√. βασιλιασ√. 6. πασαν. [εαν]. δωσω (*pro* διδωμι: Cᵃ *cum* Steph.). 7. +μοι (*post* προσκυνησησ: *improbat* Cᵃ). εμου (*pro* μου: Cᵃ *cum* Steph.). εστε√. *fin.* πασα. 8. ο ισ ειπεν αυτω. —υπαγε οπισω μου σατανα. —γαρ. κν τον θν σου προσκυνησεισ. 9. ηγαγεν δε (—και). —αυτον *secund.* —ο. 10. —γαρ (*habent* A? Cᵃ). εντελιται√. 11. αρουσιν√. 12. (οτι: *puncta ab* A *imposita, rursus erasa*). εκπιρασεισ√. 13. πιρασμον√. 14. δυναμι (*sic* v. 36)√. εξηλθεν√. χωρασ (*pro* περιχωρου). 16. —την *prim.* ναζαρα. ανατεθραμμενοσ. εισηλθεν√. 17. του προφητου ησαϊου. [αναπτυξασ]. ευρεν√. —τον. 18. ειvεκεν. εχρισεν√. ευαγγελισασθαι. απεσταλκεν√. —ιασασθαι τουσ συντετριμμενουσ την καρδιαν. αποστιλαι√. αφεσι√. 20. εκαθισεν√. οι οφθαλμοι εν τη συναγωγη ησαν. 21. λεγιν√. 22. ουχι υσ εστιν ϊωσηφ ουτοσ (—ο). 23. ειπεν (*sic* vv. 24. 43)√. εισ την καφαρναουμ. 24. ουδισ (*sic* v. 27)√. *fin.* εαυτου. 25. αληθιασ√. + οτι (*ante* πολλαι). εκλισθη√. [επι ετη τρια]. 26. ηλειασ. [σαρεπτα τησ] σιδωνιασ. 27. εν τω ιηλ επι ελισαιου του προφητου. [εκαθαρισθη]. ναιμαν. 29. —αυτον *prim.* (*habet* Cᵃ). —τησ *secund.* ωκοδομητο αυτων. εισ το (*pro* ωστε). 31. καφαρναουμ. σαββασιν√. 33. ανεκραξεν√. 34. —λεγων. 35. απ (*pro* εξ). [το *secund.*]. 36. πνασιν√. (*Pro* εξερχονται *p.m. et* Steph., A *in litura scripsit* υπακουουσιν αυτω: Cᵃ *cum* Steph.) 38. απο (*pro* εκ). —η. 39. επετιμησεν√. +ο πυρετοσ (*ante* παραχρημα δε). διηκονι√. 40. επιθεισ τασ χιρασ. [-πευσεν]. 41. εξηρχοντο. —απο. κραζοντων (Cᵃ -ντα). —ο χσ. λαλιν√. ηδισαν√. 42. —τοπον (*habet* A). επεζητουν. 43. [με δει]. το ευαγγελιον (*pro* την βασιλειαν: A *cum* Steph.). επι (*pro* εισ). απεσταλην. 44. *fin.* εισ τασ συναγωγασ τησ ϊουδαιασ (*non* γαλιλ.).

V. 1. συναχθηναι τον οχλον (*pro* τον οχλον επικεισθαι αυτω: Cᵃ *cum* Steph.). και (*pro* του *prim.*). —λιμνην (*habet* Cᵃ). γεννησαρετ'√.

2. ειδεν√.—δυο (*habet* C^a^). [πλοια]. αλεεισ (C^a^ αλειεισ). αυτων αποβαντεσ (—απ: απ αυτων αποβ. C^a^). επλυναν. 3. —του. ερωτησεν. επαναγαγιν√. καθισασ δε (—και). εν τω πλοιω εδιδασκεν τουσ οχλουσ. 4. ειπεν√. 5. ειπεν σιμων (—ο *et* αυτω: σιμ. ειπ. C^a^).—τησ. τα δικτυα. 6. συνεκλισαν√. πληθοσ ϊχθυων. διερρησσετο. τα δικτυα. 7. κατενευσεν (C^a^ -σαν).—τοισ *secund.* τουσ̇ *sic* (*pro* του: A C *cum* Steph.). συνλαμβανεσθε (συνλαβεσθε A C). ηλθαν. αμφοτεροι *primò, ut videtur*: -ρα *correctio.* 8. προσεπεσεν. γονασιν ιυ (—του).—κυριε (*habet* C^a^). 9. αυτουσ (*pro* αυτον: C^a^ *cum* Steph.). [η]. 10. ϊακωβοσ και ϊωαννησ οι υιοι. ειπεν√. [ο ισ]. 11. παντα. 12. ϊδων δε (—και). 13. εκτινασ√. τασ χειρασ *primò, ut videtur*, την χειρα A? ^λ^εγων (*pro* ειπων: λ *p.m. vel* A)√. α̇ η λεπρα (˙ *p.m.*)√. 14. παρηγγιλεν√. ειπιν√. —δειξον σεαυτον τω ιερει και (*supplet* A, *legens* διξον√ *et* ιερι√). προσενεγκαι. προσεταξεν√. μωϋσησ. 15. —περι (*habet* A).—υπ αυτου. ασθενιων√. 17. [-μενοι φαρ.].—οι (*habet* A). [εληλυθοτεσ]. *fin.* αυτον (*pro* αυτουσ). 18. ανθρωπον επι κλινησ βεβληβλημενον *sic* (*pro* επι κλ. ανθ.). 19. —δια. 20. —αυτω. αφεωντε (*non* v. 23).—σοι. σου αι αμαρτιαι. 21. διαλογιζεσθε√. γραμματισ√. [αφ. αμαρτ.]. 22. [αποκριθεισ]. ειπεν√. ταισ καρδιεσ (C^a^ -ιαισ)√. 23. —σοι. σου αι αμαρτιαι. εγειρε. περιπατι√. 24. [εξ. εχ. ο υιοσ του ανθρωπου]. [αφιεναι]. ειπεν (*sic* vv. 31. 34)√. παραλυτικω. εγειρε. αρον (*pro* αρασ). +και (*ante* πορευου). 25. αυτου (*pro* αυτων). ο (*pro* ω). 26. εκστασεισ√. [ειδομεν]. 27. εξηλθεν√. [εθεασατο]. λευειν. λεγει (*pro* ειπεν). ακολουθι√. 28. απαντασ (σ *erasum*). [ηκολουθησεν]. 29. εποιησεν√. λευεισ (—ο).—αυτω. τω οικω. πολυσ τελωνων.—και αλλων (*habet* C^a^). 30. οι φαρισαιοι και οι γραμματεισ (—αυτων). +των (*ante* τελωνων). [και αμαρ.]. εσθιεται√. 31. χριαν√. [αλλ]. 32. ασεβεισ (*pro* αμαρτωλουσ: A *cum* Steph.). 33. [ειπον]. (διατι *punctis notatum rursus erasis*). [νν]. νηστευουσιν√. εσθιουσιν√. 34. +ισ (*ante* ειπεν√). δυνανται οι ϋϊοι (C^a^ δυνασθαι τουσ ϋϊουσ). εστιν√.—ποιησαι (*habet* C^a^). *fin.* (C^a^ νηστευσαι). 35. —και (*ante* οταν). +και (*ante* τοτε). 36. ελεγεν√.—δε και (*habet* C^a^). προσ αυτουσ παραβολην (C^a^ *cum* Steph.). ουδισ (*sic* v. 39, *non* v. 37)√. +απο (*ante* ϊματιου). +σχισασ (*ante* επιβαλλει).—και (*post* μηγε: *habet* C^a^). σχισει (*pro* σχιζει). συμφωνησει το επιβλημα. 37. [ρηξει]. ο οινοσ (—νεοσ). 38. βαλλουσιν (*pro* βλητεον: A *cum* Steph.).—και αμφοτεροι συντηρουνται. 39. *init.* (και *improbat* C^a^).—ευθεωσ. χρηστοσ.

VI. 1. —δευτεροπρωτω *cum* Cod. B.—των (*habet* Cᵃ).—τουσ. [σταχ. και ησθ.]. χερσιν [*nihil additum*]. 2. —αυτοισ. ποιειται√. ουχ εξεστιν ποιειν τοισ σαββασιν (—εν: Cᵃ ουκ). 3. ο ισ̅ προσ αυτουσ ειπεν. εποιησεν δα̅δ̅√. οτε (*pro* οποτε). επινασεν√. — οντεσ. 4. (πωσ *pro* ωσ Cᵃ).—ελαβε και. εφαγεν√. εδωκεν και. εξεστιν√. 5. —οτι (*habet* Cᵃ). εστιν του σαββατου ο υσ̅ του ανθρωπου (— και *secund.*). 6. — και *prim.* εισελθιν√. διδασκιν√. ανθρωποσ εκει√. 7. [παρετηρουν δε αυτον]. θεραπευει. ευρωσιν√. κατηγοριν (κατηγοριαν κατ Cᵃ). 8. ειπεν δε (— και). ανδρι (*pro* ανθρωπω). +την (*ante* ξηραν). εγειρε. και (*pro* ο δε). 9. ειπεν δε (— ουν). επερωτω. ει (*pro* τι). εξεστιν√. τω σαββατω. 10. ειπεν√. [τω ανθρωπω]. εκτινον√. εξετινεν (*pro* εποιησεν ουτω). απεκατεστη (Cᵃ απεκατεσταθη).—υγιησ ωσ η αλλη. 11. ποιησιεν. 12. εξελθειν αυτον (*pro* εξηλθεν). επι (*pro* εν *secund.*: Cᵃ *cum* Steph.). 13. προσεφωνησεν√. ωνομασεν (*sic* v. 14)√. 14. +και (*ante* ϊακωβον). [νν]. +και (*ante* φιλιππον).—και βαρθολομαιον (ὁμοιοτ.: *habet* Cᵃ). 15. +και (*ante* μαθθαιον). +και (*ante* ϊακωβον).—τον του. 16. +και (*ante* ϊουδαν *prim.*). ϊσκαριωθ (Cᵃ -ριωτην).—και *ultim.* 17. +πολυσ (*post* οχλοσ).— του λαου (*habet* Cᵃ). +και πιραιασ (*post* ϊερουσαλημ *plenè*; *improbat* Cᵃ). σειδωνοσ. 18. ενοχλουμενοι. απο (*pro* υπο).—και *secund.* 19. εζητουν. 20. ελεγεν√. (+τω πν̅ι̅ Cᵃ *post* πτωχοι: *sed erasa*). βασιλια√. 21. πινωντεσ√. χορτασθησονται (*sic etiam* Cᵇ: *at* Cᵃ χορτασθησεσθαι√). γελασεται√. 22. [μισησωσιν]. ονιδισωσιν√. εκβαλωσιν√. [ενεκα]. 23. *init.* χαρητε. σκιρτησαται√. [ταυτα]. 24. απεχεται√. 25. + νυν (*post* εμπεπλησμενοι). πινασετε√. —υμιν *secund.* πενθησεται√. κλαυσεται√. 26. —υμιν. ειπωσιν ϋμασ. οι ανθρωποι παντεσ. (A τα αυτα *pro* ταυτα). (ψευδο: *puncta imposita sed rursus erasa*). 27. αλλα. αγαπαται√. ποιειται√. 28. ευλογιται√. ϋμασ (*pro* ϋμιν).—και. προσευχεσθαι√. περι (*pro* υπερ). 29. εισ την δεξιαν σιαγονα (επι την σιαγ. Cᵃ *cum* Steph.). 30. —δε τω. 31. και ϋμισ ποιειται√. 32. εστιν (*sic* vv. 36. 40. 43)√. αγαπωσιν√. 33. +γαρ (*ante* εαν: *improbat* Cᵃ). [-ποιητε]. χαρισ εστιν.—γαρ (*ante* οι αμαρ.). ποιουσιν√. 34. δανισηται. ελπιζεται√. λαβιν. εστιν√.—γαρ οι. δανιζουσιν√. απολαβωσιν√. εισα√. 35. αγαπαται√. αγαθοποιειται√. δανιζεται√. μηδενα (*pro* μηδεν). [απελπ.]. (*Post* πολυσ *supplet* A εν τοισ ο̅υ̅ν̅ο̅ι̅σ̅). εσεσθαι√. —του. 36. γεινεσθε√.—ουν.—και. *fin.* (+ο ουρανιοσ A: *improbat* Cᵃ). 37. [και ου μη]. +και (*post* κριθητε). καταδικασθηται√. απολυεται√. απολυθησεσθαι√. 38. διδοται√. πεπιασμενον

(Cª πεπιεσμ.).—και secund. et tert. ϋπερεκχυννομενον. ω γαρ μετρω (pro τω γαρ αυτω μετρω ω). μετριται√. [αντιμετρηθησεται]. 39. init. ειπεν δε και. ουκ (pro ουχι). [πεσουνται]. 40. —αυτου prim.—πασ. εστω (pro εσται). 42. init. πωσ δε (—η). εκβαλιν (pro εκβαλειν)√. 43. + παλιν (post ουδε). 44. γεινωσκεται√. συνλεγουσιν√. βλαστου p.m. (βαάστου, i. e. βατου A). σταφυλην τρυγωσιν. 45. —αυτου prim.—ανθρωποσ secund. (habet Cª).—θησαυρου τησ καρδιασ αυτου secund.—του (ante περισσευματοσ).—τησ (ante καρδιασ ultim.). το στομα αυτου λαλει. 46. καλειται√. ποιειται√. 47. + μου (etiam post λογων: improbat Cª). ϋποδιξω√. 48. εσκαψεν√. εβαθυνεν√. εθηκεν√. πλημμυρησ. προσερηξεν: non v. 49 (Cª προσερρ.). εκινη√. ϊσχυσεν√. δια το καλωσ οικοδομησθαι αυτην (pro τεθεμελιωτο γαρ επι την πετραν). 49. [οικοδομησαντι]. ευθυσ συνεπεσεν.

VII. 1. [επει δε]. επληρωσεν√.—παντα (habet Cª). καφαρναουμ'. 2. —κακωσ εχων (habet Cª). ημελλεν√. 3. απεστιλεν√. + αυτοσ (ante ελθων). 4. ηρωτων (pro παρεκαλουν). παρεξη. 6. —απο. επεμψεν√.—προσ αυτον (habet A). φιλουσ ο εκατονταρχοσ. —αυτω (habet Cª). [σκυλλου: sic σκυλλε viii. 49]. ϊκανοσ ᵉⁱμι (ει A et Cª). μου ϋπο την στεγην. 7. ελθειᵛ (ν A et Cª)√. αλλ. [ϊαθησεται]. 9. ειπεν (sic v. 14)√. 10. εισ τον οικον οι πεμφθεντεσ.—ασθενουντα. 11. (τω pro τη Cª). επορευθη.—καλουμενην (habet Cª).—ικανοι. 12. ηγγισεν√. [τεθνηκωσ] μονογενησ υσ. [αυτη ην χηρα]. + ην (post ϊκανοσ). 13. επ αυτην. 15. [ανεκαθισεν]. λαλιν√. [εδωκεν]. 16. ελαβεν√. [απαντασ]. ηγερθη. 17. —περι αυτου (habet A).—εν secund. 18. απηγγιλαν√. ϊωαννει. 19. [νν: sic v. 20]. επεμψεν√. [ιν]. ετερον (pro αλλον: sic v. 20). 20. —οι ανδρεσ (habet A). ειπαν. απεστιλεν (pro -ταλκεν). ετερον (pro αλλον). 21. εν εκεινη τη ημερα (—δε: ωρα pro ημερα Cª cum Steph.). εθεραπευσεν√. ακαθαρτων (pro πονηρων: Cª cum Steph.) sic viii. 2.—το (habet A). 22. —ο ισ. απαγγιλατε√. ϊωαννει.—οτι. αναβλεπουσιν√. περιπατουσιν√. + και (ante κωφοι). ακουουσιν√. + και (ante πτωχοι). 23. αν (pro εαν). 24. απελθοντ rescript p.m.?√. [νν bis in versu, sic vv. 28. 29. 33]. τοισ οχλοισ (—προσ: Cª cum Steph.). εξηλθαται (sic vv. 25. 26). θεασασθε√. 27. εστιν (sic vv. 28 bis in versu, 39)√.—εγω. 28. init. αμην.—γαρ. εν γεννηταισ (εν γεννητοισ A? Cª)√.—προφητησ.—του βαπτιστου. μεικροτεροσ√. 30. —εισ εαυτουσ. 31. —ειπε δε ο κσ. δε (pro ουν). 32. εισιν√. α λεγει (λεγοντα Cᵃ: *pro* και λεγουσιν). ωρχησασθαι√. — υμιν *secund.* 33. εληλυθεν√. μη εσθιων αρτον μηδε πινων οινον. λεγεται (*sic* v. 34)√. 34. [εσθιων]. φιλοσ τελωνων. 35. απο παντων των εργων αυτησ (— τεκνων: Cᵃ *improbat* παντων). 36. τον οικον. *fin.* κατεκειτο (Cᵃ κατεκλιθη). 37. ητισ ην εν τη πολει. + και (*ante* επιγνουσα). κατακειται. 38. οπισω παρα τουσ ποδασ αυτου. τοισ δακρυσιν ηρξατο βρεχειν τουσ ποδασ αυτου. θριξιν√. εξεμαξεν (Cᵃ εξεμασσεν√). ηλειφεν√. 39. εγεινωσκεν√. 40. ειπεν (*sic* vv. 48. 50)√. ειπιν√. διδασκαλε ειπε φησιν. 41. χρεοφιλεται. δανιστη√. ωφιλεν√. 42. [δε].— ειπε. αγαπησει αυτον. 43. [δε]. — ο. πλιον (*non* v. 42)√. 44. βλεπισ√. μου επι τουσ ποδασ. εβρεξεν√. θριξιν (— τησ κεφαλησ). εξεμαξεν√. 45. [εισηλθον]. διελειπεν. [μου τουσ ποδασ: *sic* v. 46]. 46. ηλιψασ√. ηλιψεν√. 47. ειπον (*pro* λεγω: Cᵃ *cum* Steph.). αφεονται (Cᵃ *cum* Steph.) *sic* v. 48. αυτησ αι αμαρτιαι. ηγαπησεν√. 49. [ουτοσ εστιν]. 50. σεσωκεν√.

VIII. 1. διωδευσεν. 2. ακαθαρτων (*pro* πονηρων) *sic* vii. 21. 3. [ϊωαννα]. [σουσαννα]. [αυτω]. εκ (*pro* απο). *fin.* αυτων (A? Cᵃ αυταισ *cum* Steph.). 4. συνοντοσ (Cᵃ συνϊοντοσ *cum* Steph.). ειπεν (*sic* vv. 21. 22. 25. 28. 30. 48. 52)√. 5. σπιρων√. σπιραι√. [αυτου]. σπιρειν√. επεσεν√. πετινα√. 6. [επεσεν]. + και (*ante* δια: *improbant* A? C). εχιν√. 7. συνφυεισαι. επνιξαν (Cᵃ *cum* Steph.). 8. εφυεν (*pro* επεσεν: Cᵃ *cum* Steph.). εισ (*pro* επι). εφυεν (*pro* φυεν: A C *cum* Steph.). + και (*ante* εποιησεν√: *improbat* A). 9. — λεγοντεσ. αυτη ειη η παραβολη. 10. τασ μυστηρια (· *p.m.*)√. βλεπωσιν√. + ακουωσιν και (*post* ακουοντεσ: Cᵃ *puncta imposuit ad* ακουωσιν, *sed rursus delevit*). 11. εστιν√ *bis in versu. fin.* χυ *fortasse primò, sed* θυ *p.m.* 12. ακουσαντεσ. 13. την πετραν (τησ πετρασ Cᵃ *cum* Steph.). ακουσωσιν√. + του θυ (*post* λογον: *improbat* Cᵃ).— και *prim.* (*habet* Cᵃ). πιστευουσιν√. πιρασμου√. 14. συνπνιγονται. τελεσφορουσιν√. 15. νεσ *in* οιτινεσ *bis scriptum primò: prius erasum*√. κατεχουσιν√. 16. καλυπτι√. αλλ επι την λυχνιαν τιθησιν. βλεπωσιν√. 17. εστιν√. μη γνωσθη (*pro* γνωσθησεται). 18. βλεπεται√. ακουεται√. αν γαρ (*pro* γαρ αν). [αν *secund.*]. εχιν√. 19. [παρεγενοντο]. + αυτου (*post* μητηρ). συντυχιν√. 20. απηγγελη δε (— και).— λεγοντων. + οτι (*ante* η μητηρ).— σου *prim.* ϊδιν√. [σε θελ.]. 21. [προσ αυτουσ]. — του θυ.— αυτον. 22. εγενετο δε (— και).— εν (*habet* A).— και αυτοσ (*habet* A). [ενεβη]. 23. αφυπνωσεν√. [αν. εισ τ. λ.]. 24. (επιστατα *secund. punctis notatum rursus deletis*). διεγερθεισ. επετιμησεν√. του κλυδωνι (τω κλ. C^a)√. επαυσατο. 25. — εστιν. οι δε φοβηθεντεσ.— προσ αλληλουσ. 26. κατεπλυσαν (C^a -πλευ-)√. γεογεσηνων (*pro* γαδαρηνων). αντιπερα. 27. — αυτω *secund.* εχων (*pro* οσ ειχε: C^a οσ ειχεν√). και χρονω ϊκανω (— εκ) ουκ ενεδυσατο ϊματιον (C^a *cum* Steph. *praeter* ενεδ., *sed prior lectio restituitur*). 28. — και *prim.* δαιομε√. 29. παρηγγελλεν√. εδεσμευετο. αλυσεσιν√. παιδεσ√. — και (*ante* διαρρησσων: A C^a *habent*). δεμονια *p.m.* (*pro* δεσμα: A C^a *cum* Steph.). δαιμονιου (*pro* δαιμονοσ). 30. επηρωτησεν√.— ο ι̅σ̅ λεγων (*habet* ο ι̅σ̅ C^a). ονομα εστιν√. λεγιων (C^a λεγαιων). εισηλθεν δαιμονια πολλα. 31. παρεκαλουν. απελθιν (*sic* v. 37)√. 32. βοσκομενη. (C^a παρεκαλεσαν). *fin.* — αυτοισ (*habet* C^a). 33. εισηλθον. αγγελη (· *p.m.*)√. θαλασσαν (*pro* λιμνην). 34. γεγονοσ. [εφυγον].— απελθοντεσ. απηγγιλαν (*non* v. 36)√. 35. ϊδιν√. [ηλθον]. [ευρον καθ. τον ανθ.]. εξηλθεν (*pro* εξεληλυθει: C^a εξηλθον). 36. + λεγοντεσ (*ante* αυτοισ). — και. δεμονισθεισ (C^a δαιμ.)√. 37. ηρωτησεν. παν. γεργεσηνων (C^a *cum* Steph. γαδαρ., *at* γεργεσ. *restituitur*). συνιχοντο√. — το (*ante* πλοιον). *fin.* επεστρεψαν (^{ε} A: συνεστρ.? A, υπεστρ. C^a *cum* Steph.). 38. (εδειτο A, *sed* εδεετο *restitutum*). [εξεληλυθει τα δ.]. απελυσεν√.— ο ι̅σ̅. 39. σοι εποιησεν. απηλθεν√. 40. (εν δε *pro* εγενετο δε εν C^a, *sed prior lectio restituitur*). ϋποστρεφειν. *fin.* τον θ̅ν̅ (*pro* αυτον *secund.*: A *cum* Steph.). 41. [ϊαειροσ]. [αυτοσ]. ϋπηρχεν√.— του (*habet* C^a). εισελθιν√. 42. — ην (*habet* C^a). [εν δε τω υπαγειν]. 43. ϊατροισ (— εισ). + εαυτησ και (*post* βιον: *improbat* C^a). [ϋπ]. ουδνενοσ (· *p.m. vel* A: ϋπ ουδν *rescripsit p.m., sublato* ουκ ισχ *per errorem scripto*)√. 45. συν αυτω (*pro* μετ αυτου). συνεχουσιν√. αποθλιβουσιν√.— και λεγεισ *ad fin. vers.* 46. εξεληλυθυῖαν. 47. — ιδουσα *usque ad* ηλθε (*supplet* A, *legens* ελαθεν√ *et* ηλθεν√). — δι ην αιτιαν ηψατο αυτου. διηγγειλεν (*pro* απηγγειλεν αυτω). ειαθη√. 48. — αυτη θαρσει. σεσωκεν√. 49. [παρα].— αυτω. μηκετι (*pro* μη). 50. ειπεν (*pro* απεκριθη: C^a *cum* Steph.).— λεγων. [πιστευε]. 51. *init.* ελθων. ουδενα αφηκεν συνεισελθειν αυτω (—ουκ). [ϊακ. και ϊωανν.]. 52. ου γαρ (*pro* ουκ). 54. —εκβαλων εξω παντασ και. εφωνησεν√. εγειρε. 55. επεστρεψεν√.— και ανεστη παραχρημα (*habet* A). 56. ειπιν√.

IX. 1. συνκαλεσαμενοσ. αποστολουσ (*pro* μαθητασ αυτου). δεδωκεν. 2. απεστιλεν√. ασθενισ (*pro* -νουντασ). 3. ειπεν (*sic* vv. 9. 13. 14. 20 *bis*. 50. 57. 59 *bis*. 60. 61. 62)√. ραβδον. μηδε (*pro* μητε *quart.*). — ανα. — εχειν (εχετε *habet* A). 4. μινατε. 5. [αν]. δεχωνται. εκ (*pro* απο *prim.*). εκινησ√. — και *secund.* αποτινασσεται. αυτοισ (επ αυτουσ C^a^, *sed* ι *pro* υ *restituitur*). 6. — τασ. 7. ηκουσεν√. — ο τετραρχησ (ὁμοιοτ.: A *habet* ο τετρααρχησ). γεινομενα√. — υπ αυτου. [ἴωαννησ] ηγερθη. 8. ηλειασ. τισ (*pro* εισ). 9. ειπεν δε (— και). — ο. [νν]. — εγω. ακοιω (C^a^ ακουω)√. ἴδιν√. 10. α (*pro* οσα). εποιησεν (-σαν A ?)√. ὑπεχωρησεν√. [τοπον ερ.]. — πολεωσ καλουμενησ βηθσαΐδα (C^a^ πολιν καλουμενην βηδ'σαΐδα, *omisso* τοπον ερ., *sed prior scriptura revocatur*). 11. αποδεξαμενοσ. ελαλησεν. βασιλιασ√. 12. ηρξαντο. (C^a^ -ατο). (τουσ οχλουσ C^a^, *sed* τον οχ. *restitutum*). πορευθεντεσ (*pro* απελθοντεσ). — τουσ (*ante* αγρ.). καταλυσωσιν√. 13. αυτοισ (*pro* προσ αυτουσ). [ὑμ. φαγ.]. ειπαν (*sic* vv. 19. 54). πλειονεσ αρτοι πεντε (C^a^ *cum* Steph. πλειον η π. αρ.). ἴχθυεσ δυο. ημισ√. 14. δε (*pro* γαρ: γαρ C^a^ *sed* δε *revocatum*). + ωσει (*ante* ανα). 15. ουτωσ√. κατεκλιναν παντασ. 16. — αυτουσ. κατεκλασεν√. παραθειναι. 17. των (*pro* αυτοισ). 18. (A *primò post* εν, *deinde post* αυτον *addit* εν τοπω, *sed erasum est*). + ο $\overline{ισ}$ (*ante* λεγων). με οι οχλοι λεγουσιν (C^a^ *cum* Steph.). 19. [νν: *sic* vv. 28. 54]. 20. λεγεται√. πετροσ δε αποκριθεισ (— ο). 21. παρηγγιλεν√. λεγειν (*pro* ειπειν). *fin.* τουτοι *forsan p.m.*√. 22. τον $\overline{υν}$ του ανθρωπου δει (C^a^ *cum* Steph.). [εγερθηναι]. 23. ελεγεν√. θελι√. ερχεσθαι (ελθειν A C^a^ *cum* Steph.). αρνησασθω. (καθ ημεραν: *puncta imposita sed rursus erasa*). ακολουθιτω√. 24. εαν (*pro* αν *prim.*). 25. ωφελει. 26. επεσχυνθη√. [λογουσ]. 27. εισιν√. αυτου (*pro* ωδε). [εστηκοτων]. γευσωνται. [ἴδωσι]. βασιλιαν√. 28. — και *prim.* (*habet* C^a^). — τον. προσευχεσθαι. 29. — εγενετο (*habet* C^a^). προσευξασθαι (-ευχεσθαι C^a^). + εγενετο (*ante* ετερον). ειματισμοσ√. 30. μωϋσησ. ηλειασ. 31. [ελεγον την]. ημελλεν. 32. ειδαν. στωτ *in* συνεστωτασ *rescripsit p m. vel* A√. 33. διαχωριζεσθε√. [ο]. ποιησομεν. τρισ√. σοι μιαν. [μωσει μιαν]. 34. επεσκιαζεν. εισελθειν αυτουσ (*pro* εκεινουσ εισ.). 35. εκλελεγμενοσ (*pro* αγαπητοσ) cf. Johann. i. 34. 36. — ο. απηγγιλαν√. [εωρακασιν]. 37. — εν. 38. εβοησεν (*pro* ανεβ.). [επιβλεψον]. μοι εστιν. 39. — ιδου. + και ρασσει (*post* κραζει). συντριβουν (-βον C^a^ *et jam ante eum*). 40. εκβαλωσιν. 41. γεναια√. μεθ υμων εσομαι (*pro* εσ. προσ υμ.). (+ μοι *ante* ωδε C^a^). 42. προσευχομενου (C^a^ προσερχομενου). επετιμησεν√. 43. μεγαλιοτητι√. εποιει (— ο $\overline{ισ}$ ειπε) *p.m.*: *addit* ειπεν A. 44. χιρασ√. 45. εσθωνται√. [ερωτησαι]. 46. εισηλθεν√. μιζον√. 47. ειδωσ (*pro* ιδων). [παιδιου]. 48. [εαν *prim.*]. πεδιον√.—εαν *secund.* δεχεται (*pro* δεξηται *secund.*). αποστιλαντα√. μεικροτεροσ√. εστιν (*pro* εσται). 49. [ο ἰωαννησ]. εν (*pro* επι).—τα. εκωλυομεν. 50. ειπεν δε (—και).—ο (*habet* Cª). εστιν√ *bis in versu.* καθ υμων ὑπερ ημων *p.m.* (Cª ημων *bis*, Cᵇ υμων *bis*). 51. [συμπλ.]. αναλημψεωσ. —αυτου *prim.* (*habet* Cª). [αυτου *secund.*]. εστηριξεν√. 52. απεστιλεν√. [αυτου]. πολιν (*pro* κωμην: Cª *cum* Steph.). σαμαριτων. ωσ (*pro* ωστε: Cª *cum* Steph.). 54. —αυτου. ειπαν. [απο].—ωσ και ηλιασ εποιησε. 55, 56. —και ειπεν *usque ad* αλλα σωσαι. 57. και (*pro* εγενετο δε). [αν].—κυριε. 58. εχουσιν√. πετινα√. 59. πρωτον απελθοντι. 60. —ο ισ̄. 62. [προσ αυτον ο ισ̄]. ουδισ√. επιβαλον? *primò* (-ων *p.m.* *vel* A *rescripsit*). [αυτου]. τη βασιλεια (*pro* εισ την β., *at* εν τη β. Cª).

X. 1. ανεδιξεν√. [και *prim.*]. [εβδομηκοντα και]. απεστιλεν√. ημελλεν. [ερχεσθαι]. 2. δε (*pro* ουν *prim.*). δεηθηται√. εκβαλη εργ. 3. —εγω. 4. βαλλαντιον. μη (*pro* μηδε).—και (*habet* Cª). 5. εισελθηται οικιαν. λεγεται√. 6. —μεν. η εκι. + ο (*ante* υιοσ: *sed eras.*). επαναπαησεται. 7. [εσθιοντεσ].—εστι. 8. —δ. 9. ασθενισ√. 10. εισελθητε (*pro* εισερχησθε). πλατιασ√. 11. ὑμιν (*pro* ημιν: A Cª *cum* Steph.). + εισ τουσ ποδασ (*ante* απομασσομεθα). γεινωσκετε υμισ οτι ηγγεικεν (υμισ *improbant* A C). —εφ υμασ. 12. [δε]. εκινη (*post quod verbum erasum videtur* ουαι)√. 13. [ουαι *bis in versu*]. χοραζειν. βηθσαιδαν. εγενηθησαν. δυναμισ√. καθημενοι. 15. καφαρναουμ. μη εωσ ουρανου ὑψωθηση (—η *et* του). ὁ αδου (· *p.m.* *et* C)√. 16. [ακουων υμων]. αποστιλαντα√. 17. [-κοντα μετα: cf. v. 1]. 18. ειπεν (*sic* vv. 23. 26. 28. 29. 37. 40)√. 19. δεδωκα.—ου μη (*habet* A). αδικησει. 20. χ̇ οτι *prim.* (· *p.m.*)√. χερετε *secund.* [μαλλον]. ενγεγραπται. 21. εν τω πν̄ι τω αγιω.—ο ισ̄. [εγενετο ευδοκια]. 22. —και στραφεισ *usque ad* ειπε. μοι παρεδοθη. ουδισ√. [εαν]. 24. ειδειν√. βλεπεται√. ιδαν. ακουεται√. 25. εκπιραζων√.—και *secund.* 'ἱνα' ζωην (' ' A *vel* *p.m.*)√. 26. αναγινωσκισ√. 27. [τησ καρδιασ]. εν ολη τη ψυχη σου και εν ολη τη ἰσχυΐ σου και εν ολη τη διανοια σου. 29. δικαιωσαι. αυτον (*pro* εαυτον: A C *cum* Steph.). εστιν√. 30. —δε (*habet* Cª). *In* ἰερουσαλημ *rescriptum est* ουσα, *quasi* ἰερειχω *primò scriptum*√. ἰσ (Cª εισ) ειεριχω.—τυγχανοντα. 32. *Deest versus ob* ὁμοιοτ. (*supplet* Cª, *omisso* γενομενοσ: *caetera cum* Steph., *praeter* αντιπαρηλθεν√). 33. σαμαριτησ. ηλθεν√. —αυτον *secund.* 34. κατεδησεν√. ελεον√. [επιβιβασασ δε]. πανδοκιον (C^a -χιον). 35. — εξελθων. εδωκεν√. πανδοκει (C^a -χει). [αυτω].— εγω. επανερχεσθε (C^a -σθαι)√. 36. — ουν.— των (*habent* A C^a). πλησιον δοκει σοι. 37. δε (*pro* ουν). σοι (*pro* συ). 38. *init.* εν δε (— εγενετο). — και. την οικιαν.— αυτησ (*habet* A). 39. *Post* και *prim.* αι *videtur esse deletum.* μαριαμ. — η (*habet* A *vel forte p.m.*). παρακαθεσθισα. προσ (*pro* παρα). κ̅υ̅ (*pro* ι̅υ̅). [ηκουε: C^a -εν√]. 40. μελι√. κατελιπεν διακονιν√. [ειπε]. συναντιλαβητε√. 41. κ̅σ̅ (*pro* ι̅σ̅). θορυβαζη. 42. *init.* ολιγων δε εστιν η ενοσ (— χρεια, *at* C^a *addit* χρια *post* εστιν) cf. Cod. B. γαρ (*pro* δε *secund.*). αφερεθησεται√.— απ (*habet* C^a).

XI. 1. ειπεν (*sic* vv. 2. 5. 28. 39. 46)√.— και ιωαννησ (*habet* C^a: A *vel p.m.* ιωαννησ *tantum*). εδιδαξεν√. 2. [προσευχησθε]. — ημων ο εν τοισ ουρανοισ. ελθατω. βασιλια√. [γεν. το θ. σου ωσ εν ουρ.]. + ουτω (*post* ουρανω: *improbat* C^a). — τησ (*habet* C^a, *sed rursus erasum: addens* και ρυσαι ημασ απο του πονηρου *post* γησ). 3. δοσ (*pro* διδου). — το (*habet* C^a). 4. ωσ και (*pro* και γαρ: C^a *cum* Steph.). [αφιεμεν]. οφιλοντι√. πιρασμον√. — αλλα ρυσαι *ad fin. vers.* (C^a αλλα ρυσαι ημασ απο τ *nec amplius, sed delevit, clausulâ ad fin.* v. 2 *translatâ*). 5. (A μεσονυκτιον, *sed* ν *secund. super* υ *rursus deletum*). [ειπη]. τρισ√. 6. επιδη√. 7. κεκλισται√. εισ την κοιτην μετ εμου. + και (*post* εισιν)√. 8. φιλον αυτου. δε (*pro* γε: A? C *cum* Steph.). αναιδιαν√. (C^a οσον). 9. ανυγησεται√. 10. ανυγησετε (C^a -ται)√. 11. τισ (*pro* τινα). + εξ (*ante* υμων). — ο υιοσ. η (*pro* ει και). ῒχθην√. [επιδωσει αυτω *secund.*]. 12. — εαν. αιτησει. 13. ϋμισ√. οντεσ (*pro* υπαρχοντεσ). οιδαται√. δοματα αγαθα. ο πατηρ εξ (— ο *secund.*). 14. — και αυτο ην. [εξελθοντοσ]. 15. [ειπον]. βεεζεβουλ (*sic* vv. 18. 19) *sic* Cod. B. + τω (*ante* αρχοντι). 16. πιραζοντεσ σημιον√. εξ ουρανου εζητουν παρ αυτου. 17. [αυτ. τα διαν.]. διαμερισθεισα εφ εαυτην. 18. εμερισθη. τι (*pro* οτι: A C *cum* Steph.). 19. [οι]. εκβαλλουσιν√. αυτοι κριται εσονται ϋμων. 20. (A C *habent* εγω *ante* εκβαλλω). 21. — ο (*habent* A? C). εσται (*pro* εστι). 22. — ο. ‘ εστιν ’ επελθων (‘ ’ A, *forsan etiam p.m.*)√. ερει√. 23. εστιν (*sic* v. 29)√. *fin.* + με (*improbat* C^a, *sed restituitur*). 24. (C^a *habet* τοτε *post* ευρισκον). 25. [ελθον]. ευρισκι (*addit* σχολαζοντα C^a). 26. πορευετε√. παραλαμβανι√. μεθ εαυτου ετερα π̅ν̅α̅τ̅α̅ πονηροτερα εαυτου επτα (μεθ εαυτου A *vel p.m. in rasurâ rescripsit: primò* επτα). [εισελθοντα]. γινετε√. 27. τισ φωνην γυνη.— η *prim.* 28. μενουν (*sine* γε). *fin.* τον λογον του θ̅υ̅ (*iterum pro* αυτον: *improbant* A C). 29. + γενεα (*ante* πονηρα).

σημιον *ter in vers.* (*non* v. 30)√. ζητει.—του προφητου. 30. —γαρ. τοισ νινευειταισ σημειον. 31. ανθρωπων (*pro* ανδρων: Cª *cum* Steph.). κατακρινι√. σολομωνοσ *bis in versu.* 32. νινευιται. κρισι√. 33. —δε. κρυπτην. [αλλ]. φωσ (*pro* φεγγοσ). βλεπουσιν. 34. + σου (*ante* οταν: *improbat* Cª).—ουν. [και *prim.*]. φωτινον (*sic* v. 36 *bis*)√. (Cª *habet* ολον *ante* το σωμα *secund.*, *sed rursus erasum*). σκοτινον (*sic* v. 36)√. 35. σκοπι√. 36. σω >> *in rasurâ rescript.*√. [τι μεροσ].—ο (*habet* Cª). (-ζηᵀ σε: τ *s.m. erasum*)√. 37. λαλησαι ερωτα.—τισ. 39. καθαριζεται√. 40. *init.* + ο (˙ *p.m.*)√. [εξ. και το εσ.]. εποιησεν√. 42. αλλα. αποδεκατουται√. ηδυσμον (C *cum* Steph.). παν (*p.m. vel* A: *at* το? *primò*). παρερχεσθαι√. (+ δε *post* ταυτα A). εδει ποισαι (*sic*: *sed* ποισει *in annotationibus*). *fin.* αφειναι (Cª παρειναι). 43. φαρισαιοι (*pro* τοισ φαρισαιοισ). [*nihil additum*]. 44. —γραμματεισ και φαρισαιοι υποκριται. μνημια√. [οι *secund.*]. 47. μνημια√. και οι (Cª οι δε *cum* Steph.). απεκτιναν (*sic* v. 48)√. 48. μαρτυρεσ εστε (*pro* μαρτυρειτε).—αυτων τα μνημεια. 49. αποκτινουσιν (-κτενουσιν√ Cª). διωξουσιν. 50. (Cª εκδηκηθη *sic*). εκχυννομενον. 51. —του *prim. et secund.* μετοξυ (Cª μεταξυ)√: *sic* Barnabas fol. 139*. 52. [κλειδα]. εισηλθατε. 53. κακειθεν εξελθοντοσ αυτου (*pro* λεγοντοσ *usque ad* προσ αυτουσ). δινωσ ενεχιν√. 54. —αυτον και ζητουντεσ.—ινα κατηγορησωσιν αυτου.

XII. 1. επισυναχθισων√. 2 —δε. κεκαλυμμενον. 3. ταμιοισ (*sic* v. 24)√. 4. αποκτεννοντων. με (*pro* μετα: *corrigit* Cª)√. [περισσοτερον]. 5. ϋποδιξω√.—δε.—φοβηθητε *secund.* εχοντα εξουσιαν εμβαλλειν. *fin.* φοβηθηται√. 6. πωλουνται. 7. [ουν]. (διαφερεται√ Cª). 8. + οτι (*ante* πασ).—των αγγελων (*ut videtur*) *p.m.* (*addit* A, των αγ *in liturâ posito*). 9. [ενωπιον *bis in versu*]. απαρνησεται (A -νηθησεται). 10. αιρει√. βλασφημουντι. 11. εισφερωσιν. μεριμνησητε. [η τι *bis in versu*]. 13. ειπεν (*sic* vv. 15. 16. 18. 20. 22. 41)√. εκ του οχλου αυτω. μερισασθε√. 14. κατεστησεν√. κριτην (*pro* δικαστην). *fin.* υμων (Cª υμασ *cum* Steph.). 15. ορασαι√. φυλασσεσθαι√. πασησ (*pro* τησ). *fin.* [αυτου: *at* αυτω Cª]. 16. [ευφ.]. 18. ανοικοδομησω˙ (Cª *cum* Steph.). [τα γενηματα μου: *at* τον σιτον μου A Cª, παντα *etiam ab* A *omisso*].—και τα αγαθα μου (*habent* A Cª). 19. ευφρενου√. 20. [θσ αφρων]. [απαιτουσιν]. 21. αυτω (Cª *cum* Steph.). 22. [αυτου]. λεγω ϋμιν. μεριμναται√.—υμων. [σωματι τι]. 23. + γαρ (*ante* ψυχη). [εστι: Cª εστιν√]. 24. ουτε σπιρουσιν ουτε θερ. εστιν ταμιον. πετινων√. 25. [μεριμνων]. [προσθ. επι την ηλ. αυτου].—ενα (*habet* A). 26. ουδε (*pro* ουτε). + τι (*ante* δυνασθαι√: *improbat* C[a]). μεριμναται√. 27. κατανοησαται√. αυξανι√. [ου κοπια ουδε νηθει]. + οτι (*post* ὑμιν). 28. *init.* ῐ (*pro* ει)√. εν αγρω τον χορτον οντα σημερον (— τω). αμφιεννησιν√. 29. — μη *prim.* (*habet* A). και (*pro* η). + 'μηδε τω σωματι' (*post* πιητε: ' ' *p.m.*)√. 30. επιζητουσιν. 31. αυτου (*pro* του $\overline{θυ}$). — παντα (*habet* A). προστεθησετε√. 32. ὑμων ο πατηρ. 33. βαλλαντια. ανεκλιπτον√. ενγιζει. 35. [ὑμων αι οσφ.]. 36. αναλυση. 37. — και παρελθων διακονησει αυτοισ (*habet* A). 38. *init.* καν εν τη δευτερα καν εν τη τριτη φυλακη ελθη. ουτωσ√. — οι δουλοι εκεινοι (A C *habent* εκεινοι *tantum*). 39. — εγρηγορησεν αν και (*habent* A C: αν *omisso ab* A). [αν *secund.*]. αφηκεν√. διορυχθηναι. 40. — ουν. 41. [αυτω]. 42. και ειπεν (— δε). δουλοσ (*pro* οικονομοσ: C[a] *cum* Steph.). [και φρον.]. κατεστησεν (*pro* καταστησει: C[a] *cum* Steph.). [του] διαδουναι (C[a] διδοναι *cum* Steph.). [το σιτομ.]. 43. ουτωσ ποιουντα. 44. πασιν√. [αυτου]. 45. μου ο $\overline{κσ}$ (C[a] *cum* Steph., *sed p.m. restituitur*). παιδισκασ√. 47. αυτου (*pro* εαυτου). η (*pro* μηδε). 48. — δε *tert.* (*habent* A C). — πολυ *secund.* (*habent* A C). 49. επι (*pro* εισ). 50. οτου (*pro* ου). (C[a] συντελεσθη, συν *eraso*). 52. — εσονται γαρ *usque ad* διαμεμερισμε, *duabus lineis propter* ὁμοιοτ. *omissis* (*supplet* A, *legens* εν ενι οικω). δυσιν√. τρισιν√. 53. διαμερισθησονται. επι (*pro* εφ). + και (*ante* μητηρ). θυγατερα. μητερα. — αυτησ *prim. et secund.* (*habent* C[a]). 54. ελεγεν√. — την. επι (*pro* απο). λεγεται (*non* v. 55)√. + οτι (*ante* ομβροσ). γεινεται (*sic* v. 55)√. ουτωσ√. 55. — οτι (*habet* C[a]). ερχεται (*pro* εσται: A C *cum* Steph.). 56. (C[a] του ουρ. και τησ γησ). οιδαται *prim.*√. ουκ οιδαται δοκιμαζειν (*pro* ου δοκιμαζετε). 58. [επ αρχ.]. παραδωσει. βαλει (> > > βαλει *in liturâ scripta*). 59. — ου (*post* εωσ). (C[a] τον *pro* το).

XIII. 1. πειλατοσ. εμιξεν√. 2. — ο $\overline{ισ}$. ταυτα (*pro* τοιαυτα). 3. [μετανοητε]. ομοιωσ (*pro* ωσαυτωσ). 4. — και *prim.* (*habet* C[a]) cf. v. 11. επεπεσεν. απεκτινεν√. δοκειται (*non* v. 2)√. αυτοι (*pro* ουτοι). οφιλεται√. + τουσ (*ante* ανθρωπουσ). 5. μετανοησητε (C[a] *improbat* ση, *sed restituitur*). ωσαυτωσ (*pro* ομοιωσ). απολεισθαι (*non* v. 3)√. 6. ελεγεν (*sic* v. 14)√. ειχεν√. πεφυτευμενην εν αμπελωνι αυτου (+ τω *post* εν C[a]). ηλθεν ζητων καρπον. 7. ειπεν (*sic* vv. 20. 23 *bis*)√. + αφ ου (*ante* ερχομαι). [-ψον αυτην]. 8. τοτο (*pro* το: *improbat* το *prim.* C[a])√. κοπρια. 9. εισ το μελλον ει δε μηγε. 10. σαββασιν√. 11. — ην *prim.* ασθενιασ√. — και *secund.* cf. v. 4, *non ita* v. 16. συνκυπτουσα. 12. προσεφωνησεν√. + απο (*ante* τησ ασθενιασ√). 13. χιρασ√. [ανωρθωθη]. εδοξαζεν *p.m.*, *at* -ον *primò, ut videtur.* 14. + οτι (*ante* εξ). — εν αισ δει εργαζεσθαι (*habet* A). αυταισ (*pro* ταυταισ). (θεραπευεσθαι Cª). 15. δε (*pro* ουν). ϋποκριται. — τω σαββατω (*habet* Cª). απαγων (Cª *cum* Steph.). 16. [θυγατερα]. εδι√. 17. πασιν√. λεγομενοισ (*pro* γινομενοισ: Cª γεινο-√). 18. ελεγεν ουν (— δε). βασιλια√. 19. εστιν√. [ον]. εισ̈βαλεν (·· *p.m.*)√. (+ τον *ante* κηπον A). αυτου (*pro* εαυτου). ηϋξησεν. — μεγα. πετινα√. 21. εστιν√. [ενεκρυψεν]. 22. πολισ√. ποριαν√. ιεροσολυμα. 24. αγωνιζεσθαι√. εισελθιν *prim.*√. θυρασ (*pro* πυλησ). 25. αποκλιση. — εξω εσταναι και (*habent* A Cª). — κ͞ε *secund.* 26. αρξησθαι. πλατιαισ√. 27. — λεγω. [ϋμασ]. αποστηται√. — οι. — τησ. 28. εστε√. ϊδητε (*pro* οψησθε). ϊσακ (Cª ϊσαακ). 29. — απο *secund.* 30. εισιν√ *bis in versu.* 31. ωρα (*pro* ημερα). [προσηλθον]. 32. αποτελω (*pro* επιτελω). 33. — και αυριον (*habet* Cª). ερχομενη. ενδεχεται (νδε *rescriptum*)√. 34. [αποκτεινουσα]. αυτον (*pro* αυτην: Cª *cum* Steph.). ορνιξ. την εαυτου νοσσιαν (εαυτησ Cª *cum* Steph.). ηθελησαται√. 35. — ερημοσ. — αμην δε (+ δε *post* λεγω Cª). — οτι. ϊδητε με. αν ειπητε (— ηξη οτε).

XIV. 1. — των *secund.* 3. ειπεν (*sic* vv. 5. 19. 20. 21. 25)√. [λεγων]. — ει. εξεστιν√. θεραπευσαι. *fin.* + η ου. 4. απελυσεν√. 5. αποκριθισ (*puncta imposita sed rursus rasa*). αυτον (αυτουσ Cª *cum* Steph.). [ονοσ]. πεσειτε. — τη (*post* εν: *habet* Cª). 6. αποκριθηναι. — αυτω. 7. ελεγεν (*sic* v. 12)√. 8. — υπ (*habet* A *vel* Bª *potius*). 9. μετα. κατεχιν√. 10. αναπεσε. -κωσ σε *rescript. p.m.?*√. ερι (*pro* ειπη). εστε√. — σοι (*habent* A C *ante* εστε). + παντων (*post* ενωπιον). 11. ταπινωθησεται√. ταπινων√. 12. διπνον√. — σου *tert.* γιτονασ√. αντικαλεσωσιν σε. ανταποδομα σοι. 13. δοχην ποιησησ. αναπιρουσ (*sic* v. 21). 14. δε (*pro* γαρ: Cª *cum* Steph.). αναστασι√. 15. — ταυτα (*habet post* τισ A). — μακαριοσ κ.τ.λ. *usque ad* ειπεν αυτω v. 16 (ὁμοιοτ.: *supplet* A, *legens* οστισ, *omittens* αυτω v. 15, *non* v. 16: *addit* αυτω Cª). 16. εποιει. διπνον√. [μεγα]. εκαλεσεν√. 17. απεστιλεν√. διπνου√. ερχεσθαι√. εισιν (*pro* εστι παντα: παντα *forsan* A, *sed planè erasum est*). 18. παντεσ παρετισθαι ο πρ. (Cª παραιτ.). [εχω αναγκ.]. εξελθων (*pro* εξελθειν και). — σε (*habet* A). 20. ελθιν√. 21. — εκεινοσ. απηγγιλεν√. (*Post* πολεωσ *addit* A και οσουσ εαν ευρητε, *sequente* και τουσ *improbato*: Cª *prorsus cum* Steph. *et p.m.*). αναπιρουσ. και τυφλουσ και χωλουσ. 22. ο (*pro* ωσ). εστιν√. 23. ί εξελθε (· *p.m.*)√. εισελθιν√. μου ο οικοσ. 24.

ουδισ√. ανθρωπων (*pro* ανδρων). διπνου√. 25. στραφισ√. 26. εμε (*pro* με). αυτου (*pro* εαυτου *prim.*). [ετι δε]. την ψυχην εαυτου. ειναι μου μαθητησ. 27. *init.*—και (*habet* Cª). [αυτου]. ειναι μου. 28. τα εισ (*pro* τα προσ). 29. αυτω εμπεζιν. 30. οικοδομιν√. 31. ετερω βασιλει συμβαλλειν. βουλευσεται. ϋπαντησαι. [εικοσι]. χειλιαδων√. 32. [αυτου πορρω]. αποστιλασ√.—τα (*habet* Cª). 33. [πασι]. ειναι μου. 34. +ουν (*post* καλον). αλα *prim.* (Cª αλασ). +και (*post* δε). αλα *secund.*

XV. 1. αυτω εγγιζοντεσ. 2. +τε (*ante* φαρισαιοι).—ουτοσ. προσδεχετε√. 3. ειπεν (*sic* vv. 11. 21. 22. 29)√. 4. απολεσασ εξ αυτων εν. καταλιπει√. ενενηκονταεννεα. cf. v. 7. +ου (*post* εωσ). 5. αυτου. 6. συνκαλει (*sic* v. 9). συνχαρητε (*sic* v. 9). 7. ουτωσ√. εν τω ουρανω εστε. ενενηκονκονταεννεα (κον *prius eras.*). χριαν√. [εχουσι]. 8. [δραχμ. *bis in versu, sic* v. 9]. απτι√. ζητι√. ου (*pro* οτου). 9. συνκαλει.—τασ *secund.* 10. ουτωσ√. γεινεται χαρα. 11. ειχεν√. 12. —πατερ (Cᵇ *habet* π̅ε̅ρ̅). (ο δε *post* ουσιασ *pro* και Cª). 13. [απαντα]. [διεσκορπισε]. εαυτου (*pro* αυτου). εισ χωραν μακραν (*pro* ζων ασωτωσ: A *cum* Steph.). 14. λειμοσ ϊσχυρα. ϋστερισθαι√. 15. πορευθισ√. πολειτων√. 16. χορτασθηναι εκ (*pro* γεμισαι την κοιλιαν αυτου απο). 17. εφη (*pro* ειπε). [περισσευουσιν]. δε λειμω ωδε. 18. +δε (*post* αναστασ: *improbat* Cª). 19. *init.*—και. 20. ηλθεν√. αυτου (*pro* εαυτου). [ειδεν]. 21. [αυτω ο υ̅σ̅].—και *secund.* *fin.* +ποιησον με ωσ ενα των μισθιων σου. 22. εαυτου (*pro* αυτου). +ταχυ (*ante* εξενεγκαται√).—την *prim.* 23. φερετε (*pro* ενεγκαντεσ). 24. ο υιοσ μου ουτοσ. ανεζησεν ην απολωλοσ (—και *secund.*: Cª *habet* απ. ην).—και *ult.* ευφρενεσθαι√. 25. ηγγισεν√. ηκουσεν√. 26. —αυτου. [τι ειη]. 28. [ηθελεν]. εισελθιν√. δε (*pro* ουν). 29. [πατρι ϊδου]. 30. [μετα πορνων]. τον σιτευτον μοσχον. 32. εζησεν (Cª ανεζησεν).—και *tert.* [απολωλωσ ην: *at* Cª απολωλοσ ην, *ut* v. 24].

XVI. 1. ελεγεν (*sic* v. 5)√.—αυτου *prim.*—οσ (*habet* Cª). 2. —αυτω. ετι δυνη οικονομιν√. 3. ειπεν (*sic* vv. 2. 7. 24. 25. 27. 31)√. αφαιριται√. σκαπτιν√. επαιτιν√. 4. αν (*pro* οταν). +εκ (*post* μετασταθω). *fin.* εαυτων. 5. χρεοφιλετων√. αυτου (εαυτου Cª Cᵇ *cum* Steph.). οφιλεισ (*sic* v. 7)√. 6. +αυτω (*ante* εκατον). βαδουσ. ο δε (*pro* και *prim.*). τα γραμματα (*sic* v. 7). 7. λεγει δε (—και). 8. φρονιμωτεροι οι υιοι του αιωνοσ τουτου. *fin.* γενεαν ταυτην εαυτων εισιν (··· *p.m.?*, *etiam* C). 9. *init.* και εγω.

εαυτοισ ποιησατε (A C *cum* Steph.). [μαμωνα: *sic* vv. 11. 13]. εκλιπη (C^a *addit* ται, *sed rursus eras.*). [*nihil additum ad finem*]. 10. εστιν✓ *bis in versu.* 11. εγενεσθαι (*sic* v. 12) ✓. 12. δωσει ὑμιν. 13. [δυσι]. ει (*pro* η *prim.*). μισησι✓. δυνασθαι✓. 14. — και οι φαρισαιοι (*habet* οι φαρ. A). 15. *fin.* — εστιν. 16. μεχρι ἰωαννου (— εωσ). — και πασ εισ αυτην βιαζεται (ὁμοιοτ.: *habet* C^a, *addens* και βιασται αρπαζουσιν αυτην: ευαγγ. *etiam mutare inceperat*). 17. εστιν✓. παρελθιν✓. καιρεαν πεσιν✓. 18. [πασ *secund.*]. 20. — ην. — οσ. ειλκωμενοσ. 21. — ψιχιων των (ὁμοιοτ.: *habet* C^a). επελειχον. 22. αποθανιν✓. — του. απεθανεν✓. 23. *init.* — και (*habet* C^a). — τον. 24. ὑδατι. 25. μνησθητι τεκνον. — συ *prim.* ωδε (*pro* οδε). [οδυνασαι]. 26. εν (*pro* επι). [πασι]. εστηριγται *primò, at* -κται *p.m.* ενθεν (*pro* εντευθεν). — οι *secund.* (*habet* C^a). 27. [ουν σε]. 29. + δε (*post* λεγει). — αυτω. [εχουσι μωσεα]. 30. αναστη (*pro* πορευθη). 31. πισθησονται✓. [*caetera cum* Steph.].

XVII. 1. ειπεν (*sic* vv. 6. 22)✓. + αυτου (*post* μαθητασ). εστιν✓. του τα σκανδαλα μη ελθιν. πλην ουαι (— δε). 2. λιθοσ μυλικοσ (*pro* μυλ. ον.). ερρειπται✓. των μικρων τουτων ενα (C^a *cum* Steph.). 3. — δε. — εισ σε. 4. [αμαρτη]. [και επτακισ]. — τησ ημερασ *secund.* προσ σε (*pro* επι σε). 5. ειπαν. 6. εχετε. — ταυτη. 7. [εξ υμων]. + αυτῳ (*ante* ευθεωσ). αναπεσε. 8. + μοι (*post* ετοιμασον). διπνησω✓. διακονι✓. φαγεσε✓. πιεσε✓. 9. εχι χαριν. — τω δουλω εκεινω (*habet* τω δουλω A). εποιησεν✓. *Post* διαταχθεντα *desunt ob* ὁμοιοτ. *omnia usque ad* διαταχθεντα v. 10 (*supplet* A, *omittens* αυτω ου δοκω v. 9 *et* παντα v. 10: *legit* ουτωσ✓ *et* ποιησηται✓: παντα *habet* C^a *post* ποιησ.). 10. [οτι *prim.*]. αχριοι✓. — οτι *secund.* ωφειλαμεν (-ομεν A C). 11. — αυτον. [και αυτοσ]. μεσον σαμαριασ. 12. ὑπηντησαν αυτω. — οι εστησαν πορρωθεν (*habet* C^a). 13. + την (*ante* φωνην). 14. επιδιξατε✓. ἱερευσιν✓. ὑπαγιν✓. 15. ὑπεστρεψεν✓. 16. σαμαριτησ (v. 16, *etiam* σαμαριτησ, *totus repetitur in Codice*: A C, *forsan etiam p.m., uncis includunt secundo loco*)✓. 17. [ουχι]. [οι δε]. 19. σεσωκεν✓. 20. βασιλια *prim. tantum*✓. 21. — ιδου *secund.* 22. [-τασ ελευσ.]. επιθυμησεται✓. *fin.* οψεσθαι✓. 23. ἰδου εκει και ἰδου ωδε (*non* η). απελθηται✓. μητε (*pro* μηδε)✓. διωξηται✓. 24. — η *secund.* ὑπο τον ουρανον *prim.* [ὑπ ουρανον *secund.*]. — και. [εν τη ημ. αυτ.]. 25. παθιν✓. 26. κασωσ *primò* ?✓. — του *prim.* [του *secund.*]. 27. εγαμιζοντο. εισηλθεν✓. ηρεν (*pro* απωλεσεν). [απαντασ: *sic* v. 29]. 28. καθωσ (*pro* και ωσ). 29. εξηλθεν✓.

εβρεξεν√. θιον√. 30. [ταυτα: Cª τα αυτα]. εστε√. 31. + αυτου (*post* οικια). — τω. 32. μνημονευεται√. 33. *init.* οσ δαν εαν (··· A? Cª)√. [σωσαι]. απολεσι (*pro* -σει)√. οσ δ αν απολεσι (*pro* και οσ εαν απολεση). — αυτην *secund.* 34. [μιασ ο εισ]. παραλημφθησεται. 35, 36. *Desunt versus: v.* 36 *deest omnino; v.* 35 A *habet, legens* εσονται δυο, *et* η μια παραλημφθησεται η δε ετ., ὁμοιοτ. 37. *fin.* εκει και οι αετοι επισυναχθησονται.

XVIII. 1. ελεγεν√.—και. + αυτουσ (*post* προσευχεσθαι: *puncta imposita sed rursus erasa*). ενκακειν. 3. [δε ην]. εκινη√. 4. ηθελεν. μετα (τα *instauratum*)√. [δε ταυτα]. ουδε ανθρωπον (*pro* και ανθρωπον ουκ). 5. παρενοχλειν μοι κοπουσ (Cª παρεχειν μοι κοπον *cum* Steph.). [ϋπωπιαζη]. 6. ειπεν (*sic vv.* 9. 19. 21. 24. 27. 28. 31. 41)√. — ακουσατε (*supplet* A). 7. ποιηση. αυτω (*pro* προσ αυτον). μακροθυμει. [επ αυτοισ]. 9. [και *prim.*]. εισιν√. εξουδενουντασ. 10. προσευξασθε√. [ο εισ]. 11. — προσ εαυτον (*habet post* ταυτα Cª). [ωσπερ]. [ουτ. ο τελ.]. 12. αποδεκατευω (Cª -δεκατω). 13. *init.* ο δε (— και). επαραι εισ τον ουρανον. ετυπτε (— εισ). [αυτου]. — ο $\overline{θσ}$ (*habet* Cª). 14. [ϋμιν κατεβη]. παρ εκινον (*pro* η εκεινοσ). ταπινωθησεται√. ο δε ταπινων. 15. επετιμων. 16. προσεκαλεσατο αυτα λεγων (*pro* προσκαλεσαμενοσ αυτα ειπεν). 17. αν (*pro* εαν). βασιλιαν√. 18. επηρωτησεν√. 19. ουδισ√. — ο (*ante* $\overline{θσ}$: *habet* Cª). 20. *fin.* [σου]. 21. εφυλαξα. [μου]. 22. — ταυτα. οτι (*pro* ετι: Cª *cum* Steph., *vix* A). λιπει√. εχισ√. δοσ. εν ουρανοισ. ακολουθι√. 23. + παντα (*post* ταυτα). εγενηθη. 24. — περιλυπον γενομενον. εισ την βασιλειαν του $\overline{θυ}$ εισελευσονται. 25. εστιν√. [καμηλον]. τρηματοσ βελονησ (*pro* τρυμ. ραφιδοσ). [εισελθειν *prim.*]. 26. ειπαν. 27. *fin.* παρα τω $\overline{θω}$ εστιν. 28. [ο]. ημισ√. (Cª αφεντεσ τα ϊδια *pro* αφηκαμεν παντα και). *fin.* (+ τι αρα εσται ημιν Cª). 29. — οτι (*habet* Cª). η γυναικα η αδελφουσ η γονισ. εινεκεν. 30. ουχι (*pro* ου). [απολαβη]. 31. ιερουσαλημ. 32. εθνεσιν√. εμπεχθησεται√. 35. [γγ]. [ϊεριχω]. επαιτων. 36. [τι ειη]. 37. οι δε απηγγιλαν (Cª απηγγ. δε).— αυτω (*habet* Cª). παρερχετε√. 38. εβοησεν√. $\overline{δαδ}$√. 39. [προαγοντεσ]. [σιωπηση]. ο δε (*pro* αυτοσ δε). $\overline{ιυ}$ $\overline{υυ}$ $\overline{δαδ}$ (*sic*) *at* $\overline{υε}$ *pro* $\overline{υυ}$ Cª. 40. [ο $\overline{ισ}$]. 41. — λεγων. 42. σεσωκεν√. 43. ανεβλεψεν√. αυτον (*pro* αυτω: Cª *cum* Steph.).

XIX. 1. ϊερειχω. 2. και ην πλουσιοσ (— ουτοσ). 3. ϊδιν√. εστιν√. 4. [προδραμων]. + εισ το (*ante* εμπροσθεν). συκομορεαν. του ϊδειν (ϊνα ϊδη Cª *cum* Steph.). — δι. ημελλεν√. 5. — ειδεν αυτον και. ειπεν (*sic* vv. 8. 9. 11. 13. 15. 19. 40)√. δι (*pro* δει)√. 7. παντεσ. ανδρι αμαρτωλω. εισηλθεν√. 8. + ο (*ante* ζακχαιοσ). τα ημισια μου των ϋπαρχοντων. τοισ πτωχοισ διδωμι. 9. αβρααμ'·√. — εστιν (*habet* Cª). 10. ηλθεν√. αποαπολωλοσ√. 11. εγγυσ ειναι ϊερουσαλημ αυτον. δοκει αυτοισ (*pro* δοκειν αυτουσ: Cª *cum* Steph.). η βασιλεια του θ̅υ̅ μελλει. 13. πραγματευσασθαι√. εν ω (*pro* εωσ). 14. πολειται√. απεστιλαν√. 15. επανελθιν√. δεδωκει. γνοι. — τισ. διεπραγματευσαντο. 16. δεκα προσηργασα (δ. προσειργασατο Cª). 17. [ευ]. δουλε αγαθε. 18. η μνα σου κ̅ε̅ (*at* μνασ *prim.* Cª). εποιησεν√. 19. επανω γεινου. 20. οτεροσ (*pro* ο ετεροσ, *quod habet* Cª). ηλθεν√. (μνασ *pro* μνα Cª: cf. v. 18). 21. αιρισ√. εσπιρασ√. 22. — δε. ηδισ√. εσπιρα√. 23. μου το αργυριον. — την. καγω. + ουν (*post* ελθων: *improbat* Cª). αυτο επραξα. 24. αρε (Cª αρατε). 25. ειπαν (*sic* vv. 33. 34. 39). 26. — γαρ υμιν (A *habet* υμιν). — απ αυτου (*habet* Cª). 27. τουτουσ (*pro* εκεινουσ). κατασφαξετε αυτουσ εμπ. 29. [βηθφαγη]. βηθανια (¯ *super* α Cª). ελεων (*non* v. 37)√. απεστιλεν√. — αυτου. 30. λεγων (*pro* ειπων). ουδισ√. εκαθισεν λυσ. 31. (Cª + αυτον *post* λυετε: *sed rasum est*). — αυτω. χριαν (*sic* v. 34)√. 34. + οτι (*post* ειπαν). 35. επιριψαντεσ. αυτων (*pro* εαυτων). 36. [αυτων]. 37. αινιν√. [πασων]. 38. — ερχομενοσ (*habet* Cª). εν ουρανω εν ϊρηνη (εν *ante* ϊρ. *improbat* Cª). 40. — αυτοισ. [οτι]. σιωπησουσιν. κραξουσιν. 41. επ αυτην. 42. — και συ και γε. — σου *prim. et secund.* + και συ (*post* ταυτη). ϊρηνην√. 43. παρεμβαλουσιν. περικυκλωσουσιν√. — σε *secund.* (*habet* Cª). συνεξουσιν√. — σε *tert.* (*habet* Cª). 44. εδαφιουσιν√. λιθον επι λιθον εν σοι. 45. — εν αυτω και αγοραζοντασ (ὁμοιοτ.). 46. (Cª *habet* και εσται *post* γεγραπται). — εστιν. ληστον (ληστων Cª)√. 47. — ιερω οι δε (*unâ lineâ omissâ*: *habent* A C)√. απολεσε√. 48. [ευρισκον]. [το τι]. εξεκρεμετο.

XX. 1. — εκεινων. ευαγγελιζομενοι (Cª -μενου)√. 2. ειπαν λεγοντεσ προσ αυτον. — ειπε ημιν (*habent* ειπον ημιν A C). 3. ειπεν (*sic* vv. 13. 17. 19. 23. 25. 41. 45)√. αυτον (*pro* αυτουσ: Cª *cum* Steph.). — ενα. 4. + το (*ante* ϊωαννου). 5. συνελογιζοντο. αυτουσ (*pro* εαυτουσ: Cª *cum* Steph.). [ερει διατι]. — ουν. επιστευσαται√. 6. ο λαοσ απασ. πεπισμενοσ√. [νν]· 7. — μη (*habent* A C). 8. — ο ι̅σ̅ (*habet* Cª). ουδ (ουδε A *vel forsan p.m.*). 9. — λεγειν (*habet* A *post* λαον). — τισ. [α̅ν̅ο̅σ̅ εφ. αμπ.]. εξεδετο (Cª εξεδοτο). απεδημησεν√. 10. — εν. κερω√. απεστιλεν√. — καρπου του (*habet* Cª). δωσουσιν (*pro* δωσιν). *fin.* εξαπεστιλαν αυτον διραντεσ καινον.

11. εθετο (A *cum* Steph. προσεθετο). ετερον πεμψαι. κακινον διραντεσ√. εξαπεστιλαν καινον. 12. τριτον πεμψαι. [και τουτον]. 13. — ιδοντεσ. 14. — αυτον (*habet* Cᵃ). [διελογιζοντο]. αλληλουσ (*pro* εαυτουσ). [δευτε]. αποκτινωμεν√. [γενηται]. 15. απεκτιναν√. 16. — τουσ γεωργουσ (*habet* Cᵃ). [ακουσαντεσ δε]. ειπαν. 17. εστιν√. 18. εκινον√. 19. [εζητησαν οι αρχ. και οι γρ.]. χιρασ√. — εγνωσαν γαρ (*habet* A). ειπεν την παραβολην ταυτην. 20. απεστιλαν√. ενκαθετουσ. αποκρινομενουσ (Cᵃ υποκρ.). [λογου]. ωστε (*pro* εισ το). — τη *secund.* 21. οιδαμεν (οιδ *rescript. p.m.*)√. διδασκισ√ *bis in versu.* 22. ημασ (*pro* ημιν). 23. — τι με πειραζετε. 24. δειξατε. + οι δε εδειξαν αυτω και ειπαν (*ante* τινοσ: *at* ειπεν Cᵃ). οι δε ειπαν (— αποκριθεντεσ). 25. προσ αυτουσ (*pro* αυτοισ). τοινυν αποδοτε. [-ροσ και-]. 26. του (*pro* αυτου *prim.*). 27. λεγοντεσ. 28. [μωσησ: *sic* v. 37]. — και ουτοσ *usque ad* γυναικα *secund.* (ὁμοιοτ.: *supplet* A, *habens* ην *et* C η *pro* αποθανη)√. 29. (+ παρ ημιν *post* ησαν A). 30. *Deest omnis versus praeter* και ο δευτεροσ. 31. (ελαβον *ob* v. 30 Cᵃ). [ωσαυτωσ *semel tantum*]. [επτα ου κατ.]. [απεθανον]. 32. — δε παντων (*habet* δε Cᵃ). και η γυνη απεθανεν. 33. εν τη αναστασι (— ουν: *habet* Cᵃ). — αυτων (*habet* Cᵃ). εσται (*pro* γινεται). 34. — αποκριθεισ. [γαμουσι]. γαμισκονται. 35. γαμιζονται. 36. [ουτε]. αποθανιν√. ἑσιν *prim.* (ι *supra p.m. vel* A: *instauravit* C)√. θ̅υ̅ εισιν (— του). 37. — τον *secund. et tert.* ῐσακ (Cᵃ ῐσαακ). 38. εστιν√. 39. ειπαν. + αυτω (*ante* διδασκαλε). 40. γαρ (*pro* δε). 41. [λεγουσι]. ειναι δ̅α̅δ̅ υ̅ν̅. 42. αυτοσ γαρ δ̅α̅δ̅ (— και). [-λω ψαλ.]. [ο] (42. 43. >> *citationis signa per* A). 44. [δ̅α̅δ̅ ουν κ̅ν̅ αυτον]. [υ̅σ̅ αυτου]. 45. [τοισ μαθ. αυτου]. 46. εν στολαισ περιπατειν. διπνοισ√. 47. [οι κατεσθιουσι]. [προσευχονται]. λημψονται.

XXI. 1. ειδεν (*sic* v. 2)√. εισ το γαζοφυλακιον τα δωρα αυτων. 2. — και. λεπτα δυο. 3. αυτη η πτωχη πλεον 4. παντεσ. — του θ̅υ̅. παντα. εβαλεν√. 5. (μεγαλοισ *pro* καλοισ A, *sed* καλ *restitut.*). αναθεμασιν. ειπεν (*sic* vv. 8. 29)√. 6. θεορειτε (Cᵃ θεωρ.). + ωδε (*post* λιθω: *at* λιθον Cᵃ). 7. σημιον√. γεινεσθαι√. 8. — οτι. — ο κ̣ροσ ηγγικεν μη ουν (*unâ lineâ praetermissâ: supplet* Cᵃ, ουν *omisso*). πορευθηται√. 9. ακουσηται√. [ταυτα γεν.]. 10. εγερθησετε√. επ εθν. 11. και κατα τοπουσ λειμοι και λοιμοι. [φοβητρα]. σημια μεγαλα απ ουρανου. 12. παντων. επ αυτουσ (*pro* εφ υμασ: A *cum* Steph.). χιρασ√. διωξουσιν√. + τασ (*ante* συναγωγασ). απαγομενουσ. 13. — δε (*habet* Cª). 14. θετε. — ουν (*habet* Cª). εν ταισ καρδιαισ. 15. αντιστηναι η αντειπιν παντεσ. 17. εσεσθαι√. [*ordo cum* Steph.]. 19. κτησασθαι√. 20. στρατοπαιδων ιηλμ (— την). 21. εκχωριτωσαν√. 22. — εισι. πλησθηναι. 23. [δε]. εστε√. + εν εκιναισ ταισ ημεραισ (*post* γαρ: *improbat* Cª). — εν *ultim.* 24. [μαχαιρασ]. τα˙εθνη παντα. ιηλμ√. αχρι ου πληρωθωσιν. 25. εσονται σημια. + και (*post* εθνων). ηχουσ (*pro* ηχουσησ). 26. επαρχομενων (Cª επερχ.). δυναμισ√. 27. τοτετ (˙ *p.m.*)√. [νεφελη]. 28. γεινεσθαι√. 30. + αυτων (*ante* αφ εαυτων: *improbat* A: απ αυτων Cª *pro* αφ εαυ. *sed prior lectio restituitur*). γεινωσκετε *bis scriptum* (*posterius notatum a* Cª)√. εγγυσ εστιν ηδη το θεροσ. 31. ουτωσ√. ϋμισ√. γεινομενα γεινωσκετε√. 32. — αν. 33. παρελευσονται *bis in versu* (*secund. pro* παρελθωσι). 34. — δε. βαρηθωσιν [ϋμ. αι καρ.]. κρεπαλη√. επιστη εφ υμασ εφνιδιοσ. 35. επισελευσεται γαρ (ισ *erasum*). 36. (αγρυπνειται√ Cª) δε (*pro* ουν). κατισχυσητε (*pro* καταξιω.). — ταυτα (*habet* Cª *ante* παντα). γεινεσθαι√. 37. [εν τω ϊερ. διδ.]. 38. ωρθριζεν√.

XXII. 1. ηγγιζεν√. 2. γραμματισ√. [το πωσ: *sic* v. 4, *et* το τισ vv. 23. 24]. 3. εισηλθεν√. — ο. καλουμενον. 4. συνελαλησεν√. αρχιερευσιν√. — τοισ *secund.* αυτοισ παραδω αυτον. 6. — και εξωμολογησε (*habet* Cᵇ, *at* -σεν√). [του παραδουναι]. ατερ οχλου αυτοισ. 7. ηλθεν√. [εν]. 8. απεστιλεν√. [ϊωαννην]. 9. ειπαν (*sic* vv. 38. 49. 70. 71). θελισ√. [*nihil additum*]. 10. συναντησι√. κεραμειον√. — υδατοσ (*habet* Cᵇ). ακολουθησαται√. εισ ην (*pro* ου). 11. + λεγοντεσ (*ante* λεγει). εστιν (*sic* vv. 19. 38)√. + μου (*ante* οπου). 12. αναγαιον. κακει (*pro* εκει). 13. ειρηκει. 14. ανεπεσεν√. — δωδεκα (*habet* Cᵇ, *at* δωδεκα *pro* αποστολοι Cª). 15. ειπεν (*sic* vv. 17. 31. 34. 52. 56. 60. 67)√. 16. — ουκετι. αυτο (*pro* εξ αυτου). 17. [-αμενοσ ποτηρ.]. — τουτο (*habet* Cª). αλληλοισ (*pro* εαυτοισ: Cª εισ εαυτουσ). 18. [οτι]. + απο του νυν (*post* πιω). γενηματοσ. ου (*pro* οτου). 19. εκλασεν√. ποιειται√. 20. και το ποτηριον ωσαυτωσ. διπνησαι√. εκχυννομενον. 22. οτι ο υσ (— και *et* μεν: Cª *habet* μεν). κατα το ωρισμενον πορευεται. 23. συνζητειν. ειη εξ αυτων ειη (*alterum* ειη *notat* Cª). 24. — και. φιλονικια√. εισ εαυτουσ (*pro* εν αυτοισ: Cª *cum* Steph.). μιζων (*non* v. 26)√. 25. *Post* αυτων *prim. habet* και οι αρχοντεσ των εξουσιαζουσιν αυτων και ευεργεται καλουνται (*unâ lineâ post* των ε *forsan praetermissâ: at* Cª *improbat* αρχοντεσ των *et* και *ante* ευεργεται, *legens etiam* εξουσιαζοντεσ). 26. γεινεσθω√. 27. + ο (*ante* μειζων: *improbat* Cª). εν μεσω ὑμων ειμι. 28. πιρασμοισ√. 30. εσθιηται√. πινηται√. καθησεσθε. (Cª *habet* $\overline{\iota\beta}$ *ante* θρονων). 31. [ειπ. δε ο $\overline{\kappa\sigma}$].—σιμων *semel*. ξινιασαι (σ *supra p.m.*)√. 32. εκλιπη. στηρισον. 34. ειπεν√.—μη *prim.* εωσ (*pro* πριν η). τρεισ√. με απαρνηση ειδεναι (—μη *secund.*). 35. απεστιλα√. βαλλαντιου. μηρασ (πηρασ Cª *et forsan ante eum*)√. τι (*pro* τινοσ: Cª *cum* Steph.). ὑστερησαται√. [ειπον ουδενοσ]. 36. ο δε ειπεν (—ουν: *at* ειπεν δε Cª). βαλλαντιον. [*caetera cum* Steph.]. 37. —ετι. [το *secund.*]. [γαρ]. το (*pro* τα). 38. —κυριε (*habet* Cª). μαχαιρε (-ραι Cª)√. 39. —αυτου. 40. προσευχεσθαι (*sic* v. 46)√. πιρασμον (*sic* v. 46)√. 41. απεσπαθη (-πασθη A C). προσηὔξατο. 42. βουλι παρενεγκαι. τουτο το ποτηριον τουτο (τουτο *alterum notat* A *vel p.m.*)√. γεινεσθω. 43, 44. *Habet p.m.: improbat* A, *restituit* C. 44. γεναμενοσ. και εγενετο (—δε). —ο. ωσι√. καταβαινοντοσ. 45. [-τασ ευρεν]. κοιμωμενουσ αυτουσ. 46. εισελθηται√. 47. —δε. αυτουσ (*pro* αυτων). ηγγισεν√. 48. $\overline{\iota\sigma}$ δε (—ο).—ιουδα (*habet* Cª). 49. ειδοντεσ√. ειπαν (—αυτω). μαχαιρη. 50. του αρχιερεωσ τον δουλον. αφιλεν το ουσ αυτου. 51. —αυτου. 52. —ο. προσ αυτον (*pro* επ αυτον: Cª *cum* Steph.). εξηλθαται. 53. εξετινατε√. [αλλ].—υμων *secund.* (Cª *habet post* εστιν). 54. —αυτον *secund.* την οικιαν. ηκολουθι√. 55. περιαψαντων. συνκαθισαντων.—αυτων. [εν μεσω]. 57. —αυτον *prim.* ουκ οιδα αυτον γυναι. 58. (+παλιν *post* βραχυ A: *improbat* C). εφη (*pro* ειπεν). 59. αληθιασ√.—ην (*habet* A). 60. τι (*pro* ο *ante* λεγεισ). (+αυτου *post* ετι A, *sed delevit*)√.—ο (*ante* αλεκτωρ). 61. ενεβλεψεν√. ρηματοσ (*pro* λογου). +σημερον (*post* φωνησε√). 62. —ο πετροσ. εκλαυσεν√. 63. αυτον (*pro* τον $\overline{\iota\nu}$). ενεπεζαν (Cª -ζον). 64. —αυτον ετυπτον αυτου το προσωπον και. [αυτον *secund.*]. 66. ημερα εγενετο. γραμματισ√. απηγαγον. αυτων (*pro* εαυτων). 67. ειπον (*pro* ειπε *prim.*).—υμιν (*habet* Cª). 68. —και.—μοι η απολυσητε. 69. +δε (*post* νυν). 70. ειπαν (*sic* v. 71). χριαν εχομεν μαρτυριασ.

XXIII. 1. ηγαγον. [πιλατον]. 2. κατηγοριν√. [ευρομεν]. +ημων (*post* εθνοσ). φορουσ καισαρι. +και (*ante* λεγοντα). 3. [πιλατοσ: *sic* vv. 4. 12. 13. 20. 24]. ηρωτησεν. λεγει (*pro* εφη). 4. ειπεν (*sic* vv. 14. 22. 28. 46)√. αρχιερισ√. 5. ανασι (Cª ανασιει).—διδασκων (*habet* Cª). +και (*ante* αρξαμενοσ). 6. πειλατοσ. —γαλιλαιαν. εστιν√. 7. [προσ ηρ.]. κατ αυτον *p.m.* (*at* και αυτον C? *post* οντα). αυταισ (*pro* ταυταισ: Cª *cum* Steph.).

8. — δε (*habet* Cᵃ). εξ ικανων χρονων θελων. ῒδιν✓ *bis in versu.* — πολλα. [ηλπιζε: *at* -ζεν✓ Cᵃ]. σημιον✓. γεινομενον✓. 9. — δε *prim.* (*habet* Cᵃ). ουκ (*pro* ουδεν). απεκριναντο (C -νατο)✓. 10. ῒστηκεισαν✓. 11. [εξουθενησασ]. τε και (*pro* δε).— αυτον *prim.* (*habet* Cᵃ *post* τε). ενπεξασ.— αυτον *secund.* αισθητα✓. επεμψεν (Cᵃ *cum* Steph.). [πιλατω]. 12. ο τε ηρωδησ και ο πιλατοσ. προϋπηρχοντο (Cᵃ *cum* Steph.). αυτουσ (*pro* εαυτουσ). 13. συνκαλεσαμενοσ. 14. ουθεν. — κατ. 15. ανεπεμψε γαρ αυτον προσ ημασ (*pro* ανεπεμψα γαρ υμασ προσ αυτον). ειδου *vel* οιδου *p.m.* (*primâ literâ erasâ, legitur* ῒδου *s.m.*). εστιν✓. 17. [*Habet versum*]. *fin.* ινα (ε *p.m.*)✓. 18. ανεκραγον. πανπληθει. [τον]. 19. — βεβλημενοσ (βεβλημενοσ A C). *fin.* εν τη φυλακη. 20. δε (*pro* ουν). + αυτοισ (*post* προσεφωνησεν). 21. σταυρου σταυρου. 22. αιτιον (ιτ *rescript.*, ν *primò*?)✓. 23. εκειντο. — και των αρχιερεων. 24. *init.* και (*pro* ο δε). επεκρινεν✓. 25. απελυσεν✓. — αυτοισ. — την. παρεδωκεν✓. 26. σιμωνα τινα κυρηναιον ερχομενον απ (— του). επεθηκεν (Cᵃ -καν)✓.— φερειν (*habet* C, *at* αιρειν A). 27. — αι και. 28. — ο (*habet* Cᵃ, *sed iterum improbat*). θυγατεραισ✓. 29. ημεραι ερχονται. ερουσιν✓.— αι *prim.* + αι (*ante* κοιλιαι). [μαστοι]. εθρεψαν (*pro* εθηλασαν). 30. ορεσιν✓. (πεσατε Cᵃ). 31. [τω]. ξυλω (˙ *p.m.*)✓. 32. κακουργοι δυο. 33. ηλθον. 34. *Habet omnia p.m., at ab* ο δε $\overline{ισ}$ *usque ad* ποιουσιν *uncos apposuit* A (?), *rursus deletos.* ελεγεν✓. οιδασιν✓. ποιουσιν✓. [κληρον]. 35. ῒστηκει✓.— και *secund.*— συν αυτοισ. εσωσεν✓. ȯ του $\overline{θυ}$ ο εκλεκτοσ (˙ A C). 36. ενεπεξαν. — και *prim. et secund.* 37. [ει]. 38. — γεγραμμενη. — και *secund. et tert.* ο βασιλευσ των ῒουδαιων ουτοσ (— εστιν). (Cᵃ *ad* γραμμ. ελλ. ρωμ. εβρ. *uncos apposuit, rursus erasos*). 39. εβλασφημι✓. [λεγων]. ουχι (*pro* ει). 40. επιτιμων αυτω εφη (*pro* επετιμα αυτω λεγων). ου (*pro* ουδε: Cᵃ *cum* Steph.). 41. ημισ✓. επραξεν✓. 42. ελεγεν. — τω (*habet* Cᵃ). — κυριε. εν τη βασιλια✓. 43. — ο $\overline{ισ}$. [λεγω σοι]. παραδισω✓. 44. *init.* και ην ωρα ωσει (— δε). — και (*ante* σκοτοσ: *habet* Cᵃ). ενατησ. 45. του ηλιου εκλιποντοσ (*pro* και εσκοτισθη ο ηλιοσ). εσχισθη δε (— και). χιρασ✓. παρατιθεμαι. τουτο δε (*pro* και ταυτα). 47. εκατονταρχησ (-χοσ Cᵃ). εδοξαζεν. + οτι (*ante* οντωσ). 48. συνπαραγενομενοι. εισ (*pro* επι). θεωρησαντεσ. — εαυτων. 49. ειστηκισαν✓. + απο (*post* αυτου). συνακολουθουσαι. 50. + και (*post* ϋπαρχων). 51. συνκατατιθεμενοσ.— και (*post* οσ). — και αυτοσ. 52. [πιλατω]. 53. — αυτο *prim.* αυτον (*pro* αυτο

tert.). ουδεισ ουδεπω. 54. παρασκευησ και. επεφωσκεν√. 55. δε γυναικεσ (—και). εκ τησ γαλιλαιασ αυτω. μνημιον√. 56. [μεν].

XXIV. 1. [δε]. ορθου βαθεωσ. επι το μνημιον ηλθον. — και τινεσ συν αυταισ. 2. μνημιου (*sic* v. 9)√. 3. εισελθουσαι δε (—και). ουκ (*pro* ουχ). [του κυ ιυ]. 4. απορισθαι√. [και ἰδου]. ανδρεσ δυο. εσθητι αστραπτουση. 5. τα προσωπα. ειπαν (*sic* vv. 19. 32). 6. αλλα. μνησθηται√. [ωσ]. 7. τον υν του ανου οτι δει (Cª *cum* Steph.). χιρασ√. 9. απηγγιλαν√. παντα ταυτα. πασιν√. 10. [ησαν δε]. μαριαμ *prim.* [ἰωαννα]. + η (*post* μαρια *secund.*). — αι (*habet* Cª). 11. ταυτα (*pro* αυτων *secund.*). 12. *Habet versum.*— κειμενα μονα (*habet* μονα Cᵇ). απηλθεν√. [εαυτον]. 13. εξ αυτων εν τη αυτη ημερα ησαν δε πορευομενοι (δε *improbant* A? C: *post* αυτων C *scripturus* ησαν, *addiderat* η *sed rursus delevit*). + εκατον (*ante* εξηκοντα). 15. συνζητειν. — ο. 16. *init.* + ϊν (¨ *p.m.*)√. 17. ειπεν (*sic* vv. 18. 25. 44)√. αντιβαλλεται√. αλληλουσλουσ (λουσ *secund. improbat* Cª)√. εσταθησαν (*pro* εστε). 18. —ο. ονοματι (*pro* ω ονομα). [κλεοπασ]. — εν *prim.* + ταυτα (*ante* ουκ εγνωσ). 19. ναζαρηνου. εν λογω και εργω. 20. [παρεδωκαν αυτον]. 21. ελπιζομεν. + και (*post* γε). [πασι]. — αγει σημερον (Cª *habet* αγι)√. 22. γενομεναι ορθριναι. μνημιον (*sic* v. 24)√. 23. [ηλθον]. 24. ουτωσ (*sic* v. 46 *prim.*)√. [καθωσ και]. 27. [μωσεωσ]. και διερμηνευειν (*pro* διηρμηνυεν: Cª διερμηνευσεν, και *omisso*). + τι ην (*post* αυτοισ). — πασαισ. *fin.* [εαυτου]. 28. προσεποιησατο. πορρωτερωτερω (τερω *secund. improbat* Cª) cf. v. 17. 29. μινον√. εστιν√. + ηδη (*post* κεκλικεν). εισηλθεν√. μιναι√. 30. + και (*ante* λαβων). ηϋλογησεν. εδιδου. 31. διηνυγησαν (Cª -νυχθησαν). — και επεγνωσαν αυτον (*habent* A C). 32. κεομενη√. [εν ημιν]. — και *secund.* διηνυγεν√. 33. ηθροισμενουσ. 34. οντωσ ηγερθη ο κσ. + τω (*ante* σιμωνι). 36. — ο ισ. [και λεγει αυτοισ ειρηνη ὑμιν: *nihil additum*]. 37. φοβηθεντεσ (*pro* πτοηθεντεσ). 38. [ταισ καρδιαισ]. 39. ειδετε *prim.* τουσ ποδασ μου και τασ χιρασ μου. εγω ειμι αυτοσ. σαρκασ (σ *erasum*). θεωρειται√. 40. *Habet versum.* εδιξεν√. χιρασ√. 41. [απο τησ χ. και θαυμ.]. ωδε (*pro* ενθαδε: Cª *cum* Steph.). 42. — και απο μελισσιου κηριου. 44. προσ αυτουσ (*pro* αυτοισ). [λογοι ουσ]. [μωσεωσ]. — και *prim.* + εν τοισ (*ante* προφηταισ). ψαλμοι (A? Cª *addunt* σ)√. 45. διηνυξεν√. (συνειεναι? Cª: Cᵇ *cum p.m. et* Steph.). 46. — και ουτωσ εδει. 47. εισ (*pro* και *secund.*). αρξαμενοι. 48. — δε. [εστε]. 49. καγω (*pro* και ιδου εγω). (εξ-αποστελλω Cᵃ). — ιερουσαλημ. εξ υψουσ δυναμιν. 50. εξηγαγεν√. — εξω. προσ (*pro* εισ). χιρασ√. ηϋλογησεν. 51. ευλογιν√. — και ανεφερετο εισ τον ουρανον (*habet* Cᵃ). 52. [προσκυνησαντεσ αυτον]. ιερουσαλημ'. 53. — αινουντεσ και. [ευλογουντεσ]. — αμην.

Subscr. ευαγγελιον κατα λουκαν.

κατα ϊωαννην.

Cap. I. 3. ουδεν (Cᵃ ουδε εν *cum* Steph.). ο γεγονεν *initio lineae.* 4. εστιν (*pro* ην *prim.*). 6. + ην (*ante* ονομα: ην *improbant* A? Cᵃ). [νν: *sic passim*]. 7. πιστευσωσιν√. 8. εκινοσ√. 9. αληθεινον√. 10. δι αυτον (δι αυτου Cᵃ *cum* Steph.). 11. ηλθεν√. 12. [ελαβον]. γενεσθε√. 13. — εκ (*ante* θελ. ανδρ.: *habet* Cᵃ). 14. αληθιασ√. 15. μαρτυρι√. κεκραγεν. — λεγων (*habet* A). — ον ειπον (*habet* A ο ειπων, B? ον ειπων, Cᵇ ον' ειπον). + οσ (*ante* εμπροσθεν: *improbat* C). 16. *init.* οτι (*pro* και). 17. μωϋσεωσ. αληθια√. — $\overline{χυ}$ (*habet* Cᵃ). 18. εωρακεν√. — ο *prim.* (*habet* Cᵃ). $\overline{θσ}$ (*pro* $\overline{υσ}$). — ο ων (*habet* B?). 19. απεστιλαν οι. ϊερισ√. λευειτασ. επερωτησωσιν. 20. ωμολογησεν *prim.*√. — και ωμολογησεν *secund.* εγω ουκ ιμι. 21. επηρωτησαν (A C *cum* Steph.). — αυτον (*habet* Cᵃ). + παλιν (*ante* τι). — συ *prim.* — και *secund.* — ο (*habet* Cᵃ): *non* v. 25. 22. [ειπον ουν]. 24. — οι (*habet* Cᵇ). 25. — και ηρωτησαν αυτον. [ειπον]. ουδε (*pro* ουτε) *bis in versu.* 26. + τω (*ante* ϋδατι: *improbat* C). — δε. εστηκει. 27. — αυτοσ εστιν ο (*habet* ο Cᵃ). — οσ εμπροσθεν μου γεγονεν. — εγω. [ειμι αξ.]. 28. εγενετο εν βηθανια (Cᵇ βηθαραβα: *sic*). + ποταμου (*ante* οπου). + ο (*ante* ϊωαννησ). 29. βλεπι√. — ο ιωαννησ. ο *ult. p.m. in rasurâ*√. ερων√. 30. εστιν. ϋπερ (*pro* περι: B? Cᵃ *cum* Steph.). 31. [ηλθον εγω]. — τω *secund.* 32. — λεγων (*habet* B?). ωσ περιστεραν καταβαινον εκ του ουρανου. μενον (*pro* εμεινεν). 33. και εγω. + τω (*ante* ϋδατι). εκινοσ√. [ουτοσ]. 34. εκλεκτοσ (*pro* $\overline{υσ}$: Cᵃ *cum* Steph.) cf. Luc. ix. 35. 35. ϊστηκι√. [ο ϊωανν.]. 36. [*nihil additum*]. 37. *init.* — και (*habet* Cᵃ). οι δυο μαθηται αυτου. 38. — δε (*habet* A *vel* B). — αυτοισ (*habet* Cᵃ). 39. [ειπον]. ραββει (*sic* v. 50). (Cᵃ μεθερμηνευομενον). 40. [ϊδετε]. + ουν (*post* ηλθον). ϊδον√. μαινει√. εμιναν√. — δε. 41. [ην ανδ.]. — των *secund.* (*habet* Cᵃ). 42. (Cᵃ πρωτον). εστιν√. — ο (*ante* $\overline{χσ}$). 43.

init.—και.—δε. ειπεν√. ϊωαννου (*pro* ιωνα). 44. —ο $\overline{ισ}$. εξελθιν√. + $\overline{ισ}$ (*ante* ακολουθι√: ο $\overline{ισ}$ Cª). 45. — δε ο (*habet* Cª). βηθσαϊδαν (-δα Cª).—εκ (*habet* Cª, *sed rursus erasum*). 46. εγραψεν√. [μωσησ].—τον *secund.* [ναζαρετ: *sic* v. 47]. 47. *init.*—και. ναθαναηλ'√. αγαθον τι (Cª *cum* Steph.). [αυτω φιλ.]. 48. ϊδων (*pro* ειδεν: Cª ϊδεν√). [ο $\overline{ισ}$].—και (*habet* Cª). του ναθαναηλ (*pro* αυτου: Cª *cum* Steph.). ϊσδραηλειτησ. εστιν√. 49. [ο $\overline{ισ}$]. ϊδον√. 50. [-θη ναθαν.]. και ειπεν (*pro* και λεγει αυτω). [ει ο βασ.]. 51. + οτι (*ante* ειδον). μειζονα. οψη. 52. —απαρτι. οψεσθαι√. ηνεωγοτα (Cª ανεωγ.).

II. 1. [τη ημ. τη τρ.]. κανα (*sic* v. 11). 3. *Habet p.m. initio versûs* και οινον ουχ ειχον οτι συνετελεσθη ο οινοσ του γαμου ειτα λεγει κ.τ.λ.: *at* A, *sublato* οινον ουχ ειχον οτι συνετ, *reponit* υστερησαντοσ οινου: Cª *uncis inclusa* ελεσθη *usque ad* ειτα *etiam punctis improbat. fin.* οινοσ ουκ εστιν (Cª οινον ουκ εχουσιν√). 4. (+ και *ante* λεγει Cª, *sed* και *erasum*). 5. οτι ο (*pro* ο τι). 6. λιθιναι ϋδριαι.—κειμεναι (*habet* κιμεναι Cª *post* ϊουδαιων). 7. *init.* + και. 8. οι δε (*pro* και *tert.*). 9. αρχιτλικινοσ (Cª αρχιτρικλ.)√, *non* vv. 8. 10. 10. —αυτω. τιθησιν√. μεθυσθωσιν√. —τοτε (*habet* Cª). + δε (*post* συ). 11. εποιησεν την. σημιων√. + πρωτην (*post* γαλιλαιασ: *improbant* A *vel* B *et* C). εφανερωσεν√. —αυτου (*habet* Cª). οι μαθηται αυτου εισ αυτον (Cª *cum* Steph.). 12. καφαρναουμ. [αυτου *secund.*].—και οι μαθηται αυτου. εμιναν. 13. εγγυσ δε (—και). ϊσ (*pro* εισ)√. 14. και τα προβατα και βοασ (Cª *cum* Steph.). 15. εποιησεν (*pro* και ποιησασ: Cª *cum* Steph.). + και (*ante* παντασ: *delet* Cª).—τε (και *pro* τε Cª, *sed rursus ab ipso* [?] *erasum*). [κολλ]. εξεχεεν το κερμα. *fin.* κατεστρεψεν. 16. [-θεν μη]. ποιειται√. 17. —δε. καταφαγεται. 18. [ειπον: *sic* v. 20]. σημιον δικνυεισ√. 19. [ο]. [εν]. 20. τεσσερακοντα. οικοδομηθη√. —εν. 21. ελεγεν√. —αυτου (*habet* Cª). 22. —αυτοισ. ον (*pro* ω). 23. + τοισ (*ante* ϊεροσολυμοισ). [εν *tert.*]. σημια√. 24. [ο]. αυτον (*pro* εαυτον: Cª *cum* Steph.). —αυτον. γινωσκιν√. 25. χριαν ουκ. [του]. εγινωσκεν√. .τι ην εν *bis scriptum: prius notat. per* C *et ante eum.*

III. 1. —αυτω (*habet* B). 2. νυκτοσ προσ αυτον (—τον $\overline{ιν}$). ραββει. και ουδισ δυναται ταυτα τα σημια. 3. [ο $\overline{ισ}$: *sic* v. 10]. —και ειπεν αυτω (*habet* Cª). 4. [ο]. γερων ων γεννηθηναι. εισελθιν√. 5. —ο. (+ και ειπεν *post* $\overline{ισ}$ Cª, *sed erasum*). εξ υδατοσ και $\overline{πνσ}$ γεννηθη. ειδειν (*pro* εισελθειν εισ: Cª εισελθιν). βασιλιαν√.

fin. των ουρανων (*pro* του $\overline{θυ}$: C[a] *cum* Steph.). 6. [-νν- *bis in vers.*]. εστιν *bis in vers.* (*sic* v. 8)√. 7. δι√. 8. πνι√. [αλλ: *sic* v. 16]. [και που]. + του ϋδατοσ και (*post* εκ). 10. γινωσκισ√. 11. λαμβανεται√. 12. επιγια√. πιστευεται√. *fin.* πιστευσεται√. 13. — ο ων εν τω ουρανω. 14. μωϋσησ. ϋψωσεν√. ȯ ϋψωθηναι δι (˙ *p.m.*). 15. [εισ αυτον]. — μη αποληται αλλ. 16. ουτωσ√. — αυτου (*habet* C[a]). — εδωκεν (*habet* A). 17. απεστιλεν√. — αυτου *prim.* 18. — δε. 19. οι ανθρωποι ηγαπησαν το σκοτοσ μαλλον. αυτων πονηρα. 20. μεισει√. — και ουκ ερχεται προσ το φωσ (ὁμοιοτ.: *habet* C[a]). 21. — ο δε ποιων *usque ad* αυτου τα εργα (ὁμοιοτ.: *legebat enim forsan exemplar* τα εργα αυτου: *habet* C[a], *legens* αληθιαν ερχεται [ι *abscisso*] *et* τα εργα αυτου). [εν $\overline{θω}$]. ειργασμενον (A C[a] -να). 22. εισ την ϊουδαιαν γην και οι μαθηται αυτου κακει. διετριβεν√. 23. [νν: *sic* vv. 24. 25. 26. 27. iv. 1]. ενγυσ. [σαλειμ]. παρεγεινοντο√. 24. — ο. 25. δε συνζητησισ (*pro* ουν ζητησισ: C[a] *cum* Steph.). [ϊουδαιων, *at* -αιου C[a]]. 26. [ηλθον]. [ειπον]. ραββει. ωσ̇ (*pro* ω, σ *eras.*). βαπτιζι√. 27. λαβιν. 28. ϋμισ. — μοι. μαρτυριται√. [ουκ ειμι εγω]. 29. εστηκωσ αυτου και ακουων χαρα. 30. αυξανιν√. 31. + δε (*ante* ων: *improbat* C[a]). επι (*pro* εκ *prim.*: C[a] *cum* Steph.). εστιν (*post* γησ *secund.*)√. — επανω παντων εστι (*habet* C[a], *at* εστιν√). 32. — και *prim.* ον (*pro* ο: B *cum* Steph.). [εωρακε: -εν√ C[a]]. [ηκουσε: -εν√ C[a]]. — τουτο. ουδισ√. 34. απεστιλεν√. διδωσι (— ο $\overline{θσ}$). 36. — δε (*habet* C[a]). απιθων√. (εχει ζωην A[a] *pro* οψεται ζωην, *quod habet p.m. et* C[a]). επ αυτον μενει.

IV. 1. $\overline{ισ}$ (*pro* $\overline{κσ}$). [η ιωαννησ]. 3. αφηκεν√. απηλθεν παλιν. 4. σαμαριασ (*sic* v. 7). 5. — ερχεται ουν εισ πολιν τησ σαμαρειασ (ὁμοιοτ.: *habet* A, *at* σαμαριασ√). [συχαρ]. [ο]. + τω (*ante* ϊωσηφ). 6. ωσ (*pro* ωσει: C[a] *cum* Steph., *sed* ωσ *restitut.*). 7. + τισ (*ante* γυνη). πιν (C[a] πιειν): *sic* vv. 9. 10. 8. απεληλυθισαν√. αγορασωσιν√. 9. — ουν (*habet* C[a]). σαμαριτισ. αιτισ√. γυναικοσ σαμαριτιδοσ ουσησ. — ου γαρ συγχ. *ad fin. vers.* (*habet* A, *at* συνχρωνται). 10. ηδισ√. 11. εκεινη (*pro* η γυνη: C[a] *cum* Steph.). εστιν (*sic* vv. 18. 35)√. — ουν. 12. μειζον (C[a] -ζων). οστισ (*pro* οσ). αυτοσ και (C[a] και αυτοσ *cum* Steph.). επιεν√. 13. — ο *prim.* 14. ο δε πινων (*pro* οσ δ αν πιη: C[a] *cum* Steph., *sed* πινη C[a]). διψησει. + εγω (*ante* δωσω *secund.*). — αυτω *secund.* 15. δειψω√. διερχωμαι ωδε (*pro* ερχωμαι ενθαδε: C[a] *cum* Steph., *at legit* ερχομαι√). 16. — ο (*habet* C[a]). + κα̇λ̇ (*post* $\overline{ισ}$: *notant p.m. et* C).

[τον ανδ. σου]. 17. — και ειπεν (*habet* Cᵃ). ανδρα ουκ εχω. ειπεσ. *fin.* εχισ. 18. εχισ√. αληθωσ. 19. — κε (*habet* Cᵃ). 20. τω ορι τουτω. λεγεται√. — ο τοποσ. προσκυνιν δει. 21. πιστευε μοι γυναι. προσκυνησεται√. 22. ὑμισ√. ημισ√. 23. αλλα. προσκυνησουσιν√. ζητι√. *fin.* αυτω (Cᵃ *cum* Steph. αυτον). 24. — αυτον (*habet* Cᵃ). αληθειασ (*pro* και αληθεια: Cᵃ *cum* Steph.). προσκυνιν δει (Cᵃ δει πρ.). 25. (οιδαμεν Cᵃ). αναγγελλει (αναγγελει Cᵃ *cum* Steph.). απαντα. 27. εν (*pro* επι: Cᵃ *cum* Steph.). επηλθαν (Cᵃ ηλθον). εθαυμαζον. + αυτω (*post* ειπεν). ζητισ√. 29. [ειπε, *at* -εν√ Cᵃ: *sic* v. 39]. α (*pro* οσα) *sic* v. 39. 30. *init.* [*deest* και]. [ουν]. 31. — δε. ραββει. 32. φαγιν√. ὑμισ√. 33. λεγουσιν (*pro* ελεγον ουν: Cᵃ *cum* Steph.). 34. [ποιω]. τελιωσω√. 35. υμισ λεγεται√. τετραμηνοσ. εισιν√. 36. — και *prim.* συναγι√. και ο σπιρων. 37. [ο *secund.*]. σπιρων√. 38. απεσταλκα. κεκοπιακασιν√. 39. εκινησ√. — εισ αυτον (*habet* Cᵃ). σαμαριτων. α (*pro* οσα). 40. σαμαριται. *fin.* εμινεν παρ αυτοισ (— εκει) ημερασ δυο. 42. και ελεγον τη γυναικι (— τε: Cᵃ *cum* Steph.). [οτι *prim.*]. μαρτυριαν (*pro* λαλιαν: Cᵃ *cum* Steph.). + παρ αυτου (*post* ακηκοαμεν). αληθωσ ουτοσ εστιν. — ο χσ. 43. — και απηλθεν. 44. — ο. 45. ωσ (*pro* οτε: Cᵃ *cum* Steph.). — εδεξαντο αυτον οι γαλιλαιοι παντα (*habet* Cᵃ). + οι (*ante* εωρακοτεσ: *improbat* Cᵃ). + παντα (*ante* α: Cᵃ οσα, *omissis* παντα α). εληλυθισαν (*pro* ηλθον). 46. ηλθαν. — ο ισ. καναν (Cᵃ κανα). εποιησαν (Cᵃ -σεν√). ην δε (— και). ησθενι√. καφαρναουμ. 47. — ουτοσ (*habet* Cᵃ). ο ισ ηκι. ηλθεν ουν (*pro* απηλθε: Cᵃ -θεν√). — αυτον *secund.* [ημελλε, *at* Cᵃ -εν√]. 48. σημια√. πιστευσηται√. 49. αποθανιν√. τον παιδα (*pro* το παιδιον). 50. — και *prim.* του ιυ (*pro* ω ειπεν αυτω ισ: Cᵃ *legit* του ιυ ον ειπεν αυτω). 51. — αυτου *secund.* ὑπηντησαν. και ηγγειλαν (— λεγοντεσ). αυτου (*pro* σου). 52. την ωραν παρ αυτων. εσχεν√. [και ειπον]. εχθεσ. 53. — εν *prim.* (*habet* Cᵃ). — ο ισ (*habet* Cᵃ). — οτι *secund.* 54. [τουτο παλιν]. εποιησεν σημιον.

V. 1. + η (*ante* εορτη). — ο. 2. *init.* εντιν (Cᵃ εστιν√). — επι τη (*at* Cᵃ εν τη). το λεγομενον (*pro* η επιλεγομενη: Cᵃ *cum* Steph.). βηθζαθα. 3. — πολυ. — εκδεχομενων *usque ad fin.* v. 4. 5. — εκει. τριακοντα και οκτω. ασθενια√. *fin.* + αυτου. 6. ανακειμενον (Cᵃ *cum* Steph.). — ηδη. θελισ√. 7. βαλη. καταβαινι√. 8. εγειρε αρον. κραβακτον (cf. v. 9). 9. — και ευθεωσ (*habent* Cᵃ Cᵇ). + και ηγερθη (*post* ανθρωποσ). [ηρε]. κραβακτον (Cᵃ κραβαττον) *sic*

vv. 10. 11. εκινη√. 10. + και (*post* εστιν). εξεστιν√. *fin.* + σου. 11. *init.* + ο δε. απεκρινατο (Cª *cum* Steph.). υγιην (ν *eras. per* Cª). αραι (Cª *cum* Steph.).— σου (*habet* Cª). περιπατειν (Cª *cum* Steph.). 12. — ουν. αραι και περιπατιν (— τον κραβ. σου: Cª *legit* αρον *et forsan* περιπατι). 13. [ιαθεισ]. ενευσεν (Cª *cum* Steph.). μεσω (*pro* τοπω: Cª *cum* Steph.). 14. ο ισ̅ τον τεθεραπευμενον (— αυτον: Cª *cum* Steph.). λεγει (*pro* ειπεν). [τι σοι]. 15. *init.* απηλθεν (+ ουν Cª). ειπεν (*pro* ανηγγειλε). 16. οι ϊουδαιοι τον ιν̅. — και εζητουν αυτον αποκτειναι. 17. — ισ̅. απεκρινετο. εργαζετε√. 18. — ουν. αποκτιναι√. [ελυε]. [ελεγε]. 19. *init.* ελεγεν ουν αυτοισ ο ισ̅ (*pro* απεκρινατο ουν ο ισ̅ και ειπεν αυτοισ: Cª *cum* Steph., *praeter* ελεγεν *pro* ειπεν). αμην *semel tantum* (*bis* Cª *cum* Steph.). [αν εκεινοσ ποιη]. *fin.* ποιει ομοιωσ. 20. φιλι√. δικνυσιν√. μιζονα√. εργα δειξει αυτω. θαυμαζετε. 21. ωσ (*pro* ωσπερ). ουτωσ√. 22. δεδωκεν√. 23. [τιμωσι *bis in versu*]. τειμα√. 25. — και νυν εστιν (*habet* Cª). ακουσωσι. — οι *secund.* (*habet* Cª). ζησουσιν. 26. ωσ (*pro* ωσπερ: Cª *cum* Steph.). ζωην εχει. — ουτωσ εδωκε *ad fin. vers.* (ὁμοιοτ.: *habet* Cª, *legens* ουτωσ και τω ϋϊω εδωκεν ζωην εδωκεν εχιν εχιν εν εαυτω, *at* εδωκεν εχιν *eraso*). 27. *init.* και κρισιν εδωκεν αυτω εξουσιαν ποιειν (Cª *cum* Steph.: *omisso* και *secund.*). εστιν√. 28. θαυμαζεται√. μνημιοισ√. ακουσωσιν√. 29. [δε]. 30. ποιειν εγω. — και (*habent* A C, *vix p.m.*). — πατροσ. 32. οιδαται (Cª οιδα *cum* Steph.). μαρτυρι√. 33. [ϊωαννην: *sic* v. 36]. [μεμαρτύρηκε]. αληθια√. 35. ϋμισ√. — δε (*habet* Cª). ηθελησαται√. αγαλλιαθηναι. 36. — την. [μειζω]. δεδωκεν. τελιωσω√. — εγω *secund.* μαρτυρι√. εμε απεσταλκεν. 37. εκεινοσ (*pro* αυτοσ). μεμαρτυρηκεν√. πωποτε ακηκοατε. *Videtur esse* ειδοε *in facsimili, at* ειδοσ *editt. mai. et minor.* 38. εν υμιν μενοντα. απεστιλεν εκινοσ√. ϋμισ√. 39. εραυνατε. δοκειται√. εχιν√. 42. [αλλ]. ουκ εχετε την αγαπην του θυ̅ ουκ εχετε (ουκ εχετε *prius improbat* Cª). 43. — εν *secund.* λημψεσθαι√. 44. δυνασθαι√. ϋμισ√. [θυ̅]. ζητουντεσ (Cª ζητιτε). 45. δοκειται√. μωῡσησ. 46. μωσει. γεγραφεν (Cª *cum* Steph.). 47. πιστευεται√. ρημασιν√. *fin.* πιστευσετε. *Facsim., et textus editionum mai. et min., at in utriusque editionis annotationibus* "πιστευετε: Cª -εται. Sic."

VI. 2. ηκουλουθει δε (— και). πολυσ οχλοσ. [εωρων]. — αυτου. περι (*pro* επι). 3. και απηλθεν (Cª ανηλθεν δε). — ο (*habet* Cª). — εκει (Cª εκι). εκαθεζετο. 5. τουσ οφθαλμουσ ισ̅ (— ο: *habet* ο C^a). οχλοσ πολυσ.—τον. αγορασωμεν. ουτοι φαγωσιν. 6. γαρ (*pro* δε: C^a *cum* Steph.). ελεγεν (*sic* v. 71)√. πιραζων√. δε (*pro* γαρ: C^a *cum* Steph.). [εμελλε: -εν√ C^a]. 7. αποκριυεται ουν (—αυτω: C^a απεκριθη αυτω, *sine* ουν: C^b? *etiam videtur revocare* ουν). + ο (*ante* φιλιπποσ).—αυτοισ.—αυτων. [τι]. 9. εστιν√. —εν. [ο]. 10. ειπεν.—δε. αναπεσιν√. τοποσ (*pro* χορτοσ: C^a *cum* Steph.)√. ανεπεσαν. ωσ (*pro* ωσει). τρισχιλιοι (*pro* πεντακισχ.: C^a *cum* Steph.). 11. ελαβεν√. (ουν *pro* δε C^a). ευχαριστησεν και εδωκεν.—τοισ μαθηταισ οι δε μαθηται (*habet* C^b). ανακιμενοισ√. 12. λεγι√. συναγαγεται√. 13. επερισσευσεν√. 14. ο εποιησεν σημειον.—ο ισ.—οτι. εισ τον κοσμον ερχομενοσ. 15. και αναδικνυναι (*pro* ινα ποιησωσιν αυτον: C^a *cum* Steph. αυτον *omisso*). φευγει (*pro* ανεχωρησε: C^a ανεχωρησεν√). μονοσ αυτοσ. 17. —το. ερχονται. καφαρναουμ (*sic* vv. 24. 59). κατελαβεν δε αυτουσ η σκοτια (*pro* και σκοτια ηδη εγεγονει). ουπω (*pro* ουκ). ισ προσ αυτουσ (—ο]. [διηγειρετο]. 19. [ωσ]. σταδια (A *vel* B, *etiam* C, *cum* Steph.). θεωρουσιν√. 20. και (*pro* ο δε). φοβισθαι√. 21. ηλθον (*pro* ηθελον). λαβιν√. [το πλοιον εγενετο]. την γην (C^a *cum* Steph.). *fin.* ϋπηντησεν (ϋπηγον C^a *cum* Steph.). 22. εστωσ. ειδεν (*pro* ιδων). ενκεινο (*pro* εν εκεινο: · *p.m.*, C^a *verò restituit* ν: *improbant* C^a C^b κεινο εισ ο ενεβ. οι μ. του ιυ). του ιυ (*pro* αυτου *prim.*). συνεληλυθι αυτοισ (*pro* συνεισηλθε τοισ μαθηταισ αυτου: C^a *cum* Steph., *legens* -θεν√). πλοιαν (*pro* πλοιαριον: ° C *et jam ante eum*).—απηλθον (*habet* B). 23. επελθοντων ουν των πλοιων (*pro* αλλα δε ηλθε πλοιαρια). ουσησ (*pro* του τοπου: C^a *cum* Steph.). + και (*post* οπου: *improbat* C^a).—τον. 24. και ϊδοντεσ (*pro* οτε ουν ειδεν ο οχλοσ: C^a *cum* Steph., *at* ϊδεν√). ουκ ην εκει ο ισ (C^a *cum* Steph.).—αυτου (*habet* C^a). ανεβησαν (C^a *cum* Steph.).—και αυτοι (C^a *habet* αυτοι). το πλοιον (C^a τα πλοιαρια). 25. ραββει. ηλθεσ (*pro* γεγονασ). 26. —ο.—ζητειτε με (C^a ζητιται με√). σημια√. 27. εργαζεσθαι βρωσιν μη (—την *prim.*). —την βρωσιν *secund.* διδωσιν ϋμιν (*pro* υμ. δωσει).—εσφραγισεν (*supplet* A)√. 28. ποιωμεν. ιν (C^a ινα). 29. —ο. εστιν (*sic* vv. 31. 40. 63 *bis*)√. πιστευηται√. απεστιλεν√. 30. —ουν. σημιον συ. ειδωμεν. 31. —αρτον (*habet* C^a). δεδωκεν. 32. μωϋσησ. [δεδωκεν]. 33. + ο (*post* αρτοσ). [ζω. διδ.]. 34. παντοτε κε. 35. ειπεν ουν (—δε). εμε (*pro* με). πινασῃ√. διψησει. 36. —με. πιστευεται√. 37. διδωσιν√. εμε (*pro* με).—εξω (*habet* C^a). 38. ου καταβεβηκα εκ του ουρανου ϊνα ποιησω (C^a, ου *deleto*, *habet* ουχ' ἵνα π.). 39. —τουτο δε εστι *usque ad* πεμψαντοσ με (ὁμοιοτ.: πατροσ *omisso, ut conjicere licet: habet* Cᵃ, *legens* εστιν√ *sine* πατροσ, *sed omnia rursus erasa*). δεδωκεν√. [εν]. 40. γαρ (*pro* δε). πατροσ μου (*pro* πεμψαντοσ με). + εν (*post* εγω). 42. [ουχ]. ἰωσηφ'√. ημισ√. + και (*post* οιδαμεν: *improbat* Cᵃ). — και την μητερα (ὁμοιοτ.: *habet* Cᵃ). ουν ουτοσ λεγει. εγω (*pro* οτι). 43. [ουν]. — ο. αυτοισ και ειπεν. γογγυζεται√. [μετ]. 44. ουδισ (*sic* v. 65)√. ελθιν√. [με *prim.*]. καγω. [αυτον τη: *sic* v. 54]. 45. [εστι]. — του *prim.* — ουν. [ακουσασ]. εμε (*pro* με). 46. εωρακεν τισ. πατροσ (*pro* $\overline{θυ}$). εωρακεν *secund.*√. *fin.* $\overline{θν}$ (Cᵃ *cum* Steph. $\overline{πρα}$). 47. + οτι (*post* ὑμιν). — εισ εμε. 49. [το μ. εν τη ερ.]. 51. του εμου (*pro* τουτου του). ζησει. — και (*post* αιωνα: *habet* Cᵃ). — δε. ὑπερ τησ του κοσμου ζωησ η σαρξ μου εστιν (— ην εγω δωσω). 52. [προσ αλλ. οι ἰου.]. + ουν (*ante* δυναται). ημιν ουτοσ. σαρκα φαγιν. 53. αν (*pro* εαν). φαγηται√. το αιμα αυτου. + αιωνιον (*post* ζωην). 54. καγω. 55. — αληθωσ εστι βρωσισ και το αιμα μου (ὁμοιοτ.: *supplet* Cᵃ, *at legit* αληθησ εστιν βρ.). *fin.* αληθωσ εστι ποτον (Cᵃ αληθησ, *sed* -θωσ *postea revocatur:* Cᵃ *etiam* ποσισ *pro* ποτον). 57. απεστιλεν√. ζησει (*sic* v. 58). 58. — ουτοσ (*habet* Cᵃ). [εκ του]. καταβαινων (Cᵃ *cum* Steph.). οι πατερεσ εφαγον. — υμων το μαννα. 60. ο λογοσ ουτοσ. 61. *init.* εγνω ουν $\overline{ισ}$ (Cᵃ ἰδωσ δε ο $\overline{ισ}$). γογγυζουσιν√. + και (*ante* ειπεν: *improbat* Cᵃ). σκανδαλιζι√. 62. — ουν (*habet* Cᵃ). θεωρηται√. αναβενοντα τον $\overline{υν}$ του ανθρωπου. 63. — το (*habet* Cᵃ). λελαληκα. *fin.* — εστιν. 64. [αλλ] εξ υμων εισιν. απ (*pro* εξ *secund.*). σωτηρ (*pro* $\overline{ισ}$). — μη. — τισ (*habet* Cᵃ). ην ο μελλων αυτον παραδιδοναι (*pro* εστιν ο παραδωσων αυτον). 65. ελεγεν√. εμε (*pro* με). — αυτω (*habet* Cᵃ). *fin.* — μου. 66. + ουν (*ante* πολλοι). των μαθητων απηλθον (— αυτου). 67. ὑμισ θελεται√. 68. — ουν. 69. ημισ√. ο αγιοσ (*pro* ο $\overline{χσ}$ ο $\overline{υσ}$). — του ζωντοσ. 70. $\overline{ισ}$ και ειπεν αυτοισ (*pro* αυτοισ ο $\overline{ισ}$). ουχι (*pro* ουκ). εξελεξαμην δωδεκα (— τουσ: *habet* Cᵃ). — εισ (*habet* Cᵃ *ante* εξ). 71. — τον (*habet* Cᵃ). απο καρυωτου (*pro* ισκαριωτην: Cᵃ ἰσκαριωτου). + και (*post* γαρ). εμελλον (Cᵃ -λεν). [αυτον παραδιδοναι]. [ων].

VII. 1. *init.* — και (*habet* Cᵃ *sed eras.*). μετα ταυτα περιεπατει ο $\overline{ισ}$. αποκτιναι√. 3. οι αδελφοι αυτου προσ αυτον. θεωρουσιν (Cᵃ -ρησουσιν). — σου *secund.* (*habet* Cᵃ). 4. ουδισ√. τι εν κρυπτω. ποιων ζητι (— και). [αυτοσ]. 6. — ουν (*habet* Cᵃ). — ο *prim.* (*habet* Cᵃ). ου (*pro* ουπω; Cᵃ *cum* Steph.). 7. ο κοσμοσ ου δυναται (Cᵃ *cum* Steph.). — εγω. — περι αυτου. 8. αναβηται√. [ταυτην *prim.: puncta imposita, et rursus erasa*]. ουκ (*pro* ουπω *prim.*). εμοσ καιροσ (— ο *bis:* Cª ο εμ. κ.). 9. — δε. αυτοσ (*pro* αυτοισ). εμινεν√. 10. εισ την εορτην τοτε και αυτοσ ανεβη. [αλλ]. — ωσ *secund.* 11. εκινοσ√. 12. πολυσ ην περι αυτου. τω οχλω.— δε. 13. ουδισ (*sic* vv. 19. 27. 44)√. περι αυτου ελαλει. 14. ερτησ (ο *p.m.*)√. — ο. εδιδασκεν√. 15. εθαυμαζον ουν (— και). οιδεν√. 16. + ουν (*post* απεκριθη). — ο. 17. — του. 18. ζητι (*sic* v. 20)√. και ο (*pro* ο δε). εστιν√ *bis in versu.* 19. μωϋσησ. [δεδωκεν]. ζητειται√. αποκτιναι (*sic* vv. 20. 25)√. 20. — και ειπε. 21. — ο. 22. — δια τουτο (*habet* Cª). + ο (*ante* μωϋσησ). [μωσεωσ]. + οτι (*post* αλλ). [εν]. 23. λαμβανι√. + ο (*ante* μωϋσεωσ). χολαται√. 24. [κρινατε]. 25. — εκ. ϊεροσολυμειτων. ουκ (*pro* ουχ). 26. λαλι√. λεγουσιν√. μητι (*pro* μηποτε). αρχιερεισ (*pro* αρχοντεσ). — αληθωσ *secund.* 27. *Pro* ο δε $\overline{\chi\sigma}$ *habet e* v. 31 ο $\overline{\chi\sigma}$ οταν ελθη μη πλιονα σημια ποιησει η (*haec verba post* $\overline{\chi\sigma}$ *improbant* Cª Cᵇ: ο δε $\overline{\chi\sigma}$ οταν ερχεται Cª *primò, sed revocavit*)√: *post* η *sequuntur p.m.* οταν ερχεται ουδισ γινωσκει αυτον ποθεν εστιν. 28. ο $\overline{\iota\sigma}$ εν τω ϊερω διδασκων. και εμε. αλλα. αληθησ. *fin.* οιδαται√. 29. [δε]. αυτω (Cª *cum* Steph.). απεσταλκεν. 30. οι δε εζητουν (— ουν). [επεβαλεν]. 31. πολλοι δε επιστευσαν εκ του οχλου. — οτι. μη (*pro* μητι). πλιονα√. [σημεια: cf. v. 27]. — τουτων. [*non* η, *ut in* v. 27]. *fin.* ποιει (Cª *cum* Steph.). 32. + δε (*post* ηκουσαν). ταυτα περι αυτου. απεστιλαν√. τουσ ϋπηρετασ οι αρχιερεισ και οι φαρισαιοι. 33. — αυτοισ. χρονον μικρον. 34. [-σετε και: *sic* v. 36]. ϋμισ (*sic* v. 36)√. δυνασθαι·ελθιν (*sic* v. 36)√. 35. — προσ εαυτουσ (*habet* Cª). [ουτ. μελλ.]. πορευεσθε√ *bis in versu.* — ημεισ. διδασκιν√. 36. τι (*pro* τισ). [ουτοσ ο λογ.]. [ειπε: -πεν√ Cª]. 37. ϊστηκει√. εκραζεν. — προσ με (*habet* Cª). 39. ελεγεν (*pro* ειπε). ημελλον. λαμβανιν√. [πιστευοντεσ]. $\overline{\pi\nu\alpha}$ οτι (— αγιον, *nec habet* δεδομενον). — ο. *fin.* ουπω (*pro* ουδεπω) δεδοξαστο (Cª *cum* Steph.). 40. εκ του οχλου ουν (— πολλοι). αυτου των λογων τουτων (αυτου *improbat* Cª). αληθωσ ουτοσ εστιν. 41. [αλλοι ελ.]. [αλλοι *secund.*]. — δε. 42. [ουχι]. $\overline{\delta\alpha\delta}$ *prim.*√. + ο (*ante* $\overline{\delta\alpha\delta}$ *secund.*). [ο $\overline{\chi\sigma}$ ερχ.]. 43. εγενετο εν τω οχλω. 44. ελεγον (*pro* ηθελον: Cª *cum* Steph.). επεβαλεν αυτω (επ. επ αυτον Cª *cum* Steph.). χιρασ√. 45. λεγουσιν (*pro* ειπον). 46. οι δε ϋπηρεται απεκριθησαν. ουτωσ ανθρωποσ ελαλησεν ωσ ουτοσ λαλει ο ανθρωποσ (Cª *tantum* ελαλησεν ουτωσ ανθρωποσ).

47. —ουν. [αυτοισ]. ὑμισ πεπλανησθαι√. 48. πιστευει (Cª *cum* Steph.). 49. [αλλ]. επαρατοι εισιν. 50. ειπεν δε (*pro* λεγει). —ο ελθων νυκτοσ προσ αυτον (Cª *habet* ο ελθων προσ αυτον προτερον, *sine* νυκτοσ). 51. κρινι√.—παρ αυτου (*habet* Cª *post* πρ.). πρωτον (*pro* προτερον). 52. [ειπον]. εραυνησον. [προφ. εκ τησ γαλ.]. *fin.* εγειρεται. *Post* v. 52, *in eâdem lineâ legitur* παλιν viii. 12, *pericopâ de adulterâ* (vii. 53—viii. 11) *prorsus omissâ.*

VIII. 12. αυτοισ ελαλησεν ο ισ̅. φωσ ειμι (—το: Cª *cum* Steph.). [εμοι]. περιπατηση. εχει (εξει Cª *cum* Steph.). 13. μαρτυρισ√. 14. ειπεν αυτοισ ο ισ̅ (—απεκριθη *et* και). [αλ. εστ. η μαρ. μου]. ὑμισ√.—δε. οιδαται (*sic* v. 19)√. [και που *secund.*]. 16. καν (*pro* και εαν). [αληθησ].—πατηρ (*habet* Cª). 17. γεγραμμενον εστιν (*pro* γεγραπται). 19. +και ειπεν (*post* ο ισ̅). ηδειται√ *bis in vers.*—μου *secund.* [ηδ. αν]. 20. —ο ισ̅.—διδασκων εν τω ιερω (ὁμοιοτ.). ουδισ√. 21. ελεγεν (*pro* ειπεν). —παλιν.—ο ισ̅. (Cª ζητησεται)√. αποθανισθαι (*sic* v. 24 *bis*)√. ὑμισ (*sic* v. 22)√. δυνασθαι ελθιν (*sic* v. 22)√. 22. +αν (*post* οπου: *improbat* Cª). 23. ελεγεν ουν (*pro* και ειπεν: Cª και ελεγεν, *sed prior lectio restituitur*). [του κοσμ. τουτου *bis in versu*]. 24. —ουν. +μοι (*post* πιστευσηται√). 25. —ουν. ειπεν ουν (—και). [ο]. +εν (*ante* λαλω: ·· *p.m.*). 26. λαλιν√. κρινιν√. +πατηρ (*ante* αληθησ). εστιν√. αυτω (αυτου Cª *cum* Steph.). λαλω (*pro* λεγω). 27. *fin.* +τον θν̅ (*improbat* Cª). 28. [αυτοισ]. +παλιν (*post* ισ̅). γνωσεσθαι√. εδιδαξεν√.—μου. ουτωσ (*pro* ταυτα). 29. ουκ αφηκε με μονον μετ εμου εστιν (Cª *cum* Steph., *sed* αφηκεν√).—ο πατηρ. 31.—ο (*habet* Cª). ὑμισ μινητε√.—μου (*habet* Cª). 32. γνωσεσθαι√. αληθια√. 33. προσ αυτον (*pro* αυτω). 34. [ο *prim.*]. εστιν√. 35. —ο υσ̅ μενει εισ τον αιωνα (ὁμοιοτ.). 36. ελευθερωθη (Cª -ρωση). εσεσθαι (τ *ex errore, erasum*)√. 37. αποκτιναι (*sic* v. 40)√. 38. α εγω (*pro* εγω ο). [μου]. ὑμισ√. α εωρακατε (*pro* ο εωρ.: Cª ο ηκουσαται). *fin.* παρα του πατροσ ὑμων ποιειται. 39. ειπαν (*sic* vv. 41. 48. 52. 57). εστιν απεκριθη (*pro* εστι λεγει). [ο ισ̅: *sic* vv. 42. 58]. εστε (*pro* ητε). *fin.* εποιειται√ (—αν: Cª *habet* αν). 40. ζητιτε√. αληθιαν√. 41. ποιειται√. τα^{22}: *sic* Tischend., *at deest annotatio.* —ουν. ημισ√. πορνιασ√. ουκ εγεννημεθα (Cª *cum* Steph.). 42. [ουν]. [θσ̅ πατηρ]. ημων (*pro* υμων). απεστιλεν√. 43. γινωσκεται√. 44. +του (*post* εκ *prim.*). εσται√. εκινοσ√. αληθια *bis in versu*√. ουκ (*pro* ουχ). εστιν (*sic* v. 54)√. 45. αληθιαν (*sic* v. 46)√. [λεγω ου]. 46. —δε. πιστευεται√. 48. —ουν. σαμαριτησ.—συ (*habet* Cª). 49. +και ειπεν (*post* ισ̅). ϋμισ√. 51. τον εμον λογον τηρησει. θεωρησει. 52. απεθανεν (*sic* v. 53)√. γευσηται.—θανατου (*habet* Cª). 53. μιζων√.—συ *secund.* 54. +ο (*ante* ισ̅). δοξασω (Cª -ζω, *sed* -σω *restitutum*). λεγεται√. [ϋμων]. 55. εγνωκαται√. καν (*pro* και εαν). [ομοιοσ ϋμων]. [αλλ]. 56. ειδη. ειδεν√. 57. εωρακεν σε (*pro* εωρακασ: Cª *cum* Steph.). 59. —διελθων *ad fin. vers.* (*habet* Cª και διελθων δια μεσου αυτων επορευετο και παρηγεν ουτωσ: Cᵇ *delet* επορ. και παρ. ουτ.).

IX. 1. [ειδεν]. 2. ραββει. γονισ (*sic* vv. 3. 18. 20. 22. 23)√. 3. —ο. 4. ημασ (*pro* εμε: A *vel* B *cum* Steph.). ημασ (*pro* με: A *vel* B *cum* Steph.). ουδισ√. 6. επτυσεν√. εποιησεν (*sic* v. 11)√. +αυτου (*post* επεχρισεν).—του τυφλου. 7. [νιψαι]. ηλθεν√. 8. προσαιτησ (*pro* τυφλοσ). 9. —οτι *prim. et secund.* [αλλοι δε *secund.*]. +ουχι αλλα (*ante* ομοιοσ). +δε (*post* εκεινοσ: δε *et* οτι *tert. punctis notata rursus deletis*). 10. ελεγαν (Cª ελεγον): *sic* v. 16 *prim.* +'οι ϊουδαιο' (*post* ουν *prim.*: ' ' *p.m.*)√. +ουν (*post* πωσ). ηνεωχθησαν. [σου]. 11. —και ειπεν (*post* εκεινοσ). +ο (*ante* ανθρωποσ). +ο (*ante* λεγομενοσ). επεχρισεν√. ειπεν√. +οτι (*ante* ϋπαγε).—την κολυμβηθραν του. +τον (*ante* σιλωαμ). απελθων ουν και (—δε). 12. και ειπαν (—ουν). 14. εν η ημερα (*pro* οτε). 15. μου επι τουσ οφθαλμουσ. 16. ουκ εστιν ουτοσ παρα θυ̅ ο ανθρωποσ. τηρι√. +δε (*post* αλλοι). σημια√. 17. +ουν (*post* λεγουσιν). +ποτε (*ante* τυφλω). +ουν (*post* παλιν: Cª *notavit* ουν). τι συ. σεαυτου (*pro* αυτου). ηνοιξεν (*sic* v. 32)√. 18. ην τυφλοσ. οφωνησαν *p.m.* εφ. *s.m.*√. 19. ει (*pro* λεγοντεσ: Cª *cum* Steph.). λεγεται√. βλεπι αρτι√. 20. +ουν (*post* απεκριθησαν).—αυτοισ. ειπαν (*sic* vv. 12. 22. 23. 24. 26. 28. 34. 40). 21. ηνυξεν. [αυτ. ηλ. εχει].—αυτον ερωτησατε αυτοσ (*habet* Cª αυτον ερωτησαται *ante* ηλικιαν εχει αυτοσ). εαυτου (*pro* αυτου *secund.*). 22. συνετεθιντο√. 23. —εχει (Cª εχι√). επερωτησαται. 24. τον ανθρωπον εκ δευτερου. ημισ√. ουτοσ ο ανθρωποσ ȯ αμ. (˙ *p.m. vel* A: *etiam* C). 25. —και ειπεν. +δε (*post* εν: *improbat* Cª). 26. ειπαν (—δε: *at* ειπον ουν Cª).—παλιν (*habet* Cª). εποιησαν (-σεν A?). ηνυξεν√. 27. θελεται√ *bis in vers.* ϋμισ√. μαθηται αυτου. 28. *init.* +και (οι δε *pro* και Cª).—ουν. μαθητησ ει. εκινου√. μωϋσεωσ. 29. ημισ√. μωϋσει√. 30. τουτω γαρ. +το (*ante* θαυμαστον). οιδαται√. εστιν√. ηνοιξε. 31. —δε. [αμαρτ. ο θσ̅]. 35. *init.* +και (*improbat* Cª).—ο (*habet* Cª).

— αυτω (*habet* C[a]). ανθρωπου (*pro* θῡ). 36. εκινοσ√. και ειπεν κε̅ κ̇ τισ εστιν (κ̇ *p.m.*). 37. εφη (*pro* ειπε δε). [εωρακασ]. 38. *Deest versus totus, et* και ειπεν ο ισ̅ v. 39 (*habet* C[a], *o ante* ισ̅ *omisso*). 39. βλεπωσιν√. 40. — και *prim.* — ταυτα (*habet* C[a], *sed erasum est*). μετ αυτου οντεσ. 41. — ουν (C[a] αι αμαρτιαι ὑμων μενουσιν, *sed prior lectio restituitur*).

X. 1. εστιν (*sic* vv. 2. 13. 21. 29. 34)√. 3. ανυγει√. φωνει (*pro* καλει). 4. — και *prim.* — προβατα (παντα *habet* C[a], *sed rursus erasum*). ακολουθι√. οιδασιν√. 5. [ακολουθησωσιν]. [οιδασι]. 6. και (*pro* εκεινοι δε: C[a] *cum* Steph., *sed* εκινοι√). [ην]. 7. αυτοισ παλιν (*sic* A, *nam p.m. verba deesse videntur:* C[a] *improbat* παλιν, *at* C[b] *revocat*). [οτι]. 8. — προ εμου (*habet* C[a] *post* ηλθον). εισιν√. 9. εγω ή ειμι (· *p.m.*)√. 10. + αιωνιον (*ante* εχωσιν *prim.*√). 11. διδωσιν (*pro* τιθησιν: C[a] *cum* Steph.). 12. ο δε μισθωτοσ. εστιν (*pro* εισι). θεωρι√. αφιησιν√. — τα προβατα *tert.* 13. — ο δε μισθωτοσ φευγει. [μελει]. 14. γεινωσκω√. *fin.* γεινωσκουσι με τα εμα (*pro* γινωσκομαι υπο των εμων). 15. γινωσκι√. διδωμι (*pro* τιθημι: C[a] *cum* Steph.). 16. δει με. αγαγιν√. ακουσωσιν. (C[a] γενησονται). 17. με ο πατηρ. 18. ουδισ (*sic* v. 29)√. ηρεν (*pro* αιρει: C[a] ερει√). 18. λαβιν√. 19. — ουν. 20. ελεγαν (C[a] -γον). ουν (*pro* δε: C[a] *cum* Steph., *sed* ουν *restitutum*). ακουεται√. 21. + δε (*ante* ελεγον). ανυξαι. 22. ενκαινια. — τοισ. — και. 23. [ο: *sic* v. 34]. σολομωνοσ (— του: C[a] σολομωντοσ). 24. — αυτον (*habet* C[a]). ερεισ (*pro* αιρεισ)√. ειπον (C[a] ειπε, *sed* -ον *revocatum*). 25. — αυτοισ (*habet* C[a]). πιστευεται (*non* v. 26)√. — τω. μαρτυρι√. 26. αλλα. ὑμισ√. οτι ουκ εσται (*pro* ου γαρ εστε). — καθωσ ειπον υμιν. 27. ακουουσιν√. και (*pro* καγω). ακολουθουσιν√. 28. διδωμι αυτοισ ζωην αιωνιον. αποληται (C[a] -λωνται). ου μη αρπαση (*pro* ουχ αρπασει). 29. — μου *prim.* (*habet* C[a]). ο (*pro* οσ). δεδωκεν√. παντων μειζων. *fin.* — μου *secund.* 31. — ουν. αυτον *p.m. in liturâ scripsit.* 32. εργα καλα. εδιξα√. — μου (*habet* C[a]). εμε λιθαζετε. 33. — λεγοντεσ. — και. 34. — υμων (*habet* A). + οτι (*ante* ειπα, εγω *omisso: at* οτι εγω ειπα C[b] ?). 35. ειπεν√. [του θῡ εγεν.]. 36. ηγιασεν√. απεστιλεν√. βλασφημισ√. — του. 38. πιστευεται (*pro* -ευητε)√. πιστευεται (*pro* πιστευσατε). πιστευητε (*pro* -ευσητε). τω πατρι (*pro* αυτω). 39. [ουν]. — παλιν (*habet* C[a] *post* αυτον). 40. απηλθεν√. — εισ τον τοπον (*habet* C[a]). [ἰωαννησ: *sic* v. 41 *bis*]. προτερον (*pro* πρωτον). εμινεν√. 41. — οτι. σημιον√. 42. πολλοι επιστευσαν εισ αυτον εκει.

XI. 1. + τησ (*ante* μαριασ). 2. [μαρια]. αλιψασα√. ησθενι√. 3. απεστιλαν√. προσ αυτον αι αδελφαι. 4. εστιν√. + αλλ (*ante* ινα). 6. εμινεν√. 7. επιτα√. [μαθηταισ αγ.].— παλιν (*habet* C[a]). 8. ραββει. λιθασε√. 9. — ο. ωραι εισιν. του (*pro* τουτου *p.m., ut videtur: supplet* του C)√. 10. νυκτει√. 11. ειπεν (*sic* vv. 25. 34. 41)√. 12. ειπαν (*sic* v. 46). αυτω οι μαθηται (— αυτου). 13. ειρηκι√. — αυτου (*habet* C[a]). 14. [ουν]. ° ισ̅ (ο *p.m.?*). παρησια (C[a] παρρ.). απεθανεν√. 15. εκι√. αλλα. 16. συνμαθηταισ. ημισ√. 17. [ελθων]. [ισ̅ ευρ: *at* C[b] *post* ισ̅ *habet* εισ βηθανιαν]. τεσσαρεσ ημερασ ηδη. μνημιω√. 18. — η (*habet* C[a]). 19. πολλοι δε (— και). εληλυθισαν√. την (*pro* τασ περι). [μαριαν: *sic* vv. 28. 31. 45]. — αυτων. 20. — ο. 21. [η]. — τον. ουκ αν απεθανεν ο αδελφοσ μου. 22. — αλλα (*habet* C[a]). εαν (*pro* αν). αιτησει. 24. λεγι√. [αυτω μαρθα]. 25. + δε (*post* ειπεν: *improbat* C[a]). 28. τουτο (*pro* ταυτα). απηλθεν√. εφωνησεν√. [ειπουσα *secund.*]. παρεστιν√. 29. + δε (*ante* ωσ). ηγερθη (*pro* εγειρεται). ηρχετο (*pro* ερχεται). 30. + ετι (*post* ην). 31. δοξαντεσ (*pro* λεγοντεσ). + ισ̈̅ (*ante* ϋπαγει: ·· *p.m.*)√. μνημιον (*sic* v. 38)√. 32. [μαρια]. — ο (*habet* C[a]). αυτου προσ τουσ ποδασ. μου απεθανεν. 33. — ωσ (*habet* C[a]). [ειδεν]. εβριμησατο (ενεβρ. A *vel* B, *etiam* C). 34. τεθικαται√. 35. *init.* + και. — ο (*habet* C[a]). 36. ελεγαν (C[a] -γον). 37. ειπαν (C[a] -πον). [ηδυνατο]. 38. εμβριμουμενοσ. — εν (*habet* C[a]). 39. [ο]. λεγι *secund.*√. τετελευτηκοτοσ. εστιν (*sic* v. 57)√. 40. οψη. 41. — ου ην ο τεθνηκωσ κειμενοσ. ηρεν√. 42. απεστιλασ√. 43. εκραυγαζεν (C[a] -γασεν√). λαζαρ *hic* (C[a] -ρε). 44. *init.* [και]. χιρασ κιριαισ. [αυτοισ ο ισ̅]. αφεται ϋπ. 45. δε (*pro* ουν). [α: *sic* v. 46]. ισ̅ (— ο). 46. [ο]. 47. ελεγαν (*sic* v. 56). ποιει σημια. 48. ουτωσ√. πιστευουσιν (C[a] -σουσιν). 49. ϋμισ√. 50. λογιζεσθε. — ημιν. 51. εκινου√. επροφητευσεν. εμελλεν ισ̅ (— ο). αποθνησκιν√. 52. (+ δε *post* εθνουσ C[a], *sed eras.*). 53. εβουλευσαντο. αποκτινωσιν√. 54. *init.* ο ουν ισ̅. εφρεμ. εμινεν (*pro* διετριβε). — αυτου. 56. ελεγαν. 57. δεδωκισαν√. — και *prim.* αρχιερισ√. εντολασ.

XII. 1. — ο τεθνηκωσ. + ισ (*ante* εκ νεκρων: *at* ο ισ̅ C[a]). 2. διηκονι√. + εκ (*post* ην). ανακειμενων συν. 3. [μαρια]. ηλιψεν√. [του ιυ̅]. εξεμαξεν√. 4. δε (*pro* ουν). ϊουδασ ο ϊσκαριωτησ εισ εκ των μαθητων αυτου (— σιμωνοσ). 6. ειπεν (*sic* v. 38)√. [εμελεν]. εχων (*pro* ειχε). — και *secund.* 7. + ϊνα (*ante* εισ). τηρηση. 9. + ο (*ante* οχλοσ). εστιν (*sic* vv. 31. 35)√. 10. αποκτινωσιν√.

12. — ο *prim.* (*habet* Cᵃ). ερχεται ισ̅ (— ο *secund.*). 13. εκραυγαζον λεγοντεσ (*pro* εκραζον). και ο βασιλευσ (και *punctis notatum rursus erasis*). 14. [εστι]. 15. [θυγατερ]. 16. — δε. αυτου οι μαθηται. — ο. επ αυτω ην. 17. εμαρτυρι√. [οτε]. μνημιου√. 18. [και]. — ο. + πολυσ (*post* οχλοσ). ηκουσαν αυτον τουτο. 19. ειπαν. ειδε√. 20. ελληνεσ τινεσ. [προσκυνησωσιν]. 21. [βηθσαϊδα]. ϊδιν√. 22. *init.* [-ται φιλ.]. ανδραια (Cᵃ -ρεα). και παλιν ερχεται ανδρεασ. + και (*ante* λεγουσιν√). 23. αποκρινεται. 25. απολλυει (*pro* απολεσει). μεισων√. — φυλαξει αυτην (*unâ lineâ forsan omissâ: habet* A). 26. τισ διακονη. ακολουθιτω√. — και *tert.* σειμησει (τ *p.m. vel* A: *etiam* C)√. 29. [ουν]. [εστωσ]. — και. ελεγεν√. 30. — ο. — και ειπεν. η φωνη αυτη. 31. — νυν ο αρχων του κοσμου τουτου (ὁμοιοτ.: *supplent* A Cᵃ). + και (*ante* εκβληθησεται). 32. παντα (Cᵃ *cum* Steph.). 33. τουτον (˙ *p.m.*)√. ελεγεν√. εμελλεν. 34. + ουν (*post* απεκριθη). ημισ√. συ λεγισ. 35. εν υμιν (*pro* μεθ υμων). [εωσ]. (+ η Cᵃ *ante* σκοτια *prim.*). οιδεν√. 36. ωσ (*pro* εωσ). πιστευεται√. [ο ισ̅: ο *tamen videtur esse* C *correctoris*]. 37. σημια√. 38. επιστευσεν√. 40. επηρωσεν. ειδωσιν√. τη καρδια συνωσιν (— νοησωσι). στραφωσιν (*pro* επιστραφωσι). ϊασομαι. 41. οτι (*pro* οτε). ειδεν√. ελαλησεν√. 43. ϋπερ (*pro* ηπερ). 44. εκραξεν. αλλα. 46. μινη√. 47. φυλαξη (*pro* πιστευση). 49. δεδωκεν. 50. εγω λαλω. ειρηκεν√. *fin.* ουτωσ λαλω.

XIII. 1. ηλθεν (*pro* εληλυθεν). ϊουδαιουσ (*pro* ιδιουσ: Cᵃ *cum* Steph.). 2. διπνου√. γεινομενου (Cᵃ γενομ.). ϊνα παραδοι (Cᵃ -δω) αυτον ϊουδασ σιμωνοσ ϊσκαριωτησ. 3. ϊδωσ√. — ο ισ̅. εδωκεν. χιρασ (*sic* v. 9)√. εξηλθεν√. 4. διπνου√. τιθησιν√. 6. και λεγι√. — εκεινοσ κε̅ (*habet* Cᵃ, *at* εκινοσ√). νιπτισ√. 7. α (*pro* ο: Cᵃ *cum* Steph.). 8. [*omnino cum* Steph.]. 9. — κε̅ (*habet* Cᵃ). 10. [ο *prim.*]. ουκ εχι (-χει Cᵃ) χρειαν. — η τουσ ποδασ. αλλα εστιν. 11. ηδει. [ειπεν ουχι]. 12. ενιψεν√. — και. ελαβεν√. αυτων (*pro* αυτου: Cᵃ *cum* Steph.). και ανεπεσεν (*pro* αναπεσων: Cᵃ και αναπεσων). γεινωσκεται√. 13. ϋμισ (*sic* v. 15)√. λεγεται√. 14. οφιλεται√. νιπτειν αλληλων τουσ ποδδασ (˙ *p.m.?*). 15. ϋποδιγμα. δεδωκα. ποιηται√. 16. εστιν√. μιζων *prim.*√. 18. + γαρ (*post* εγω). τινασ (*pro* ουσ). [μετ εμου]. επηρκεν. 19. πιστευσηται οταν γενηται. 20. αν (*pro* εαν). λαμβανι *secund.*√. 21. — ο. εμαρτυρησεν√. 22. ουν ουν οι ϊουδαιοι εισ αλληλουσ οι μαθηται (A *uncis includit* οι ϊουδαιοι: Cᵃ Cᵇ *etiam* ουν *secund. improbant*).

23. [δε]. + εκ (*post* εισ). [πυθεσθαι τισ αν ειη]. ελεγεν (*pro* λεγει). *fin.* + και λεγει αυτω ειπε τισ εστιν περι ου λεγει. 25. (αναπεσων Cª *pro* επιπεσων). ουν (*pro* δε). [εκεινοσ επι]. 26. (+ ουν Cª *ante* ο ισ). + και λεγει (*ante* εκεινοσ). [βαψασ]. [επιδωσω]. βαψασ ουν (*pro* και εμβαψασ). (+ λαμβανι και *ante* διδωσιν Cᶜ, *sed rursus erasa*). ϊσκαριωτου. 27. — τοτε. [ο ισ]. ταχειον√. 29. επι (*pro* επει)√. — ο (*prim. et secund.*). χριαν√. 30. εξηλθεν ευθυσ. 30, 31. οτε ουν εξηλθεν λεγει ισ (— ο). 32. — ει ο θσ εδοξασθη εν αυτω (δμοιοτ.: *habet* Cª). αυτω (*pro* εαυτω: *sic* Cª, *sed* ε *rursus erasum*). 33. μεικρον√. + χρονον (*ante* μεθ). ζητησεται√. — οτι (*habet* Cª). εγω ϋπαγω. δυνασθαι ελθιν√. 34. — ινα *secund.* 35. εχηται√. μετ αλληλων (*pro* εν αλληλοισ). 36. [αυτω ο]. + εγω (*ante* ϋπαγω). ακολουθησεισ δε ϋστερον (— μοι). 37. — ο. — κυριε (*habet* Cª). δυναμε√. [ακολουθησαι]. ϋπερ σου την ψυχην μου θησω. 38. *init.* αποκρινεται. — αυτω ο. φωνηση. [απαρνηση]. (τρεισ√ Cª).

XIV. 1. πιστευεται *prim.*√. 2. — αν. + οτι (*ante* πορευομαι). 3. [και ετοιμασω] τοπον ϋμιν. παραλημψομαι. ϋμισ (*pro* υμεισ: *sic* vv. 17. 20 *bis*)√. 4. [εγω]. — και *secund.* — οιδατε *secund.* 5. και πωσ την οδον ειδεναι δυναμεθα. 6. — ο. ουδισ√. 7. εγνωκατε εμε (*pro* εγνωκειτε με). γνωσεσθαι (*pro* εγνωκειτε αν). [και *secund.*]. γνωσεσθαι (*pro* γινωσκετε). εωρακαται αυτον. 8. + ο (*ante* φιλιπποσ). 9. [ο ισ]. τοσουτω χρονω (Cª -τον -νον: *sed prior lectio revocatur*). εωρακεν√. — και *secund.* λεγισ√. + οτι (*ante* δειξον: *improbat* Cª). 10. εστιν (*sic* v. 28)√. [λαλω *prim.*]. [ο δε πατηρ ο]. ποιει τα εργα αυτου (— αυτοσ). 11. πιστευεται *prim.*√. [*deest* εστιν]. — δια (*habet* Cª). *fin.* — μοι. 12. — μου. 14. + με (*post* αιτησητε). [εγω]. 15. — με (*habet* Cᵇ). τηρησητε. 16. *init.* καγω. τηρησω (*pro* ερωτησω: Cª *cum* Steph.). μεθ υμων η εισ τον αιωνα (— μενη). 17. αληθιασ√. (ο *prim.*: Cª *habet* ον, *sed* ν *rasum*). (αυτον *pro* αυτο *prim.* Cª, *sed restitutum* αυτο). — αυτο *secund.* — δε. γεινωσκετε√. *fin.* [εσται]. 19. ζησεσθαι√. 20. εκινη√. γνωσεσθαι ϋμισ. 21. καγω. 22. + και (*ante* τι). 23. — ο. (αυτοισ Cª *pro* αυτω: *sed* αυτω *restitutum*). τηρηση. *fin.* ποιησομεθα. 24. ακουεται√. 26. ο δε παρακλητοσ πεμψει το πνα το αγιον (— ο: Cª ο δε παρ. το πν. το αγ. ον πεμψι) ο πατηρ εν κ.τ.λ. 27. + ϋμιν (*post* διδωσιν). διλιατω√. 28. — ειπον *secund.* (μου *prim.*: *puncta addita sed rursus erasa*). 29. γενεσθε√. ϊν. 30. — τουτου. 31. [και]. ενετιλατο√. ουτωσ√.

XV. 1. εστιν (*sic* v. 20)√. 2. αυτον (*pro* αυτο *secund.*). καρπον πλειω. 4. μινατε (*non* v. 9)√. μενη. ϋμισ (*sic* vv. 5. 16 *bis*)√. *fin.* μενητε. 5. δυνασθαι√. 6. μενη (Cª *cum* Steph.). αυτο (*pro* αυτα). + το (*ante* πυρ). βαλλουσιν√. 7. εν υ μινη (υμιν *pro* υ Cª). οσα (*pro* ο). [εαν]. [αιτησεσθε]. 8. φερηται√. γενησεσθαι√. μοι (*pro* εμοι). 9. ηγαπησεν√. [ηγαπησα ϋμασ]. 10. — εαν τασ εντολασ μου τηρησητε μενειτε εν τη αγαπη μου (*habet* Cª, *legens* τηρησεται μενιται√ *et* τη εμη *pro* μου: ὁμοιοτ. *fortasse*). καγω (*pro* εγω). του πατροσ μου τασ εντολασ μου (*delent* μου *secund.* A? C). ετηρησα. 11. [μεινη]. 13. ουδισ (*sic* v. 24)√. — τισ (*habet* Cª). 14. + γαρ (*post* ϋμεισ: *improbat* Cª). ποιηται√. α (*pro* οσα). 15. λεγω ϋμασ. οιδεν√. 16. εξελεξασθαι√. φερηται√. — ινα *secund.* (*habet* Cª). εαν (*pro* αν). αιτησηται√, δωσει (*pro* δω). 18. μεισει√. — υμων (*habet* Cª). εμισηκεν (Cª μεμ.). 19. ο κοσμοσ μισει υμασ. 20. μνημονευεται√. τον λογον ον. — εγω. ελαλησα (*pro* ειπον). ϋμασιν (*pro* ϋμιν: ·· *p.m.*)√. *fin.* τηρησωσιν√. 21. — υμιν (A *scripsit* ποιησουσιν *in liturâ, additis ad marg.* εισ υμασ). οιδασιν√. 22. ειχοσαν. — δε (*habet* Cª). εχουσιν√. 23. μεισων√ [*at* μισει]. 24. εποιησεν. ειχοσαν. εωρακασιν√. μεμισηκασιν√. 25. ο εν τω κοσμω (Cª νομω) αυτων γεγραμμενοσ. 26. — δε. 27. μαρτυριτε√.

XVI. 1. — μη (*habet* Cª)√. 2. + γαρ (*ante* ποιησωσιν√). αλλα. αποκτινασ√. λατριαν προσφεριν√. 3. ποιησωσιν (*sic* v. 2) ϋμιν. 4. αν (*pro* οταν: *at* εαν Cª). ωρα μνημονευηται αυτων (αυτων *punctis additis sed rursus erasis*). — υμιν *secund.* (*habet* Cª). 5. + εγω (*ante* ϋπαγω). ουδισ (*sic* v. 22)√. *fin.* ϋπαγει (Cª -γεισ). 7. [γαρ μη]. [ελευσεται]. ημασ (*pro* υμασ *prim.*: Cª *cum* Steph.)√. 9. — ου (*habet* Cª)√. 10. — μου. 11. κο *in* κοσμου *emendatum p.m.*√. 12. ϋμιν λεγειν. δυνασθαι√. — αρτι (*habet* Cª). 13. αληθιασ√. εν τη αληθεια (— πασαν: *at* Cª *habet* παση *post* αληθεια). ακουει (— αν: C *literam super* α *in* οσα *notavit et ipse delevit*). *fin.* (υμιν *p.m.* ημ. *s.m.*?)√. 14. λημψεται. αναγγελλει. 15. *Deest versus ob* ὁμοιοτ. (*habet* Cª, *legens* εχι√. εστιν√. + υμιν [*post* ειπον]. λαμβανι. αναγ'γελι). 16. μεικρον *prim.*√. ουκετι (*pro* ου). — οτι εγω *ad fin. vers.* 17. [ειπον]. εστιν (*sic* vv. 18. 32)√. — και ου θεωρειτε με και παλιν μικρον (ὁμοιοτ.: Cª *supplet post* ημιν, *legens* θεωριται√). ω (*pro* οτι εγω: Cª οτι *tantum legit*). 18. τι εστιν τουτο. — ο λεγει. (Cª *pro* το *habet* ο λεγι). 19. — ουν. [ο ισ̅]. ημελλον (*pro* ηθελον). 20. θρηνησητε (ε *p.m.*). ϋμισ *bis in versu*√. — δε *secund.* (*habet* C[a]). λυπηθησεσθαι√. [αλλ]. 21. + ο (*ante* ανθρωποσ: A? C *improbant*). 22. + νυν μεν (*ante* ουν: *at post* ουν C[a]). λυπην εχεται (— μεν νυν: εξεται C[a] *pro* εχεται). [αιρει]. 23. ερωτησηται. οτι ο αν αιτησηται (ο *pro* οσα). δωσει ὑμιν εν τω ονοματι μου. 24. ητησαται√. αιτησασθαι (*pro* αιτειτε: C[a] αιτιται√). λημψεσθε. 25. — αλλ. οπου (*pro* οτε: C[a] *cum* Steph.). απαγγελλω (*pro* αναγγελω). 26. αιτησασθαι εν τω ονοματι μου. 27. με (*pro* εμε). — του (C[a] *super* θυ *scripsit* πρσ *et ipse, ut videtur, delevit*). 28. [παρα]. 29. λεγουσιν οι μαθηται αυτω (— αυτου: C[a] αυτου, *omisso* αυτω). + εν (*ante* παρρησια). 30. χριαν√. 31. [ο ισ]. πιστευεται√. 32. — νυν. + η ωρα (*ante* ἵνα: *improbat* C[a]). καμε (*pro* και εμε). 33. εχηται√. εχετε (*pro* εξετε). θαρσειται√.

XVII. 1. λελαληκεν ισ (— ο). επαρασ. — και *secund.* ειπεν√. — και *tert.* — σου *secund.* 2. δωσω αυτω (*pro* δωση αυτοισ: C[a] *cum* Steph.). 3. [γινωσκωσι]. απεστιλασ (*sic* vv. 8. 18. 21. 23. 25)√. 4. τελιωσασ (*pro* ετελειωσα). με (*pro* μοι: C[a] *cum* Steph.). 5. ην (*pro* η: C[a] *cum* Steph.). 6. εδωκασ (*pro* δεδ.) *bis in versu.* [και εμοι]. ετηρησαν. 7. εγνων (*pro* εγνωκαν). [δεδωκασ: *sic* vv. 8. 9. 22. 24]. *fin.* εισιν. 8. — και εγνωσαν (*habet* C[a]). επιστευσασ (C[a] -σαν)√. 9. εισιν (*sic* vv. 11. 16)√. 10. και εμοι αυτουσ εδωκασ (*pro* και τα εμα παντα σα εστι και τα σα εμα). δεδοξασμεν√. 11. αυτοι (*pro* ουτοι). καγω. ω (*pro* ουσ). εδωκασ (*pro* δεδωκασ). [καθωσ ημεισ]. 12. — εν τω κοσμω. κ̇ σου (˙ *p.m.*)√. — ουσ δεδωκασ μοι (C[a] ο δεδωκασ μοι). και εφυλασσον (*pro* εφυλαξα: C[a] και εφυλαξα). ουδισ√. απωλιασ√. 13. εχωσιν√. πεπληρωκενην (C[a] -μενην)√. *fin.* [ε]αυτοισ (ε *p.m.*). 14. — εγω *secund.* (*habet* C[a]). 16. *fin.* ουκ ειμι εκ του κοσμου. 17. αληθια *prim.*√. — σου ο λογοσ ο σοσ αληθεια (ὁμοιοτ.: C[a] *habet, legens* σου *et* αληθια√). *fin.* εστιν√. 18. απεστιλασ√. απεστιλα√. 19. — εγω. ωσιν και αυτοι. αληθια√. 20. πιστευοντων. 21. ωσιν *prim.*√. [πατερ: *sic* vv. 24. 25]. εν ωσιν. πιστευη (C[a] -ση). 22. *init.* καγω. εδωκα (*pro* δεδωκα). *fin.* — εν εσμεν (*habet* C[a]). 23. ωσιν τετελιωμενοι√. [και *secund.*]. — ινα *secund.* 24. ο (*pro* ουσ). ωσιν√. θεωρωσιν√. δεδωκασ (*pro* εδωκασ). 26. αυτουσ (*pro* με).

XVIII. 1. — ο. εξηλθεν συν α̈υτοισ (¨ *p.m.*)√. χιμαρρου√. του κεδρου (C[a] *cum* Steph.). 2. — ο *secund.* 3. + εκ των (*ante* φαρισαιων: *puncta addita et rursus erasa*). — εκει (C[a] εκι√). 4. δε (*pro* ουν). [εξελθων ειπεν]. 5. ισ̅ εγω ειμι (— ο). ϊστηκει (*sic* v. 16)√. 6. — αυτοισ (*habet* Cᵃ). — οτι. απηλθαν. επεσαν. 7. αυτουσ επηρωτησεν. 8. — ο. 10. επεσεν (*pro* επαισε)√. τον δουλον του αρχιερεωσ. ωταριον. 11. — σου. δεδωκεν√. 12. σπιρα (*non* v. 3)√. 13. ηγαγον (Cᵃ *cum* Steph.). — αυτον. 14. αποθανιν (*pro* απολεσθαι). 15. ηκολουθι√. — ο *prim.* (*habet* Cᵇ). [ην γνωστοσ]. συνεισηλθεν√. 16. εξω προσ τη θυρα. [οσ ην]. [τω αρχιερει]. ειπεν√. εισηνεγκε (*pro* εισηγαγε). 17. [η π. η θ. τω πετρω]. 18. ϊστηκισαν√. + και (*ante* οι δουλοι). και ο πετροσ μετ αυτων. 19. [ηρωτησε]. 20. *init.* και απεκριθη ισ̅ αυτω (— ο: Cᵃ αυτω ισ̅). λελαληκα.— τη. παντεσ (*pro* παντοτε *secund.*). 21. ερωτασ ερωτησον. 22. παρεστηκωσ των ϋπηρετων (Cᵃ των παρεστηκοτων ϋπ.). εδωκεν√. 23. ο δε ισ̅ ειπεν αυτω (*pro* απεκριθη αυτω ο ισ̅). ειπον (*pro* ελαλησα: Cᵃ *cum* Steph.). δερισ√. 24. απεστιλεν δε αυτον (*non* ουν). 26. συνγενησ. απεκοψεν√. ιδον√. 27. [ο]. 28. πρωϊ. αλλα φαγωσιν (— ινα). 29. προσ αυτουσ ο πιλατοσ εξω. φησιν (*pro* ειπε). — κατα (*habet* A). 30. ειπαν. κακον ποιησασ (*pro* κακοποιοσ: Cᵃ κακον ποιων). παρεδωκειμεν. 31. [ουν: *bis in versu*]. [ο]. [πιλατοσ: *sic* vv. 29. 33. 35. 37. 38]. ϋμισ√. — αυτον *secund.* (*habet* Cᵃ). αποκτιναι√. *fin.* + ‘ουδενα’ (*improbant p.m.? et* Cᵇ ‘ ’)√. 32. — ον ειπε (Cᵃ ον ειπεν√). αποθνησκιν√. 33. [εισ το πρ. παλιν]. εφωνησεν√. 34. [αυτω ο ισ̅]. απο σεαυτου.— συ (*habet* Cᵃ). ειπασ (*pro* λεγεισ: Cᵃ λεγισ√). [σοι ειπον]. 35. μη (*pro* μητι: Cᵃ *cum* Steph.). ο αρχιερευσ (Cᵃ *cum* Steph.). 36. —ο. η εμη βασιλεια *prim. et tert.* η εμη βασιλια *secund.* και οι ϋπηρεται οι εμοι ηγωνιζοντο αν. 37. [ο ισ̅]. — εγω *semel.* μαρτυρηση (-σω A, *vix p.m.*). περι τησ αληθιασ (Cᵃ τη αληθια√). — εκ (*ante* τησ αληθιασ√: *habet* Cᵃ). 38. τισ (*pro* τι: Cᵃ *cum* Steph.). εξηλθεν√. [αιτ. ευρ. εν αυτω]. 39. εστιν√. συνηθια√. απολυσω ϋμιν *prim.* + ϊνα (*ante* απολυσω ϋμιν *secund.*). 40. — παντεσ. [βαραββ. *bis in versu*].

XIX. 1. λαβων. [πιλατοσ *passim*]. — και. εμαστιγωσεν√. 2. επεθηκεν (Cᵃ -καν)√. [τη κεφαλη]. *fin.* + και ηρχοντο προσ αυτον. 3. βασιλευ (— ο). ἐδιδοσαν. 4. εξηλθεν (— ουν). ο πιλατοσ εξω. *fin.* αιτιαν ουχ ευρισκω (— εν αυτω ουδεμιαν: *at* Aᵃ αιτιαν ουδεμιαν ευρισκω εν αυτω). 5. [ο ισ̅]. — το. ϊδου. 6. ϊδον√. εκραξαν (Cᵃ *cum* Steph. εκραυγασαν). — λεγοντεσ. + αυτον και (*ante* λεγει). 7. — αυτω.— ημων. οφιλει αποθανιν√. υν̅ θυ̅ εαυτον. 8. τον λογον τουτον. 9. — παλιν (*habet* A). 10. — ουν (*habet* Cᵃ). λαλισ√.

fin. απολυσαι σε και εξουσιαν εχω σταυρωσαι σε. 11. + αυτω (*ante* ο $\overline{ισ}$). εχισ (*pro* ειχεσ). κατ εμου ουδεμιαν. δεδομενον σοι. παραδουσ. 12. ο πιλατοσ εζητει. ελεγον (*pro* εκραζον λεγοντεσ: Cª *cum* Steph.). εαυτον (*pro* αυτον *secund.*). 13. των λογων τουτων. — του. γολγοθα (*pro* δε γαββαθα: Cª *cum* Steph.). 14. ην ωσ (*pro* δε ωσει). (τριτη *pro* εκτη Cª). 15. οι δε ελεγον (*pro* οι δε εκραυγασαν: Cª εκραυγασαν ουν εκινοι). (αρον *prim. punctis notatum rursus erasis*). 17. οι δε λαβοντεσ (*pro* παρελαβον δε: Cª παραλαβοντεσ ουν). — και *prim.* + αυτον (*post* απηγαγον). εαυτω τον σταυρον (— αυτου). ο (*pro* οσ). 19. εγραψεν√. 20. *Deest versus totus et* v. 21 *usque ad* ιουδαιων *secund.* (ὁμοιοτ.: *supplet* A *legens* v. 20: ο τοποσ τησ πολεωσ. ρωμαϊστι· ελληνιστι·). 21. ειπεν (*sic* v. 30)√. *fin.* [ειμι των ϊουδαιων]. 23. οι σταυρωσαντεσ (*pro* οτε εσταυρωσαν). τεσσερα. — και τον χιτωνα (*habet* Cª). αραφοσ. 24. ειπαν. αυτουσ (*pro* αλληλουσ: Cª εαυτουσ). — η λεγουσα. μου τα ϊματια. 25. ϊστηκισαν√. μαριαμ (*pro* μαρια) *bis in versu.* 26. — $\overline{ισ}$ ουν ιδων την $\overline{μρα}$ (*unâ lineâ forsan omissâ: supplet* A, *sed habet* δε *pro* ουν). + και (*ante* λεγει: *improbant* A? Cª). — αυτου. [ϊδου]. 27. ειδε (*pro* ιδου). εκινησ√. [αυτην ο μαθητησ]. 28. πληρωθη (*pro* τελειωθη) cf. v. 36. [*caetera cum* Steph.]. 29. δε (*pro* ουν). σπογγον ουν μεστον οξουσ ϋσσωπω (*pro* οι δε *usque ad* υσσωπω: Cª του οξουσ). 30. ελαβεν√. — ο $\overline{ισ}$ (*habet* Cª). κλειναs√. παρεδωκεν√. 31. επει παρασκευη ην *transfert in locum ante* ϊνα μη. μινη√. — η. [εκεινου]. + ουν (*post* ηρωτησαν: *improbat* Cª). 32. συνσταυρωθεντοσ. 33. ευρον (*pro* ωσ ειδον: Cª ωσ ϊδον√). [αυτον ηδη]. + και (*post* τεθνηκοτα: *delet* Cª). 34. ενυξεν√. εξηλθεν ευθυσ. 35. μεμαρτυρηκεν√. αληθησ (*pro* -θινη). [αυτου εστιν]. [κακεινοσ]. + και (*post* ϊνα). ϋμισ√. πιστευητε (A -σητε). 36. + απ (*ante* αυτου). 38. [δε]. ηρωτησεν√. — ο *prim.* [*non secund.*]. *fin.* ηλθον ουν και ηραν αυτον (— το σωμα του $\overline{ιυ}$: Cª ηλθεν ουν και ηρεν το σωμα αυτου). 39. ηλθεν√. [τον $\overline{ιν}$]. εχων ελιγμα (*pro* φερων μιγμα: Cª *cum* Steph.). σζμυρνησ. ωσ (*pro* ωσει). 40. [αυτο οθονιοισ]. ην (*pro* εστι: Cª εστιν√). 41. μνημιον (*sic* v. 42)√. ουδισ ουδεπω. ην τεθειμενοσ (*pro* ετεθη). 42. + οπου (*ante* εθηκαν: *improbat* Cª).

XX. 1. μαριαμ (*sic* vv. 11. 16. 18). + απο τησ θυρασ (*ante* εκ του μνημιου√). 2. + τον (*ante* σιμωνα). μνημιου√. 3. — και ηρχοντο εισ το μνημειον (*habet* Cª, *at* μνημιον√). 4. *init.* και ετρεχον (*pro* ετρεχον δε: Cª *cum* Steph.). προεδραμεν δε (— και ο αλλοσ μαθητησ : *habet* C^a, *sine* ο *et* δε *sequent.*). ηλθεν εισ το μνημιον πρωτοσ. 5. τα οθονια κειμενα. 5, 6. — ου μεντοι *usque ad fin.* v. 6 (ὁμοιοτ.: *supplet* C^a, *legens* v. 6 + και *ante* σιμων. μνημιον√. θεωρι√). 8. εισηλθεν√. μνημιον (*sic* v. 11)√. ειδεν√. 9. ηδει (C^a *cum* Steph.). 10. αυτουσ (*pro* εαυτουσ: C^a *cum* Steph). 11. ιστηκει√. εν τω μνημιω (*pro* προσ το μν.). — εξω (*habet* C^a *ante* κλαιουσα). εκλαιεν√. 12. — δυο (*habet* C^a). καθεζομενουσ εν λευκοισ. 13. *init.* — και. 14. *init.* — και. — ο. εστιν (*sic* vv. 15. 30)√. 15. — ο *prim.* + δε (*post* εκεινη: *improbat* C^a). ει ο βαστασασ (*pro* εβαστασασ: C^a *cum* Steph.). εθηκασ αυτον. 16. [ο ισ̅: *sic* vv. 17. 19. 29]. + δε (*ante* εκεινη). + εβραιστι (*ante* ραββουνι). *fin.* (C^a + και προσεδραμεν αψασθαι αυτου, *improbante* C^b). 17. — μου *secund.* (ουν *pro* δε C^a, *sed* δε *restitutum*). — μου *tert.* (*habet* C^a). + ϊδου (*ante* αναβαινω). 18. αγγελλουσα (C^a *cum* Steph.). εωρακα (*pro* -κε). 19. — τη *secund.* (*habet* C^a). — των *prim.* κεκλισμενων (*sic* v. 26)√. — συνηγμενοι (*habet* A). — αυτοισ (*habet* C^a). ϊρηνη (*sic* v. 26)√. 20. εδιξεν√. τασ χιρασ και την πλευραν αυτοισ (— αυτου). 21. *init.* (και ειπεν C^a, *sed* ειπεν ουν *restitut.*). — ο ισ̅. απεσταλκεν√. πεμψω (αποστελλω C^a, πεμπω C^b *cum* Steph.). 22. ενεφυσησεν√. 23. [αν τινων *prim.*]. αφηται√. αφεθησεται (*pro* αφιενται: C^a αφεωνται). εαν δε τινων *secund.* (C^a *cum* Steph.). κρατηνται (C^a κρατηται√, *pro* κρατητε). 24, 25. οτε ουν ηλθεν ισ̅ ελεγον αυτω οι μαθηται (— ο *et* αλλοι: C^a *cum* Steph., ο *tantum omisso*). 25. [εωρακαμεν]. ειδω. — αυτου *prim.* (*habet* C^a). μου τον δακτυλον. την χειραν αυτου (*pro* τον τυπον των ηλων *secund.*: C^a *cum* Steph.). μου την χειρα (*secund.*). 26. — αυτου. 28. *init.* — και. [ο *prim.*]. 29. ειπεν δε (*pro* λεγει: C^a λεγι δε). — θωμα. + και (*ante* πεπιστευκασ: *improbat* C^a). + με (*post* ϊδοντεσ: *improbat* C^a). 30. [αυτου]. 31. πιστευητε (C^a -σητε). — ο *prim.* — και (*habet* C^a). + αιωνιον (*post* ζωην).

XXI. 1. εφανερωσεν παλιν εαυτον ο ισ̅. εφανερωσεν *secund.*√. 2. υιοι (*pro* του). 3. σοι εξηλθον ουν και ενεβησαν. — ευθυσ. εκινη√. εκ̈οπιασαν (A C *cum* Steph.). 4. — ηδη (*habet* C^a). [γενομενησ]. — ο. επι (*pro* εισ). εγνωσαν (*pro* ηδεισαν). εστιν (*sic* vv. 7 *bis.* 25)√. 5. ισ̅ (— ο). — τι (*habet* C^a). 6. λεγει (*pro* ο δε ειπεν: C^a *cum* Steph., *sed p.m. restitut.*). (*Post* ευρησετε C^a *habet* οι δε ειπον δι ολησ τησ νυκτοσ εκοπιασαμεν και ουδεν ελαβομεν επι δε τω σω ρηματι βαλουμεν *ex Lucâ* v. 5: *improbat* C^b). + οι δε (*ante* εβαλον). — ουν. ϊλκυσαι ϊσχυον. 8. + αλλω (*ante* πλοιαριω). αλλα. 9. ανεβησαν (C *cum* Steph.). (επι την γην C^a, *sed* εισ *restitutum*). [βλεπουσιν]. 10. [ο $\overline{\iota\sigma}$: *sic* vv. 12. 13. 14]. ενεγκαται√. 11. ενεβη ουν (*pro* ανεβη). ειλκυσεν√. εισ την γην. [ῒχθ. μεγαλων]. 12. ουδισ δε. 13. — ουν. 14. + δε (*ante* ηδη). — αυτου. 15. — ιωνα (A C ἰωανου). πλεον. 16. παλιν λεγει αυτω. — δευτερον (A C *habent* το $\overline{\beta}$). ἰωαννου. — ναι (*habet* C^a). [προβατα: *sic* v. 17]. 17. ἰωαννου. + δε (*post* ελυπηθη: *delet* C^a). + και (*ante* φιλεισ *secund.*: A C *improbant*). και λεγει (*pro* και ειπεν). παντα συ. + και (*ante* λεγει *ultim.*). — ο $\overline{\iota\sigma}$. 18. εκτενισ√. την χιραν (C^a τασ χιρασ√). *fin.* αλλοι ζωσουσιν σε και ποιησουσιν σοι οσα ου θελισ (C^a αποισουσιν *pro* ποιησουσιν: σε οπου *pro* σοι οσα). 19. ειπεν√. ακολουθι√. 20. [δε]. βλεπι√. — ακολουθουντα οσ (ακολ. *habet* A, C οσ *addit*)√. λεγει αυτω (*pro* ειπε: C^a ειπεν αυτω). 21. + ουν (*ante* ἰδων). ειπεν (*pro* λεγει). — $\overline{\kappa\epsilon}$. 22. μενιν (*non* v. 23)√. μοι ακολουθι. 23. ουτοσ ο λογοσ. ουκ ειπεν δε (— και). — τι προσ σε (*habet* A). 24. (*Post* τουτων A C^b *habent* ο). [εστιν η μαρ. αυτ.]. 25. α (*pro* οσα). ουδ. χωρησειν. — αμην.

V. 25 *et subscr.* ευαγγελιον κατα ἰωαννην *judicat* Tischendorf. (*dissentit* Tregellesius, *testis oculatus*) *esse correctoris* A^a, *qui idem Codicis ipsius scriba est* D: *cf. annotationem cum Tab.* xix. *editionis majoris. Inde conjicere licet subscriptionem, ut ad finem S. Matthaei, primâ manu defuisse.*

In Evangeliis longè plurimas secundae manûs correctiones praebet C^a *vel* C, *ad textum receptum ferè accommodatas*: *post* C^a *creberrimus est* A: *post eum* C^b, B, A^a, B^a. C^c *ad* Johann. xiii. 26, E *ad* Matth. xix. 3 *tantum reperiuntur;* A obliq. *et* D *nusquam.*

προσ ρωμαιουσ

Cap. I. 1. [ι̅υ̅ χ̅υ̅]. 2. προεπηγγιλατο√. 3. θ̅υ̅ passim√. 4. δυναμι√. 5. πασιν√ (sic v. 7). 6. υμισ√. 8. —δια ι̅υ̅ χ̅υ̅ (*habet* A). περι (*pro* υπερ). 9. μνιαν√. 10. ευοδωθησομε√. ελθιν√ (*sic* v. 13). 11. ἴδιν√. 12. εστιν√. συνπαρακληθηναι ε|ν (*initio lineae*): *sic p.m.* 13. τινα καρπον. 14. ελλησιν√. οφιλετησ√. 15. (ουτωσ C, ουτω *p.m.*√). 16. —του χριστου. ἰουδε πρωτον *p.m.* (ἰουδαιω τε πρωτον A). 18. αληθιαν√ (*sic* v. 25). 19. ο θ̅σ̅ γαρ. εφανερωσεν√. 20. ποιημασιν√. καθορατε√. 21. ηΰχαριστησαν. 23. πετινων√. 24. —και. *fin.* αυτοισ. 27. [τε και οι αρρενεσ]. αρρενεσ εν αρρεσι (ρσ *bis* A). 28. επιγνωσι√.—ο θεος (*addit* A). 29. —πορνεια. πονηρια· κακια· πλεονεξια. κακοηθιασ√. 30. απιθεισ√. 31. —ασπονδουσ (*addit* C). 32. [ποιουσιν]. συνευδοκουσιν√. πρασσουσιν√.

II. 1. ι (*pro* ει)√. -ρινις *bis*√. 2. γαρ (*pro* δε). εστιν√. 4. καταφρονισ√. 5. (C *addit* και *post* -ψεωσ.). 7. ζητουσιν√. 8. απιθουσι√. —μεν (-σιν μεν C). αληθια√. πιθομενοισ√. ·οργη· και θυμοσ. 11. εστιν√. προσωπολημψια. 13. —του *bis*. [τω]. 14. ποιωσιν. [ουτοι]. εισιν√. 15. ενδικνυνται√. καρδιεσ (C·-αισ)√. συνμαρ. 16. [οτε]. *fin.* χ̅υ̅ ι̅υ̅ (*sine* δια) *p.m.* (δια ι̅υ̅ χ̅υ̅ A). 17. *init.* ει δε.—τω. 18. γινωσκισ√. 19. σκοτι√. 21. κλεπτιν κλεπτισ√. 22. ἴδωλα√. 24. βλασφημιται√. εθνεσιν√. 25. ωφελι√. -βυστια *p.m.*, at -βιστια *primò*√. 26. ουχ. 29. [αλλ].

III. 1. —η (*habet* C). ωφελια√. 2. [γαρ]. 4. καθαπερ. γεγραπτε√. νικησεισ. 5. συνιστησιν√. + αυτου (*post* οργην): *delet* C. 6. κρινι√. 7. αληθια√. 8. φασιν√. λεγιν√. εστιν√ (*sic* vv. 10. 18. 23). 11. [*sic*]. 12. ηχρεωθησαν. εστιν ο ποιων. *fin.* αινοσ√. 13. χιλη√. 14. [στομα αρασ]. 17. ιρηνησ√. 19. λαλει (*pro* λεγει): C λεγει. 21. νυνει√. 22. —και επι παντασ (*addit* C). 25. —τησ *prim.* ενδιξιν√. 26. + την (*ante* ενδιξιν). [*fin.* ι̅υ̅]. 27. εξεκλισθη√. 28. γαρ (*pro* ουν). δικαιουσθαι πιστι (πισ. δικ. C). 29. —δε. 30. ειπερ (επειπερ C). 31. μη (μ *rescript.*)√. ἴστανομεν (ἴστωμεν C).

IV. 1. ευρηκεναι αβρααμ τον προπατορα ημων (*sic etiam* C: π̅ρ̅α̅ α). 2. —τον. 3. + γαρ (*post* τι) *erasum, sequente* γαρ√. επιστευσεν (*sic* v. 17)√. 4. —το. οφιλημα√. 5. ασεβην. 8. ου (*pro* ω) *p.m.* [*sic* Cod. B] (ω C). 9. —οτι. 11. σημιον ελαβεν√. [δι].—και (*ante* αυτοισ): *habet* C.—την. 12. —τοισ ουκ εκ περιτομησ (ὁμοιοτελ.: *habet* A). στοιχουσιν√. ϊχνεσιν√.—τη.—πιστεωσ (*habet* A). 13. —η (*habet* η A).—του. 15. δε (*pro* γαρ: γαρ C). εστιν√ (*sic* vv. 16. 21). 16. ειναι√. 17. τεθικα√. 18. [επ]. κατα *eras. ante* κατα√. 19. πιστι√ (*sic* v. 20).—ου. κατενοησεν√. [ηδη]. 21. *init.* [και], *sic* v. 22. 24. λογιζεσθε√. εγιραντα√. 25. δικεωσιν√.

V. 1. εχωμεν (εχομεν A). 2. (A *habet* εν *ante* τη, *at eras.*). πιστι√. [επ]. 3. χαυχωμεθα√. 5. καρδιεσ√. ὑμων *p.m.* (ημων C). 6. [*init.* ετι] + ετι (*ante* κατα). απεθανεν√ (*sic* v. 8). 7. μογισ (μολισ A). αποθανιται√. αποθανιν√. 8. συνιστησιν√. [εισ η. ο. θ.]. 9. *Post* δικαιωθεντεσ *p.m. habet* ε̄ (*eras. p.m.*)√. 12. [η αμ. εισ τ. κ.]. [ο θαν.]. 13. ενελογειτο (A *marg.* ελλογαται: *at* C ενλογειται). 14. [αλλ]. μωϋσεωσ. εστιν√. 15. ουτωσ√ (*sic* vv. 18. 19. 21). επερισσευσεν√. 16. αμαρτητοσ√ (-σαντος C). 17. [τω του ενοσ]. εβασιλευσεν√. [τησ δωρ.]. βασιλευσουσιν√. 18. + ανθρωπου (*ante* παραπτωματος), *delet* C.

VI. 1. επιμενομεν. 2. [ζησομεν]. 4. ουτωσ√ (*sic* v. 11). ημισ√. 8. συνζησομεν. 10. απεθανεν *bis*√. 11. ειναι νεκρουσ μεν (ν. μ. ε. C). [τω κ̅ω̅ ημων]. 12. —αυτη εν. 13. ωσει. 14. ουκετι (*pro* ου *prim. Delet* ουκετι C). αλλα (*sic* v. 15) *p.m.* αλλ *s.m.* 15. αμαρτησωμεν. 18. ουν (*pro* δε): C *habet* δε. 19. ασθενιαν√. [ουτω]. 21. επεσχυνεσθε√. (C *habet* μεν *ante* γαρ). εκινων√. 22. δε *secund. p.m.*, *at* τε *primò.*

VII. 2. [*sic*]. 3. εταιρω *bis*√ (*non* v. 4). 4. και ὑμεισ αδελφοι μου. (χ̅ρ̅υ̅ *p.m.* χ̅υ̅ C). 6. [-τεσ]. [ημασ]. 7. ηδιν√. 8. [κατειρ.]. (+ η *ante* αμαρτια *secund.* C). 11. εξηπατησεν√. απεκτινεν√. 13. εγενετο (*pro* γεγονεν). [αλλα]. 14. [γαρ]. σαρκινοσ (-κοσ C). 15. [*sic*]. 16. συνφημι. 17. [αλλ η] ενοικουσα. 18. θελιν√. κατεργαζεσθε√. *fin.* ου (*pro* ουχ ευρισκω). 19. αλλα. 20. [θελω εγω]. 23. μελεσιν *bis*√. + εν (*post* με). 25. (A *habet* χαρισ δε *pro* ευχαριστω).—μεν (*habet* C).

VIII. 1. —μη κατα σαρ. *ad fin. vers. p.m.* (*habet* C). 2. ηλευθερωσεν√. σε (*pro* με). 3. εαν[7]: *sic Tischendorf.*, *at deest annotatio.* [κατεκρινε]. 7. ουναται (δυναται C)√. 9. αλλα. 10. [δι]. 11. εγιραντος√. + τον (*ante* ι̅ν̅: *non* C). ο εγειρασ (*sic*) εκ νεκρων χ̅ν̅ ι̅ν̅ (C *cum Steph.*),—και. του ενοικουντοσ. π̅ν̅σ̅. 12. οφιλεται√. 13. πραξισ√. 14. ϋιοι θ̅υ̅ εισιν. 15. δουλιασ√ (*sic* v. 21). αλλα.

16. συνμαρτυρει. 17. συνκληρονομοι. συνπασχομεν. 21. *init.* εφ. διοτι (*pro* οτι). 22. [συστ]. 23. εχοντεσ ημεισ και αυτοι. 24. και ϋπομενει (*pro* τι και ελπιζει: C *habet* τι και ελπιζι). 26. τη ασθενεια. [-ξωμεθα]. αλλα.—υπερ ημων (*habet* C). 27. εραυνων. οιδεν√. εντυγχανι√. 28. αγαπωσιν√. [-γει εισ]. 29. προωρισεν√. συνμορφουσ. 30. προωρισεν√. εκαλεσεν√ *bis.* εδικαιωσεν√ *bis.* εδοξασεν√. 32. εφισατο√. αλλα. 34. + ισ (*post* χσ.) μαλλον δε εγερθεισ εκ νεκρων οσ εστιν (— και *prim. et secund.*): C — εκ νεκρ. *et* + και (*post* οσ *prim.*). 35. θυ (*pro* χυ) *solum in lineâ.* Cod. B addit τησ εν χω ιυ: cf. vv. 1. 5. 36. ενεκεν. 38. πεπισμαι√. ουτε δυναμεισ *ponit post* μελλοντα. 39. [τω κω].

IX. 2. εστιν√. αδιαλιπτοσ√. 3. ειναι αναθεμα αυτοσ εγω. 4. ϊσραηλειται√. [αι διαθ.]. 6. ιηλ' *prim.* ιηλ *secund.*√ (*sic* v. 27 *bis.* v. 31). 7. εισιν√. ισακ (C ϊσαακ, *sic* v. 10 *p.m.*). 8. (+ οτι C *post* τουτεστι, *sic* Cod. B *s.m.*). 9. εστε√. 11. φαυλον (*pro* κακον). προθεσισ του θυ. 12. ερρεθη. μειζον (-ων C). 15. τω μωϋσει γαρ. οικτιρησω√. οικτιρω√. 16. ελεωντοσ. 17. ενδιξωμαι√. 18. [ελεει]. 19. ερισ μοι ουν τι ετι. [γαρ]. ανθεστηκεν√. 20. ω ανθρωπε μενουνγε (μ. ω α. C). 22. ενδειξασθε√. απωλιαν√. 25. λεγι√. 26. ω (ου A?) ερρεθη αυτοισ. 27. ϋπολιμμα (καταλιμμα A). 28. — εν δικ. οτι λογον συντετμημενον (C εν δικ. οτι λογ. συν.). 29. σαβαωθ' ενκατελιπεν. [ωμοι.]. 30. κατελαβεν√. 31. — δικαιοσυνησ *secund.* (*addit* C). εφθασεν√. 32. — νομου (*addit* C). προσεκοψεν (-αν C). — γαρ (*addit* C). 33. — πασ. κατεσχυνθησεται√.

X. 1. — η *tertium* (προσ τον θν *p.m. super ras.*). αυτων (*pro* του ιηλ εστιν: C *habet* αυτων εστιν). 3. [*sic*]. 5. μωυσησ. οτι *transfert in locum post* γραφει (*at* C *cum* Steph.).—του.—αυτα (*habet* C). *fin.* αυτη (C αυτοισ). 6. ουτωσ√. [τη]. τουτεστιν√ (*sic* vv. 7. 8). 9. [κν ιν]. 11. κατεσχυνθησεται√. 12. εστιν√. 14. επικαλεσωνται. πιστευσωσιν. ακουσονται (C ακουσωσιν). 15. κηρυξωσιν. αποσταλωσιν√. ωρεοι√—των ευαγγ. ειρηνην (*habet* C των ευ. ϊρ.). [τα αγ., *at* —τα C]. 16. + εϋ *ante* τω ευ. (. . *p.m.*). επιστευσεν√. 17. χυ (*pro* θυ: A *et* C θυ). 19. ιηλ ουκ εγνω. μωϋσησ. (αυτουσ C *bis in versu, pro* υμασ). εθνι *bis*√. 20. [ευρεθην τοισ *et* εγενομην τοισ]. επερωτωσιν√. 21. λεγι√. απιθουντα√.

XI. 1. (C *habet* ον προεγνω *ante* μη γεν.). ϊσδραηλειτησ√ βενιαμειν√. 2. (—λεγων C). 3. απεκτιναν√.—και *prim.* (*habet* C).

ὑπελιφθην√. ζητουσιν√. 4. βααλ'√. 5. λιμμα√. 6. επι *prim.*√. γεινεται√.—ει δε εξ εργ. *ad fin. vers.* (*habet* C: *at* εστιν *bis*). 7. τουτο. 8. καθαπερ (*pro* καθωσ). ο οθσ√. 10. συνκαμψον. 11. πεσωσιν√. 13. δε (*pro* γαρ). + ουν (*post* μεν). 15. προσλημψισ. 17. αγριελεοσ√. συνκοινωνοσ.—και *secund.* (*habet* C). ελεασ√. 18. αλλα. 19. ερισ√. — οι. ενκεντρισθω. 20. πιστιν√. υψηλα φρονει. 21. ει γαρ *in rasura p.m.* εφισατο√. — μηπωσ. φισεται. 22. αποτομια *p.m.* (*pro* -αν *secund.*: C -αν, ν *deleto*). χρηστοτητοσ θυ εαν επιμενησ. 23. κακεινοι. επιμενωσιν (επιμεινωσιν C). ενκεντρισθησονται (*sic* v. 24). ενκεντρισαι. 25. θελω γαρ. [παρ]. 26. [ουτω].—και *secund.* ασεβιασ√. 28. πρασ (α *supplet* A ?)√. 30. *Deest vers. p.m.* (*supplet* A, *omisso* και, *quod supplet* C). 31. ουτωσ√. ηπιθησαν√. [υμετ.]. νυν (*pro* αυτοι), *at* A αυτοι νυν. ελεηθωσιν√. 32. συνεκλισεν√. απιθιαν√. 33. ανεξεραυνητα. 35. ανταποδοθησετε√.

XII. 1. τω θω ευαρεστον (C *cum* Steph.). λατριαν√. 2. συνσχηματιζεσθε. μεταμορφουσθαι. [υμων]. 3. δοθισησ√. ὑπερφρονιν√. φρονιν√ *bis.* σωφρονιν√. εμερισεν√. 4. πολλα μελη. 5. το (*pro* ο). καθισ√. 6. δοθισαν√. προφητιαν√. 7. (C ειτ ο διακονων *pro* ειτε διακονιαν). 8. προιστανομενοσ. ελαιων√. 11. κω (*pro* καιρω). 12. θλιψι√. υπομενοντεσ (*sic p.m.*)√. 13. χριαισ. 14. [ὑμασ]. 15. — και. 16. ταπινοισ√. γινεσθαι. 17. [*sic*]. 19. εκδικησεισ√. 20. αλλ εαν πινα (—ουν).

XIII. 1. ὑπο (*pro* απο).—εξουσιαι.—του (*habet* C). 2. λημψονται. 3. εισιν√. τω αγαθω εργω. τω κακω. φοβεισθε√. εξισ√. 4. εστιν√. εισ οργην εκδικοσ (εκδ. εισ ορ. C). 5. συνιδησιν√. 6. λιτουργοι√. 7. —ουν [πασι] *at* C ουν πασιν *habet.* οφιλασ√. 8. οφιλοντεσ (οφιλητε C). αλληλουσ αγαπαν. πεπληρωκεν√. 9. μοιχευσισ√. ψευδομαρτυρησισ. + εστιν (*ante* εντολη: *non* C). τω λογω τουτω. [εν τω] αγαπησισ√. σεαυτον. 11. ηδη ὑμας (ημ. *pro* υμ. C). 12. — και (*ante* ενδυσ: C *addit* και). [οπλα]. 13. ασελγιαισ√. [εριδι]. 14. [αλλ]. ποιεισθαι.

XIV. 1. πιστι√. 2. φαγιν√. 3. εξουθενιτω√. ο δε (*pro* και ο: C *cum* Steph.). 4. δυνατι γαρ ο κσ (*pro* δυν. γαρ. εστιν ο θσ). 5. + γαρ (*post* μεν: *non* C). νοει√. πληροφορισθω√. 6. — και ο *usque ad* φρονει. + και (*ante* ο εσθιων). ευχαριστι√ *bis.* 7. ουδισ *bis*√. αποθνησκι√. 8. αποθνησκωμεν *ter in vers.* 9. — και *prim.* (*habet* C). — και ανεστη (*habet* C). εζησεν. 10. εξουθενισ√. *fin.* θυ (χυ C *cum* Steph.). 11. [*sic*]. 12. [*sic*]. 14. πεπισμαι√. 15.

γαρ (*pro* δε). απεθανεν√. 16. βλασφημισθω√. 18. τουτω (C *cum* Steph. τουτοισ). [τω χ̅ω̅]. [δοκιμοσ]. 19. διωκομεν. 20. απολλυε (C καταλυε). (+τοισ καθαροισ *post* καθαρα C). 21. *fin.* λυπειται (*loco* προσκ. *ad fin. vers. p.m.* A *habet* προσκ. *pro* λυπειται. C *addit* η σκαν. η ασθενι). 22. + ην (*post* πιστιν).. σεαυτον.—ενωπιον του θ̅υ̅ (*habet* A). 23. —παν δε ο ουκ εκ πιστεωσ (*addit* A) *ob* ὁμοιοτελευτον.

XV. 1. οφιλομεν√. ημισ√. αρεσκιν√. 2. —γαρ.—εισ το αγαθον (*habet* A). 3. ονιδισμοι√. ονιδειζοντων√. επεπεσαν. 4. εγραφη *secund.* (προεγ. C). +δια (*ante* τησ παρακ.). 5. φρονιν√. ι̅ν̅ χ̅ν̅. 7. προσλαμβανεσθαι√. ϋμασ (*pro* ημασ). +του (*ante* θ̅υ̅). 8. γαρ (*pro* δε).—ι̅ν̅. [γεγενησθαι]. αληθιασ√. 9. δια του προφητου *p.m.* (A δια τουτο ‘φητου’ *uncinis incluso*). εθνεσιν√.—και *p.m.* (*habet* C). 11. και παλιν αινειται παντα τα εθνη τον κ̅ν̅. επαινεσατωσαν. 12. λεγει ησαϊασ. ανισταναμενοσ. 13. δυναμι√. 14. πεπισμαι√. +τησ (*ante* γνωσεωσ). 15. —αδελφοι (*habet* C). δοθισαν√. απο (*pro* υπο: C ϋπο). 16. λιτουργον χυ ι̅υ̅. 17. +τον (*ante* θ̅ν̅). 18. (τολμω C). τι λαλιν. [κατειρ.]. 19. [θ̅υ̅]. ι̅η̅λ̅μ̅√ (*sic* vv. 25, 26). 20. ουτωσ√. [-μενον]. 21. ανηγγελλη√. ακηκοασιν συνησουσιν√. 22. [τα πολλα]. ελθι̅√. 23. [κλιμασι]√. [του] ελθιν. [πολλω̅]. 24. αν (*pro* εαν).—ελευσομαι προσ υμασ (*habet* C). [υφ]. 25. διακονησων (C διακονων). 26, 27. ηϋδοκησαν. 26. μακαιδονια√. 27. οφιλεται√. εισιν αυτων. οφιλουσιν√. λιτουργησαι√. 28. σφραγισαμενοισ (*ob* αυτοισ *seq.*)√.—την (*habet* C). 29. —του ευαγγελιου του (*habet* C). 30. [αδ.]. 31. απιθουντων√.— ινα *secund.* (*habet* C). [διακονια]. ισ ιερουσαλημ (*plenè*)√. τοισ αγιοις γενηται. 32. ελθω̅ εν χαρα (C *cum* Steph.). ι̅υ̅ χ̅υ̅ *et* —και (*pro* θ̅υ̅ και: C *cum* Steph.). 33. ϊρηνησ√. [αμην].

XVI. 1. [ημων]. (+και *ante* διακονον C). κε̅χραιαισ. 2. *fin.* και αυτου και εμου [*caetera cum* Steph.]. 3. ασπασασθαι√ (*sic* vv. 5. 7, 8. 12 *bis*). πρισκαν. 5. ασιασ (*pro* αχαϊασ). 6. [-αμ]. *fin.* υμασ. 7. συνεχμαλωτουσ√.—οι (C οι *addit*). γεγοναν. 8. αμπλιατον. 9. [χ̅ω̅]. 11. ηρωδιωνα. 12. τρυφεναν√. [ασπ. περσ. κ.τ.λ. *cum* Steph.]. 14. ασυνκριτον. ερμην πατροβαν ερμαν. 15. [*sic*]. 16. +πασαι (*post* εκκλησιαι). 17. εκκλινετε (-ατε C). 18. —ι̅υ̅. [-τωσι]. 19. εφ υμιν ουν χαιρω (—το: C *cum* Steph.). [μεν]. ακαιρεουσ√. 20. συντριψι√ ταχι√.—χ̅υ̅. [αμην *deest*].

21. ασπαζεται. 23. ολησ τησ εκκλησιασ. ασπαζετε *secund.* 24. *Deest versus.* 25. κ̅υ̅ (*pro* το κηρυγμα: A *cum* Steph.). 27. + των αιωνων (*ante* αμην).

Subscr. προσ ρωμαιουσ.

προσ κορινθιουσ α.

Cap. I. 1. [*sic:* ι̅υ̅ *p.m. at* αυ *primò*]. 2. —τε (*habet* C: *caetera cum* Steph., *etiam* πασι). 4. —μου *p.m.* (*habet* A). δοθισῃ√. 5. ἐν ἐν (..*p.m.*) *primum*√. 7. ὑστερισθαι√. 8. *Bis scriptus hic versus, ob* ι̅υ̅ χ̅υ̅ v. 7: *delet* A√. 11. εισιν√. 13. [ὑπερ]. 14. —τω θ̅ω̅ (*habet* C). πρισκον (κρ. C). 15. εβαπτισθητε. 17. απεστιλεν√. αλλα. ευαγγελιζεσθε√. 18. εστιν *bis*√. σωμενοισ√. 20. συνζητητησ.—τουτου (*addit* C). 21. επιδη√ (*non* v. 22). 22. σημια αιτουσιν√. 23. εθνεσιν (*pro* ελλησι). 24. ελλησιν√. 25. εστιν *prim.*√. *fin.* —εστι (*at* εστιν C). 26. βλεπεται√. ευγενισ√. 27. κατεσχυνη τουσ σοφουσ. κατεσχυνη *secund.* [*caetera cum* Steph.]. 28. ασθενη (*pro* αγενη: A *cum* Steph.).—και *tert.* (*habet* C). 29. [-σηται]. του θ̅υ̅ (*pro* αυτου: *at* αυ θ̅υ̅ C, αυ *eras.*). 30. σοφια ημιν.

II. 1. μυστηριον (*pro* μαρτυριον: C *cum* Steph.). 2. —του. [ειδ. τι]. 3. καγω. ασθενια√. 4. πιθοισ√.—ανθρωπινησ (*habet* C). λογοσ (-οισ A?? C)√. 5. δυναμι√. 6. τελιοισ√. 7. θ̅υ̅ σοφιαν. 9. ειδεν√. ηκουσεν√. 10. [δε] απεκαλυψεν ο θ̅σ̅.—αυτου (*habet* C). ερευνα. 11. ουτωs√. εγνωκεν (*pro* οιδεν). 12. ημισ√. 13. (λογοισ α *rescript. p.m.*).—αγιου. συνκρινοντεσ. 14. εστιν√. 15. *Deest versus ob* ὁμοιοτελ. (*habet* A, *etiam* μεν). 16. [συμβ. *et* χ̅υ̅].

III. 1. καγω. σαρκινοισ. 2. —και. εδυνασθε. ουδε [ετι]. 3. [σαρ. εστε]. —και διχοστασιαι. 4. ουκ α̅ν̅ο̅ι̅ (*pro* ουχι σαρκικοι: C *cum* Steph.). 5. τι ουν εστιν απολλωσ· τι δε εστιν παυλοσ (τισ C *bis*).—αλλ η. 6. αλλα. 7. εστιν√. ουδε (*pro* ουτε *secund.*: C *cum* Steph.). 8. λημψεται (*sic* v. 14). 10. δοθισαν√. εθηκα (C τεθικα). 11. ι̅σ̅ χ̅σ̅ (—ο). 12. —τουτον (*habet* C). αργυριον. 13. εστιν√ (*sic* v. 19; *caetera cum* Steph.). 14. εποικοδομησεν√.

15. ουτωσ√. 17. [τουτον]. ῦμισ√. 19. [τω]. 20. γινωσκι√. εισιν√. 21. μηδισ√. 22. *fin.* —εστιν.

IV. 2. ωδε (*pro* ο δε). + τι (*post* λοιπον: *non* A?? C). ζητειτε√. 4. γαρ (*pro* δε: C *cum* Steph.). 5. κρινεται√. 6. —δε (*habet* A). απολλων (ν *delent* A?? C). α (*pro* ο). γεγραπτε√. —φρονειν (φρονιν C). φυσιουσθαι√. 8. ημισ√. συνβασιλευσωμεν. 9. —οτι (*habet* C). απεδιξεν√. 11. πινωμεν√. γυμνιτευομεν. 12. χερσιν√. 13. δυσφημουμενοι (βλασφ. C). 14. νουθετω̄. 17. +αυτο (*post* τουτο: *delet* C). εστιν√. μου τεκνον. + ῑῡ (*post* χ̄ω̄). 20. δυναμι√. 21. [πραοτ.].

V. 1. ακουετε√. πορνια√ *bis.*—ονομαζεται (*habet* C). εχιν√. 2. ῦμισ√. αρθη. πραξασ. 3. —ωσ *prim.* ουτωσ√. 4. ημων *prim.* [χ̄ῡ, *primo loco*]. δυναμι√. [ημων *secund.*].—χ̄ῡ *secund.* 5. [ῑῡ]. 7. —ουν (*habet* C).—υπερ ημων (*habet* C). [ετυθη]. 8. [-ζωμεν]. ειλικρινιασ√. αληθιασ√. 10. *init.*—και (*habet* C). και (*pro* η *secund.*: C η). ωφιλετε√. εξελθιν√. 11. [νυνι *p.m.*, *at* νυν C]. 12. —και. κρινειτε (A κρινετε). 13. —και. εξαρατε.

VI. 2. *init.* +η. κρινουσιν√. 5. [λεγω]. ενι (*pro* εστιν). ουδεισ σοφοσ. ανακριναι (C διακρ.). 7. —ουν (*habet* C).—εν. κριμα. 8. τουτο. 9. θ̄ῡ βασιλειαν. κληρονομησουσιν√ (*sic* v. 10). πλανασθαι√. 10. ου μεθυσοι (*pro* ουτε μ.).—ου *ult.* 11. [αλλα]. αλλα εδικ. κ̄ῡ ῑῡ χ̄ῡ. 13. πορνια√. 14. ηγειρεν√. [ημασ εξεγερει]. δυμεωσ√* (* in MS.). 15. ημων (C ῦμων). 16. [η]. 17. εστιν√. 18. πορνιαν√. αμαρτανι√. 19. οιδαται. (+ τον [*ante* θ̄ῡ] C). *fin.* αυτων (εαυτων C). 20. —δη (*habet* A).—και εν τω π̄ν̄ῑ *ad fin. vers.*

VII. 1. —μοι. 2. πορνιασ√. 3. οφιλην (*pro* οφ. ευνοιαν). [δε]. 4. αλλα *bis.* 5. αποστεριτε√. σχολασητε.—τη νηστεια και (C τη νηστια και). ητε (*pro* συνερχησθε). πιραζη√. 6. [γγ]. 7. δε (*pro* γαρ: C *cum* Steph.). [αλλ]. εχει χαρισμα. ο (*pro* οσ *bis*: C *cum* Steph.). 8. —εστιν. μινωσιν√. 9. κριττον. εστιν γαμιν (γαμησαι C) η πυρουσθε√. 10. γεγαμηκοσιν√. αλλα. [-ρισθηναι]. 12. λεγω εγω. [αυτη]. 13. ει τισ (*pro* ητισ). ουτοσ (*pro* αυτοσ). *fin.* αῦτον ανδρα (. . *p.m.?* *et* C). 14. απι[στος A] *secund.* √. αδελφω (*pro* ανδρι: C *cum* Steph.). εστιν√ *bis.* 15. χωριζετε√.—η *inter* η *et* αδελ. (*habet* C). ῦμασ (C ημασ). 16. σωσισ *prim.* √. 17. μεμερικεν ο κ̄σ̄ (εμερισεν C: *deest* θ̄σ̄). θ̄σ̄ (*pro* κσ *sequente*). πασαισ ταισ εκκλησιαισ. 18. κεκληται τισ. 19. εστιν *bis*√. 22. — και. *fin.* χυ εστιν (C *cum* Steph.). 23. γεινεσθε√. 24. —τω. 27. δεδεσε√. ζητι√ *bis*. 28. γαμησησ. [η]. ημαρτεν√. φιδομαι√. 29. συννεσταλμενος εστι τολοιπον. [οι εχ.]. ωσιν√. 31. τον κοσμον (— τουτω), *at* C *cum* Steph. 32. αρεση (*sic* vv. 33. 34). 34. *init.* και μεμερισται και + η αγαμοσ (*post* γυνη). και τω σωματι και τω πνι. 35. συμφορον (C *cum* Steph.). ευπαρεδρον. 36. ασχημονι√. οφιλει γινεσθε√. γαμιτωσαν√. 37. εν τη καρδια αυτου εδραιοσ (C εδρ. εν τη καρ. αυτ.). ιδια καρδια τηριν (—αυτου του). *fin.* ποιησει. 38. γαμιζων την εαυτου παρθενον (*pro* εκγαμιζων). και ο (C *et* Steph. ο δε). γαμιζων *secund.* (C *et* Steph. εκγαμιζων). κρισσον ποιησει. 39. —νομω (*habet* C). [*deest* και].—αυτησ. 40. ουτωσ μινη√.

VIII. 1. ϊδωλοθυτων (*non* v. 4). 2. — δε. εγνωκεναι (*pro* ειδεναι). ουπω εγνω (—ουδεν). 3. — υπ αυτου (*habet* C). 4. ουδισ√. —ετεροσ (*habet* C). 5. εισιν√ *bis*.—τησ. 6. [αλλ].—θσ (*habet* A). ημισ√ *bis*. 7. συνηθια (*pro* συνειδησει: *at* C συνϊδησι). εωσ αρτι του ειδωλου. εστιν (*pro* εσθιουσιν *quod legit* A). συνιδησεισ√ (*sic* v. 10). 8. υμασ (ημασ C) ου παραστησει (παριστησιν C).—γαρ. [*caetera cum* Steph.] 9. ασθενεσιν. 10. γνωσιν εχοντα (εχ. γν. C). ιδωλιω√. ϊδωλοθυτα√. 11. απολλυται γαρ (και απολλυται C). εν τη ση γνωσει ο αδελφοσ (C αδ. εν τη ση γν.). 12. ουτωσ√. συνιδησιν√. 13. κρεασ (C κρεα).

IX. 1. ουκ ειμι ελευθεροσ ουκ ειμι αποστολοσ.—χυ. εορακα. 2. μου τησ αποστολησ. 3. εστιν αυτη. 4. πιν (C πιϊν). 6. — του. 7. τον καρπον (—εκ: C *cum* Steph.). [η]. 8. και ο νομοσ ταυτα ου. 9. μωϋσεωσ. [-σεισ]. 10. οφιλει επ ελπιδι (C *cum* Steph.). επ ελπιδι του μετεχειν (—τησ ελπιδοσ αυτου: C *cum* Steph., *praeter* μετεχιν). 11. ημισ *bis*√. εσπιραμεν√. [-σομεν]. 12. ϋμων εξουσιασ. (ουχι *pro* ου C). ημισ√. τινα εκκοπην. 13. + τα (*ante* εκ). παρεδρευοντεσ (προσεδ. C). [μμ]. 14. ουτωσ√ (*sic* v. 15). διεταξεν√. 15. ου κεχρημαι ουδενι (ουκ εχρησαμην ουδενι C). αποθανιν√. ουδισ κενωσει (—ινα τισ: C ινα τισ κενωσει). 16. χαρισ (*pro* καυχημα: A *cum* Steph.). γαρ (*pro* δε: C *cum* Steph.). [-ζωμαι]. 18. μου (*pro* μοι: C *cum* Steph.). ευαγ: *rescript.*√. ε *deest p.m.?*—του χυ. + εν̈ (*ante* τη εξουσια: . . *p.m.?*). 19. πλιονασ√. 20. + μη ων αυτοσ ϋπο νομον (*ante* ινα *secund.*). 21. θυ. χυ. κερδανω τουσ (C κερδησω *sine* τουσ). 22. —ως (*habet* C). [πασι: πασιν C].—τα. 23. παντα (*pro* τουτο). [γκ]. 24. λαμβανι√. βραβιον√. ουτωσ√ (*sic* v. 26 *bis*). 25. *fin.* ᵃφθ (*a minutum, at p.m.*). 27. [υπωπια-].

X. 1. γαρ (*pro* δε: C *cum* Steph.). 2. [μωσην] εβαπτισθησαν. 3. —το αυτο *prim.* (*habet* C). π̄ν̄ικον βρωμα (C *cum* Steph.). π̄ν̄ικον επιον πομα. 4. πετρα δε. 5. [ευδ.]. 7. ωσπερ (*pro* ωσ). πιν. πεζιν√. 8. επεσαν.—εν (*habet* C). εικοσιτρισ√. 9. εκπιραζωμεν√. κ̄ν̄ (*pro* χ̄ν̄).—και *prim.*—αυτων (*habet* C). εξεπιρασαν. απωλλυντο (*non* v. 10). 10. γογγυζωμεν καθαπερ.—και *prim.* 11. παντα δε ταυτα. τυπικωσ συνεβαινεν. εισ (*pro* προσ: C *cum* Steph.). κατηντηκεν. 13. πιρασμοσ√. πιρασθηναι√. δυνασθαι√. πιρασμω√.—υμασ *tert.* (*habet* C). 14. ϊδωλολατριασ√. 15. ϋμασ (ϋμεισ A. Steph.). 16. κοινωνιασ *prim.* (-ια A). [του αι. του χ̄ῡ]. εστιν√. [*caetera cum* Steph.]. 18. ουχ (C *cum* Steph.). εισιν√. 19. τι ουν φημι οτι ειδωλοθυτον εστιν *tantum.* (A ειδωλοθυτον τι εστιν η οτι ειδωλον τι εστιν). 20. α θυουσιν τα εθνη δαιμονιοισ και ου θ̄ω̄ θυουσιν. γεινεσθαι√. 21. πινιν√. μετεχιν√. 23. —μοι *bis* (*habet* C). 24. —εκαστοσ. 25. συνϊδησιν√ (*sic* vv. 27. 28. 29). 26. κ̄ῡ γαρ. 27. —δε. θελεται πορευεσθε√. 28. ϊεροθυτον (*pro* ειδωλ.). εστιν√ (τιν μη *rescripsit p.m. vel* A).—του γαρ κ̄ῡ *ad fin. vers.* 30. —δε. 32. και ϊουδαιοισ γεινεσθε (γειν. και ϊου.). ελλησιν√. 33. συμφορον (C *cum* Steph.). σωθωσιν√.

XI. I. *Jungit* σωθωσιν *cum* μιμηται. γεινεσθαι√. 2. —αδελφοι. μεμνησθαι√. παραδεδωκα. 3. εστιν√ (*sic* vv. 5. 13. 14. 20). +του (*ante* χ̄ῡ). 5. αυτης (*pro* εαυτησ). 7. οφιλει√ (*sic* v. 10). (C *habet* η *ante* γυνη). 11. ουτε γυνη χωρισ ανδρος ουτε ανηρ χωρισ γυναικοσ. 12. ουτωσ√. 14. *init.*—η. η φυσισ αυτη. +γαρ (*post* μεν) *delet forsan p.m.* 15. [*sic*]. 16. φιλονικοσ√. συνηθιαν√. 17. [-λλων ουκ επαινω]. κρισσον. αλλᵃ (*a minut. p.m.*)√. ησσον. 18. —τη. 19. αιρεσισ√. [ινα οι]. 20. διπν̄ō√ (*sic* v. 21). φαγει (-ειν C *alii ?*)√. 21. φαγιν√. πινα√. 22. πινιν√. καταφρονιτε√. κατεσχυνετε√. ειπω ϋμιν. [-νεσω]. 23. παρεδιδετο. 24. εκλασεν√. ειπεν√.—λαβετε φαγετε. εστιν√.—κλωμενον (*addit* C). ποιειται√. 25. διπνησαι√. εαν (*pro* αν), *sic* v. 26 *prim.* 26. —τουτον (*habet* C), *at habet* τουτο και το ποτηριον πινητε (C *cum* Steph.). αχρι.—αν *secund.* (αχρισ ου αν C). 27. —τουτον. [η]. +του κ̄ῡ (*post* του κ̄ῡ αναξιωσ). εστε√. +του (*ante* αιματοσ). 28. [ανθ. εαν]. (+πρωτον *post* εαυτον *in* C). 29. —αναξιωσ (*habet* C). πινι√.—του κ̄ῡ (*habet* C). 30. ασθενισ√. 31. δε (*pro* γαρ: C *cum* Steph.). 32. + του (*ante* $\overline{κυ}$). 33. φαγιν√. 34. —δε (*habet* C). πινα√. [-ξομαι].

XII. 2. + οτε (*ante* εθνη). ϊδωλα√. 3. ουδισ√ *bis*. $\overline{ισ}$ *prim*. $\overline{κσ}$ $\overline{ισ}$. 4, 5. εισιν√. 6. διερεσεισ√ *hic tantum*. [ο δε].—εστι (*habet* εστιν C). 9. —δε *prim*. (*habet* C). [αυτω *secund*.]. 10. [δε *secund*. *et tert*.]. προφητια√. διακρισισ√.—δε *quart*. (*habet* C). ερμηνια√. 11. ενεργι√. 12. εστιν *bis*√. πολλα εχει. μεληλη *secund*.√.—του ενοσ (*habet* C). ουτωσ√. 13. — εισ *secund*. 15. εστι^ν (ν *p.m.*, στ *rescript*: *forsan ab* A: *primò* ειμι)√. 18. [νυνϊ δε] *p.m.*? *vel* νυν ϊδε. 19. [τα]. 20. [μεν]. 21. + ο (*post* δε). ειπιν√. χριαν *bis*√ (*sic* v. 24). ποσιν√. 22. εστιν√. 23. [ατιμοτερα]. 24. αλλα. συνεκερασεν√.—το (*habet* C.). ϋστερουμενω (C *cum* Steph.). 25. σχισματα. [μεριμνωσι]. 26. [ειτε *bis*]. συνπασχει.—εν *secund*. (*habet* C). [συγχ.]. 28. δυναμισ√ (*sic* v. 29). επειτα (*pro* ειτα). αντιλημψεισ. κυβερνησισ√.—γενη (*habet* A). 30. λαλουσιν√. διερμηνευουσιν√. 31. μιζονα (*pro* κρειττονα). δικνυμι√.

XIII. 1, 2. ὁμοιοτελ.—γεγονα *usque ad* μη εχω v. 2 (*supplet* A: *legens* προφητιαν. μεθιστανα, *at* αλαλαζον και εαν). 2. [ουθεν]. 3. [και εαν *bis*]. καυχησωμαι (*pro* καυθ.). ουθεν (*pro* ουδεν). 4. [*sic*]. 5. ζητι√. 6. συγχαιρι√. αληθια√. 8. πιπτει (C *cum* Steph.). προφητιαι√. [γνωσισ]. καταργηθησονται. 9. [γαρ]. 10. τελιον√.—τοτε. 11. ελαλουν ωσ νηπιοσ· εφρονουν ωσ νηπιοσ· ελογιζομην ωσ νηπιοσ.—δε (*habet* C). 12. το^τε δε (τε A: το δε *p.m.*). 13. μιζων√. (*Jungit* διωκετε την αγαπην XIV. 1, *cum cap*. XIII.)

XIV. 2. ουχ.—τω (*habet* C). ουθισ (*pro* ουδεισ). 5. λαλιν√. δε (*pro* γαρ: C *cum* Steph.). 6. νυν.—η *prim*. προφητια√ (*sic* v. 22).—εν *ult*. (*habet* C). 7. [*sic*]. 8. σαλπιγξ φωνην. 9. ουτωσ√ (*sic* v. 12). ϋμισ√. 10. εισιν.—αυτων (*habet* C). 12. επι√. ζητιτε√. 13. διο (διοπερ C). 14. [γαρ]. 14, 15. εστιν√. 15. προσευξωμαι *prim*. [-ομαι *secund*.]. [ψαλω δε και τω]. 16. ευλογησ (+ εν C).—τω. οιδεν√. 17. ευχαριστισ√. 18. —μου. γλωσση λαλω. 19. —αλλ [*habent* A? C]. τω νοϊ (—δια). 20. γεινεσθε√. φρεσιν *bis*√. 21. + τι (*ante* γεγραπται: *improbat* C). ετερων. 22. σημιον√. 23. [συνελθη]. π. λαλωσιν γλωσσαισ. εισελθωσιν√. 25. —και ουτω. γεινεται√. ουτωσ *secund*.√. οντωσ $\overline{θσ}$ (—ο: *habet* C). εστιν√. 26. —υμων (*habet* C). αποκαλυψιν εχει γλωσσαν εχει. ερμηνιαν√. γινεσθω. 27. λαλι√. πλιστον τρισ√. 28. [διερμ.]. 29. τρισ√. 30. ο̇π̇^{κα}θημενω (*p.m. omnia*)√. 31. μανθανωσιν√. 33. αλλα. 34. —υμων. επιτρεπεται. αλλα ϋποτασσεσθωσαν. 35. μανθανειν (μανθειν C). εστι γυναικι (εστιν γυναιξι C) λαλειν εν εκκλησια. 37. —του. εντολη εστιν (εστιν εν. C). 38. αγνοειται (-τω C). 39. +μου (*post* αδελφοι). μη κωλυετε γλωσσαισ. 40. +δε (*post* παντα).

XV. 1. γνωριζω ἀ (ἀ *p.m.*)√. 4. τη ημερα τη τριτη. 6. πλιονεσ.—και (*habet* C). 7. επειτα (*pro* ειτα: C *cum* Steph.). 9. ιμι *secund.*√. 10. απαντων (α *eras.*). αλλα *secund.*—η *ult.* (*habet* C). 11. ουτωσ *bis*√. πιστευσατε (επισ. C). 12. κηρυσσετε√. [οτι εκ ν.]. λεγουσιν εν υμιν τινεσ. 13. —ει δε *usque ad* εστιν (ὁμοιοτ. *supplet* A). 14. +και (*post* αρα: *improbat* C). καινη.—δε *secund.* 15. ηγειρεν√ *bis*. +αυτου (*post* $\overline{\chi\nu}$: *improbat* C). 16. εγιρονται *hic*√. 17. ϋμω̄ και ετι (και *improbat* C). 19. εν $\overline{\chi\omega}$ ηλπικοτεσ εσμεν. 20. —εγενετο. 21. επιδη√.—ο. 22. υσιν *p.m. in rasura.—addito ad explendum spatium.* Tisch.√. ουτωσ√. 23. δε *supra, p.m.* +του (*ante* $\overline{\chi\nu}$). 24. παραδιδω. βασιλιαν√. του $\overline{\theta\upsilon}$ (τω $\overline{\theta\omega}$ C). 25. αχρι (αχρισ C).—αν (*habet* C). [-ρουσ ϋπο]. 27. —παντα γαρ *usque ad* ποδασ αυτου (*habet* C: *in* A *transfertur in locum ante* v. 26). ειπ. οτι τα παντα. 28. —οταν δε υπ. αυτ. τα παν. (ὁμοιοτ.: *habet* A). [τοτε και]. [τα π. *tert.*]. 29. εγιρονται√. αυτων (*pro* των ν. *secund.*). 30. ημισ√. 31. ϋμετεραν. +αδελφοι (*ante* ην). 33. πλανασθαι√. χρηστα. 34. εχουσιν√. λαλω (*pro* λεγω). 35. [αλλ]. ερι√. 36. αφρων. σπιρεισ√. +εισ την (*ante* εαν: ... ... *p.m.*)√. 37. σπιρεισ *prim.*√.—σπειρεισ *secund.* (*habet* A). 38. διδωσιν αυτω. ηθελησεν√.—το (*habet* C). 39. —σαρξ *tert.* αλλη δε σαρξ πτηνων αλλη δε ϊχθυων. 40. [αλλ]. 42. ουτωσ√ (*sic* v. 45). σπιρεται *et* εγιρεται (*non* v. 43)√. 43. ασθενια√. δυναμι√. 44. ε' εστιν *prim.* (ε' *p.m.? instauravit* C). *fin.* εστιν και $\overline{\pi\nu}$ικον (—σωμα *quart.*). 45. [ανθρωποσ]. 47. —ο $\overline{\kappa\sigma}$ (*habet* C). 49. φορεσωμεν. 50. [-νομει]. 51. παντεσ μεν κοιμηθησομεθα ου π. δε. 52. [ριπη]. [εγερ.]. 54. —το φθαρτον *usque ad* αφθαρσιαν και (*habet* C: *at* και το, *superante* το). +την (*ante* αθανασιαν). 55. κεντρον *et* νικοσ *transferuntur:* θανατε (*pro* αδη). (C *improbat* που σου θ. το νικ.: *at post* κεντρον *addit* που σου αδη το νικοσ, *prorsus cum* Steph.) 57. νεικοσ√. 58. γεινεσθε√. εστιν√.

XVI. 1. γαλατειασ√. ουτωσ√. υμισ√. 2. σαββατω (ου A, ων C). (ευοδωθη C). 3. [εαν]. δοκιμασηται√. απενεγκιν√. ισ ι̅η̅λ̅μ̅√. 4. (αξιον η C). 5. μακαιδονιαν *bis*√. 7. ειδιν√. γαρ (*pro* δε). επιτρεψη. 9. ανεωγεν√. αντικιμενοι√. 10. βλεπεται√. καγω. 11. —δε (*habet* C). ιρηνη√. [με]. 12. —απολλω (*habet* A). + δηλω ὑμιν οτι (*ante* πολλα: *improbat* C). ευκερηση√. 13. πιστι√. -ζέσθε κρατεουσθαι√. 15. —δε (*habet* C). (+ και φορτουνατου *post* στεφανα C). 17. φορτουνατου (ρ *instaurat* C). [ὑμων]. [ουτοι]. 18. επιγινωσκεται√. 19. ασπαζεται (*pro* ασπαζονται *secund.*). πρισκα. 22. —ι̅ν̅ χ̅ν̅ (*habet* C). 23. —χ̅υ̅ (*habet* C). [αμην].

Subscr. προσ κορινθιουσ α.

προσ κορινθιουσ β.

Cap. I. 1. χ̅υ̅ ι̅υ̅. πασιν√. 5. ουτωσ√ (*sic* v. 7). + του (*post* δια). 6. ειτε παρακαλουμεθα *usque ad* παρακλησεωσ *transfert in locum ante* τησ ενεργουμενησ κ.τ.λ.— και σωτηριασ *secund.* ημισ√. [*fin.* και η ελπισ κ.τ.λ.]. 7. ωσ (*pro* ωσπερ). 8. περι (*pro* υπερ).— ημιν (*habet* C). ὑπερ δυναμιν εβαρηθημεν. 9. αλλ. εγιροντι√. 10. [ρρ]. ρυσεται (*pro* ρυεται). [οτι και ετι]. 11. $\overset{η}{υ}$μων (η *etiam p.m.*, *pro* ημων *prim.*). *fin.* [ημων]. 12. εστιν√. ημων *secund. p.m. at* υ *primò*. αγιοτητι (*pro* απλοτητι: C *cum* Steph.). ειλικρινια√. + του (*ante* θ̅υ̅ *prim.* ·· *eras.*). 13. [αλλ]. αναγεινωσκεται√. [επιγινωσκετε].—και *secund.* 14. ὑμισ√. + ημων (*ante* ι̅υ̅). *fin.* (+ χυ C, *at eras.*). 15. (+ προτερον A, *post* εβουλομην). [πρ. υμ. ελθ.].—προτερον. (χαραν *pro* χαριν C). σχητε. 16. διελθιν√. μακαιδονιαν√. μακαιδονιασ√. 17. βουλομενοσ. 18. εστιν (*pro* εγενετο: C *cum* Steph.). 19. του θ̅υ̅ γαρ. χ̅σ̅ ι̅σ̅ (C ι̅σ̅ χ̅σ̅). 20. διο και δι αυτου (*pro* και εν αυτω).—το *secund.* (*habet* C). 21. χρεισασ√. 22. —ο (*habet* C). αραβωνα. καρδιεσ (-αισ C)√. 24. πιστι√.

II. 1. εν λυπη προσ ὑμασ ελθειν. 2. $\overset{ε}{ι}$ γαρ εγω $\dot{ο}$ (^{ε} *et* · *p.m.*). —εστιν (*habet* C). 3. —υμιν (*habet* C). σχω (εχω C). 5. αλλα. 10. καγω (C^{a} και εγω). ο κεχαρισμαι ει τι κεχαρισμαι. 13. τω μη ευριν (*at* τω C). μακαιδονιαν√. 14. τη^{σ} (σ *p.m.* ? *vel* A). 16. + εκ (*ante* θανατου). εκ ζωη$\overset{σ}{ν}$ εισ (σ *p.m.*). 17. [πολλοι]. ιλικρινιασ√. κατεναντι θ̅υ̅ (C ενωπιον του θ̅υ̅).

III. 1. συνισταναιν✓. η (*pro* ει). [ωσ τινεσ].—συστατικων *secund.* 2. ενγεγ. καρδιεσ ῦμων γινωσ. 3. διακονηθισα✓. ενγεγ. πλαξιν✓ *bis.* [αλλ]. καρδιαισ. 5. αφ εαυτων ἴκανοι εσμεν λ. τι. [εαυτων]. 6. αποκτεννι. 7. του θῦ *p.m.* (του [θανα]του A). [γραμμασιν].—εν *secund.* (*habet* C). δυνασθε✓. ἴηλ̅✓. μωῦσεωσ. αυτου προσωπου αυτου (¨ *p.m.*)✓. 8. ουδι (χ *p.m. vel* A). εστε✓. 9. τη διακονια *prim.* δικεοσυνησ✓. δοξα (*pro* εν δοξη: C *cum* Steph.). 10. ου (*pro* ουδε). εινεκεν. 13. μωῦσησ. [εαυτου]. 14. +ημερασ (*post* σημερον). επει✓. 15. αν αναγεινωσκηται μωῦσησ. 16. δε εαν (C δ' αν). 17. — εκει (εκι C). 18. μεταφορμορφουμεθα (. . . *p.m.*).

IV. 1. εγκακουμεν. 2. αλλα. αληθιασ✓. συνισταντεσ. συνιδησιν✓. 3. εστιν✓ *bis.* 4. ετυφλωσεν✓. [αυγασαι].—αυτοισ. *fin.* (+του αορατου C). 5. ῑν̄ χ̄ν̄. ημων (*pro* υμων). *fin.* ῑῡ (A χ̄ῡ). 6. ο ειπων ȯ (˙ *p.m.*)✓. λαμψει (-αι C). [του θῡ]. [ῑῡ]. 10. —κ̄ῡ. τοισ σωμασιν (*pro* τω σωματι *secund.*). 12. ωστε° (ο *p.m.*?)—μεν. 13. +και (*post* διο *prim.*). ημισ✓. 14. συν (*pro* δια: C *cum* Steph.). ἰ ῑῡ✓. 16. εγκακουμεν. διαφθιρεται✓. εσω ημων (*pro* εσωθεν). 17. —εισ υπερβολην (*habet* A: ὁμοιοτ.).

V. 1. επιγιοσ✓. αχιροποιητον✓. 3. [ειγε]. [ενδυσ.]. 4 σκηνι✓. εφ ω (*pro* επειδη). αλλα. 5. ο θσ̄ ο δουσ (—και: θσ̄ ο και δ. C). αραβωνα. 8. θαρρουντεσ (*pro* θαρρουμεν).—εκ (εκ' C). 10. ἑκομισηται (˙ *p.m.*)✓. [δια]. φαυλον (*pro* κακον). 11. συνιδησεσιν✓. 12. —γαρ. ῦμων (*pro* ημων). μη εν (*pro* ου *secund.*). 15. —ει (*habet* C). απεθανεν (*pro* -νον: C *cum* Steph.)✓. 16. ημισ✓.—δε (*habet* C). 17. γεγονεν✓.—τα παντα. 18. —ῑῡ. 19. καταλασσων✓. 21. —γαρ (*habet* C). ημισ✓. γενωμεθα.

VI, 1. καινον✓. *fin.* ημασ (ῦμασ A C). 2. δε[κτω] (κτω A)✓. 4. συνισταντεσ (συνΐστωντεσ C). 5. νηστιαισ✓. 6. γνωσι✓. 7. αληθιασ✓. δυναμι✓. 11. ανεωγεν✓. ῦμων (*pro* ημων *secund.*). 12. στενοχωρισθαι *secund.*✓. 13. ῦμισ✓. 14. η τισ (*pro* τισ δε). 15. [συμφ]. χ̄ῡ. [βελιαρ]. 16. συγκαταθεσεισ✓. ημεισ γαρ ναοι θ̄ῡ εσμεν (υμεισ γαρ ναοσ εστε θ̄ῡ C). [εμπ]. μου (*pro* μοι). 17. εξελθαται✓.

VII. 2. εφθιραμεν✓. 3. προσ κατακρισιν ου. +εστε (*post* οτι: . . . . *p.m.*). ῦμων (ημων C). συναποθανιν✓. συνζην. 4. παρακλησι✓. (*non* vv. 7. 13). 5. μακαιδονιαν✓. [εσχ. ανεσ.]. 6. ταπινουσ✓.

7. ὑμιν (*pro* ημιν: C *cum* Steph.). 8. [γαρ]. εκινη✓. 9. —αλλ οτι ελυπηθητε (*habet* A obliq.: ὁμοιοτελ.). 10. εργαζεται (κατεργ. C) *prim.* 11. —υμασ (*habet* C). [κατειρ]. (+εν *ante* ὑμιν C). ανακτησιν (C αγανακτησιν). επιποθιαν (C επιποθησιν). αλλα εκδικησιν. —εν *ult.* 12. ενεκεν *ter.* (+αλλ' *post* αδικησαντοσ C). ὑμων την ὑπερ υμων. 13. + δε (*post* επι). ημων (*pro* υμων).—δε (*ante* μαλλον). 14. αυτω̅ (*pro* -τω). [π. εν αλ. ελ.]—ὑμιν (A obliq. *habet*). ουτωσ✓. ημων επι (—η: *habet* C). 15. —παντων (*habet* C). εδεξασθαι✓. 16. [*deest* ουν].

VIII. 1. μακαιδονιασ✓. 2. το πλουτοσ (C *cum* Steph.). 3. παρα (*pro* υπερ). αυθερετοι✓. 4. —δεξασθαι ημασ. 5. [αλλ]. 6. ουτωσ✓ (*sic* v. 11). 7. εν πιστι (*improbat* εν C). 8. [ὑμετερασ]. 9. επτωχευσεν✓. πτωχια✓. 11. επιτελεσαται✓. επιτελεσε✓. εχιν✓. 12. αν (*pro* εαν). —τισ. 13. —δε (*habet* C). 14. ^το εκεινων (τ *p.m.*)✓. επλεονασεν✓. ηλαττονησεν✓. 16. (C *habet* δοντι). 17. εξηλθεν✓. 18. τον αδελφον μετ αυτου (C *cum* Steph.). 19. [συν]. [αυτου]. *fin.* ημων. 21. *init.* προνοουμεν γαρ.—ενωπιον *secund.* (*habet* C). 24. τη^ν ουν ενδιξιν (^ν *p.m. vel* A). ενδιξασθαι✓.—και *secund.*

IX. 1. εστιν✓. 2. παραεσκευασται (˙ *p.m.*)✓. το ὑμων ζηλοσ (—εξ). [ηρεθισε]. 3. μερι✓. ελεγον *p.m.* (-εν *primò*)✓. 4. ελθωσιν✓. μακαιδονεσ✓.—τησ καυχησεωσ (*habet* C). 5. [εισ *et* -σωσι]. προεπηγγελμενην.—και *secund.* (*habet* C). ωσ (*pro* ωσπερ). 6. σπιρων *bis*✓. φιδομενωσ *secund. tantum.* 7. προηρηται. 8. δυνατει. 9. εδωκεν✓. 10. [σπερμα]. χορηγησει (-αι C). πληθυνει (-αι C). αυξησει (-αι C). γενηματα. 11. [τω θ̅ω̅]. 12. λιτουργιασ✓. εστιν✓. 14. ὑπερ η^υμων (υ *p.m.*). (C *habet* ἴδιν *additum ante* δια). 15. —δε (*habet* C).

X. 1. πραΰτητοσ (C *cum* Steph.). επιεικιασ✓. ταπινοσ✓. 4. στρατιασ✓. καθερεσιν✓. 7. εφ (*pro* αφ). ουτωσ✓. ημισ✓. *fin.* —χ̅υ̅. 8. —και *prim.* (*habet* C). καυχησομαι.—ημιν (*habet* C). 9. εκφοβιν✓. 10. επιστολαι μεν (C *cum* Steph.). φησιν✓. [-ουθεν-]. 12. [εγ- *et* συγ- *bis*]. τισιν✓. (A obliq. *addit* εαυτουσ *post* μετρουντεσ). *fin.* συνισασιν (A *et* C συνιασιν). 13. ουκ (*pro* ουχι). 14. [ου γαρ ωσ]. ὑπερεκτινομεν✓.—γαρ *secund.* (*habet* A). 15. ὑμων (*pro* ημων). περισσιαν✓. 18. ^υο γαρ ^οεαυτον συνιστανων (υ ο *p.m.*). δοκιμοσ εστιν (εστ. δοκ. C). [αλλ].

XI. 1. [ανειχεσθε]. + τι (*post* μικρον).—τη. αφροσυνησ. ανα-
εναν
σχεσθε (*pro* ανεχ.). 3. εξηπατησεν ὑμιν (εναν *p.m.? evidentius* C).—ουτω. + και τησ αγνοτητοσ (*post* απλοτητοσ): *uncis inclusit* C.—τον. 4. ετερον ‘ετερον’ (‘ ’ *p.m. vel* A)√. *fin.* ανειχεσθε. 5. [γαρ]. 6. φανερωσαντεσ (C *cum* Steph.). 7. ταπινων√. 8. εκλησιασ√. ουθενοσ. 9. μακαιδονιασ√. εμαυτον ὑμιν (C *cum* Steph.). 10. φραγησεται. [κλιμασι]. 12. ευρεθωσιν√. ημισ√. 13. αποστ. χ̅υ̅ *p.m., at rescript.*√. 14. θαυμα. 16. καγω μικρον τι. 17. κατα κ̅ν̅ λαλω. 18. — την (*habet* C). 20. εισ προσωπον ὑμασ δερι. 21. ημισ ησθενηκαμεν.—λεγω *secund.* (*habet* A obliq.). 22. εβρεοι√. εισιν√ *ter.* ἰσδραηλιται. 23. εισιν√. εν πληγ. περισσοτερωσ εν φυλ. ὑπερβαλλοντωσ (C *cum* Steph.). 24. τεσσερακοντα. 25. τρεισ *bis*√. εραβδισθην. 27. *init.*—εν (*habet* C, *forsan* A). λειμω√. νηστιαισ√. ψυχι√. 28. επιστασισ. μοι (C μου). 29. ασθενι√. σκανδαλειζεται√. 31. — ημων.— χ̅υ̅. 32. εφρουρι√. πολιν δαμασκηνων. [θελων]. 33. τιχουσ√. χιρασ√.

XII. 1. (*init.* + ει C). καυχασθαι δε ου συμφερον μεν ελευσομαι δε (— γαρ). 2. [του]. τρυτου (*p.m., at primò* του *pro* τρυ)√. 3.
ου
[*cum* Steph.]. 4. παραδισον√. 5. εμαυτου καυχησομαι (ου *p.m.*?). ασθενιαισ μου. 6. — τι (*habet* C). 7. -ψεων·. + διο (*ante* ἱνα). σατανα (C *cum* Steph.).—ἱνα μη υπεραιρωμαι (*habet* C). 9. ειρηκεν√.—μου *secund.* (*habet* C). ασθενια√. τελειται (C τελειου-
α
ται). ασθενιαισ√ (*sic* v. 10). 10. και εναγκαισ (α *p.m.*?: C *habet* εν *pro* και). και στενοχ. (εν *pro* και C). 11. — καυχωμενοσ. 12. [κατειρ.]—εν *tert.* (τε *pro* εν C). σημιοισ√. + τε (*post* σημιοισ: *punctis notavit* A). [τερασι]. δυναμεσιν√. 13. ησσωθητε (ηττηθητε C). 14. + τουτο (*post* τριτον).—υμων *prim.* αλλα *prim.* οφιλει√. [γονευσι]. αλλα οι γονισ. 15. — και *secund.* (*habet* C). αγαπω ησσον αγαπ. (C *cum* Steph.). 16. κατεναρκησα ὑμων αλλα (*pro* κατεβ. υμασ αλλ). 18. συναπεστιλα√. ἰχνεσιν√. 19. παλαι (παλιν C). κατεναντι.—του (*habet* C). 20. ερισ. [ζηλοι]. εριθιαι√. 21. ελθοντοσ μου (C *cum* Steph.). ταπινωση√. + με (*post* ταπ.). πορνια√.

XIII. 1. (*init.* + ιδου C). + ἱνα (*ante* επι): *delet* C. η (*pro* και). 2. — γραφω. προημαρτηκοσιν√. φισομαι√. 4. — ει (*habet* C). [-ειασ]. [και γαρ ημ.]. συν (*pro* εν). ζησομεν. 5. πιραζετε√. πιστι√.—η (*habet* C). χ̅σ̅ ι̅σ̅. [εστιν]. 6. ημισ ε ουκ (· *p.m.*). 7. ευχομεθα. ημεισ (*pro* υμεισ: *emendant* A? C)√. ποιειτε√.

8. αληθιασ *bis*√. αλλα. 9. —δε (*habet* C). 10. ο κσ εδωκεν μοι. 11. καταρτιζεσθαι√. ϊρηνευετε√. ϊρηνησ√. 12. [αγ. φιλ.]. 13. *fin.*—αμην (*habet* C).

Subscr. προσ κορινθιουσ β.

στιχων χιβ *s.m.*

προσ γαλατασ.

CAP. I. 1. εγιραντοσ αυτων (ο A *vel p.m.*). 3. *Transfert* ημων *in locum post* πατροσ *plenè scriptum.* 4. περι (*pro* υπερ: C *cum* Steph.). του αιωνοσ του ενεστωτος (C *cum* Steph.).—το (*habet* C). 6. ουτωσ√. μετατιθεσθαι√. 7. —και θελοντεσ (*habet* A obliq.). 8. ευαγγελισηται.—υμιν *prim.* (*habet* C). 9. προειρηκα (C *cum* Steph.). 10. πιθω√. αρεσκιν√.—γαρ *secund.* 11. (γαρ A, δε *p.m.*, C, Steph.). εστιν√. 12. ουδε (*pro* ουτε). 14. γενι√. 15. [ο θσ]. 17. [ανηλθον]. αλλα. 18. τρια ετη. κηφαν (*pro* πετρον: C *cum* Steph.). 19. ιδον√. 21. —τησ *secund.* (*habet* A obliq.).

II. 1. συνπαραλαβων. 2. εθνεσιν√. δοκουσιν√. 4. παρισακτουσ√. καταδουλωσουσιν. 5. αληθια√. [διαμεινη]. 6. ποτ (ποτε C). διαφερι√. +ο (*ante* θσ). 7. ειδοντεσ√. 8. —ο γαρ εν. *usque ad* περιτομησ (ὁμοιοτ.: *supplet* A[2]). ενηργησεν√. [και εμοι]. 9. [νν]. (A obliq. + μεν *post* ημεισ). 11. ηλθεν κηφασ (—πετροσ). αντιοχιαν√. 12. ελθιν√. ηλθεν. ϋπεστελλεν√. 13. + παντεσ (*ante* ωστε: *improbat* C). (συνυπ. C *partim scriptum pro* συναπ.). ϋποκρισι√. 14. [-δουσι]. κηφα (*pro* πετρω]. εθνικωσ και ουχ ϊουδαϊκωσ ζησ (ουχει C). πωσ (*pro* τι). 15. ϊουδεοι√. 16. +δε (*post* ειδοτεσ). [ιυ χυ]. ημισ√. [χν ιν]. οτι εξ εργων νομου ου δικαιωθησεται. 18. συνιστανω. 20. νυν σζω (. *p.m.*)√. πιστι√. [του ϋιου του θεου του αγ.].

III. 1. εβασκανεν.—τη αληθεια μη πειθεσθαι.—εν υμιν. 3. επιτελεισθαι√. 5. δυναμισ√. 6. επιστευσεν√. 7. ϋιοι εισιν (C *cum* Steph.). 8. τα εθνη δικαιοι. -ααμ'. [ενευλογ.]. 10. εισιν√ *bis.* +οτι (*ante* επικατ.).—εν *prim.* (*habet* C). πασιν√. 12. αλλα.—ανθρωποσ. 13. [*cum* Steph.]. 14. εν ιιυ χυ *sic* (ι *eras.*). 15. ουδισ√. αθετι√. 16. ερρεθησαν. εστιν√. 17. —εισ χν. τετρακοσια και τριακοντα ετη. 19. χιρι√. 21. [*habet* του θυ]. εκ *νομου ην αν. δικεοσυνη*√. 22. *συνεκλισεν*√. [*ὑπο*]. *πιστευουσιν*√. 23. *ελθιν*√. *συνκλιομενοι*. 26. + *οι* (*ante* $\overline{θυ}$: A *vel forsan p.m. delevit*)√. *χω* (*sic*)√. 28. *αρρεν. απαντεσ. ἐν* $\overline{χυ}$ $\overline{ιυ}$ (" A: *at* C *habet εισ εστε εν* $\overline{χω}$), *cf.* v. 14. 29. — *και. κατα.*

IV. 1. *διαφερι*√. 2. [*εστι*]. 3. *ουτωσ*√. *ημισ*√. *στοιχια*√ (*sic* v. 9). *ημεθα* (*pro ημεν secund.*). 4. *ηλθεν*√. *εξαπεστιλεν*√ (*sic* v. 6). 6. *ημων* (*pro υμων*). 7. *αλλα. fin. -νομοσ δια* $\overline{θυ}$ ($\overline{θυ}$ *δια* $\overline{χυ}$ C, Steph.). 8. *φυσει μη ουσι*. 9. *δουλευσε* (i. e. *-σαι*). 12. *ὑμισ*√. *ηδικησαται*√. 13. *οιδαται*√. *ασθενιαν*√. 14. *πιρασμον ὑμων εν* (C *-μον τον εν, ὑμων improbato*).—*ουκ* (*habet* A obliq.)√. [*αλλ*]. 15. *που* (*pro τισ*).—*ην*.—*αν* (*habet* C). 17. *εκκλισαι ὑμασ*. 18. — *το. ζηλουσθε*√. 19. *τεκνα* (*τεκνια* C). *μεχρισ* (*αχρισ* C). 21. [*cum* Steph.]. 23. [*μεν*]. *ελευθεριασ. δι.*—*τησ tert.* 24. [*habet αι*: *improbat* C]. *δουλιαν*. 25. — *αγαρ. εστιν* ō *εν* (*sic*)√. [*συστ.*]. $\overline{ιλημ}$ ($\overline{ιλημ}$ v. 26). *γαρ* (*pro δε secund.*). 26. — *ητισ εστι.*—*παντων* (*at ητισ εστιν* A, *παντων* C). 27. *στιρα*√. 28. *ἰσακ* (C *cum* Steph.). [*caetera cum* Steph.]. 29. [*εδιωκε*]. *ουτωσ*√. 30. *κληρονομησει.*—*του υιου* (*habent* A C). 31. *διο* (*pro αρα*). *πεδισκησ*√.

V. 1. — *ουν η. ημασ* $\overline{χσ}$ (C *cum* Steph.). *ηλευθερωσεν*√. *στηκετε ουν. δουλιασ*√. 2. — *παυλοσ* (*habet* A obliq.). 3. — *οτι* (*habet* C). *οφιλετησ*√. 4. *κατηργηθηται*√.—*του*. [*-σατε*]. 5. *εκδεχομεθα* (*απεκ.* C). 7. *ενεκοψεν.*—*τη* (*habet* C). *αληθια*√. *πιθεσθαι*√. 8. *πισμονη*√. *καλουντασ*√. 10. [*εγω πεπ.*]. *εαν* (*pro αν*). 13. *δουλευεται*√. 14. *πεπληρωται. σεαυτον*. 15. *καταισθιετε*√. *ὑπ* (*ὑπο* C). 17. *γαρ* (*pro δε secund.*: C *cum* Steph.). [*αντ. αλλ.*]. *εαν* (*pro αν*). 18. (*ουκετι pro ουκ* C). 19. *εστιν*√ *bis.*—*μοιχεια* (*μοιχια* C). *πορνια*√. *ασελγια*√. 20. *φαρμακια*√. *ερισ*. [*ζηλοι*]. *αιρεσισ*. 21. — *φονοι. ἁ p.m. καθωσ ειπον* (— *και*: C *cum* Steph.). *βασιλιαν*√. 23. *πραΰτησ. εστιν*√. 24. $\overline{κυ}$ $\overline{χυ}$ $\overline{ιυ}$ ($\overline{κυ}$ *improbant* A C). [*-μασι*]. 26. [*cum* Steph. *-μενοι rescr.* A *vel p.m.*].

VI. 1. *προλημφθη. ὑμισ*√. *πραυτητοσ. πιρασθησ*√. 2. *βαστασετε* (C *-ζετε*). [*-σατε*]. 3. *φρεναπατα εαυτον*. 7. *μυκτηριζετε*√. [*εαν σπειρη*]. 8. *σπιρων*√ *bis. θερισισει prim.* (*σι delet* A: *τησ σαρκ. rescript.*)√. *θερισι secund.*√. 9. *εγκακωμεν. θερισωμεν*. 10. *εχωμεν*. 12. *περιτεμνεσθε*√. *τω σταυρω* (*sic*) *του* $\overline{χυ}$ *μη διωκωνται*. 13. [*περιτεμν.*]. 14. [*καυχασθαι*].—*τω secund.* 15. *εστιν* (*pro ισχυει*: *praecedentia cum* Steph.): (*εισχυϊ* C). 16.

[στοιχησουσιν]. ῐρηνη√. 17. μηδισ√. κυ ιυ χυ. 18. — ημων. [αμην].

Subscr. προσ γαλατασ.

στιχ. τιβ *s.m.*

προσ εφεσιουσ.

Cap. I. 1. [ιυ χυ]. [ουσι].—εν εφεσω (*habet* C: *etiam* πασιν *post* αγιοισ *addito*). 3. + και σωτηροσ (*post* κυ: *improbat* C).—ημασ (*habet* A). + εν (*ante* χω). 6. ησ (*pro* εν η: C *cum* Steph.). 7. εσχομεν (εχομεν C). το πλουτοσ (*non* v. 18: C *cum* Steph.). 10. εισ εισ (··· *p.m.*). ανακεφαλαιωσασθε√. τα επι (τα τε εν C *cum* Steph.). 11. [εκληρωθημεν]. 12. — τησ. 13. ῡμισ (η *pro* υ C *primò*)√. αληθιασ√. 14. [οσ]. [ρρ].—τησ *tert.* 15. — την αγαπην (C εισ την αγαπ. την εισ). 16. μνιαν√.—υμων *secund.* 18. καρδιασ (*pro* διανοιασ).—και (*habet* C). τησ κληρονομιασ τησ δοξησ. 19. ενεργιαν√. 20. [ενηργησεν]. καθισασ (*pro* εκαθισεν). + αυτον (*ante* εν δεξια). [επουρ.]. 22. εδωκεν√. 23. εστιν√. + τα (*ante* παντα). πασιν√.

II. 1. παραπτωμασιν√ (*sic* v. 5). *fin.* + ῡμων. 2. απιθιασ√. 3. ημισ√. ημεθα. [τεκ. φυ.]. *fin.* -ποι ȯ ο (ȯ *leviter abstersum*)√. 4. — εν (*habet* C). 5. συνεζωοποιησεν τω. 6. συνηγειρεν√. 7. *Deest versus ob* ὁμοιοτελ. (*habet* A: αιωσιν: το ῡπερβαλλον πλουτοσ: *caetera cum* Steph.). 8. — τησ. 10. θυ (*pro* αυτου: A *cum* Steph.). 11. ποτε ῡμεισ (C *cum* Steph.). 12. — εν. επαγ. (π *p.m.*, *at* λ *primò*)√. 13. εγενηθητε εγγυσ. 15. δογμασιν√. αυτω (*pro* εαυτω: C *cum* Steph.). ιρηνην√. 16. αποκτινασ√. 17. ῐρηνην√. + ῐρηνην (*ante* τοισ εγγυσ). 18. + 'οι αμφοτεροι εν ενι' (*ante* εχομεν: ' ' A)√. (A εσχομεν). 19. αλλα εστε συνπολιται. 20. — αυτου. του χυ (*pro* ιυ χυ: A *habet* αυτου χυ ιυ). 21. — η (*habet* A). 22. ῡμισ√.

III. 1. — ιυ (*habet* A). 2. δοθισησ√. 3. [οτι]. εγνωρισθη. προεγραψ^α (α *p.m.*). 5. — εν *prim.* 6. συνκληρ. συνσω. συνμετ. —αυτου. *fin.* εν χω ιυ. 7. εγενηθην. τησ δοθισησ. 8. — των.— εν. το ανεξ. πλουτοσ (C *cum* Steph.). 9. [*init.* και]. —παντασ (*habet* C). οικονομια (*pro* κοινωνια).—εν (*habet* C).—δια ιυ χυ.

11. (+ τω *ante* $\overline{χω}$ A: *delet* C). 12. — την *secund.* (*habet* C). 13. εγκακιν√. θλιψεσιν√. εστιν√. 14. — του $\overline{κυ}$ *ad fin. vers.* (*habet* C). 16. δω. το πλουτοσ. δυναμι√. 18. εξισχυσηται√. [πασι]. [β. και ὕψ.]. 21. + και (*post* εκκλησια).

IV. 1. $\overline{χω}$ (*pro* $\overline{κω}$). εκληθηται√ (*non* v. 4). 2. ταπινοφροσυνησ√. πραΰτητοσ. 3. τηριν√. 6. *fin.*—υμιν. 7. [η]. 8. — και (*habet* C). εδωκεν√ (*sic* v. 11). 9. — πρωτον (*habet* C). 10. εστιν√. 13. τελιον√. 14. κυβια√. μεθοδιαν. 15. — ο (*habet* C). 16. συνβιβ. ενεργιαν√. αυτου (*pro* εαυτου). 17. — λοιπα (*habet* C). 18. εσκοτωμενοι. 21, 22. $\overline{ιυ}$ απ *rescript. p.m. super rasuram.* 22. φθιρομενον√. 23. [ανανεουσθαι δε]. 24. ενδυσασθε. οσιοτητι και δικαιοσυνη (C *cum* Steph.). 25. λαλειτε (ε *in* ει *p.m.*, ι *primò*). εκαστοσ αληθειαν (C *cum* Steph.). προσ τον πλ. (μετα του πλ. A C). 26. — τω (*habet* C). 27. μηδε (*pro* μητε). 28. ταισ ἴδιαισ χερσιν το αγαθον (— ιδιαισ C). εχηται (εχη C). χριαν√. 29. [αλλ]. χριασ√. ακουουσιν√. 31. συμπαση (*pro* συν π.)√. 32. γεινεσθε√. [δε]. [*fin.* υμιν].

V. 1. γεινεσθε√. μιμητε√. 2. ὕμασ (ημασ C). [ημων]. θυσιαν και προσφοραν. 3. πορνια√. ακαθαρσια πασα. 4. [*init.* και]. η (*pro* και *secund.* A *cum* Steph.). ευτραπελεια√. α ουκ ανηκεν. 5. ἴστε (*pro* εστε). ο (*pro* οσ). 6. καινοισ.—γαρ (*habet* A? *min.*). απιθιασ√. 7. γεινεσθαι√. συνμ. 9. φωτοσ (*pro* $\overline{πνσ}$). 10. δοκέιμαζοντεσ√. 11. συνκ. ελεγχεται√. 12. εστιν√ (*sic* v. 13). 14. λεγι√. εγιρε√. επιφαυσι√. 15. ακριβωσ πωσ (C αδελφοι πωσ ακρ.). 16. εισιν√. 17. συνιετε τι το φρονημα του $\overline{κυ}$ (θελημα C). 18. μεθυσκεσθαι√. πληρουσθαι√. 19. [-τοισ ψαλ-]. κα̈ $\overline{πνικαισ}$ (¨ *p.m.*).—εν (C εν ταισ καρδιαισ). 20. — ημων. 21. $\overline{χυ}$ (*pro* $\overline{θυ}$). 22. ὑποτασσεσθωσαν. 23. — ο *prim.* εστιν *prim.*√.—και *secund.* (*habet* C). + ο (*ante* σωτηρ *plenè*: *improbat* C).—εστι *secund.* (*habet* C). 24. [αλλ]. ωσ (*pro* ωσπερ). ουτωσ√.—ιδιοισ. 25. — εαυτων. ηγαπησεν√. 27. αυτοσ αυτω (*pro* αυτην εαυτω: C εαυτω).—η τι (*habet* A obliq.). 28. οφιλουσιν οι αν. τεκνα (*pro* σωματα: C *cum* Steph.). 29. ουδισ√. την σαρκα αυτου (C *cum* Steph.). [αλλ]. $\overline{χσ}$ (*pro* $\overline{κσ}$). 30. — εκ τησ σαρκοσ *ad fin. vers.* (*forsan ob* ὁμοιοτ.: *habet* C). 31. καταλιψι√. [τον πατ.].—αυτοι *prim.* (*habet* C). [την μητ.]. τη γυναικι (— προσ *et* αυτου *secund.*): (τη γυν. αυτου A, *at* C κολλ. προσ την γυν. αυτ.). 32. [εισ την]. 33. ὕμισ√. (ἵνα εκαστ. C).

VI. 1. [εν $\overline{κω}$]. εστιν√. 3. *Versus bis scriptus p.m.* (*secundo loco uncis inclusit* A)√. 4. αλλα. εκτρεφεται√. παιδια√. 5. κατα σαρκα κυριοισ.—τησ. 6. οφθαλμοδουλιαν√.—του *prim.* 7. + ωσ (*ante* τω $\overline{κω}$). 8. εαν ποιηση εκαστοσ (— ο *et* τι: C *habet* ο εαν π. ε.). κομισεται (C *cum* Steph.).—του. 9. απιλην√. εαυτων και ῦμων (*pro* υμων αυτων: ῦμων και εαυτων C). ουρανω. προσωπολημψια. εστιν *secund.* 10. του λοιπου.—αδελφοι μου (C το λ. αδ. μου). ενδυναμουσθαι√. + τω (*ante* $\overline{κω}$): *improbant* A? C. κρατι√. 11. μεθοδιασ√. 12. [ημιν].—του αιωνοσ (*addit et absterget* C). 14. αληθια√. 16. εν (*pro* επι). δυνησεσθαι√. [τα πεπ.]. 17. εστιν√. 18. — τουτο. 19. δοθη μοι (μοι δοθη C). [του ευαγ.]. 20. παρρησιασωμαι εν αυτω. 21. και ῦμεισ ἴδητε. ὐ γνωρισει ῦμιν (· *p.m.*: C υμιν γν. *sed delevit*).—διακονοσ (*habet* A). 24. — αμην (*habet* C).

Subscr. προσ εφεσιουσ.

στιχων $\overline{τιβ}$ *s.m.*

προσ φιλιππησιουσ.

Cap. I. 1. $\overline{χυ}$ $\overline{ιυ}$. [πασι]. 4. + τη (*ante* δεησει: *improbat* C). 5. + τησ (*ante* πρωτησ). 6. επιτελεσι√. αχρι. [$\overline{ιυ}$ $\overline{χυ}$]. 7. εστιν√. + εν (*ante* τη απολογ.). συνκ. 8. — εστιν (*habet* C: *instaurator* μοι? *pro* μου). $\overline{χυ}$ $\overline{ιυ}$. 9. [περισσευη]. 10. — υμασ (*habet* C). αλικρινεισ (ει *pro* α *p.m. vel* A)√. 11. καρπον. τον. 12. γεινωσκιν√. 13. + τω (*ante* $\overline{χω}$: *improbat* C). γεγονεναι (γενεσθαι A? C). πασιν√. 14. + του $\overline{θυ}$ (*ante* λαλ$\overline{ι}$). 15. (— και *prim.* C). *fin.* κηρυσσειν (A *minut.* κηρυσσουσιν). 16. οι μεν εξ αγαπησ κ.τ.λ. *e vers.* 17. 17. οι δε εξ εριθειας κ.τ.λ. *e vers.* 16 (*ad* τον *puncta apposita sed rursus erasa*). εγειρειν (*pro* επιφερειν). 18. + οτι (*post* πλην). ειτε ε̇ αληθεια (· *p.m.*?). 23. δε (*pro* γαρ). (A obliq. *addit* γαρ *post* πολλω). κρισσον√. 24. επιμενιν√.—εν. 25. παραμενω. + ῦμων (*post* πιστεωσ: *improbat* C). 27. — του $\overline{χυ}$ (*habet* A). πολιτευεσθαι√. ειδων√.—ειτε απων (*habet* A obliq.). ακουω (ακουσω A obliq.). πιστι√. 28. εστιν αυτοισ (— μεν). ενδειξεισ√. απωλιασ√. ῦμων (*pro* υμιν). 30. ειδετε.

II. 1. τισ (*pro* τινα). 2. [συμψ.]. αυτο (*pro* εν: C *cum* Steph.). 3. κατ εριθιαν μηδε κατα κενοδ. (κατα *improbat* C). ταπινοφροσυνη√. 4. εκαστοσ σκοπουντεσ.—εκαστοσ *secund.*: *at* v. 5 *init.* εκαστοι τουτο φρονειτε (— γαρ: τουτο γαρ C). 7. αλλα. εκενωσεν√. 8. εταπινωσεν√. + του (*ante* σταυρου *plenè*). 9. ϋπερυψωσεν. + το (*ante* ονομα *prim.*). 10. + χ̅υ̅ (*post* ι̅υ̅: *delet* C). επιγιων√. 11. εξομολογησητε√. 12. (C *improbat* εν *prim.*). 13. — ο *prim.* 15. [γενησθε]. ακαιρεοι√. αμωμα μεσον (— εν). 16. εχοντεσ (επεχοντεσ A). 17. [αλλ]. λιτουργια√.—και συγχαιρω (A *habet* και συνχ.): ὁμοιοτελ.? 18. δε. ϋμισ√. [συγχ.]. 19. [κ̅ω̅]. 21. ι̅υ̅ χ̅υ̅ (— του). 23. αφιδω. 24. (+ εγω *ante* ταχεωσ A). *fin.* + προσ ϋμασ (*improbat* C). 25. [συστρ.]. λιτουργον√. 26. + ἴδειν (*post* ϋμασ: *improbat* C). ησθενησεν√ (*sic* v. 27). 27. (θανατου C). αλλα. ηλεησεν αυτον. λυπην (*pro* λυπη). 28. ειδοντεσ√. 29. προσδεξασθαι√. 30. κ̅υ̅ (*pro* του χ̅υ̅). ηγγισεν√. παραβολευσαμενοσ. αναπληρωσει. εμε (με C). λιτουργιασ√.

III. 1. ταυτα (τα αυτα C *cum* Steph.). [δε ασφ.]. 3. θ̅υ̅ (θ̅ω̅ C *cum* Steph.). 4. πε (*pro* εγω *secund.*: *corrigit* A). 5. βεμαμειν. 6. ζηλοσ (C *cum* Steph.). 7. — αλλ (*habet* C). [ην μοι]. 8. — και *prim.* (*habet* C). [-εωσ χ̅υ̅]. [κ̅υ̅ μου].—ειναι *secund.* (*habet* C). 9. δικαιοσυνην εμην (C *cum* Steph.). πιστι√. 10. γνωσεωσ (*pro* αναστασεωσ: A obliq. *cum* Steph.). και κοινωνιαν παθηματων (*habet* την *et* των C). συνμορφιζομενοσ (συνμορφουμενοσ C). 11. την εκ (*pro* των). 12. τετελιωμαι√.—και *prim.* (*habet* C). ει (*pro* και *secund.*: *corrigit* A). κατελημφθην. ϋπο χ̅υ̅ ι̅υ̅ (— του). 13. ουπω (*pro* ου). 14. επεκτινομενοσ·√. εισ (*pro* επι). βραβιον√. 15. τελιοι√. + ουν (*ante* φρονουμεν [*sic*]: *improbat* C). 16. — κανονι *ad fin. vers. forsan ob* ὁμοιοτελ. (C καν. το αυτο φρονιν). 17. συνμιμητε√. [ουτω]. 19. απωλια√. επιγια√. 20. [σωτηρα *plenè*]. 21. ταπινωσεωσ√.—εισ το γενεσθαι αυτο. συνμορ. αυτω (*pro* εαυτω: C *cum* Steph.).

IV. 1. κ αγαπητοι (κ *notat. p.m.*)√. ουτωσ√. 2. ευοδιαν. φρονιν√. 3. ναι (*pro* και *prim.*). γνησιε συζηγε *sic edit. min.* (*at in not. et edit. mai.* συζυγε: C συνζυγε). συνλαμβανου. και των συνεργων μου και των λοιπων (C *cum* Steph.). 6. μετ. 8. επενοσ√. 9. ἴρηνησ√. 10. φρονιν√. ηκαιρισθε√. 12. και (*pro* δε). ταπινουσθαι√. πασιν√. πιναν√. ϋστερισθαι√. 13. — χ̅ω̅ (*habet* C). 14. [συγκ.]. 15. οιδαται√. ϋμισ√ *bis*. μακαιδονιασ√. λημψεωσ. 16. [εισ]. χριαν√ (*sic* v. 19). 17. [αλλ]. 18. παρα (A απο) επαφροδειτου. 19. το πλουτοσ (C *cum* Steph.).—εν *prim.* (*habet* A obliq.). 20. + ω (*ante* η δοξα: *delet* C). 21. ασπασασθαι√. 23. —ημων. του πνσ (*pro* παντων: C *cum* Steph.). [αμην].

Subscr. προσ φιλιππησιουσ.

στιχοι ω (*i. e.* σ) *s.m.*

προσ κολοσσαεισ.

Cap. I. 1. χυ ιυ. 2. κολοσσαισ. [χω χαρισ]. [και κυ ιυ χυ]. 3. [*cum* Steph.]. 4. κω ιυ (χω ιυ C). ην εχετε (*pro* την *tert.*). 5. αληθιασ√. 6. —και *secund.* εστιν (*sic* v. 7)√. + και αυξανομενον (*ante* καθωσ). αληθια√. 7. —και. εμαθατε. ημων (*pro* ὑμων: C *cum* Steph.). 9. ημισ√. 10. —υμασ (*habet* C). αρεσκιαν√. τη επιγνωσει (εν τη επ. C). 12. + θω (*ante* πατρι). ὑμασ (*pro* ημασ). 13. [ρρ]. 14. —δια του αιματοσ αυτου. 16. —τα *secund. et tert.* (*habet* C). 17. εστιν (*sic* v. 27)√. συνεστηκεν√. 18. —εκ (*habet* C). 19. ευδοκησεν (υ *p.m.*). 20. [δι αυτου]. 22. [αποκατηλλαξεν]. + αυτου (*post* θανατου). 23. πιστι√.—τη *secund.* (*habet* C). κηρυξ και αποστολοσ (*pro* διακονοσ: C *cum* Steph.). 24. παθημασιν υμων (—μου υπερ: C *cum* Steph.: A *omittit* μου *tantum*). [ο]. 25. + παυλοσ (*post* εγω: *improbat* C). δοθισαν√. 26. νυν. 27. [τισ ο]. του (*pro* τουτου: C *cum* Steph.). [οσ]. 28. —ιυ (*habet* C). 29. ενεργιαν√.

II. 1. ὑπερ (*pro* περι). λαοδικια√. εορακαν (-κασιν C).—εν σαρκι (*habet* C). 2. συμβιβασθεντεσ (-ων C, *sed rursus abstersit*). παν πλουτοσ (C *cum* Steph.). *fin.* του θυ πατροσ χυ (C και πατρ. του). 3. εισιν√.—τησ *secund.* (*habet* C). γνω *rescript. ab* A *vel p.m.* 4. —δε (*habet* C). μηδεισ (C μητεισ) *pro* μη τισ. 7. —εν αυτω (*habet* A). [εν τη π.].—εν αυτη (εν αυτω *legit* C). 8. βλεπεται√. εσται ὑμασ. συλαγων (-γωγων C)√. στοιχια√. 10. [οσ]. + τησ (*ante* αρχησ). εκκλησιασ (*pro* και εξουσιασ: C *cum* Steph.). 11. —των αμαρτιων (*habet* C). [-ματι *p.m.*, *at* βαπτισμω C]. 12. [συνηγερθητε].—των. 13. —εν (*habet* A). παραπτωμασιν√. συνεζωοποιησεν ὑμασ (ὑμασ *improbat* C). [ημιν, *at* C υμιν]. 14. εξαλιψασ√. τοισ (τ *p.m. in ras.*)√. ημων (*pro* ημιν: A *cum*

Steph.). 15. εδιγματισεν√. 16. βρωσι√. [νουμ-]. 17. [α]. εστιν√. (— του C). 18. μηδισ√.— εν (*habet* A). ταπινοφροσυνη (*sic* v. 23)√. ' μελλοντων ' αγγελων (' ' A).—μη (*habet* C). εορακεν. *fin.* αυτων (-ου A C). 19. [συμβ.]. αυξη (A αυξει). 20. αποθανετε (*sic*) ουν (— ουν A? ουν απ. C).—τω. στοιχιων√. 21. εστιν (*sic* v. 23)√. 23. εθελοθρησκια√. [και *secund.*]. αφιδια√.

III. 1. εν (*pro* τω: A *cum* Steph.). $\overline{θσ}$ (*pro* $\overline{χσ}$ *primò:* χ A *vel p.m.*)√.— εστιν (*habet* A). 4. ὑμων (*pro* ημων). ὑμισ (*sic* v. 7)√. 5. — υμων (*habet* C). πορνιαν√. πλεονεξειαν√. ειδωλολατρια√. 6. απιθιασ√ [*caetera cum* Steph.]. 7. τουτοισ (*pro* αυτοισ). 8. — και ὑμεισ (*habet* A). 10. επενδυσαμενοι (ενδ. C). 11. [-λοσ ελευ-].—τα (*habet* C). πασιν√. 12. [του]. οικτιρμου. ταπινοφροσυνην√. πραυτητα. 13. $\overline{θσ}$ ($\overline{χσ}$ A? C *cum* Steph.). (C *correcturus* ημιν *pro* υμιν, *rursus* η *abstersit*). ουτωσ√. ὑμισ√. 14. [πασι]. οσ (*pro* ητισ: C *cum* Steph.). 15. $\overline{χυ}$ (*pro* $\overline{θυ}$: C *cum* Steph.). 16. $\overline{κυ}$ (*pro* $\overline{χυ}$: C *cum* Steph.). ενοικιτω√.—και *secund. et tert.* (C *habet* τη *ante* χαρ.). ταισ καρδιεσ. *fin.* $\overline{θω}$ (*pro* $\overline{κω}$). 17 [αν]. $\overline{κυ}$ $\overline{ιυ}$ $\overline{χυ}$ (+ του *ante* $\overline{κυ}$ C).—και *secund.* 18. ὑποτασσεσθαι√.—ιδιοισ. 19. (+ εαυτων *ante* γυν. C). πικρενεσθε√. 20. γονευσιν√. ευαρεστον εστιν εν $\overline{κω}$. 21. παροργιζεται (*pro* ερεθιζετε). 22. οφθαλμοδουλιαισ√. *fin.* $\overline{κν}$ (C $\overline{θν}$). 23. — και παν (C *habet* παν). ο (*pro* ο τι). 24. απολημψεσθε (λημψ. C).— γαρ. 25. γαρ (*pro* δε). (C κομισεται). ηδικησεν√. εστιν√. προσωπολημψια.

IV. 1. [παρεχεσθε: (-θαι C)]. ουρανω (-οισ C). 2. προσκαρτεριτε√.—εν αυτη (*habet* A). 3. αμα (ῑν *primò:* αμα *vix p.m.*)√. [δι ο]. 4. δι (*non* v. 6)√. 6. ενει√. 7. + δε (*ante* κατ: *improbat* C).—και συνδουλοσ (*habet* C). 8. γνω τε (*sic Tischendorf.:* γνω C). [ὑμων *prim.:* C ημ. *sed abstersit*]. τ^α^σ (α *p.m.*?)√. 9. [υμων: C ημ. *sed rursus abstersit*]. γνωριουσιν (C γνωρισουσιν). 12. ασπαζετε√. + $\overline{ιυ}$ (*post* $\overline{χυ}$). ημων (*pro* υμων *secund.:* υμ. C *post* στιχων *scriptorem*). σταθητε (C στητε). τελιοι√. πεπληροφορημενοι (*pro* πεπλ.). 13. πολυν πονον (*pro* ζηλον πολυν). λαοδικια (*sic* v. 15)√. 15. αυτων (*pro* αυτου). 16. λαοδικαιων√. λαοδικιασ√. ὑμισ√. 18. — αμην (*habet* C).

Subscr. προσ κολασσαεισ.

στιχων τ. *s.m.*

προσ θεσσαλονικεισ α.

Cap. I. 1. [*cum* Steph.]. **2.** μνιαν√.—υμων *secund.* (*habet* C). **3.** αδιαλιπτωσ√. **4.** + του (*ante* θυ). **5.** + του θυ (*ante* ημων). [εισ ὑμ.]. δυναμιν√.—εν *tert.*—εν *quart.* **6.** μιμητε√. **7.** [τυπουσ]. πασιν√. μακαιδονια (*sic* v. 8)√. + εν (*ante* τη αχ.). **8.** — γαρ (*habet* A). θυ (*pro* κυ: C *cum* Steph.). + εν τη (*ante* αχαια). αλλα ε (— και: ε *addunt* A? C: αλλα *p.m.*). χριαν εχιν ημασ. **9.** εσχομεν. **10.** αναμενιν√. + των (*inter* εκ *et* νεκρων). εκ (*pro* απο).

II. 1. οιδαται (*sic* v. 2)√. **2.** — και *prim.* **3.** ουδε (*pro* ουτε). **4.** ουτωσ√.—τω *prim.* (*habet* C). **5.** κολακιασ√. (— εν *secund.* C). **7.** αλλα. νηπιοι (ηπιοι C). (εαν *pro* αν C). **8.** ομειρομενοι. εγενηθητε. **9.** — γαρ *secund.* ὑμιν (*pro* εισ ὑμασ: A *cum* Steph.). **11.** μαρτυρομενοι. **12.** περιπατειν. καλεσαντοσ. **13.** *init.* + και. αδιαλιπτωσ√.—αληθωσ (*habet* A *ante* εστιν√). ημιν (*pro* υμιν). **14.** ὑμισ√ (*bis in vers.*). *Post* θυ *propter* δμοιοτ. *addit p.m.* εδεξασθε κ.τ.λ. v. 13 ... καθωσ εστιν λ.... ενεργιται ... ημιν ... v. 14 μιμηθητε *usque ad* του θυ v. 14: *improbat* A√. τα αυτα. **15.** αποκτιναντων√.—ιδιουσ. ημασ (*pro* υμασ). **16.** εθνεσιν√. εφθασεν√. **18.** διοτι. **19.** —η *tert.* (*habet* C).—χυ. **20.** εσται√.—η *secund.* (*habet* C).

III. 1. ηυδοκησαμεν. καταλιφθηναι√. **2.** [διακ.].—και συνεργον ημων.—υμασ *secund.* ὑπερ (*pro* περι). **3.** *init.* το. [μηδενα σαινεσθαι εν τ. θλιψεσι]. **6.** + υμων (*ante* πιστιν: νπ *separat* C??). μνιαν√. **7.** αναγκη και θλιψει. **8.** (C στηκετε). **9.** κω (*pro* θω: C *cum* Steph.). κυ (*pro* θυ: C *cum* Steph.). **11.** — χσ. ὑμων (*pro* ημων *tert.*: C *cum* Steph.). **13.** — χυ. *fin.* + αμην (*improbat* C).

IV. 1. — το. + τω (*ante* κω). [ιυ καθωσ]. + καθωσ και περιπατειτε (*post* θω). **2.** δεδωκαμεν. **3.** εστιν√. [-ιν θελ-]. (πασησ *pro* τησ C). **4.** [εκαστον]. + εν (*ante* τιμη: *improbat* C). **6.** — ο (*habet* C). [*caetera cum* Steph.]. **7.** [αλλ]. **8.** και διδοντα το πν. αυτ. (C δοντα). *fin.* ὑμασ. **9.** (εχομεν *pro* εχετε C). **10.** ὑμων (*pro* τουσ *secund.*: C *cum* Steph.). [μακεδ-]. **11.** (— ιδιαισ C). ὑμιν παρηγγιλαμεν√ (παρηγγ. ὑμιν C). **13.** θελομεν. κοιμωμενων. [λυπησθε]. (ωσ *pro* καθωσ C). **14.** επιστευομεν (C *cum* Steph.). απεθανεν√. ουτωσ (*sic* v. 17)√. **17.** περιλιπομενοι√.

V. 1. του γραφεσθαι υμιν (του *improbat* C). 2. ακρειβωσ√. —η. 3. — γαρ (*at* δε C). επισταται. ωδειν√. 4. εσται√. [η ημ. υμ.]. [κλεπτησ]. 5. + γαρ (*post* παντεσ). εσται (ε *p.m.*)√. 6. — και *prim.* (*habet* C). 7. καθευδουσιν√. 8. — και αγαπησ (*post* πιστεωσ: *habet* C). 9. αλλα. 10. περι (*pro* υπερ: C *cum* Steph.). 12. προϊσταναμενουσ. 13. + και (*ante* ειρην.: *improbat* C). *fin.* αυτοισ. 15. αποδοι (-δω C).—και *prim.* (*habet* C). 17. αδιαλιπτωσ√. 18. [γαρ θελ.]. + του (*ante* $\overline{\theta\upsilon}$: *improbat* C). 19. [σβεννυτε]. 21. [*sic, cum* Steph.: *at* C παντα δε]. 25. [και *deest*]. 27. [ορκιζω]. [πασι].—αγιοισ (*habet* C). 28. [αμην].

Subscr. προσ θεσσαλονικεισ α.

προσ θεσσαλονικεισ β.

Cap. I. 1. + και (*ante* $\overline{\pi\rho\iota}$: *improbat* A, *forsan p.m.*). 2. [ημων]. 3. οφιλομεν√.—υμων *tert.* (*habet* C). 4. αυτουσ ημασ. εγκαυχασθαι. [πασι, *sic* v. 10]. 5. ενδιγμα√. 7. υμων (*pro* ημων: C *cum* Steph.). 8. [πυρι φλ.]. [ειδοσι]. (+ τον *ante* $\overline{\theta\nu}$, C). ὑπακουουσιν√. [$\overline{\chi\upsilon}$]. 9. [ολεθρον]. 10. πιστευσασιν. 12. — $\overline{\chi\upsilon}$ *prim.*

II. 1. (ερωτωμ[εν] *p.m. super ras.*)√. 2. μηδε (*pro* μητε *prim.*). *fin.* $\overline{\kappa\upsilon}$ (*pro* $\overline{\chi\upsilon}$). 3. ανομιασ (*pro* αμαρτιασ). 4. — και υπεραιρομενοσ (*habet* A obliq.) *ob* ὁμοιοτ.—ωσ $\overline{\theta\nu}$. αποδικνυντα√. εστιν√. 6. οιδαται√. αυτου (εαυτου C). 7. + γαρ (*post* ηδη: *improbat* C). 8. $\overline{\kappa\sigma}$ $\overline{\iota\sigma}$ αναλοι (C ανελοι). 9. ενεργιαν√. δυναμι√. σημιοισ√. τερασιν√. 10. — τησ *prim.* (*habet* C).—εν *secund.* (*habet* C). 11. πεμπει (-ψει C). 12. κριθωσιν απαντεσ. αλλα.—εν (*habet* C). αδικεια√. 13. οφιλομεν√. ευχαριστιν√. + του (*ante* $\overline{\kappa\upsilon}$). ειλατο. ημασ (*pro* ὑμασ: C *cum* Steph.). [απ αρχησ]. πιστι√. 14. + και (*ante* εκαλεσεν). [ὑμασ]. ὑμων (*pro* ημων *prim.*: A C *cum* Steph.). 16. $\overline{\iota\sigma}$ $\overline{\chi\sigma}$ και ο $\overline{\theta\sigma}$ ο πατηρ (και *p.m.*: C *delet* ο *ante* πατηρ).—ο αγαπησασ ημασ (*addit* A). 17. τασ καρδιασ ὑμων.—υμασ. εργω και λογω.

III. 1. προσευχεσθαι√. 3. ο $\overline{\kappa\sigma}$ εστιν (εστιν ο $\overline{\kappa\sigma}$ C). 4. — υμιν.—και *prim.* (*habet* C). 5. + την (*ante* ὑπομονην). 6.

[ημων]. παρελαβοσαν (παρελαβον C). 7. οιδαται√. μιμισθαι (*sic* v. 9)√. 8. αλλα. νυκτοσ και ημερασ. 10. — τουτο (*habet* C). εργαζεσθε√. 12. εν κω ιυ χω (C *cum* Steph., δια κ.τ.λ.). 13. εγκακησητε. 14. σημιουσθαι.—και. συναναμιγνυσθαι. 15. νουθετιται√. 16. [τροπω]. 17. εστιν σημιον√. ουτωσ√. 18. — αμην (*addit* C αμην·).

Subscr. προσ θεσσαλονικεισ.

στιχων ρπ. *s.m.*

προσ εβραιουσ.

Cap. I. 1. πατ *super ras.* 2. εσχατου. εθηκεν√. εποιησεν τουσ αιωνασ. 3. — δι εαυτου. των αμαρτιων ποιησαμενοσ (— ημων: *at* υμων C). 4. κριττων√. 5. ειπεν√.—αυτω (*habet* A). 7. λιτουργουσ√. 8. + και (*post* αιωνοσ).—ραβδοσ ευθυτητοσ (*habet* A η ραβδοσ τησ ευθυτητοσ ραβδοσ τησ β.)√. *fin.* αυτου (*pro* σου). 9. αδικιαν (*pro* ανομιαν). εχρισεν√. 12. αλλαξεισ (ειλιξεισ C). + ωσ ἱματιον (*post* αυτουσ). + και (*ante* ο αυτος: ··· *p.m.*). εκλιψουσιν√. 13. ειρηκεν√. 14. εισιν√. λιτουργικα√.

II. 1. περισσοτερωσ δει. προσεχιν ημασ. ακουσθισι√ (-σιν C). παραρυωμεν. 3. λαλισθαι√. 4. σημιοισ√. [τερασι]. θερισμοισ (A μερισμοισ). 5. ὑπεταξεν√. 6. [τι]. 7. σασ αυτο *secund. in rasur. rescript. p.m.? vel* A√. [*Habet* και κατεστησασ *ad fin. vers.*]. 8. ὑπεταξα^{σ} (σ *forsan p.m.*). τω γαρ. [αυτω *prim.*]. 10. επρεπεν√. τελιωσαι√. 14. κεκοινωνηκεν√. αιματοσ και σαρκοσ. μετεσχεν√. τουτεστιν√. 15. δουλιασ√. 17. ωφειλεν√. 18. — πειρασθεισ (*habet* πιρασθισ C). πιραζομενοισ√.

III. 1. — χν. 2. [μωσησ]. 3. ουτοσ δοξησ. μωϋσην. 4. — τα. 5. μωϋσησ. 6. καν (*pro* εανπερ: ᵉ *i.e.* εαν *p.m.*: C *cum* Steph.). [μεχ. τελ. βεβ.]. 8. πιρασμω: *non* v. 15 (*pro* παραπικρ.). πιρασμου√. 9. επιρασαν√.—με *prim.* (*habet* C). εν δοκιμασια (*pro* εδοκιμασαν με: C *cum* Steph.). τεσσερακοντα (*sic* v. 17). 10. ταυτη (*pro* εκεινη). [ειπον]. 12. εστε√. 13. [τισ εξ υμων]. 14. του χυ γεγοναμεν. 16. εγυπτου√. μωϋσεωσ. 17. τισιν (*sic* v. 18)√. δε προσωχθισεν√. 18. ωμοσεν√. απιθησασιν√. 19. εισελθιν (*sic* iv. 1)√. [δι].

IV. 1. καταλιπομενησ√. 2. συνκεκερασμενοσ. πιστι√. 3. ουν (*pro* γαρ). 4. ειρηκεν√. ουτωσ√. 6. [δι] απιστιαν (απιθιαν C). 7. οριζει τινα (τινα οριζει C). δαυειδ. προειρηται. σκληρυνηται√. 8. $\overline{ισ}$ (*sic*). 9. *Deest versus* (*habet* A, *legens* απολιπεται√). 10. πα των (πα C *scripsit et abstersit: i. e.* παντων *pro* των *prim.*). 11. ειναι√.—τισ (*habet* C). ϋποδιγματι√. απιθιασ√. 12. —ψυχησ (*supplet forsan p.m.*).—τε *prim.* [ενθυμησεων]. 13. εστιν√. 14. διεληλυθα√. 15. συνπαθ. ασθενιαισ√. πεπιρασμενον√. 16. ελεοσ.

V. 1. [τε]. 2. [αγνοουσι]. ασθενιαν√. 3. δι αυτην. ουτωσ (*sic* v. 5)√. [εαυτου]. περι (*pro* υπερ). 4. —ο *bis*. καθωσπερ (C *cum* Steph.). 5. εδοξασεν√. 8. επαθεν√. 9. πασιν τοισ ϋπακουουσιν αυτω. 12. χριαν *prim.*√. στοιχια√.—και *ultim.* (*habet* C). 13. εστιν√.

VI. 2. [διδαχησ]. [τε *bis*]. 3. [ποιησομεν]. 6. παραδιγματιζοντασ√. 7. ερχομενον πολλακισ. 9. αδελφοι (*pro* αγαπητοι: C *cum* Steph.). κρισσονα√. ουτωσ (*sic* v. 15)√. 10. —του κοπου. ενεδειξασθαι√. 12. μειμηται√. 13. επαγγιλαμενοσ√. ειχεν√. ωμοσεν√. 14. ει (*pro* η). 15. επετυχεν√. 16. —μεν. ομνυουσιν√. 18. + τον (*ante* $\overline{θν}$: *improbat* C). προκιμενησ√. 19. [ασφαλη]. 20. μελχεισεδεκ (*non* v. 6. 10; vii. 10. 11. 17; *at sic* vii. 1. 15).

VII. 1. σαλημ' (*non* v. 2). [του υψ-]. οσ (*pro* ο *secund.*). 2. εμερισεν απο παντων. εστιν√. 3. [αφωμοι.]. 4. [και]. 5. [υιων] λευει (*sic* v. 9)√. ϊερατιαν√. [αποδεκατουν]. τουτεστιν√. 6. δεδεκατωκεν (—τον *prim.*: *habet* C). ευλογηκεν√. 7. κριττονοσ (*sic* v. 19)√. 9. [ειπειν]. δι. λευει (C -εισ). 10. ετι γαρ *inter lineas p.m.*√. —ο. 11. λευειτικησ√. επ αυτησ νενομοθετηται. 13. προσεσχηκεν√. 14. περι ϊερεων μωυσησ ουδεν ελαλησεν (ουδ. μωυσ. C). 16. σαρκινησ. 17. μαρτυρειτε [*i. e.* -αι]. 19. [-ζομεν]. 21. (C μετ'). ωμοσεν√.—εισ τον αιω. *ad fin. vers.* (*habet* C *in marg.*, *legens* μελχισεδεκ'). 22. τοσουτο και (C τοσουτον *sine* και). κριττονοσ√. 23. εισιν√. [γεγ. ϊερ.]. 26. [ημιν επρ-]. 27. *fin.* προσενεγκασ.

VIII. 2. λιτουργοσ√.—και *secund.* 3. τι ⁊ (⁊ *p.m. vel* A). 4. ουν (*pro* γαρ).—των ιερεων.—τον (*habet* C). 5. ϋποδιγματι√. λατρευουσιν√. μωϋσησ. φησιν√. ποιησισ. 6. [νυνι]. τετυχε (C τετευχε). λιτουργιασ√.—εστι διαθ . . . επι κρειττοσ (ob ὁμοιοτ.). *Supplet* A διαθηκησ εστιν μεσειτησ ητισ επι κριττο(σ *deest*): *textus p.m. procedit* ιν επαγγ. 8. αυτουσ (-τοισ C). $\overline{ισλ}$ ($\overline{ιηλ}$

v. 10). οικον *secund.* κον *supplet* C).√. 9. [-μενου μου]. ενεμιναν√. 10. [-θηκη ην]. εκινασ√. καρδιαν (-ασ C). μοι *p.m.*, *at primò* μου, *ante* εισ λαον. 11. πολιτην (*pro* πλησιον). ειδησουσιν√.—αυτων *prim.* 12. —και των ανομιων αυτων (*habet* C) *ob* ὁμοιοτ. 13. κενην√ (*non* v. 8). [πεπαλαιωκε].

IX. 1. [ειχε].—σκηνη. λατριασ√. 3. τα αγια των αγιων. 5. χερουβιν. ενεστιν (*pro* εστι: εν *eras.*). 6. ουτωσ√. 9. ην (*pro* ον). συνιδησιν τελιωσαι√. 10. βρωμασιν√. πομασιν√. δικαιωματα (—και: *habet* και C). 11. [μελλ.]. 12. εισ τα αγια εφαπαξ εισ τα αγια (εισ τα αγια *prim. improbat* A)√. [ευραμ-]. 13. τραγων και ταυρων. 14. (C αγιου *pro* αιωνιου). [*p.m. omnino cum* Steph.]. 17. τοτε (*pro* ποτε: C *cum* Steph.). ισχυϊ√. 18. [ουδ]. ενκεκενισται. 19. (+ τον *ante* νομον C). + των (*ante* τραγων: *improbat* C). εραντισεν (*sic* v. 21). 20. ενετιλατο√. 21. λιτουργιασ√. 23. ϋποδιγματα√. κριττοσι√. 24. χιροποιητα√. εισηλθεν αγια.—ο. 25. (+ των αγιων *post* αγια C). 26. νυνι. + τησ (*ante* αμαρτιασ). 28. + και (*post* ουτωσ).

X. 1. + αυτων (*ante* ασ). δυνανται. τελιωσαι√. 2. [ουκ]. εχιν√. συνιδησιν√. κεκαθαρισμενουσ. 4. τραγων και ταυρων. αφεριν (ρ *p.m.*, λ *primò*)√. 6. [ευδ., *sic* v. 8]. 7. —ηκω (*habet* A). 8. θυσιασ και προσφορασ (C *cum* Steph.).—τον. 9. —ο $\overline{θσ}$ (*habet* C). 10. —οι.—του *secund.* 11. [ϊερευσ]. εστηκεν λιτουργων καθ ημεραν (εστ. καθ ημ. λιτ. C). 12. ουτοσ (*pro* αυτοσ). εκ δεξια (εν δ. C)√. 14. τετελιωκεν√. 15. ειρηκεναι. 16. την δ:ανοιαν. 17. μνησθησομαι (C -σθω). 18. αφει^{σ}σ (^{σ} *p.m.* ? C). —τουτων (*habet* C). 20. τουτεστιν√. 22. ρεραντισμενοι (C ερραν-). συνιδησεωσ√. 23. λελουσμενοι. + ημων (*post* ελπιδοσ: *improbat* C). 25. εγκαταλιποντεσ. αυτων (C εαυτων). οσον (C οσω). 26. τησ (*pro* την: C την)√. επιγνωσιαν (α *delet* A). απολιπεται√. 28. μωϋσεωσ. τρισιν√. 30. εκδικησεισ√.—λεγει $\overline{κσ}$ (C λεγι $\overline{κσ}$). κρινει $\overline{κσ}$ (C *cum* Steph.). 31. εμπεσιν√. χιρασ√. 32. (C *habet* αναμιμνησκεσθαι). αμαρτιασ ϋμων (*pro* ημερασ: A C ημερασ:—ϋμων C). 33. ονιδισμοισ√. θλιψεσιν√. 34. [δεσμοισ μου]. γινωσκο̄√ (*sic*). εαυτουσ κρισσονα (—εν *prim.*).—εν ουρανοισ (*habet* C). 35. μεγαλην μισθαποδοσιαν. 36. χριαν εχετε (εχ. χρ. C). κομισασθαι. 37. χρονισει (-ιει C). 38. + μου (*post* δικαιοσ). ϋποστιληται√. 39. απωλιασ (-λιαν A C).

XI. 1. εστιν√. 3. πιστι (*non* vv. 5. 7. 27; *at sic* vv. 4. 8. 9. 11.

21. 22. 23. 24. 28. 29. 30. 31)√. φαιν[ομενω̅ *supplet* A]√. τα βλεπομενον. 4. προσηνεγκεν√. τω θω̅ (*pro* του θυ̅: C *cum* Steph.). *fin.* λαλει. 5. ηὑρισκετο. οτι (*pro* διοτι: A C *cum* Steph.). μετετεθηκεν (μετεθηκεν A? C).—αυτου (*habet* C). [ευηρ.]. 6. —τω (*habet* C). εστιν√. γεινεται√. 7. κατεσκευασεν√. [κατεκρινε]. 8. [-τι καλ-].—τον (*habet* C). ημελλεν κληρονομιαν λαμβανιν (—εισ: *supplet post* ημ. A *vel p.m.*: *at* C. λαμ. εισ κλ.). 9. —την. συνκλ.—τησ *ult.* (A τησ αυτησ επαγγ. C τησ επ. τησ αυτησ *cum* Steph.). 11. ελαβεν√.—ετεκεν (*habet* C). 12. [-εννη-]. ωσ η (*pro* ωσει). χιλοσ√. 13. κομισαμενοι (*pro* λαβοντεσ: C *cum* Steph.).—και πεισθεντεσ. 14. [εμφ.]. επιζητουσιν√. 15. μνημονευουσιν (C *cum* Steph.). εξεβησαν (εξηλθον C *cum* Steph.). 16. νυν. κριττονοσ√. επεσχυνεται√. ητοιμασεν√. 17. πειστι (*sic* v. 20)√. ἴσακ (*sic* v. 18). πιραζομενοσ√. 19. εγιρειν δυνατοσ. 20. πειστι περι. ευλογησεν (—ισαακ: A *supplet* ἴσακ, C ἴσαακ). 21. ἴωσηφ' (*non* v. 22). ευλογησεν√. 22. ισηλ̅√. εμνημονευσεν√. ενετιλατο√. 23. μωϋσησ (*sic* v. 24). αστιον√. [διαταγμα]. 25. συνκακουχισθαι√. 26. μιζονα√. αιγυπτου (—εν). απεβλεπεν√. 27. εκαρτερησεν√. 28. πεποιηκεν√. [ολοθρευων]. 29. + γησ (*post* ξηρασ). 30. ἴερειχω επεσαν. 31. ρααβ'√. + επιλεγομενη (*ante* πορνη: *improbat* C). απιθησασιν√. 32. επιλειψι√. με γαρ.—τε και *prim.*—και *secund.* δαυειδ'√. -ουηλ'√. 33. ηργασαντο (ειργ- C). 34. μαχαιρησ (*sic* v. 37). εδυναμωθησαν (C ενεδ.). 35. γυναικασ (C *cum* Steph.). κριττονοσ√. 36. ενπεγμων√. πιραν√. 37. επιρασθησαν επρισθησαν. αιγιοισ√. 38. επι (*pro* εν). [ορεσι]. 39. [την επ.]. 40. κριττον√. τελιωθωσιν√.

XII. 1. ημισ√. τηλικουτον (C τοσουτον *cum* Steph.). 2. ὑπεμινεν√.—του θυ̅ (ὁμοιοτ.). κεκαθικεν. 3. εαυτουσ (*pro* αυτον: αυτουσ C). 4. [αντικ-]. ανταγω^{ν}ιζομενοι (^{ν} *et* αγω *in liturâ scripsit* A, *ut videtur*)√. 5. εκλελησθαι√. παιδιασ√. 7. εισ παιδιαν ὑπομενετε· (—ει).—εστιν (*habet* C). 8. παιδιασ√. [γεγονασι]. και ουχ' ὑϊοι εστε. 9. [ενετρ.]. πολυ (*pro* πολλω). (+ δε *post* πολυ C). 10. *init.* ο (C οι)√. επεδευον√.—εισ το (*habet* C). 11. μεν (*pro* δε *prim.*: δε C). παιδια√. ἴρηνικον√. αποδιδωσιν√. 12. χιρασ√. 13. ποιειτε. 14. ουδισ√. 15. [δια ταυτησ]. μιανθωσιν οι π. 16. [απεδοτο]. *fin.* εαυτου (αυτου C *cum* Steph.). 17. ευρεν√. 18. —ορει. ζοφω (*pro* σκοτω: C *cum* Steph.). 19. —μη (*habet* C). 20. *init.* ουκ (*primò* θ *loco* ο?)√.—η βολιδι κατατοξευθησεται. 21. [ουτω, ουτωσ C]. η (*pro* ην). μωϋσησ.—ειμι (*habet* C). *fin.* ει ...οσ. 22. ῑηλμ√. 23. απογεγραμμενων εν ουρανοισ. [πνασι ...)]. τελιων δεδικαιωμενοισ (C δικαιων τετελιωμενων). 24. κ... ον. [τον αβ.]. 25. εξεφυγον επι γησ (—τον *et* τησ: C ... *et* εφυγον τον). + τον (*ante* χρηματιζοντα: *improbat* C). ...λυ (*pro* πολλω). 26. εσαλευσεν√. σισω (*pro* σειω). 27. την των σαλευομενων ^την^ μεταθεσιν (την *supra* C). μινη√. 28. εχομεν. λατρευομεν. *fin.* μετα ευλαβιασ και δεουσ (C αιδουσ *pro* δεουσ, *sed restitutum* δεουσ).

XIII. 2. την φιλοξενιαν (τησ -ιασ C). 3. μιμνησκεσθαι√. 4. πασιν (*sic* v. 18)√. γαρ (*pro* δε). κρινι√. 5. εγκαταλειπω. 6. —και (*habet* C). 7. μιμεισθαι√. 8. εχθεσ. 9. παραφερεσθε. βεβαιουσθε√. περιπατουντεσ (C *cum* Steph.). 10. [εξουσιαν]. 11. [αιμα περι αμαρτιασ]. 12. (επαθεν C *marg.*).—επαθε *p.m.* 15. —ουν (*habet* C). τουτεστιν√. 16. ευαρεστιται√. 17. (C + αυτοισ *ante* αυτοι). ποιωσιν√. 18. *Loco* πεποιθαμεν (*quod habet* C) *p.m. legit errore* οτι καλη̄ θα: *sequente* γαρ κ.τ.λ. *Constat autem exemplar, quod describebat p.m., legisse* πειθομεθα *cum* Codd. A C D M. συνῑδησιν√. 19. ταχειον√ (*non* v. 23). 21. —εργω. + αυτω (*ante* ποιων: *improbat* C). ημιν (*pro* υμιν). [των αιωνων]. 22. [ανεχεσθε]. —γαρ (*habet* C). επεστιλα√. 23. γεινωσκετε√. + ημων (*post* αδελφον: *improbat* C). ερχησθε (ερχηται C *cum* Steph.). 24. ασπασασθαι√. 25. *fin.* —αμην (*habet* C).

Subscr. προσ εβραιουσ.

στιχοι ψν *s. m.*

προσ τιμοθεον α.

Cap. I. 1. χ̄ῡ ῑῡ. επαγγελιαν (*pro* επιταγην). σ̄ρ̄σ̄ (ii. 3)√. [κ̄ῡ ῑῡ χ̄ῡ]. 2. πιστι√ (*non* v. 4). ῒρηνη.—ημων *prim.* (*habet* C). 3. μακαιδονιαν√. παραγγιλησ√. τισιν√. ετεροδιδασκαλιν√. 4. εκζητησεισ. [παρεχουσι]. [οικονομιαν]. 7. λεγουσιν√. 8. [χρηται]. 9. κιται√. [ασεβεσι]. πατρολωαισ. μητρολωαισ. 12. *init.* —και. ενδυναμουντι (—με: *at* -μωσαντι με C). 13. *init.* το (*pro* τον). [-τα βλ-]. αλλα. 14. ϋπερεπλεονασεν√. 15. —τον. 16. ενδιξηται√. [ῑσ̄ χ̄σ̄]. απασαν. + 'αγαθων' (*ante* πιστευειν: ' ' *p.m.* ?).

17. —σοφω (*habet* C). 18. στρατευση (C *cum* Steph.). 19. συνιδησιν√. 20. ϋμενεοσ√. [παιδευθωσι]. βλασφημιν√.

II. 2. ευσεβια√. 3. —γαρ (*habet* C). 4. ελθιν√. 5. μεσειτησ√. 6. και μαρτυριον (το *pro* και C). 7. κηρυξ'√. (εν $\overline{\chi\omega}$ *improbat* C). γνωσι (*pro* πιστει). 8. χιρασ√. [διαλογισμου *p.m.*, -σμων C). 9. —και *prim.* (*habet* C).—τασ. (C κοσμιωσ). κοσμιν√. και χρυσω (—η *prim.*). 12. διδασκιν δε γυναικι. [αλλ]. 14. εξαπατηθεισα (C *cum* Steph.). γεγονεν√. 15. μινωσιν√. πιστι√.

III. 2. δι√. ανεπιλημπτον. νηφαλιον (C -λαιον). 3. —μη αισχροκερδη. αλλα. 4. προϊστανομενον (*non* v. 12). 5. οιδεν√. 7. —αυτον. εχιν√. ονιδισμον√. 8. —σεμνουσ (*habet* C). 9. και καθαρασ συνειδησεωσ (*pro* εν κ. σ.: C *cum* Steph., *at* καθαρασ C *errore*). 10. δοκειμαζεσθωσαν√. διακονιτωσαν√. 11. νηφαλιουσ. πασιν√. 13. πιστι√. 14. ελθιν√. [ταχιον]. 15. αληθιασ√. 16. εστιν√. οσ (*pro* $\overline{\theta\sigma}$: *at* θεὸσ *sic plenè* E [XII *cent.*] *antiquissimâ scripturâ salvâ: cf. ed. maj. tab.* xvii). ανελημφθη.

IV. 1. [$\overline{\pi\nu\alpha\sigma\iota}$]. διδασκαλειασ (-λειαισ C). 2. κεκαυστηριασμενων. συνιδησιν√. 3. μεταλημψιν. [επεγνωκοσι]. αληθιαν√. 6. $\overline{\chi\upsilon}$ $\overline{\iota\upsilon}$. [παρηκολουθηκασ]. 7. ευσεβιαν√. 8. —προσ *prim.* (*habet* C). 9. —πασησ (*habet* C). 10. —και *prim.* αγωνιζομεθα (C ονιδιζομεθα: Steph. ονειδ.). εστιν√. 12. μηδισ√. καταφρονιτω.—εν πνευματι. πιστι√. αγνια√. 14. πρεσβυτερου (-τεριου C *cum* Steph.). 15. —εν *secund.* 16. *fin.*—σου (*habet* C).

V. 1. —ωσ πατερα (*habet* C). 2. αγνια√. 4. ευσεβιν√. εστιν. —καλον και. 5. επι $\overline{\kappa\nu}$ (C *cum* Steph. επι τον $\overline{\theta\nu}$). δεησεσιν√. 6. τεθνηκεν√. 7. *init.* (και *improbat* C). ανεπιλημπτοι. 8. —των *secund.* οικιων√. προνοειται (C *cum* Steph.). 10. επηκολουθησεν√. 11. καταστρηνιασωσιν√. γαμιν (*sic* v. 14)√. 13. μανθανουσιν√. 14. οικοδεσποτιν√. 15. [τινεσ εξετραπησαν]. 16. —πιστοσ η. επαρκεισθω. 18. γραp (˙*p.m.*)√. [β. α. ου φ.]. ου μισθου *rescripsit* A: "Non dubito quin antea [i. e. *p.m.*] τησ τροφησ scriptum fuerit, licet prorsus rasum sit" Tischend. 20. [τουσ αμαρ-]. εχωσιν√. 21. $\overline{\chi\upsilon}$ $\overline{\iota\upsilon}$ (—$\overline{\kappa\upsilon}$). [προσκλισιν]. 23. αλλα. —σου *prim.* 24. εισιν√. τισιν√. 25. [-τωσ και]. τα εργα τα καλα. —εστι. [δυναται].

VI. 1. π τουσ (˙*p.m.*)√. 2. καταφρονιτωσαν√.—οτι αδελφοι εισιν (*habet* C). εισιν *secund.*√. 3. προσεχετε (C *cum* Steph.). [ϋγιαινουσι]. ευσεβιαν (*sic* v. 5)√. 4. [ερισ]. 5. διαπαρατριβαι.

— αφιστασο απο των τοιουτων. 6. εστιν√. 7. — δηλον (*habet* C). 8. [αρκεσθησομεθα]. 9. πλουτιν√. πιρασμον√. [βυθιζουσι]. απωλιαν√. 10. ποικιλαισ (*pro* πολλαισ: C *cum* Steph.). 11. — του (*habet* C). — ευσεβειαν (C *habet* ευσεβιαν). *fin.* πραυπαθιαν (C πραυτητα). 12. — και *prim.* 13. — σοι (*habet* C). — του *prim.* [ζωοποι-]. $\overline{ιυ}$ $\overline{χυ}$. 14. ανεπιλημπτον. $\overline{χυ}$ $\overline{ιυ}$. 15. διξειν√. 16. + το (*ante* κρατοσ). 17. καιρω (*pro* αιωνι: C *cum* Steph.). ὑψηλα φρονιν. επι (*pro* εν *secund.*). — τω *secund.* — τω ζωντι. ημιν παντα πλουσιωσ. 18. πλουτιν√. 19. οντωσ (*pro* αιωνιου). 20. παραθηκην. 21. μεθ υμων (*pro* μετα σου). — αμην (*habet* C).

Subscr. προσ τιμοθεον α.

στιχ^ω αν *s. m.*

προσ τιμοθεον β.

Cap. I. 1. $\overline{χυ}$ $\overline{ιυ}$. επαγγελιασ. 2. ἱρηνη√. $\overline{κυ}$ $\overline{ιυ}$ $\overline{χυ}$ τον $\overline{κυ}$ (*at* C $\overline{χυ}$ $\overline{ιυ}$ του $\overline{κυ}$). 3. συνιδησιν√. μνιαν√. δεησεσιν√. 5. λαβων (C λαμβανων *cum* Steph.). ενωκησεν√. ευνικη. πεπισμαι√. 6. θελημα (*pro* χαρισμα: C *cum* Steph.). χιρων√. 8. επεσχυνθησ√. — ημων (*habet* A). συνκακ. 9. κατα ἰδιαν. δοθισαν√. αιωνιὰν (-ιων C *cum* Steph.). 10. $\overline{χυ}$ $\overline{ιυ}$ ($\overline{ιυ}$ $\overline{χυ}$ *vult* C). 11. — εθνων (*habet* C). 12. — και *prim.* (*habet* C). πεπισμαι√. εστιν√. [παραθηκην]. εκινην√. 14. παραθηκην. 15. εστιν√. φυγελοσ. 16. ανεψυξεν√. [επησχυνθη: *at* C *primò* επαισ.]. 17. σπουδαιωσ. εζητησεν√. ευρεν√. 18. διηκονησεν√.

II. 3. συγκακοπαθησον (— συ ουν). $\overline{χυ}$ $\overline{ιυ}$. 4. εμπλεκετε√. πραγματιαισ√. 6. πρὼτερον (· *p.m.*: *at* πρωτον C). μεταλαμβανιν√. 7. ο (*pro* α: C *cum* Steph.). δωσει. πασιν√. 8. $\overline{δαδ}$. 9. αλλα. — ου (*habet* C). 10. τυχωσιν√. 11. συνζησομεν. 12. συνβασιλευσομεν. αρνησομεθα (C *cum* Steph.). 13. εκινοσ√. + γαρ (*post* αρνησασθαι: *improbat* C). 14. $\overline{θυ}$ (*pro* $\overline{κυ}$). [λογομαχειν]. επ (*pro* εισ: C *cum* Steph.). 15. ανεπεσχυντον√. 17. εξι√. 18. αληθιαν√. — την *secund.* ανατρεπουσιν√. την πιστιν τη̄ τινων (την π. τινων C). 19. $\overline{κυ}$ (*pro* $\overline{θυ}$: C *cum* Steph.). 19. + παντωσ (*ante* τουσ οντασ: *improbat* C). *fin.* $\overline{κυ}$ (*pro* $\overline{χυ}$). 20.

εστιν√. **21.** ***— εσται σκευοσ (habet*** **A).** ***— και (habet*** **C).** **22.** ***[μετα των].*** **23.** ***απεδευτουσ√. ζητησισ√. [γεννωσι].*** **24.** ***αλλα.*** **25.** ***πραΰτητι. πεδευοντα√. δωη (δω*** **C** ***cum*** **Steph.).** ***— μετανοιαν (habet*** **C).**

III. 1. ***[γινωσκε].*** **2.** ***— οι. απιθεισ√.*** **3.** ***— αστοργοι (ὁμοιοτ.).*** **5.** ***ευσεβιασ√.*** **6.** ***αιχμαλωτιζοντεσ.— τα.*** **7.** ***αληθιασ√ (non*** **v. 8).** **8.** ***ουτωσ√.*** **9.** ***εκινων√.*** **10.** ***παρηκολουθησασ. πιστι√.*** **11.** ***αντιοχια√. εικονιω√. [ερρυσατο].*** **12.** ***ζην ευσεβωσ.*** **14.** ***τινων (pro τινοσ).*** **15.** ***— τα prim.*** **16.** ***ελεγμον. παιδιαν√.***

IV. 1. ***— ουν εγω.*** $\overline{\chi\upsilon}$ $\overline{\iota\upsilon}$ ***(— του*** $\overline{\kappa\upsilon}$***). κρινιν√. και (pro κατα:*** **C** ***cum*** **Steph.).** **2.** ***παρακαλεσον επιτιμησον (*****C** ***cum*** **Steph.).** ***μαση (pro παση)√.*** **3.** ***ἴδιασ επιθυμιασ (pro επ. τασ ιδ.). επισωρευσουσιν√.*** **4.** ***αληθιασ√.*** **5.** ***πασιν.— κακοπαθησον (habet*** **C).** **6.** ***τησ αναλυσεωσ μου. εφεστηκεν√.*** **7.** ***τον καλον αγωνα.*** **8.** ***εκινη√. [πασι:*** **C** ***-ιν]. — τοισ ηγαπηκοσι (*****C** ***habet τοισ ηγαπηκοσιν).*** **9.** ***ελθιν√.*** **10.** ***[-λιπεν]. γαλλιαν (pro γαλατιαν). [δαλμ.].*** **11.** ***εστιν√ bis. [αγε].*** **12.** ***απεστιλα√.*** **13.** ***φελονην. [απελιπον].*** **14.** ***ενεδιξατο√. αποδωσει. fin. — αυτου (habet*** **C).** **15.** ***αντεστη (*****C** ***ανθεστηκεν).*** **16.** ***παρεγενετο (*****C** ***συνπαρ.). ενκατελιπον. λογισθιη√.*** **17.** ***ενεδυναμωσεν√. ακουσωσιν. ερυσθην.*** **18.** ***init. — και. ρυσετε√.*** **20.** ***εμινεν√.*** **21.** ***ασπαζετε√. fin. — παντεσ (habet*** **C).** **22.** ***—*** $\overline{\iota\sigma}$ $\overline{\chi\sigma}$ ***(habet*** **C).** ***— αμην (habet*** **C).**

Subscr. προσ τιμοθεον.

στιχων ρπ s.m.

προσ τιτον.

Cap. I. 1. [$\overline{\iota\upsilon}$ $\overline{\chi\upsilon}$]. **3.** ***εφανερωσεν√.*** **4.** ***και (pro ελεοσ).*** $\overline{\chi\upsilon}$ $\overline{\iota\upsilon}$ (— $\overline{\kappa\upsilon}$). **5.** ***απελιπον (κατελιπον*** **C** ***cum*** **Steph.).** ***λιποντα. [-θωση].*** **6.** ***ανἡεγκλητοσ (ʽ p.m., η eras.)√.*** **7.** ***ωσ*** $\overline{\theta\upsilon}$ ***οικονομον p.m. vel*** **A** ***rescripsit.*** **9.** ***ελεγχιν√.*** **10.** ***εισιν√. — και prim. [-στα οι]. + τησ (ante περιτομησ).*** **11.** ***ανατρεπουσιν√. δι√.*** **12.** ***ειπεν√. + δε (ante τισ: improbat*** **C).** **13.** ***— εν (habet*** **A).** ***πιστι√.*** **14.** ***αληθιαν√.*** **15.** ***— μεν (habet*** **C).** ***μεμιαμμενοισ. συνϊδησισ√.*** **16.** ***απιθεισ√.— και (ante προσ: habet*** **C).** ***— αγαθον (habet*** **A,** ***αγαθ in liturâ scribens).***

II. 1. α λαλει α (*sic*). πρεπι√. 2. [-λιουσ]. πιστι√. 3. ἱεροπρεπισ√. μηδε (*pro* μη *secund.*: C *cum* Steph.). 4. σωφρονιζουσι (-ζωσι C). 5. οικουργουσ (C *cum* Steph.). ὑποτασσομεναι *p.m.* (-ασ *s.m.*). 7. τυπον παρεχομενοσ (C *cum* Steph.). αφθοριαν (αδιαφθ. C *cum* Steph.).—αφθαρσιαν. 8. εχων (ν *p.m.*?)√. λεγειν περι ημων (*non* υμων). 10. —πιστιν (C *habet post* πασαν). ενδικνυμενουσ√. την του σρσ ημων (*non* υμων). 11. —η *secund.* σωτηροσ (C *cum* Steph.). 12. πεδευουσα√. 13. χυ ιυ (ιυ χυ C) [*caetera cum* Steph.]. 14. αυτον (*pro* εαυτον: C *cum* Steph.]. 15. μηδισ√.

III. 1. —και. πιθαρχιν√. αγαθουσ (C *cum* Steph.). 2. βλασφημιν√. ενδικνυσθαι. σπουδητα (*sic p.m., diversas lectiones* σπουδην *et* πρα .... τα *intermiscens*: Tischend. Proleg. p. xxiii: C ενδικνυμενουσ πραοτητα). 3. απιθεισ√. + εν (*ante* επιθυμιαισ: *improbat* C). στυγηται (-τοι C). μεισουντεσ√. 5. α (*pro* ων). το αυτου ελεοσ. παλινγενεσιασ. 7. δικαιωθεντοσ (*sic*). γενηθωμεν (C *cum* Steph.). 8. διαβεβεουσθαι√. φροντιζωσιν√.—τω. εστιν√.—τα. 9. ζητησισ√. εριν (C ερισ). εισιν√. ανωφελισ√. 10. [και δευ. νουθ.]. 12. νεικοπολιν√. παραχιμασαι√. 13. απολλω. λιπη. 14. χριασ√. 15. πιστιν√.—αμην (*habet* C).

Subscr. προσ τιτον.

στιχων ϙϛ *s.m.*

προσ φιλημονα.

Ver. 2. αδελφη (*pro* αγαπητη). συνστρατιωτη (συ: *et p.m. et* C ‾). 3. —ημων (*habet* C). 4. μνιαν√. [προσ τον κν]. 6. διακονια (*pro* κοινωνια). επιγνωσι√. [του εν υμιν].—ιυ (*habet* C). 7. *init.* χαραν. πολλην εσχον.—και παρακλησιν. 8. επιτασσιν√. 9. χυ ιυ. 10. *fin.* —μου (*habet* C). 11. ·νυ νι√. + και (*ante* σοι *secund.*: *delet* C, *sed rursus restitutum*). 11, 12. ανεπεμψα σοι (—δε: C *cum* Steph.). 12. τουτεστιν√.—προσλαβου (*habet* C). 13. ηβουλομην. κατεχιν√. μοι διακονη. 16. αλλα.—αδελφον (*habet* C). 17. με (*pro* εμε). 18. ηδικησεν√. οφιλει√. ελλογα (C? ελλογι, *at a iterum restitutum*). 19. προσοφιλεισ√. 20. *fin.* χω (*pro* κω *secund.*). 21. α (*pro* ο). 23. ασπαζεται. 25. —ημων. [αμην].

Subscr. προσ φιλημονα.

στιχων [*deest numerus*] *s.m.*

In Epistulis Paulinis longè plurimas secundae manus correctiones praebet C, *ad textum receptum praecipuè accommodatas.* A *post* C *creberrimus est:* A obliq. *rarò occurrit;* A[a] *et* C[a] *bis terve;* E *tantum ad* 1 Tim. iii. 16; B D *haud semel.*

πραξεισ.

Cap. I. 1. [ο ισ]. διδασκιν√. 2. εντιλαμενοσ√. ανελημφθη. 3. τεσσερακοντα. 4. περιμενιν√. 5. [ϊωαννησ *pass.*]. εν πνι βαπτισθησεσθαι αγ. (C *cum* Steph.). 6. ελθοντεσ (C *cum* Steph.). ηρωτων. 7. ειπεν√. εστιν√. 8. λημψεσθαι√. μού (*pro* μοι). [εν *secund.*]. σαμαρια. αισχατου√. 9. ειποντων (C ειπων). 10. παριστηκισαν√. εσθησεσι λευκαισ. 11. ειπαν (*sic* v. 24). βλεποντεσ (C εμβλ.). αναλημφθεισ. εθεασασθαι√. 12. ελεωνοσ. 13. —ανεβησαν (*habet* C). και ϊωαννησ και ϊακωβοσ. βαρθολομεοσ. μαθθαιοσ.—ο (*ante* ζηλωτησ: *habet* C). 14. ομοθυμαδον προσκαρτερουντεσ ομοθυμαδον (ομοθ. *secund. improbat* C)√.—και τη δεησει. γυναιξιν√. [μαρια].—συν *secund.* 15. αδελφων (*pro* μαθητων). ωσει (*pro* ωσ). εικοσι. 16.—ταυτην. προειπεν√. δαδ√. συλλαβουσιν ιν (—τον). 17.—ην (*habet* C). εν (*pro* συν). ελαχεν√. 18.—του. πρινησ (C πρηνησ)√. ελακησεν√. 19. *init.* +ο (ο *eras.*). [πασι].—ιδια. αχελδαμαχ'. τουτεστιν√. 20. λαβετω. 21. δι√.—εν *secund.* (*habet* C). εισηλθεν√. 22. αχρι (*pro* εωσ). ανελημφθη. συν ημιν γενεσθαι. 23. βαρσαββαν. [ματθιαν]. 24. ον εξελεξω εκ τουτων των δυο ενα. 25. [κληρον]. αφ (*pro* εξ). 26. αυτοισ (*pro* αυτων). ματ'θιαν. κατεψηφισθη.(C συνκ.).

II. 1. [συμπληρουσθαι].—απαντεσ (παντεσ C). ομου (*pro* ομοθυμαδον). 2. [καθημενοι]. 3. γλωσσει (*pro* γλωσσαι ωσει: C *cum* Steph.)√. +και εκαθισαν (*pro* εκαθισε τε: C και εκαθισεν). 4. παντεσ. λαλιν√. αποφθεγγεσθαι αυτοισ. 5. εισ ϊηλμ (*pro* εν ιηλμ:

C *cum* Steph.). — ιουδαιοι. 6. [συνηλθε]. ηκουσεν. — εισ. 7. απαντεσ *prim.* (παντεσ C *cum* Steph.). — προσ αλληλουσ. ουχ (*pro* ουκ). απαντεσ *secund.* 8. ημισ√. 9. — και ελαμιται (*habet* C). 12. διηπορουντο. — αν. [θελοι]. 13. διαχλευαζοντεσ. εισιν√. 14. + ο (*ante* πετροσ). επηρεν√. παντεσ. ενωτισασθαι√. 15. ϋπολαμβανεται√. εστιν (*sic* v. 16)√. 16. [ϊωηλ']. 17. *init.* και εστε. ενυπνιοισ. 18. επι τασ δουλασ μου και επι τουσ δουλουσ μου. εκιναισ√. προφητευσουσιν√. 19. σημια√. 20. — η (*ante* ελθιν√). — την *prim.* (*habet* C). — και επιφανη. 21. *Deest versus* (*habet* A, *legens* εστε√. αν επικαλεσητε√). 22. ισδραηλειτε. ναζοραιον (C ναζωρ.). αποδεδιγμενον απο του θῡ. [δυναμεσι και τερασι]. σημιοισ√. εποιησεν√. — και *ultim.* οιδαται√. 23. — λαβοντεσ (*habet* C). χειροσ. ανειλατε. 24. ανεστησεν√. ωδεινασ√. κρατισθαι√. 25. δᾱδ (*sic* vv. 29. 34)√. προορωμην. + μου (*post* κ̄ν̄). 26. ηϋφρανθη. μου η καρδια (C *cum* Steph.). εφ ελπιδι (*pro* επ. ε.). 27. εγκαταλιψεισ√. αδην. 29. ετελευτησεν√. 30. — το κατα σαρκα αναστησειν τον χ̄ν̄. καθισε√. τον θρονον. 31. ελαλησεν√. οτι ουτε ενκατελιφθη εισ αδην ουτε η σ. (— η ψυχη αυτου). ειδεν√. 32. εσμεν ημεισ. 33. του π̄ν̄σ̄ του αγιου. εξεχεεν√. ο ϋμεισ βλεπετε (— νυν). 34. ειπεν κ̄σ̄ (— ο: *habet* C: ψαλμω ρθ *in marg. et* >> > > *s.m.*: *sic* v. 28 >>). 36. [πασ οικοσ]. και κ̄ν̄ αυτον και χ̄ν̄ εποιησεν ο θ̄σ̄. 37. την καρδιαν. ειποντεσ (— τε). ποιησωμεν. 38. προσ αυτουσ μετανοησατε φησιν (— εφη). [επι]. των αμαρτιων ϋμων. λημψεσθαι. 39. [πασι]. [οσουσ]. προσκαλεσητε√. 40. πλιοσιν√. διεμαρτυρατο. + αυτουσ (*ante* λεγων). σωθηται√. 41. — ασμενωσ. + εν (*ante* τη ημερα). εκινη√. ωσ (*pro* ωσει: C *cum* Steph.). 42. [-τεσ τη διδ.]. — και *secund.* (*habet* C). κλασι√. 43. *init.* εγινετο. δε (*pro* τε). σημια√. *fin.* + εν ῑη̄λ̄μ̄ φοβοσ τε ην μεγασ επι παντασ: cf. V. 5. 11. 44. και παντεσ δε οι πιστευσαντεσ. 45. πασιν√. χριαν ειχεν√. 47. — τη εκκλησια. (καθ ημεραν επι *in eodem versu*, το αυτο *in sequente*: *in novâ pericopâ habet* πετρ. δε . .).

III. 1. πετροσ δε και ϊωαννησ. ενατην. 2. του αιτιν. 3. λαβιν. 4. προσ (*pro* εισ *prim.*). ειπεν (*sic* v. 6)√. 5. λαβιν√. 6. ουκ (*pro* ουχ). ναζοραιου (C ναζωρ.). — εγειραι και. 7. + αυτον (*post* ηγειρεν). αι βασισ αυτου. στα σφυδρα (*pro* τα σφυρα: *s.m.* δ *eras.*)√. 8. εισηλθεν√. [και αινων]. 9. ειδεν πασ ο λαοσ αυτον. 10. δε (*pro* τε). — αυτον (αυτον *habet* A *inter* δε *et* οτι: *inceperat scribere post* οτι). αυτοσ (*pro* ουτοσ). ελαιημοσυνην√. την ωραιαν πυλην (C τη ωραια, *praetermisso* πυλην). 11. αυτου (*pro* του *καθεντοσ χωλου*). +*τον* (*ante ἰωαννην*). *συνεδραμεν πασ ο λαοσ προσ αυτουσ*. [*σολομωντοσ*]. 12. +*ο* (*ante πετροσ*). *ἰσδραηλειται*. *ει* (*pro η prim.*). *ατενιζεται*√. *δυναμι*√. *ευσεβια*√. *πεποιηκοσιν* (*π prius p.m., at τ primò*)√. 13. +*ο θσ* (*ante ἰσαακ* [*sic*] *et ἰακωβ*). *τω πρων* (*sic*)√. *εδοξασεν*√. *πατερα* (*pro παιδα*: E? *demum παῖδα*)√. + *μεν* (*post ὑμεισ*). —*αυτον*. *εκινου απολλυειν*√. 14. *ητησασθαι*√. 15. *απεκτινατε*√. *ημισ*√. 16. —*επι* (*habet* C). *οιδαται εστερεωσεν*√. 18. *προκατηγγιλεν*√. *παθιν τον χν αυτου*. *ουτωσ*√. 19. *μετανοησαται*√. *επιστρεψαται*√. *προσ το εξαλιφθηναι* (*προσ pro εισ*). *ελθωσιν*√. 20. *αποστιλη*√. *προκεχειρισμενον* (*pro προκεκηρ.*). *χν ιν*. 21. *δι*√. *των* (*pro παντων secund.*). (C +*των post αγιων*). *απ αιωνοσ αυτου προφητων*. 22. [*μωσησ*: *in marg. s.m. δευτ*]. —*γαρ προσ τουσ πατερασ*. *ημων* (*pro υμων prim.*: C *cum* Steph.). 23. *εαν* (*pro αν*). [*εξολοθρευθησεται*]. 24. *οι* (*pro οσοι*). *κατηγγιλαν*. 25. +*οι* (*ante ὑιοι*). [*διεθετο ο θσ*]. (*υμων pro ημων* C). + *εν* (*ante τω σπερματι*: *marg. s.m. habet δευτερ*). 26. *αναστησασ ο θσ*. —*ιν*. *απεστιλεν*√. *αποστρεφιν*√. *fin.* [*ὑμων*].

IV. 2. *καταγγελλιν*√. 3. *χιρασ*√. *γ αυριον* (· *p.m., γ postea rasum*). 4. —*ο*. —*ωσει*. 5. +*τουσ* (*ante πρεσβυτερουσ et γραμματεισ*). [*εισ ἰηλμ*]. 6. *αννασ*. *ο αρχιερευσ*. *καϊαφασ*. *ἰωαννησ*. *αλεξανδροσ*. 7. [*τω*]. *δυναμι*√. *fin.* *τουτο εποιεησατε ὑμισ* (*sic p.m.*: *ποιειτε primò*). 8. *πλησθισ*√. *ειπεν*√. —*του ισραηλ*. 9. *ημισ*√. *σεσωται*. 10. *παν* (*pro παντι*: C *cum* Steph.)√. *ναζοραιου* (C *ναζωρ.*). *ὑμισ*√. 11. *εξουθενηθισ*√. *οικοδομων*. 12. *ουδε* (*pro ουτε*). *ετερον ονομα εστιν*. 13. *εισιν*√. 14. *τε* (*pro δε*). *αντειπιν*√. 15. *κελευσαντοσ p.m.* (-*τεσ s.m. instauratoris*)√. *συνεβαλλον*. 16. *ποιησωμεν*: cf. ii. 37. *γεγονεν*√. [*πασι*]. *αρνισθαι*. 17. —*απειλη*. *απιλησωμεθα*√. *λαλιν* (*sic* vv. 20. 29)√. 18. *παρηγγιλαν* (-*λαντο* C)√. —*αυτοισ το*. 19. *ειπον προσ αυτουσ*. *κριναται*√. 20. *ειδαμεν*. 21. *προσαπιλησαμενοι*. [*το πωσ*]. 22. *τεσσερακοντα*. [*εγεγονει*]. *σημιον*√. 23. *ανηγγιλαν*. *αρχιερισ*√. *ειπαν* (*sic* v. 24). 24. —*ο θσ*. 25. *ο του πατροσ ημων δια πνσ αγιου στοματοσ δαδ παιδοσ σου* (—*του post δαδ*). (*ψαλμ. β in marg. s.m.*). *fin.* *καινα*√. 27. +*εν τη πολι ταυτη* (*post αληθειασ*). [*πιλατοσ*: *sic* iii. 13]. *εθνεσιν*√. 28. *χιρ*√. [*σου secund.*]. *προωρισεν*√. 29. [*επιδε*]. *απιλασ*√. 30. *χιρα σου εκτινιν σε ισ ἰασιν* (*εισ pro ισ* A; —*σε posterior manus*). *σημια*√. *γεινεσθαι*√. 31. *παντεσ* (C *cum* Steph.). *του αγιου πνσ*. 32. —*η prim. et secund.* [*ουδε εισ*]. [*απαντα*]. 33. *δυναμι μεγαλη*. *τησ αναστασεωσ ιυ χυ του*

$\overline{\kappa\upsilon}$. 34. ην (*pro* υπηρχεν). — υπηρχον (*habet* C). 35. διεδιδετο. χριαν√. 36. ϊωσηφ. απο (*pro* υπο). εστιν√. [λευϊτησ]. 37. ηνεγκεν√. εθηκεν√. προσ (*pro* παρα).

V. 1. [ανανιασ ονοματι]. παμφιρη (C σαμφιρη). επωλησεν√. 2. *init.* και ενοσφ. (και *p.m.*?). συνϊδυησ. — αυτου. 3. ειπεν (*sic* vv. 8. 19. 35)√. + ο (*ante* πετροσ). επηρωσεν (επληρωσεν C *cum* Steph.). [-σασθαι απο]. 4. ἑμενον σοι εμενεν (· *p.m.*)√. ϋπηρχεν√. 5. + ο (*ante* ανανιασ). εξεψυξεν√. — ταυτα (*habet* C). 6. συνεστιλαν√. 7. εωσ (*pro* ωσ: C *cum* Steph.). ϊδυια√. 8. δε προσ αυτην πετροσ (— ο). απεδοσθαι√. 9. — ειπε. + ουν (*post* τι: *improbat* C). εξοισουσιν√. 10. επεσεν√. προσ (*pro* παρα). [ευρον]. 12. χιρων√. εγινετο. σημια√. πολλα εν τω λαω. [απαντεσ]. σαλομωντοσ. 13. ουδισ√. 15. και εισ (*pro* κατα). πλατιασ√. ασθενισ (*sic* v. 16)√. κλιναριων. κραβαττων. *fin.* αυτω (C αυτων)√. 16. — εισ. 17. αιρεσεισ√. 18. χιρασ√. — αυτων. 19. — τησ (*habet* C). ανοιξασ. 21. απεστιλαν√. 22. παραγενομενοι ϋπηρεται. απηγγιλον. 23. — μεν. κεκλισμενον√. — εξω. επι (*pro* προ). 24. — ιερευσ και ο. + το (*ante* τι: *improbat* C). 25. απηγγιλεν√. — λεγων. — οι (*habet* C). εθεσθαι√. — εστωτεσ και (εστωτεσ A, και *addit* C). 26. ηγεν. — ινα. 28. — ου (*habet* C). παρηγγιλαμεν√. διδασκιν√. επληρωσαται. βουλεσθαι√. 29. — ο. ειπαν. πιθαρχιν δι√. 30. + δε (*ante* $\overline{\theta\sigma}$). διεχιρισασθε√. 31. ϋψωσεν√. + του (*ante* δουναι: *improbat* C). 32. εσμεν μαρτυρεσ (— αυτου). — δε. πιθαρχουσιν√. 33. [εβουλευοντο]. αναιλειν√. 34. τουσ ανθρωπουσ (*pro* τι τουσ αποσ.). 35. ϊσδραηλειται. μελλεται√. πραττειν. 36. προσεκλιθη ανδρων αριθμοσ ωσει τετρακοσιοι (ωσ τετρακοσιων C). επιθοντο. 37. απεστησεν√. — ικανον. κακινοσ√. επιθοντο. 38. — υμιν (*habet* A). αποστηται√. αφετε (*pro* εασατε). 39. δυνησεσθαι. αυτουσ (*pro* αυτο). 40. επισθησαν√. παρηγγιλαν√. λαλιν√. — αυτουσ. 41. κατηξιωθησαν ϋπερ του ονοματοσ (— αυτου). 42. *fin.* τον $\overline{\chi\nu}$ $\overline{\iota\nu}$.

VI. 2. [ειπον]. καταλιψαντασ√. διακονιν√. 3. επισκεψασθαι√. δε (*pro* ουν). [αδελφοι]. — αγιου και (και *tantum habet* C). [καταστησομεν]. χριασ√. 5. εξελεξαν τον (*pro* εξελεξαντο). πληρησ. $\overline{\pi\nu\sigma}$ και πιστεωσ αγιου (C *cum* Steph.). 7. ηϋξανεν√. ϊουδαιων (*pro* ιερεων: C *cum* Steph.). πιστι√. 8. χαριτοσ (*pro* πιστεωσ). σημια√. 9. — των *prim.* των λεγομενων (*pro* τησ λεγ.). [και ασιασ]. συνζητουντεσ. 11. λεγοντεσ (*pro* -τασ). λεγοντοσ (*pro* λαλουντοσ: C *cum* Steph.). βλασφημιασ *primò*, *at p.m. mutatum in* βλασφημααε, *priusquam ad* εισ *pergeretur.* μωϋσην. 12. — επισταντεσ (*habet* C). 13. λεγοντεσ (*pro* -τασ: cf. v. 11). λαλων ρηματα (— βλασφημα). — τουτου. 14. [μωϋσησ]. 15. — εισ (*habet* A). παντεσ. [ειδον].

VII. 1. ειπεν (*sic* vv. 3. 7. 33)√. — αρα. 3. [εκ *secund.*]. συγγενιασ√. + την (*ante* γην). εαν (*pro* αν: C *cum* Steph.). διξω√. 4. αποθανιν√. κατοικιτε√. 5. επηγγιλατο√. δουναι αυτην εισ κατασχεσιν αυτω. 6. ελαλησεν√. αυτω (*pro* ουτωσ). 7. εαν δουλευσωσιν. ο $\overline{θσ}$ ειπεν. λατρευσουσιν√. 8. εγεννησεν√. ϊσαακ' *prim.* εβδομη (C *cum* Steph. ογδοη). — ο *prim. et secund.* [ϊσαακ *secund.*]. ϊακωβ' *prim.*√. 10. εξιλατο. εναντι. + εφ (*ante* ολον). 11. ηλθεν√. αιγυπτον (*pro* γην αιγυπτου). θλιψεισ√. 12. σιτια εισ αιγυπτον. εξαπεστιλαν (C -στιλεν)√. 13. ϊωσηφ'· *prim.*√. — τω *secund.* αυτου (*pro* του ιωσηφ). 14. αποστιλασ√. ϊακωβ' τον πατερα αυτου. — αυτου *secund.* 15. και κατεβη (— δε). ϊακωβ' [εισ αιγυπτον]. 16. ω (*pro* ο). εμμωρ εν συχεμ (— του: + του *ante* εν C). 17. ομολογησεν (*pro* ωμοσεν). 18. [αχρισ]. + επ εγυπτον (*post* ετεροσ: C αιγ.). 19. εκακωσεν√. — ημων *secund.* τα βρεφη εκθετα. 20. μωϋσησ. αστιοσ√. μου (*pro* αυτου: ··· *p.m.*). 21. εκτεθεντοσ δε αυτου ανειλατο. 22. επεδευθη√. μωϋσησ. + εν (*ante* παση). — εν *ultim. fin.* + αυτου. 23. τεσσερακονταετησ. 25. ενομιζεν√. — αυτου. [διδωσι] σωτηριαν αυτοισ. οι δε *p.m., sed* υ *pro* ι *primò.* 26. [τε]. συνηλλασσεν. — υμεισ. αδεικειτε√. 27. δικ *prim. in rasurâ scriptum.* ημων (*pro* ημασ). 28. αναιλειν√. εχθεσ. 29. εφυγεν√. μωϋσησ (*sic* vv. 31. 32. 40). 30. τεσσερακοντα (*sic* vv. 36. 42). — $\overline{κυ}$. [φλογι πυροσ]. 31. εθαυμαζεν. — προσ αυτον. 32. — ο $\overline{θσ}$ *tert. et quart.* ϊσαακ'. ϊακωβ'√. μωϋσησ γενομενοσ. ετολμησεν. 33. εφ (*pro* εν). 34. [αυτων]. αποστιλω (*i. e.* -στειλω). 35. + εφ ημων (*post* δικαστην *prim.*). (+ και *post* $\overline{θσ}$ A *potius quam p.m.*). δικαστην (*pro* λυτρωτην: C *habet* λυτρωτην *post* αρχοντα και *secund.*). απεσταλκεν [εν]. 36. σημια√. γη αιγυπτω. 37. ειπασ. $\overline{ιηλ}$'√. αναστησι√. — $\overline{κσ}$. — υμων *prim.* — υμων *secund.* (*habet* C). — αυτου ακουσεσθε. 38. ορι√. ϋμων (*pro* ημων). ϋμιν (*pro* ημιν). 39. αλλα. και εν ταισ καρδιεσ αυτων (··· *p.m.*: καρδιαισ C). 40. + ο ανθρωποσ (*ante* οσ). εγενετο (*pro* γεγονεν). 42. εστρεψεν√. $\overline{ϊηλ}$'√. 43. [ϋμων] ρομφαν (*at* C ραιφαν). προσκυνιν√. επεκινα√. 44. — εν *prim.* εταξατο (C *cum* Steph.). μωϋση. αυτη (*pro* αυτην). 45. εξεωσεν (ε *med. eras.*). $\overline{δαδ}$√. 46. ευρεν√.

— ητησατο (*habet* C). ευριν√. οικω (*pro* $\overline{θω}$: C *cum* Steph.). 47. σαλομων. 48. χιροποιητοισ√. — ναοισ. κατοικι√. (*Marg. s.m.* ησαιασ). 49. οικοδομησεται√. λεγι√. 50. εποιησεν√ [ταυτα παντα]. 51. ταισ καρδιαισ ὑμων. αντιπιπτεται√. [ωσ]. υμισ *secund.*√. 52. απεκτιναν√. προκαταγγιλαντασ√. φονισ√. *fin.* εγενεσθαι. 54. — ταυτα (*habet* C). 55. + πιστεωσ και (*ante* $\overline{πνσ}$). ειδεν√. 56. διηνοιγμενουσ (*pro* ανεωγ.). εστωτα εκ δεξιων (C *cum* Steph.). 58. [αυτων]. 60. εκραξεν√. — φωνη μεγαλη (*habet* C). [την αμαρτιαν ταυτην]. *Jungit* viii. 1 *usque ad* αναιρεσι√ αυτου *cum* cap. vii.

VIII. 1. εκινη√. — τε (*at* και παντεσ C). σαμαριασ. 2. εποιησαν. 3. + τουσ (*ante* ανδρασ: *improbat* C). 4. ηλθον (διηλθον C *cum* Steph.). 5. + την (*ante* πολιν). καισαριασ (*pro* σαμαρειασ, cf. v. 40; xxi. 8: C σαμαριασ). 6. δε (*pro* τε). αυτου *forsan p.m.* (σ *addito a* C?). βλεπιν√. σημια√. 7. πολλοι. φωνη μεγαλη εξηρχοντο. 8. εγενετο δε πολλη χαρα (— και *et* μεγαλη). πολι (*sic* v. 9)√. 9. εξιστανων. σαμαριασ. 10. προσειχαν (*non* v. 11). [παντεσ]. + καλουμενη (*ante* μεγαλη). 11. μαγιαισ√. 12. του φιλιππου ευαγγελιζομενου (C *cum* Steph.). — τα. βασιλιασ√. $\overline{κυ}$ (*pro* $\overline{θυ}$: C *cum* Steph.). — του (*ante* $\overline{ιυ}$ $\overline{χυ}$). 13. επιστευσεν√. θεορων τε σημια και δυναμισ μεγαλασ γεινομενασ εξισταντο (C εξΐστατο). 14. σαμαρια. $\overline{χυ}$ (*pro* $\overline{θυ}$: C *cum* Steph.). απεστιλαν√. — τον *secund.* 15. λαβωσιν√. 16. ουδεπω (*pro* ουπω). εβαπτισμενοι (C βεβαπ.). 17. επετιθεσαν. χιρασ (*sic* v. 19)√. 18. ἴδων (*pro* θεασαμενοσ). χιρων√. — το αγιον. 19. εαν (*pro* αν). 20. ειπεν (*sic* vv. 24. 29. 31. 34)√. αυτουσ (*pro* αυτον: C *cum* Steph.). απωλιαν√. 21. εστιν√ (*bis in versu*). ευθια√. εναντι (*pro* ενωπιον). 22. $\overline{κυ}$ (*pro* $\overline{θυ}$). 24. δεηθηται ὑμισ√. 25. διαμαρτυρομενοι. ὑπεστρεφον. ιεροσολυμα. σαμαριτων√. ευηγγελιζοντο. 26. ελαλησεν√. [πορευου]. + καλουμενην (*ante* καταβαινουσαν: *improbat* C). 27. — τησ *prim.* — οσ *secund.* (*habet* C). 28. — και *secund.* (*habet* C). ανεγινωσκεν√. 30. ησαιαν τον προφητην. 31. οδηγησει. παρεκαλεσεν√. καθισε√. 32. κιραντοσ. ανυγει√. 33. ταπινωσει√. — αυτου *prim.* — δε. 35. + και (*ante* ευηγγελισατο: *improbat* C). 36. ἴδωρ (C ὕδωρ) *secund.* 37. *Deest versus.* 38. εκελευσεν√. 39. ηρπασεν√. 40. πολισ√. του ελθιν. καισαριαν.

IX. 1. — ετι (*habet* C). ενπνεων. απιλησ√. 2. επιστολασ παρ αυτου. αν (*pro* εαν). οντασ τησ οδου. ιερουσαλημ'·√. 3. εξεφνησ τε (— και). αυτον περιηστραψεν. εκ (*pro* απο). 4. ηκουσεν√. 5.

ειπεν *prim.* (*sic* vv. 10 *prim.* 15. 17. 40)✓. — κσ. [*habet* ειπεν *secund.*]. [ισ ον]. 5, 6. —σκληρον σοι *usque ad* και ο κσ προσ αυτον. 6. + αλλα (*ante* αναστηθι). ο τι (*pro* τι *post* σοι). 7. ϊστηκεισαν✓. ενεοι. ορωντεσ (*pro* θεωρουντεσ: C θεορουντεσ✓). 8. — ο. ηνυγμενων (*pro* ανεωγμενων: C ηνεωγμ.). ουδεν (α *super* ν *s.m.*, *sed revocatum*). εβλεπεν✓. 9. τρισ✓. 10. εν οραματι ο κσ. 11. [αναστασ]. ευθιαν✓. 12. ϊδεν✓. — εν οραματι. ανανιαν ονοματι. χιρασ (C τασ χιρασ). 13. — ο. ηκουσα. τοισ αγιοισ σου εποιησεν. ϊερουσαλημ'✓. 15. εστιν μοι. ενωπιον εθνων τε. 16. ϋποδιξω✓. 17. απηλθεν✓. χιρασ✓. απεσταλκεν✓. —η ηρχου (*habet* A). 18. απεπεσαν. [απο των οφθ. αυτου]. ωσ (*pro* ωσει: C *cum* Steph.). ανεβλεψεν✓. δε (*pro* τε).—παραχρημα. 19. — ο σαυλοσ. 20. εκηρυσσεν✓. ιν (*pro* χν). 21. εξισταντο (ν *p.m.*?). εισ (*pro* εν). [εληλυθει]. 22. συνεχυννε ϊουδαιουσ (— τουσ: *habet* C). [συμβιβ.]. 24. παρετηρουντο. δε και (*pro* τε *prim.*). αυτον αναιλωσιν (αναιλ. αυτον C). 25. οι μαθηται αυτου (— αυτον). δια του τιχουσ καθηκαν αυτον. σφυριδι. 26. — ο σαυλοσ [εισ ιηλμ]. επιραζεν (*pro* επειρατο). εστιν✓. 27. ηγαγεν✓. ειδεν✓. — και (*ante* πωσ *secund.*: *habent* A C). [του ιυ]. 28. εισ (*pro* εν). 29. *init.* — και (*ante* παρησιαζομενοσ✓). — ιυ (*habet* C). + τε (*ante* προσ τουσ ελληνιστασ: ·· *p.m.*). επεχιρουν✓. ανελειν αυτον✓. 30. καισαριαν. εξαπεστιλαν αυτον. 31. η μεν ουν εκκλησια. σαμαριασ ειχεν. οικοδομουμενη και πορευομενη. επληθυνετο. 32. κατελθιν✓. εν λυδδα (·· *p.m. vel* A). 33. ευρεν✓. ονοματι αινεαν. κραβακτου (C κραβαττου). 34. — ο *secund.* 35. [ειδον]. λυδδα. —τον *prim.* (*habet* C). σαρρωνα. 36. [αγαθ. εργ.]. ελαιημοσυνων✓. 37. εκιναισ✓. αποθανιν✓. εθηκαν αυτην (C *cum* Steph.). [εν υπερ.]. 38. λυδδασ (C λυδδα). απεστιλαν✓. οκνησησ. διελθιν✓. ημων (*pro* αυτων). 39. κλεουσαι✓. επιδικνυμεναι✓. 40. + και (*ante* θεισ). [ηνοιξε]. ανεκαθισεν✓. 42. επιστευσαν πολλοι. 43. ημερασ ϊκανασ μιναι (—αυτον: *ante* ημερ. *habet* C).

X. 1. — ην. ʼκαισαρια. [σπειρησ]. 2. — τε. 3. *init.* ωεδεν (ω *notat. p.m.*: ειδεν *demum* C).—εν. ωσ (*pro* ωσει: C *cum* Steph.). + περι (*ante* ωραν). ενατην. 4. ειπεν *bis in vers.* (*sic* vv. 14. 19)✓. εστιν (*sic* vv. 34. 35. 36)✓.—εισ μνημοσυνον (*habet* C). εμπροσθεν (*pro* ενωπιον). 5. ανδρασ εισ ιοππην. [σιμωνα οσ]. 6. — ουτοσ λαλησει *usque ad fin. vers.* 7. αυτω (*pro* τω κορνηλιω). — αυτου. 8. απαντα αυτοισ. απεστιλεν✓. 9. αυτων (*pro* εκεινων). προσευξασθε✓. (ενατην *pro* εκτην C). 10. προσπινοσ✓. ηθελεν γευσασθε√. αυτων (*pro* εκεινων). εγενετο (*pro* επεπεσεν). 11. θεωρι√. — επ αυτον. — δεδεμενον και. 12. ὑπηρχεν√. τετραποδα και ερπετα τησ γησ (— και τα θηρια *et* τα *ante* ερπετα) cf. xi. 6. — τα (*ante* πετινα√). 14. και (*pro* η). 15. εκαθαρισεν√. 16. τρεισ√. ευθυσ (*pro* παλιν). ανελημφθη. 17. ειδεν√. — και. ὑπο (*pro* απο). + του (*ante* σιμωνοσ). 19. διενθυμενου√. το πνα αυτω. τρισ√. ζητουντεσ. 20. οτι (*pro* διοτι). 21. — τουσ απεσταλμενουσ απο του κορνηλιου προσ αυτον. 22. ειπαν. 23. εξενισεν√. αναστασ (*pro* ο πετροσ). εξηλθεν√. — τησ. 24. τη δε (*pro* και τη: *lineae contra* v. 23 τη δε επ. *positae ad* v. 24 *lectorem referunt*). εισηλθαν. κεσαριαν. συνκαλεσαμενοσ. 25. + του (*ante* εισελθιν√). 26. ηγειρεν αυτον. και εγω. 27. εισηλθεν√. 28. ὑμισ√. επιστασθαι√. καμοι εδιξεν ο θσ. 29. πυνθανομε√. μετεπεμψασθαι√. 30. — νηστευων και. ενατην. — ωραν. εμου (*pro* μου *secund.*). 31. φησιν√. 32. — οσ παραγενομενοσ λαλησει σοι. 33. *fin.* ὑπο του κυ (απο *pro* ὑπο C). 34. (+ αυτου *post* στομα C). προσωπολημπτησ. 35. εθνι√. 36. ὸν (·· A *potius quam p.m.*). απεστιλεν√. 37. αρξαμενοσ απο. 38. ναζαρεθ. ωσ (*pro* οσ: C *cum* Steph.). 39. ημισ√. — εσμεν. [εν *secund.*]. + και (*ante* ανιλαν *sic*). 40. ηγειρεν εν τη τρ. (*improbat* εν C). 41. [μαρτυσι]. προκεχιροτονημενοισ. 42. παρηγγιλεν√. [αυτοσ]. 43. λαβιν√. 44. [επεπεσε]. 45. οσοι συνηλθαν. [αγιου πνσ]. 46. — ο. 47. δυναται κωλυσαι. ωσ (*pro* καθωσ). 48. προσεταξεν√. δε (*pro* τε). αυτοισ (*pro* αυτουσ). εν τω ονοματι ιυ χυ βαπτισθηναι (— του κυ).

XI. 2. οτε δε (*pro* και οτε). ῗηλμ. 3. εισηλθεσ προσ ανδρασ ακροβυστιαν εχοντασ. 4. — ο. 5. πολι√. — προσευχομενοσ (*habet* C). εκστασι√. αχρι. 6. ^ερ^πετα (ερ *p.m.*)√. 7. + και (*post* δε). 8. — παν. ακα *p.m.* (θαρ *supplet* A, τον C), *at* κοινον η α *rescriptum* *p.m.*√. 9. — μοι. εκαθαρισεν. 10. ανεσπασθη παλιν. 11. τρισ√. ημεν (*pro* ημην). καισαριασ. εμε (*pro* με: C *cum* Steph.). 12. ειπεν√. το πνα μοι. συνελθιν√. μηδεν διακρινοντα (C -ναντα). 13. απηγγειλεν√. δε (*pro* τε). ειδεν√. — αυτω. αποστιλον√. — ανδρασ. 14. λαλησι√. 15. λαλιν√. [επεπεσε]. 16. + του (*ante* κυ). (+ οτι *ante* ϊωαννησ C). βαπτισθησεσθαι√. 17. δεδωκεν. — δε. 18. εδοξασαν. αρα (— γε). εισ ζωην εδωκεν. 19. [στεφανω]. αντιοχιασ (*non* v. 22). *fin.* ϊουδαιοι. 20. ελθοντεσ. αντιοχιαν (*sic* v. 26, *non* v. 27). + και (*post* ελαλουν: *improbat* C *sed restitut.*). ευαγγελιστασ (*pro* ελληνιστασ: C ελληνασ). 21. + ο (*ante* πιστευσασ). 22. τησ ουσησ εν ιερουσαλημ (*pro* τησ εν ιεροσολυμοισ). εξαπεστιλαν√.—διελθειν. 23. + την (post χαριν). προσμενιν√. 24. ανηρ ην. 25. εξηλθεν√. — ο βαρναβασ. 26. — αυτον prim. et secund. αυτοισ και (pro αυτουσ). πρωτωσ. αντιοχια. χρηστιανουσ p.m. (χριστ. s.m.). 28. εσημανεν√. μεγαλην (pro μεγαν). μελλιν√. ητισ (pro οστισ). — και. — καισαροσ. 29. ευποριτο. 30. init. ο και ο (ο secund. improbat A). αποστιλαντεσ√.

XII. 1. ο βασιλευσ ηρωδησ. χιρασ√. 2. ανιλεν√. μαχαιρη. 3. ἴδων δε (— και). — εστι (C εστιν√). συλλαβιν√. [δε ημεραι]. 4. τεσσαρσιν√. αναγαγιν√. 5. ετηριτο√. εκτενωσ. περι (pro υπερ). 6. ημελλεν προσαγειν αυτον. αλυσεσιν δυσιν√. 7. εξεπεσαν. 8. ειπεν (sic vv. 11. 17)√. [τε]. ζωσαι. εποιησεν√. ουτωσ√. λεγιν√. ακολουθι√. 9. ηκολουθι√.—αυτω (habet C). ηδι√. [εστι]. [δια]. εδοκι√. — δε (habet C). βλεπιν√. 10. ηλθαν. ηνυγη (pro ηνοιχθη). 11. εν εαυτω γενομενοσ. εξαπεστιλεν√. εξειλατο. 12. + τησ (ante μαριασ). 13. αυτου (pro του πετρου). προηλθε. ὑπακουουσα (A cum Steph.). 14. ηνυξε√. απηγγιλεν√. 15. ειπαν. οι δε ελεγον αγγελοσ εστιν αυτου (—ο: habet ο C, et αυτ. εστ.). 16. [επεμενε]. [ειδον]. 17. κατασισασ√. χιρι√.— αυτοισ secund. τε (pro δε secund.). απαγγιλατε√. 18. ουχ (pro ουκ). 19. —την. καισαριαν. 20. — ο ηρωδησ. πισαντεσ√. 21. αισθητα√. — και. 22. [θυ φωνη]. ανθρωπων (C cum Steph.). 23. [εδωκε την δ.]. 24. ηὔξανεν√. 25. εισ (pro εξ: nihil additum). συνπαραλαβοντεσ. — και secund. επικαλουμενον.

XIII. 1. — τινεσ. αντιοχια. τετρααρχου (a alterum eras. s.m.?) cf. Matth. xiv. 1; Luc. iii. 1. 19. 2. ειπεν (sic v. 22)√. — τε. (τον secund. improbat A). 3. χιρασ√. 4. αυτοι (pro ουτοι). του αγιου πνσ.—την prim. et secund. σελευκιαν. 5. εισ σαλαμινη (εν pro εισ C). 6. + ολην (post δε). + ανδρα (ante τινα). βαριησου. 8. ουτωσ√. 9. — και secund. 10. + του (ante κυ: improbat C). ευθιασ√. 11. χιρ√. — του. τε επεσεν (pro δε επεπεσεν). εζητι χιραγωγουσ√. 13. — τον. ὑπεστρεψαν (C -ψεν)√. 14. την πισιδιαν. ελθοντεσ (pro εισελ.: C cum Steph.). 15. απεστιλαν√. ει τισ εστιν εν υμιν λογοσ. 16. κατασισασ√. ἴσδραηλειται. 17. ἴσηλ'. αιγυπτου. βραχειονοσ√. 18. τεσσερακονταετη. [ετροποφορησεν]. 19. κατεκληρονομησεν. — αυτοισ. 20. init. ωσ ετεσι τετρακοσιοισ και πεντηκοντα και μετα ταυτα. εδωκεν√.—του. 21. κακιθεν√. κεισ. βενιαμειν. τεσσερακοντα. 22. τον δαυειδ αυτοισ. δυδ secund. (sic vv. 34. 36). 23. — απο του σπερματοσ (habet C). ηγαγεν (pro ηγειρε). 24. 'ιη' λαω ιηλ ('' p.m.)√. 25. — ο.

ελεγεν√. τι εμε. ὑπονοειται√. ειδου√. ερχετε√. λυσε√. 26. ημιν (*pro* υμιν *secund.*). εξαπεσταλη. 27. ἱερουσαλημ'√. 28. ητησαν τον πιλατον (C *cum* Steph.). 29. παντα. μνημιον√. 31. πλιουσ√. + νυν (*post* εισι *sic*). 32. την προσ τουσ *rescripsit in rasura* A *vel p.m.*√. εκπεπληρωκεν√. ημων (*pro* αυτων ημιν). 33. τω ψαλμω γεγραπται τω δευτερω (*marg. s.m.* ψαλμω β̄). 34. ὑποστρεφιν√. 35. διοτι (*pro* διο: *marg. s.m.* ψαλμω *tantum*). ειδιν√. 36. ειδεν (*sic* v. 37)√. 38. ὑμιν εστω. 39. — και. — τω. μωϋσεωσ (μωϋσ *rescripsit p.m.*). *fin.* δικαιωθηναι *primò, at* -ουται *p.m.*√. 40. απελθη (C επελθη). — εφ υμασ. (*marg. s.m.* ἰωηλ). 41. ειδετε√. καταφρονησατε (C -νητε)√. θαυμασετε. ο εγω εργαζομε εγω (*pro* εγω εργαζομαι: C *delet* ο *tantum*). ο (*pro* ω). πιστευσηται√. 42. αυτων (*pro* εκ τησ συναγωγησ των ιουδαιων). — τα εθνη. 43. λυθισησ√. + αυτοισ (*post* δε: *improbat* C). [αυτοισ]. επιθον. προσμενιν. 44. [τω δε ερχομενω]. κ̄ῡ (*pro* θ̄ῡ). 45. — του. λαλουμενοισ (*pro* λεγομ.). — αντιλεγοντεσ και. 46. τε (*pro* δε *prim.*). ειπαν. επιδη√. — δε *secund.* (*habet* C). απωθισθαι√. κρινεται√. 47. [ουτω].—ο (*habet* C). τεθικα√. σαι (*pro* σε *prim.*)√. 49. καθ (*pro* δι). 50. (και *ante* τασ ευσχ. *improbat* C). επηγιραν√.— τον *secund.* 51. — αυτων. 52. [δε].

XIV. 1. εικονιω. — των ιουδαιων (*habet* C). 2. απιθησαντεσ. επηγιραν√. 3. + επι (*ante* τω λογω: *improbat* C). διδοντοσ (*pro* και διδοντι). σημια√. γεινεσθαι√. χιρων√. 6. [-νιασ λυστραν]. 7. ευαγγελιζομενοι ησαν. 8. αδυνατοσ εν λυστροισ (C *cum* Steph.). — υπαρχων. περιεπατησεν. 9. + ουκ (*ante* ηκουσεν *sic*). λεγοντοσ (C *cum* Steph. λαλουντοσ). εχει πιστιν. 10. ειπεν√. — τη. [*nihil additum*]. ηλατο. 11. τε (*pro* δε). ειδοντεσ. — ο (*ante* παυλοσ). — αυτων (*habet* C). ανθρωποι (C *cum* Steph.). 12. — μεν. [δια]. επι (*pro* επειδη: C επιδη√). 13. *init.* ο τε (*pro* ο δε). — αυτων. ηθελεν√. 14. βαρναβ *forsan p.m.* (ασ *supplet* A?)√. (C εαυτων *pro* αυτων). εξεπηδησαν. 15. [εσμεν ὑμιν]. επιστρεφιν√.— τον *prim.* (*improbat* C τον *secund.*). εποιησεν√. 16. ἰασεν√. πορευεσθε√. 17. (γε *improbat* C). αυτον (*pro* εαυτον: C *cum* Steph.). αγαθουργων. ὑμιν (*pro* ημιν: *improbat* ὑμιν C). διδουσ ὑετουσ. *fin.* ὑμων (*pro* ημων: C *cum* Steph.). 19. επηλθαν. αντιοχιασ√. πισαντεσ√. [εσυρον].—εξω (*habet* C). νομιζοντεσ. τεθνηκεναι. [*nihil additum in hoc versu*]. 20. των μαθητων αυτον. 20, 21. — και τη επαυριον *usque ad* πολιν v. 21 (ὁμοιοτ.: *habet* C, *legens* εξηλθεν√ *et* ευαγγελισαμενοι: *punctis positis rursusque deletis*)√. 21. + εισ (*ante* εικονιον *et* αντιοχιαν). 22. (+ τε *post* παρακαλουντεσ C).

ενενμενιν√. εισελθιν√. 23. κατ εκκλησιαν πρεσβυτερουσ. νηστιων√. πεπιστευκισαν√. 24. + εισ (*ante* την πισιδιαν). + την (*ante* παμφυλιαν). 25. εισ την περγην (C *cum* Steph., *at ipse forsan revocavit* εισ την π.). + του $\overline{κυ}$ (*post* λογον). ατταλιαν. 26. *init.* κακ *rescripsit p.m.*√. 27. ανηγγελλον. ο $\overline{θσ}$ εποιησεν. ηνυξεν√. εθνεσιν√. 28. — εκει. ουχ (*pro* ουκ: *sic ante* ολιγ. xii. 18; xix. 23. 24; *at non* xv. 2; xvii. 4. 12; xxvii. 20).

XV. 1. περιτμηθητε. εθνι (*pro* εθει: ν *eras.*). + τω (*ante* μωϋσεωσ). δυνασθαι√. 2. δε (*pro* ουν). ζητησεωσ (*pro* συζητησεωσ). αναβαινιν√. εξ αυτων αλλουσ. 3. + τε (*ante* φοινικην). σαμαριαν. διηγουμενοι (A C *cum* Steph.). [πασι]. 4. παρεδεχθησαν. [ὑπο]. — και *prim.* (*habent* A C). ανηγγιλαν√. — τε (*habet* C). εποιησεν√. 5. παραγγελλιν√. τηριν√. 6. [δε]. ειδιν√. 7. ζητησεωσ. ειπεν (*sic* v. 36)√. επιστασθαι√. — οτι (ὅτι C). εν υμιν εξελεξατο ο $\overline{θσ}$ (*non* ημιν). 8. — αυτοισ *secund.* 9. [ουδεν]. διεκρινεν√. πιστι√. 10. πιραζετε√. — ζυγον (*habet* A?). ημισ√. 11. + του (*ante* $\overline{κυ}$). — $\overline{χυ}$. πιστευσομεν. 12. εσιγησεν√. σημια√. εθνεσιν√. 13. ακουσαται√. 14. λαβιν√. — επι. 16. (*marg. s.m.* αιωσ). $\overline{δαδ}$√. κατεστραμμενα. 17. — ο (*habet* C). — παντα (ταυτα *jungit cum* γνωστα απ αιωνοσ·). 18. — εστι τω $\overline{θω}$ *usque ad fin. vers.* 20. επιστιλαι√. — απο. πορνιασ√. [του πνικτου]. 21. μωυσησ. αυτου (ν *p.m.*). 22. [εδοξε]. αντιοχιαν (*sic* v. 23, *non* v. 30). καλουμενον βαρσαββαν. ηγουμενοισ (-ουσ C). 23. — ταδε (*habet* C). — και οι (*ante* αδελφοι: *habet* C). 24. επι δε (*i. e.* επει δε *pro* επειδη: C επιδη√). υμων (*pro* ημων: C *cum* Steph.). — εξελθοντεσ (*habet* C). — λεγοντεσ *usque ad* τον νομον. διεστιλαμεθα√. 25. [εκλεξαμενουσ: *sic* v. 22]. 26. [παραδεδωκοσι]. 28. εδοξεν√. τω $\overline{πνι}$ τω αγιω. κ μηδεν (· *p.m.*)√. τουτων επ αναγκαισ *nisi mavis* επαναγκαισ *cum* Tischend. (— των: *habet* C *ante* επ). 29. πνικτων (C *cum* Steph.). πορνιασ√. ερρωσθαι√. 30. κατηλθον. 32. [τε]. — και επεστηριξαν (*habet* A). 33. αποστιλαντασ εαυτουσ (ε *eras.*: *pro* αποστολουσ). 34. *Deest versus.* 36. προσ βαρναβαν παυλοσ. δε (*pro* δη: C *cum* Steph.). — ημων. πολιν πασαν. κατηγγιλαμεν√. εχουσιν√. 37. εβουλετο συνπαραλαβιν και τον ἰωαννην. (C *scripturus* επικαλουμενον *rursus abstersit* επ). 38. συνπαραλαμβανιν. 39. δε (*pro* ουν). 40. εξηλθεν√. $\overline{κυ}$ (*pro* $\overline{θυ}$). 41. [και κιλ.].

XVI. 1. κατηντησεν√. [δε εισ]. + εισ (*ante* λυστραν). — τινοσ.

2. εμαρτυριτο√. ϊκονιου√. 3. εξελθιν√. εκινοισ√. απαντεσ οτι ελλην ο πατηρ αυτου ϋπηρχεν. 4. παρεδιδοσαν. φυλασσιν√.—των *secund.* ιεροσολυμοισ. 5. πιστι√. 6. διηλθον (*pro* διελθοντεσ). —την *secund.* 7. +δε (*post* ελθοντεσ). επιραζον√. εισ (*pro* κατα *secund.*). πορευθηναι. ιασεν√. *fin.* +$\overline{ιυ}$. 9. [τησ]. τω παυλω ωφθη. μακαιδων τισ ην. +και (*ante* παρακαλων). 10. εξητησαμεν (*pro* εζητ.). εξελθιν√.—την. μακαιδονιαν. [συμβιβ.].—ημασ (*habet* C). $\overline{θσ}$ (*pro* $\overline{κσ}$). 11. δε (*pro* ουν).—τησ. δε (*pro* τε). νεαν πολιν. 12. κακειθεν (—τε). εστιν√.—τησ *secund.* μακαιδονιασ. [κολωνια]. [ταυτη]. 13. πυλησ (*pro* πολεωσ). ενομιζεν προσευχην. +ημιν (*ante* γυναιξιν√: *improbat* ημιν C). 14. διηνυξεν√. 15. (+αυτη *post* εβαπτισθη C). παρεκαλεσεν√. μενετε (*pro* μεινατε). *fin.* ϋμασ (C *cum* Steph. ημασ). 16. +την (*ante* προσευχην). οχουσαν (C εχουσ.)√. πυθωνα υπαντησαι. ϋμιν (*pro* ημιν: C *cum* Steph.)√. παρειχεν√. 17. κατακολουθουσα. [εκραζε]. ϋμιν (*pro* ημιν *secund.*). 18.—ο. ειπεν√.—τω *secund.* εξελθιν√. 19. [τον σιλαν]. 20. ειπαν (*sic* v. 31). 21. ουσιν√. 22. περιρηξαντεσ. 23. παραγγιλασ τε (C παραγγιλαντεσ√). τηριν√. 24. λαβων (*pro* ειληφ.). ησφαλισατο αυτων. 25.—το. 26. σισμοσ√. ηνοιχθησαν δε (*pro* ανεωχθησαν τε). ανελυθη (ανεθη C *cum* Steph.). 27. δεσμοφυλασ (*non* v. 36). [-μενοσ μαχ.]. ημελλεν. 28. εφωνησεν√. φωνη μεγαλη παυλοσ (—ο). 29. εισεπηδησεν√. προσεπεσεν√. [τω σιλα]. 30. προαγων (προαγαγων C *cum* Steph.). 31. πιστευσαν (-σον C)√.—$\overline{χν}$. 32. $\overline{θυ}$ (*pro* $\overline{κυ}$: C *cum* Steph.). συμ πασι (*pro* και πασι). 33. εκινη√. απαντεσ. 34. [αυτου]. παρεθηκεν√. [ηγαλλιασατο]. πανοικει. 35. απεστιλαν√. 36. απηγγιλεν√. [τουτουσ]. απεσταλκαν. *fin.* εισ ϊρηνην. 37. διραντεσ√. [εβαλον]. 38. απηγγιλαν. τε (*pro* δε *prim.*). εφοβηθησαν δε (—και). εισιν√. 39. απελθιν απο (*pro* εξελθειν). 40. απο (*pro* εκ). προσ (*pro* εισ). παρεκαλεσαν τουσ αδελφουσ (—αυτουσ). *fin.* εξηλθαν.

XVII. 1. πολιν (*pro* αμφιπολιν: A *cum* Steph.). +την (*ante* απολλωνιαν).—η. 2. εισηλθεν√. διελεξατο. 3. παθιν√. $\overline{ισ}$ $\overline{χσ}$ (—ο). 4. επισθησαν√. σεβομενων ελληνων πληθοσ πολυ. 5. —απειθουντεσ. και επισταντεσ (—τε). προαγαγειν. [*caetera cum* Steph.). 6. ευρον (*pro* εσυρον: C *cum* Steph.).—τον. 7. πρασσουσι (C -σιν√). ετερον λεγοντεσ. 10. εξεπεμψαν δια νυκτοσ (—τησ). [των ϊουδ. απηεσαν]. 11.—το. 13. +και ταρασσοντεσ (*post* σαλευοντεσ). 14. εξαπεστιλαν√. εωσ (*pro* ωσ). ϋπεμιναν. τε (*pro* δε *secund.*). 15. καθισπαντεσ (C -στωντεσ)√.—αυτον *prim.* +τον (*ante* τιμοθεον). ελθωσιν√. 16.—αυτουσ (*habet* C).

αυτου (*pro* του παυλου : C *cum* Steph.). θεωρουντοσ. κατιδωλον√. 18. + και (*ante* των επικουριων *sic*). — των *secund.* στοικων. καταγγελλευσ. — αυτοισ (C *habet post* ευηγγ.). 19. αριον. [η ῦπο]. 20. εισφερει (C *cum* Steph.). τινα θελει (— αν). 21. ηυκερουν. η λεγειν τι η ακουειν τι (— και *secund.*). 22. — ο. αριου. ειπεν (*pro* εφη). δισιδεμονεστερουσ√. 23. σεβαστα. ο (*pro* ον : C *cum* Steph.). τουτο (C *cum* Steph. τουτον). 24. ῦπαρχων κσ̄. χιροποιητοισ√. 25. ανθρωπινων χιρων. + ωσ (*ante* προσδεομενοσ: *improbat* C). [πασι]. και (*pro* κατα : C και τα). 26. εποιησεν√. — αιματοσ. κατοικιν√. παντοσ προσωπου (*deest articulus*). προστεταγμενουσ. 27. θν̄ (*pro* κν̄). ψηλαφησειεν. [και ευροιεν καιτοιγε]. 28. ειρηκασιν√. 29. οφιλομεν√. χρυσιω. θιον√. 30. απαγγελλει (C *cum* Steph.). παντασ (*pro* πασι). 31. καθοτι (*pro* διοτι). κρινιν√. ωρισεν√. 32. ειπαν. 32, 33. σου περι τουτου και παλιν ουτωσ. 34. [ο αρεοπαγιτησ].

XVIII. 1. — δε. — ο παυλοσ. 2. γενι√. [πρισκιλλαν]. τεχεναι (*ob* δια το *praeced.*? C *cum* Steph. διατεταχεναι)√. απο (*pro* εκ). 3. εμενεν√. ηργαζοντο (C *cum* Steph. ειργαζετο). τη τεχνη. 4. επιθεν. 5. μακαιδονιασ. λογω (*pro* πνευματι). + ειναι (*ante* τον χν̄). 6. ειπεν (*sic* v. 9)√. 7. εισηλθεν. + τιτου (*ante* ιουστου). 8. επιστευσεν√. 9. εν νυκτι δι οραματοσ. 10. + 'αλλα' (*ante* διοτι *prim.* : ' ' *p.m.*)√. ουδισ√. κακωσε√. [εστι]. πολι√. 11. εκαθισεν√. δε (*pro* τε). + κ̇ ενα (*post* ενιαυτον : · *p.m.*). 12. ανθυπατου οντοσ (*pro* ανθυπατευοντοσ). παρα (*pro* επι). 13. αναπειθει ουτοσ. 14. ανοιγιν√. — ουν. ανεσχομην (C ηνεσχ. *cum* Steph.). 15. ζητηματα. εστιν√. — γαρ. 17. — οι ελληνεσ. *fin.* εμελλεν. 18. + εφη (*ante* ετι : *delet* C)√. προσμινασ√. εν κενχραιαισ την κεφαλην. ειχεν√. 19. κατηντησαν. εκει (*pro* αυτου). διελεξατο. 20. (επιμειναι C). — παρ αυτοισ. 21. αλλα αποταξαμενοσ (— αυτοισ) και ειπων. — δει με παντωσ *usque ad* ιεροσολυμα. — δε (*post* παλιν). ανηχθη δε (— και : *etiam* δε *improbat* C). 22. καισαριαν. 23. εξηλθεν√. + και (*ante* καθεξησ: *improbat* C). στηριζων. 24. απελλησ (*pro* απολλωσ : C *cum* Steph.) cf. xix. 1. 25. + ω (*ante* ελαλει : *delet* C). ιῡ (*pro* κῡ *secund.*). 26. παρησιαζεσθαι (*non* xix. 8)√. πρισκιλλα και ακυλα. *fin.* την οδον του θῡ. 27. πεπιστευκοσιν√. 28. επιδικνυσ√.

XIX. 1. απελλην (*pro* απολλω : C *cum* Steph.). κατελθιν (*pro* ελθειν). ευριν (*i. e.* -ειν). 2. ειπεν τε (*pro* ειπε). — ειπον. ουδ. 3. ο δε ειπεν (*pro* ειπε τε προσ αυτουσ). ειπαν (*pro* -ον). 4.

ειπεν√.—μεν. εβαπτισεν√. πιστευσωσιν√.—χ̅ν̅. 6. χιρασ (—τασ). [ηλθε]. επροφητευον. 7. δωδεκα. 8. τρισ√. πιθων√. [τα]. 9. ηπιθουν√. αφωρισεν√.—εν *primò* (*supplet p.m.*)√.—τινοσ. 10.—ι̅υ̅. 11. δυναμισ√. ο θ̅σ̅ εποιει. χιρων√. 12. αποφερεσθαι. εκπορευεσθαι (*pro* εξερχεσθαι). — απ αυτων. 13. επεχιρησαν√. και (*pro* απο). ορκιζω. + κ̅ν̅ (*ante* ι̅ν̅ : *delet* C).—ο. 14. [τινεσ]. υιοι *transfert in locum post* επτα.—οι. 15. + αυτοισ (*post* ειπεν). (+ μεν *ante* ι̅ν̅ C). 16. εφαλομενοσ (C εφαλλ-). ο ανθρωποσ επ αυτουσ. (και *secund. improbat* C). αμφοτερων (*pro* αυτων *prim.*). ενισχυσεν (C ϊσχυσεν√). 17. ελλησιν√. κατοικουσιν√. + ο (*post* επεπεσεν : C *delet* ο). 19. κατεκεον√. 20. ουτωσ√. του κ̅υ̅ ο λογοσ (C *cum* Steph.). ηΰξανεν√. ϊσχυσεν. 21. [διελθων]. μακαιδονιαν. [και αχ.]. ιεροσολυμα. 22. αποστιλασ√.—την. μακαιδονιαν. + εισ (*ante* τιμοθεον : ··· *p.m.*)√. επεσχεν√. 23. εκινον√. ουχ (*pro* ουκ). 24. ναον αργυρουν (C *cum* Steph.). [παρειχετο]. ουχ ολιγην εργασιαν. 25. τοιαυτασ√. επιστασθαι√. ημιν (*pro* ημων). εστιν√. 26. [αλλα σχ.]. — πεισασ. εισιν. — οι (*habet* C). 27. κινδυνευσι. — αλλα (*habet* C). [αρτεμιδοσ ϊερον]. εισ ουθεν λογισθηναι μελλειν τε (— δε *secund.*). τησ μεγαλιοτητοσ. 28. πληρισ√. 29. — ολη. + τησ (*ante* συγχυσεωσ : *improbat* C). μακαιδονασ. — του. 30. παυλου δε (—του : C του παυλου δε). εισελθιν√. ιων (*pro* ειων : C *cum* Steph.)√. 31. αυτον (*pro* εαυτον : C *cum* Steph.). 32. συνκεχυμενη. ενεκα. συνεληλυθισαν. 33. συνεβιβασαν. [προβαλοντων]. ο δ ουν (*pro* ο δε : C *cum* Steph.). κατασισασ√. (τη̄ χειρι C). ηλθεν (*pro* ηθελεν : C *cum* Steph.). 34. επιγνοντεσ. εστιν√. κραζοντεσ. 35. καταστιλασ√. αδελφοι (*pro* εφεσιοι : C *cum* Steph.). ανθρωπων. γινωσκι√. + και (*post* ουσαν : *improbat* C). — θεασ. 36. — τουτων (*habet* C). ϋπαρχιν√. (+ τι *post* προπετεσ C). πρασσιν. 37. θεον ημων (*pro* θεαν υμων). 38. εχουσιν προσ τινα λογον. 39. [περι ετερων]. επιζητειται√. 40. εγκαλισθαι√. + ου (*post* περι ου). [αποδουναι]. + περι (*post* λογον). 41. [απελυσε].

XX. 1. μεταπεμψαμενοσ (*pro* προσκ.). + παρακαλεσασ και (*inter* και *et* ασπασαμενοσ). εξηλθεν√. πορευεσθαι. — την. μακαιδονιαν. 3. επιβουλησ αυτω. γνωμησ. ϋποστρεφιν√. [μακεδ.]. 4. — αχρι τησ ασιασ. σωπατροσ πυρρου βεροιοσ (C βεροιεοσ). θεσσαλονικαιων. 5. + δε (*post* ουτοι). προσελθοντεσ. εμεινον (ι *eras.*). τρωαδει. 6. απο (*pro* αχρισ). οπου (*pro* ου). 7. ημων (*pro* των μαθητων). — του. παρετινεν√. 8. ημεν (*pro* ησαν *secund.*). 9. καθεζομενοσ.

πλιον√. 10. συνπεριλαβων. ειπεν (*sic* v. 35)√. 11. + τον (*ante* αρτον: *improbat* C). αχρι αυτησ (*ex* τ C *fecit* γ). 13. επι (*pro* εισ). αναλαμβανιν√. ουτωσ√. διατεταγμενοσ ην. 14. συνεβαλλον (-λλεν C). επι (*pro* εισ: C *cum* Steph.). 15. αντικρυσ.—και μειναντεσ εν τρωγυλλιω. + δε (*ante* εχομενη). 16. κεκρικει. εσπευδεν√. ειη (*pro* ην). *fin.* ιερουσαλημ. 18. [αυτον ειπεν]. επιστασθαι√. 19. ταπινοφροσυνησ√.—πολλων. πιρασμων√. 20. ϋπεστιλαμην√. αναγγιλαι√. 21. [ελλησι].—τον *prim.*—την *secund.* [ιν χν]. 22. δεδεμενοσ εγω. πορευομε√. εμοι (*pro* μοι: C *cum* Steph.). 23. (διεμαρτυρατο C). + μοι (*ante* λεγον). και θλιψισ με. 24. λογου (*pro* λογον).—ουδε εχω. (C λογον εχω ουδε ποιουμαι).—μου *prim.* (εωσ *pro* ωσ C). τελιωσω.—μετα χαρασ. 25.—ετι.—του θυ. 26. διοτι (*pro* διο). ειμι (*pro* εγω). 27. ϋπεστιλαμην√. αναγγιλαι√. ϋμιν *transfert ad fin. vers.* (C *cum* Steph.). 28. —ουν. ποιμενιν√. [θυ]. του αιματοσ του ϊδιου. 29.—γαρ (δε *pro* γαρ C).—τουτο. βαρισ√. φιδομενοι√. 30. *fin.* εαυτων. 31. γρηγοριται√. 32. ϋμιν (*pro* υμασ).—αδελφοι. οικοδομησαι.—υμιν. + την (*ante* κληρονομιαν). 33. ουθενοσ. 34.—δε. χριαισ√. [ουσι]. χιρεσ√. 35. ουτωσ√. εστιν√. μαλλον διδοναι. λαμβανιν√. 36. θισ√. 37. τε (*pro* δε). κλαυθμοσ εγενετο. κατεφιλων (C *cum* Steph.). 38. μελλουσιν√. θεωριν√.

XXI. 1. αναχθεντασ (*pro* αναχθηναι: C *cum* Steph.). κω. 2. (C διαπερον). 3. [αναφαναντεσ]. κατηλθομεν (*pro* κατηχθημεν). το πλοιον ην. 4. ανευροντεσ δε (—και). επεμιναμεν αυτου. επιβαινιν ϊσ ιεροσολυμα (εισ *pro* ϊσ C). 5. [ημασ εξαρτισαι]. [γυναιξι].—εωσ. + 'προσευξαμενοι' (*post* γονατα: ' ' *p.m.* ? *et* C)√. 5, 6. προσευξαμενοι απησπασαμεθα (*pro* προσηυξ. και ασπ.). 6. και ανεβημεν (*pro* επεβημεν: C και ενεβ.). 7. (κατεβημεν *pro* κατηντησαμεν C). πτολεμαϊδαν (C *cum* Steph.). εμιναμεν (*non* v. 8)√. 8.—οι περι τον παυλον. σ̇ ηλθομεν (*pro* ηλθον: · *p.m.*). καισαριαν. —του *secund.* 9. τεσσαρεσ παρθενοι. 10. αυτων (*pro* ημων: C *cum* Steph.). κατηλθεν√. 11.—τε. εαυτου τουσ ποδασ και τασ χιρασ. ειπεν (*sic* vv. 13. 39)√. λεγι√. ουτωσ√. + τασ (*ante* χιρασ√ *secund.*: *improbat* τασ *s.m.*). 12. ημισ√. αναβαινιν√. ιερουσαλημ'·√. 13. *init.* τοτε απεκριθη (—δε). + και ειπεν (*post* παυλοσ).—κλαιοντεσ και (C κλεοντεσ κ√). αποθανιν√. εν ϊερουσαλημ'· (εισ *forsan p.m.*). 14. πιθομενου. του κυ το θελημα γεινεσθω. 15. επισκευασαμενον (*pro* αποσκευασαμενοι: -νοι *pro* νον *s.m.* ? *super ras.*).—ανεβαινομεν (*habet* C). ϊεροσολυμα. 16. καισαριασ. ϊασονι (*pro* μνασωνι). 17. ϊσ (C εισ)√. απεδεξαντο. 18. τε (*pro* δε). 19. εθνεσιν√. — δια. 20. εδοξασαν. θν̄ (*pro* κν̄). ειπαν τε. θεωρισ√. — ιουδαιων. ϋπαρχουσιν√. 21. — δε (*habet* C). διδασκισ√. μωυσεωσ. [παντασ]. λεγω (C *cum* Steph. λεγων). περιτεμνιν√. εθεσιν περιπατιν√. 22. εστιν√. συνελθειν πληθοσ. — γαρ οτι (*habet* C). 23. [τεσσαρεσ]. αφ (*pro* εφ). 24. ξυρησονται. γνωσονται. φυλασσων τον νομον. 25. επεστιλαμεν√. — μηδεν *usque ad* ει μη. — το *secund.* πορνιαν√. 27. συντελισθαι√. [συνεχεον]. επεβαλαν (C *cum* Steph.). επ αυτον τασ χιρασ. 28. ϊσδραηλειται. βοηθιται√. τουτουσ (*pro* τουτου: ˙*p.m.*)√. πανταχη. κεκοινωνκεν (˙ *p.m.*)√. 29. — τον. 30. εκεινηθη√. — και *tert.* εκλισθη^σαν ευθεωσ (σαν *p.m.*). — αι θυραι (C και ευθεωσ εκλισθησαν αι θυραι). 31. τε (*pro* δε). αποκτιναι√. σπιρησ√. συνχυννεται (C συνκεχυται). ϊηλμ̄√. 32. [παραλαβων]. εκατονταρχασ. 33. [εκελευσε]. [αλυσεσι δυσι]. — αν. εστιν√. 34. επεφωνουν (*pro* εβοων). δυναμενου δε αυτου (*pro* δυναμενοσ δε). 36. κραζοντεσ. 37. εξεστιν√. [τι]. γινωσκισ√. 39. — ειμι (*habet* C). + λογον (*ante* λαλησαι: *improbat* C). 40. κατεσισε√. [γενομενησ]. προσεφωνησεν√.

XXII. 1. νυνι. 2. [προσεφωνει]. 3. — μεν. ανηρ ειμι. ακριβιαν√. 5. μαρτυρι√. 7. επεσα. σαουλ' σαουλ'·√. 8. + και ειπα (*ante* τισ). ειπεν (*sic* vv. 10. 13. 21. 25)√. εμε (με C). ναζοραιοσ (ναζωρ. C)√. 9. εθεατο (C *cum* Steph. εθεασαντο)√. — και εμφοβοι εγενοντο. (C ηκουον). 10. κακι√. 12. ευλαβησ (*pro* ευσεβησ). 13. εμε (*pro* με). 14. προσεχειρησατο (σ *eras.*). ϊδιν√. 16. αυτου (*pro* του κῡ). 17. ϊσ ιερουσαλημ'√. γενεσθαιθαι√. εκστασιν√. 18. ϊδον (*pro* ιδειν). ταχι√. — την. 20. εξεχυννετο. — τη αναιρεσει αυτου. 22. καθηκεν. 23. [δε]. αεραν (C *cum* Steph.). 24. ο χιλιαρχοσ εισαγεσθαι αυτον. ειπασ (*pro* ειπων). 25. προετιναν√. εστιν (*pro* εξεστιν: C *cum* Steph.). 26. εκατονταρχησ (C -ρχοσ): *non* v. 25. τω χιλιαρχω απηγγιλεν. — ορα. εστιν (*sic* v. 29)√. 27. — μοι (*habet* C). — ει *prim.* 28. δε (*pro* τε). πολιτιαν√. — δε (*post* εγω *secund.*: *habet* C). 29. αναιταζειν (C *cum* Steph.)√. — δε (*habet* C). αυτον ην. 30. [το τι]. κατηγοριται√. ϋπο (*pro* παρα). — απο των δεσμων. συνελθειν (*pro* ελθειν). παν (*pro* ολον). — αυτων.

XXIII. 1. τω συνεδριω ο παυλοσ. συνιδησει√. 2. [επεταξε]. — αυτω (*habet* C). τυπτιν (*sic* v. 3)√. 3. προσ αυτον ο παυλοσ. ειπεν (*sic* vv. 11. 20)√. 4. ειπαν (*sic* v. 14). 5. ηδιν√. + οτι (*ante* αρχοντα). ερισ√. 6. εστιν (*sic* v. 34)√. εκραζεν. φαρισαιων (*pro* -αιου). 7. ειπαντοσ (*pro* λαλησαντοσ: C ειποντοσ). των σαδδουκαιων και φαρισαιων. [εσχισθη το]. 8. σαδδουκαι (-καιοι C)√. [μεν]. λεγουσιν√. μητε (*pro* μηδε). ομολογουσιν√. 9. τινεσ των γραμματεων του μερουσ (— οι). + προσ αλληλουσ (*ante* λεγοντεσ).—εν (*habet* C).—μη θεομαχωμεν. 10. γινομενο$^{\eta}$σ στασεωσ (η C *post p.m. vel* A). φοβηθισ (*pro* ευλαβηθεισ). εκελευσεν√. — εκ μεσου αυτων (*habet* C). 11. — παυλε. [ουτω]. 12. συστροφην οι ϊουδαιοι (— τινεσ). (λεγοντεσ *improbat* C). φαγιν (*sic* v. 21)√. [πιειν: *sic* v. 21]. αποκτινωσιν√. 13. τεσσερακοντα. ποιησαμενοι. 14. [αρχιερευσι]. [μηδενοσ]. γευσασθε√. αποκτινωμεν√. 15. — αυριον. καταγαγη αυτον. εισ (*pro* προσ). διαγινωσκιν√. —του *secund.* (*habet* C). 16. την ενεδραν. [παραγενομενοσ]. απηγγιλεν√. 17. απαγε. τι απαγγιλαι. 18. [ηγαγε]. ηρωτησεν√. νεανισκον (*sic* v. 22). 19. επιλαβομενου (C *cum* Steph.). χιροσ√. εχισ√. 20. τον παυλον καταγαγησ εισ το συνεδριον. μελλοντι *seu mavis* μελλον τι (*pro* μελλοντεσ τι: C μελλοντων τι). 21. πισθησ√. [ενεδρευουσι]. τεσσερακοντα. εισιν ετοιμοι. 22. [απελυσε]. παραγγιλασ√. εμε (*pro* με). 23. τινασ δυο. καισαριασ. 24. [διασωσωσι]. φιλικα (C *cum* Steph. φηλικα), *hic tantum*. 25. εχουσαν. 27. συλλημφθεντα. αναιρεισθε√. εξειλαμην. — αυτον. εστιν√. 28. τε επιγνωναι (*pro* δε γνωναι). — αυτον. 29. εχοντα εγκλημα. 30. μηνυθισησ√. — μελλειν. — υπο των ιουδαιων. εξ αυτων (*pro* εξαυτησ). παραγγιλασ√. λεγιν√. αυτουσ (*pro* τα προσ αυτον). [ερρωσο]. 31. — τησ. 32. απερχεσθε (*pro* πορευεσθαι). επεστρεψαν. 33. καισαριαν. 34. — ο ηγεμων. επαρχειασ√. *fin.* + εστιν (*puncta jam ante* C *imposita*). 35. διακουσομε√. κελευσαντοσ (*pro* εκελευσε τε αυτον: C κελευσασ). [του ηρ.]. *fin.* + αυτον.

XXIV. 1. πρεσβυτερων τινων (—των). 3. διορθωματων. εθνι√. 4. ενκοπτω. επιεικια√. 5. στασισ (*i. e.* -εισ). [πασι: *sic* v. 14]. ερεσεωσ√. 6. επιρασεν√. 6—8. *Desunt omnia ab* και κατα τον ημ. ν. v. 6 *usque ad* ερχεσθαι επι σε v. 8. 9. συνεπεθεντο. 10. τε (*pro* δε). εθνι√. ευθυμωσ. 11. επιγνωναι. εισιν√. — η. δωδεκα. εισ (*pro* εν). 12. επιστασιν. 13. ουδε (*pro* ουτε). — με. + σοι (*post* δυνανται). νυνι. κατηγορουσιν√. 14. ουτωσ√. + τοισ εν (*ante* τοισ προφηταισ: *delet* C). 15. προσ (*pro* εισ). — ουτοι. μελλιν√.—νεκρων. 16. και (*pro* δε). συνϊδησιν√. 17. *Transfert p.m.* παρεγενομην *in locum post* μου, *at* C *post* προσφορασ. 18. αισ (*pro* οισ). [τινεσ δε]. 19. εδει. εμε (*pro* με). 20. — ει. — εν εμοι.

21. εκεκραξα εν αυτοισ εστωσ. [ὑφ]. **22.** *init.* ανεβαλετο δε ... αυτουσ ο φηλιξ (— ακουσασ *et* ταυτα). ειπασ. κατεσθ (*pro* καθ: ··· *p.m.*, *at pro* θ *scripserat* ε *primò*)√. **23.** —τε. χιλι *pro* εκατοντ *primò: correxit p.m. vel* A√. τηρισθαι√. αυτον (*pro* τον παυλον). εχιν√. ὑπηρετιν√. — η προσερχεσθαι. **24.** [ημ. τινασ]. [τη γυναικι αυτου *p.m.*: *at* ιδια *ante* γυν. A, ιδια *erasum per* C ?]. + και (*ante* μετεπεμψατο: *improbat* C). + $\overline{ιυ}$ (*post* $\overline{χυ}$: *improbant* A *et* C ?). **25.** εγκρατιασ και δικαιοσυνησ. — εσεσθαι. **26.** — δε. — οπωσ λυση αυτον. **27.** πληρωθισησ ελαβεν√. τε χαριτα (δε χαριν C). (κατελιπεν C, -πε *p.m.* ?)√.

XXV. **1.** τη επαρχιω (-χια C). τρισ√. καισαριασ. **2.** τε (*pro* δε). οι αρχιερεισ. ϊουδεων√. **4.** τηρισθαι (*sic* v. 21)√. εισ καισαριαν (*pro* εν καισ.). μελλιν√. (C εκπορευεσθαι εν ταχει). **5.** οι ουν εν ημιν φησιν δυνατοι καταβαντεσ (*non* υμιν). ατοπον (*pro* τουτω). κατηγοριτωσαν√. **6.** ου πλειουσ ημερασ οκτω η δεκα. κεσαριαν. εκελευσεν√. προαχθηναι (προ *improbat* C). **7.** + αυτον (*ante* οι). αιτιωματα καταφεροντεσ (— κατα του παυλου). ισχυσαν (C *cum* Steph.). αποδιξαι√. **8.** του παυλου απολογουμενου (— αυτου). **9.** θελων τοισ ϊουδαιοισ. ειπεν (*sic* v. 10)√. κριθηναι. **10.** εστωσ επι του βηματοσ καισαροσ ειμι (C *cum* Steph.). δι (*pro* δει)√. ηδικηκα. **11.** ουν (*pro* γαρ). παραιτουμε√. αποθανιν√. κατηγορουσιν√. **12.** συνλαλησασ. **13.** καισαριαν. ασπασαμενοι. **14.** εστιν√. καταλελιμμενοσ√. **15.** ϊσ (C εισ)√. *fin.* καταδικην. **16.** — εισ απωλειαν. εχοι κατα προσωπον. **17.** [αυτων]. ποιησαμενοι (C -νοσ)√. **18.** εφερον. εγω ὑπενοουν. *fin.* + πονηρα (*jungitne cum* v. 19 ?, *at* πονηρων C). **19.** δισιδαιμονιασ√. **20.** — εισ *prim.* τουτων (*pro* τουτου). κρινεσθαι (*pro* πορευεσθαι: C *cum* Steph.)√. ιεροσολυμα. **21.** αναπεμψω. **22.** — εφη (*scripsit* C ε *abstersitque*). — ο δε. **23.** ακρωτηριον (C *cum* Steph.). — τοισ *prim.* [ανδρασι]. — ουσι. **24.** συνπαροντεσ. απαν. βοωντεσ. αυτον ζην. **25.** (C κατελαβομην). [θαν. αυτ.]. — και. πεμπιν√. — αυτον *secund.* **26.** — σου (*habent* A C). *fin.* γραψω.

XXVI. **1.** [επιτρεπεται]. περι (*pro* ὑπερ). εκτινασ την χιρα απελογιτο. **2.** επι σου μελλων σημερον απολογισθαι. **3.** σε οντα (C *cum* Steph. οντα σε). (+ επισταμενοσ *post* ζητηματων C). — σου. **4.** [την εκ]. εθνι√. + τε (*ante* ϊεροσολυμοισ). [ϊσασι]. [οι ϊουδ.]. **5.** [θελωσι]. μαρτυριν√. θρησκιασ√. **6.** εισ (*pro* προσ). + ημων (*post* πατερασ). **7.** [εκτενεια]. ελπιζι√. ὑπο ϊουδαιων βασιλευ (— των *et* αγριππα). **9.** + του (*ante* $\overline{ιυ}$: *improbat* C). ναζοραιου. **10.**

εποιησαν (ν *erasum*). + τε (*post* πολλουσ). + εν (*ante* φυλακαισ). κατεκλισα√. κατηνεγκαν. 11. βλασφημιν√. εμμενομενοσ√. 12. — και *prim.* (τησ: *puncta imposuit* C *sed rursus abstersit*). — παρα. 13. — ημερασ (*habet* C). κατην (*pro* κατα την)√. 14. τε (*pro* δε). λεγουσαν (*pro* λαλουσαν). — και λεγουσαν. σαουλ' σαουλ√. 15. [ειπον]. + $\overline{κσ}$ (*post* ο δε). 16. σοι (*pro* σε: C *cum* Steph.). οφθησομε√. 17. εξερουμενοσ√. + εκ (*ante* των εθνων). εγω αποστελλω σε (— νυν). 18. ανυξαι√. πιστι√. 19. απιθησ√. 20. + τε (*post* πρωτον). [και ῒερ.]. — εισ. απηγγελλον (*pro* απαγγελλων). επιστρεφιν√. 21. — οι (*habet* C). συλλαβουμενοι. + οντα με (*ante* εν τω ῒερ: με *improbat* C). επιρωντο√. διαχιρωσασθαι (C -ρισασθαι). 22. απο (*pro* παρα). μαρτυρομενοσ. μωϋσησ. 23. (> > *in marg.*)√. μελλῑ (¯ *i. e.* ν *eras.* α C?)√. + τε (*ante* λαω). εθνεσιν√. 24. φησιν (*pro* εφη). 25. + παυλοσ (*post* ο δε). μαινομε√. φησιν√. αλλα. αληθιασ√. 26. λανθανιν√. πιθομαι√. ουθεν (*improbat* C) *pro* ουδεν. 28. — εφη. πιθεισ√. χρηστιανον *p.m.* (χριστ. *s.m.*) cf. xi. 26. ποιησαι (*pro* γενεσθαι). 29. — ειπεν. ευξαμην (C *cum* Steph. -αιμην). μεγαλω (*pro* πολλω). 30. — και ταυτα ειποντοσ αυτου. + τε (*post* ανεστη). συνκαθημενοι. 31. η δεσμων αξιον. + τι (*ante* πρασσει). 32. [εδυνατο]. [επεκεκλητο].

XXVII. 1. [εκατονταρχη]. ῒουλιω ονοματι ῒουλιω (*delet* ῒουλιω *prim.* C)√. [σπειρησ]. 2. [αδραμυττηνω]. μελλοντι. + εισ (*post* πλειν). αρισταρχοσ (-χου C)√. μακαιδονοσ. 3. (δε *pro* τε *prim.* C). σιδονα (C *cum* Steph.). [επετρεψε]. + τουσ (*ante* φιλουσ). πορευθεντι. επιμελιασ√. 5. κατηλθαμεν. λυστραν (*pro* μυρα). 6. εκατονταρχησ (*sic* vv. 11. 43). *fin.* + τουτο (*improbat* C). 7. προσεεωντοσ√. 8. πολισ ην. λασσαια (C λαϊσσα). 9. νηστιαν√. 10. θεορω (C θεωρω). φορτιου. (υμων *pro* ημων C). 11. μαλλον επιθετο. — του. 12. πλιονεσ. εκειθεν. λειμενα√. 13. ῠποπνευσαντεσ√. 14. εβαλεν√. κατα ταυτησ. ευρακυλων. 15. αντοφθαλμιν√. 16. κλαυδα (λ *eras.*). ῒσχυσαμεν μολισ. περικρατισ√. 17. βοηθιαν (-θιαισ√ C). εκπλεσωσιν (λ *delet* C)√. — το *secund.* (*habet* C). 19. εριψαν. 20. πλειουσ (C *cum* Steph.). [πασα ελπισ]. 21. τε (*pro* δε). σταθισ√. πιθαρχησαντασ√. κερδησε√. 22. ευθυμιν√. ουδεμια ψυχησ (C *cum* Steph.). 23. τηδε τη νυκτι (C ταυτη τη νυκτι). αγγελοσ *transfert in locum post* λατρευω. + εγω (*post* ειμι). 25. ευθυμειται√. 27. [εγενετο]. προαγαγειν (*pro* προσαγειν: C *cum* Steph.). 28. οιτινεσ (*pro* και *prim.*: C *cum* Steph.). 29. δε (*pro* τε). μη ^{που} (*pro* μηπωσ: που *p.m. vel* A, *etiam* C). κατα (*pro* εισ). εμπεσωμεν (*pro* εκπεσωσιν). τεσσαρεσ. [ηϋχοντο]. 30. πλωρησ (C πρωρησ). [μελλ. αγκ.]. εκτινειν√. 31. εν τω πλοιω μινωσιν (C μιν. εν τω πλ.). 32. απεκοψαν οι στρατιωται. ϊασαν√. 33. ημερα εμελλεν. γεινεσθαι√. διατελειται√. μηθεν (C δ *pro* θ, *sed abstersit*). [προσλαβομενοι]. 34. παρακα√. μεταλαβειν τι (*pro* προσλαβειν: τι *delet* C). [ουδενοσ]. [εκ]. απολειται (*pro* πεσειται). 35. ειπασ. ευχαριστησασ. 36. απαντεσ (α *prius eras.*). μεταλαβαν. 37. ημεθα δε αι πασαι ψυχαι εν τω πλοιω. *fin.* εξ'. 38. — την (*habet* C). 39. εβουλευοντο. [δυναιντο]. 40. προελοντεσ (C περιε.). επαραντεσ (επα *rescript. p.m.*)√. αρτεμωνα. 41. επεκειλαν. ελυτο. απο (*pro* υπο: C *cum* Steph.). — των κυματων (*habet* C). 42. αποκτινωσιν√. (+ ινα *iterum ante* μητισ C). εκκολυβησασ διαφυγη. 43. βηματοσ (C βουληματοσ)√. εκελευσεν√. αποριψαντασ. τησ γησ (*non* v. 44).

XXVIII. 1. επεγνωμεν. 2. [δε]. παρειχαν. αψαντεσ. προσανελαμβανον (C *cum* Steph.). — δια *secund.* (*habet* C). 3. σ̇φρυγανων (˙ *p.m.*). (+ τι *ante* πληθοσ: *suppletum forsan p.m.*). επιθεντεσ√. απο (*pro* εκ). [εξελθουσα καθηψε]. χιροσ (*sic* v. 4)√. 4. [ειδον]. προσ αλληλουσ ελεγον. — τησ (*habet* C). ιασεν√. 5. [αποτιναξασ]. — κακον (*habet* C). 6. μελλιν√. εμπιπρασθαι (C *cum* Steph.). καταπιπτιν√. θεωρωντων (C -ρουντων). γεινομενον√. [λλ]. αυτον ειναι θ̄ν̄. 7. εκινον√. [ϋπηρχε]. τρισ (*sic* vv. 11. 12: *non* v. 17)√. 8. δυσεντεριω. επιθισ√. χιρασ√. 9. δε (*pro* ουν). οι εν τη νησω εχοντεσ ασθενειασ. 10. — τα (*habet* C). τασ χρειασ. 12. ημερασ τρισ. 13. περιελοντεσ (C *cum* Steph. περιελθ.). δευτερεοι√. 14. παρ (*pro* επ). εισ την ρωμην ηλθαμεν. 15. ηλθαν (*pro* εξηλθον). υπαντησιν ϋμιν (C *cum* Steph. απ. ημιν). αχρι π̇ αππιου (˙ *p.m.*)√. [ελαβε: C -εν√]. 16. εισηλθομεν. + την (*ante* ρωμην: *improbat* C). — ο εκατοντ. *usque ad* στρατοπεδαρχη. επετραπη τω παυλω (— δε). μενιν√. 17. συνκαλεσασθαι. αυτον (*pro* τον παυλον). δε *secund. bis scriptum* (*notat* C *altero loco*)√. ελεγεν√. + λεγων (*ante* ανδρεσ αδελφοι: εγω *pro* λεγων *s.m.*). — εγω (*post* αδελφοι). [εθεσι]. χιρασ√. 18. ανακρινοντεσ (C *cum* Steph.). + με (*ante* απολυσαι: *improbat* C). 19. κεσαρα. + ου̇̇ (*ante* εχων: ˙˙ *p.m.*)√. κατηγορειν. 20. παρεκαλεσαν (ν *eras.*)√. ϊδιν√. εινεκεν (ι *eras.*). ϊσδραηλ. 21. ειπαν. ημισ√. κατα σου εδεξαμεθα (κατα *pro* περι *prim.*). απηγγιλεν√. ελαλησεν√. 22. ακουσαι παρα σου. φρονισ√. ημιν εστιν. 23. ηλθον (*pro* ηκον). διαμαρτυραμενοι (C -νοσ)√. πιθων. — τε *prim.* (*habet* C). — τα. μωϋσεωσ. 24. + ουν (*post* μεν: *delet* C). επιθοντο. 25. τε (*pro* δε: C *cum* Steph.). ελαλησεν√. περι (*pro* δια: C *cum* Steph.). ϋμων (*pro* ημων).

26. λεγων. ειπον (*pro* ειπε). (C βλεψητε). 27. εβαρυνθη (*pro* επαχυνθη: C *cum* Steph.). + αυτων (*post* ωσιν *prim.*). ἴδωσιν√. ακουσωσιν√.—και τη καρδια συνωσι (ὁμοιοτ.: *habet* C, *at* συνωσιν√). επιστρεψωσιν√. ἴασομαι. 28. + τουτο (*post* απεσταλη: *improbat* C). 29. *Deest versus.* 30. ενεμιναν (ε *p.m. suprascriptum videtur:* εμινεν√ C). — ο παυλοσ. διαιτιαν (C *cum* Steph.)√. 31. — $\overline{\chi\upsilon}$ (*habet* C).

Subscr. πραξεισ αποστολων.

In Actibus Apostolorum e correctoribus A *rarò occurrit,* C *saepissimè: de reliquis* E *tantum, ut videtur,* παῖδα iii. 13. *In margine porrò interiore hujus libri inveniuntur subinde literae, manu secundâ sed perantiquâ scriptae* [cf. $\overline{\text{H}}$ Tab. xiii, col. 3, l. 47 mai. edit.], *numeros pericoparum seu sectionum designantes. Notandum verò est has sectiones cum Vaticanis* (Cod. B) *minoribus apud Maium* (N. T. 1859) *ferè per omnia concinere, nec alibi, quod novimus, reperiri. In Cod. Sinaitico hae leguntur:* $\overline{\text{B}}$ cap. i. 15; $\overline{\text{H}}$ iii. 1; $\overline{\Theta}$ iv. 1; $\overline{\text{I}}$ *ibid.* 13; $\overline{\text{IA}}$ *ibid.* 23; $\overline{\text{IB}}$ *ibid.* 32; $\overline{\text{I}\Gamma}$ v. 1; $\overline{\text{I}\Delta}$ *ibid.* 12; $\overline{\text{IE}}$ *ibid.* 21; $\overline{\text{Iϛ}}$ *ibid.* 34; $\overline{\text{IZ}}$ vi. 1; $\overline{\text{IH}}$ *ibid.* 9; $\overline{\text{I}\Theta}$ vii. 11; $\overline{\text{K}}$ *ibid.* 35; $\overline{\text{KA}}$ viii. 1; $\overline{\text{KB}}$ *ibid.* 9; $\overline{\text{K}\Gamma}$ *ibid.* 18; $\overline{\text{K}\Delta}$ *ibid.* 26; $\overline{\text{KE}}$ *ibid.* 34 [*at* ix. 1 *apud* Cod. B]; $\overline{\text{Kϛ}}$ ix. 10 [*sic etiam* Cod. B]; $\overline{\text{KZ}}$ *ibid.* 32; $\overline{\text{KH}}$ x. 1; $\overline{\text{K}\Theta}$ *ibid.* 19; $\overline{\Lambda}$ *ibid.* 30; $\overline{\Lambda\text{A}}$ *ibid.* 48 τοτε ηρ. [xi. 1 Cod. B]; $\overline{\Lambda\text{B}}$ xi. 27; $\overline{\Lambda\Gamma}$ xii. 1; $\overline{\Lambda\Delta}$ *ibid.* 18; $\overline{\Lambda\text{E}}$ xiii. 1; $\overline{\Lambdaϛ}$ *ibid.* 13; $\overline{\Lambda\text{Z}}$ *ibid.* 26; $\overline{\Lambda\text{H}}$ xiv. 1; $\overline{\Lambda\Theta}$ *ibid.* 8; $\overline{\text{M}}$ xv. 1 [*at* xv. 23 Cod. B]; $\overline{\text{MA}}$ *ibid.* 23 [*at* $\overline{\text{M}}$ Cod. B]; $\overline{\text{MB}}$ *ibid.* 40 [at $\overline{\text{MA}}$ Cod. B]. *Post* $\overline{\text{MB}}$ *in Cod. Sinait. desinunt omninò hae sectiones, idque ad quaternionis finem, ut opportunè notat Tischendorfius.*

Deest titulus. Jacob. Cap. I. 2. ηγησασθαι√. πιρασμοισ περιπεσηται√. 3. δοκιμειον√. 4. τελιον√. τελιοι√. 5. αιτιτω (*non* v. 6)√. ονιδιζοντοσ√. 6. πιστι√. εοικεν√. 7. λημψετε.—τι. 9. ταπινοσ√. 10. ταπινωσει√. 11. ανετιλεν√. εξηρανεν√. εξεπεσεν√. ευπρεπια√. ουτωσ√. ποριαισ√. 12. υπομενι√. λημψεται. επηγγιλατο√. — ο $\overline{κσ}$. 13. μηδισ πιραζομενοσ√. ὑπο (*pro* απο του). εστιν (*sic* v. 17 *prim.*)√. 14. πιραζετε√. 15. αποτελεσθισα√. 16. πλανασθαι√. 17. καταβενον√. εστιν (*pro* ενι). αποσκιασματοσ (C *cum* Steph.): *sic* Cod. B. 18. βουληθισ√. αληθιασ√. (εαυτου *pro* αυτου C). 19. ἴστω (*pro* ωστε: *at* ἴστε C). ·εστω δε πασ (*sic*). 20. ουκ εργαζεται. 21. περισσιαν√. εμ πραΰτητι√. δεξασθαι√. 22. γεινεσθαι√. [μον. ακρ.]. 23. εστιν√. κατανοουντεσ (-ουντει C). 24. κατενοησεν√. απεληλυθεν√. 25. [παρακυψασ]. παραμινασ√. — ουτοσ *prim.* 26. [ει τισ]. — εν υμιν. [αυτου *bis in versu*]. αλλα. του *p.m.* (*pro* τουτου: C *cum* Steph.)√. 26, 27. θρησκια√ *bis.* 27. — τω (*habet* C). επισκεπτεσθε√. τηριν√.

II. 1. προσωπολημψιαισ. 2. — την (*habet* C). αισθητι√ *bis in versu* (*non* v. 3). 3. και επιβλεψηται. — αυτω. [*habet* ωδε *secund.*]. ὑποποδιον (ὑ *p.m.* Tisch., *s.m.* Tregelles.). 4. *init.* — και. διεκριθηται√. εγενεσθαι√. 5. ουκ (*pro* ουχ). τω κοσμω (*sine* εν). — τουτου. πιστι√. επαγγελιασ (*pro* βασιλειασ: C βασιλιασ√). 6. [ουχ]. ὑμασ (*pro* ὑμων: C *cum* Steph.). 7. βλασφημουσιν√. 8. τελιται√. ποιειται√. 9. προσωποληματιται. εργαζεσθαι√. 10. τηρηση. πταιση. γεγονεν√. 11. μοιχευσισ (*pro* -σησ). ειπεν√. [φονευσησ]. μοιχευεισ φονευεισ. 12. ουτωσ *prim.* (*sic* v. 17)√. [ουτω *secund.*]. 13. ανελεοσ. — και. (+ δε C, *sed iterum abstersit, post* κατακαυχαται). 14. [τι το οφ.: *sic* v. 16]. [λεγ. τισ]. 15. — δε. ὑπαρχωσιν√. — ωσι. 16. ειπει Tisch., ειπε Tregelles. (C *cum* Steph.). τι (τισ C *cum* Steph.). ὑπαγεται√. ιρηνη√. θερμαινεσθαι√. χορταζεσθαι√. επιτηδια√. 17. εχη εργα. εστιν√. 18. ερι√. διξον√. χωρισ (*pro* εκ *prim.*). — σου *secund.* σοι δειξω. *fin.* — μου *secund.* 19. εισ εστιν ο $\overline{θσ}$. πιστευουσιν√. φρισσουσιν√. 20. γνωνε√. καινε√. [νεκρα]. 21. [ἴσαακ]. 22. συνεργει (C *cum* Steph.). 23. $\overline{επιστευσεν}$ (*sic*)√. 24. — τοινυν. 26. ουτωσ√. — των. *fin.* εστιν√.

III. 1. λημψομεθα. 2. δυναμενοσ (*pro* δυνατοσ). 3. *init.* ει δε γαρ των (γαρ *improbat* C). εισ (*pro* προσ). πιθεσθαι√. [*caetera cum* Steph.]. 4. ανεμων σκληρων. — αν. βουλεται. 5. ουτωσ (*sic* v. 10)√. εστιν√. [μεγαλαυχει]. ηλικον (*pro* ολιγον). αναπτι√. 6. *init.* — και (*habet* C). — ουτωσ (ην *post* αδικιασ *scripsit* C, *sed abstersit*). και (*pro* η *tert.*: C *cum* Steph.). + ημων (*post* γενεσεωσ). 7. πετινων√. 8. δυναται δαμασαι $\overline{ανων}$. ακαταστατον. 9. $\overline{κν}$ (*pro* $\overline{θν}$). 12. ελεασ√. ουτωσ ουδε αλυκον γλ. π. υ. (— ουδεμια πηγη *et* και). 13. [πραυ-]. 14. εριθιαν√. ταισ καρδιαισ. κατακαυχασθαι τησ αληθιασ και ψευδεσθαι (*at* + κατα *ante* τησ C).

15. ανοθεν (*sic* v. 17: C ανωθεν)√. αλλα επιγιοσ. 16. εριθια√. + και (*post* εκει). 17. ϊρηνικη√. — και. 18. ο (*pro* τησ: *at* ο *eras.* — τησ). σπιρεται√.

IV. 1. + ποθεν (*ante* μαχαι). 2. δυνασθαι√. και ουκ εχετε *secund.* (— δε). αιτισθαι√. 3. αιτιτε√. αιτισθαι√. καταδαπανησητε (C *cum* Steph.). 4. — μοιχοι και (*habet* C). μοιχαλειδεσ√. + τουτου (*post* κοσμου). εστιν τω θω̅. εαν (*pro* οσ αν: C *cum* Steph.). (βουληθησ C *primò*, *sed abstersit*). εχθρα (*pro* εχθροσ: C *cum* Steph.). 5. δοκειται√. κατωκισεν√. 6. μιζονα√. διδωσιν√ *bis in versu.* ταπινοισ√. 7. + δε (*post* αντιστητε). φευξετε√. 9. — και *secund.* κατηφιαν√. 10. ταπινωθητε√. + ουν (*ante* ενωπιον). — του. 11. καταλαλειται√. η (*pro* και *prim.*). κρινι√. κρινισ√. 12. + και κριτησ (*post* νομοθετησ). + δε (*post* συ). *fin.* ο κρινων τον πλησιον. 13. η (*pro* και *prim.*). πορευσομεθα. [ποιησωμεν]. — ενα. εμπορευσομεθα. κερδησομεν. 14. [το]. — γαρ *prim.* (*habet* C). — ατμισ γαρ εστιν. και (*pro* δε). 15. λεγιν√. [ζησομεν]. [ποιησομεν]. εκινο√. 16. κατακαυχασθε√. αλαζονιαισ√. απασα. καυχησεισ√.

V. 1. ταλαιπωριεσ (-ριαισ C)√. *fin.* + ϋμιν. 2. σεσηπεν√. 3. εστε√. φαινετε (*pro* φαγεται: C φαγετε√). (C *habet* ο ϊοσ *ante* ωσ πυρ). 4. αφυστερημενοσ (*pro* απεστ.). σαβαωθ'· εισεληλυθασι̅. 5. ενι *pro* επι *p.m.*, *at* π A? C√. — ωσ (*habet* C). 7. [αν]. καρπον (*pro* υετον). + τον (*ante* προϊμον [*sic*]: *improbat* C). 8. + ουν (*ante* και ϋμισ√). ηγγικεν√. 9. κατα αλλ. αδ. κριθητε. + ο (*ante* κριτησ). 10. υποδιγμα√. αδελφοι μου τησ καλοκαγαθιασ (— κακοπαθειασ). (C *habet* εχεται *ante* τουσ προφ.). εν (*pro* τω). 11. ϋπομιναντασ. [ειδετε]. [πολυσπλ. εστ. ο κσ̅]. οικτειρμων√. 12. ουν (*pro* δε *prim.*: C δε). + ο λογοσ (*ante* ϋμων: *improbat* C). ϋπο κρισιν (— εισ). 13. ευθυμι√. 14. ασθενι τισ α̈σ (¨ *p.m.*)√. επ αυτουσ (επ αυτον C *cum* Steph.). αλιψαντεσ√. [του κυ̅]. 15. εγερι√. 16. εξομολογισθαι ουν. τασ αμαρτιασ (*pro* τα παραπτωματα). ευχεσθαι√. 17. τρισ√. *fin.*: 18. εδωκεν τον ϋετον. εβλαστησεν√. 19. + μου (*post* αδελφοι). + τησ οδου (*ante* τησ αληθιασ√). 20. + αυτου (*post* ψυχην). *fin.*:

Subscr. επιστολη ϊακωβου.

πετρου επιστολη α.

Cap. I. 1. + και (*ante* παρεπιδ., *at* και *eras.*). γαλατειασ. καππαδοκειασ. — ασιασ (*habet* C: ὁμοιοτ.). 2. πληθυνθιη√. 3. [ημασ].

δια. 4. και αμαραντον και αμιαντον. τετηρημενον (-ην C cum Steph.). *fin.* εν ουρανω εισ ῦμασ. 5. δυναμι√. ετοιμωσ (-μην C *cum* Steph.). 6. — εστι (εστιν C√). λυπηθενταϲ (-τεσ C)√. πιρασμοισ√. 7. πολυτιμοτερον. επενον√. και δοξαν και τιμην. 8. ιδοντεσ. αγαλλιασθαι√. 9. [ῦμων]. 10. εξηραυνησαν. 11. εραυνωντεσ. 12. ῦμιν (*pro* ημιν). [εν]. 13. τελιωσ√. 14. [συσχ.]. 16. *init.* διο. [-πται αγ.]. εσεσθαι (*pro* γενεσθε). διοτι (*pro* οτι). — ειμι. 17. επικαλεισθαι√. απροσωπολημπτωσ. *fin.* αναστρεφομενοι Tisch., αναστραφομενοι Tregelles. (-στραφητε C *cum* Steph.). 18. φθαρτου αργυριου (C *cum* Steph.). ελὼυτρωθητε (· *p.m. et* C)√. 19. αλλα (λ *prim. instaurat* C: *sic* v. 20 σ *in* ῦμασ, v. 23 υ *in* ουκ)√. 20. ανεγνωσμενου (προεγ. C *cum* Steph.). επ εσχατου του χρονου (-του των χρονων C). 21. [πιστευοντασ]. εγειροντα (-ραντα C *cum* Steph.). 22. αληθιασ√.—δια πνευματοσ. [καθ. καρδ., *at* C καρδ. αληθινησ]. 23. φθορασ (*pro* σπορασ), *sic* Codd. A C. — εισ τον αιωνα. 24. ωσι (*pro* ωσ *prim.: at* ὠσει C). πασα η δοξα αυτου (— ανθρωπου: *at* π. δ. αυτησ *sine* η C). ανθοσ εξεπεσεν (— αυτου). 25. εστιν√.

II. 1. ῦποκρισισ (-σεισ *vel* -σειν? C). πασαν καταλαλιαν (C *cum* Steph.). 2. *fin.* αυξηθηται εισ σωτηριαν. 3. ει (ειπερ C) εγευσασθαι. [χρηστοσ]. 5. λιθοσ οντεσ (C *cum* Steph.). εποικοδομεισθαι√. πνσ (πνικοσ C *cum* Steph.). + ῑσ (εισ C) *ante* ιερατευμα. ανενεγκασ (-και C *cum* Steph.). — πνευματικασ. — τω (*habet* C *cum* Steph.). 6. διοτι (*pro* διο και). — τη. επ αυτον (επ αυτω C *cum* Steph.). 7. *init.* ημιν (υμιν C, *fortasse etiam p.m.*). απιστουσιν (*pro* απειθουσι). (λιθοσ C). 8. πετραν. (C *habet* και *ante* προσκοπτουσιν√). απιθουντεσ√. 9. βασιλιον√. εξαγγιληται√. 11. [-θαι των]. 12. ῦμιν (*pro* υμων *prim.*). εποπτευοντεσ. δοξασουτρεμουσιν *sic* (δοξασωσιν√ C)√. *Mixtae lectiones:* cf. Tit. iii. 2: Proleg. p. xxiii. *edit. min.* 13. — ουν. — ανθρωπινη (*habet* C). 14. — μεν. 15. εστιν√. φιμοιν (-μουν C *cum* Steph.). 16. θυ δουλοι. 17. παντεσ. φοβεισθαι√. 18. εν παντι φοβω ῦποτασσομενοι. + ῦμων (*ante* ου). 19. συνιδησιν√. 20. (κολαζομενοι C, *pro* κολαφ.). (ῦπομενετε C, *pro* -ειτε *prim.*). [τουτο χαρ.]. 21. + ο (*ante* χσ). απεθανεν (*pro* επαθεν) cf. iii. 18; iv. 1. υμων ῦμιν. (21, 22. ησαΐασ A *marg.*). 22. ηῦρεθη. 23. ελοιδορει (αντελ. C *cum* Steph.). ηπιλει√. 24. — εν (*habet* C). (αυτου *secund. improbat* C). 25. πλανωμενοι. επιστραφητε.

III. 1. — αι (*habet* C). απιθουσιν√. κερδηθησονται. 2. εποπτευοντεσ (C *cum* Steph.). 3. ουκ ο. [τριχων και]. 4. — τω (*habet* C).

πραεωσ. — και (*habet* C). ησυχιουσ̇. 5. ουτωσ√. εκοσμουν εαυτασ αι ελπιζουσαι επι τον θ̅ν̅. 6. ϋπηκουσεν. 7. συνομιλουντεσ (συνοικ. C *cum* Steph.). — κατα γνωσιν (*habet* C). γυνεκειω (C *cum* Steph.)√. συνκληρονομουσ (-μοισ C). + ποικιλησ (*ante* χαριτοσ) cf. iv. 10. ενκοπτεσθαι. 8. ταπινοφρονεσ (*pro* φιλοφρονεσ). 9. — ειδοτεσ. (10. ψαλ λγ A *marg.*). 10. ϊδιν√. [αυτου *prim.*]. χιλη (χ *supplet* A)√. — αυτου *secund.* 11. [-τω απο]. ϊρηνην√. 12. — οι. 13. ζηλωται (*pro* μιμηται). γενεσθαι (γενησθαι C√). 14. αλλα ει (ει δε C). + εσται (*post* μακαριοι). φοβηθηται√. 15. χ̅ν̅ (*pro* θ̅ν̅). — δε *secund.* (απαιτουντι C). + αλλα (*ante* μετα πραΰτ-). 16. συνιδησιν√. καταλαλουσιν [ϋμ. ωσ κακοπ.]. κατεσχυνθωσιν√. εισ χ̅ν̅ (C *cum* Steph. εν χ̅ω̅). 17. κριττον√. θελοι. ει (*pro* η: C η). 18. — και. + των (*ante* αμαρτιων: *improbat* C). ϋπερ ημων απεθανεν (*pro* επαθε: cf. ii. 21; iv. 1).—ημασ (*habet* C). σαρκει√.—τω *secund.* 19. π̅ν̅α̅σ̅ι̅ν̅. 20. απιθησασιν√. απεξεδεχετο την του θ̅υ̅ μακροθυμιαν (η *pro* την *s.m.*:—απαξ). ολιγοι. 21. *init.* — ο (*habet* C). ϋμασ (*pro* ημασ). νυν αντιτυπον. 22. — του (*habet* C).

IV. 1. αποθανοντοσ (παθοντοσ C *cum* Steph.: cf. ii. 21; iii. 18). υμων (*pro* ημων: C *cum* Steph.). — εν. (*fin.* αμαρτιαισ C). 2. ανθρωπον (*pro* -ων: C *cum* Steph.)√. ανθρωπου (*errore pro* θ̅υ̅: C *cum* Steph.)√. 3. ϋμιν (*pro* ημιν: *improbat omninò* C). παρεληλυθοσ (-θωσ C)√. — του βιου. βουλημα (*pro* θελημα). κατιργασθε. πορευομενουσ. ασελγιαισ√. οινοφρυγιαισ (-φλ- C *cum* Steph.). ειδωλολατριαισ√. 4. και βλασφημουσιν (C *cum* Steph.). 5. — οι αποδωσουσι λογον (*habet* C: -σιν√). οτ^ω (*o eras. et ω p.m.: forsan οι pro τω p.m. primò*)√. 6. [κριθωσι]. [ζωσι: *at* ζησωσι C]. 7. ηγγικεν√. — και (*habet* C). — τασ. 8. — δε. [οτι αγαπη καλυψει]. 9. γογγυσμου. 10. ελαβεν√. 11. πασιν√. δοξαζητε√. 12. πιρασμον√. 13. [καθο]. παθημασιν√. 14. ονιδιζεσθαι√. — εν (*habet* C). + και τησ δυναμεωσ αυτου (*post* δοξησ: αυτου *improbat* C). (επαναπεπαυται C *apud* Tisch., *at* επαναπαυεται *teste* Tregellesio: *p.m. cum* Steph.). — κατα μεν αυτουσ κ.τ.λ. *ad fin. vers.* (ὁμοιοτ.?). 15. αλλοτριεπισκοποσ. 16. χρηστιανοσ (χριστ. *s.m.*) cf. Act. xi. 26; xxvi. 28. εσχυνεσθω (αισχ. C)√. ονοματι (*pro* μερει). 17. — ο. υμων (ημων C *cum* Steph.). απιθουντων√. τω 'λογω' του θ̅υ̅ ευαγγ. (' ' *p.m.*)√. 18. [ο ασ.]. + ο (*ante* αμαρτωλοσ). φανειτε√. 19. — ωσ. αυτων (*pro* εαυτων). [-ποιια].

V. 1. + ουν (*ante* τουσ: ο *in* ουν *p.m. super* τ *primò*). συνπρ.

2. ποιμαναται✓. υμνιον (*pro* υμιν ποιμνιον: *corrigit* C)✓. — επισκοπουντεσ (*habet* C). αλλα. + κατα θν (*post* εκουσιωσ). [μηδε]. 4. αρχιποιμαινοσ✓. κομιεισθαι✓. 5. + δε (*post* ομοιωσ: *improbat* C). + τοισ (*ante* πρεσβυτεροισ). — υποτασσομενοι. ταπινοφροσυνην✓. ενκομβωσασθαι✓. ταπινοισ✓. διδωσιν✓. 6. ταπινωθητε✓. χειραν. κερω [*nihil additum*]. 7. επιριψαντεσ. *fin.* ημων (υμων C *cum* Steph.). 8. — οτι (*habet* C). περιπατι✓. καταπιν· (C καταπιειν). 9. πιστι✓. τὴν (*pro* τη *secund.*: · *p.m.* Tisch., *at s.m.* Tregelles.)✓. + τω (*ante* κοσμω). επιτελεισθε✓. 10. ὑμασ (*pro* ημασ). — ιυ. καταρτισει. — υμασ. στηριξει. σθενωσι. θεμελιωσει. 11. [*cum* Steph.]. 12. [του *prim.*]. + και (*ante* ταυτην: *improbat* C). *fin.* στητε. 13. ασπαζετε✓. + εκκλησια (*ante* συνεκλεκτη). 14. ειρηνησ (σ *eras.*)✓. πασιν✓. [ιυ αμην].

Subscr. πετρου α.

πετρου β.

Cap. I. 1. [συμεων]. λαχουσιν✓. εισ δικαιοσυνην του κυ ημων και σωτηροσ ιυ χυ (— θυ). 2. πληθυνθιη✓. επιγνωσι✓. + χυ (*post* ιυ). 3. + τα (*ante* παντα). θιασ✓. + τον θν και (*post* προσ: *improbat* C). ευσεβιαν✓. ἴδια δοξη και αρετη (— δια). 4. τα τιμια ημιν και μεγιστα. φυσεωσ κοινωνοι. την εν τω κοσμω επιθυμιαν. 5. και αυτο δε τουτο. [επι]χορηγησατε (επι *p.m. et* C). πιστι✓. 6. γνωσι✓. εγκρατιαν✓. εγκρατια✓. 7. την ευσεβια (*sic*)✓. 8. [ὑπαρχοντα]. ‘ουδ’ καθιστησιν (‘’ *p.m. et* C). 9. παρεστιν✓. εστιν✓. *fin.* αμαρτηματων. 10. + ἵνα δια των καλων εργων (*ante* βεβαιαν). [ποιεισθαι]. πτεσητε✓. 11. ουτωσ✓. — η. βασιλιαν✓. 12. μελλησω (*pro* ουκ αμ.). αει περι τουτων ὑπομιμνησκιν ὑμασ. — καιπερ *usque ad* υμασ v. 13 (ὁμοιοτελ. *Habet* C: *at* ἴδοτασ . . αληθια . . διεγιριν✓). 13. + τη (*ante* ὑπομνησει). 14. ταχεινη✓. — καθωσ και ο κσ ημων. εδηλωσεν✓. 15. σπουδαζω. 17. + του (*ante* θυ). ενεχθισησ (*non* v. 18)✓. [*caetera cum* Steph.]. 18. εκ του ουρανου. ουν (*pro* συν *p.m.*: σ C)✓. ορι τω αγ. 19. ποιειται✓. + η (*ante* ημερα). ανατιλη✓. 20. προφητια (*non* v. 21)✓. 21. [ποτε προφ.]. αλλα. — οι. [αγιοι θυ].

II. 1. (— εν τω λαω C). παρισαξουσιν✓. απωλιασ✓. απωλιαν (*non* v. 3)✓. 2. ασελγιαισ (*pro* απωλειαισ). (δοξα *pro* οδοσ C).

αληθιασ√. 3. εκπορευσονται (ενπ. C). 4. *init.* ει *p.m.*, *at* η *primò*√. εφισατο (*sic* v. 5)√. σιροισ. ζοφοισ (*pro* ζοφου: C *cum* Steph.). κολαζομενουσ τηριν (*pro* τετηρημενουσ). 5. αλλα. εφυλαξεν√. κοσμον (κοσμω C *cum* Steph.). 6. πολισ√. ὑποδιγμα√. τεθικωσ√. 7. ασελγια√. [ρρ]. 8. [ο δικ.]. ενκατ. 9. οιδεν√. πιρασμων (-μου C). + πεφυλακισμενουσ Tisch., *at* περιφυλακισμενουσ Tregelles. (*ante* εισ ηραν *sic*: *improbat* C). τηριν√. 10. εν επιθυμιασ (-μια C)√. αυθαδισ√. τρεμουσιν√. 11. ἴσχυει√. δυναμι μιζονεσ√. φερουσιν√. [παρα $\overline{κω}$]. 12. αυτοι (*pro* ουτοι). γεγεννημενα φυσικα. αγνοουντεσ βλασφημουσιν. και φθαρησονται (*pro* καταφθ.: C *cum* Steph.). 13. αδικουμενοι (*pro* κομιουμενοι: C *cum* Steph.). [απαταισ]. 14. μοιχαλιασ. [ακαταπαυστουσ]. αμαρτιαισ. πλεονεξιασ. 15. καταλειποντεσ.—την. βεωορσορ (—οσ: βοσορ οσ C). [*lectio mixta*; Proleg. p. xxiii. *edit. min.*: Tit. iii. 2; 1 Pet. ii. 12; 1 Jo. iv. 17?; Apoc. iv. 11]. 16. ελεγξειν√. — εν (*habet* C). εκωλυσεν√. 17. εισιν√. και ομιχλαι (*pro* νεφελαι). λελαποσ√.—εισ αιωνα. 18. μαθηταιωτητοσ (¨ *p.m. et* C)√. ασελγιαισ [*sine* εν]√. του οντωσ (τουσ ολιγωσ C)√. αποφευγονταſ. 18, 19. ελευθεριαν ελευθεριαν (*prius improbat* C). 19. — και (*habet* C). 20. + ημων (*post* $\overline{κυ}$). 21. κρισσον√. εισ τα οπισω ανακαμψαι απο (*pro* επιστρεψαι εκ). παραδοθισησ√. 22. συμβεβηκεν√. — δε (*habet* C). [κυλισμα].

III. 1. υπομνησι√. 2. ὑμων (*pro* ημων). 3. εσχατων. + εν εμπεγμονη (*ante* εμπεκται√). [αυτ. επιθ.]. 4. ουτωσ διαμενι√. 5. δια. συνεστωτα (-ωσα C *cum* Steph.). 7. τω αυτου λογω. εισιν√ 8. $\overline{κυ}$ (*pro* $\overline{κω}$). — και χιλια ετη (ὁμοιοτ.). 9. — ο. μακροθυμι√. δι ὑμασ (*pro* εισ ημασ). παντεσ√. 10. [η ημ. Tisch., *at* — η Tregelles.]. — εν νυκτι. — οι. + μεν (*ante* ρυζηδον√). λυθησεται. — και *prim.* (*ante* γη). ευρεθησεται (*pro* κατακαησεται). 11. [ουν]. ημασ (*pro* υμασ: C *cum* Steph.). 12. — και σπευδοντασ (*habet* C: ὁμοιοτ.). στοιχια√. [τηκεται]. 13. κενην γην. κατα τα επαγγελματα. 15. αγειfeatured σθαι (C ηγεισθ.)√. δοθειαν αυτω (σ *p.m. et* C). 16. [ταισ]. αισ (*pro* οισ). εστιν√. 17. φυλασσεσθαι√. 18. γνωσι√. [αμην].

Subscr. πετρου β.

ϊωαννου επιστολη α.

Cap. I. 1. [εωρ.: *sic* v. 2]. 3. ο ακηκοαμεν και εωρακαμεν. και απαγγελλομεν ' ϊ' και ϋμιν ϊνα και (' ' *p.m.: at* απαγγελομεν Tregelles.). υμισ √. εχηται√. + ϋμων (*post* ημετερα: *improbat* C). 4. ημεισ (*pro* υμιν). [ημων]. 5. εστιν αυτη. η απαγγελιασ (γαπη τησ ε) (*sic p.m.:* C η αγγελια *tantum*). εστιν *secund.*√. 6. σκοτι√. αληθιαν (*non* v. 8)√. 7. — $\overline{χυ}$. [8. *cum* Steph.]. 9. — εστι (εστιν√ *habet* C). + ημων (*post* αμαρτιασ *secund.*). 10. ουκ ημαρ.

II. 2. ϊλασμοσ εστιν. 3. φυλαξωμεν (*pro* τηρωμεν: C *cum* Steph.). 4. + οτι (*post* λεγων). εστιν *prim.*√. — εν τουτω. + του $\overline{θυ}$ (*post* αληθια√). 6. μενιν οφιλει√. περιεπατησεν√. ουτωσ√. 7. αγαπητοι (*pro* αδελφοι). ην *p.m., at* $\bar{η}$ (*deleto* ν) C√.— απ αρχησ *secund.* 8. + και (*post* αληθεσ). τον αληθ. (το C)√. 9. μεισων (*non* v. 11)√. + ψευστησ εστιν και (*post* μεισων). 10. ουκ εστιν εν αυτω. 11. εστιν√. οιδεν√. ετυφλωσεν√. 12. αφεονται (C *cum* Steph.). 13. το πονηρον (*pro* τον π.: *non* v. 14). εγραψα (*pro* γραφω *tert.*). 16. αλαζονια√. [αλλ]. *fin.* εστιν√. 18. εστιν√. — ο (*habet* C). 19. [-θον]. [ησαν εξ ημων *bis in versu*]. μεμενηκισαν√. εισιν√. 20. ϋμισ√. οιδαται√. παντεσ (*pro* παντα). 21. αληθιαν√. οιδαται√. αληθιασ√. εστιν√. 22. + καὶ (*ante* τον $\overline{πρα}$: · *p.m., et* και *eras.*). 23. *fin.* + ο ομολογων τον $\overline{υν}$ και τον πατερα εχει. 24. — ουν. ακηκοατε *prim.* — εν *secund.* (*habet* C). μινη√. [*Inscriptio paginae* πετρου $\overline{β}$]√. ακηκοατε απ αρχησ *secund.* εν τω πατρι και εν τω υιω. 25. επηγγιλατο√. 26. + δε (*post* ταυτα). 27. ϋμισ√. μενει εν υμιν. χριαν√. το αυτου $\overline{πνα}$ (*pro* το αυτο χρισμα: C το αυτου χρ.). αληθησ εστιν√. εστιν *secund.*√. μενετε. 28. — και νυν τεκνια μενετε εν αυτω (δμοιοτ.). εαν (*pro* οταν). [εχωμεν, *at* C σχωμεν]. *fin.* + απ αυτου. 29. εστιν√. + και (*post* οτι).

III. 1. ειδετε√. + και εσμεν (*post* κληθωμεν). ϋμασ (*pro* ημασ: C *cum* Steph.). 2. — δε. εστιν (*sic* v. 3)√. 3. αγνιζι√. εκινοσ (*non* v. 5)√. 4. [η αμαρ.]. + και (*post* εστιν: *improbat forsan p.m.*). 5. οιδαμεν. [ημων]. ουκ εστιν εν αυτω. 6. αμαρτανι (*sic* v. 8)√. [εωρ.]. 7. — την (*habet* C). εστιν *bis in versu*√. 9. αμαρτανιν√. 10. εστιν *bis in versu*√. ποιων δικεοσυνην. 11.

επαγγελια. ηκουσαται√. 12. εσφαξεν *prim.*√. εσσφαξεν *secund.*√. 13. *init.* + και. — μου. μισι√. 14. μεταβεβηκεν√. + ημων (*post* αδελφουσ). — τον αδελφον. 15. εστιν√. εαυτω. 16. εθηκεν√. ημισ√. *fin.* θειναι. 17. χριαν√. κλιση√. 18. — μου. και γλωσση (— μηδε). αλλα εν εργω. αληθια√. 19. [*init.* και]. γνωσομεθα. εκπροσθεν (*sic*)√. 20. καταγιγνωσκη. [οτι *bis in vers.*]. γινωσκι√. 21. αδελφοι (*pro* αγαπητοι). [ημων *prim.*]. καταγινωσκω Tisch., *at* -σκιν Tregelles. (-σκη C)√. 22. αιτωμεθα. απ (*pro* παρ). τηρωμεν. [ποιουμεν]. 23. πιστευωμεν. *fin.* [ημιν]. 24. — και *tert.* (*habet* C). εδωκεν ημιν.

IV. 1. γευδοπροφηται (C ψευδ.)√. 2. γινωσκομεν (C -σκετε, *cum* Steph.). *fin.* εστιν√. 3. — τον. κ̅ν̅ (*pro* χ̅ν̅). [εν σ. ελ.]. εστιν *ter in versu*√. οτι (*pro* ο *secund.*). ακηκοαμεν. 5. εισιν√. 6. ημισ√. 7. εστιν√. 8. — ο μη αγ. *usque ad* τον θ̅ν̅ (ὁμοιοτ.). *Habet* C ο μη αγαπων ουκ εγνωκεν (*sic*). 9. ζωμεν (ζησωμεν C *cum* Steph.). 10. + του θ̅υ̅ (*post* αγαπη). ημισ ηγαπησε̅ (-πησαμεν C *cum* Steph.)√. απεσταλκεν. 11. ημισ οφιλομεν. 12. τετελειωμενη εν ημιν εστιν. 14. απεσταλκεν√. 15. μενι (*sic* v. 16 *bis*)√. 16. ημισ√. εστιν√. — ο *quart.* *fin.* + μενι. 17. + εν ημιν (*ante* ἵνα: *lect. mixt.*). εχομεν√. αγαπη (*pro* ημερα)√. εστιν√. εσομεθα (*pro* εσμεν). 19. ημισ αγαπ. τον θ̅ν̅ (*pro* αυτον). [αυτοσ]. 20. τισ ^{ειπη} αγαπω (— οτι: ειπη A *potius quam p.m.*). μειση (*s.m.* μεισι)√. εωρακεν√ *bis in versu.* ου (*pro* πωσ). δυνατε√.

V. 1. και το (τον Tregelles.) γεγεννημενον. 2. γεινωσκομεν√. [τηρωμεν]. 4. αυτησ (αυτη C *cum* Steph.). 5. + δε (*post* τισ). νεικων (*non* v. 4)√. 6. δια. + και π̅ν̅σ̅ (*post* αιματοσ). — ο *secund.* [και τω αιμ.]. εστιν *bis in versu*√. 7. + οι (*ante* τρεισ: *refert ad* v. 6). 7, 8. — εν τω ουρανω *usque ad* εν τη γη. 9. του θ̅υ̅ (*pro* των ανθρωπων: C *cum* Steph.)√. οτι (*pro* ην). μεμαρτυρηκεν√. 10. [-ριαν εν εαυτω]. [θ̅ω̅]. ουκ επιστευκεν√. εμαρτυρηκεν√. 13. — τοισ πιστευουσιν εισ το ονομα του υιου του θ̅υ̅. αιωνιον εχετε. τοισ πιστευουσιν (*pro* και ινα πιστευητε: *at* οι πιστευοντεσ C). 14. [οτι εαν τι]. 15. — και εαν οιδαμεν οτι ακουει ημων (ὁμοιοτ. *Supplet* C και εαν ἴδωμεν οτι ακ. η.). εαν (*pro* αν). εαν εχωμεν (*pro* εχομεν: *improbat* εαν C). απ (*pro* παρ). 16. [ιδη]. αιτησισ *et* δωσεισ (σ *fin. in utroque eras.*). αμαρτανουσιν√. *fin.* (C ερωτησησ). 17. εστιν *bis in versu*√. 18. αμαρτανι√. [αλλ]. τηρι√. [εαυτον]. 20. [οιδαμεν δε]. γινωσκομεν.

το αληθινον (*τον αλ.* C *cum* Steph.). *χυ* (*χω* C *cum* Steph.). — *ῃ*. 21. *εαυτα* (*-τουσ* C *cum* Steph.). — *αμην*.

Subscr. ιωαννου α.

ιωαννου β.

1. *αληθια* (*non* vv. 2. 3. 4)√. 2. *μεν ουσαν* Tischend. (*aliquantum spatii post μεν in facsimili*, Tab. XIV.). 3. [*ημων*]. *απο* (*pro παρα prim.*: C *cum* Steph.). —*παρα secund.* (*habet* C). [*κυ*]. + *αυτου* (*ante του πατροσ*: *improbat* C). 4. *ελαβον*. 5. [*ουχ ωσ*: *errat* Scrivener.]. *καινην γραφων σοι*. + *εντολην* (*post αλλα*). *ειχαμεν*. 6. + ‘ *ϊνα καθωσ* ’ (*ante αυτη εστιν η εντο* [*sic*]: ‘ ’ *p.m.*: *εντο non correctum*)√. + *αυτου ϊνα* (*ante καθωσ*). [*ϊνα repetitum*]. *περιπατησητε*. 7. *εξηλθον* (*pro εισηλθον*). — *ο secund.* 8. *απολησθε* (C *απολεσητε*). *ειργασασθαι*√. *απολαβητε*. 9. *προαγων* (*pro παραβαινων*). *και μη μενων* ‘ *και μη* ’ (‘ ’ *p.m.*)√. — *του χυ secund.* [*τον π. και τον υ.*]. 10. *την εδιδαχην* (· *p.m.* ?)√. *φερι*√. 11. *ο λεγων γαρ αυτω*. *κοινωνι*√. 12. *εχω* (*εχων* C *cum* Steph.). *εβουληθην*. [*αλλα ελπιζω*]. *γενεσθαι* (*pro ελθειν*). *στοματι* (*pro στομα prim.*: C *cum* Steph.): *non* 3 Jo. 14. [*ημων*]. *πεπληρωμενη ην* (C *ῆ* [*sic*]: *ν eraso*). 13. *ασπαζετε*√. — *αμην*.

Subscr. ιωαννου β.

ιωαννου γ.

1. *αληθια* (*non* v. 4)√. 2. *ευχομε*√. *ευοδουσθε*√. 3. — *γαρ*. 4. *μιζοτεραν*√. [*εν αλ.*]. 5. [*εργαση*]. *τουτο* (*pro εισ τουσ secund.*). 7. *γαρ γαρ*√. *ονοματοσ εξηλθαν*. *fin. εθνικων*. 8. *οφιλομεν*√. *ϋπολαμβανιν*. *fin. εκκλησια* (*pro αληθεια*: C *αληθια*√). 9. + *τι* (*post εγραψα*: C *legit εγραψα αν sine τι*: *αν p.m.* Tregelles.). 10. *φλοιαρων*√. *επιδεχετε*√. — *εκ*. 11. — *δε*. *εωρακεν*√. 12. *ϋπο* (*pro υπ*). *αληθιασ*√. *οιδασ*. *fin. εστιν*√. 13. *γραψαι σοι* (*pro γραφειν*). *fin. σοι γραφειν*. 14. [*ϊδειν σε*]. *λαλησαμεν* (*ο p.m.* ?)√. 15. *ασπασαι* (*pro ασπαζου*).

Subscr. ϊωαννου γ.

ϊουδα.

1. [$\overline{ιυ}$ $\overline{χυ}$]. ηγαπημενοισ (*pro* ηγιασμενοισ). 2. πληθυνθι|η αγαπητοι· ‖ (*sic divis.*). 3. + του (*ante* γραφειν). + ημων (*ante* σωτηριασ). + και ζωησ (*post* σωτηριασ). γραφιν (*pro* γραψαι). πιστι✓. 4. + και (*ante* παλαι). [χαριν]. ασελγιαν✓. — $\overline{θν}$. 5. [υμασ *bis in versu*]. παντα (*pro* απαξ τουτο). — ο. + απαξ (*post* $\overline{κσ}$). 7. τροπον τουτοισ. προκινται✓. + δε (*ante* διγμα✓). ουκ εχουσιν (*pro* υπεχουσαι: C υπεχουσιν). 8. μιαινουσιν✓. κυριοτητασ. αθετουσιν✓. 9. [ο δε]. [οτε]. μωυσεωσ. ετολμησεν✓. [αλλ]. *fin.* επιτιμησε σοι ο $\overline{θσ}$ ($\overline{κσ}$ *pro* $\overline{θσ}$ C *cum* Steph.). 10. οιδασιν✓. 12. *Post* ουτοι εισιν *ob idem initium habet e* v. 16. γογγυσται μεμψιμυροι κατασεπιθυμιασ (*sic*) αυτων πορευομενοι (*improbat* C, *at legit* κατα τασ *pro* κατασ) ✓. *Sequuntur* εν ταισ αγ. ϋμ. (*at* C *ante* εν *legit* οι). [-μενοι αφοβ-]. παντι ανεμω (— υπο). παραφερομεναι. φθινοπωρικα (-ρινα C *cum* Steph.). 13. αγρια κυματα. — τον. 14. προεπροφητευσεν (*sic*) ✓ Tisch., *at* Tregelles. προεφητευσεν. ηλθεν ο $\overline{κσ}$. αγιων αγγελων (*pro* αγιαισ αυτου). 15. ελεγξαι. πασαν ψυχην (*pro* πανταο τουσ ασεβεισ αυτων). — ασεβειασ αυτων. + λογων (*post* σκληρων). 16. εισιν✓. μεμψιμυροι *iterum*✓. 17. [ρημ. των προειρ.]. 18. — οτι *secund.* επ εσχατου του χρονου. (ελευσονται C *pro* εσονται). εμπεκται✓. επιθυμιασ αυτων (-μιασ εαυτων C). 19. αποδιοριζοντεσ ψυχ. (··· C, *sed rursus eras.*). 20. εποικοδομουντεσ εαυτουσ τη αγιωτατη ϋμων πιστι. 22. ελεατε διακρινομενουσ. 23. — εν φοβω. — του. αρπαζοντεσ (ον *p.m.*, *at* ε *primò*). + ουσ δε ελεατε εν φοβω (*ante* μισουντεσ). 24. ϋμασ (*pro* αυτουσ). απτεστουσ✓. αγαλλιασι✓. 25. — σοφω. + δια $\overline{ιυ}$ $\overline{χυ}$ του $\overline{κυ}$ ημων ω (*ante* δοξα: C *delet* ω). — και *prim.* + προ παντοσ του αιωνοσ (*post* εξουσια). — παντασ. [αμην·].

Subscr. ϊουδα.

> αποκαλυψισ > ϊωανου >.

Cap. I. 1. αγιοισ (*pro* δουλοισ: C[a] *cum* Steph.). ϊωανει (C[a] *cum* Steph.). 2. εμαρτυρησεν✓. οσα ϊδεν (— τε). 3. τον λογον τησ προφητιασ. 4. ϊωανησ. — του. των (*pro* α εστιν). 5. — εκ. βασειλειων (ι *notat. p.m.*) — τω *prim.* (*habet* C[a]). αγαπωντι. λυσαντι. — ημασ *secund.* (*habet* Cª). εκ (*pro* απο *secund.*). 6. [εποιησεν ημασ]. βασιλειαν. — και *secund.* (*habet* Cª). τον αιωνα (Cª *cum* Steph.). [των αιωνων]. 7. οψονται. παρ (πασ Cª)√. — αυτων *secund.* (*habet* Cª). — επ (*habet* Cª). 8. το αλφα και εγω και το ω (και εγω *improbat* C). [αρχη και τελοσ: Cª *expunxit et ipse forsan rursus restituit*]. — ο (*ante* $\overline{κσ}$). + ο $\overline{θσ}$ (*post* $\overline{κσ}$). 9. ιαννησ (ω *p.m.*, *at* -αννησ Cª). — και *prim.* συνκοιν. θλιψι√. — εν τη *secund.* + εν (*ante* $\overline{ιυ}$ *prim.* ι *priore eraso*). — $\overline{χυ}$ *prim.* (Cᶜ $\overline{ιυ}$ $\overline{χω}$). [δια *bis in versu*]. *fin.* — $\overline{χυ}$ (*habet* Cᶜ). 10. [ο. μ. φ.]. 11. (Cᶜ λεγουσαν). — εγω ειμι το α *usque ad* εσχατοσ και. — ο βλεπεισ (Cª *habet* ο βλεπισ√). + το (*ante* βιβλιον). — και (*ante* πεμψον: *habet* Cª). + επτα (*ante* εκκλησιαισ). — ταισ εν ασια. και εισ περγαμον και εισ θυατειρα και εισ ζμυρναν. — και εισ σαρδεισ. φιλαδελφιαν. λαοδικιαν (+ και εισ σαρδισ Cª). 12. [*deest* εκει]. βλεπιν (Cᶜ *cum* Steph. -πειν). ελαλει. (Cª ϊδον). 13. μεσον (*pro* εν μεσω). [επτα]. $\overline{υν}$. [ποδηρη]. μασθοισ. χρυσαν (Cª *cum* Steph. -σην). 14. ωσ (*pro* ωσει). 15. πεπυρωμενω. 16. ειχεν (*pro* εχων: Cª *cum* Steph.). χειρι αυτου. φαινει ωσ ο ηλιοσ. 17. [ειδον]. [επεσα]. εισ (*pro* προσ). ωσι (Cª ωσει: *pro* ωσ). επεθηκεν. — χειρα (*habet* Cᶜ). — μοι. — μη φοβου (*habet* Cª). 18. *init.* — και (*post* εσχατοσ: *habet* Cª). — αμην (*habet* Cª). [κλεισ]. θανατου και του αδου. 19. + ουν (*post* γραψον). [ειδεσ]. εισιν√. δει μελλειν (*pro* μελλει: Cª *cum* Steph.). γενεσθαι (Cª γειν.). 20. ουσ (*pro* ων). [επι τησ δ.]. — εισι *prim.* (εισιν√ Cª). — αι (*habet* Cª). [επτα λ.]. — ασ ειδεσ. *fin.* εισιν√.

II. 1. τησ εν εφεσω (*pro* τησ εφεσινησ). + χειρι (*ante* ο περιπ.: *improbat* Cª). [εν μεσω *et* χρυσων]. 2. [σου *secund.*]. [και οτι]. επιρασασ. λεγοντασ εαυτουσ αποστολουσ (*pro* φασκ. ειν. αποστ.). (+ ειναι Cᶜ *post* αποστολουσ). εισιν√. 3. και ϋπομονην εχισ και θλιψισ πασασ και εβαστασασ (*pro* και εβαστασασ και υπομονην εχεισ και: Cª *improbat* και θλιψ. πασ.). *fin.* και ουκ εκοπιασασ (*pro* κεκοπ. και ου κεκμηκασ). 4. αλλα. αφηκεσ (-κασ Cᶜ *cum* Steph.). 5. πεπτωκεσ. — ταχει. 6. -λαιτων (-λαϊτων Cª: *sic p.m.* v. 15). 7. [ταισ εκ-]. νεικωντι (ε *eras.*)√. — αυτω. τω παραδισω (*pro* μεσω του παραδεισου: *at* μεσω τω π. Cᶜ). [*fin.* $\overline{θυ}$ *tantum*]. 8. τησ εν ζμυρνη εκκλησιασ (ν *p.m.*). 9. [τα εργα και]. πτωχιαν√. αλλα πλουσιοσ (— δε). + την εκ (*post* βλασφημιαν). ϊουδαιων (-ουσ Cª *cum* Steph.). (*fin.* + εισιν Cᶜ). 10. *init.* [μηδεν]. [πασχειν]. [ιδου μελλ-]. βαλλειν βαλιν (*sic*: βαλιν *im-*

probat Cª) √. [εξ υμ. ο δια.]. πιρασθηται √. εξεται √. [ημερων]. — γινου (*habet* Cª). 13. — τα εργα σου και. σου (*pro* μου *prim.*: Cᶜ *cum* Steph.). — και *quart.* εν ταισ (εν αισ Cª *cum* Steph.). (αντειπασ Cᶜ). [-τοσ οσ]. ο σατανασ κατοικει. 14. [αλλ]. — κατα σου (*habet* Cª). [οτι εχεισ]. βαλααμ' √. [εδιδασκεν]. — εν τω βαλακ (*at* Cª τον βαλακ). (βαλλειν Cª). [ῑσλ' φαγ.]. 15. [των νικο.]. ομοιωσ (*pro* ο μισω). 16. [-ησον ει]. συ (*pro* σοι: Cª *cum* Steph.) √. 17. λεγι √. [νικωντι]. — αυτω φαγειν. εκ (*pro* απο). — δωσω αυτω *secund.* — ο (*ante* ουδεισ: *habet* Cª). οιδεν (*pro* εγνω). 18. [τησ εν θυατειροισ]. [αυτου *prim.*]. φλοξ (*pro* φλογα). 19. — και την διακονιαν (Cª *habet* και διακονιαν, Cᶜ και την δια., *sed uterque post* πιστιν). [την ϋπομ.]. — σου *secund.* — και *ult.* (Cª εσσχατα √). 20. [αλλ]. πολυ (*pro* ολιγα). αφεισ (*pro* εασ: Cª αφηκασ). γυναικα ϊαζαβελ (ϊεζαβελ' Cª). η λεγουσα (την λεγουσα[ν Cᶜ] Cª). αυτην προφητειαν ειναι (προφητιν Cªᶜ). και διδασκει και πλανα. + τουσ (*ante* εμουσ). φαγειν ειδωλοθυτα. 21. (*post* μετανοηση Cª *habet* και ου θελι μετανοησαι). εκ τησ πορνιασ ταυτησ (— αυτησ και ου μετενοησεν). 22. — εγω. καλω (*pro* βαλλω: Cª βαλω). μετανοησουσιν. αυτησ (*pro* αυτων). 23. [ερευνων]. *fin.* — υμων (*habet* Cª). 24. τοισ εν (*pro* και *prim.*: *improbat* εν Cª). — ουκ (θυατειρη οι ουκ Cª: + ουκ *tantum* Cᶜ). εχουσιν √. — και *secund.* [βαθη]. [βαλω]. 25. εχεται κρατησαται √. αχρι ου. 26. — επι (*habet* Cª). 27. ποιμανι √. 28. [πρωϊνον]. 29. λεγι √.

III. 1. + επτα (*ante* πνατα). — το. [οτι ζησ]. 2. εγρηγορων (ε *not. et ras.*) √. [στηριξον]. εμελλον αποθανιν. [τα εργ.]. *fin.* + μου. 3. — ουν *prim.* [και ηκ. και τηρ.]. μετανοησησ (*pro* γρηγορησησ: Cªᶜ *cum* Steph.). [επι σε *prim.*]. γνωση οιαν (*pro* γνωσ ποιαν). 4. αλλα εχισ ολιγα. — και *prim.* [α]. περιπατησουσιν √. 5. ουτωσ (Cª *cum* Steph. ουτοσ). εξαλιψω √. ομολογησω. εμπροσθεν (*pro* ενωπιον *prim.*). 7. φιλαδελφια √. εκκλησιαισ (*alterum* ι *eras.*). ο αληθινοσ ο αγιοσ. — την (*habet* Cª). κλιν (*pro* κλειδα). [του]. δαδ. και ανυγων (*pro* ο ανοιγων). και ουδισ κλισει και κλειων και ουδισ ανυξει (και κλειων *cum punctis, at iterum rasis*). 8. τα εργα σου. ηνεωγμενην. ην (*pro* και *prim.*). — αυτην. 9. δεδωκα (*pro* διδωμι). ηξουσιν. προσκυνησουσιν. γνωση (*pro* γνωσιν). 10. *init.* [οτι]. — τηρησω. πιρασμου √. ερχεσθε √. πιρασαι √. 11. — ιδου. κρατι √. εχισ √. μηδισ √. 12. αυτω (*pro* αυτον *prim.*: Cª *cum* Steph.). — εν (Cª *habet*). — ετι. [εκ αυτον]. κενησ ϊηλμ' √. (Cª τησ καταβαινουσησ). (*Ex* ου *priore in* ουρανου Cª θυ *fecerat*, *sed* ου *ipse restituit*)√. [μου το καινον]. 13. ° εχων (ο *p.m.*?). λεγι√. 14. εν λαοδικια εκκλησιασ. + και (*post* αμην: *improbat* C[a]). + ο *ante*, + και *post* αληθινοσ. εκκλησιασ (*pro* κτισεωσ: C[a] *cum* Steph.). 15. — ει (*habet* C[a]). ησ (*pro* ειησ). 16. οτι ουτωσ. χλιεροσ *p.m.* (χλιαροσ C[a] *cum* Steph.). ζεστροσ ουτε ψυχροσ ει (ρ *eras.* C[a] *vel* C[c] *transfert* ει *post* ψυχροσ, *ubi legitur p.m.*, *in locum post* ζεστροσ). παυσε του στοματοσ σου (*pro* μελλω σε εμεσαι *ad fin. vers.* C[a] *habet* μελλω σε εμιν εκ του στοματοσ μου). 17. — οτι *secund.* [ουδενοσ]. χριαν√. οτι ταλαιπωροσ ει (— συ *et* ο: C[a] *cum* Steph.). [και ελεεινοσ]. 18. [παρ εμου χρ.]. κολλυριον. ενχρισαι. 19. αν (*pro* εαν). [ζηλωσον]. 20. ανοιξω. + και (*ante* εισελευσομαι). διπνησω√.

IV. 1. ἴδον. [ηνεωγμενη]. + ἴδου (*ante* η φωνη). λαλουσαν. λεγων (C[a] *cum* Steph. λεγουσα). [αναβα]. διξω√. [α] δι√. 2. *init.* — και (ευθεωσ δε C[a]). + ο (*ante* επι τον θρονου καθ.: ο *eras.*). 3. [και ο καθημενοσ]. — ην. σαρδιω. ἴερεισ (ε *priore raso, pro* ιρισ). 3, 4. — ομοι. ορασ. σμαραγ. και κυκλ. του θρον. (ὁμοιοτ.: *supplet* C[a], *legens* ομοιωσ ορασι κ.τ.λ.). 4. θρονουσ (*pro* θρονοι). εικοσιτεσσαρεσ (*primo loco*)√. — [*habet* και] επι τουσ θρ. ειδον τουσ εικ. και τεσσ. (ὁμοιοτ.: *non suppletum*). εν λευκοισ (— ιματιοισ). — εσχον. χρυσεουσ. 5. και φωναι και βρονται. — αι εισι *ad* θρονου *prim.* v. 6 (ὁμοιοτ.: *supplet* C[a] α εισιν τα επτα πνευματα του $\overline{\theta υ}$ και ενωπιον του θρονου). 6. + ωσ (*ante* θαλασσα). [ϋαλινη]. [εν μεσω]. [τεσσαρα]. ενπροσθεν. 7. ωσ ομοιον ανθρωπω (*pro* ωσ ανθρωποσ). πετομενω. 8. και τα τεσσερα ζωα εν εκαστον αυτων ειχον. εσοθεν (C[a] εσωθεν)√. γεμουσιν. ουχ εξοσαν (*pro* ουκ εχουσιν: C[a] *cum* Steph.). λεγοντεσ. αγιοσ *octies* (*improbat* C[a] *post tertium*). $\overline{κσ}$ $\overline{θσ}$ παντοκρατωρ (*at* + ο *ante* $\overline{θσ}$ C[a]). 9. δωσωσιν. — δοξαν (*habet* C[a]). τω θρονω. *fin.* + αμην (cf. v. 10). 10. *init.* + και. εικοσιτεσσαρεσ. προσκυνησουσιν. + αμην (*post* αιωνων). βαλλουσιν (*alterum* λ *eras.*)√. *fin.* εντεσ (*pro* λεγοντεσ: C[a] *cum* Steph.). 11. + ο $\overline{κσ}$ και $\overline{θσ}$ ημων (*post* $\overline{κε}$). — την *secund.* [*habet tert.*]. ησαν (*pro* εισι).

V. 1. (ειτι? *pro* επι *prim. vetus instaurator, errore*)√. [ειδον: *sic* vv. 2. 6. 11]. — βιβλιον γεγραμμενον (*habet* C[a]). εμπροσθεν (*pro* εσωθεν). (+ και *ante* κατεσφ. C[a]). επτα (ε *p.m.*)√. 2. κηρυσσοντα ἴσχυρον εν φ. μ. — εστιν. ανοιξε (*sic* v. 3; *non* vv. 4. 9)√. 3. εδυνατο. ουτε (*pro* ουδε *prim. et tert.*). — ουδε υποκατω τησ γησ (ὁμοιοτ.). 4. — εγω. εκλααν πολυ (*at* εκλεον π. C[a]). ευρεθησεται (C^a *cum* Steph. ευρεθη). — και αναγνωναι (ὁμοιοτ.). 5. — ο ων. δᾱδ. [λυσαι]. 6. — και ιδου. [εν μεσω *bis in versu*]. εστηκωσ. εχων. εισιν√. τα επτα πνατα του θυ αποσταλμενα (— τα *secund.*). 7. ηλθεν√. ειληφεν√. — το βιβλιον. τησ καθημ. (του κ. C^a *cum* Steph.)√. 8. ελαβεν√. τεσσερα√. [εικοσιτεσσαρεσ]. επεσαν. εκαστοσ εχοντεσ.. κιθαραν. χρυσεασ. α (*pro* αἵ). — αι (*ante* προσευχαι: C^a *habet*). 9. λαβιν√. [ημασ *sic*]. 10. αυτουσ (*pro* ημασ). [τω θω ημων]. βασιλιαν (*pro* βασιλεισ). ϊερατειαν (*pro* ϊερεισ). βασιλευσουσιν. 11. + ωσ (*ante* φωνην). κυκλω. + και ην ο αριθμοσ αυτων μυριαδεσ μυριαδω̄ (*ante* και χιλ.). 12. εστιν√. λαβιν√. 13. το (*pro* ο εστιν). επι τησ γησ. — και υποκατω τησ γησ (ὁμοιοτ.). και τα εν τη θαλασση (— α εστι). + και (*post* παντα). [λεγοντασ]. (και *post* του θρονου *improbat* C^a). παντοκρατοροσ (*pro* και το κρατοσ: C^a *cum* Steph.). 14. [τεσσαρα]. [ελεγον]. — εικοσιτεσσαρεσ. [επεσαν]. — ζωντι *ad fin. vers.*

VI. 1. ϊδον. [οτε]. ηνυξεν (*sic* vv. 3. 7)√. μιαν εκ των επτα (— σφραγιδων: *supplet* C^a). ενοσ ^{εκ} (εκ *p.m.*). λεγοντων. φωνην. ϊδε (*pro* βλεπε: *sic* vv. 3. 5. 7). 2. [και ειδον: *sic* v. 5]. επ αυτον (*littera* ο *vel* ε *sequens eras.*). εξηλθεν√. ενικησεν (*pro* ινα νικηση). 3. την σφραγιδα την δευτεραν. 4. + ϊδον και ϊδου (*ante* εξηλθεν). [πυρροσ]. επ αυτον. (αυτω *post* εδοθη *prim. improbat* C^a). εκ (*pro* απο: *improbat* εκ τησ γησ C^a). ειva. σφαξωσιν√. 5. ηνυξε√. την σφραγιδα την τριτην. επ αυτον. χιρι√. 6. + ωσ (*ante* φωνην). [εν μεσω]. (σιτου *improbatum sed rursus restitutum*). τρισ√. κριθων. 7. [φωνην]. λεγοντοσ. 8. *init.* και ϊδον. — ο *secund.* ηκολουθι αυτω (— μετ). [αυτοισ]. επι το τεταρτον τησ γησ αποκτειναι. — εν *secund. et tert.* 9. ηνοιξεν√. την σφραγιδαν την ειδον (*sic p.m., at in exemplari suo procul dubio pro* ειδον *erat* ε̄ ιδον: C^a *habet* ε̄ σφραγιδα). + των ανθρωπων (*post* ψυχασ). και δια την μαρτυριαν *bis script.* (*secund. notavit* C^a). εσχον (ειχον C^a *cum* Steph.). 10. εκραξαν. — ο *tert.* εκδικησεισ. εκ (*pro* απο). 11. εδοθη αυτοισ εκαστω στολη λευκη. ερεθη. [αναπαυσωνται]. επι χρονον μικρον (— ετι). εωσ πληρωσωσιν (— ου). αποκτεννεσθαι. + ϋπο αυτω̄ (*ante* ωσ και αυτοι: *improbat* C^a). 12. [ειδον]. ενυξεν (ηνυξεν C^a)√. — ιδου. σισμοσ√. [μεγ. εγ.]. μελασ εγενετο. + ολη (*post* σεληνη). 13. [επεσαν]. επι (*pro* εισ). βαλλουσα. απο (*pro* ϋπο). ανεμου μεμειγαλου (··· *p.m.*?). σιομενη√. 14. + ο (*ante* ουνοσ). ελισσομενοσ. βουνοσ (*pro* νησοσ). — αυτων. εκινησαν (C^a *cum* Steph.). 15. και οι χιλιαρχοι και οι πλουσιοι. ϊσχυροι (*pro* οι δυνατοι). — και πασ ελευθεροσ (*habet* Cª: ὁμοιοτ.?). σπηλεα√. 16. λεγουσιν√. ορεσιν√. πεσεται√. κρυψεται. τω θρονω. επι (*pro* απο *secund.*: Cª *cum* Steph.). 17. αυτων.

VII. 1. και μετα τουτο ἰδον δ̄ αγγ. [τεσσαρασ γων.]. [τεσσαρασ αν.]. πνευση. [επι τησ γησ]. [παν δεν.]. 2. [ειδον]. αναβαινοντα. [ανατολησ]. σφαγιδα (Cª σφρα.)√. εκραξεν√. τοισ τεσσαρεσ αγγελοισ (Cª *cum* Steph. τεσσαρσιν). 3. αδικησεται. μηδε (*pro* μητε) *bis in versu*. αχρισ σφραγισωμεν (—ου). 4. ηκουσαν. εκατο̄ τεσσερακοντα χιλιαδεσ (— τεσσαρεσ). ισ̄λ̄√. 5—8. δωδεκα *decies*. εσφραγισμενοι *prim. et duodecimum retinentur: deest* εσφρ. *decies*. 5. — εκ φυλησ γαδ ιβ̄ χιλ. εσφ. (ὁμοιοτ.). 6. νεφθαλι. 7. — εκ φυλησ συμεων ιβ̄ χιλ. εσφ. (ὁμοιοτ.). λευει. δωδεκα χειλιαδεσ (*post* λευει: *item post* βενιαμιν *et* ἰωσηφ v. 8). ἰσσαχαρ. 8. βενιαμιν *ante* ἰωσηφ. 9. ἰδον. [και ἰδου οχλοσ πολυσ]. οσ (*pro* ον: Cª *cum* Steph.). [αυτον]. ουδισ εδυνατο. περιβεβλημενουσ (-νοι Cª *cum* Steph.). φοινικασ (-κεσ Cª *cum* Steph.). 10. κραζουσιν. η σωτηρια τω θ̄ω̄ ημων (— τω καθημενω: *habet* Cª *post* ημων) επι τω θρονω (Cª του θρονου). (Cª του αρνιου, *at p.m.* τω αρνιω). *fin.* + εισ τουσ αιωνασ των αιωνων αμην (*improbat* Cª). 11. — οι (*habet* Cª). ἰστηκισαν. επεσαν. τα προσωπα. 12. [και η σοφια]. — η *quart.* (*habet* Cª). *fin.* [αμην: *sic*]. 13. — εκ. εισ των πρεσ. λεγ. μοι *bis script.* (*secundum delet* Cª)√. ^σ^τολασ (^σ^ *p.m.*? *silet* Tischend.). εισιν√. 14. + μου (*post* κ̄ε̄). ειπεν (— μοι). [εκ τ. θλ. τ. μ.]. αυτασ (*pro* στολασ αυτων *secund.*). 15. [του θρονου]. γινωσκει (*pro* σκηνωσει επ: επ *inserit* Cª, σκηνωσει Cᶜ *marg.*). 16. πινασουσιν√. — ετι *prim.* ουδε διψασουσιν. [ουδε μη π.]. + ετ̇ι̇ (*post* ηλιοσ: ⋯ *p.m.*). 17. [ποιμανει]. [οδηγησει]. ζωησ (*pro* ζωσασ). εξαλιψει√. δρακυον, cf. xxi. 4 (Cª δακρ.)√. [απο τ. οφ.].

VIII. 1. [οτε]. ηνοιξεν√. ειμιωριον√. 2. ἰδον√. εστηκασιν√. 3. ηλθεν√. του θυσιαστηριου. δωσει (*pro* δωση). — το (*ante* ενωπιον). 4. αναβη καπνοσ (ανεβη ο καπ. Cª *cum* Steph.). χιροσ√. 5. τον (*pro* το). αυτον (*pro* αυτο). βρονται και φωναι και αστ. 6. [αγγελοι εχοντεσ]. αυτουσ (*pro* εαυτουσ: Cª *cum* Steph.). σαλπισωσιν√. 7. — αγγελοσ. εσαλπισεν√. μεμιγμενον εν αιμ. + και το τριτον τησ γησ κατεκαη (*post* γην). 8. — αγγελοσ (*non* vv. 10. 12). εσαλπισεν (*sic* vv. 10. 12). εγενηθη (*pro* εγενετο). 9. [απεθανε]. + μεροσ (*post* τριτον *prim.*). ψυχην. διεφθαρησαν. 10. + των (*ante* ὑδατων). 11. αψινθιον (Cª αψινθοσ *cum* Steph.) *sine articulo*.

λεγεται και εγενετο (*pro* γινεται: C^a *improbat* και λεγεται). + των ϋδατων (*post* τριτον). αψινθιον *secund.* + των (*ante* ανων). 12. φανη. 13. [ειδον]. — ενοσ. αετου (*pro* αγγελου). πετομενου. — εν. τουσ κατοικουντασ.

IX. 1. [αγγελοσ: *sic* v. 13]. εσαλπισεν (*sic* v. 13)√. [ειδον]. αστερασ (-ρα C^a *cum* Steph.). πεπτωκοτασ (-τα C^a *cum* Steph.). κλισ√. 2. — και ηνοιξε το φρεαρ τησ αβυσσου (ὁμοιοτ.). επι (*pro* εκ *prim.*: *habet* εκ C^a). καμινοσ *primò, at* καπινοσ *p.m.* (*pro* καπνοσ *secund.*)√. [εσκοτισθη]. vv. 2, 3. — του φρεατοσ και εκ του καπνου (C^a του φρεατοσ και εκ το[υ *partim abscis.*] καπνου) ὁμοιοτ.√. 3. αυτοισ (*pro* -αισ): *sic* vv. 4. 5. ^σκορπιοι (σ *p.m.*). 4. αυτοισ (*pro* -αισ). αδικησωσιν√. — ουδε παν χλωρον (ὁμοιοτ.). ουδε̄ *i. e.* ουδεν *ante* παν δενδρον *in facsimili* Tab. XV., *sed* ουδε *in editione utrâque.* (*Super* δενδ C^a χλω, *rursusque abstersit*). — μονουσ. εχουσιν√. σφραγιδαν (ν C^a *instauravit*). *fin.* — αυτων. 5. αυτοισ (*pro* -αισ). αποκτινωσιν√. βασανισθησονται. πεση√. 6. ου μη ευρησουσιν. αποθανιν√. φυγη. 7. ομοιοι. 8. ειχαν (*non* v. 9). 10. ομοιοισ. και (*pro* ην). — και (*ante* η εξουσια). 11. *init.* — και. εχουσιν εαυτων τον βασιλεα τον αγγ. (— εφ). + ω (*ante* ονομα αυτω). [αβαδδων]. και εν τη ελληνιδι εχι ονομα απολλυων. 12. — η *bis* (η μια C^a). ερχεται (C^a *cum* Steph.). 13. *init.* — και. (φωνησ C^a). — μιαν εκ των τεσσαρων κερατων (C^a μιασ εκ των κερατων). 14. λεγοντα (C^a λεγουσησ). ο εχων (*pro* οσ ειχε). τεσσαρεσ (*sic* vii. 2). 15. — οι *secund.* — και ημεραν (ὁμοιοτ.). ἵνα μη αποκτινωσιν. 16. + των (*ante* στρατευματων). δυο μυριαδων μυριαδασ. — και *secund.* 17. [ειδον]. επανω (*pro* επ). θυωδεισ (*levi rasura s.m.?* θιωδεισ). *fin.* θιον (*non* v. 18)√. 18. απο (*pro* υπο). πληγων (*pro* τριων). — εκ *secund. et tert.* των^ου στομ. (ου C^a, *at rursus abstersit*)√. 19. *init.* η γαρ εξουσια των ἵππων εν τω στοματι αυτων εστιν και εν ταισ ουραισ αυτων αι γαρ ουρ. κ.τ.λ. [οφεσιν]. εχουσασ (εχουσαισ C^a). αδικουσιν√. 20. + αυτων (*ante* ταυταισ). ουδε (*pro* ουτε). χιρων√. προσκυνησουσιν. + τα (*ante* ἴδωλα√). χρυσαια. χαλκεα. και τα ξυλινα και τα λιθινα. δυναντ^οαι. 21. φωνων (ο *minutâ formâ*: *p.m. an s.m.?*)√. φαρμακων. πονηριασ (C^a *vel* C^c *cum* Steph., *at* πορνιασ√).

X. 1. [ειδον: *sic* v. 5]. [αλλ. αγγ. ισχ.]. η θριξ (*pro* ιρισ: C^a ἶρισ). + αυτου (*post* κεφαλησ). 2. εχων (*pro* ειχεν). βιβλαριδιον (λι C^a, *sed abstersit*). ηνεωγμενον. εθηκεν√. τησ θαλασσησ. τησ γησ. 3. εκραξεν√. μυκατε√. + ωσ (*ante* ελαλησαν: Cª *improbat*).—αι. φωναι (*pro* βρονται: *at* Cª αι ε. βρονται *cum* Steph.). *fin.* ταισ εαυτων φωναισ. 4. οσα (*pro* οτε). — τασ φωνασ εαυτων. [εμελλον].—μοι. οσα (*pro* α). [επτα *secund.*]. αυτα (*pro* ταυτα). 5. ηρεν√. + την δεξιαν (*ante* εισ τον ουρανον). 6. ωμοσεν τω ζ. (— εν: *habet* Cᶜ). εκτισεν√. — και την θαλασσαν και τα εν αυτη (*habet* Cª). *fin.* ουκετι εστιν (ουκετι εσται Cª). 7. αλλ. του αγγελου του εβδομου. ετελεσθη. ευηγγελισεν√. τουσ εαυτου δουλουσ και τουσ προφητασ. 8. λαλουσαν. λεγουσαν. [βιβλαριδιον]. + του (*ante* αγγελου).—επι τησ θαλασσησ και (*habet* Cª). 9. [απηλθον]. δουναι. βιβλιον (*pro* βιβλαριδιον): *sic* v. 10. λαβε αυτο και καταφαγε και πικρανι (*post* καταφαγε Cª *addit* αυτο). αλλα. 10. ωσ μελει γλυκυ. εγεμισθη (*pro* επικρανθη). *fin.* (+ πικριασ Cª). 11. λεγουσιν (*pro* λεγει). δι√. και εθνεσιν. βασιλευσιν√.

XI. 1. λεγει (Cª Cᶜ* λεγων: + και εστηκει ο αγγελοσ *ante* λεγων Cᶜ*). εγειρε. 2. *init.* και τησ αυλησ τησ εσωθεν του ναου και εκβαλε εσω (*corrigit* Cª την αυλην την: *pro* ναου *primò* λαου *p.m.*, *corrigit* Cª, *qui etiam* και *ante* εκβαλε *improbat*: *pro* εσω Cª *legit* εξωθεν). + και (*ante* τοισ εθνεσιν√: *improbat* Cª). πατησουσιν√. τεσσερακοντα δυο. 3. δυσιν μαρτυσιν√. (+ πεντε *post* εξηκοντα Cᶜ*). περιβεβλημενουσ (Cª *cum* Steph. -νοι). 4. οι δυο ελαιαι (Cª αι, *qui etiam legit* και αι δυο λυχνιαι).—αι (*ante* ενωπιον). του $\overline{κυ}$ (*pro* του $\overline{θυ}$). εστωτεσ (Cᶜ *cum* Steph.). 5. θελει αυτουσ *prim.* ητισ (*pro* ει τισ *secund.*: Cª *cum* Steph.). θελησῃ αδικησαι αυτουσ ουτωσ. δι√. 6. [-σιν εξου. κλ. τον ουρ.]. ϋετοσ βρεχη τασ ημερασ τησ προφητιασ αυτων.—και (*ante* παταξαι: *habet* Cª). + εν (*ante* παση). [εαν θελησωσι]. 7. τελεσωσιν√. τοτε (*pro* το *secund.*: Cª το). μετ αυτων πολεμον. 8. [τα πτωματα]. (+εσται Cᶜ* *ante* επι). πλατιασ√. + τησ (*ante* πολεωσ). (+ και εγγυσ ο ποταμοσ *post* σοδομα Cª). και ο $\overline{κσ}$ (—ημων: *at improbat* και Cª, *post* $\overline{κσ}$ *addens* αυτων). 9. βλεπουσιν. των φυλων και λαων ^και^ γλ. (^και^ *p.m.*). το πτωμα *prim.* [τρεισ και]. αφιουσιν (αφησουσιν Cª *correcturus*, *non absolvit*). μνημα (Cª *cum* Steph.). 10. χαιρουσιν. ευφραινονται. πεμπουσιν (Cª *cum* Steph.). οι προφηται οι δυο. 11. —τασ. τρισ√. ημισου (ο *eraso*)√. εισ (*pro* επ). [επεσεν]. θεορουντασ (Cª θεωρ.)√. 12. [ηκουσαν, ν *erasum*]. φωνησ μεγαλησ. λεγουσησ. αναβατε. 13. *init.* [και]. εκινη√. [ωρα]. σισμοσ (*non* v. 19)√. επεσεν√. σισμω√. εν φοβω (*pro* εμφοβοι). 14. (— η *prim.* Cª). παρηλθεν. ιδου ερχεται η ουαι η τριτη τ. 15. εσαλπισεν√. εγενετο (*pro* εγενοντο *prim.*: C[a] *cum* Steph.). [λεγουσαι]. εγενετο η βασιλια. *fin.* + αμην. 16. — οι *prim.* (*habet* C[a]). εικοσιτεσσαρεσ. [οι ενωπ.]. οι καθηνται (*pro* καθημενοι: *improbat* οι C[a]). + και (*ante* επεσαν). 17. $\overline{κσ}$ (*pro* $\overline{κε}$). — ο (*ante* παντοκρατωρ: *habet* C[a]). — ο ερχομενοσ (και *praecedens improbat* C[a]). [ειληφασ]. 18. ωργισθη (C[a] *cum* Steph.). — τοισ (*ante* φοβουμενοισ). τουσ μικρουσ και τουσ μεγαλουσ (C[c] *cum* Steph.). [-ροντασ]. 19. ηνυγη. [$\overline{θυ}$ εν]. + ανω (*post* ουρανω: *improbat* C[a]). του $\overline{θυ}$ (*pro* αυτου *prim.*). εγενετο (C[a] *cum* Steph.). [και σεισμ.].

XII. 1. σημιον (*sic* v. 3)√. την σεληνην (C[a] *cum* Steph.). 2. + και (*ante* κραζει). 3. πυρροσ μεγασ. επτα διαδηματα. 4. συρι√. + το τριτον (*etiam post* των αστερων: C[a] *notavit*)√. 5. [αρρενα]. ποιμενιν√. ηρπαγη. + προσ (*ante* τον θρονον). 6. + εκει (*post* εχι√). [απο]. τρεφουσιν. αυτον (*pro* αυτην: C[a] *cum* Steph.). (*fin.* + πεντε C[c*]: cf. xi. 3). 7. [ο μιχ.]. πολεμησαι μετα (*pro* επολεμησαν κατα). επολεμησεν√. 8. + προσ αυτον (*post* ισχυσαν). ουδε (*pro* ουτε). τοτε (*pro* τοποσ: C[c] *cum* Steph.). — αυτων (αυτοισ *sine* ετι C[c]). 9. — ο *tert.* — και (*post* διαβολοσ). [ο σατ.]. 10. εν τω $\overline{ουνω}$ λεγουσαν. βασιλια√. [χριστου *plenè*]√. εβληθη. [κατηγοροσ]. [αυτων]. 11. ουτοι (*pro* αυτοι). [ουκ ηγ.]. (εαυτων C[a] *pro* αυτων *secund.*). 12. ευφρενεσθε√. — οι *prim.* κατοικουντεσ εν αυτοισ (*pro* εν αυτοισ σκηνουντεσ). εισ (*loco* τοισ κατοικουσι). — μεγαν. 13. [ειδεν]. (οτι εβληθη ο δρακων εισ C[a]). εδωκεν (*pro* εδιωξε: *at* C[a] εξεδιωξεν). ετεκεν τον αρσενα. 14. (C[a] εδοθη). [-κι δυο]. — του *prim.* — τον. [οπου τρεφεται]. — καιρον (και καιρον C[a]). κερουσ√. ημισου (-συ C[a]: cf. xi. 11). 15. εκ του στοματοσ αυτου οπισω τησ γυναικοσ. αυτην (*pro* ταυτην). 16. [κατεπιε]. 17. [επι]. απηλθεν πολεμον ποιησαι. επιλοιπων. *fin.* του $\overline{θυ}$ (*pro* του $\overline{ιυ}$ $\overline{χυ}$: *at* $\overline{ιυ}$ *tantum* C[a]). 18. εσταθη (*sic*).

XIII. 1. [ειδον: *sic* vv. 2. 11]. κερατα δεκα και κεφαλασ επτα. αυτων (*pro* αυτου *prim.*: C[a] *cum* Steph.). διαδηματα δεκα. [ονομα]. 2. παρδαλι√. αρκου. λεοντων. — ο (*ante* δρακων: *habet* C[a]). 3. — ειδον. + εκ (*post* μιαν). [ωσ]. θανατου θανατου (··· ν *p.m.*) εθερ.√. εθαυμασεν ολη η γη (— εν). 4. τω δρακοντι. οτι (*pro* οσ). εδωκεν την εξου. τω θηριω (*pro* το θηριον). + και (*ante* τισ *secund.*). [δυναται]. 5. [βλασφημιασ]. αυτω ποιησαι (— εξουσια: *habet* C[a]). + ο θελει (*ante* μηνασ). τεσσερακοντα δυο. 6. [ηνοιξε]. βλασφημιασ. αυτον (*pro* το ονομα αυτου: C[a] *cum* Steph.). — και *ult.* (*habet* Cᵃ). σκηνουντεσ√. 7. ποιησαι πολεμον [*nihil omissum*]. εξουσιαν (· Cᵃ)√. + και λαον (*post* φυλην). 8. [αυτω]. ων γεγραπται (— ου: *habet* Cᵃ). + αυτων (*post* ονοματα: *improbat* Cᵃ). εν βιβλω (— τη: *at* εν τω βιβλω Cᵃ). + του (*ante* εσφαγμενου). 10. — αιχμαλωσιαν συναγει. [-ρα: *bis in versu*]. αποκτεινει. ὑ η πιστισ (· *p.m.*)√. 11. ειχεν√. 12. [ποιει *bis in versu*]. εν αυτη κατοικουντασ. προσκυνιν (— ινα). 13. σημια (*sic* v. 14)√. [ινα και πυρ ποιη καταβ. εκ τ. ουρ. εισ (*pro* οι *p.m. scripsit* υ *primò*)]. 14. + και (*ante* ποιησαι *secund.*). [εικονα]. [ο εχει]. πληγησ (*pro* την πληγην). μαχαιρησ και εζησεν. 15. [αυτω δου. πν.]. ποιησει οσοι αν [*deest* ινα *post* ποιησει]. προσκυνησουσιν τη εικονι. — ινα (*ante* αποκτανθωσιν√). 16. (Cᵃ ποιησει). — τουσ *secund.* τουσ πτωχουσ και τουσ πλουσιουσ. ἵνα δωσιν αυτω (*at* ἵνα δωσι αυτοισ Cᵃ). [χαραγμα]. το μετωπον. 17. *init.* — και (*habet* Cᵃ). [δυνηται]. το χαραγμα του θηριου η το ονομα αυτου η. 18. ουσ (*pro* τον νουν: Cᶜ νουν *tantum*). εστιν *secund.* — και ο αριθμοσ αυτου. εξακοσιαι (*sic*) εξηκοντα εξ'.

XIV. 1. [ειδον: *sic* v. 6]. το αρνιον εστοσ. τεσσερακοντα τεσσαρεσ. + ^αυ^του και το ονομα (*post* ονομα: αυ *p.m.*). *fin.* αυτω (Cᵃ *cum* Steph. αυτων). 2. — μεγαλησ (*habet* Cᵃ). η φωνη ην ηκουσα ωσ κ. (*pro* φωνην ηκουσα κ.) κιθ^α^ραισ (α *p.m.*)√. 3. — ωσ. + και ^ην^ *sic* (*post* καινην: ^ην^ *p.m.*). τω̄ των τεσσαρων (*sic*)√. + ενωπιον (*ante* των πρεσβ.). εδυνατο. (αι *improbat* Cᵃ). εκατον τεσσερακοντα μιαν (τεσσαρεσ *pro* μιαν Cᵃ). 4. — εισιν *tert.* — οι (*ante* ακολου.). [α ὑπαγη]. [ουτοι ηγορ.]. απ αρχησ (*pro* απαρχη). + εν (*ante* τω αρνιω *secund.*: *improbat* εν Cᵃ). 5. [ουχ ευρ. ψευδ.]. ψευδοσ (*pro* δολοσ). [γαρ]. — ενωπιον του θρονου του θ̄ῡ. 6. — αλλον (*habet* Cᶜ). πεταμενον. μεσωουρανηματι (ω *delet* Cᵃ). ευαγγελισασθε επι. καθημενουσ (*pro* κατοικουντασ). + επι (*ante* παν). 7. — λεγοντα. [εν φ. μ.]. [θ̄ν̄]. π^ο^ριησαντι (π̄ρ̄ι *primò*, *at* ποι *p.m.*)√. + την (*ante* θαλασσαν). 8. — αγγελοσ (*habet* Cᶜ). + δευτεροσ (*ante* ηκολουθησεν√). — λεγων επεσεν *usque ad* v. 9 ηκολουθησεν (ὁμοιοτ.: Cᵃ *supplet*, *sic varians*: — επεσε: — η πολισ: — οτι: πορνιασ√: πεπτωκαν: + τα *ante* εθνη: και αλλοσ αγγελοσ ηκολουθησεν τριτοσ). 9. προσκυνι το θηριον. λαμβανι√. τω μετωπω. 10. [εκ του οινου του θ. του θ̄ῡ]. αγγελων αγιων (— των). 11. εισ εωνασ των αιωνων αναβαινει (Cᵃ αιωνασ). 12. + η (*ante* ὑπομονη). — ωδε *secund.* των τηρουντων. [-τιν ῑῡ]. 13. λεγουσησ εκ του ουρανου.

— μοι. [εν κ̄ω̄]. — ναι (*habet* C^a). αναπαησονται. γαρ (*pro* δε). ακολουθι√. 14. — και ειδον. καθημενον ομοιον ϋῑο. εχοντα (C^a εχον). [τησ κεφαλησ]. 15. + αυτου (*post* ναου). φωνη μεγαλη. ηλθεν (— σοι). του θερισμου (*pro* του θερισαι). 16. τησ νεφελησ. 17. [*cum* Steph.]. 18. [εξηλθεν]. [-ριου εχ-]. εφωνησεν√. φωνη (*pro* κραυγη). λεγω (C^a *cum* Steph. λεγων)√. το δρεπανον (*secund.*) σου το οξυ. + τησ αμπελου (*post* βοτρυασ). [ηκμ. αι στ. αυτ.]. 19. επι τησ γησ (*pro* εισ την γην). ετρυγησεν√. σου θ̄ῡ την μεγαλην (τ *p.m.*)√. 20. [εξω]. διακοσιων (*pro* εξακοσιων: C^a *cum* Steph.).

XV. 1. ἴδον. σημιον√. 2. [ειδον: *sic* v. 5]. [ϋαλινην *bis in vers.*]. [νικωντασ]. — εκ *secund.* — εκ του χαραγματοσ αυτου (ὁμοιοτ.??: *habet* και). αυτου *ult.* (υ *in ras.*: *utrum autem?*)√. *fin.* + κ̄ῡ (*ante* του θ̄ῡ). 3. αδοντασ (*pro* αδουσι). μωϋσεωσ. + του (*ante* δουλου). [λεγοντεσ]. βασιλευ των αιωνων (*pro* ο βασιλευσ των αγιων: C^a βασιλευσ, *forsan* ο βασιλευσ, υ *in* σου *eraso*: *pro* αιωνων *etiam* C^a *habet* εθνων, *at idem forsan restituit* αιωνων). 4. τισ σε ου φοβηθη (— μη). [δοξαση]. [οσιοσ]. [π. τα εθ.]. ηξουσιν√. — τα *secund.* + ενωπιον (*post* δικαιωματα). 5. — ιδου. ηνυγη√. 6. [εξηλθον]. [-γοι εχον.]. [εκ του ναου ενδεδ.]. καθαρουσ λινουσ (— και) λαμπρουσ. 7. — εν (*habet* C^a). εδωκεν√. — επτα *secund.* *fin.* + αμην. 8. [ναοσ καπνου]. ουδισ√. [ηδυνατο]. εισ τον ναον εισελθειν.

XVI. 1. [φωνησ μεγαλησ εκ του ναου]. ϋπαγεται√. και εκχεεται. + επτα (*ante* φιαλασ). 2. — και απηλθεν *usque ad* την γην (ὁμοιοτ.: C^a *supplet, at* εξεχεεν√ *et* εισ *pro* επι). ελκον πονηρον και κακον (C^a *primò* ελκοσ κα *i. e.* κακον: *at rursus delevit* κα). επι (*pro* εισ). *fin.* προσκυνουντασ την εικονα αυτου. 3. εισ (*loco* και ο δευτεροσ αγγελοσ εξεχεεν: C^a *cum* Steph., αγγελοσ *omisso*). ωσι (*pro* ωσ). ζωσα απεθανεν επι τησ θαλασσησ. 4. — αγγελοσ. εξεχεεν√. επι (*pro* εισ *prim.*).— εισ *secund.* [εγενετο]. 5. των αγγελου (οι *p.m.*)√.—κυριε. [ο ην]. ο οσιοσ (— και). 6. αιματα *prim.* εδωκασ αυτοισ πιειν. οπερ αξιοι εισιν (— γαρ). 7. — αλλου εκ. κρισισ√. 8. [αγγελοσ]. εξεχεεν√.— εν. 9. [-μησαν το ονομα]. (υ θ̄ῡ του C^c *rescripsit*: *latent p.m.* Α *vel* Λ [*unâ litterâ sequente*] ΑΥ [?]√). + την (*ante* εξουσιαν). 10. — αγγελοσ (*sic* v. 12). εξεχεεν (*sic* v. 12)√. (εσκοτισμενη C^c). εμασωντο. απο (*pro* εκ). 11. — και εκ των ελκων αυτων (ὁμοιοτ.).— εκ των εργων αυτων. 12. — τον *tert.* ανατολησ. 13. εδοθη (*pro* ειδον). — εκ του στοματοσ του δρακοντοσ και εκ του στοματοσ του θηριου και (*idem initium*: cf. x. 8; xvi. 14: C^a *supplet*). [τρια ακαθ.]. ειω̈σει (*pro* ομοια: ¨ *p.m.*) βατραχουσ (-χοι C^a). 14. εισιν√. δαιμονιων. [εκπορευεσθαι: *at* C^a -ρευονται *sine* α *vel* και]. εισ (*pro* επι). — τησ γησ και (*idem init.*). + τον (*ante* πολεμον). — εκεινησ [ημ. τησ μεγ.]. 15. ερχ^{ομ}εται (ομ *p.m.?*). ο τε γρηγορων (τε *delet* C^a). βλεπωσιν√. 16. συνηγαγον. — τον *prim.* αρμαγεδω̄ (C^a αρμε-, *at rursus abstersit*). 17. οτε (*pro* ο εβδομοσ αγγελοσ: C^a ο ζ̄ αγγελοσ). εξεχεεν√. επι (*pro* εισ). εξηλθεν√. [μεγαλη]. εκ (*pro* απο *prim.*). του θ̄ῡ (*pro* του ουρανου απο του θρονου). γεγονεν√. 18. βρονται και αστραπαι και φωναι και βρονται (*sic*: *improbat* C^c βρονται *secund.*, *non* και). σισμοσ√ *bis in versu*. [εγενετο *prim.*]. οισ ουκ εγενοντο (*pro* οιοσ ουκ εγενετο: C^a *cum* Steph.). — οι. [ανθρωποι εγενοντο]. [ουτω]. 19. η πολισ (*pro* αι πολεισ: C^a αι πολισ√). επεσεν (C^a επεσαν). + του (*ante* δουναι). — το. — του (*ante* οινου). *fin.* — αυτου. 20. εφυγεν√. 21. ^{ωσ} ταλαντιαια (ωσ *p.m.*).

XVII. 1. — εκ. ελαλησεν√. — μοι. διξω√. — των *tert. et quart.* 2. εποιησαν πορνιαν (*pro* επορνευσαν). οι κατοικουντεσ την γην εκ του οικου (οινου C^a) τησ πορνιασ αυτησ. 3. απηνεγκεν√. [ειδον]. γεμοντα ονοματα *vel* γεμον τα ονοματα (C^a γεμον ονοματα). εχοντα (*ergo* γεμοντα). 4. ην (*pro* η *secund.*). πορφυρουν. κοκκινον. [και κεχρ. χρυσω]. ποτηριον χρο̇υσουν (˙ *p.m.?*). γεμων (γεμον C^a?). *fin.* τα ακαθαρτα τησ πορνιασ αυτησ και τησ γησ. 6. ειδα. — εκ *prim.* τω αιματι (*at* του αιματοσ *sine* εκ C^a). θαυμα μεγα ειδων αυτην. 7. ειπεν√. [σοι ερω]. 8. *init.* + το. [ειδεσ]. εστιν√ *bis in vers.* αναβαινιν√. απωλιαν (*sic* v. 11)√. [ϋπαγειν]. [θαυμασονται]. [ου γεγ. τα ον.]. βλεποντων. [οτι ην]. και παλιν παρεστε (*pro* καιπερ εστιν: C^a και παρεστιν). 9. επτα ορη εισιν. 10. επτα βασιλεισ ε^{ι}σιν (^{ι} C^a, *forsan etiam p.m.*). [επεσαν]. — και *secund.* ηλθεν√. μινε ζει (δει C^a). 11. ουκ εστιν ουτοσ ο ογδοοσ εστιν (— και αυτοσ). εστιν *tert.*√. 12. καιρατα√. βασιλιαν√. ουτω (*pro* ουπω: C^a *cum* Steph.). αλλα. εξουσιν (εξουσιαν C^a *cum* Steph.). ωσ βασιλεισ βα̈ (¨ *p.m.*)√. λαμβανουσιν√. 13. γνωμην εχουσιν. την εξουσιαν αυτων (*pro* τ. ε. εαυτων). διδοασιν. 14. πολεμησουσιν√. νικησι√. εστιν√. 15. [λεγει]. ταυτα (*pro* τα υδατα: *at* C^c ταυτα τα υδατα). ειδε^{σ} (σ *p.m.*)√. — η (*habet* C^a). + και (*ante* λαοι). εισιν√. 16. και (*pro* επι). μισησουσιν√. — εν. 17. αυτου (*pro* αυτων *prim.*: C^a *cum* Steph.). (αυτου Steph. *et p.m.*: αυτων C^a^). και ποιησε μι. γν. (και ποιησε *tantum improbat* C^a^). βασιλιαν (*non* v. 18)√. τελεσθησονται οι λογοι. 18. [ειδεσ]. — η *quart.* βασιλειων (*pro* βασιλεων).

XVIII. 1. *init.* — και. [ειδον]. + αλλον (*ante* αγγελον). 2. ἴσχυρα φωνη (— εν ισχυι *et* μεγαλη). — επεσε. δαιμονιων. [ακαθαρτου και φυλακη]. [ορνεου]. 3. [του οινου]. πορνιασ√. πεπτωκασιν. *Post* τησ γησ *secund.* 'με' 'τ αυτησ επορνευσα' (υ *p.m.*, *etiam* '' ' ' *p.m.*: ὁμοιοτ.)√. [στρηνουσ]. 4. [αλλην φωνην]. εξελθαται. ο λαοσ μου εξ αυτησ. συνκοινωνησηται. *fin.* εκ των πληγων αυτησ ἵνα μη λαβηται. 5. εκολληθησαν (*pro* ηκολ.). 6. — υμιν και. — αυτη. + τα (*ante* διπλα). + αυτησ (*post* ποτηριω). εκερασεν√. κερασαται√. [αυτη]. 7. αυτην (εαυτην C^c^ *cum* Steph.). εστρηνιασεν√. + οτι (*ante* καθημε√ βασιλισσα). *fin.* ειδω. 8. ο $\overline{\theta\sigma}$ ο $\overline{\kappa\sigma}$ ο κρινασ (C^a^ *cum* Steph.). 9. [κλαυσονται]. — αυτην *prim.* επ αυτην. — και στρηνιασαντεσ (ὁμοιοτ.: *habet* C^a^, *praetereaque* C^c*^ *adjecit* και στεναξωσιν). ἴδωσιν (*pro* βλεπωσι). πτωσεωσ (*pro* πυρωσεωσ: C^a^ *cum* Steph.). 10. — εν. 11. + σου (*ante* κλαιουσιν√). επ αυτην. 12. μαργαριτων. βυσσινων. [πορφυρασ]. σιρικου. [ξυλον]. — και μαρμαρου (ὁμοιοτ.). 13. κι̅ναμωμου· (*i. e.* κινν.) + και αμωμον (*ante* και θυμιαματα: *improbat* C^a^). [κ. κτ. κ. προβ.]. (ἵππον C^a^, *sed rursus abstersit*). [ρεδων]. 14. [η]. σου τησ επιθυμιασ τησ ψυχησ. ριπαρα (C^a^ *cum* Steph. λιπαρα).√ — τα *secund.* απωλοντο (*pro* απηλθεν *secund.*). ου μη αυτα ευρησουσιν. 16. *init.* — και. — η μεγαλη η περιβεβλη (*deest unus* στίχοσ, *ut videtur, in exemplari*, cf. xix. 12; xxii. 2: *supplet* C^a^). [β. και π. και κ.]. κεχρυσωμενον [εν χρυσω]. μαργαριτη. 17. ο επι τον τοπον πλεων (*pro* επι των πλοιων ο ομιλοσ). 18. [εκραζον]. ^β^λεποντεσ (*sic p.m., at primò* λεγοντεσ, *pro* ορωντεσ). πολι τη μ. 19. [εβαλον]. τησ κεφαλησ. [εκραζον κλ. και πενθ. λεγ.]. — ουαι *semel.* + τα (*ante* πλοια). 20. ευφρενου√. επ αυτη. ουρανει√. + ·και οι (*ante* αποστολοι). 21. λιθον ἴσχυρον (C^c^ ἴσχυροσ *pro* λιθον *primò, deinde* λιθον ἴσχυροσ *legit*). λιθον (*pro* μυλον: *i. e.* λιθον *bis in versu*). + οτι (*ante* ουτωσ). 21, 22. ετι εν αυτη φωνη κιθαρωδων· (— και). 22. σαλπιγγων. — πασησ τεχνησ. — και φωνη μυλου *ad fin. vers.* (ὁμοιοτ.). 23. [εν *prim.*]. φωνην νυμφιου (C^a^ *cum* Steph. φωνη). [οι *prim.*]. φαρμακια√. 24. [αιμα].

XIX. 1. *init.* — και. ωσ φωνην μεγαλην οχλου πολλου. λεγοντων. — και η δοξα και η τιμη (C^a^ *habet* και η δοξα *tantum*). του $\overline{\theta\upsilon}$ (*pro* $\overline{\kappa\omega}$ τω $\overline{\theta\omega}$). 2. εκρινεν√. πορνην (η *p.m.?*)√. εφθιρεν. πορνια√.

εξεδικησεν√. δουλων αυτησ εκ χιροσ αυτησ (*pro* αυτησ *post* δουλων Cª *cum* Steph. αυτου). 3. [ειρηκαν]. 4. [επεσαν οι πρ. οι] εικοσιτεσσαρεσ. τεσσερα.—ζωα (*habet* Cª). τω θρονω. 5. και φωναι εξηλθον εκ του θρονου λεγουσαι (Cª φωνη εξηλθεν *et* λεγουσα). αινειται τω $\overline{\theta\omega}$.—και *secund. et tert.* 6. [ωσ *ter in versu*]. λεγουσων. εβασιλευσεν ο $\overline{\theta\sigma}$ ο $\overline{\kappa\sigma}$ ημων (Cª $\overline{\kappa\sigma}$ ο $\overline{\theta\sigma}$ ημων). 7. αγαλλιωμεν. (δωσομεν Cª *pro* δωμεν). αυτων (*pro* αυτω: Cª *cum* Steph.). (νυμφη Cᶜ *pro* γυνη). 8. λαμπρον καθαρον (—και *secund.*). των αγιων εστιν. 9. λεγε' *prim.* (ι *p.m.*? *et* Cª). διπνον√.—του γαμου (*habet* Cª).—και λεγει μοι *secund.* (Cª και λεγι μοι *habet*). +μου (*post* λογοι: Cª *cum* Steph.). εισιν√. (Cª *habet* του $\overline{\theta\upsilon}$ αλ. εισιν). 10. επεσα.—σου *secund.* (*habet* Cª).—του *bis in versu.* εστιν√. προφητιασ√. 11. [ειδον]. ηνεωγμενον. πιστοσ καλουμενοσ. πολεμι√. 12. *init.* οι δε οι οφθ. (δε *errore punctatum, sed rursus restitutum*).—ωσ. [εχων ονομα].—γεγραμμενον ο ουδεισ (*deest unus* στίχοσ *in exemplari*, cf. xviii. 16; xxii. 2: *pro* ονομα Cª *habet* ονοματα γεγραμμενα α ουδισ)√. η μη (*pro* ει μη: Cª *cum* Steph.)√. 13. περιρεραμμενον (*pro* βεβαμμενον: *at* Cᶜ περιρεραντισμενον). κεκλητο (*pro* καλειται το: Cª κεκληται το). 14. [-ματα εν τω]. ηκολουθι√. [εφ]. ενδεδυμενοισ (σ *eras.*). [και καθ.]. 15. παταξει. τησ οργησ του θυμου (—και *quart.*: τησ οργησ *punctat. sed rursus restitut.*). 16.—επι *secund.*—το *secund.* 17. [ειδον]. αλλον (*pro* ενα). +εν (*post* εκραξεν). πασιν√. πετομενοισ.—και *tert.* συναχθητε. διπνον√. το μεγα (*pro* του μεγαλου). +του (*ante* $\overline{\theta\upsilon}$). 18. φαγηται√. επ αυτοισ. +τε (*post* ελευθερων). *fin.* και μικρων και των μεγαλων. 19. ἴδον. κατα τα στρατευματα αυτων (και τα *pro* κατα τα Cª *cum* Steph.). (συ|νηγ *p.m.*: συν|ηγ Cª: *et sic* C *haud rarò*). +τον (*ante* πολεμον). 20. μετ αυτου ο (*pro* μετα τουτου ο). σημια√. επλανησεν√. την εικονα (Cª *cum* Steph. τη εικονι). τησ κεομενησ εν θιω (—τω). 21. εξελθουση (*pro* εκπορευομενη).

XX. 1. και ειδον αγγε καταβαινοντα (*at* αλλον αγγελον Cª)√. —εκ του ουρανου (*habet* Cª). κλιν√. αλυσεσιν (Cª *cum* Steph. αλυσιν)√. εν τη χειρι (*pro* επι την χ.). 2. εκρατησεν√. [τον οφ. τον αρ.]. ο εστιν ο διαβολοσ (ο *pro* οσ). + ο (*ante* σατανασ). 3. —χιλια ετη και εβαλεν αυτον (ὁμοιοτ.). εκλισεν (—αυτον *sequens*). πλανησει ετι τα εθνη.—και *ultim.* δι (Cª δει)√. [αυτον λυθηναι]. 4. [ειδον: *sic* vv. 11. 12].—και (*post* $\overline{\theta\upsilon}$). ει τινεσ (*pro* οιτινεσ). ουν^ου^ (*pro* ου: ^ου^ *p.m.*). το θηριον. ουδε (*pro* ουτε). [την εικονα].—αυτων *prim.* + του (*ante* $\overline{\chi\upsilon}$). — τα (*ante* χιλια). 5. — οι δε λοιποι *usque ad* χιλια ετη (ὁμοιοτ.). 6. αναστασιν√. ο δευτεροσ θανατοσ. αλλα. + και (*post* ϊερεισ). βασιλευσουσιν√. + τα (*ante* χιλια). 7. σ̈ε τα χιλ. (·· *p.m.*)√. 8. + παντα (*post* πλανησαι). — τα *secund.* τετρασι. — τησ γησ (*habet* C[a]). — τον *bis in versu* (*habet* C[a]). τωγ' *primò*?√. γωγ' *p.m.*: μαγωγ'. + και (*ante* συναγαγειν). + τον (*ante* πολεμον). + αυτων (*post* αριθμοσ). 9. [εκυκλωσαν]. 9, 10. — πυρ v. 9 *usque ad* λιμνην v. 10 (*supplet* C[a] πυρ απο του $\overline{\theta\upsilon}$ κ.τ.λ. *cum* Steph.). 10. + του (*ante* θιου√). [οπου το]. + οπου (*ante* ο ψευδοπ.). 11. μεγαν λευκον. επανω (*pro* επ). [αυτου]. + του (*ante* προσωπου). 12. + και (*ante* μεγαλουσ: *at* τουσ *pro* και C[a]). μεγαλουσ και τουσ μικρουσ. επι (*pro* ενωπιον: C[a] ενωπιον επι). θρονου (*pro* $\overline{\theta\upsilon}$). ηνεωχθη. — και βιβλιον αλλο ηνεωχθη (*habet* C[a], *at* αλλο βιβλιον: ὁμοιοτ.). εστιν√. ταισ βιβλοισ (*pro* τοισ βιβλιοισ). 13. τουσ νεκρουσ τουσ εν αυτη. τα̈ θανατοσ (·· *p.m.*)√. [εδωκαν]. τουσ νεκρουσ τουσ εν αυτοισ. κατεκριθησαν. *fin.* και ουτοσ ο δευτεροσ θανατοσ εστιν η λιμνη του πυροσ. 15. ευρεθησεται (C[a] *cum* Steph.).

XXI. 1. [ειδον]. κενον√. κενην√. απηλθαν (*pro* παρηλθε). 2. — εγω ιωαννησ. ειδον *transfertur in locum ante* καταβαινουσαν. $\overline{ϊηλμ}$' κενην√. εκ του $\overline{ουνου}$ απο του $\overline{\theta\upsilon}$. 3. — ηκουσα (*habet* C[a]). φωνη μεγαλη (φωνησ μεγαλησ C[a] *cum* Steph.). θρονου (*pro* ουρανου). λεγουσα (C[a] *cum* Steph. -σησ). εσκηνωσεν (C[a] *cum* Steph. σκηνωσει). [λαοι]. — και *ultim.* [εσται μετ αυτων]. — θεοσ αυτων (ὁμοιοτ.). 4. εξαλιψει√. — ο $\overline{\theta\sigma}$. δρακυ (C[a] δακρυον)√ cf. vii. 17. εκ (*pro* απο). — ο (*ante* θανατοσ). ουτε κραυγη ουτε πενθοσ. — ουτε πονοσ (ὁμοιοτ.). οτι (*pro* ετι *secund. p.m.*, *at* ετι *primò*). τα προβατα (*pro* οτι τα πρωτα: C[a] τα πρωτα *sine* οτι *repetit.*). απηλθεν. 5. τω θρονω. κενα ποιω παντα. [μοι]. πιστοι και αληθινοι εισιν. 6. λεγει (*pro* ειπε). γεγονα (γεγοναν C[a] *primò*, *sed rursus totum verbum improbavit*). — ειμι. αλφα [*at* $\overline{\omega}$]. [δωσω εκ]. δωρεασ (C[a] *cum* Steph. -εαν). 7. κληρονομησι√. ταυτα (*pro* παντα). — ο (*ante* $\overline{\upsilon\sigma}$). 8. *init.* τοισ δε ω̈σ διλοισ (·· *p.m.*). π̇ φονευσει (· *p.m.*)√. φαρμακοισ. ϊδωλολατραισ√. πασιν√. ψευδεσιν. θιω√. εστιν ο θανατοσ ο δευτεροσ. 9. ηλθεν√. — προσ με. + εκ (*post* εισ). των γεμοντων των (C[a] των γεμουσων των). ελαλησεν√. διξω√. την γυναικα του αρνιου. 10. απηνεγκεν√. επι. εδιξεν√. — την μεγαλην. [$\overline{ιηλμ}$]√. [απο του $\overline{\theta\upsilon}$]. 11. + απο (*post* δοξαν).

— και. 12. εχοντι (*pro* εχουσαν τε). τιχοσ√. εχοντασ (*pro* εχουσαν *secund.*: Cª εχουσασ). δωδεκα και επι τουσ πυλωνασ αγγελουσ $\overline{ιβ}$. + αυτων (*post* ονοματα). γεγραμμενα. εστιν√. [$\overline{ιβ}$ φυλ.].—των *ultim.* [$\overline{ισλ}$]. 13. *init.* απο. [ανατολησ]. και απο βορρα πυλωνεσ $\overline{γ}$· *bis script.* + και (*ante* απο νοτου). — απο δυσμων πυλωνεσ τρεισ (ὁμοιοτ.: Cª *pro* βορρα *secund.* νοτου *habet, pro* νοτου *sequente* δυσμων *legit*). [τρεισ *prim. et quart.*: $\overline{γ}$ *secund. et tert.*]. 14. τιχοσ (*non* v. 15)√.—εχον (*habet* Cª). [$\overline{ιβ}$ *prim. et tert.*]. εκ αυτων. + δωδεκα (*ante* ονοματα). 15. + μετρον (*post* ειχεν√). (Cª καλαμου). 16. + αυτησ (*ante* τετραγωνοσ).—αυτησ τοσουτον εστιν.—και *tert.* εμετρησεν (*sic* v. 17)√. [σταδιων δωδεκα: Cª σταδιου (*pro* -ιουσ)]. *fin.* εισα εστιν√. 17. χιλοσ (*pro* τειχοσ). εκατον $\overline{μδ}$ πηχεων. 18. [ην].—η *prim.* εν δωμασι του τιχουσ (Cª η ενδωμησισ *sine* ην). ειασπισ (*non* v. 19)√. ομοιον. [ϋαλω: *sic passim*]. 19. *init.* (και *improbat* Cª). τιχουσ√. εισ (*pro* πρωτοσ). + και (*ante* ο δευτεροσ). + και (*ante* ο $\overline{γ}$). [$\overline{δ}$]. 20. ο $\overline{ε}$ σαρδονυξ˚. ο $\overline{ς}$ σαρδιον· [$\overline{ζ}$ *et* $\overline{η}$]. ο $\overline{εθ}$ τοπαδιον (ε *eras.*: -ζιον Cª). [$\overline{ι}$ *et* $\overline{ια}$ *et* $\overline{ιβ}$]. [χρυσοπρασοσ, *at* -σιοσ Cª]. αμεθυστινοσ (Cª αμεθυσοσ). 21. [$\overline{ιβ}$ *prim.*].—δωδεκα *secund.* (Cª *habet* $\overline{ιβ}$). μαργαρειται√. + ων (*ante* ην: *improbat* Cª). πλατια√. *fin.* διαυγησ (-τησ *primò, levi rasurâ mutat. in* Γ). 22. [ειδον]. οτι ο $\overline{κσ}$ ο $\overline{θσ}$ (*pro* ο γαρ $\overline{κσ}$ ο $\overline{θσ}$: Cª ο γαρ ο $\overline{κσ}$ $\overline{θσ}$). [-ωρ να-]. εστιν√. 23. χριαν√.—εν (*habet* Cª). 24. περιπατησουσιν δ̇ τα εθνη δια του φωτοσ αυτησ (— των σωζομενων: δ̇ *notat. p.m. et* Cª). φερουσιν√.—και την τιμην. 25. ημερα (Cª *cum* Steph. -ρασ). [νυξ˚]√. εστε√. 26. οισουσιν√. 27. εισελθωσιν. κοινον. ο ποιωσει (*pro* ποιουν: Cª ποιων, ωσει *improbato*). $\overline{ουνου}$ (*pro* αρνιου).

XXII. 1. εδιξεν√.—καθαρον.—του *prim.* 2. [εν μεσω]. πλατιασ√. ενθεν (*pro* εντευθεν *prim.*: *habet* και *sequens*).—εντευθεν ξυλον ζωησ, *unâ lineâ forsan omissâ*: cf. xviii. 16; xix. 12 (Cª ενθεν και ενθεν και, *sine* ξυλ. ζω.). [ποιουν]. [$\overline{ιβ}$]. κατα μηνα εκαστον αποδιδουσ (— ενα). τουσ καρπουσ (*pro* τον καρπον). των ξυλων. — των (*ante* εθνων). 3. καταγμα (*pro* καταναθεμα: Cª καταθεμα).—ετι (*habet* Cª).—ο. 4. + και (*ante* επι). 5. ετι (*pro* εκει). ουκ εχουσιν χρειαν. + φωτοσ (*ante* λυχνου). [ηλιου]. φωτιει επ (*pro* φωτιζει). 6. ειπεν√. + ο (*ante* $\overline{κσ}$). $\overline{πνατων}$ των (*pro* αγιων). απεστιλεν√. + με (*ante* τον αγγελον:

improbat C^a^). διξαι√. δι√. 7. *init.* + και. (ερχονται C^a^ *pro* ερχομαι). προφητασ (ι *p.m.*?)√. 8. καγω. [ϊωαννησ]. ο βλεπων και ακουων ταυτα. [εβλεψα επεσα]. δικνυντοσ. 9. —γαρ. 10. + τουτουσ (*post* λογουσ: *improbatur jam ante* C^a^). ο καιροσ γαρ εγγυσ (— οτι). 11. ρυπαροσ ρυπανθητω. δικαιοσυνην ποιησατω (*pro* δικαιωθητω). 12. *init.*—και. αποδοθηναι (C^a^ *cum* Steph.). *fin.* εστιν αυτου. 13. — ειμι. αλφα. [ω]. ο πρωτοσ και ο εσχατοσ η αρχη και το τελοσ. 14. πλυνοντεσ τασ στολασ αυτων (*pro* ποι. τασ εντ. αυτ.). + ωσ δε η εξουσια (*ante* επι: *improbat* C^a^). 15. — δε. ϊδωλολατραι√. — ο. ποιων και φιλων. 16. [επι]. δαδ (—του). ο πρωϊνοσ (*pro* και ορθινοσ). 17. — το. π πνα (· *p.m.*)√.— η. ερχου (*pro* ελθε) *bis in vers.* ερχεσθω (*pro* ελθετω). — και *ultim.* λαβετω ΰδωρ (— το). 18. η μαρτυρω εγω (*pro* συμμαρτυρουμαι γαρ) + τω (*post* παντι). επιθησει επ αυτον (*pro* επιτιθη προσ ταυτα). — επιθησει *sequens.* — επ αυτον *sequens.* (*inter* εαν τισ επιθησει *et* επ αυτον C^a^ *habet* επ αυτα επιθησι: *p.m.* ὁμοιοτ.). + τω (*ante* βιβλιω). 19. αν (*pro* εαν). αφελη (*pro* αφαιρη). + τουτων (*post* λογων). του βιβλιου (*pro* βιβλου *prim.*). προφητιασ√. αφελι (*pro* αφαιρησει). του ξυλου (*pro* βιβλου *secund.*). [εκ τησ πολ.]. — και *ultim.* + τω (*ante* βιβλιω). 20. λεγι√. + ειναι (*ante* ναι *prim.*: *improbat* C^a^). — αμην. — ναι *secund.* (*fin.* + χε *post* ιην C^a^). 21. — ημων. — χυ. των αγιων (*pro* παντων υμων). [αμην: *sic*].

Subscr. αποκαλυψεισ ϊωαννου.

ERRATA

IN TISCHENDORF'S EDITION OF THE CODEX SINAITICUS.

See Introduction, p. xii.

The text of the larger edition can be corrected only by comparison with the original MS., as by the aid of Tregelles we have been enabled to do in the Catholic Epistles: he now reads *αναπεπαυεται p.m.* 1 Pet. iv. 15; *κατα τασ p.m.* Jude 12. We note besides in Mark i. 23 the second *εν* is found in both editions, but is wanting in the *Notitia Cod. Sin.* p. 31.

John v. 37 *ειδοε* in the *facsimile*, *ειδοσ* in both editions. *Ibid.* xi. 9 *του* should be placed for *τουτου* in both, since the note assigns *τουτου* to C. Apoc. ix. 4, *ουδε̄* (*i. e. -εν pro ουδε secund.*) in the *facsimile*, *ουδε* in both editions.

The text of the smaller edition should thus be corrected from the larger:

Cancel the dot over *κ̇αι secund.* Matt. i. 25, over *αφανιζουσ̇ι ibid.* vi. 16, and over *οικιαν* Luke x. 5.

Matt. xiii. 32 *for πετιπα read πετινα. Ibid.* xxi. 28 *for ε read ε̄* (*i. e. εν*). Luke xv. 27 *for σιτευτο read σιτευτο̄* (*i. e. -ον*). Rom. vi. 8 *for συνζησομε read συνζησομε̄* (*i. e. -εν*). Phil. iv. 3 *for συζηγε read συζυγε* (so even notes of smaller). 1 Tim. vi. 20 *for φυλαζον read φυλαξον.* Acts x. 3 *read ὠ̇εδεν. Ibid.* xxvi. 18 *for τηο read τησ. Ibid.* xxviii. 15 *for αρχι read αχρι.* Apoc. v. 11 *for χιλιαδω read χιλιαδω̄* (*i. e. -ων*). *Ibid.* v. 12 *for δυναμι read δυναμῑ* (*i. e. -ιν*). *Ibid.* xviii. 3 *place a point over τ in the second μετ.*

In John ix. 26 the larger has *εποιησαν*, the smaller *εποιησαν*, and there is no note on the word in either edition: also in John

iii. 25 Fol. XXXXIX, the figures 16, 17 are placed one line too high in both editions: in John xxi. 25 the stop before and aspirate over the first *a* in the *facsimile* Tab. XIX, being dropped in both editions, must be deemed *s.m.*

ERRATA IN THE ANNOTATIONS

ERRATA

IN THE ANNOTATIONS TO BOTH EDITIONS (UNLESS THE CONTRARY BE EXPRESSED).

Fol. I, note 18, *read* μνηστευθισησ. Fol. II, notes 19, 20 *refer to* Tab. XVIII. Fol. II*, notes 1, 2 *not found in* Tab. XIX. Fol. IV, notes 7, 8, *transpose* ουν *and* εαν *in smaller edit. and refer to* Tab. XVIII. *Ibid.* note 10 *refer to* Tab. XVIII. Fol. VI. Matt. xi. 4. ο ισ̅[9] text., *at deest annotatio.* Fol. VI*, note 10, *read* text βηδσαιδαν. Fol. VII, note 9, *read* text δεμονιων. Fol. XVI, note 1, *read* text γυνεκι. Fol. XVI*, note 11, *read* text λεγιωνων. Fol. XVII*, note 9, *refer to* Tab. XIX. Fol. XVIII, note 2, *refer to* Tab. XIX. Fol. XX, note 15, *read* text ακουωσι. Fol. XXII*, Mark vii. 29 δεμονιον[13] *text, at deest annotatio.* Fol. XXXI*, note 1, "θ medium" *in* μαθθαθ *ambiguè dictum.* Fol. XXXVIII*, note 10, *read* text ποισαι. Fol. XXXVIIII*, note 3, "inter ε et ι" *ambiguè. Ibid.* note 27, *read* το prim. in smaller edit. Fol. XXXXIIII*, note 1, *add from larger edit. to smaller* "ι prima manus vel A supplevit." Fol. XXXXV*, note 4, *read* των *for* αυτ. Fol. XXXXVI*, note 3, *read* βεβλημενοσ *in smaller edition.* Fol. XXXXVIII*, note 14—18, line 5, *for* συνετε *read* συνετ: see Tab. XVIII. Fol. LI, note 6, *read* text πιστευσετε. *Ibid.* note 14, *read* C^b *for* C^a *secund.* Fol. LIII. John viii. 41. τα[22] text, *at deest annotatio.* Fol. LVII*, note 7 occurs *twice.* Fol. LXIIII*, Rom. viii. 3, εαν[7] text, *at deest annotatio.* Fol. LXX*, 1 Cor. vi. 14 δυμεωσ̊ text., *at deest annotatio.* Fol. LXXX, note 4, *refer to* Tab. XVIII. Fol. LXXXII, note 8, *refer to* Tab. XVIII. Fol. LXXXIX, note 5, *erase* C? Fol. C, note 8, *read* ομοθυμαδον *in smaller edit.* Fol. CV, note 12, *read* s.m. *after* α? Fol. CVI, note 7, *for* 129 *read* 130. Fol. CVII, note 9, *read* "ο secund." *in the smaller edit.* Fol. CX, note 5, *for* C επ. *read* C εβ. *in the smaller edit.* Fol. CXVI, note 8, *insert* C *before* κατελαβομην *in the smaller edit. Ibid.* note 14, *read* "του prim." *in the smaller edit.* Fol. CXVIIII, note 3, "ειπει (ει primae manus est)" *ambiguè dictum.* Fol. CXXVI*, note 4, *read* βασειλειων. Fol. CXXVIII*, note 3, 4 *insert* και *before* δια. Fol. CXXVIIII, Apoc. vii. 13 ^σ^τολασ τασ* *text., at deest annotatio.* Fol. CXXX, note 10, *refer to* Tab. XVIII. Fol. CXXXI*, note 8, "αυτου: υ in rasuram incidit" *ambiguè dictum.* Fol. CXXXIII*, note 18, 19, *for* αγγελον *read* αγγε. Tab. XVIII, column 3, ll. 14—16 *larger edit., for* 129 *read* 130.

In the Prolegomena to both editions (Section V) Tischendorf (apparently in error) cites several readings otherwise than his text represents: such are Matt. x. 15 γομορρασ *for* -ων; *ibid.* xxvi. 65 ιδου *for* και λεγει ϊδε *p.m.;* Mark iv. 28 ειτεν σταχυν, *but* —σταχυν *p.m.; ibid.* iv. 36 πλοιαρια *for* πλοια; Luke xix. 38 εν ουραν. ειρην. *for* εν ουρανω εν ϊρηνη *p.m.;* John i. 6 ην αυτω ονομα *for* ην ονομα αυτω *p.m.; ibid.* vii. 22 θαυμαζετε μωυσησ *for* θαυμαζετε ο μωϋσησ; Apoc. xix. 13 ρεραμμενον *for* περιρεραμμενον; *ibid.* xxii. 5 ουχ εξουσιν *for* ουκ εχουσιν. There occur also several false references which the student will easily rectify, except ειδα Apoc. xvii. 3 *for* xvii. 6.

In the following passages the words are susceptible of a different division from that adopted by Tischendorf in his smaller edition: Acts ix. 6, Apoc. xvii. 8 οτι T. *or* ο τι; Acts xv. 28 επ αναγκαισ *or* επαναγκαισ (*itacism for* -εσ) T.; *ibid.* xvi. 32 συμ πασι T. *or* συμπασι; *ibid.* xxiii. 20 μελλοντι *or* μελλον τι T.; Col. iv. 8 γνω τε T., *rather* γνωτε; Apoc. xiv. 6 μεσω ουρανηματι *p.m., rather than* μεσωουρανηματι T.; *ibid.* xvii. 3 γεμοντα *or* γεμον τα; *ibid.* xx. 4 ειτινεσ T., *rather* ει τινεσ; *ibid.* xxi. 18 ενδωμασι T., *rather* εν δωμασι.

ΤΩι ΘΩι ΔΟΞΑ

CPSIA information can be obtained
at www.ICGtesting.com
Printed in the USA
LVHW040021180422
716440LV00005B/531

9 783752 593600